Outstanding praise for
HALLOWEEN PARTY MURDER!

"There are parties and then there are parties, as this trio of treats by Maine authors proves. Readers may never look at Halloween parties the same way."
—*Kirkus Reviews*

"Entertaining . . . All three charming novellas are enlivened by appealing characters. These puzzling cases are a seasonal treat for cozy readers."
—*Publishers Weekly*

"A zany, fun-filled collection of holiday stories that will turn cozy mystery enthusiasts into armchair sleuths as they help detect alongside their favorite amateur detectives in this stellar holiday-themed anthology."
—*The Press-Republican* (Plattsburgh, New York)

"Fun, creepy, holiday mayhem."
—*Kennebec Journal*

Books by Leslie Meier

MISTLETOE MURDER
TIPPY TOE MURDER
TRICK OR TREAT
MURDER
BACK TO SCHOOL
MURDER
VALENTINE MURDER
CHRISTMAS COOKIE
MURDER
TURKEY DAY MURDER
WEDDING DAY MURDER
BIRTHDAY PARTY
MURDER
FATHER'S DAY MURDER
STAR SPANGLED
MURDER
NEW YEAR'S EVE
MURDER
BAKE SALE MURDER
CANDY CANE MURDER
ST. PATRICK'S DAY
MURDER
MOTHER'S DAY MURDER
WICKED WITCH
MURDER
GINGERBREAD COOKIE
MURDER
ENGLISH TEA MURDER
CHOCOLATE COVERED
MURDER
EASTER BUNNY
MURDER
CHRISTMAS CAROL
MURDER

FRENCH PASTRY
MURDER
CANDY CORN MURDER
BRITISH MANOR
MURDER
EGGNOG MURDER
TURKEY TROT MURDER
SILVER ANNIVERSARY
MURDER
INVITATION ONLY
MURDER
YULE LOG MURDER
HAUNTED HOUSE
MURDER
CHRISTMAS SWEETS
IRISH PARADE MURDER
EASTER BONNET
MURDER

Books by Lee Hollis

Hayley Powell Mysteries
DEATH OF A KITCHEN
DIVA
DEATH OF A COUNTRY
FRIED REDNECK
DEATH OF A COUPON
CLIPPER
DEATH OF A
CHOCOHOLIC
DEATH OF A CHRISTMAS
CATERER
DEATH OF A CUPCAKE
QUEEN

Published by Kensington Publishing Corp.

HALLOWEEN
PARTY
MURDER

Leslie Meier
Lee Hollis
Barbara Ross

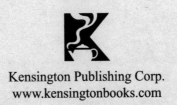

Kensington Publishing Corp.
www.kensingtonbooks.com

Contents

HALLOWEEN PARTY MURDER

MURDER

Leslie Meier

For Stella Rose Levitt
and
Abigail Meldrim Meier,
because they know everything!

Chapter One

"Lucy, you were really wrong about Ty Moon," said Bill, stepping into the kitchen and taking off the barn coat that was his autumn uniform. "He's a really nice guy," he continued, hanging the tan jacket on one of the hooks beside the kitchen door. He crossed the kitchen to the fridge and took out a beer, then joined his wife at the round golden-oak table.

Lucy, who had been doing a crossword puzzle, looked up and smiled at her husband, even though she felt the slightest bit defensive. "I wasn't the only one who suspected he was up to no good," she said, remembering how most people in town had reacted to the strange noises and flashing lights emanating from the old Victorian house Ty and his wife, Heather, had bought a year or so ago. "I admit I may have overreacted," she continued, thinking back to the frightening afternoon when her grandson Patrick disappeared inside the Moons' house, a once-grand Victorian that had become so derelict that townsfolk suspected it was haunted. "But it wasn't all my fault. Things kind of spiraled out of control."

"You can say that again," said Bill, popping the top on his can of beer. "It's a miracle nobody got shot once the SWAT team arrived."

Lucy put down her pencil. "All's well that ends well," she said. "If Ty hadn't been so unfriendly and downright secretive about his work, people wouldn't have been so suspicious."

"He's been real successful; he told me he's got a huge job coming up that's gonna make him a lot of money."

Lucy knew that Ty created computer-generated special effects for TV and movies, and was able to work from home in the quaint seaside town of Tinker's Cove, Maine. "And I think I was entirely justified in thinking he was abusing Heather," she said, warming to her subject. "How could we know she was undergoing chemo for cancer?"

"Well, she's in remission now, and they're ready to start a family," said Bill. "And they've hired me to renovate that old monstrosity of a house and restore it to its former grandeur." He took a long swallow. "With some modern improvements."

Lucy was definitely interested. She and Bill had recently expanded their former bedroom into a luxurious master suite, and she was nurturing plans for a kitchen reno, obsessively watching the home improvement shows on TV. "What have they got in mind?" she asked.

"Well, they want to keep all the old moldings, the doors and fireplaces, all the stuff that gives the place character. The rooms are big and have high ceilings, which is great.

We can't go all-out open plan, but there are double door-ways between the two living rooms and also from the hall into the dining room. I'm thinking of moving the kitchen into one of the living rooms, making the dining room a living room, and turning the old kitchen into a solarium." He paused. "What do you think?"

"I'm jealous," said Lucy, glancing around at their an-tique farmhouse, with its small rooms, cramped stair-cases, and dormered bedrooms where they had raised their four children, who were now grown. "I love our house, I always have, but it would be nice to have a kitchen island, and a laundry room instead of having to go down to the basement, and," she looked at the messy collection of coats and boots by the kitchen door, "a real mud room, with plenty of storage."

"Well," said Bill, shrugging philosophically, "if the Moons go ahead with this reno, maybe all your champagne dreams will come true." He fingered his beer can. "They're talking big, and that means a big paycheck for me."

"When will you know?" asked Lucy.

"Soon, I hope. I've got to draw up a plan and give them an estimate, but I don't anticipate any problems. They were very clear about what they want, which makes it easy for me." He drained his beer. "And, oh, you'll love this, Lucy. Before we start demo, they want to have a big Halloween party. They said everybody thought the house was haunted, so why not throw a big bash? Heather said it could even be a fundraiser for your Hat and Mitten Fund."

Lucy was definitely revising her opinion of the Moons. "That's a great idea." She and three friends had created the fund years ago to provide warm winter clothing for the town's less-fortunate kids, collecting outgrown cloth-

ing and distributing it to those in need. Through the years,
the fund had grown, and it now provided back-to-school
backpacks, holiday parties, and even summer-camp scholar-
ships, in addition to its original mission of providing gently
used jackets, boots, hats, and mittens.

"Yeah, Heather said you should give her a call, see
what you can work out."

"Will do," said Lucy, reaching for her phone. She was
still talking to Heather, inviting her to the next Hat and
Mitten Fund meeting, when her youngest child, and the
only one still living at home, arrived. Zoe was finally finishing up her degree at nearby Winchester College, ending a protracted higher-education career in which she'd
sampled practically every major the small liberal-arts institution offered, finally settling on communications. She
dropped her backpack on the floor and shrugged out of
her bright pink Winchester hoodie, hanging it on the hook
beside her father's jacket.

"What was that all about?" she asked, extracting a yogurt from the fridge and leaning against the kitchen
counter to eat it. "I didn't know you were friends with
Queen Heather."

"I don't know what you mean," said Lucy. "As it happens, your father got a job fixing up the Moons' old Victorian, and they want to have a big Halloween party there
before the demo starts. A haunted house in the haunted
house! It should be really popular, and it's going to be a
fundraiser for the Hat and Mitten Fund; that's why I
called her."

"Wow, Mom, I guess your suspicions about Ty Moon
were way wrong," she said, causing Bill to chuckle as he
beat a hasty retreat to the family room.

Lucy took a deep breath. "As I told your father, I was

not the only person who had doubts about Ty Moon. If you remember, everybody thought he was abusing Heather and probably conducting all sorts of ungodly goings-on in that spooky house."

"Yeah, well, now he and Heather are the most popular couple in town," said Zoe, licking the last of the yogurt off her spoon and tossing the cup into the trash.

"Really?"

"Yeah. They're part of this young crowd of smart, hip creative types."

This was news to Lucy, who thought she and her friends were the smart, young crowd. After all, the population in Tinker's Cove definitely skewed upward, with a large percentage of elderly citizens in their eighties and even nineties, which allowed Lucy and her friends to think of themselves as comparative youngsters. "Who are these people?" she asked.

"Oh, you know. There's Matt and Luisa Rodriguez, from the Cali Kitchen restaurant. That's where they all hang out, especially for Sunday brunch. The Moons are regulars, and Juliette Duff shows up if she's in town."

Lucy knew the Rodriguezes, a brother and sister who ran the restaurant created by their father, renowned chef Rey Rodriguez. Juliette Duff was a supermodel who had inherited her extremely wealthy grandmother's estate on Shore Road, where it occupied a spectacular piece of property overlooking the ocean. "Who else?"

"Well, Rosie Capshaw, she's always there."

Lucy, who was a reporter for the *Courier* weekly newspaper, had interviewed Rosie, a recent arrival who was distantly related to Juliette and was living on the estate, where she created spectacular puppets in a disused barn.

"What about Brendan Coyle?" Lucy knew the director of the local food pantry was a good friend of Rosie's.

"Yup, he's there a lot, and so is Kevin Kenneally. They give the place a real happening vibe; you'd almost think you were in Portland or Boston."

"Kevin doesn't seem to fit in with the others; they're all creatives, and he's pretty conservative, being the assistant DA and all," said Lucy, trying to picture the group.

"They love teasing him, and he's a really good sport about it all."

Lucy suddenly wondered how her cash-strapped student daughter had come by this knowledge. She certainly couldn't afford to frequent the expensive Cali Kitchen Sunday brunch. "How do you know all this?" she asked. "Since when have you been eating brunch?"

"I wish," said Zoe, sighing and rolling her eyes. "Don't you remember? I filled in at Cali Kitchen for my friend Catie a couple of weeks ago. It was brutal hard work; that bunch had me running my feet off getting them mimosas and Bloody Marys, but they were generous tippers. Especially Ty."

"Well, I better get supper started," said Lucy, pressing her hands on the table and pushing herself up off her chair. She had to admit it; she wasn't as young as she used to be, what with her aching back and diminished energy. "I could use some help," she suggested, hopefully.

"Sorry, Mom, I've got a paper due," said Zoe, zipping up the back stairs and leaving Lucy to peel the potatoes.

Lucy and her Hat and Mitten Fund friends had been meeting at Jake's Donut Shack on Thursday mornings for years, beginning when their kids had gone off to college and they no longer ran into each other at sports practices and school events. The four women had shared advice and offered emotional support as their kids entered their tricky twenties and launched their own careers and families. But now, as she glanced around the table, she realized they were no longer the young, hip bunch she'd always considered them to be.

Nowadays, they were on the far side of middle age, and it was beginning to show. There were streaks of gray in Rachel Goodman's shoulder-length black hair; Pam Stillings still wore her reddish hair in a ponytail, but bags had begun to appear under her eyes. Sue Finch, always the most stylish member of the group, worked hard to maintain her slim figure, but Lucy had noticed the slightest beginnings of a muffin top around her waist, and one day her chic ballet shoe slipped off, revealing an orthotic arch support. As for herself, Lucy knew she was fighting a losing battle when she smoothed on her drugstore moisturizer every morning and faithfully applied night cream before going to bed.

The years were definitely taking a toll, but they'd also given the four friends the gift of friendship. They formed a tight group, having shared so many experiences, and Rachel was quick to remind them when they gathered at their usual table that Heather might find them a bit intimidating. "She's a newcomer," began Rachel, who had majored in psychology in college and had never gotten over it, "and we need to make her feel welcome. No inside jokes, no references to past events she knows nothing about, that sort of thing. Also, I would imagine she's still dealing with the emotional effects of her cancer diagnosis and treatment, even though she's now in remission and may even be cured."

"I don't know about that," said Lucy, signaling to Norine, the waitress, that she wanted a cup of coffee. "Zoe calls her 'Queen Heather' and says she and Ty are the most popular couple in town. They're part of a group of bright young things that regularly gather for Sunday brunch at Cali Kitchen."

Lucy felt Sue bristle beside her as Norine approached to fill their mugs and take their orders: a sunshine muffin for Rachel, hash and eggs for Lucy, granola and yogurt for Pam, and black coffee for Sue. When Norine went off to the kitchen, Sue practically exploded.

"Queen Heather? That's ridiculous!" she exclaimed, tucking a glossy lock of hair behind one ear with a perfectly manicured hand. "And since when did these upstart social climbers—millennials who, I can guarantee, don't know the first thing about writing a thank-you note or a proper letter of sympathy—when did they become the most popular social set in town? And who decided that anyway?"

"Shhh," cautioned Pam, nodding toward the door, where Heather had paused, checking out the room. "Remember," she whispered, "this fundraiser could mean some big bucks for the fund." Then she lifted her head and made eye contact with Heather, waving her over.

"I'm so glad you could come," she said, as Heather seated herself. "Are you famished? Do you want to order?" she asked, looking for Norine.

"Oh, no. Nothing for me. No food," replied Heather, sounding horrified at the thought. "I wouldn't mind some herbal tea, if they have that here."

Sue snorted. "It's a donut shop. They have coffee."

"I guess then I'll just have a glass of water," said Heather, shrugging out of her stylish fake fur coat to reveal a painfully slim body and tossing back her long, silvery hair. "As you probably all know, I'm Heather Moon, and I live in that big, old haunted house on School Street."

"We're so glad you could come this morning," began Rachel, "and we're so excited about the fundraiser, which is so generous of you." She smiled. "I'm Rachel Goodman, and I know you've met Lucy . . ."

"We've met," said Heather, without much enthusiasm.

"I just want to say that I'm sorry about any misunderstandings in the past," offered Lucy. "I'm looking forward to working with you and publicizing the haunted house. I know Ted is always eager to promote local events, right, Pam?"

"Absolutely," said Pam. "I'm Pam Stillings, I own the *Courier*, along with my husband Ted, and I can guarantee that the paper will provide plenty of free publicity."

"That's great," said Heather, turning to Sue with a questioning expression.

Sue took a sip of coffee, narrowed her eyes, and gave Heather a tiny smile. "I'm Sue Finch," she said, "and it's an absolute pleasure to meet you."

"Same here," said Heather, as Norine arrived with their orders.

"Ohmigosh, I didn't see you," she apologized to Heather, distributing the plates and then pulling her order book out of her apron pocket. "What can I get you, hon?"

"Chamomile tea with lemon," said Heather.

"Oh, sorry. No can do. We've got Tetley."

"I'll just have a glass of water. Thank you."

"Okay." From her tone, it was clear that Norine did not approve of her choice.

Heather pressed her lips together, but whether she was

suppressing a smile or a thought wasn't clear. She glanced around the table, then began speaking. "Well, as you know, my husband and I are hosting a grand Halloween party, including a haunted house, before we start modernizing the old place."

"It's the perfect venue for a haunted house," said Pam, enthusiastically.

"That's what we thought," said Heather. "And my husband has the technical skills to provide amazing special effects. You wouldn't believe what he can do with light and sound."

"Oh, I think we have an idea," said Sue, as Norine arrived with a tall glass of water. A clear plastic straw topped with a white paper casing was in the glass.

"Oh, oh. No plastic straws!" exclaimed Heather. "But what can I do with it? It's already been opened, and now it's going to go in the ocean . . ."

"No big deal," said Norine, extracting the offending straw.

"But it is a big deal. Some sea turtle will eat it and die, and they'll all become extinct."

"I'll make sure it doesn't get in the ocean," promised Norine, furrowing her brow.

"But how?" demanded Heather.

"I just will," said Norine, hurrying off to the kitchen.

"Plastics, they're terrible," said Heather. "They last forever."

"So true," agreed Pam. "But we really need to talk about the fundraiser. Do you have a date in mind?"

"Well, I certainly don't want it to conflict with the children's party you ladies always have for the elementary school kids."

"That will be on Halloween, which is a Friday this year," said Pam.

"I think the haunted house party should be on a weekend, but maybe not the weekend just before Halloween. If we hold it a week earlier, it will kind of set the tone and get people in the mood, if you know what I mean."

"I assume you'll need lots of volunteers to help construct the scary effects, and it will take some time to organize, too," said Rachel.

"Absolutely. Maybe Lucy can put out a call for volunteers in this week's paper," said Heather.

"We'll all be glad to help," said Pam.

"Well, I'm not sure how much I can do," said Rachel. "My husband is running for state rep, and I'm pretty busy with his campaign."

"You get a pass," said Sue. "But for the rest of us, it's all hands on deck, right?"

"Righto," said Lucy, as they all nodded their heads. "And don't worry," she told Rachel. "I've been covering the campaign and Bob's a shoo-in, running as an independent. Nobody ever heard of the Democrat, Andi Nardone, and George Armistead, the Republican, is ninety years old if he's a day."

"I hope you're right," said Rachel. "You can't ever be too sure; things can change in a minute in a campaign."

Chapter Two

Lucy decided Rachel's fears were unwarranted when she stood outside the IGA grocery store on Saturday morning, handing out leaflets for Bob. It was a brisk fall morning, and she enjoyed being out in the fresh air and sunshine, which she knew would soon be only a memory, along with the bright yellow and orange leaves that were already starting to fall. The store was busy; many shopping carts were loaded with pumpkins, potted chrysanthemums, and jugs of apple cider. She knew most of the shoppers, who were friends and neighbors, and everybody seemed pleased to learn that Bob was running for state rep.

"It's about time George Armistead took to his rocking chair," said retired kindergarten teacher Lydia Volpe. "He's been a state rep for over forty years, and I don't think he even bothers to attend the sessions, or vote. And when he does vote, it's always against anything that might raise taxes, like improving the schools or health care. I'll gladly vote for Bob; I think he'll be a great state rep."

"That's great. I know he'll appreciate your vote. And while I've got you, Heather and Ty Moon have offered to hold a haunted house fundraiser for the Hat and Mitten Fund, and we're looking for volunteers . . ."

"Say no more," said Lydia. "I'll be happy to help, but you know I'm already on the committee for the children's party, and I really don't want to go to any more meetings."

Lucy laughed. "Anything you can do would be appreciated. How about taking tickets on the night of the event; that's just a couple of hours."

"Okay, put me down for that," said Lydia, giving her cart a push and heading across the parking lot to her car.

As Lucy watched Lydia's progress, her attention was caught by a young mother struggling with a toddler on one hand and what looked like a four-year-old girl on the other. The toddler kept going limp, impeding their progress, and the mom finally just picked up the tot, telling the little girl to hang on to her jacket.

"Why, Mom?" asked the girl.

"Because I don't have a free hand. I've got to carry Benjy, and I want you to be safe in the parking lot."

"Why does Benjy have to be carried?"

"He's little and gets tired."

"Well, I'm big, and I can take care of myself." With that, the little girl darted away from her mother and ran ahead, just as a zippy sports car rounded the line of parked cars.

Seeing that the little girl was directly in front of the approaching car, Lucy ran into the parking lot, waving her arms and screaming "Stop!" The car braked and stopped mere feet from the girl, who burst into tears and ran back to her mother. She fell to her knees and enfolded the girl into her arms, along with the toddler brother.

"It's okay, you're okay," crooned the mom, smoothing the little girl's hair.

The driver of the car climbed out, and Lucy was surprised to recognize Kevin Kenneally, whom she'd frequently covered at press conferences. Kenneally, who was dressed in freshly ironed jeans and a North Face windbreaker, angrily confronted the little family. "You know, lady, you really ought to keep that kid under control."

"Well, maybe you should drive a little more carefully. If it wasn't for this lady here, we would've had a real tragedy," declared the mom.

"This is a parking lot, not a playground," insisted Kevin, turning to Lucy. "That girl was in no danger. I saw her and was braking."

Lucy was trembling, and her heart was pounding, but she wasn't about to let Kevin have the last word. "Maybe so, but it didn't seem like that to me. There's no excuse for speeding in a parking lot where there are elderly folks and children. If a cop was here, you would've been cited."

"I'm not so sure about that, Lucy," he said, with a knowing smile. On second thought, Lucy figured he was right; it was doubtful that a local cop would cite an assistant district attorney. "And if I were you," he added, "I wouldn't be so quick with the accusations." Having said his piece, he hopped back in his fancy sports car, backed away too fast into a three-point turn, and zoomed out of the parking lot. As she watched him go, Lucy wondered exactly how much assistant district attorneys made these days, and whether his salary would stretch to cover such an expensive car.

"Well, I never . . ." said the shocked mom, picking up the toddler.

"What a reckless driver," said Lucy, rolling her eyes. She took the little girl's hand and began walking to the entrance. "My name's Lucy, what's yours?"

"Stella. Stella Rose Levitt."

"And how old are you, Stella?"

"Four."

"Well, remember to be extra careful in parking lots and to mind your mom, okay?"

Stella scowled. "I'm a big girl."

"Yes, you are, but cars are bigger." Lucy turned to the mom. "By the way, I'm campaigning for my friend Bob Goodman. He's running for state rep. Can I give you a brochure?"

"Sure, thanks," said the woman, who was settling the toddler into the seat of a shopping cart. "And thanks so much for stopping that car and saving Stella. I can't even imagine . . ."

Lucy gave her a big smile. "No problem. And don't forget to vote for Bob."

Lucy recounted the episode that afternoon at a meeting of the Hat and Mitten Fund planning committee at Sue's antique captain's house on Parallel Street. "I'm pretty confident I got at least one sure vote for Bob," she said, ending the tale. All the members of the breakfast group were there, as well as Heather Moon and Rosie Capshaw, who Lucy suspected had come to offer moral support to Heather.

"I should think so," said Heather, in her soft voice. "You saved that little girl's life."

Rosie Capshaw didn't hesitate to express her opinion. "I like Kevin and all, but sometimes he can be a big jerk."

"What kind of car was it?" asked Pam.

"I dunno. Some sort of sports car," answered Lucy, with a shrug.

"It's a second-hand Corvette, and he loves it," said Rosie.

"Men and their toys," sighed Sue.

"Well, I hope that mother will take better care of her children," said Heather, sounding a bit wistful. "They're really a gift from God, you know, and not everyone gets them."

Lucy's ears perked up at this. Bill had told her that Ty and Heather wanted to start a family, and she wondered if they'd run into difficulties. She and the others were seated at Sue's prized wine-tasting table in her breakfast nook, and were nibbling on home-baked madeleines and sipping chamomile tea in Heather's honor.

"Right," added Pam. "I'm sure that near-accident was a real wake-up call for her." She pressed her lips together thoughtfully. "Did you get her name? Maybe she could help with the fundraiser or the kids' party."

"No. Her last name is probably Levitt; that's what Stella said her name was," said Lucy, reaching for another madeleine even though she knew she shouldn't. "And in the poor woman's defense, I have to say she really had her hands full with those kids."

"Families aren't what they used to be," offered Sue. "Lots of women keep their birth names; kids have different fathers and different surnames. It can be hard to keep it all straight."

Sue spoke from experience; she used to be engaged full-time as the part-owner, executive director, and head teacher at Little Prodigies Child Care Center, but was now semi-retired and acted mostly as a silent partner, helping out occasionally.

"Well, let's turn our attention to the matters at hand," urged Rachel, draining her cup and setting it in the saucer. "I think the kids' party is pretty much under control. We've done it so many times, it doesn't require much thought."

"Can you do the fortune-telling?" Pam asked Rachel. "Or will you be too busy with the campaign?"

Rachel traditionally put on a pair of oversized hoop earrings, wrapped herself in colorful scarves and shawls, seated herself in a little tent with a garden globe as a crystal ball, and pretended to tell the future. Her fortunes, really advice for good behavior couched in mystical terms, were terribly popular, especially with the older kids.

"Absolutely, I wouldn't miss it for the world. And the fortunes may include advising the kids to tell their parents to vote for Bob." She furrowed her brow. "Would that be wrong?"

"Actually, we could include his brochures in the treat bags," suggested Lucy.

"You can even get specially wrapped candies. Vote for Bob Bars or something," said Rosie, who admitted skipping breakfast as an excuse for eating most of the madeleines. She was dressed in a plaid shirt and jeans and was much sturdier than her fragile friend, Heather; as a puppeteer, she was used to the hard physical labor that constructing and working her oversized creations required.

"Thanks, Rosie, I'll look into that," said Rachel, impressed with the idea. "So the kids' party is all set?"

"Yup," said Pam. "I've got plenty of refreshments, the DJ is booked, the soccer moms are doing the decorations, the PTA is organizing games, posters are up . . . can anybody think of anything I've missed?"

"Sounds great," said Sue. "Let's move on to the haunted house. Any thoughts?"

"I guess we could have one of those gruesome operating rooms; those are pretty popular," said Lucy.

"Oh, yeah," said Pam, enthusiastically, reaching for one of the rapidly disappearing madeleines. "And surprises. Like a ghost that pops out of a closet, something like that. And I'm sure Ty will come up with lots of eerie noises and spooky lighting effects."

"You can count on him," said Rosie, getting a big smile from Heather.

Heather didn't smile often, thought Lucy, biting into her madeleine, but when she did, she looked even more angelic than usual. Lucy tried to figure out how she did it, what made her look so ethereal, like a fairy or some other-worldly creature. Was it the long, ash-blond hair? Her big blue eyes? The fluttery clothes she chose, always in shades of white and dripping with lace and ruffles. And, of course, she was fine-boned and very thin, really too thin. Somewhat guiltily, she put down the rest of her madeleine on her saucer.

"Actually," continued Heather, speaking rather hesitantly, almost whispering, "Ty and Rosie had some thoughts about the tableaux that would elevate the haunted house above the usual stuff people expect."

Pam wasn't sure she liked the sound of this. "Really? Like what?" she asked, in a challenging tone.

"Oh, it was just an idea," said Heather, shrinking into her lacy tablecloth shawl.

"Don't let Pam put you off," said Sue, patting her hand. "Tell us how you want to do it. It's your house, after all." She stood up. "More tea, anyone?"

Getting a few nods, she refilled the cups and then sat down, tenting her hands expectantly. "Go on, Heather," she invited.

"Well, we thought—" she began, looking to Rosie for approval and getting a nod. "Well, it's really Ty, he's the one with the ideas. He suggested we might base the tableaux on famous books and paintings. For instance," she said, warming to her subject and speaking somewhat less hesitantly, "I thought I could portray Ophelia, but with a twist. You know, there's a famous painting of Ophelia floating in a river by an artist named Millais. He painted the creek *en plein air*, out in the woods, and that's how he got all the beautiful plants and nature in the background. But he had his model for Ophelia pose in a bathtub, so that's what I thought I would do. What do you think?"

"I think that might be rather chilly," offered Pam.

"And damp," said Lucy.

"Oh, I wouldn't use real water. I'm going to use plastic sheeting and bubbles, and Ty will fix the lights, so it will look quite realistic. He says he can create the illusion of rippling water."

"It's easy-peasy with the right equipment," offered Rosie. "And I have some ideas for recycling the plastic in my puppets."

"I suppose someone will portray the artist, Millais?" asked Rachel.

"Yes. Kevin Kenneally has offered to play the artist; he'll wear a smock and a beret, and since he's the assistant DA, I think I'll be in very good hands."

Lucy was tempted to say something like "as long as he's not driving," but bit her tongue. She didn't want to strain her fragile relationship with Heather.

"Right," said Pam, thoughtfully. "You'll be in a rather vulnerable position, and you don't want anybody messing with you."

Heather hadn't considered this and was alarmed. "Do you think they would?"

"I wouldn't put it past some. Teen boys, for example, might try to get a rise out of you just to break the illusion."

"I'm pretty sure Kevin can keep me safe," said Heather.

"One thing I can tell you," said Sue, tucking a stray lock of midnight-black hair behind one ear with her perfectly manicured hand, "is that posing as Ophelia didn't work out very well for Elizabeth Siddall, the model. Millais did have her in a bathtub of water, which he tried to keep warm with oil lamps, but one of the lamps went out, and she caught a chill and was seriously ill for months."

"Really?" asked Heather, sounding doubtful.

"It's true," said Sue, responding to her friends' skeptical expressions.

"How on earth do you know this?" asked Lucy.

"I took art history in college, and the professor told us all about it. He really despised the pre-Raphaelites, of which John Everett Millais was one. He said it was a sad and pathetic attempt to idealize the past when the art world was moving forward into exciting new ways of seeing, like impressionism, and painting speeding trains, trying to capture movement and light, and, well," she grinned naughtily, "that professor made a big impression on me." She took the teapot over to the stove and added some hot water. She was smiling at the memory when she apologized, saying, "I'm sorry. I got carried away down Memory Lane."

"Not at all, that's very interesting," said Heather. "But I won't be chilly. No real water." She smiled. "And I'll wear my long johns."

"Actually, I like this idea of yours," said Pam. "We could reference all sorts of classics. Hamlet and poor Yorick, along with the witches."

"The witches were in *Macbeth*," said Rosie.

Pam was not about to be put off. "Well, just Hamlet and Yorick's skull then, in a graveyard. And how about Dr. Jekyll and Mr. Hyde? Maybe with a mirror and a strobe sort of light that flicks from one to the other? Wouldn't that be cool?" She paused momentarily. "Oh, and what about Van Gogh? Slicing his ear off!"

"Maybe we should leave the choice of scenes to Ty and Rosie," suggested Rachel.

"Right." Pam took a deep breath. "I was letting my imagination run away with me."

"All good ideas," said Heather, politely.

"What else do you have in mind, apart from Ophelia?" asked Lucy. "Is there anything for us?"

Heather smiled, one of those "butter wouldn't melt in her mouth" smiles. "Actually, we do. Don't we, Rosie?"

Rosie was grinning broadly and could hardly contain her excitement. "It's terrific!"

"What is it?" asked Pam, eagerly.

"Well, remember, you don't have to do it," said Heather. "It's just a suggestion."

Sue returned to the table with the fresh pot of tea.

"We're all dying to hear," she said, setting it down. "Tell us while it steeps."

"Okay." Heather bit her lip. "It was Ty's idea, really. He thought we could have a guillotine, and the blade would come down and a head would roll." Her eyes had grown quite bright, and her face became animated as she went on to describe the special effects. "He can create the illusion of blood with lights, and he'd add the sound of the blade whooshing and thumping down."

"It would be like that scene from *A Tale of Two Cities*, you know, the book by Dickens," said Rosie.

"'Tis a far, far better thing that I do than I have ever done,'" quoted Lucy, with a dramatic flourish. "I guess I could be that guy."

"Oh, no," said Heather, hastily. "No. We thought you'd make a perfect Madame Defarge, Lucy."

Lucy felt rather deflated. "Madame Defarge?"

"Yes," continued Heather brightly. "And you could all be *tricoteuses,* the women who knitted and chortled gleefully while the guillotine did its grisly work in the French Revolution."

"Well, that would certainly be interesting," said Sue, rather coolly. "More tea?"

Nobody seemed interested in tea. The mood in the room had suddenly changed; the enthusiasm was gone. Silent glances were exchanged, and suddenly, as if with one accord, they were all beginning to gather up their things and preparing to leave. Thank-yous were offered, goodbyes were said, and the women quickly departed.

Rosie and Heather were standing together on the porch when Lucy went outside, but when she tried to say goodbye, they didn't respond, but ignored her and continued their conversation. Walking down the brick path to her car, Lucy had the unnerving sensation that she was becoming invisible. And when Rosie and Heather actually deigned to acknowledge her, she fumed, they thought she would make a perfect Madame Defarge. Settling herself behind the steering wheel, she came to the unwelcome conclusion that it wasn't a compliment.

Chapter Three

L ucy was still fretting about Heather's assertion that she would make a perfect Madame Defarge when she went, along with Bill, on Sunday afternoon to work on setting up the haunted house. As luck would have it, she was assigned to work with Ty on painting the walls in the upstairs hallway black, and she felt uncomfortable, worrying that he might harbor some resentment toward her. She decided to tackle the problem head-on, while he was bent over, stirring the paint.

"Ty," she began, "I want you to know that I'm really sorry about that whole thing with my grandson. I was terrified when I couldn't find him, and when the kids said he'd gone into your house, I called the police, but honestly, I never dreamed they'd bring the SWAT team. I thought one of the officers would knock on your door, that was all."

He looked up at her, a smile playing on his lips. "Listen, that's all water under the bridge. I can understand how terrifying it is to lose track of a kid, and, well, to be honest, that whole situation was a much-needed wake-up call for me and Heather. We were so involved with her treatment and my work that we didn't realize the impression we were making on other people, like our neighbors and the school kids." He put the paint-covered stirring stick down carefully on a sheet of newsprint and stood up, facing her. "That's one reason we want to do the haunted house. We want folks in Tinker's Cove to know that we're really rather nice, and we want to be good neighbors."

Lucy was struck by his sincerity, and if she was honest with herself, his remarkable good looks. Ty was tall and broad-shouldered, with tousled dark hair and dramatic eyebrows, and he wore his ripped jeans and paint-daubed sweatshirt with casual flair. Maybe it was those boat shoes, held together with duct tape, which reminded her of boys she'd been smitten with in college. "You and Heather are not only good neighbors, you're exceptionally generous, and if this haunted house is successful, it will give the Hat and Mitten Fund a much-needed boost."

"That's what we're hoping." He squatted down and poured some of the paint into a roller tray, then unwrapped a roller and stuck it on a holder. "I've recruited some of my special-effects and theater pals, and"—he stood up and shrugged—"well, if it all goes according to plan, this will be like nothing this little town has seen before."

She picked up a roller and smiled at him. "So where do we start?"

"Just pick a spot," he said, grinning broadly. "And remember, you don't have to be too careful. There'll be special lighting, and we want it to look kind of shabby and creepy anyway."

"Hey!" protested Lucy, smiling. "I'm practically a pro. I've painted every room in my house several times over!"

"So you've lived here in Tinker's Cove for quite a while?" he asked, climbing on a step ladder and brushing paint on the crown molding.

Lucy had started in the middle of the opposite wall, hoping to leave the baseboards to younger and spryer volunteers. "Yup, we were living in New York and hating it. Bill was making a lot of money on Wall Street, but it wasn't what he wanted to do, so we took the plunge and bought an old farmhouse here in Tinker's Cove. He gradually built up his restoration contracting business. We have four kids, but they've pretty much flown the nest now . . ." Lucy was enjoying spreading the black paint on the faded wallpaper that clung to the old cracked plaster surface using the W strokes she'd learned from one of Bill's painter subcontractors.

"So you've become real Mainers?" he asked, moving the stepladder.

"I wouldn't say that," admitted Lucy. "We'll always be washashores. Even our kids, who were all born here, aren't considered natives. You have to have ancestors going back at least a hundred years, maybe longer, to be a real Mainer."

He climbed up on the ladder and extended the line of black. "Wow, Heather and I have our work cut out for us."

"I wouldn't let it bother me," advised Lucy. "You might not be accepted by the old guys in the o-five-hundred club . . ."

"The what?" he asked, stretching as far as he could with the brush.

"The good old boys who gather at the gas station for coffee every morning when it opens at five a.m."

"Trust me, I'm not getting up before seven at the earliest."

"Me, either," said Lucy. "And I doubt you'd have much in common with them anyway. But there are a lot of newcomers, younger people like yourselves, moving into town now." She dabbed her paint roller in the tray. "I really enjoyed interviewing Rosie Capshaw, and Matt and Luisa Rodriguez; they're like a breath of fresh air, if you ask me." She picked up where she left off, rolling the paint onto the wall and obliterating the faded flowers on the wallpaper. "And this town can use some new, young blood."

"I have noticed that there are a lot of old people . . ." he said.

"It's a real problem in these coastal towns," said Lucy, pushing her roller back and forth. "Property values are keeping young people out of the market, so they move away. Pretty soon, we're not going to have any teachers or cops or firemen . . . just a lot of old folks."

"Well, Heather and I hope to stick around and start a family; we're not going anywhere."

"Good for you," said Lucy, putting down her roller and pressing her hands on her behind and arching her back. "How did you two meet?"

Ty hopped down from the stepladder and moved it along once again. "Pretty typical story, I guess. We were both working in an off-Broadway theater in New York, but supporting ourselves by working in restaurants, temporary jobs, anything we could find. We were killing ourselves and not feeling like we were making any progress, so one day we decided to head out to LA, kind of a do-or-die kind of thing. We didn't hit the big time, like we'd hoped, but I discovered I really liked special effects, and Heather got steady work as an assistant to one of the big makeup artists. She was doing great until she got sick. Her doctor recommended a treatment program at Dana-Farber in Boston, so we decided to move back East. Boston was real expensive, but we were able to arrange for her to get her chemo in Portland, so we rented there for a while until we found this house." He climbed back on the ladder and slapped some paint on the molding. "It's been a big adjustment, but, thank God," he said, his voice husky, "she's doing fine now. We did the right thing."

"It must have been hard for you," said Lucy, wishing she'd been a bit more charitable toward Ty and Heather when they moved into town.

"Well, it's all in the past now," said Ty, jumping down from the ladder. "You know what we need? Some music!"

He disappeared, and soon the old house was rocking with upbeat disco tunes that pepped everybody up. Lucy found herself smiling and humming along as she rounded the corner and started on a fresh wall.

The days until the Haunted House flew by in a whirl. October was Lucy's favorite month anyway; she loved the crisp weather, the gorgeous reds and yellows of the changing trees, and the swirling leaves caught by the breeze. Most of all, she enjoyed the relaxed, blowsy look of many gardens and backyards as late bloomers like Montauk daisies and autumn clematis took over and lawns were dotted with colorful fallen leaves. She found the cooler weather energizing and fully enjoyed spending every spare moment working with the other volunteers at the Moon house.

Excitement was palpable when the big day finally arrived and the cast and crew assembled for the fundraiser. Rachel, who frequently directed shows for the town's amateur little-theater group, said it felt just like an opening night. "I'm nervous and excited, all at the same time," she said, with a little shiver, checking her makeup in a little mirror.

She was seated, along with Lucy, Pam, and Sue, behind a fake guillotine in an upstairs bedroom painted a lurid red-orange shade. They were all costumed in long skirts and shawls, and Heather had used her theatrical makeup skills to horrifying effect, giving them sooty eyes and dark parentheses around their mouths. They'd each brought along a knitting project.

"I've been working on this scarf for about six years," confessed Sue, who was working with a lovely shade of lavender angora yarn. "You know how it is, you get the yen to knit when it starts to get chilly, so I dig it out and add a few rows, but then the holidays roll around, and I get too busy, and it gets put away." She sighed. "At this rate, I'll never finish it."

"All I ever make are kids' hats and mittens," confessed Pam, who was working on a few inches of ribbing. "For the fund, of course."

"I'm almost finished with this vest for Bob," said Rachel, holding up a length of navy yarn worked into a cable design.

"Wow, that's beautiful," said Lucy, who was holding her needles awkwardly and trying to remember if she was supposed to go into the stitches from the front of the needle or the back. "I don't really know how to knit," she confessed, setting the tangled mess into her lap.

"Just pretend," advised Rachel, as the masked executioner joined them. The women all gasped at the sight of the hooded man, who was carrying a stuffed cloth dummy under one arm and its head under the other.

"Hi," he said, lifting his hood and revealing a big smile. It was Matt Rodriguez, dressed in blood-stained knee breeches and shirt, with a red scarf around his neck.

"Wow, that's quite a getup," admitted Lucy, when her heart resumed beating.

"Anybody have any idea how this thing works?" he asked, approaching the guillotine and arranging the dummy.

"I think there's a rope that lowers the blade," offered Lucy.

"That's right," agreed Pam, putting down her knitting and going into a corner, where she bent down. "And Ty showed me that all we have to do for the special effects is flip this little switch." She looked up. "Everybody ready?"

Matt took his place behind the guillotine, the women nodded, and Rachel turned on the switch. The room immediately became darker, and a stomach-turning thud was heard, followed by a flash of red light that simulated blood gushing from the dummy. "I guess that's the sound of the guillotine," she said, in a tone of professional detachment. "You'll need to coordinate dropping the blade with the sound effect."

Pam, however, had a different reaction. "I think I'm going to be sick," she said.

"Put your head between your knees," advised Rachel. "Trust me, stage fright often has that effect on people."

"It was awfully realistic," said Lucy, patting Pam's back.

Pam's reply was muffled. "I'll be okay in a minute."

An air horn went off, announcing that the doors were opening, and Rachel hurried back to her seat. "It's show time!" she announced, picking up her knitting. "Remember, we're *tricoteuses*, and we're enjoying this! The rich and stuck-up, the oppressors who've been lording it over us, are finally getting what they deserve!"

"I'm just not going to look," whispered Pam, raising her head.

"That's the spirit," said Lucy, encouraging her. "*Aux armes, citoyens!*" she proclaimed, struggling to remember the rest of *La Marseillaise*. Coming up empty, she improvised, saying, "Let the blade fall and the blood flow!"

"Whuh?" moaned Pam, as the waiting crowd could be heard entering the hallway below.

People were soon jostling each other in the doorway to see the tableau, some in costume and others not, and Lucy was interested to see their reactions as the blade thudded down. Some laughed nervously, some gasped in horror, and others scurried away, eager to see what terrors the next room held, or perhaps hoping for something a bit tamer to show their kids. Lucy wished she had thought to explore a bit before settling in to her assigned role; she was curious about the other tableaux, but from the screams and giggles and moans, it seemed as if the haunted house was a big success.

The four friends found themselves getting into the spirit of the thing, whooping and cheering and muttering insults as the blade fell again and again, even adding some spirited dialogue. "Ah, the marquis! He deserves to lose his head! What about the king? When will it be his turn? And that filthy whore, the queen? That will be the day, eh?" All too soon, it seemed, the air horn sounded again, signaling that the haunted house was over and the party would begin.

They all joined the crowd of revelers streaming downstairs to the living and dining rooms, where the Lobster Claws were already playing covers of rock classics. From the buzz in the room, it was obvious that everyone was having a great time. Some were dancing, others were talking with friends, and everybody seemed to be finding plenty to eat and drink. Lucy was helping herself to the generous buffet, filling a plate with zombie fingers, batty wonton bites, and a mini mummy pepperoni pizza, discovering that she'd built up quite an appetite witnessing all those faux decapitations. She was also thirsty and helped herself to a mad scientist's potion, which appeared to be rum and ginger beer served up in a lab beaker and garnished with a gummy worm.

She stood along the wall while enjoying her refreshments, watching the costumed crowd of partiers and trying to figure out who was who. Some were easy, like her friend Sgt. Barney Culpepper, who was the largest man in town by far and had decided to come as the Michelin Man. Others were harder, like the mummy she suspected was actually Bob Goodman, and a classic ghost in a white sheet, who could have been anybody. She'd just polished off her potion when Bill appeared, costumed as a green-tinted Frankenstein carrying a red plastic cup of draft beer.

"Having a good time?" he asked.

Lucy gave him her last zombie finger. "Yeah. This is

fun, and I'm really happy that it's so successful. It was a lot of work, but I think we pulled it off."

He bit into the crunchy baked pastry, helped it down with a gulp of beer, and nodded in agreement. "Have you seen Ty and Heather?" he asked. "I want to congratulate them . . ."

Lucy finished the sentence for him: "And find out when you can start demo?"

"That too," he said, laughing.

She scanned the crowd and spotted a tall, gangly scarecrow from the *Wizard of Oz* movie. "I think that's Ty over there," she said, pointing him out. She continued to search for Heather, who, she was sure, would have remained in her flattering Ophelia costume, but saw no sign of a small woman wearing a long, red wig and a medieval robe. "But I don't see Heather."

"The party was her idea," said Bill. "She wouldn't miss it."

"I didn't see her come downstairs with the rest of us," said Lucy, growing concerned. "I think I better go up and make sure she's all right. That bathtub arrangement's a bit tricky, and she might've fallen trying to get out."

"Okay," said Bill, studying his empty cup. "I'll get a refill and go talk to Ty."

Lucy gave him her empty plate and beaker and headed for the stairs, which were now littered with scraps from people's costumes as well as a number of discarded paper plates and cups. She made her way through the mess, clucking with disapproval, and along the dimly lit hall to the bathroom.

Oddly, she thought, the door was shut. Well, maybe somebody was using the toilet, which still worked and was disguised behind a screen. Just in case, she knocked on the door with a few polite taps.

Receiving no reply, she turned the knob and cautiously opened the door, half expecting a voice to say, "Occupied, just a minute, please."

Hearing no such warning, she pushed the door open wider and reached for the string dangling from the old-fashioned ceiling light. Giving it a yank, and blinking from the sudden brightness, she spotted an arm hanging limply over the side of the tub. Dashing across the small room, she found Heather, eyes closed, still lying amid the plastic sheeting, fake bubbles, and stringy green reeds. For a moment, she feared the worst, that Heather was dead, but wrapped her hand around that dangling wrist and discovered a pulse. She was alive, but barely. Lucy dashed for the stairs, and help, before it was too late to save her.

Chapter Four

Returning to the party, Lucy searched frantically among the costumed revelers for a first responder and finally spotted Barney helping himself to refreshments. She told him about Heather, and he produced his official walkie-talkie from beneath his costume and called for help, at the same time making his way through the crowd and pounding up the stairs. Reaching the bathroom, he handed the device to Lucy and immediately began CPR.

"Tell 'em it's a drug overdose," he said, panting a bit as he compressed Heather's bird-like chest. "We need 'em fast."

Lucy obliged, learning from the dispatcher that the ambulance was already on its way. Moments later, she heard the siren, growing louder as the ambulance grew closer; then it abruptly ceased when it arrived at the haunted house. The party was still in full swing but fell silent as the rescuers entered; Lucy went to the top of the stairs and yelled for them to come on up.

Then she and Barney stepped aside as Heather was quickly examined. An oxygen mask was fixed to her face, and she was then lifted from the tub and laid on a stretcher. One of the EMTs quickly established an IV line, and then they were off, carrying her downstairs. Lucy watched from the upstairs hall, which gave her a bird's-eye view of the scene below. She saw them pause at the bottom of the stairs, where they popped open the legs to raise the gurney, which they wheeled through the watching crowd to the door. There they were suddenly confronted by Ty, still dressed in his scarecrow costume. "What's going on?" he demanded. Recognizing Heather beneath the oxygen mask, he reeled a step or two backward, then gathered himself together and followed them out to the waiting ambulance.

Lucy turned back, expecting to see Barney, but he was already searching the bathroom for evidence, along with several other officers, including police chief Jim Kirwan, who was dressed as a magician in top hat and tails. Seeing her, Kirwan joined her in the hall. "So tell me what happened," he coaxed, recording her on his cell phone.

"I was at the party," began Lucy, speaking rapidly, "and realized I hadn't seen Heather, so I came upstairs to check on her. I found her in the tub, unconscious, so I grabbed Barney—he was the first person I saw—and he called for help and started CPR."

"Why did you think you should check on her?"

"Well, these tableaux are all kind of patched together, there's wiring and lights and scenery, and when I didn't see her at the party, I thought she might have tripped on a cable or got tangled up and fell climbing out of the tub.

She was supposed to be the model for a famous painting of Ophelia. Kevin Kenneally was the artist. He might know something . . ."

"Kevin was here?"

"Yeah. He was there at the easel," said Lucy, pointing at the easel, now folded and propped against the wall. His palette was there, too, on the floor.

"And she was unconscious when you found her?"

"Yeah. Still in the tub." Lucy pictured the scene in her mind. "I was afraid she was dead. One arm was out, hanging over the side, and I felt it for a pulse. I thought I felt something, so I ran downstairs for help . . ."

"You did the right thing," said the chief, patting her shoulder. "You've probably saved her life."

Barney came to the bathroom door, and Kirwan turned to him. "You oughta see this, Chief," he said.

"Thanks for your help, Lucy," said the chief, with a nod, dismissing her. Lucy was dying to know what the investigators had found, but the chief had closed the bathroom door behind him, shutting her out.

Sighing, she went back downstairs, slowly. The Lobster Claws had toned down the volume and were playing a James Taylor tune; a few people were slow-dancing, but most were gathered in small groups, talking quietly. After searching through the living room area, Lucy found Sue and her husband, Sid, standing with Bill in the dining room, just outside the kitchen door.

Bill quickly wrapped her in his arms. "How are you?"

"I'm okay."

"That was real quick action," said Sid. "The minute I saw you, I knew something was up."

"Barney said it was a drug overdose," she said, speaking slowly and sounding doubtful. She turned to Sue. "Do you think that's likely? Do you think Heather was a user?"

Sue shrugged. "Who knows what people do in their spare time? It's possible, I guess, but I have to say I never thought that Ophelia gig was a good idea. Too many things could go wrong."

"Well, something did," said Sid, taking his wife's hand. "I guess we'll call it a night."

"Us, too," said Bill, wrapping his arm around Lucy's waist and leading her through the nearly empty rooms, where the Lobster Claws had begun packing up their instruments. The once-festive rooms were now nearly deserted, the floor strewn with fallen paper streamers and crushed cups.

"Hell of a party," said Bill, opening the door.

Lucy didn't respond. In her mind, she was back in that bathroom, replaying the awful moment when she'd found Heather.

Next morning, she went to the IGA to do her weekly grocery shopping and ran into Barney's wife, Marge, at the deli counter. Marge was tall and carried a few extra pounds, but they didn't slow her down. She was a brisk, no-nonsense woman who kept her curly gray hair clipped in a short cut and wore comfortable plus-size knits. After requesting two pounds of ham, two pounds of American cheese, and one pound of roast beef, she greeted Lucy.

"Terrible news about that poor Heather Moon." She clucked her tongue and shook her head. "Drugs."

"I guess she's got a long road ahead. I hope she goes straight into rehab and gets herself straightened out."

Marge pressed her lips together. "Haven't you heard?"

Lucy had a horrible sinking feeling in her stomach. "Heard what?"

Marge wasn't one to beat about the bush. "She died. She was DOA. Fentanyl, they say."

Lucy reached for the glass-fronted deli case to steady herself. "She didn't make it to the hospital?"

Marge reached up and took the packs of cold cuts off the counter. "Thanks," she told the clerk, with a little smile, then turned to Lucy. "They gave her Narcan, did everything they could, but . . ." She shrugged and put the packs of meat and cheese in her cart. "I'm sorry, Lucy. I thought you'd heard. It was on the radio."

"No, I hadn't heard," said Lucy, who could almost feel Heather's fluttery pulse beneath her fingers, and could still see the way her long hair fell across her pale face, her colorless lips.

"It's a terrible thing; she was so young," said Marge. "What a waste." She sighed heavily and put her hands on the cart's handle. "Imagine going through all that chemo and beating cancer and then," she lifted one hand in a little wave, "pffft."

"Can I get you something?" asked the clerk.

Lucy couldn't remember what she'd intended to buy. "Uh, no, thanks," she said, turning back to Marge. "Her poor husband. They had such plans. They were going to fix up the house and start a family." She paused, remembering how happy and excited Ty had seemed when they were working together to paint the hallway. "He must be devastated."

"I don't know about that," said Marge. "The police brought him in for questioning, took him straight from the hospital."

"They did?"

"Of course. Those were illegal drugs, and they want to know how she got them." She leaned close to Lucy and lowered her voice. "They suspect he actually supplied them."

Lucy didn't like the way this was going. "But that means . . ."

Marge nodded. "That means he could be tried for manslaughter—even murder, if they can prove a motive."

Lucy wandered through the store, shopping list in hand, but even though she knew the store like the back of her hand, she couldn't seem to find anything. The products all merged together in a blur; she couldn't tell the Raisin Bran from the Froot Loops, the toilet paper from the paper towels, and the wall of yogurt completely baffled her. Her cart was only half full when she went to the checkout.

The cashier, Dot Kirwan, noticed right away. "Light week?" she asked, scanning a loaf of bread, then moving on to some canned goods.

"I'm not myself," admitted Lucy. "I just heard about Heather Moon."

"Jim told me you found her and called for help." Dot was the police chief's mother and related to numerous other Kirwans who worked in the police and fire department. She plopped a bunch of bananas on the scale. "Must have been upsetting."

"I thought they'd be able to save her."

Dot reached for a pound of butter. "These drugs are so risky, I don't know why people do it. They call it 'recreational,' but I don't get it; I don't see how it's worth risking your life to get high." She shook her head, scanning a pack of ground beef. "My Danny, he's an EMT, he tells me half the time you save somebody from an overdose on

Friday, and on Saturday you get another call and have to do the same thing all over again. You'd think they'd learn from a close call like that, but they don't; the first thing they do when they get out of the hospital is get more drugs." She hit the TOTAL button rather harder than necessary. "That'll be forty-three nineteen."

On the way home, Lucy detoured down School Street past the Moon house. She drove slowly, noticing that the sign advertising the haunted house fundraiser was still in place, the black-painted plywood cutout of a witch on a broomstick still rode above the roof, and strips of yellow crime-scene tape fluttered from the porch. That yellow tape would have been a nice touch yesterday, a sort of macabre flourish, thought Lucy. Today, however, it had an entirely different meaning. It was for real.

She went through the rest of her weekend chores in a sort of haze: She changed the sheets on the beds and cleaned the bathrooms; she cooked up a big batch of chili and raked leaves off the lawn. She yanked the dying tomato plants out of the garden, but left the leeks and the kale, which benefited from cool weather. She did these things automatically; it was as if her brain had split in two. One half took care of these familiar tasks, while the other half struggled to understand why Heather had indulged in such risky behavior. Why would she take possibly lethal drugs after surviving a grueling battle with cancer? Why?

That question was still on her mind when she went to work at the newspaper on Monday morning.

Phyllis greeted her with a small smile, and Lucy noticed she hadn't dressed with her usual flair. Phyllis enjoyed dressing to suit the holiday, all holidays, and in October went in for sweaters and sweatshirts trimmed with falling leaves, jack-o'-lanterns, and witches on broomsticks, occasionally even going so far as to dye her hair orange. Today, however, she'd opted for a plain, navy-blue turtleneck and jeans; a pair of dangling black cat earrings was her only reference to the coming holiday. "Heck of a thing, a young woman dying like that," she said, adding a big sigh.

"You said it," agreed Lucy, starting to unzip her lightweight parka.

"I wouldn't bother to settle in. Aucoin's announced a press conference at nine at the police station, and Ted wants you to cover it."

Lucy glanced at the antique Regulator clock on the wall, which informed her it was a quarter to. "I guess I might as well go now. Maybe I can get some background." She paused at the door. "Have you heard anything?"

Phyllis shrugged. "I saw Franny at church yesterday, and she said she hasn't seen hide nor hair of Ty since he went off with Heather in the ambulance."

Lucy knew that Franny Small was the Moons' next-door neighbor. "That doesn't mean anything," said Lucy, unwilling to admit that Ty might have had anything to do with Heather's death. "The house was a mess; he might be staying with friends."

"You'd think he'd come by to check on it."

"He's got a lot to deal with right now," said Lucy. "His wife just died. The house is probably the last thing on his mind."

"You're probably right."

"I'll know soon enough," said Lucy, pushing the door open. The little bell was still jangling as she crossed the sidewalk and made her way to the police station on the other side of the street.

"You can go straight down to the Emergency Control Center," said the dispatcher, buzzing her through. The Emergency Control Center in the basement did double duty as a meeting space in the cramped police station. Lucy knew the way, taking the stairs located just beyond the locked steel door that sealed the lobby off from the rest of the station.

A number of chairs had been set up in the underground bunker, and they were already filled by a handful of other reporters. NECN and the Portland news station had set up cameras, which Lucy took to be a bad sign indicating that the DA was prepared to make a major announcement.

Aucoin and Kenneally entered on the dot of nine, along with Jim Kirwan, and all three took their places, lining up behind a podium containing a couple of waiting microphones. Aucoin was first to speak, thanking everyone for coming. He then cleared his throat and began reading from a sheet of paper. "After a thorough investigation, this department is charging Tyler Monteith Moon, age thirty-three, with first-degree murder in the death of his wife, Heather Moon, age twenty-nine, on Friday evening. It is believed that Moon caused his wife's death by substituting a lethal dose of fentanyl for the opioid painkillers she occasionally used."

Lucy had been expecting this, after her conversation with Marge, but it still came as a shock. She sat for a minute, trying to process this development, trying to reconcile the Ty she'd worked alongside painting the haunted house with Ty the accused murderer. She was struggling to imagine how Ty—or anyone, for that matter—could even dream of killing the fragile, ethereal, beautiful creature that was Heather.

"And now, I'm passing the mic to my colleague, Assistant District Attorney Kevin Kenneally," said Aucoin, stepping back so Kenneally could take the podium.

"I would now like to speak to motive," he began. "We believe Ty Moon was motivated by the fact that Heather Moon, who had recently undergone chemotherapy for non-Hodgkin's lymphoma, had recently come into a large inheritance. Ty Moon wanted the good life, he wanted a family, and he didn't want to be tied to a sickly wife." He paused. "Any questions?"

Lucy's hand shot up, and she got a nod from Kenneally. "Has Ty Moon confessed to any of this?"

"No. He denies the charges."

Another reporter jumped in. "When's the arraignment?"

"Later this morning."

"What's the evidence?" demanded another.

Kenneally turned to the chief, who stepped up to the mic. "I'm not free to disclose details, but I can say that our investigation found ample evidence that clearly links Moon to his wife's death."

The questions and answers flew fast and furiously, but Lucy just sat there, scribbling it all down in her notebook. Her ears were hearing, her mind was processing the data, and her hand was writing it all down, but her heart was not accepting the information. She simply couldn't believe that Ty was guilty.

Chapter Five

Lucy was just leaving the police station when she got a text from Ted informing her that Ty had hired Bob Goodman to defend him and assigning her to write a profile of Ty. Bob was already at the courthouse, awaiting the arraignment, so she decided to start by calling Rosie Capshaw.

Rosie wasn't eager to talk. "This is for the paper, right?" she asked.

"Yeah. I'm just looking for some perspective from the people who knew Ty and Heather best." Lucy was at her desk, staring at the photos of her kids, taken when they were still in elementary school, and wondering how well she knew them now that they were adults living out in the world. "Did you know that Heather was into drugs?"

"Pot's legal now, you know, so sure. I've been growing my three plants, and so are a lot of other people.

Heather was dealing with a lot, you know, with the chemo and cancer and moving into a new community. She said that grass really helped with the pain and anxiety she was experiencing."

"She didn't die from using grass," said Lucy. "What about heavier drugs?"

"I wouldn't know about that," said Rosie, in a clipped tone.

Lucy decided to change her tactics. "Would you say that Ty and Heather were a happy couple?"

Rosie took her time before answering, and Lucy was beginning to wonder if she was still on the line when she finally spoke. "Who knows what really goes on in a marriage?"

"What do you mean by that?"

"Exactly what I said. They seemed happy, but now Ty's been charged with killing her. The cops must've found some evidence; I don't think they just made up a charge like that. It makes you wonder if what you thought was happening was actually what was going on." She paused. "I'll say this, I always thought Ty was the dominant partner. Heather always seemed to defer to him. She wouldn't do anything unless he approved. Like if I asked her to meet me for lunch or to come by for a glass of wine, she'd always say she had to check with Ty."

"And did Ty ever say no?"

There was another long pause. "Yeah. Sometimes he did."

"Did she give a reason for that? Like she forgot they made plans or something?"

"No. She'd say something like 'Ty doesn't think I should.'" She paused. "Sometimes I wondered if that was just an excuse, something Heather made up because she didn't feel like going out."

"Interesting," said Lucy, remembering her initial suspicion about Ty when she first met him and thought he was extremely controlling and even suspected he was abusing his wife. As she got to know him better, she'd changed her opinion, but now she was wondering if her first impression was possibly correct. "Anything else you'd like to add?"

"Uh, no. I've probably said too much already."

"I don't have to use your name," offered Lucy, hoping to get more information.

"Thanks. That makes me feel better."

"No problem," said Lucy. "Who else should I call?"

"Matt and Luisa, maybe? Brendan? We all hung out together. Kevin, too, but as assistant DA, he's prosecuting . . ."

"Right," said Lucy. "Thanks for your help."

Lucy's next call was to Luisa Rodriguez, but she said she was too upset about Heather's death to talk. Her brother, Matt, claimed he knew nothing about any illegal drugs in Tinker's Cove and declared he believed Ty was one hundred percent innocent. Brendan Coyle said only that he refused to judge people. "My mother used to say that if you want to know someone, you should walk a mile in their shoes."

That caused Lucy to smile. "That's what my mother used to say, too."

"Well, it's good advice."

Figuring that she'd struck out in her conversations with Ty's friends, Lucy decided to tap into a richer source of information and dialed Franny Small.

After exchanging pleasantries, Lucy got down to business. "You were the Moons' next-door neighbor, after all. How did they seem to you?"

"Weird, that's how they seemed. There was all that business with the moans and noises and flashing lights when they moved in, but that was all connected to his work, so I got used to it. But they were never friendly. Not at all, not even a wave if you happened to see them coming or going. And that's the only time I saw them outside the house. They didn't use their backyard at all; they were always either in the house or leaving to go somewhere. They didn't work in the yard or garden, nothing like that. They had landscapers mow the grass, but they never even sat outside of a summer evening, say, to relax and enjoy the fresh air." Pausing a moment for breath, she added her most damning observation. "They didn't even feed the birds!"

"Did they have company? Did people come for dinner or anything?"

"Not until they started working on that haunted house party. That was the first time I saw other folks at the house."

"Did they give you and the other neighbors a heads-up about the haunted house? You know, do the neighborly thing and let you know what was going on, and maybe even ask for your help?"

Franny laughed. "Not a peep. Even after that whole thing with your grandson and the SWAT team, not a word. He just kept on doing what he did, noises and lights and all. I mean, sometimes it was impossible to sleep."

"Did you approach him? Tell him he was disturbing you?"

"No," admitted Franny. "To tell the truth, I was afraid of him. I didn't want to get involved, if you know what I mean."

Lucy thought she did. Some people were approachable, and some weren't, and Ty Moon was one of the latter. There was something about him that was like a big warning sign—danger, falling rocks, something that made you want to keep your distance. She'd thought she'd broken through the barrier and discovered there was nothing to fear, after all, but now she was beginning to wonder if she'd been fooled. Abusers were often master manipulators, and maybe he'd simply told her what she wanted to hear and convinced her of what she already wanted to believe.

At home that night, she asked Bill if he thought Ty was guilty and got a strong denial. "No way. He adored Heather. Remember, I saw them together when we worked out the plans for the remodel, and he always included her, always asked for her opinion. That's not always the case, you know. A lot of men shut their wives out of the planning or demean their ideas. But not Ty. He sincerely wanted to give Heather everything she wanted."

Lucy had done numerous stories about domestic abuse and was familiar with the abuser's cycle of violence, which often included a period of contrition and even apology. She found herself wondering if Ty had a guilty conscience and was trying to make amends with Heather for something he had done.

"Do you think he was afraid of losing her?" she asked.

"What kind of question is that?" demanded Bill, who was seated at the kitchen table. "A guy treats his wife nicely, and you start suspecting his motives?"

"Well, it's not an unreasonable reaction," said Lucy, putting a pot away in the cabinet. "He has been charged with killing her."

"Sorry, but I just don't see the guy as a wife killer."

"Maybe that's what he was counting on," said Lucy, standing behind her husband and stroking his hair. "Maybe he was just playing the part of a loving husband."

First thing on Tuesday morning, Lucy got a call from Bob Goodman. "I just want to let you know that I'm planning to mount a strong defense for Ty Moon, who is definitely not guilty of murdering his wife. And I'm happy to say the judge was not impressed by the prosecution's argument that Ty was a flight risk and a danger to the public. He pointed to Ty's absolutely clean record, not even a parking ticket, and decided to grant bail. I'm happy to report that Ty has been released from custody and is now eagerly awaiting trial and the opportunity to prove his innocence of these outrageous charges."

"Thanks for the update," said Lucy, wondering how the community would take this news. She had a feeling that many people would not be happy with the judge's decision. "So is he going back to the house on School Street?"

"Not just yet," said Bob. "We decided it would be best for him to lay low for a while, until things die down."

"So where's he going?"

"I'm not free to give you that information. But I will remain in constant touch with him, and he will appear for trial. The date has not been set yet, but I will let you know when it is."

"Well, thanks, Bob. Anything you want to add about your client?"

"Only that he is devastated by the loss of his wife; he's grieving, and he won't rest until the truth about her death is known."

"Okay," said Lucy, who had been clicking away on her keyboard, getting every word.

"And, oh, before I go, Rachel wanted me to remind you about the Hat and Mitten Fund party on Friday. Make sure there's a notice in the paper, okay?"

"I haven't forgotten; it's on page one," said Lucy, smiling.

When Friday rolled around, Lucy was ready for some welcome distraction from the Moon story. She understood why readers were fascinated by the sensational tale involving drugs and murder that was unfolding in their own town, but for the most part, they had the advantage of a certain distance. Ty and Heather were like actors on a stage to them, but she actually knew them and found the whole story terribly depressing. As she drove through town to the Community Church, where the annual Hat and Mitten Fund Halloween party took place, she resolutely tucked all thoughts of the Moons into the back of her mind and focused instead on all the various holiday decorations people had put out. It seemed that staid, reserved Mainers who limited Christmas décor to a simple swag on the front door tended to go overboard for Halloween. Maybe it was the riot of fall color in the forest that inspired them, or maybe it was the hint of the macabre that impelled them to set out scarecrows and harvest figures on their lawns. Not to mention huge, inflatable jack-o'-lanterns, enormous purple spiders perched on porch roofs, and fluttering ghosts hanging from trees. And there was always the classic witch that had unfortunately crashed into a tree or even a chimney.

The party was just getting started when she arrived, and a line of costumed kids and their caregivers were entering the basement room. She could hear the DJ playing "Monster Mash," and the cries of the kids as they discovered the games and treats inside. She slipped past the line with an apologetic smile and popped into the kitchen to change into her witch costume. Sue was not impressed.

"You're not going to be a witch again?" she said, watching as Lucy wiggled into the long black dress.

"Why not? It's a classic." Lucy noticed that Sue was dressed entirely in gray and had added a necklace of paint chips, also all gray. "What in the world are you supposed to be? A foggy day?"

"Think, Lucy, think."

"Gray Gables?"

Sue exhaled and rolled her eyes. "Come on, Lucy. You've certainly heard of *Fifty Shades of Grey*, haven't you?"

Lucy plopped her pointy witch's hat on her head and grinned broadly. "That is clever! I wish I could think of something like that."

"Once more into the fray," said Sue, as they left the quiet of the kitchen and entered the madhouse beyond the swinging door.

The music was pounding, kids were dancing and dashing from game to game, dropping candy and spilling drinks in their haste to see and do everything. There were all sorts of games: bean bag tosses, bobbing for apples, a marshmallow shooting gallery, a ball toss, and, of course, Rachel's Madame Zenda. Lucy took her place behind the refreshment table, which was covered with a colorful assortment of ghoulish treats: zombie fingers, meringue ghosts, eyeball cupcakes, mummy pretzel rods, jack-o'-lantern cookies, and devil's food Draculas. Lucy was particularly impressed by the Franken-munchies, Rice Krispies treats that had been dyed purple and trimmed with fruit leather and marshmallows to resemble Frankenstein's monster.

Stella Rose Levitt, however, was not impressed. "There's no such thing as purple Rice Krispies," she declared, stamping her foot and making her curly hair bounce. She was dressed as a fairy, in a gauzy dress complete with wings and a little sparkly wand.

"Wouldn't you like to try one?" asked Lucy, smiling down at the little four-year-old. "Give them a taste test?"

"No! I know everything, and I know there's no such thing as purple Rice Krispies! Yuck!"

"Perhaps you'd like a smiling skeleton cookie?" offered Lydia Volpe, taking her place beside Lucy at the table. "They're just plain cookies with some sugar icing."

"Sugar's not good for you, you know."

"It's all right to have a treat once in a while," said Lucy.

"No. My mom says sugar makes me crazy."

"Your mother may have a point," said Lydia, who was a retired kindergarten teacher. "Why don't you try bobbing for apples?"

"I don't wanna get wet!"

"Do you see that little tent over there?" asked Lucy, pointing. "There's a very wise fortune-teller in there, who can see the future and tell you all about it."

"My mom says nobody can see the future."

"Well, you might try dancing to the music, or what about the bean bag toss," suggested Lydia.

"This party is dumb," said Stella Rose, turning on her heel and running off.

"Wow," said Lucy, turning to Lydia. "She's a tough little cookie."

"They all are; kids are a lot smarter than they used to be. I retired just in time, before the screen generation arrived."

"I was so shocked one day when I saw a tiny toddler in a stroller swiping away on her mother's cell phone," said Lucy.

"It was probably the tyke's own cell phone," said Lydia, offering a tray of cupcakes to a little boy in a superhero costume and watching with dismay as he took two. "Hey, it's one to a person," she informed him in her teacher voice.

"Not if you can't catch me!" he cried, dashing off with a cupcake in each hand.

"Typical," said Pam, joining her two friends. "Kids today."

"The winds of change do seem to be blowing, even here in Tinker's Cove," said Lucy.

"And not in a good way," offered Lydia. "I've seen young people wearing pajamas in the supermarket!"

"And the cars, have you noticed the cars?" said Lucy. "I was happy to have a second-hand Subaru when I was a young mom, but now they're all driving Audis and Volvos and Range Rovers."

"Not everybody," said Lydia. "A lot of kids qualify for reduced lunch, you know."

"And I bet a lot of others are bringing fancy whole-grain goodies in their reusable, organic lunch bags," said Pam.

"Face it," said Lucy, "house prices around here are out of reach unless you're a professional with a big income. That means we've got yuppie newcomers with plenty of money and the poor folks who are living with Mom and Dad in the old family farmhouse, or maybe they've plunked down a trailer in the front yard."

"Ted says it's not sustainable," offered Pam. "He worries about the future of towns like Tinker's Cove. He says we're losing the sense of community and shared values that made us special."

"I think he's right," said Lydia, with a sigh. "It's getting harder and harder for folks to raise a family here."

Looking out across the room at all the children in their Halloween costumes, Lucy hoped Lydia and Pam were wrong. Times changed, but kids were kids, weren't they?

Chapter Six

Lucy was out campaigning for Bob at the IGA again on Saturday morning, distributing handouts and chatting up potential voters. She found it quite a pleasant experience, as she discovered she knew more people than she thought and was enjoying catching up with folks she hadn't seen in a while, like her Prudence Path neighbor Frankie LaChance, whose daughter, Renee, was pursuing graduate studies at the University of St. Andrews in Scotland. She was enjoying a vicarious glow of pride over Renee's accomplishments when she spotted Rosie Capshaw, dressed in her usual uniform of paint-stained farmer's overalls, pushing an empty cart across the parking lot.

"Hi, Rosie," she called, adding a little wave. "Have you got a minute?"

Rosie didn't seem inclined to linger. "Actually, I'm in a bit of a rush . . ."

Lucy suspected Rosie might be trying to avoid further questions about Ty and Heather and was quick to inform her that she was campaigning for Bob Goodman. "Can I give you one of these flyers? It's full of good information about Bob."

"Sure, thanks," said Rosie, giving the cart a push and then stopping in mid-stride, as if she suddenly remembered something. "Hey, you know, I've got the money from the haunted house party, and I don't know what to do with it."

"Oh, golly," exclaimed Lucy, horrified that the money had been overlooked in the excitement about Heather. "I never gave it a thought. I figured whoever was supposed to have it actually had it."

"No. The kitty was sitting there by the door after everybody left, so I grabbed it to keep it safe. What should I do with it?"

"I don't really have a clue," said Lucy, who knew the Hat and Mitten Fund hadn't been involved in the financial arrangements. "I suppose there were expenses and donations and all. Who was keeping track of all that?"

"It was actually Heather. Well, she was supposed to do it, but she found it was too much, so I was helping her."

"So you've got all the figures?" asked Lucy. "Why don't you just tote it up, pay any outstanding bills, and give whatever's left over in a check to the Hat and Mitten fund?"

"I'm really not comfortable doing it all by myself." Rosie glanced down at her black-and-white-checked Vans. "I'm no bookkeeper; I can't actually balance my checkbook," she confessed. "And considering everything that's happened, I'd really appreciate some oversight, in case there are any questions." She glanced around. "I don't want anybody to think that the finances weren't, well, you know, aboveboard."

"I don't think you need to worry about that! After all, you're the one who saved the cash," said Lucy, giving her a reassuring smile. "But I do see your point. Why don't Pam and I meet with you and go over it all? Out of an abundance of caution? Pam's the fund treasurer."

"That would be a big relief. That cash box just weighs on me every time I see it," said Rosie, letting out a huge sigh. "When do you want to meet?"

"I'll check with Pam and get back to you."

The three women met a few days later, choosing the morgue in the newspaper office as the most practical spot. There they had plenty of room to spread out all the various invoices and checks on the big conference table, and the locked door made it a secure place to count up the cash. Lucy was amused to see that Rosie and Pam hit it off immediately; it turned out that they both had been high school cheerleaders. When they were finally done, Pam gave a quick rah-rah cheer and announced that they'd made a tidy profit, thanks to some unexpected donations from Hollywood movie people, including a few celebrities.

"Well, at least something good came out of that nightmare," said Rosie, grabbing the museum tote bag she used as a purse and standing up, ready to leave.

"Before you go, I want to ask about something," said Pam. "This is quite a bit of money. I've been thinking that perhaps we should set it aside in a separate fund; we could name it after Heather and use it for a special scholarship."

Rosie sat back down, dropping the bag on her lap. "That's such a nice idea," she said. "Could you do that?"

"The committee would have to vote, but I think they'd support it," said Pam. "What do you think, Lucy?"

"I think it's a great idea, and I don't think there'd be any problem getting it approved. It would be nice to have some recognition of Heather's contribution. After all, the party was her idea, wasn't it?"

"Absolutely," declared Rosie, excited about Pam's proposal. "Ty wasn't for it at first, you know. She had to convince him it would be good for his career, which had actually kind of fizzled out. He wasn't getting work, and she thought it would be a way to get his name out there. It's the new thing, you know. Get yourself associated with a good cause, like Prince Harry and Meghan Markle."

"I don't think they donated," said Pam, with a naughty grin.

"I don't think they were asked," said Rosie. "Heather stuck to people she and Ty had worked with, or friends of friends, that sort of thing."

Lucy was trying to process this new information; she remembered Bill saying that Ty had landed a big contract that enabled him to renovate their house. "But you say Ty wasn't getting work? How were they going to pay for the renovations?"

"This is completely off the record, Lucy," began Rosie, giving Lucy a stern warning, "but the haunted house was a last-ditch effort by Heather to save her marriage. Ty was jealous of all the attention she received because she was sick, and then she got that inheritance, and he somehow got the idea that she didn't need him anymore, that she thought he wasn't pulling his weight."

"So she came up with the haunted house to show her support for his career?" asked Pam.

"More than that. It was all to prove to him that she loved him," said Rosie.

"I guess that didn't work," observed Pam, "since he killed her."

"You said it," said Rosie, lowering her voice and leaning forward, making eye contact with Pam and Lucy. "I heard, from one of his best friends, that he suspected she was having an affair."

"Was she?" asked Lucy, finding this hard to believe. First it was drugs, now infidelity.

Rosie shrugged. "Not that I knew about. If she was fooling around, she was being very discreet."

"But Ty was suspicious?" asked Lucy.

"More than that, he was determined to find out. And word is, from this friend, that Ty said he could forgive her if she ended the affair, but he'd never let her leave him. He said he'd rather see her dead."

Lucy wasn't convinced that Rosie was telling the truth; she suspected that this so-called friend had concocted the story, but she also couldn't imagine why. She also wondered why Rosie believed it and would pass along such damaging gossip about her friends. On the other hand, Ty's alleged sense of failure and his suspicions about his wife were typical behaviors of abusers. "Do you think that's what happened? Do you really think Ty killed her?"

Rosie nodded and stood up, pausing at the door to put on her jacket. Then she twisted the button that unlocked the door. "That's what it looks like, and if he's guilty, I never want to see Ty again. I hope he goes to jail for-ever," she said, opening the door and marching through the newsroom.

The little bell on the outer door was still jangling when Lucy turned to Pam and asked, "Do you think she's telling the truth?"

Pam's eyes were large with amazement. "I dunno. That was, well, pretty weird."

"Quite a performance, I'd say," said Lucy, remember-ing that Rosie was a puppeteer, skilled at manipulating an audience's emotions. "I worked side by side with Ty, and I got no bad vibes at all. He was a hard worker, and I really got to like him."

"I don't know, Lucy." Pam spoke slowly. "I've done some volunteer work on the domestic abuse hotline, and I know that it's often the people you least suspect who are actually abusers."

"I know," said Lucy, who'd covered terrible stories of abuse, one of which involved a very popular local pedia-trician. She gave a wry smile. "Actually, I don't know. I'm really confused."

"Well, the one thing I believe is the need to really lis-ten to victims of abuse, especially women. For too long, their stories have been disbelieved, or mocked, or turned against them. We've all heard 'she asked for it,' right? Or accusations that she was lying because of some ulterior motive, like getting a decent, hardworking fellow into trouble." She paused to stuff the money into a blue leatherette bank wallet for deposit, then zipped it shut. "I'm not saying we have to believe every word, but I do think we have to listen and take these stories seriously."

Lucy nodded in agreement, but she was determined to keep an open mind about Rosie's accusations. The more she thought about it, the more she thought Rosie, or more probably the mysterious "friend," was simply trying to muddy the waters. On one hand, Heather was portrayed as a loving wife trying to save her marriage, while on the other, she was the unfaithful wife of an abuser. Was it possible that Heather was both?

After Pam left the office, Lucy settled herself at her desk, preparing to write up a story about new recycling regulations at the town's disposal area. It wasn't exactly riveting material, and her mind kept returning to the moment she'd discovered Heather lying unconscious in the tub. In the end, she decided, all she knew for certain was that Heather's death seemed monstrously unfair. She was young, she'd successfully battled cancer to regain her health, and she should have been looking forward to a nice, long life.

She had finally finished up summarizing the new regulations, including the fact that pizza boxes would absolutely not be accepted henceforward, when her phone rang. It was Bob, inviting her to interview Ty Moon, who was now eager to share his side of the story. "He's at your disposal, Lucy, any time you want."

"The sooner, the better," replied Lucy, who was ready to drop everything in order to talk to Ty. Maybe now she'd finally get the answers she was looking for.

As arranged, Lucy went to Bob's law office that evening to interview Ty, bringing with her a list of questions. Bob himself greeted her at the doorway, explaining that since his secretary had left at five, they'd have plenty of privacy. "It's not that I don't trust her, but Ty is understandably nervous these days. There have been threats and nasty phone calls, and he feels as if he has a target on his back."

Lucy wasn't sure how to take this bit of information. Was Bob expecting her to write a flattering puff piece? If so, she decided, he'd chosen the wrong girl for the job. "I've been a reporter for a long time, but people never cease to amaze me," she said. "Just when you think they couldn't go any lower, down they go."

"So true," agreed Bob, helping her take off her jacket and hanging it in the closet. "Come on into my office."

Ty was sitting in one of the two captain's chairs arranged in front of Bob's desk, and he stood up when Lucy came in. "Thanks for coming," he said, looking very serious. It seemed to Lucy that he had shrunk a bit in the last few days, and there were dark circles under his eyes.

"Always interested in a good story," said Lucy, taking the other chair.

Bob settled himself in his usual spot behind the desk, but tilted his chair back and propped his feet on an open drawer, signaling that he was merely an onlooker. Lucy wasn't fooled; she knew it was a pose and that he wouldn't hesitate to jump in and intervene if he felt they were getting into dangerous territory.

"Well, I'm very grateful for the opportunity to clear things up," said Ty. "Thanks for coming, Lucy."

"Let's get started then," began Lucy. "How have you been?"

Ty seemed a bit surprised by the question. "What do you mean? My wife's dead, and I'm accused of killing her. How do you think I am?"

"I don't know; you have to tell me," prompted Lucy.

He let out a huge sigh and slumped forward. "I'm sad; I miss Heather terribly. And I'm angry. I'm angry that somebody took her from me, and I'm angry that I've actually been accused of killing her, and mostly I just want things to go back the way they were, but I know that can never happen." He stared at Bob's framed diplomas from Colby College and the University of Maine School of Law that hung on the wall behind his desk. "Nothing can bring Heather back."

"Did you know she was using drugs?" asked Lucy.

"Yeah. Because of the chemo. She said marijuana really helped her; she had a prescription for medical marijuana."

"But that didn't kill her," said Lucy. "What else was she using?"

"Recreational stuff, nothing serious. A little cocaine now and then. To perk her up, she said."

"Where did she get it?" asked Lucy.

Ty shrugged. "Friends. There's plenty of stuff around."

"You didn't know about any other drugs? Like opioids?"

"Looking back, I should've been more suspicious, I guess. She was tired and depressed a lot, and I figured it was from the chemo and everything. I should've paid closer attention, but I was busy, working. You know how it is."

"I heard you weren't getting much work," said Lucy. "Is that true? Was the haunted house fundraiser designed to promote your career?"

"I don't know where you got that idea," said Ty. "I've been busier than ever, actually turning away work." He looked down at his hands. "Well, until this happened. I've been open with my clients, letting them know that I'm finishing up my current projects, but I'm not taking on anything new, pending the trial."

"And how are they reacting?"

Ty sat up a bit straighter. "I've been surprised. Really quite supportive. They all say they don't believe a word of it, and they're sure I'm innocent." He gave her a half grin and shrugged. "That's what they say; I don't know if it's what they really believe. It's Hollywood, after all."

"There's also a rumor that your marriage was in trouble," said Lucy, uncomfortably aware that she was venturing onto thin ice.

Bob took his feet off the open drawer and sat up, ready to protest, but Ty waved his hand.

"It's okay. There are always rumors, and the DA thinks I was trying to get my hands on Heather's inheritance. It's stupid; we were married. My stuff was hers, and hers was mine; it was always like that with us. We were going to use part of that money to renovate the house. We were happy; we had plans." His voice broke. "We were going to start a family."

Bob gave Lucy an *I hope you're happy now* look, and she felt a bit ashamed of herself, but only a bit. Ty had requested the interview, and if he wasn't ready to answer the tough questions, well, that was just too bad.

"I think we should wrap this up," said Bob, standing up.

"Before I go, is there anything you'd like to add?"

Ty glanced at Bob, then began. "I just want to say that I'm innocent; they've got the wrong guy. I would never do anything to harm Heather, never. And the thing that really bothers me is the fact that while I'm waiting for trial, a dangerous killer is at large and may be ready to strike again."

Bob cleared his throat. "I'd like to add something. I want to make it very clear that Ty is looking forward to the trial, and we are planning a strong defense that will prove beyond any question that he is entirely innocent." He paused. "Did you get that, Lucy?"

"Every word," said Lucy, turning off the cell phone she'd been using to record the interview. There were smiles and thanks all around, but when she left the office and walked to her car, she had mixed feelings. Who should she believe? Was Ty telling the truth? Or was Rosie?

Chapter Seven

Lucy checked her phone for messages when she left Bob's office and noticed a text announcing that Andi Nardone, one of Bob's opponents in the state rep race, was holding a press conference the next morning. Andi hadn't been getting much traction in the campaign so far; her platform was similar to Bob's, but she wasn't as well known, so Lucy was intrigued. Did Andi have some sort of trick up her sleeve?

She was sitting front and center next morning at the Gilead Senior Center, where Andi was scheduled to speak at ten o'clock, but there was no sign of Andi. "Par for the course," said Luke Halloran from the *Portland Press Herald*. He was a veteran reporter who'd pretty much seen it all and wasn't shy about sharing it. "All these candidates run late because they want to look as if they're in great demand and campaigning hard, when what they're mostly doing is deciding what to wear and checking that nothing is stuck in their freshly whitened teeth."

Lucy couldn't help laughing, and he continued. "Andi, for instance, has got to do something about that frizzy hair of hers, and she's got that New York accent, which doesn't fly in Maine. Of course, her biggest handicap is that she's got two X chromosomes; don't ask me why, but voters don't seem to like women much."

Lucy knew there was some truth in Luke's observations but, as a feminist, felt she had to stick up for her gender. "We're making progress, especially in state and local races. There are quite a few women governors these days and growing numbers of women reps in Washington, along with a handful of senators."

"True enough," he admitted, "but, by and large, politics is a man's game."

Lucy was about to challenge that assertion when Andi arrived, accompanied by her campaign manager and sister, Haley Glass. They were both smiling broadly, greeting individual reporters by name as they made their way to the mics in the front of the room. Haley did a quick sound check and then handed the mic over to Andi.

She hadn't straightened her hair, observed Lucy, but she had adopted a blue blazer and red-and-white-striped shirt as her campaign outfit, along with a tight blue skirt and red high heels. It was quite a change from the jeans and duck boots Andi usually wore for her work as owner of Green Thumb Landscaping.

"Thank you all for coming," she began. "As you know, I'm a candidate for state rep, eager to bring some fresh air into that stale old state house."

A good beginning, thought Lucy, and it earned some chuckles from the assembled reporters.

"It's definitely time to weed out some of those non-producers," she continued, getting a few more chuckles. "I think many voters will agree that the incumbent, George Armistead, began to wilt a long time ago."

By now, the media audience was definitely with her, appreciating the quotable material she was serving up for them, and Andi was ready to dish. "While George is stuck back in the nineteen-fifties, I have to say my other opponent isn't much better. Bob Goodman claims to be a progressive, but the fact that he has chosen to defend Ty Moon, an alleged domestic abuser accused of murdering his wife, reveals that his so-called progressive agenda is nothing of the sort. Bob Goodman is a walking, talking example of male privilege, and I challenge him to prove otherwise."

That accusation didn't go over very well, and when Andi paused for breath, hands shot up all over the room. Andi chose Lucy to ask the first question.

"Aren't you forgetting that defendants have the right to a lawyer, and that they are considered innocent until proven guilty?" she asked.

"I have no quarrel with the American system of justice, when it's applied equally and fairly, which we all know it is not. Just ask any African-American or Hispanic citizen who's been forced into a plea deal," declared Andi. "But every attorney also has the right to decide who he or she is going to defend. I submit that by choosing to defend Ty Moon, Bob Goodman has revealed himself to be a misogynist committed to perpetuating male dominance."

"Don't you think you're oversimplifying the situation?" asked Bob Mayes, who was a stringer for the *Boston*

Globe. "We don't know what really happened to Heather Moon."

Andi bristled at this challenge. "Don't know! Heather Moon is dead! What more do we need to know? This young woman was victimized by a society that encourages and permits men to abuse and mistreat women. A society that refuses to take women seriously when they find the courage to speak up and accuse a man of sexual misconduct. Even today, if a woman accuses a man of abusing her, she often finds the tables are turned, and she becomes the defendant."

Catching a warning glance from her sister, Andi realized her voice had risen and she was beginning to sound shrill. She took a moment to catch her breath, then pivoted to a safer topic.

"It's simply true," she continued, in a lower-pitched conversational tone, "that this society discriminates against women across the board, whether it's career advancement, health care, or education. Do you know that women pay double what men do for a haircut? Check out the prices at the dry cleaner for women's and men's clothing; you'll find that women are charged more. And what about drugs? If a menopausal woman needs a little hormone lift, she has to pay ten times more than a man pays for his Viagra! All this at the same time that women earn only eighty cents compared to the dollar that men take home."

As she listened to Andi's back and forth with the reporters, Lucy had to admit that Andi had earned her grudging respect. She'd certainly managed to revive her lackluster campaign with new energy by accusing Bob Goodman of being a male chauvinist, but Lucy wondered if the accusation would stick or if the issue would actually matter to voters. George Armistead had held his seat for decades, and he could hardly be described as a feminist. Eventually, the questions died down, and Andi closed the press conference by declaring that she was ready, willing, and able to take on both George Armistead and Bob Goodman at the upcoming debate.

As Lucy gathered up her things and made her way to the door, she was met by Haley Glass. "Lucy, I'm so glad you could come," she said, blocking the exit.

"Just part of the job," said Lucy.

"I know you and Bob Goodman are friends," said Haley, "and your publisher, too, I think."

Lucy didn't like the sound of this. "I don't know what you're insinuating."

"Nothing at all. I'm sure you and Ted strive to maintain the highest journalistic standards." She paused. "But it would sure look funny if Ted endorsed his friend as the best candidate, wouldn't it?"

Lucy found herself laughing. "Readers know and trust Ted; they know he's fair and honest, and his endorsements are thoughtful and well-reasoned. He will endorse the candidate he feels will best serve the community." She paused. "Satisfied?"

"Of course, that's all I'm asking for."

"Well," said Lucy, climbing on her high horse, "you didn't need to ask. It's a given." And with that, she brushed past Haley and marched out the door.

When she got back to the office, however, her sense of satisfaction at putting down Haley quickly evaporated. "A new poll from Winchester College is just out," said Ted, looking glum. "Bob's lead has dropped five percent."

"But he's still ahead?" asked Lucy. It occurred to her

that even though professional ethics required impartial reporting, it was impossible for journalists to remain personally impartial, especially when they were covering friends. Or, she realized with a sense of dismay, enemies.

"Barely," said Ted. "Believe it or not, George Armistead is gaining. His 'old-fashioned morals' issue is working for him. Never mind income disparity, climate change, institutional racism, and voter suppression; according to George, the most pressing issue facing the nation is moral decay."

That was a bit of a surprise to Lucy. "What about Andi?"

"Her numbers are flat."

"I have a feeling they're going to start climbing; she's accusing Bob of perpetuating male dominance by defending Ty Moon."

"Smart move," said Phyllis, playing with the orange bead necklace resting on her ample bosom. "Combines the moral issue and a play to women voters."

"Time will tell," said Ted, philosophically. "Write it up, Lucy, okay? Run the poll as a sidebar with the Andi Nardone press conference."

"Okay, boss." Lucy got to work, resolutely shelving her fondness for Bob and striving to present Andi's accusations in a completely straightforward manner, even though they angered her. Her instinct was to defend Bob, a man she knew well and highly esteemed, but that wasn't her job. Besides, she had every confidence that Bob was more than capable of defending himself at the debate and would score an easy win over both his opponents.

Her confidence was shaken, however, when a press release arrived from the DA announcing he was dropping all charges against Ty; Lucy feared Andi would claim that as further proof of the old boys' network in action. "We simply don't have enough evidence to go forward," said Phil Aucoin, when Lucy called to follow up on the announcement. "A supply of drugs, including various opioids, cocaine, and heroin, was found in the bathroom vanity, but there were no prints and no evidence at all linking them to Ty Moon. That house was like a sieve, people were in and out for weeks preparing for the fundraiser. Anybody could have stashed them there."

"Why would they do that?"

"Maybe somebody was dealing; all those volunteers coming and going would have been great cover for a dealer. Remember, this was an artsy crowd, probably not averse to a little recreational drug use. Or maybe the drugs were going to be distributed at the party." He sighed. "All I know is, the forensics simply weren't there. And as for motive, that didn't pan out either."

Her next call was to Bob, who shared her fears that voters would take Aucoin's action as proof that Andi Nardone's accusations rang true. "Now people will think there's some sort of underhanded dealing between me and the DA's office. All us guys sticking together . . ."

"That's outrageous," said Lucy, who knew that Bob and Phil Aucoin had their differences, which sometimes erupted in contentious conflicts in and out of court.

"Honestly, I'm happy for Ty, but this couldn't have come at a worse time for me, what with Andi Nardone's claims of sexism and the debate only days away."

It was after one o'clock when Lucy hit the SEND button and decided to treat herself to a couple of cider donuts from MacDonald's farm stand. Not the most nutritious lunch, she reminded herself, but she hadn't had even one cider donut this fall, and she knew they would soon be gone, along with the brightly colored foliage on the maple trees.

It was only a short drive to the farm stand, which offered a corn maze, pick-your-own pumpkins, and dozens of varieties of apples. Apple cider was also featured, along with the delicious donuts. Lucy found herself browsing among the bins of apples, eventually deciding on a peck of winesaps, and it was there that she spotted Juliette Duff.

Lucy had helped Juliette during a family tragedy a few years ago, so she didn't hesitate to greet the famous supermodel. While some models looked marvelous in photographs but tended to be gaunt and emaciated in real life, Juliette looked terrific all the time, whether she was posing for *Vogue* in a designer ball gown or shopping for apples in jeans and a sweatshirt. She had perfect proportions, and each feature was exactly where it should be; her gorgeous blond hair looked natural, even though it wasn't, and she had an easy-going, friendly attitude that seemed to say, "I'm just a regular girl."

"Hi, there," said Lucy, greeting her with a big smile. "Are you here for long?" She knew that Juliette's career kept her away from her home in Tinker's Cove for much of the time.

"I've got a week off, and this is my favorite season. I love the apples and"—she sighed and rolled her eyes— "the cider donuts."

"Me, too," said Lucy. "I'm having a late lunch. Want to join me?"

"Sure." The two women supplied themselves with a half-dozen donuts to share, along with a jug of apple cider, and seated themselves on a convenient bale of straw.

"I'm sorry about Heather," began Lucy, "I know you were friends."

"It's terrible, and they accused Ty! I felt so bad for him."

"They've dropped all charges," said Lucy, biting into her donut.

"That's a relief." Juliette was studying her donut, as if considering where to begin eating it. "He adored Heather; he would never hurt her."

"That was my impression, too," said Lucy, polishing off her first donut. "I got to know him a little bit when we were working to set up the haunted house. I really liked him. He was fun and so creative. And a hard worker."

"That's Ty." Juliette took a tiny bite of her donut and chewed thoughtfully. "I'll give him a call."

"I know he'd love to hear from you. He really needs his friends now." Lucy was considering eating a second donut but didn't want to seem piggy in front of Juliette, who still had only taken a few tiny bites of hers.

"I suppose people are being terrible," said Juliette, who'd experienced the hate mail that was the downside of a high-profile career.

"He's been lying low," said Lucy, deciding that the donuts really were rather small and reaching into the bag for another. "I gotta say, I never suspected Heather of using drugs, especially after all she'd been through with chemo. Did you?"

"I think a lot of people use medical marijuana during chemo," said Juliette, speaking slowly and thoughtfully.

"She was doing more than that," said Lucy, realizing that she'd almost finished that very small donut. "The cops found cocaine, oxy, all sorts of bad stuff, including heroin, in the bathroom."

Juliette sighed. "There's a lot of drugs in the modeling world, I'm afraid. Mostly diet pills, amphetamines, stuff like that, but I've always stayed clear of them. I don't even take aspirin."

Juliette was wrapping up the remaining half of her donut in a paper napkin, and Lucy wondered if she was actually saving it for later. "If I have a headache, I go for a walk, get some fresh air. Or do some yoga, something like that. I know myself pretty well, and if I have aches and pains, I know just what to do. Or if I'm anxious, I go for the deep breathing. I concentrate on the in and out and clear my mind."

"What if you're hungry?" asked Lucy, thinking about a third donut.

Juliette laughed. "I'm always hungry. That's just the way it is."

"Wow," said Lucy, unscrewing the cap on the cider and filling the paper cup decorated with the MacDonald Farm logo that was offered with cider purchases. "I wish I could be like that."

"Believe me, when I retire, I'm going to eat everything, and I mean everything! Every darn thing that I've been denying myself, starting with pizza!"

Lucy laughed. "Good for you." She drank some cider, savoring its delicious tangy taste and the slight fizz that tickled her tongue. "I don't suppose you know where Heather got her drugs, do you?"

Juliette filled her cup halfway with cider and took a sip, then stared into the cup, running her finger around the rim. "No idea," she said. "If I did, I'd be tempted to commit murder myself."

"I know how you feel," said Lucy, biting into that third donut.

Chapter Eight

Okay, thought Lucy, starting her car. So Juliette pleaded complete ignorance about illegal drugs—good for her. She drove carefully through the busy parking lot and paused at the road, wondering which way to go. Left would take her back to town and the office, but right would take her to Shore Road and Rosie Capshaw's studio at the Van Vorst estate. She drummed her fingers on the steering wheel, uncertain about what to do, and then, impulsively, turned left. She'd only interviewed Matt and Luisa Rodriguez briefly, on the phone, and hadn't really pressed them for information. Now, she decided, she could put it off no longer and headed for their restaurant, Cali Kitchen, where she knew the lunch rush would be ending and the staff would be preparing for the dinner crowd.

Reaching the restaurant, which was located on the harbor, Lucy parked in the town parking lot, which was now filling up with white-shrink-wrapped yachts stored high and dry for the winter. Making her way to the restaurant, Lucy remembered when it had been an Irish pub that had fallen on hard times and had attracted a rough crowd. That had all changed when Rey Rodriguez, Matt and Luisa's father, bought the place and transformed it into a trendy eatery offering an international fusion menu. Gone were the gingham curtains, sticky tables, and dusty fake geraniums, replaced with blond wood, gleaming chrome, and uncluttered windows offering harbor views. Also gone were the four-dollar beers; now a craft brew would cost eight or nine bucks, and a glass of white wine would set you back a cool twelve dollars.

Stepping inside, Lucy saw a handful of diners were lingering over their lunches and enjoying the view of the cove and the lighthouse perched out at Quissett Point; a couple of servers were clearing away the ketchup bottles and lunch menus and setting the empty tables with white cloths and candles. Matt was behind the bar, staring at a computer screen, and he greeted her with a big smile. "Kitchen's closed, Lucy, but I could make you a sandwich," he offered.

"I'm not here to eat, Matt. I'm working on a story, and I've got a few questions I'm hoping you can help me with."

"Sounds like trouble," he said, biting his lip and giving a half-smile.

"Just background stuff, completely off the record."

"Now I am worried," he said, closing the laptop. "Shall we sit in a booth?"

"Good idea," replied Lucy, following him to the far corner of the dining room.

Sliding onto the salmon-colored leather banquette, Lucy thought she and Bill really ought to eat out more. It would be lovely to come here of an evening and relax, have a delicious dinner without the bother of deciding what to make and gathering the ingredients, cooking it all, and cleaning up afterward. Of course, it would cost a lot more than one of her homemade meatloaf dinners, so she pushed that thought aside and smiled at Matt, who was seated opposite her.

"I'm sure you know about Heather's overdose," she began.

"That was awful," said Matt. "Luisa and I were at the party . . ."

"I don't remember seeing you there . . ."

"She was Wonder Woman, and I was a bumble bee . . ."

Lucy could easily picture Luisa as Wonder Woman but couldn't quite see tall, dark, and handsome Matt as a bumble bee. "I wish I'd seen you buzzing around," she said, shaking her head.

"I was mostly in the kitchen, keeping the platters filled." His expression was serious. "And then, well, you know what happened. All of a sudden, the party was over. We cleaned up and left."

Lucy remembered the sense of desolation and shock that had befallen the revelers after Heather was taken away in the ambulance. "The DA has dropped all charges against Ty."

Matt's dark eyebrows rose in surprise. "I hadn't heard."

"Yeah," admitted Lucy, "but it opens the question of who gave Heather the drugs? And did that person know it was fentanyl?"

"And why do you think I know the answers to those questions?" As Lucy had feared, Matt's tone was challenging, defensive.

She knew she was venturing into sensitive territory and had to be as diplomatic as possible. "Well, it's no secret that restaurant work is demanding, and sometimes people, um, well, self-medicate . . ."

Matt laughed. "So you think I've got a drug dealer on my list of contacts?"

Lucy was quick to backtrack. "Listen, I'm not making any judgments. I just thought you might have heard something from an employee, or maybe had to let somebody go . . ."

"Luisa and I have worked very hard to keep this a drug-free establishment. We're very clear about our policies when we hire somebody, and if there's the least sign that somebody is using, we give them a warning and offer help with treatment. If the problem persists, we regretfully let them go."

Lucy glanced around the restaurant, now empty of diners, where there was a sense of quiet purpose as the workers went about setting the tables. Soothing jazz played on the sound system, and one server was at the bar, filling small glass vases with fresh clusters of chrysanthemums. "I know how seriously you take this issue," said Lucy, making eye contact. "I'm asking because of Bob, Bob Goodman. Andi Nardone is accusing him of sexism because he was defending Ty. If I can prove somebody else supplied the drugs to Heather, her accusation will be groundless; Bob was simply defending an innocent man."

"But you said the charges against Ty have been dropped."

"Right. But suspicions linger, especially when it's the

husband. The spouse is almost always the prime suspect. And the charges were dropped because there wasn't enough evidence to prove the case, not because the DA decided Ty is innocent."

Matt nodded. "You and Bob are friends, right?"

"For a long time," said Lucy, smiling at Luisa, who had come out of the kitchen and was distributing the flower arrangements. "Bob's a good man. I'd really like to see him win this election."

"Andi Nardone's a good woman," countered Luisa, setting one of the vases of bronze chrysanthemums on their table. "And electing her will help even the balance of power in the male-dominated legislature."

"She's not as qualified as Bob . . ."

"She'll bring a fresh point of view and represent women's interests . . ."

"So will Bob."

"Be realistic, Lucy," said Luisa, with a nod toward her brother. "A man can claim to support women's rights; he can even actually do it, but it's not the same. How can a man know what's really important to women? I bet Bob's wife takes care of all the nitty-gritty details of life so that Bob can concentrate on his work, right? Does Bob go the dry cleaner? Does he remember to pick up bread and milk? Prescriptions? I bet his wife makes sure his under-wear drawer is full and dinner's on time every night, right? How would he manage without her?"

Lucy found herself smiling at this description of Rachel, which was spot-on. "I see your point," she admitted. "But it does seem a bit unfair to accuse a lawyer of chauvinism simply because he defended a person accused of a crime who happened to be a man. Wasn't Ty entitled to have a strong defense, and his rights protected? If you ask me, Andi is implying he's guilty when everybody is presumed innocent until proven otherwise."

Luisa rolled her eyes. "It's never quite like that, now, is it? And one big reason is people like you, the media, who seize on sensational crimes and dig up every nasty little salacious detail."

"Only because we're trying to discover the truth!"

"Wouldn't that be better left to the courts?"

Lucy felt deflated; she didn't like to argue, especially when she wasn't scoring many points. She didn't want to give up, though, and desperately reached for something, anything that would convince Luisa and Matt to help her. "Well, it looks as if the courts aren't interested in finding out the truth about Heather's death, so it's up to people like you and me." She paused. "Do you really think Ty gave Heather the lethal drugs?"

Matt shook his head. "No, but I'm pretty sure he knew where she was getting them, and he certainly wasn't trying to get her to stop. There's a term for what he was doing; he was an *enabler*, right?"

Lucy didn't like the idea but had to admit the possibility that Ty had enabled Heather's drug use. Husbands and wives often had shared secrets that they kept to protect each other. Ty had admitted knowing that Heather used marijuana and occasionally cocaine, but had denied knowing that she was into heavier drugs. Now Lucy was rethinking the truth of that claim, which seemed increasingly unlikely. She pressed on, pleading with them: "C'mon, you must have some suspicions, some idea who she was getting them from?"

"I don't know for sure," began Luisa, letting out a big sigh, as if she was finally getting a weight off her chest, "but I got the feeling it wasn't some random dealer, some stranger. I think it was somebody she knew, somebody she trusted."

"Why do you think that?"

"Just because of Heather's personality. She really wasn't very adventurous. She had a small circle of friends; she wasn't spontaneous. She wasn't comfortable leaving home; she refused to use public transportation or stay in motels. She didn't even like the hospital; she wasn't convinced it was really clean." She paused. "It's just a hunch, but I don't think she would have taken any drugs unless whoever gave them to her looked her in the eye and told her they were perfectly safe."

"So you think she got the drugs from someone in that small circle of friends?" asked Lucy, turning to Matt.

He picked up a salt shaker and ran his fingers down the smooth ceramic cylinder. "Look, I don't know for sure. My drug of choice is a nice, cold IPA, but it's no secret that illegal drug use is practically an epidemic around here. People die of overdoses all the time; just check the obits. And like the social workers say, it involves people in every class, including college-educated professionals with high incomes. So do I think somebody I know is dealing? I think it's more than likely, but I don't know who."

"Not even a suspicion?" prompted Lucy.

Luisa turned to her brother and shrugged. "I've got enough to think about. I just don't let my mind go there. I try to take people at face value. What you see is what you get." She picked up the vase and adjusted the flowers. "Now that's better, isn't it?" she asked, stepping back and cocking her head to one side.

"Thanks for the chat," said Lucy, who knew when it was time to quit. "See you at the debate."

Luisa smiled mischievously. "May the best woman win."

Leaving the restaurant, Lucy was struck with the fact that in Tinker's Cove, as in many coastal Maine towns, the town fathers had seen fit to locate the parking lot in a piece of prime, waterfront real estate. A strip of grass with a few benches was a recent addition, and she paused to snap a photo of an old gentleman who was enjoying the fine day and watching a flock of geese heading south. After getting his permission to use the photo and jotting down his name, she continued on her way back to the office, trying to decide if Matt and Luisa had been telling her the truth. Now that she thought about it, it seemed that Luisa had rather smoothly managed to change the subject when she joined the conversation. They had given her one bit of interesting information, however, and that was their belief that Heather had gotten the fatal drugs from someone she trusted, someone in her close circle of friends.

Driving the short distance to the *Courier* office, Lucy's thoughts turned to Brendan Coyle, another member of the group, who ran the local food pantry. He provided healthy food for an ever-increasing number of families who struggled to make ends meet by juggling several part-time jobs in the new "lean" economy. She'd interviewed Brendan often, learning that the great majority of pantry clients were working at low-paying jobs that didn't offer guaranteed hours, which meant that shifts were only allocated as needed. A cashier or stock clerk who was expected to work overtime in the busy tourist season would only get fifteen or twenty hours a week, at minimum wage, come winter.

She'd always enjoyed talking to Brendan, who was passionate about his work and seemed to her to have a generous, kind spirit. He was a big man, with a full beard and a huge smile, who laughed a lot. Now, as she drove along, she wondered if she'd missed something.

Was the pantry a convenient cover for the distribution of illegal drugs? Was Brendan himself a user?

Pulling up at a stop sign, she decided she was being ridiculous. Brendan was a salt-of-the-earth kind of guy; it was absurd to think otherwise. Perhaps she ought to take Luisa's advice and start accepting people at face value, instead of suspecting them of all sorts of devious behavior.

Turning on to Main Street, and parking in front of the police station, she found herself wondering about Kevin Kenneally. He was a member of the group, and he'd portrayed the artist Millais in Heather's tableau. She knew he must have been present at the haunted house, but now that she thought about it, she didn't remember seeing him at the party afterward. That didn't mean he wasn't there; the party had been crowded and spread throughout several rooms. Or he might have left early, moving on after doing his duty in the tableau. He'd certainly had the opportunity to give Heather the fentanyl, but motive and means? He was an assistant district attorney, clearly a man with an eye on the future. He was active in community organizations like the Hibernian Knights and other clubs; he was always available for a quote or interview, and was clearly laying the foundation for either a run for public office or a successful private practice. More importantly, she thought, he had the trust of DA Phil Aucoin, who often said he had complete confidence in Kevin. That was something Aucoin didn't give easily; he certainly didn't take people at face value. He thought the worst of everyone, and Lucy admitted ruefully that everyone included her!

Gathering up her bag and getting out of the car, she stopped at the police department to pick up the weekly log. The log was a popular feature of the weekly paper, and whenever Ted tried to discontinue printing it, considering it a waste of space, he got complaints from readers. They apparently enjoyed reading the carefully worded notations that suspicious activity was reported on Parallel Street or that a traffic violation had occurred on Route 1. Details such as the name of the offender or the exact description of suspicious activity were never included, offering readers plenty of opportunity to speculate about who among their neighbors was involved.

The log was always waiting for her at the dispatcher's desk, and it was there in the lobby that she bumped into Kevin Kenneally, who was on his way out. He greeted her warmly and seemed in no rush to leave, so Lucy took advantage of the situation to ask him about the steps his department was taking to stop drug trafficking in the county.

"Well, you know DA Aucoin created the Drug Task Force to tackle that very problem, and they've had terrific success seizing more than a ton of illegal drugs and hundreds of thousands of dollars," he said.

Lucy knew all about the task force, which in her opinion worked at an exceedingly slow pace. Investigations were inevitably drawn out and took years, which was difficult to understand since she herself had witnessed drug deals in broad daylight, often in public parking areas. That was her next question.

"Well, the task force has to operate very carefully and must abide by strict legal guidelines or their cases get thrown out of court," said Kenneally. "Any sort of undercover activity or phone tapping, anything like that must be closely and carefully supervised. And, of course, it takes time to build the trust of suspected offenders."

"But I've seen drug deals take place in the parking lot at Blueberry Pond," protested Lucy, mentioning a popular swimming spot.

"Those folks are low-level bottom feeders," said Kenneally. "The task force is after much bigger fish."

"I understand that, but isn't there a community policing theory about broken windows, that if police stop petty crimes, it changes the environment in which more serious crimes can take place?"

"I think that's been discredited," said Kenneally, giving her a rather patronizing smile. "That sort of thing involves racial profiling, stop and frisk, and we certainly don't want to perpetuate that sort of discrimination. Besides, here in Tinker's Cove, I don't think you'll find many broken windows."

"We have some pretty run-down areas," said Lucy.

"Well, poverty is always with us, but just because a family doesn't have much money doesn't mean it's involved in criminal activity."

Lucy could think of several exceptions to this rule that everybody in town knew about, but decided not to press the issue.

Kenneally had taken a step toward the door and seemed

ready to end the interview. "I guess I'll see you at the debate," he said. "Should be interesting."

"I'll be there," said Lucy, giving him a little wave. "Thanks for the interview."

"Always happy to chat with you, Lucy." He pushed the door open, holding it for Lucy, and the two walked down the steps together. He strode down the sidewalk to his car, and Lucy paused at the curb, preparing to cross the street to the newspaper office on the other side. She was waiting for a pickup truck to pass when she heard a female voice calling her name. Turning around, she saw Officer Sally Kirwan waving at her from the station steps. She waved back and waited for Sally, who was in a hurry to talk to her.

"What's up?" she asked, as Sally met her.

"Let's move along a bit," said Sally, casting an eye at the police station. "This is a bit sensitive."

Lucy knew that Sally handled a lot of confidential matters, especially domestic disputes and crimes against women. She expected to hear about something along those lines as she accompanied Sally for a little stroll down the street. Reaching the alley between the hardware store and the fudge shop, she stepped inside and Lucy followed, eager to hear whatever tip Sally was so eager to share.

"This is on the QT, and you can't say it came from me, but I really think people ought to know what's going on," began Sally.

"No problem," said Lucy. "I'm always grateful for background information."

"It's about the evidence room in the station. It seems that some illegal drugs that were seized and stored there have gone missing." Sally paused, giving Lucy a meaningful look. "That's why Kenneally was at the station today. He met with the chief to discuss the problem."

"If these drugs are missing, they must have been taken by somebody in the department," said Lucy. "They're the only ones with access, right?"

Sally gave a knowing nod. "That's right."

"But won't they be missed? I imagine they're evidence needed for a trial, right?"

"A lot of defendants end up plea bargaining. The court's backed up, and instead of waiting months for a trial, they want to get on with their lives, so they plead to a lesser charge and take a couple of months in the county jail, sometimes just probation."

"What happens to the evidence then?"

"It sits there, piling up, and when they run out of space, they destroy it."

"How much is missing?" asked Lucy.

"Heroin, hundreds of tabs of oxy, some fentanyl, a lot of pot."

"Any suspects?"

Sally pressed her lips together, thinking. Finally, she spoke. "A couple of officers have had issues with drugs in the past—went to rehab and recovered—and I imagine they'll start with them." She paused. "I'm not going to name names; I'm sure you understand."

"Of course not," said Lucy, who would have given anything to get those names. "You've been a great help. Thanks."

Sally looked a bit uneasy, already regretting what she'd done. "Don't tell anybody where you got this, right?"

Lucy took her hand. "Don't worry. I never reveal my sources." She smiled. "Besides, I'm not exactly sure how to use this. I'll have to talk it over with Ted."

"Do whatever you think is best," said Sally, straightening her heavy utility belt. "Just keep me out of it."

"Right," said Lucy, watching as Sally marched down the road in her blue uniform. Not many women could carry it off, thought Lucy, but Sally had a trim little figure and looked rather smart as she marched along.

Chapter Nine

On the night of the debate, the high school auditorium was packed; it was standing-room only. The Hat and Mitten Fund always held a bake sale at these civic events, and Lucy was pleased to see they were doing a brisk business, selling homemade treats and hot coffee. She stopped and bought some shortbread and coffee, which she figured would provide the energy she needed to cover the event and write it up before heading home to bed.

Walking down the aisle to the front of the auditorium, where she had been assured there would be a reserved seat for her, she paused here and there to greet friends and neighbors. Finding the promised seat, she didn't have long to wait for the debate to begin. Roger Wilcox, a veteran local politician who had chaired the town's board of selectmen for eons, was moderating the event and was a stickler for promptness. When the hands on the clock over the stage clicked into place at 7:00 p.m., he tapped the microphone, calling for silence.

"Welcome, all," he began. "It's great to see so much interest in the upcoming election for state rep. We have three highly qualified candidates: incumbent George Armistead, and two challengers: businesswoman Andi Nardone and attorney Bob Goodman." Roger was a tall man, well into his sixties, with gray hair and wire-rimmed spectacles, and Lucy knew from experience that he always held the door for a lady. So she wasn't at all surprised when he gave Andi a gentlemanly bow of the head and invited her to be the first speaker. "Ladies first," he said, adding a brief introduction summarizing her qualifications for office, which included a college education, community involvement, and a successful business career.

Andi didn't seem pleased with his choice of words, however. "I don't know that I'd call myself a lady. Ladies stay home and drink tea like this," she said, miming taking a sip from a tea cup with her pinky raised.

The audience laughed, enjoying her little joke at Roger's expense.

"I don't spend my days drinking tea," she continued, "I bet you've seen my Green Thumb Landscaping trucks around town. I started that business from scratch, and I now employ dozens of workers and have hundreds of satisfied customers.

"But why am I running to be your state rep, you may wonder, when I have so many other responsibilities?" She paused and looked at the audience. "Well, it's because my experience starting a business opened my eyes to the many hurdles women face in our society. When I applied for my first small-business loan, I had to ask my father to co-sign for me. The bank wasn't willing to grant me a loan based on my business plan; I had to be sponsored by a man.

"Nowadays, they're practically begging me to borrow money," she continued, with a naughty smile that got a laugh from the audience. "So I have to admit that women are making progress, but it's slow. We're a long way from being treated equally with men, and that's especially true when it comes to state government. Women are fifty-one percent of the population, they say, but we do not have fifty-one percent representation in the legislature.

"In closing, I don't want you to think I am a one-issue candidate. It's true that I'm a feminist and will work to establish equal rights for women, but I am a citizen of Tinker's Cove, and I will work hard for all of you, for this very special, unique community. So I humbly ask for your votes come Election Day. Thank you."

Andi got a healthy round of applause, and not just from the women. A lot of men, she noticed, were nodding along in agreement and clapping. Lucy was relieved that Andi hadn't attacked Bob directly, but that sense of relief faded when Andi took the first question, which Lucy suspected had been planned all along.

The questioner was Lori Johnson, a mom who coached youth soccer and was a strong advocate of equal funding for girls' athletics. "You've spoken about your strong feminist convictions, but can't men also be feminists? Do you think you will do more for women than the other candidates?"

"I'm so glad you asked that question, Lori," said Andi, moving into an obviously carefully prepared answer. "I have to say I have seen no evidence at all that George Armistead supports women's rights; in fact, he has consistently voted to reduce funding for women's health programs. He has also voted against legislation designed to extend the time period in which victims of sexual abuse of both sexes can take legal action against their abusers."

Lucy glanced at George, who she suspected wasn't the least bit bothered by these accusations but instead regarded Andi as little more than an annoying upstart.

Moving right along, Andi turned her attack on her primary target, Bob. "As for Attorney Bob Goodman, I was very surprised when he chose to defend a man charged with murdering his wife. Bob claims to support women's rights, he calls himself a feminist, but when push comes to shove, I fear he's just as much a member of the old boys club as George Armistead."

This caused quite a buzz in the audience, and Bob raised his hand, demanding an opportunity to rebut Andi's charges. Roger Wilcox demurred, saying he would have a chance to explain his views shortly, and allowed Andi to take a few more questions.

When Bob took the podium, he abandoned his prepared speech and instead defended his decision to represent Ty Moon, reminding the audience that the DA had dropped all charges against him. He argued forcefully for the right of the accused to a strong legal defense, regardless of sex, religion, or race. "Everyone is presumed innocent until proven otherwise," he declared, "and I am innocent of these aspersions on my character. If you vote for me, you will find I will do everything in my power to represent the interests of all citizens in this district, whether boy or girl, man or woman, cat or dog!"

That got quite a laugh from the assembled crowd, but Bob soon found himself answering some tough, even hostile questions. "Why haven't you spoken out before in support of increased funding for girls' athletics at the high school?" "How do you intend to make sure women in Maine don't lose access to abortion clinics?" "Can we really trust you to defend a woman's right to choose?" "You're on the board of directors of Seamen's Bank, which has a dismal record of promoting women to executive positions and has been challenged in court by female employees claiming they are paid less than male employees. What have you done to change these policies?"

Bob did his best to explain his positions and to defend his actions, but his questioners were not satisfied with his responses and persisted in peppering him with questions that were thinly veiled accusations of male chauvinism. Lucy suspected he was in trouble when Andi's campaign manager, Haley, stepped up to the microphone provided for audience questions. "As a white, heterosexual male, wouldn't you say you've been blind to the many advantages and privileges you've had throughout your life?"

Bob sighed, seemingly defeated. "All I can say is that I find it hard to imagine myself as anybody except myself. Perhaps I have been blind," he admitted, then rallied a bit. "But I would like to say that I've always followed the advice my mother gave me . . . to treat everyone as I'd like to be treated myself."

"And with that," said Roger Wilcox, "let's hear from our incumbent state representative, George Armistead."

George was the very picture of a prosperous member of the establishment, with a head of snowy white hair; he was dressed in the regulation navy-blue suit, white shirt, and red tie. He made no bones about his old-fashioned views, calling for a return to traditional Yankee values like thrift and hard work, and lamented dwindling memberships at local churches. He called for stricter drug laws and tougher sentencing of convicted criminals, and reminded everyone that he was a strong supporter of Second Amendment gun rights. "Moral turpitude is this country's biggest problem," he insisted, "and I, for one, am not afraid to stand up, as I always have, for the American family and this great country, one nation under God. Thank you."

George got a warm round of applause, mostly from older members of the audience, but Lucy wasn't entirely convinced that the support would translate into enough votes to return him to the state house. On the other hand, it seemed that Andi's attack on Bob had lost him some votes, and she now doubted he was the shoo-in she'd believed him to be before the debate. Andi had managed to change the direction of the campaign, and it seemed that any one of the three might win the election.

She lingered afterward to offer some words of support to Bob and Rachel, then joined the crowd heading out to the parking lot and home. She found herself next to Officer Sally in the crush, and when they were outside, Sally drew her aside into a shadowy spot. "Golly, I feel like I'm in a spy movie," said Lucy, laughing.

"I know; I'm paranoid," admitted Sally. "Working in the department will do that to you. As a woman, I'm an outsider. I'm not in the club, and there are some who'd love to see me fall on my face."

"But you're related to most of the guys in the department," said Lucy. As a Kirwan, Sally was a member of a large family that included many workers in the town's police and fire departments, as well as the Department of Public Works.

"That's the problem," said Sally, with a rueful sigh. "I was supposed to be a dispatcher, or an admin, but silly

Sally went all out and got a degree in criminal justice. Just who did I think I was, hunh?"

"Well, I think you do a hell of a job; I think you're the best cop on the force."

"I try," said Sally. "So listen, I got a peek at the ME's report on Heather, and it seems she was no amateur when it came to drugs. She had needle tracks up and down her arms."

Lucy remembered that Heather always wore long sleeves, mostly fluttery chiffon, and sometimes even added lacy gloves. She'd thought it was a fashion statement, a preference, but now it seemed she was hiding her addiction.

"Couldn't it have been from the chemo?" asked Lucy. "Those IVs can be brutal."

"No. According to the ME, they were quite recent."

"That's a bit of a surprise," said Lucy. "I never would have guessed."

"That's how it goes," said Sally. "I've been in a state of constant surprise since I started this job. You wouldn't believe some of the stuff I've seen."

Lucy saw an opportunity for a story. "Well, maybe, one of these days, you can tell me all about it," she coaxed, with a naughty smile.

"No way," said Sally, chuckling. "That would certainly get me chucked out of the department, and the family!"

Chapter Ten

Next morning, when Bill barged into the bathroom, looking for a toenail clipper when she was brushing her teeth, Lucy came to a conclusion. The more she thought about Heather's addiction, the more she thought that Ty must have known. It would have been impossible for Heather to keep it a secret, especially since she was mainlining. It was one thing to sniff up some powder, quite another to manage an injection that required a syringe and other equipment. Unless a married woman had a room and bath of her own, it was very difficult to keep secrets from a husband; she'd discovered with some dismay that even her much-desired en suite master bath didn't give her all the privacy she craved because she had to share it with Bill. But even if Ty hadn't discovered Heather's drug paraphernalia, he must have noticed mood swings and changes in behavior that would have led him to suspect that she was using. That meant there was a good chance he knew who was supplying the drugs. The trick was to convince him to tell her.

She waited until mid-morning to call him, figuring that, like her, he might be taking a break. You could only sit at a computer for so long before you had to get up and stretch, give your eyes a rest by looking out the window, and recharge with some caffeine. So she took her coffee and her phone over to the big plate-glass window in the *Courier* newsroom that overlooked Main Street and dialed his number.

"I was just thinking about you," she began, when he answered. "You've been through so much. How are you doing?"

"Okay," he replied, in a noncommittal voice.

"I'm just calling as a friend," she continued. "I really enjoyed working with you on the haunted house. It was all so shocking. I'm having a hard time processing it all, and I know it must be much harder for you."

"It's no picnic," he confessed. "I've got my work. It's a good distraction, but I find my mind wanders. I can't say I'm being very productive."

"It's important to keep up the routine, even if you're pretending. It will get easier with time. Trust me." Lucy took a deep breath, remembering some scary moments. "I've been through some things that I'd rather forget—I was even captured by a religious cult once. It takes time; you need to be patient with yourself. Maybe talk to a therapist, even. But eventually you find you're more in control of your emotions and you begin to feel better."

"If you say so," said Ty, unconvinced.

"I do." Lucy paused. "Say, can I take you out to lunch? I bet you haven't been eating much or seeing other people."

"You would be right. But believe me, I'm not good company. I don't know anybody here in Portland, I've become a bit of a loner."

"I have some errands in Portland anyway," said Lucy, fibbing in an attempt to persuade him to meet with her.

Much to her surprise, he accepted her invitation, saying, "Thanks, Lucy. To tell the truth, I've got to start seeing people again. I've heard there's a great little small-batch brewery near here. It's called Blackbeards. Want to meet me there?"

"Great. I'll meet you there around one."

Ending the call, Lucy wondered how on earth she was going to get Ty to confide in her, but figured it was worth a try. She didn't like the way Andi Nardone was using him to smear Bob in the campaign, and the best way to end it was to prove his innocence by finding the real killer.

That's what she planned to tell Ty, when she found him in the brewery, sitting at a small table against an exposed brick wall, with a half-drunk glass of beer. The actual brewing machinery, including huge stainless-steel vats, was enclosed behind a glass partition.

Spotting her, he stood up and gave her a little wave. Lucy hurried to meet him, smiling broadly. As she made her way to the table, she noticed that he was much thinner, his face had acquired some lines, and he needed a haircut. His smile, however, was welcoming.

"Thanks for coming; it's good to see a friendly face," he said, indicating a chair.

When she'd taken it, he added, "This seasonal pumpkin ale is quite good."

When the waiter arrived, he ordered one for Lucy and another for himself, along with a fried-fish sandwich. Lucy chose her usual BLT. The drinks came first, and they chatted about a range of topics: his work, the scene in Portland, news from Tinker's Cove. They were both hungry, and conversation halted while they tackled their sandwiches and fries. Once their plates were bare, the waiter returned to remove them and asked if they'd like another drink. Lucy chose tea, but Ty went for a third beer.

"I hope you don't have to drive home," said Lucy, somewhat concerned.

"Nope. I walked. My place is just round the corner."

"You know, when we moved to Tinker's Cove, I thought I'd be able to walk everywhere because it's a small town, but I soon discovered that our house was too far out, and I had to drive. I walked a lot more when I lived in New York City."

"The walking is one of the things I like about Portland." He looked up as the waiter set down his beer and Lucy's tea, along with the folder containing the bill. "That and the anonymity."

"Yeah, I can appreciate that," said Lucy, spooning out the tea bag and setting it on the saucer. "Especially since Andi Nardone won't let it rest."

He took a slurp and set down his glass. "What do you mean?"

Lucy took a cautious sip of her tea and discovered it was actually barely warm. "Oh, you know, in the campaign. She's calling out Bob as anti-feminist because he defended you. The implication is that you're really guilty but got off because of some technicality."

Ty looked shocked. "That's terrible. It's unfair to Bob, and it's slanderous to me. Why does she think she can do that?"

"It's pretty clever, in a nasty way. She knows how suspicious people can be in a small town, and she's exploiting that and manipulating them. It's very hard for Bob to defend himself since the police haven't charged anybody else."

"He's such a great guy; I'm really grateful for everything he did for me. I wish there was some way I could help."

This was her chance, thought Lucy. "Well, actually, there is a way."

Ty sat up a bit straighter. "How? How can I help? I've already said I didn't do it; I wouldn't hurt Heather. I've said it over and over, but nobody believes me."

Lucy caught his gaze and held it. "Come on, Ty. You must've known Heather was using. How come you didn't tell Bob who she was getting the drugs from?"

He turned away, looking out the window at the loading dock, where a truck was being filled with metal kegs of beer. "It was Pretendsville," he said. "Heather pretended she wasn't using; I pretended I didn't know."

"I guess I can see that," admitted Lucy, thinking of the things she knew about Bill but never mentioned, like the money he spent on lottery tickets and the occasional winnings he kept for himself. As for herself, she had a few secrets, too, like the exorbitant amount she spent getting her hair professionally colored at the salon, following Sue's advice. "But you really knew, and you must have some idea who was supplying the drugs, don't you?"

Ty hesitated for a few minutes, then the dam seemed to break, and he blurted out Kevin Kenneally's name. "He stole them from the police evidence locker, said nobody'd ever suspect, and I guess he was right."

"Why didn't you tell Bob?"

"Because of Heather. I didn't want anyone to know. She'd been through such a bad time with the cancer, and she was so fragile." He paused, his eyes brimming, then let out a big sigh. "She was so beautiful . . ." He sniffed and wiped his eyes with the back of his hands. "I loved her so much." He screwed up his mouth. "I still do."

Lucy sipped her awful tea, then decided it wasn't worth the bother and shoved the cup and saucer away from her. "I understand that you wanted to protect Heather, but the secret is out. She OD'd. And Kenneally is sending people to jail for doing the exact thing he's been doing. He even fingered you for murder."

If she'd expected outrage and indignation from Ty, she was about to be disappointed. "So what's new?" he asked, rhetorically. "There's always people like him who think they're better and smarter than everybody else and they don't have to play by the rules. It's always been that way, and it always will be." He flipped open the leatherette folder, glanced at it, and stood up, pulling a fifty from his wallet.

"Oh, let me," said Lucy, protesting. "I invited you."

"We're all set," he said, snapping the folder shut and tossing it on the table. "It was great catching up, Lucy."

"No chance you'll name Kenneally?" she asked, in a last-ditch effort.

He shook his head. "Nah. I'm just trying to get through one day at a time."

Lucy remained at the table, watching as he made his

way to the door. Then she gathered up her things and headed for the ladies room; it was a long drive home.

On the ride back to the office, Lucy struggled with her emotions. On one hand, she sympathized with Ty's reluctance to tarnish his wife's reputation by admitting she was an addict. As things stood now, her death was the result of an accidental one-time overdose. People might speculate that she was a user, but the ME's findings were only known to law enforcement and hadn't been released to the public. Her addiction would remain a private matter unless there were further legal proceedings, such as a demand for the release of public records by a media organization or a wrongful death lawsuit, or if criminal charges were pressed against another individual. All of which were unlikely at the moment. Ted certainly didn't want to jeopardize his relationship with local police authorities by taking them to court, and Ty, who would be the logical person to pursue a wrongful death lawsuit, certainly wasn't interested in exposing Heather's life to further examination. Most frustrating of all to Lucy was his reluctance to identify Kenneally as the person responsible for giving her the tainted drugs, but she understood that any decent defense attorney would do everything possible to implicate Heather in her own murder. The victim would be put on trial, too.

She had almost reached Tinker's Cove when she got a text from Ted informing her that something was going on over at the county courthouse complex and instructing her to find out what it was all about. Lucy loved covering breaking news, so she flipped down the visor with her PRESS card on it and stepped on the gas.

As she negotiated the back roads leading to Gilead,

she speculated about what was going on. A fire? Auto accident? Those were certainly possibilities, but the fact that whatever was occurring was taking place at the county complex, which included the county jail as well as the district and superior courthouses, implied some sort of criminal activity. Sometimes prisoners attempted to escape, sometimes defendants attacked their accusers, and sometimes the losing parties expressed their disappointment in the justice system in carefully orchestrated statements. There was also the possibility of some sort of disorder in the county jail itself, like prisoners attacking a guard or holding a hunger strike. Anything could happen, really, and Lucy was eager to find out what was going on.

Gilead seemed peaceful enough when Lucy crossed the town line and cruised down Main Street, past the usual shops and restaurants. She had the road to herself when she turned into the access road for the county complex, and she was beginning to think Ted had gotten bad information, but when she arrived at the parking lot, she found several police cruisers were parked, blue lights flashing, outside the DA's office building. Closer examination revealed that two of the cruisers were state police vehicles and another was from Tinker's Cove, which she suspected might mean that the jig was up for Kevin Kenneally.

Whatever was taking place was happening inside, she decided as she noted the absence of any police presence in the parking lot apart from the cruisers. No snipers were posted on the rooftops; there was no SWAT team lurking in the shadows, waiting to strike. Concluding that she was not likely to be caught in any crossfire, she got out of her car and started walking to the DA's office, which was a small brick building tucked alongside the stately granite county courthouse that was listed on the National Register of Historic Places.

She was just stepping out from the first row of parked cars when the courthouse door burst open and Kenneally dashed out, looking rather frantic. Lucy stared at him, wondering why he hadn't bothered to put on his coat. It took a few seconds for her to figure out that he must be making a run and trying to escape, and that's when he saw her. Lucy looked around for help, thinking she could use that SWAT team about now, and that's when Kenneally grabbed her arm and shoved something that sure seemed like a gun into her side.

"Let's go," he growled, shoving her between two parked cars toward the empty row of spaces where her car with its PRESS card proudly displayed was parked. "Get in your car."

Behind them, Lucy heard the sound of a door banging open and thudding feet. Then somebody yelled, "Stop where you are! Put your hands up, Kenneally!"

Kenneally looked back over his shoulder, and his grip on her arm weakened. Lucy seized the opportunity to pull away from him and ran as fast as she could. Terrified they would begin shooting at Kenneally, she wanted to get as far away from him as she could, and she sheltered behind a large green metal dumpster.

Kenneally ducked down and scooted behind the parked cars, hunched over. This maneuver was observed by several cops who had their guns out but were holding fire. This enabled Kenneally to reach his sporty Corvette and climb in; he backed out right into a parked Volvo and, shifting gears with an audible grind, zoomed straight toward Lucy. She was boxed in; the dumpster was enclosed by fencing, and Kenneally's car was blocking the opening. "Get in!" he ordered, waving the gun at her. Lucy knew that would be a fatal mistake and leaped behind the dumpster just as Kenneally fired a shot; then he hit the gas and zoomed up the hill toward the county jail and the access road.

Now sirens could be heard as more cruisers started pouring into the parking lot, blocking all the exits. Kenneally circled around the perimeter, desperately looking for an escape that didn't exist; finally, returning back to the little brick DA's office building, he stopped his car. He got out, raised his hands over his head, and was arrested by Tinker's Cove police chief, Jim Kirwan, who read him his rights.

The election took a back seat to Kenneally's arrest at Cali Kitchen, where Bob's friends and supporters had gathered to await the results of the vote. The mood was generally upbeat, albeit with a tingle of nervous anticipation. But even the possibility of victory couldn't top the scandalous revelation that one of the county's assistant district attorneys had been stealing drugs from various local police department evidence rooms and selling them, which was followed by the even more disturbing news that the DA was preparing to charge Kenneally with Heather Moon's murder, presumably because he feared she would expose him.

"Those kids get paid peanuts," observed Sid Finch, helping himself to a handful from one of the bowls on the bar. "They've got tons of student loan debt from law school; they're trying to get started in life, you know, buying cars, paying rent, getting married." He paused to enjoy a big swallow of beer. "Of course, that doesn't excuse what he did. And now they're saying he killed Heather Moon, who thought he was her friend. I just don't get it."

"Stealing was bad enough, but actually selling the drugs and taking advantage of desperate people, that really stinks," observed Zoe.

"Zoe's right," said Rachel. "Addiction is a disease, an effort to treat psychic pain, which is every bit as serious as actual physical pain."

"You can't dismiss actual physical pain as a causal factor," volunteered Eddie Culpepper, who, as an EMT on the town's rescue squad, had responded to countless overdoses. "That's how a lot of users get started."

"It's the hypocrisy that gets me," said Pam. "You wouldn't have thought butter melted in Kenneally's mouth."

"You said it," chimed in high school teacher Charlie Zeigler, his voice trembling with outrage. "He actually did an entire assembly presentation on the dangers of addiction and illegal drugs. I guess we were lucky he didn't give the kids his phone number in case they wanted to try some oxy or pot."

"And he actually tried to convict Ty of killing Heather, when he was the murderer. It's unbelievable." Sue shook her head. "Wow."

"I think we do deserve a certain level of integrity in public officials like district attorneys," observed Franny Small, neat and prim as ever in a crisp white blouse with a gold bar pin clipped to both sides of her Peter Pan collar. "Don't forget he was prosecuting Ty Moon for the very crime he committed." She took a very small sip of white wine. "I find that unforgivable."

"I'm pretty sure the bar association agrees," said Bob.

"Have you heard from Ty?" asked Lucy. "What was his reaction?"

"Mostly relief, I guess," replied Bob. "He did say he never really took to Kenneally."

"I do hope he continues renovating the house," said Franny, who lived next door. "I miss him. He wasn't actually such a terrible neighbor. Not like the woman on my other side, who lets her cats out to kill the birds at my feeder and use my hydrangea bed as a potty."

"I think he wants to finish the reno and sell the house," said Bob, giving Bill a nod. "He's thinking of going back to LA."

"I don't blame him," said Sue. "Why would he stay here where there must be so many bad memories?"

"I do hope he finds a good therapist," observed Rachel, picking up her phone. "We have some early results . . ."

Lucy clanked her spoon against a glass, and conversation paused. Everyone remained silent as Rachel stood, finger in the air, listening intently to her cell phone; more than a few people were holding their breath. Then she smiled broadly and announced, "Bob took Tinker's Cove, getting seventy-two percent of the vote!"

Cheers and clapping erupted; there was back slapping, and someone called for a speech.

"Too early for a victory speech," said Bob, blushing with pleasure. "We've got to hear from the other precincts, but we're off to a good start!"

Unfortunately, the numbers soon turned as other districts were counted. Andi Nardone had a surprisingly strong showing in Gilead and got the college vote, too.

But it was the more conservative inland areas that finally dominated and returned George Armistead to the assembly.

"I guess that male privilege issue was a non-starter," grumbled Zoe, who Lucy suspected had voted for Andi Nardone.

"Oh, well, you can't win 'em all," proclaimed Sue. "Let's have a toast for our Bob, anyway."

Glasses were raised, somebody started singing "For He's a Jolly Good Fellow," and there were hugs all around. "There's always next time!" proclaimed Bob, raising his glass.

His significant other and major supporter wasn't quite as enthusiastic, however. Rachel, gathered with Sue, Pam, and Lucy in a corner, rolled her eyes. "Over my dead body," she muttered. "One campaign was enough. Over my dead body."

DEATH OF A HALLOWEEN PARTY MONSTER

Lee Hollis

Chapter One

"Wait, don't tell me!" Reverend Ted exclaimed, stopping Hayley as she passed by with a plate of hors d'oeuvres. "Prom Night Carrie!"

"Bingo," Hayley said with a wink. Although pretty much everyone at the party had nailed her costume on the first guess. There were only so many movie-monster characters who would wear a cheap metal tiara and a satin, white prom gown splattered with fake pig's blood. She had set down the flower bouquet that completed her look earlier so she could serve more food to her guests.

Hayley was excited to be hosting her first-ever private function at her new restaurant.

Hayley's Kitchen.

She still could not believe it, even with the beautifully stenciled signage outside.

Hayley Powell officially owned her own business.

After she'd opened the doors to her new eatery, just two months ago, in the small coastal tourist town of Bar Harbor, Maine, Hayley's Kitchen had quickly become the new local hot spot. Although most of the island summer visitors had departed immediately after Labor Day, Hayley had remained open, hoping to serve the town until at least Thanksgiving. And given the unexpected support from the community, she was now considering possibly even staying open until Christmas, almost unheard of in a tiny New England tourist town. But Bar Harbor desperately needed a year-round place for friends and families to enjoy a nice dinner out during the cold, unforgiving winter months, and Hayley was itching to fill that void.

She had decided to celebrate her newfound success by throwing a party. Halloween was her favorite holiday of the year, and so, with the help of her BFFs Liddy and Mona, she'd e-mailed invitations for what she hoped would be her first annual Halloween party at Hayley's Kitchen, with many more in the years to come.

Once word got out that Hayley was having a soirée at her new restaurant, half the town had clamored for invites. But Hayley had insisted on keeping the guest list down to a manageable thirty attendees, at least for her first time out. But, of course, to no one's surprise, about a third of those invited asked if they could bring a guest, and Hayley just couldn't say no, so at last tally, thirty-nine people in a wide variety of colorful Halloween costumes were packed into her restaurant's main dining room.

"What about me? Can you guess who I am?" Reverend Ted asked eagerly as he struck a pose, arms out.

Hayley smirked.

This was hardly a huge mental challenge.

Reverend Ted was in a tunic and sandals, wearing a gray wig and fake beard, holding a tablet made of Styrofoam with the Ten Commandments printed on the front of it.

"Um, wild guess, Moses?" Hayley shrugged.

The invitation had specifically requested, in the spirit of Halloween, that everyone come dressed as their favorite *movie monster*. Reverend Ted had obviously missed the memo. Moses was a far cry from the Creature from the Black Lagoon.

Reverend Ted relaxed. "I know, it's a little on the nose. Local pastor comes as religious figure, but I didn't have time to go buy a new costume, so I recycled this one from last year. I'm still new to town, so no one has ever seen me wear it before. By the way," he said, snatching one of the hors d'oeuvres off her silver tray, "these little cheese pumpkins are delicious."

"Thank you, Ted," Hayley said, not wanting to be rude, but quickly moving on. She had so much to do. The party had only started a half hour ago, and she was already running low on food. She had spent the past week cooking and baking in the few hours she was not busy running the restaurant. She was closed on Mondays, so that finally gave her a full day to finish preparing. Although she was not about to admit it to anyone, Hayley was using her guests as guinea pigs. She had made a wide array of recipes from her card file for the party, and she was hoping to see what was popular and what was not before she decided whether or not to add them to her permanent menu or nightly specials.

Suddenly, there was a loud crash.

Hayley spun around to see Freddy Krueger, with the iconic molded face mask, hat, striped shirt, and glove with fake steel claws. He had dropped his cocktail glass, and it had shattered all over the floor. His eyes were bulging out at the sight of a giant shark standing next to him.

"Sorry, Cappy," the shark said.

Hayley instantly recognized the voice inside the big bulky foam shark costume.

It was Mona.

As if reading her thoughts, Liddy was suddenly at Hayley's side. "Why on earth would she choose such a cumbersome costume, knowing the room would be so packed with people? I tried to warn her, but since when does she listen to me? That's the fourth person she has bumped into in fifteen minutes. If this keeps up, you'll have no glassware left by the end of the party!"

Freddy Krueger bent down to pick up the shards of glass off the floor. Feeling guilty, Mona bent down to help, but she was weighted down by her unmanageable costume and pitched forward, landing flat on the floor, facedown.

"Shark down! Shark down!" Mona cried, her voice muffled. She rolled over onto her back, arms and legs sticking out of the costume, flailing.

Liddy couldn't help but giggle, and Hayley nudged her, flashing an admonishing look. Mona's greatest fear was anyone laughing at her. She dreaded embarrassment of any kind.

Freddy Krueger tried to lift her up but couldn't do it on his own, so he signaled a couple of buddies, a sexy vampire and a furry thing—maybe the Wolfman, was Hayley's best guess—who bounded over to help with the heavy lift. Together, they managed to haul Mona back up to her feet; they could see her red, puffy face inside the shark's mouth, a border of shark teeth surrounding it, almost as if she was inside a big, round picture frame.

"Thanks, guys," Mona barked as she marched over to Hayley and Liddy. "He should have watched where he was going!"

"Oh, it's *his* fault?" Liddy gasped, incredulous.

They could see Mona glaring at them from inside the shark's mouth. "At least I came as a famous movie monster! Liddy, you didn't even bother dressing up! You just came as yourself!"

"What are you talking about?" Liddy scoffed. "I did not come as *myself*!"

"You're wearing your own wedding dress, the one you had custom-made for your big wedding day that blew up in your face! Who else could you possibly be?" Mona argued.

Poor Liddy's ill-fated wedding day had involved the groom not showing up, but that was another story that neither Hayley nor Liddy were anxious to revisit anytime soon.

Liddy put her hands on her hips. "And I suppose the green makeup, black lipstick, and giant fright wig don't give you *any* clues as to who I'm supposed to be?"

Mona casually shook her head. "The green complexion did give me pause, but I figured you just ate too many of those gravestone-shaped sugar cookies and were feeling nauseous . . ."

"*Bride of Frankenstein*!" Liddy wailed. "I'm supposed to be the Bride of Frankenstein!"

Mona studied her from inside the shark's mouth. "Oh . . . I see it now . . . I guess . . ."

Liddy was coming to a slow boil.

Hayley put her hand on Liddy's shoulder to help calm her down. "She's just messing with you, Liddy."

"I know. I guess I just don't get Mona's peculiar sense of humor. Maybe it works on some other level, some different frequency, like one that only dogs can understand."

Liddy brushed some cookie crumbs off her white wedding dress. She had lent the same dress to Hayley's daughter, Gemma, the year before when she wanted to go to a Halloween party as Glinda the Good Witch from *The Wizard of Oz*. At least they were getting some good use out of the dress after Liddy was forced to box it up and store it in her attic, since it had been custom-made and she was unable to return it to the dress shop.

"Food's getting pretty low; people are scarfing it down faster than I can put it out. Would you two mind helping me restock?" Hayley asked.

"Lead the way, Carrie," Liddy said before turning back to Mona. "Come on, Jaws."

"I'm not Jaws, I'm Meg," Mona protested.

"Who's Meg?" Liddy asked, puzzled.

"Meg! The megalodon from that Jason Statham movie!" Mona sighed.

"The mega-what?" Liddy laughed, shaking her head.

"A megalodon, which means big tooth, a giant extinct shark! My kids *loved* that movie!"

"Whatever happened to a simple great white like Jaws? I wouldn't even get in a swimming pool for two years after seeing that movie!" Liddy said.

"Jaws is old news, so twentieth century," Hayley joked.

As the three women made their way to the kitchen, they passed a woman with flat brown hair, wearing a flannel shirt underneath a denim coverall dress, filming the party with her phone while lugging around a large sledgehammer.

Liddy cranked her head around to get a good look. "Hayley, who is that woman? I don't recognize her."

"That's Randy," Hayley answered, chuckling.

"*What*?" Liddy gasped, surprised. "Who is he supposed to be, the mother from *Psycho*?"

"Oh, come on, Liddy, it's so obvious. He's Annie Wilkes," Mona howled.

"Who?"

"From *Misery*, the Stephen King book. Kathy Bates won the Oscar for playing her?" Hayley said.

"Oh, right," Liddy said. "What's the sledgehammer for?"

"You really are not a movie person, are you?" Hayley remarked as they headed through the swinging doors into the kitchen.

Hayley stopped suddenly.

From the moment she'd stepped foot into the kitchen, she'd sensed something was amiss.

Liddy instantly noticed her tensing. "Hayley, what is it?"

"Some food's missing," Hayley said ominously.

"What do you mean? I see plenty of it on the table over there," Mona shouted from inside the shark's mouth.

Hayley nodded. "Yes, but I also had several pans of my Mummy Meat Sliders and Pepperoni Pizza Pockets shaped like jack-o'-lanterns that I took out of the freezer to thaw so I could pop them in the oven. But now they're gone."

They heard rummaging coming from behind the pantry door.

"Who's in there?" Hayley shouted.

The rummaging suddenly stopped.

"There is nowhere to go!" Hayley warned. "You better just come out here right now!"

There was a little stalling, but finally, the evil Chucky doll emerged from the pantry.

Or at least it was someone dressed like the evil Chucky doll.

It was actually Mona's sixteen-year-old son, Chet.

"Chet, what the hell are you doing? You know you're not supposed to be back here!" Mona yelled.

"I know," Chet mumbled. "But Hayley's out of those little Thai-Spiced Deviled Pumpkin Eggs, which were awesome, so I came to see if there were any left."

"I'm sorry, Chet, we're totally out. I should have made more," Hayley said with an apologetic smile.

"Did you move the pans that were sitting right over there?" Mona demanded to know.

Chet quickly shook his head. "I didn't touch anything!" He paused for a moment, then reached into the pocket of his Chucky-inspired overalls. He withdrew his hand, which held some cookies—one bat, one ghost, one black cat. "Except these. But I only took three for later. Okay, five. I already ate two . . ."

Suddenly, they heard a bloodcurdling scream.

It echoed throughout the kitchen but had come from the dining room. Hayley, Mona, Liddy, and Chet all dashed out of the kitchen to investigate.

The main dining room had quieted down, everyone shocked by the ear-splitting outburst.

Hayley stepped forward to address her shocked guests. "What happened? Who screamed?"

There was silence as everyone waited for the guilty party to confess, but no one stepped forward.

Finally, Annie Wilkes, or Randy, stepped forward and pointed a finger. "It was the Mummy."

All eyes fell upon someone dressed as the Mummy, who stared down at the floor, embarrassed.

Hayley gasped. "Sergio?"

The Mummy nodded slightly.

"But it sounded like a *woman* screaming," Liddy said.

The Mummy sighed again, now utterly humiliated. "No, Liddy, it wasn't a woman; it was me. I apologize for startling everybody. I got scared, and I lost it for a second and yelled."

"That was no yell," Mona said. "That was a full-on, damsel-in-distress scream if I ever heard one!"

All the party guests erupted in laughter.

Sergio was normally the brave, macho chief of police of Bar Harbor, and so it was quite disconcerting that such a high-pitched cry had come flying out of his mouth.

Although wrapped up like a mummy, Sergio Alvares's handsome face was still exposed, and he looked as if he wished he was anywhere else in the world at this moment.

"What scared you so badly, Sergio?" Hayley asked.

Sergio again did not want to admit anything. He just stared at the floor, lips pursed.

"Pennywise," Randy, his husband, answered for him.

Suddenly, Pennywise the Clown, from the *It* movies and another popular Stephen King novel, proudly stepped forward, white-gloved hand raised. He certainly looked exactly like the creepy killer with the white painted face, large forehead, gray crinkle clown suit with ruffled pant legs and puffed sleeves. In one hand, he held a red balloon. Pennywise moved slowly, eerily toward Sergio, holding out his balloon.

Sergio shrieked again and jumped back.

The partygoers erupted in laughter, even louder and more raucous this time.

"So I hate clowns! Sue me!" Sergio bellowed.

In an effort to alleviate her brother-in-law's supreme embarrassment, Hayley recruited everyone nearby to help set out whatever food was left and not missing. Pretty soon her guests forgot all about the Pennywise incident and were focused on the appetizers fresh out of the oven, while Hayley, Liddy, Mona, and Randy gathered around Sergio, who was shaking slightly, more than a little discombobulated.

Hayley gently patted his back.

"He just snuck up behind me and scared me half to death. I'm fine now, please don't everyone make a fuss," Sergio said, waving them off.

Liddy turned to Pennywise. "Who are you anyway?"

He gave her an awful, shiver-inducing, I'm-going-to-kill-you-in-your-sleep wide grin. "I'm Pennywise."

Liddy was hardly spooked. "Okay, cut the crap, clown. I mean, who are you *really*?"

"You don't recognize me? It's Boris. Boris Candy."

The high school music teacher.

At first, Hayley forgot she had even invited him. But then she remembered that it had been Mona who had strong-armed her into e-mailing him a last-minute invitation. Mona wanted to stay on his good side because she was afraid Mr. Candy might flunk her son, Chet. Apparently Chet, who played the trombone in Mr. Candy's jazz band, had had a few truancy issues and was also having trouble in his music appreciation class. Hayley barely knew the music teacher since both her kids had long graduated before Mr. Candy started at the school, but she had decided to grant Mona's request. Hayley had to admit, Boris Candy's Pennywise costume was well thought out and highly effective. It had made Bar Harbor's chief of police scream like a frightened little baby.

And, frankly, Boris was quite proud of that fact.

"I should get some kind of prize for scariest costume, right? Let's face it! If the big, strong, strapping Chief Alvares was so spooked by me as Pennywise that he screamed at the top of his lungs and nearly ran to the bathroom and locked himself inside, that deserves something!" Boris excitedly turned to Hayley. "What do I win? Might I suggest a free dinner at Hayley's Kitchen?"

"I'll figure something out," Hayley said, politely brushing him off.

Sergio had finally managed to calm his nerves. "This all started when I was a boy . . ."

"Back in Brazil?" Liddy asked.

"Yes. There was this crazy old man in our village who sat on his porch every day drinking cachaça and yelling at all the kids who passed by. Then, when he was drunk, he would dress up as a clown and take a perverse pleasure in hiding until we were close enough, and he would pop up and terrorize us," Sergio solemnly explained. "I was so scared every time it happened. Finally, one day, I could not take it anymore, and so I went to the local municipal guards and complained, and he was given a warning to stop. Well, that just chickened him on even more . . ."

Hayley, Mona, and Liddy exchanged confused looks.

"*Egged* him on, Sergio. Not chickened. The warning just *egged* him on even more . . ." Randy said softly, correcting his husband.

English was not Sergio's first language.

Sergio sighed. "Chicken, egg, who cares? Anyway, because I had dared to stand up to him, he decided to exact his revenge. One night while I was asleep in my bed, I heard tapping on the window, and when I turned over to see what it was . . ." He stopped, quivering at the horrible memory. "There was that evil clown staring at me. I screamed bloody murder until my parents came running in to see what was happening. I pointed at the window, but the clown was gone, and my parents thought I had just had a bad dream. But I never forgot the terror I felt, and I have been afraid of clowns ever since."

"Well, I can certainly see why," Liddy said. "That's terrible. Whatever happened to the old man?"

"As far as I know, he's still alive in the village; he's just a *really* old man now, probably still yelling at the kids and dressing up as a clown at night to scare them."

Somebody tapped Sergio on the shoulder.

He turned around and was face-to-face with Pennywise again.

"Boo," Pennywise blurted out, wearing that grotesque evil grin.

Sergio yelped, but thankfully this time didn't scream.

It looked as if he wanted to punch Boris in the clown face, but as a law-enforcement officer, he refrained and just stalked off, trying to get away from him.

"Who knew this costume would be such a big hit and so much fun?" Boris gushed, chasing after Sergio.

"Randy, he's not going to stop needling Sergio. You should do something," Hayley suggested.

"You're right," Randy said. "I missed recording Sergio screaming earlier on my phone; maybe Boris will be able to get him to do it again, so I get it on video!"

"You are not being a good husband right now, Randy," Hayley scolded.

Randy nodded. "I know, but Sergio says we can't afford to go to Provincetown next summer on vacation. He's being pretty stubborn about it actually, but if I have him screaming like Janet Leigh in the *Psycho* shower scene on a phone video that I can post on YouTube at any time, well, then maybe I'll have more leverage to convince him!"

Randy excitedly trotted off.

Hayley felt the burning need to remind him one more time, "Not a good husband!"

Chapter Two

"You're late," Hayley said, clutching her phone to her ear as she supervised Liddy and Mona setting out the last few remaining trays of food for the guests.

"I know, sorry, babe," Hayley's husband, Bruce, said on the other end of the call. "I was leaving the office when a report came over the police scanner about a residential break-in on Hancock Street."

"*Another* break-in?"

There had been an unsettling rash of home burglaries over the past several months. Well, "rash," in a town as small as Bar Harbor, actually meant *four* break-ins. But that was still a lot and was a developing pattern, especially since the summer tourist season, which ordinarily caused a spike in local crimes, was long over.

"There was no one else around to go cover it; all the reporters are probably at your party, so it was left to me.

You know only a late-breaking story would keep me away," Bruce said apologetically.

"Is it the same M.O. as the others?" Hayley asked.

"No," Bruce said solemnly.

Hayley immediately tensed up. "How is this one different?"

"All of the previous break-ins occurred at empty houses; the residents were either not home at the time or out of town," Bruce quietly explained.

"Oh, dear . . ." Hayley heard herself saying.

"Apparently the thief broke in thinking no one was inside the house, but the elderly widow who lives there was upstairs taking a nap. She heard some kind of commotion, and when she came out her bedroom to investigate, she came face-to-face with the burglar."

Elderly widow.

Hancock Street.

"Was it Clara Beaumont?" Hayley gasped.

"Yes," Bruce said quietly.

Clara Beaumont was about eighty-six years old, widowed fifteen years ago when her husband Irving died at seventy-six following complications from a stroke. Clara had lived in Bar Harbor her entire life, married Irving straight out of high school, and had one daughter, who went on to give her three grandchildren, all of whom lived in California but visited once a year for the holidays. Hayley had had the pleasure of interacting with Clara at the Congregational Church services, a number of library bake sales, and at the village green during the summer band concerts, since Clara was an avid music lover. She was a sprightly, happy woman, and still remarkably sharp for her age.

Hayley held her breath. "Is she all right?"

There was a long pause on the other end of the phone. "Bruce?"

"I'm afraid not, babe."

Hayley's heart sank. "Oh, no . . ."

"From what the cops can gather, Clara suddenly appearing out of nowhere spooked the guy. One of the neighbors walking his dog past the house at the time heard Clara screaming and called 911. What happened next is a little fuzzy. Either Clara slipped and fell down the stairs, trying to get away, or there was a struggle and the guy pushed her," Bruce said. "The police found her lying at the foot of the staircase when they arrived. At that point, she was still conscious."

"Did she know the man who broke into her house?"

"Hard to say. All she managed to get out was that the thief took off with her diamond wedding ring. I guess she saw it in his hand when she came out of her bedroom. But she passed out before she had a chance to identify him. She's at the hospital in intensive care right now. The cops are still combing the house for clues."

"Poor Clara . . ." Hayley moaned.

"I'm still waiting to talk to one of the officers at the scene, but I will get to the party just as soon as I can," Bruce promised.

Bruce continued talking, but Hayley could not hear what he was saying due to an argument happening right behind her just a few feet away.

"What was that, Bruce?" Hayley asked, holding the phone closer while pressing a finger into her other ear.

"I said I've got my King Kong costume in the trunk of my car so I can change in the parking lot and make a grand entrance."

"I can hardly wait," Hayley laughed. "See you when you get here." She ended the call, then spun around to discover Annie Wilkes and the Mummy, or Randy and Sergio, snapping at each other in a heated exchange.

"You're completely overreacting," Randy insisted.

"No, I am not," Sergio griped, his hand held out. "Now give me the phone."

Hayley quickly interceded. "Please, you guys, I really want this party to go off without a hitch, so I'm begging you, don't fight. Not tonight."

Her emotional appeal seemed to do the trick and brought the temperature down a bit between the bickering couple.

"He wants me to erase the video I've been recording of the party because he can't stand the thought of anybody seeing him scream like a little girl," Randy sighed.

"I am the chief of police in this town, and so I have a certain image to maintain. I do not want that video getting passed around and making me look like a fool!"

"I'm not going to post it on social media, Sergio, I promise; it's just for family and friends," Randy said with a Cheshire-cat-like grin.

Sergio glared at him, skeptical.

"Don't you think he's making too much of this, Hayley?" Randy asked, turning to his sister to back him up.

"I think it's none of my business, and so I plead the fifth."

Sergio's phone buzzed. He glanced at the screen. "It's Donnie. I better take this."

Randy turned to Hayley. "He's been calling all night. There was another break-in on Hancock Street . . ."

"I just heard. Bruce is covering the story for the paper. I pray Clara Beaumont recovers," Hayley said.

"What's the status, Donnie?" Sergio asked, listening intently.

Officer Donnie, after eight years with the Bar Harbor Police Department, had finally been promoted to lieutenant. It had been a long time coming. Sergio had been grooming him, putting him in charge when he was out of town on vacation. Donnie had grown quite a bit from his early days as a wet-behind-the-ears rookie and was now ready to do the chief proud. Hayley was not surprised that Sergio had not immediately rushed out of the party to the crime scene the moment he heard about the 911 call, because Donnie was anxious to prove his mettle and run an honest-to-goodness police investigation all on his own without the chief there to look over his shoulder. This was Donnie's big chance, but Hayley could tell just from Sergio's agitated tone and gestures that staying out of it was killing him.

"Are you sure you don't need me there, Donnie? Not in any supervisory capacity, just as an observer? No, I promise, you are point man on this, but I can just be there if you have any questions," Sergio said, pausing to allow Donnie to argue his point. Sergio nodded. "Okay, if you are sure. But you will call me the minute you are done sweeping the house for evidence, or if Mrs. Beaumont's condition changes? I can be over at the house or at the hospital in less than five minutes!"

Hayley smiled to herself. Sergio was obviously desperate for any excuse to ditch this party and the embarrassing moment he had endured earlier.

"No, Donnie, I trust you. Just keep me updated, that's all I ask," Sergio said before ending the call. With a half-smile, he cracked, "I just promoted him to lieutenant last month, and I think he's already gunning for *my* job."

"Donnie's loyal to you, Sergio, and he's developed into a good cop over the years. Give him a chance to spread his wings a little," Randy said.

Sergio nodded. "You're right."

"Now relax, and enjoy the party," Randy said, aiming his phone at a nearby gaggle of guests in a wide variety of colorful Halloween-movie-monster costumes. "Everyone looks so great. Although if there was a costume contest, I would be a shoo-in to win. You have to admit, I make an awesome Annie Wilkes."

"It's like you're channeling Kathy Bates. Hey, what happened to your sledgehammer?" Hayley noticed.

"It was too heavy to carry around, so I left it in the kitchen," Randy said, swiveling his phone around to capture all the revelers in his video.

"Just keep the camera away from me, or the Mummy here will mummify you," Sergio warned.

"Promises, promises," Randy joked.

Hayley busted up laughing.

Chapter Three

What sounded like a woman's bloodcurdling scream pierced the air, startling Hayley, who was in the kitchen, lining a garbage bin with a big plastic bag in order to begin the clean-up effort. She raced back out into the dining room to see what was happening, stopping short at the sight of Sergio confronting Pennywise, who had snuck up behind him yet again.

"I warned you, Candy! If you don't stop following me around, I will arrest you for stalking!" Sergio yelled.

Mona, who was sweeping the floor with an industrial broom, and Liddy, who was folding up a linen tablecloth, both suppressed smiles. Mona's son, Chet, was slumped down in a chair in the corner, eyes glued to his phone but with a smirk on his face. Randy gulped down the last of the spiked punch, red-faced, trying not to laugh too hard. There were no other guests left at the party.

Pennywise, who had been stacking leftover cookies and brownies on a paper plate, just stared at Sergio without saying a word.

"Don't look at me like that!" Sergio warned.

Pennywise didn't budge.

It was almost as if he wasn't sure what to do.

Sergio pointed a finger at his clownish, exaggerated, scary red lips. "Did you hear me? This is *not* funny!"

"It's a little funny . . ." Randy interjected.

Sergio threw him a fierce glare, and Randy mimed zipping his lips. He was not going to say another word and upset his husband any more than he already was. Randy also held up his phone to show Sergio he was not still recording.

Sergio returned his attention to Pennywise. "Would you at least take off that mask?"

Again, Pennywise stood frozen, not moving a muscle.

Sergio took a deep breath, collected himself, and then said calmly, "Look, Boris, the party's over. Unless you're going to help us clean up, maybe you should consider just going home."

Pennywise continued to stand motionless a few more seconds, ratcheting up the tension.

Hayley stepped forward. "Boris, is everything all right?"

He then nodded his head slightly, grabbed the last few remaining cookies off the table, piled them onto his paper plate of leftover desserts, and lumbered away. But he did not head for the front door. Instead, he wandered toward the kitchen, passing by Chet, who reached out and snatched a praline square off the plate and stuffed it in his mouth.

"Chet, stealing sweets from your music teacher is not

going to help get you a better grade! Now get off your duff and help us clean up!" Mona ordered.

Chet stood up and sighed, annoyed, then reluctantly took the garbage bin from Hayley and began half-heartedly dumping empty cups and paper plates into it.

Pennywise disappeared out the back of the restaurant.

"What was that all about?" Hayley wondered. "And why isn't he leaving out the front door?"

"Front door, back door, who cares? As long as he's gone. What an odd seagull," Sergio said, shaking his head.

"Duck," Randy corrected him. "Odd duck."

"Fine. Whatever," Sergio snorted. "We are on an island off the coast of Maine. I do not understand why the saying just cannot be a seagull!"

Liddy chuckled. "You know, Sergio does make sense in his own strange way."

Randy crossed to Sergio and gently patted his back. "I'm sorry for laughing at you earlier. I'm sure it wasn't easy to talk about your fear of clowns. Forgive me?"

Sergio glanced at Randy, appearing to soften, but then spit out an emphatic, "No!"

Hayley wasn't too worried. Her brother and his husband rarely stayed mad at each other for too long. Sergio would probably forget why he was even upset by morning. Still, she was confused by Boris Candy's bizarre behavior. She was about to follow him out the back to see if she might find out what, if anything, was wrong with him when suddenly the front door burst open and Cruella de Vil blew in, looking wild-eyed and discombobulated. She wore an oversized fake fur coat, a black dress, long, red gloves that stretched out to her elbows, and a half-black, half-white wig. Her face was caked with white makeup, and her lips were painted a ruby red. The costume was spot-on.

"I can't find Pia!" Cruella roared.

"Is Pia one of your dalmatian puppies?" Randy cracked.

"No! My daughter!"

Cruella was actually Dr. Mira Reddy, a physician at the Jackson Lab, a biomedical research facility founded in Bar Harbor, Maine, way back in 1929. Although she was smart as a whip and at the forefront of her field—mammalian genetics and human genomics research—the common opinion around town was that Dr. Reddy's personality was no match for her brains. Many in town found her snobbish and dismissive. In fact, Hayley would never have even thought about inviting the doctor to her Halloween party, especially since she had culled the guest list to only include a small number of close family and friends, but Mona had begged Hayley to include her, just like she had with Boris Candy.

Dr. Reddy's daughter, Pia, was Mona's youngest child Jodie's best friend, and Jodie was desperate to have her BFF at the party so she had someone to play with. Unfortunately, Pia had told Jodie that her mother refused to allow her to come on her own, that she would have to accompany her as a chaperone, so Hayley was left with no choice but to include Dr. Reddy on the final guest list. The irony of her showing up dressed as Cruella de Vil was not lost on anybody.

"Well, has anyone seen her?" Cruella huffed. "It's late, and it's a school night! I want to go home!"

Everyone exchanged blank looks.

Except for Chet, who stopped picking up paper plates off the table and asked quietly, "Was Pia dressed as a witch?"

"Yes," Dr. Reddy said. "She and Jodie came as characters from that old movie *Hocus Pocus*, which they saw recently. Did you see them? Where are they?"

"In the back, near the storeroom," Chet said. "But that was a while ago."

Everyone fanned out to find the girls, no one having a clue what was about to turn up.

Chapter Four

After bumping into tables and knocking over a few chairs, Mona mercifully shed her bulky foam shark costume to lead the search for her daughter, Jodie, and her friend Pia. Sergio slipped out of his Mummy getup as well, and Liddy continued with the cleanup. But the rest of the remaining group were already spread out in the restaurant, checking everywhere for the missing girls.

Not two minutes passed before they heard Randy call out, "Found them!"

They all raced in the direction of Randy's voice, which, as Chet had already told them, was coming from the storeroom in the back. Hayley, with Dr. Reddy breathing heavily down her neck, was the first to enter after Randy. The two girls sat in the middle of the floor, opposite each other, in their *Hocus Pocus* costumes. Jodie had a red wig on and was wearing a green dress, like the Bette Midler character Winifred in the movie, and Pia, who was smaller, wore a blond wig and pink dress, presumably the Sarah Jessica Parker character, aptly named Sarah. Between them was a large hardcover tome embossed with the title *Witchcraft: A Book of Spells*, along with lit candles and various potion bottles.

"Girls, what are you doing in here?" Hayley asked.

They stared up nervously at her.

Finally, Jodie squeaked out, "Nothing."

Dr. Reddy pushed her way past Hayley and gasped. She reached down, picked up the book, and began thumbing through it. "What exactly is going on here? Where did you get this book?"

Another long pause.

This time Pia spoke. "Amazon."

By now, Mona and Sergio had joined Hayley, Dr. Reddy, and Randy in the storeroom with the girls.

Dr. Reddy slammed the book shut, her mouth open in shock. When she finally managed to collect herself, she kneeled down, took her daughter by the arm, and said firmly, "Were you two practicing *witchcraft*?"

The girls glanced at each other, not wanting to get themselves into any trouble, but after some tortured hesitation, Pia ultimately nodded slightly and broke down, her eyes pooling with tears. "Yes. I'm sorry, Mommy."

Dr. Reddy released her grip on her daughter and shot back up to her feet. "This is outrageous! What kind of party is this, allowing little girls to engage in this kind of behavior?"

"Oh, come on, they're just having a little harmless fun," Mona snapped, rolling her eyes.

This did nothing to tamp down the mounting tension.

Dr. Reddy whipped around to Mona and marched up

to her until their noses were almost touching. "I can't say I'm surprised to hear you say that, Mona Barnes. You've unleashed an army of misbehaved troublemakers onto the streets of this town over the years, so why should I expect some decent parenting with the last runt in the litter?"

Absolute silence.

Except perhaps the sound of Mona's blood boiling.

Mona rolled up the sleeves of her sweatshirt in a threatening manner and took a step toward Dr. Reddy. "I think I have put up with enough of you, you sanctimonious, snobby—"

"Let's just *all* calm down," Hayley pleaded.

Sergio instinctively reached out and grabbed Mona, pulling her back by his side, gripping her tightly by the arm and preventing a potential all-out brawl.

Mona struggled a bit to free herself from his iron grip, but thankfully she slowly cooled down and stopped fighting him.

Still, Sergio wasn't taking any chances. He casually threw an arm around Mona's shoulders, so he was in a good position to take her down in case she unexpectedly tried to lunge at Dr. Reddy and attack her, which, given Mona's legendary quick temper, was not a difficult scenario to imagine.

"I find it reprehensible that anyone would think something like this is acceptable behavior. Come on, Pia, we're going home right now," Dr. Reddy spit out.

Pia grabbed the book and scrambled to her feet.

"No, you give that back to Jodie. I will not have my daughter reading that blasphemous filth!"

"B-but . . ." Pia sputtered.

"But *what*?" Dr. Reddy snapped.

"It's my book," Pia muttered, eyes downcast.

Mona snorted through her nose, trying to suppress a laugh.

Dr. Reddy's nostrils flared. She snatched the book out of her daughter's hand and tossed it in a nearby garbage bin. "We'll talk about you ordering items off the internet without my permission when we get home. Now come on, Pia!"

Liddy suddenly popped her head in the storeroom, carrying a casserole dish wrapped in tinfoil. "Hayley, there was half a Chicken Cordon Boo casserole left over. No sense letting it go to waste. Should I put in the fridge for later?"

"No, take it to the freezer; thanks, Liddy," Hayley said, returning her attention to a rattled Dr. Reddy and a remorseful, teary-eyed Pia.

"Where's your coat?" Dr. Reddy asked her daughter.

Pia shrugged. "I don't know."

Dr. Reddy sighed. "Well, go find it, so we can get out of here."

Pia dashed off.

Hayley knelt down to Mona's daughter, Jodie, who had remained tight-lipped since they had first been caught. "Jodie, do the candles and bottles belong to you?"

Jodie shook her head, eyes glued to the floor, and said quietly, "No, Pia brought them, too. It was her idea to be real witches and cast spells."

Mona relished this moment by throwing a self-satisfied smile in Dr. Reddy's direction, which the doctor willfully ignored.

Randy surreptitiously leaned in and whispered in Hayley's ear, "I only see one real witch here," as he nodded toward Dr. Reddy, stifling a chuckle.

Hayley was about to ask Dr. Reddy if she would like them to put the candles and bottles in a paper bag so she could take them home with her, too, when suddenly they heard another woman's high-pitched, bloodcurdling scream.

All eyes turned to Sergio.

"It was *not* me!" Sergio protested.

"Liddy . . ." Hayley said under her breath as she shoved her way out of the storeroom and ran toward the walk-in freezer located in the opposite far corner of the kitchen.

The large, stainless-steel freezer door was open when Hayley arrived on the scene, with Sergio, Randy, Mona, and Dr. Reddy bringing up the rear.

Hayley suddenly came to an abrupt stop.

The casserole dish had slipped out of Liddy's hands, shattering the glass and sending Hayley's Chicken Cordon Boo Halloween recipe flying everywhere. Just past Liddy, on the floor in the freezer, was a man's body, sprawled out on his back, limbs akimbo.

Hayley's eyes zeroed in on the man's pale ghostly face, his glassy, lifeless eyes staring up at her, his crooked mouth wrenched open as if frozen in a silent scream.

"Oh, no . . ." she moaned.

There was no mistaking who it was.

The dead man was Boris Candy.

Chapter Five

Liddy couldn't stop screaming.

The shock of stumbling over a corpse had been too much for her.

Hayley whipped around and grabbed her by the arms. "Liddy, please, get a hold of yourself!"

Liddy managed to catch her breath, heaving gulps of air and fanning herself in an attempt to calm down, but then her eyes would drop back down to Boris Candy's corpse, and she would start screaming all over again.

Hayley shook her by the arms. "Liddy, I don't want to slap you!"

That seemed to do the trick.

Liddy finally managed to get herself under control, grabbed Hayley's hand, poised to strike, and growled, "Don't you dare . . ."

Sergio was already circling the body, inspecting the

scene. He knelt down to examine the back of Candy's head.

Hayley pushed Liddy toward the door. "Go and make sure Jodie and Pia stay far away from here. I don't want them to see anything!"

But it was too late.

Hearing Liddy's terrified scream, Jodie had already rushed to the freezer and pushed her way through the group to see what was causing such a commotion. The little girl's eyes popped open wide, and she emitted a frightened gasp.

Mona instantly covered her daughter's eyes with her hands and hustled her out. "Come on, Jodie, there is nothing to see here!"

"I'm going to go check on Pia," Dr. Reddy said, mostly to herself, before taking one last glance at the dead body and shaking her head in distress before rushing out.

Sergio sprang back up when he was done investigating. "There is a bloody wound on the back of Candy's head."

Hayley gasped, even louder than Jodie. "*What?*"

"It appears as if someone bludgeoned him to death with some kind of blunt object. Near as I can tell, Mr. Candy must have decided to change out of his clown costume back here before going home, and while he was distracted, someone came up behind him, whacked him good in the back of the head, then dragged the body into the freezer, hoping to hide it long enough for him . . . or her . . . to escape out the back door."

Randy bolted from the freezer, only to return a few moments later. "There is one problem with your theory, Sergio. The back door is locked from the inside. The killer could not have gone out the back, unless someone locked it *after* he left."

"No," Liddy whispered. "It was already locked when I came back here to clean up after the party. I know because I checked. Boris Candy was still in the main dining room."

"Then the killer had to have left out the front door, but most of the party guests had already left by the time we all last saw Mr. Candy alive," Hayley noted. "Which means . . ."

Sergio nodded, a solemn look on his face. "It would have to be one of us still at the party . . . me, you, Randy, Mona, Liddy, Dr. Reddy, Mona's boy, Chet . . ."

"No, that's preposterous!" Hayley protested. "Why would any one of us want to harm poor Mr. Candy?"

Sergio shrugged. "I don't know. But it's all we've got at this point."

Mona appeared at the freezer door, her face ashen and her whole body trembling. "You all better come out to the dining room, right now!"

"Why? What's happened now?" Hayley groaned, almost dreading to find out.

Mona didn't answer her. She just whipped around and led them all out of the freezer, leaving behind the body and taking them back out front to the dining room.

There they saw Dr. Reddy pacing back and forth in full Cruella de Vil mode, sucking on a cigarette and rubbing her tired eyes with her black-gloved fingertips. Chet sat in a corner, legs stretched out, arms folded, obviously wishing he was anywhere else. Jodie and Pia were sitting cross-legged on the floor, close together, shoulders touching, sticking together, both with long, solemn faces.

Mona marched over to the two little girls, bent down, and said gently, "Okay, Jodie, repeat to Sergio exactly what you just told me."

Sergio eagerly stepped forward. "Did you girls see something? Do you know who killed Mr. Candy?"

Jodie and Pia exchanged petrified looks.

Then Jodie turned back to the Chief and nodded slightly.

Sergio rested a hand on Mona's shoulder, signaling for her to get up. Mona rose and took a step back, allowing Sergio to kneel down and take her place. He smiled at the girls and said in a warm, reassuring voice, "It's okay, girls. You're not in any trouble. Everything is going to be okay. Just tell me who it was. Who killed Mr. Candy?"

Another nervous glance between the girls.

Pia was now on the verge of tears. "Tell him, Jodie!"

Finally, Jodie, after a lot of wriggling and hemming and hawing, stared down at the floor and whispered under her breath, "We did. We killed Mr. Candy."

Island Food & Cocktails
by
Hayley Powell

It's never been a secret that Halloween has always been my kids' favorite holiday, probably because every year their father made such a big deal out of it when they were growing up. Every October, my husband, Danny, would try to top himself by going bigger with his scary costumes and elaborate pranks. The kids loved it. I just found myself exhausted. Mostly because, nine times out of ten, I was the target of his pranks. One year involved dressing up in a giant raccoon costume and hiding in the laundry room, so when I came to get the towels out of the dryer, he could jump out at me. The kids, of course, were in on it and fell to the floor holding their sides and laughing hysterically as I came screaming out of the laundry room, frantically waving my hands in the air. But I never complained too much because I had long accepted the fact that it had become a family tradition.

That is, until the year Danny and I separated and he moved out of state a couple of months before Halloween. The kids were heartbroken, and as Halloween drew closer, I could tell they just didn't have the same spirit without their dad around to get them excited. I didn't want them sulking at home, so I convinced the kids to dress up in their favorite costumes and march in the middle-school Halloween parade. I also rallied them to go trick-or-treating with me, Mona, and her kids in the early evening. I was certainly no substitute for their father, but I did my best to whip up a little enthusiasm.

It seemed to work. Dustin dusted off his go-to Batman costume, and Gemma transformed herself into Hermione Granger from the *Harry Potter* books for the next day's parade. The kids had set off for school, and that's when things took a decidedly dark turn.

As I was leaving for work, I noticed that the pumpkins I had placed on the railing of the deck were gone. I cursed to myself, assuming some kids must have smashed them on the road. So I went down the street to investigate, but I didn't see any pumpkin guts anywhere. When I returned, both pumpkins had mysteriously returned. They were sitting on the front steps unscathed, except they were now each wearing a clown's hat, which I found somewhat disconcerting.

Later, when I arrived home for lunch to let my dog, Leroy, outside to take care of his midday business, I opened the refrigerator to get some turkey and cheese for a sandwich, and screeched at the sight of a sandwich already made, sitting on a plate, with a knife plunged into the middle of it, sticking straight up. It *had* to be the kids. Who else could have done it? They had learned from the best, and as the saying goes, the apples don't fall far from the tree, and let's face it, my ex, Danny, was that mighty big tree!

Then, after work, when I went to grab the mail out of the box in front of the house, waving to my neighbor Jim across the street, who was already raking the fall leaves in his yard, I reached inside the box and felt something thick and fuzzy brush across my hand. I instantly yanked my hand out, peeked inside, and let out a shriek loud enough to wake the dead! Poor Jim dropped his rake and came running across the street to help me. A few curious neighbors peered out their windows. My kids raced out the front door as I stood there blubbering about a giant spider in the mail box. Jim peeked inside, then reached in and pulled out a big, black, fake fuzzy spider with a note attached that said, "Boo!"

Jim couldn't stop himself from busting up laughing; Dustin thought the spider looked cool and wanted to keep it; Gemma just rolled her eyes and moaned that I was embarrassing her in front of the neighbors. I knew right then by their reactions that the kids had had nothing to do with this bizarre series of pranks.

I marched inside and called Danny, who swore he was still in Iowa and had not snuck back to town to engage in his typical Halloween revelry.

So who was behind this unexpected reign of terror?

That's when I opened the kitchen cabinet for a box of pasta to make for dinner and was met with a giant ghoul face bobbing up and down and laughing maniacally. More screaming. More running around. Both hands in the air. Not my most calm and composed moment.

That was the last straw. After taking a few deep breaths, I dragged the kids out to the car and drove straight over to my brother Randy's house, hoping to coerce an invitation to stay for dinner because I was not about to spend another moment in my own home, dreading what might happen next.

Randy and his husband, Sergio, were more than happy to host us, and we all gorged on one of Randy's specialty dishes, Chicken Cordon Bleu—or Boo, as he liked to call it around Halloween—a name I adopted for my own Chicken Cordon Boo Bites appetizer, but more on that later. I spent most of the meal breathlessly recounting the day's heart-stopping pranks, and how I was clueless as to who could be behind them! Sergio promised to have a squad car patrol the neighborhood to be on the lookout for anything out of the ordinary. I thanked him profusely. I was determined to get to the bottom of this.

The next day was Halloween. I made plans with Mona, who offered to pick up my kids and her own brood and take them back to her house for a quick dinner before we would all meet up to go trick-or-treating. After a long day at work, including a mid-morning break to step outside on the sidewalk of the *Island Times* office to watch the parade pass by and wave at all the children in their costumes, I rushed home to feed Leroy and grab a quick bite to eat before Mona arrived with the car full of kids, ready to load up on trick-or-treat sweets.

I tossed my purse on the kitchen table and glanced around for Leroy, who, oddly, was nowhere to be seen. I started to get an eerie feeling. The house was so quiet, almost too quiet, as I stood in the middle of the kitchen, just listening for a moment.

I slowly walked out of the kitchen toward the living room when I thought I heard soft music playing. I strained to hear what it was as I silently crept down the hallway. As it seemed to slowly grow in volume, I recognized the tune. It was the theme from that creepy 1960s supernatural soap *Dark Shadows*! My stomach was in knots as I rounded the corner and suddenly saw a man sitting in a chair facing away from me. I covered my mouth to muffle my gasp. I quietly backed away, keeping my eye on the man in the chair, and then spun around to make a run for it. That's when I found myself face-to-face with a lumbering, black-eyed, decaying zombie with pieces of skin hanging off his face. I screamed and turned to see the man in the chair stand up and turn around. It was *another* zombie! Perhaps I had woken the dead with all my screaming outside at my mailbox the day before!

I was just about to faint dead away when the zombies began chuckling and snorting, softly at first, then building to all-out guffawing. That was the moment I knew I had been had. The zombie masks came off. It was Randy and Sergio!

Suddenly, the basement door flew open and Dustin and Gemma, who apparently had not gone to Mona's, came running out, with Leroy yipping at their heels, laughing and yelling, "We got you! We got you!"

When Randy and Sergio finally managed to stop howling, they explained that the kids were very sad about their dad not being here to play a Halloween trick on Mom like they did every year. Danny had decided that if he couldn't be there to supervise the prank personally, he would enlist a little help from their two uncles, who were more than happy to lend a helping hand to scare the living daylights out of their poor mother. Why I am always the target, I will never know. But I have to admit, they got me good!

Later that night, after trick-or-treating, Gemma and Dustin called their dad to fill him in on how well the plan had worked and how terrified I was, and then they handed me the phone. Danny rather sheepishly asked me if I was mad, but I told him no. I couldn't be upset when I saw how excited the kids were to be doing something with their dad, even if he was 1,500 miles away. But as I hung up the phone, I thought to myself, *You better watch out next year, Danny Powell. What goes around comes around.*

Then I went to make myself a Hot White Russian, hoping that might do the trick in getting my heart rate to come down.

Hot White Russian

Ingredients
4 ounces hot coffee
2 ounces Kahlua
2 ounces milk
1 ounce vodka
Whipped cream (optional)

Pour all the ingredients into a coffee mug and stir, topping with whipped cream, if you like. Sit back and enjoy!

Chicken Cordon Boo Bites

Ingredients
2 boneless chicken breasts
⅓ to ¾ cup vegetable oil
1 cup flour
2 tablespoons Cajun seasoning
1 teaspoon granulated garlic
1 cup milk
1½ cup seasoned Panko bread crumbs
4 slices of ham cut into 1-inch squares
4 slices of Swiss cheese cut into 1-inch squares

Dipping sauce
⅔ cup mayonnaise
1 tablespoon mustard

Instructions
Mix the two ingredients for the dipping sauce in a small bowl, and set aside.

Pound the chicken breasts with a kitchen mallet to equal thickness.

Heat the oil to medium heat.

Add the flour, Cajun seasoning, and garlic to a 1-quart ziplock bag.

Cut the chicken into bite-size pieces. One by one, dip the chicken bites into the milk, then into the flour mixture. Shake off excess flour and dip back into the milk, then roll each bite around in the panko bread crumbs, making sure it is fully coated. Add the coated chicken to the heated oil, and cook until golden brown and cooked through (7–10 minutes), turning as needed. Remove from oil and place on a cooling rack placed on a baking pan.

To each bite, add a piece of cheese, a piece of ham, and another piece of cheese, and secure with a toothpick. When ready to serve, you can warm for a bit in the oven or even for a few seconds in the microwave, just long enough to melt the cheese. Put out the bowl with the dipping sauce, and you are in business!

Chapter Six

"This is preposterous! The girl is obviously making up stories to get attention!" Dr. Reddy cried.

"Please, let the girl speak," Sergio demanded, before swiveling back around and kneeling down so he was eye-to-eye with Jodie. "Now, Jodie, are you saying you hit Mr. Candy in the back of the head with something?"

Jodie shook her head, blinking back tears.

Sergio nodded. "Okay, then why do you think you killed him?"

Jodie turned to glance at Pia, who was sucking her thumb nervously, eyes wide with fright. Jodie then returned her gaze to Sergio and whispered, barely loud enough for the others to hear, "We cast an evil spell on him."

"I have heard enough!" Dr. Reddy sighed, marching

forward and grabbing her daughter by the hand, dragging her toward the door. "Come on, Pia, we're leaving."

Sergio sprang back to his feet, chasing after her until he managed to insert himself in front of her and her daughter and block their exit. "I'm sorry, Dr. Reddy, but I cannot allow you to leave until we figure all this out."

"You can't force me to stay! I will not be held prisoner!"

"Then I will consider your refusal to cooperate as an obstruction of justice, and I will call Judge Crowley to issue an arrest warrant."

Dr. Reddy gasped. "You wouldn't dare!"

"Try me," Sergio threatened.

Hayley suspected Sergio was bluffing, but Dr. Reddy appeared convinced enough that he would make good on his threat that she plopped down at a table near the door, still squeezing Pia's hand, keeping her firmly by her side. She sat there pouting, refusing to make eye contact with anyone.

Sergio walked back and knelt down next to Jodie again. "Okay, dear, I want you to tell me exactly what happened. Start from the beginning."

Jodie looked toward her mother, not sure what to do.

"Go on, tell him, Jodie. Sergio wants to help you," Mona said as gently as the irascible Mona was capable of.

"Mr. Candy came to the storeroom, where we were playing with the spell book, and he accidentally stepped on one of our candles, and his costume nearly caught on fire before he stamped it out. He got really mad at us and called us 'silly, stupid little girls,' and then he grabbed a bottle of wine and stormed out. He was so mean, and he made us so mad . . . that's when we . . ."

"Cast your spell?" Sergio asked.

Jodie nodded.

Sergio put a comforting hand on Jodie's shoulder. "What kind of spell did you cast?"

Jodie stared at the floor, ashamed. "A death spell . . . We didn't think it would actually work, we were just playing around . . . But then . . . then he died."

Tears streamed down Jodie's face.

Dr. Reddy piped up. "Well, I certainly hope you are proud, Mona Barnes! You've managed to spawn your very own *bad seed*!"

"I swear, if she doesn't button it, I am going to knock her head to kingdom come!" Mona seethed under her breath.

"Violence is never the answer," Liddy warned.

"Since when?" Mona groused.

Pia tugged on her mother's Cruella de Vil fake fur coat. She also had tears pooling in her eyes. "It was me, Mama . . ."

"What do you mean?" Dr. Reddy snapped.

"I was the one who went to the chapter on black magic in the book and found the death spell. Jodie just went along with it."

"Why on earth would you ever do something like that, Pia?" Dr. Reddy cried.

"Because Mr. Candy called us names and hurt our feelings, and we just wanted to get back at him. But it was just a game! We didn't really want him to *die*!" Pia wailed.

Dr. Reddy hugged her daughter, trying to comfort her as the girl sobbed uncontrollably, while still glaring at Mona, refusing to believe her poor daughter was at fault in the slightest despite the girl's full confession. In the doctor's mind, no matter what Pia was willing to admit, she had to be under the bad influence of the juvenile delinquent Barnes girl.

Hayley walked over to Jodie and gingerly put a hand underneath her chin, raising it up so she could offer the distraught child a reassuring smile. "It was wrong to cast a nasty spell on anyone, even someone who mistreated you, but, Jodie, believe me when I tell you, your spell did *not* kill Mr. Candy—"

"That's right! He died from a blow to the back of the head!" Dr. Reddy yelled. "Obviously, neither girl is big enough, or tall enough, or strong enough to do that kind of damage, so that puts Pia in the clear. Are we free to go now?" Dr. Reddy said as she stood back up.

"Sit!" Sergio barked, pointing a finger at her as if she was a misbehaving Great Dane.

Dr. Reddy dropped back down in her chair again, still gripping Pia tightly by the hand.

"It was just a coincidence," Hayley promised Jodie, who used the back of her hand to wipe away the tears streaking her apple cheeks.

"But the spell could have made him trip and fall and crack his head open!" Jodie sniffed.

Sergio pulled Hayley aside and said in a low tone, "That's not possible. The wound is not consistent with him tripping and falling. This is definitely a homicide. Someone whacked him pretty hard in the back of the head."

"I know," Hayley whispered back to Sergio. "I just don't want to scare the girls. They're upset enough as it is without having to worry about an actual murderer being among us."

"So what do we do now, call the police?" Liddy asked.

"I am the police, Liddy, in case that little fact slipped your mind," Sergio sighed. "All of my officers have their hands full with the break-in at Clara Beaumont's house at the moment, so I want you all to just sit tight until I have had a chance to question everyone."

"Uh oh . . ." a man squeaked.

All eyes turned to Randy, still in his Annie Wilkes overall denim dress and flat, brown stringy-haired wig.

"What is it?" Sergio asked.

"Has anyone seen my sledgehammer?"

They all looked around the dining room, but there was no sign of it.

"I remember putting it down in the kitchen earlier because it got too cumbersome to lug around, but then I lost track of it, and now I can't find it," Randy said quietly.

"What were you doing carrying around a sledgehammer?" Dr. Reddy howled.

"It was part of my costume! Annie Wilkes from the Stephen King novel *Misery*! Didn't you read the book or see the movie?"

Dr. Reddy shook her head. "No, I am not a fan of Stephen King. Too much unbelievable supernatural nonsense. I'd rather live in the real world."

"What about Hayley's awesome costume? You didn't know she was prom-night Carrie in a blood-soaked dress from King's very first novel?" Randy gasped.

Dr. Reddy shrugged and snorted, "I just thought she had a lousy dry cleaner."

Sergio was losing patience. "Okay, let's table the Halloween costume contest for later. We need to locate that sledgehammer. Hayley, why don't you and Liddy fan out and see if you can find it. The rest of us will stay here and try to remember if one of us saw anything unusual during the time leading up to Candy's mur—"—he stopped himself, eyeing the two visibly distraught moppets—"Candy's death."

Randy suddenly gasped. "We don't have to try to remember. I have it all right here." He held up his phone. "I was recording a video of the party for most of the night."

Sergio charged across the room to his husband and snatched the phone out of his grasp. They both began to intently watch the playback of the evening.

As Hayley and Liddy headed toward the back of the restaurant again, in search of the sledgehammer, Dr. Reddy and Mona remained behind, glaring at each other.

Dr. Reddy opened her mouth to say something, but Mona quickly cut her off with a stark warning. "If you say one more disparaging word about my daughter, it will be the end for you."

"I wasn't going to say anything," Dr. Reddy sniffed, pausing, waiting; then, unable to resist, she added, "Except that I'm surprised you know such a big word as *disparaging*."

Hayley winced, glancing back, half-expecting to see Mona flying across the room at Dr. Reddy, but Mona surprisingly didn't go on the attack. She held back, hugging her shaken daughter, whispering some soothing, comforting words in her ear.

Hayley and Liddy decided to split up in the back of the restaurant, in their frantic hunt to track down the possible murder weapon. But after a thorough search, the sledgehammer failed to turn up.

It was as if it had just vanished into thin air.

Or someone had taken great pains to hide it.

But where?

Chapter Seven

Sergio sat at a table in the dining room with Jodie and Pia, going over their story one more time as Dr. Reddy and Mona hovered nearby and Randy watched the video he had recorded on his phone for any obvious clues.

"After you cast this spell on Mr. Candy, did you see anyone else wandering around near the storeroom?"

"No," Jodie said quietly.

"Were you in the storeroom the whole time until we came to find you?" Sergio asked gently.

"Yes," Jodie said, nodding.

Pia tugged on the sleeve of Jodie's witch costume. "No, Jodie, remember, after Mr. Candy yelled at us, we went to get some cookies because we were hungry."

Jodie nodded, then turned back to Sergio. "Oh, yeah. That's right. We went back out front to the party for a little while."

"So you never saw Mr. Candy come back, and you never saw him talking to anyone else?"

Both girls shook their heads.

"They didn't see anything!" Dr. Reddy sighed. "Stop badgering them!"

"Please, Dr. Reddy, I am just trying to do my job, which would be a whole lot easier if you would stop interrupting me!" Sergio snapped.

Dr. Reddy threw her hands up in the air in surrender.

Liddy had now joined Randy, whose eyes were focused on his phone, and started watching the video of the party over his left shoulder.

Hayley decided to do one more sweep of the whole restaurant just in case she and Liddy had failed to spot the missing sledgehammer, which must be hidden somewhere, during their initial search. She looked in all of the cupboards, under the sink, in every corner—still with no luck.

That's when she realized there was one place where she had not looked.

The walk-in freezer.

Where Boris Candy's body was still lying on the floor.

Hayley took a deep breath, steeled herself, and pulled the freezer door all the way open. Fortunately, Mr. Candy's body was exactly where they had left it. Nothing supernatural had spirited it away. Hayley took a tentative step inside, shivering from the cold, and scanned every nook and cranny.

There was no sign of the sledgehammer.

Just poor Mr. Candy, who would probably die of frostbite if he had not already been dead.

That's when it dawned on her.

Where was his Pennywise costume?

The current theory was that he had changed out of his costume right before he was attacked. If so, then what had happened to the costume? Hayley poked around, but she could not locate it.

Maybe he had already stored the costume in his car but, for some reason, had come back inside before driving home, perhaps having forgotten something.

Hayley then unlocked the back door and walked outside, circling around the building to the parking lot, where only a few cars remained. She knew Mr. Candy drove a red Prius and spotted it instantly, parked next to Liddy's black Mercedes.

Hayley turned on the flashlight on her phone as she approached Mr. Candy's car. She first tried the door handle. It was unlocked. She opened it and scanned the seats and floor with the light. No sign of the costume. Then she popped open the trunk and searched there. Still no costume. What had he done with it?

She walked back inside, bolted the door shut again from the inside, and returned to the dining room.

Liddy quickly noticed the troubled look on her face. "What's wrong? What did you find?"

Hayley shrugged. "That's just it. I didn't find anything. Mr. Candy's Pennywise costume is missing. The mask, the clown costume, the big red shoes, everything."

"Sit tight, girls, I will be right back," Sergio told Jodie and Pia before standing up and crossing over to Hayley. "Are you sure he didn't put it in his car after he changed?"

"No, I just checked; it wasn't there. And he was wearing it right up until the end of the party, after most of the guests had gone, so it should be around here somewhere," Hayley said.

"The sledgehammer, the costume, what else has disappeared without a trace?" Liddy pondered.

Randy marched over to them, clutching his phone.

Sergio turned to his husband. "See anything on your video that was out of the ordinary?"

"No, and I watched it three times," Randy said, holding up the phone so Hayley and Sergio could see the video for themselves. "I started recording pretty early on during the party, and you can plainly see Mr. Candy walking around, mingling with the other guests, generally having a good time."

They watched the video, following Candy, sometimes in the background, sometimes just for a flash as Randy moved the camera around, before stopping on Candy as Pennywise, towering behind Sergio, who casually turns around and screams.

Hayley glanced at the Chief, who grimaced.

"Can you fast-forward through this part, please?" Sergio groaned.

Randy snickered but did as he requested, before slowing the video back down to normal speed. "Now wait, here comes the interesting part. He's having a perfectly good time, and then something changes. Wait, here it comes . . ."

They watched as Mr. Candy suddenly reacts to something, stopping in the middle of the room and spinning his head around frantically, before dashing out toward the kitchen.

Randy pressed pause on the video. "Something just spooked him real bad!"

"Why does he suddenly run to the kitchen?" Hayley asked.

Randy shrugged. "I have no idea." He pressed the fast-forward button up to the point when Pennywise returned to the party. "But he comes back about ten minutes later as if nothing had happened."

"That's strange," Hayley observed, watching as Pennywise threaded his way through all the costumed guests, as if on the hunt again to scare a few unsuspecting people. "Right about here, the party begins to wind down." He paused the video again. "There you can see Jodie and Pia by the dessert table. They did come out to the dining room to get cookies, just like they said. And Mr. Candy is still alive and well. He's right there, loading up on food as the other guests begin to file out."

"When do you lose track of him?" Sergio asked.

Randy continued playing the video. "Right up to this moment, with only a small handful of people left at the party, you can see him heading out again by himself toward the kitchen and storeroom . . ."

The video froze.

"And that's when I stopped recording because the party was pretty much over at that point," Randy said.

Sergio paced back and forth, trying hard to put the pieces of the puzzle together. "So the murder had to have occurred after the point when Mr. Candy changed out of his costume. The back door was locked from the inside, so no one could have entered from there. And the only people left in the restaurant are the ones who are still here now . . ."

Cruella de Vil.

The Mummy.

Annie Wilkes.

Carrie.

Bride of Frankenstein.

A giant land shark.

Chucky the killer doll.

And two pint-sized witches from *Hocus Pocus*.

One of those movie monsters was definitely a killer.

But which one?

And how did the murderer manage to get rid of the clown costume and the sledgehammer, the presumed murder weapon?

"Well, I, for one, find it difficult to believe that any of us here could be some kind of maniacal butcher!" Dr. Reddy sniffed, adjusting her half-white, half-black Cruella wig. "It's just too ridiculous to even consider!"

"Then who else could it be?" Randy wanted to know.

There was a long silence.

"A ghost . . ." a tiny voice squeaked.

It came from Pia, who hid behind her mother's massive fur coat. Dr. Reddy turned, taking a step away from her. "Pia, there are no such things as ghosts!"

"Jodie and I conjured up an evil spirit that murdered Mr. Candy, and then it must have just floated away . . ."

Dr. Reddy opened her mouth to protest but stopped short of speaking, because the more they all pondered the little girl's outlandish theory, the more they realized that, at this point, it was the only theory that made sense.

If everyone in the dining room was as innocent as they claimed, then the only other possible explanation had to be rooted in the supernatural.

And with no clues pointing in a more grounded direction, no one present in Hayley's restaurant at this moment was prepared to rule out a ghost with an ax to grind.

Chapter Eight

"If you are finished tormenting my daughter with your barrage of questions, Chief Alvares, I would like to take her home now, because it is well past her bedtime," Dr. Reddy said, grabbing Pia by the hand, anxious to bolt out the front door.

"I am done with Pia, Dr. Reddy, but not with you, so I would appreciate it if you would just take a seat and be patient," Sergio sighed, at his wit's end. "I do not want to have to ask you again."

Dr. Reddy huffed and muttered to herself, but did as she was told, sitting back down at one of the dining tables, Fendi bag in her lap, while gesturing to Pia to take a seat as well.

Hayley held her hand out to Randy. "Mind if I take a look at the video?"

Randy gave her the phone. "Be my guest."

Hayley pressed PLAY and reviewed the video footage of the party again while half-listening to Sergio.

"Liddy, you're up," the Chief said.

"*Me*? Why me? You certainly don't consider me a suspect, do you?"

"I consider everyone here a suspect," he said pointedly.

"Including *yourself*?" Dr. Reddy cracked, annoyed, as Pia stared at the floor, embarrassed by her mother's obstinance.

Sergio chose not to respond. He just flashed her an annoyed look before turning his attention back to Liddy. "Liddy, it's late; we're all tired. Just try to be cooperative, will you?"

Liddy dramatically sighed. "Fine. You can ask me anything you want. I have nothing to hide. I scarcely knew Boris Candy. I hardly had any interaction with him whatsoever."

"Ha!" Mona piped in.

Liddy turned to Mona, right eyebrow raised. "You have something to say, Mona?"

"Yes! What about the blind date you had with Boris when he first moved to town? Did you conveniently forget about *that*?"

There was a long dramatic silence.

"No, I did not forget about that, Mona," Liddy spit out with a furious look. "I have just tried to bury that awful memory and put it behind me."

Everyone in the room seemed to lean forward, curious.

"It happened a couple years ago, right before Boris started as the new music teacher at the high school. Mona, for some inexplicable reason, decided to play matchmaker. He had only been in town for about a week or so when he came into Mona's lobster shop—"

"He had never tasted a Maine lobster before in his life; can you believe that?" Mona interrupted. "So I set him up good with a three-pack and gave him tips on the best way to steam them. He told me later that it was the best meal he'd ever tasted. He was hooked. He came back every week after that. He seemed like such a nice, decent guy; I don't know what I was thinking, fixing him up with Liddy!"

"Mona, Sergio is questioning me, not you. I do not need your needless and unsolicited color commentary," Liddy seethed.

"Whatever," Mona shrugged. "The floor's yours."

"Thank you," Liddy said evenly, before turning back to Sergio. "In Mona's cluttered, confused mind, she somehow thought the two of us would actually hit it off."

"I'm assuming the two of you didn't?" Sergio asked.

"No!" Liddy scoffed. "From the moment we sat down at the restaurant, there was this underlying tension between us. I knew right away the date was going to be a disaster!"

"What did he say that set you off?" Sergio asked.

"It's not what he said. It was the rude looks he kept giving me as I told him about myself, like he was judging me. I found it very off-putting and uncomfortable."

"Did you ask him about it?"

"Yes, finally I couldn't take it anymore. I asked him why he was being so quiet. And do you know what that obnoxious, rude man said? He had the gall to tell me that he found me self-involved, that I had been talking nonstop about myself for thirty minutes without showing even the tiniest bit of interest in *him*! Can you believe that?"

Mona involuntarily gave a snort, but quickly pretended it hadn't come from her when Liddy shot her a glowering stare.

Sergio tried getting Liddy back on track. "Was Mr. Candy right about that?"

"Of course, he was right! Why should I show interest in a completely nondescript, boring, utterly humorless human being? If I am going to get all gussied up for a date, I want the man I'm meeting to have a little kick to him, like a spicy chili, but Boris Candy was basically a bland bowl of applesauce!"

"So am I safe in assuming there was no second date?" Sergio asked, suppressing a smile.

"No, we didn't even get through the first date. I was so insulted, I threw my glass of merlot at him. He got up from the table to go clean himself off in the bathroom, but then he never came back! Can you believe that?"

There were a few nods about the room that Liddy willfully chose to ignore.

"He ditched me! We had driven to the restaurant in his car! I was stranded!" Liddy wailed. "At least he had the good manners to pay the bill on his way out, but I had to call a taxi to take me home. We were at Jack Russell's, which is outside of town. I couldn't walk all the way home!"

"She called me the next day and demanded that I reimburse her for the cab fare," Mona said, chuckling. "Which I did, because, I admit, it was my fault for thinking those two might get along."

"Oh, I could have killed the man for abandoning me like that . . ." Liddy said, before realizing the implications of her remark and quickly adding, "But I didn't! It was a long time ago, and everyone knows I am never one to hold grudges!"

There was more quiet snickering in the room over Liddy's bogus claim about not holding grudges, enough for her to feel the need to add another caveat, "At least not in this case! Anyway, Mona was right about one thing! It was all *her* fault!"

"I was just trying to cheer you up after you got ditched at the altar!" Mona protested.

"Must we bring *that* up?" Liddy sighed.

"You're the one still wearing the wedding dress!" Mona said.

"How many times must I say this? It's my Halloween costume! I'm the Bride of Frankenstein!"

Randy wandered over to address Mona. "I am a little surprised you called Boris a nice, decent guy, Mona."

"Why is that?" Mona asked.

"Because I remember you two having an altercation at my bar not too long ago," he said.

"That was *nothing*!" Mona snapped.

"What is he talking about, Mona?" Sergio pressed.

"It was just a minor disagreement, that's all! I went in for Chet's parent-teacher conference at the school, and Candy told me that Chet had been acting out in his music-appreciation class lately, and that if he didn't adjust his behavior, he was going to take disciplinary action."

"And you thought he was being unfair to Chet?" Sergio asked.

"What? No," Mona scoffed, glancing over at Chet,

who was still slumped down in a chair in the corner, texting. "We all know the kid can be a hellion. I had no problem with making him pay for his bad behavior. But he insinuated that *I* was to blame for failing to keep him in line at home. Well, I stewed about that all day, and then I ran into him at Drinks Like a Fish, and yes, okay, I admit, I had a few beers in me when I approached him. I started yelling at him that maybe if he was a better teacher, he might be able to keep Chet interested in his boring class! It was not one of my prouder moments."

"Imagine an education professional questioning your parenting skills," Dr. Reddy whispered under her breath.

Mona whirled around, eyes blazing. "Lady, you are *this* close to a whole world of hurt!"

Dr. Reddy pointed an accusing finger at Mona. "See, if anyone is capable of causing bodily harm, it's *her*!"

"Dr. Reddy, please stay out of this," Sergio warned.

"The bottom line is, we resolved our differences shortly after that," Mona insisted. "I even brought him free lobsters at the school as a peace offering because I knew how much he loved them. And we haven't had a problem since. I actually like the guy . . . I mean *liked*."

The dining room fell silent again.

And then Hayley let out a gasp as she watched the video on Randy's phone.

"What is it, Hayley?" Sergio asked.

"How did we miss this?" Hayley whispered, running the video back a few seconds and playing it again.

Sergio and Randy rushed over to her, surrounding her on each side to see what had suddenly piqued her interest.

The scene on the phone was Boris Candy walking up behind Sergio and scaring him, causing him to scream.

Sergio sighed, annoyed. "Yes, Hayley, we have already had a good laugh over it. We do not have to watch it yet again."

"No," Hayley insisted. "Look, in the background. We were all laughing at you screaming, and we completely missed what was happening just a few feet away."

Behind Sergio and Candy, they could clearly see Mona's son, Chet, holding a cup of hot chocolate and distinctly dropping some kind of white pill into it. Moments later, he approached Mr. Candy, offering it to him. Mr. Candy happily accepted and chugged the hot chocolate down in a couple of gulps.

"Chet, get over here right now!" Sergio demanded.

Chet looked up from his phone, worried. "What?"

"Now!" Sergio roared.

Chet hauled himself up out of the chair, pocketed his phone, and shuffled slowly over to Sergio with a heavy sigh.

Sergio walked up to Chet so he was inches from him, towering over him in an intimidating manner. "What did you put in the hot chocolate you gave to Mr. Candy?"

There was a flicker of panic on Chet's face.

"Nothing," he said, obviously lying.

Sergio gestured toward Randy's phone. "We have it all recorded. You spiked the hot chocolate with something. Now tell us what it was!"

Mona barreled over to her son, sticking a finger in his face in a threatening manner. "What did you do, Chet? Come clean now, and you may live to see your high school graduation!"

Chet stuffed his hands in his pants pockets and shuffled his feet some more, staring at the floor, and then finally said in a tiny, defeated voice, "Mr. Candy kicked me off my trombone spot in the jazz band . . ."

Mona's eyes widened in surprise. "What? When?"

"A few weeks ago. He said I wasn't taking music seriously. I didn't want to tell you and make you mad," Chet said, hemming and hawing before mumbling, "I wanted to pay him back, so I slipped some Ex-Lax in the hot chocolate, and I sort of gave it to him as a peace offering."

Hayley wanted to laugh, but stopped herself.

"That would explain why he ran out of the party so fast," Randy said, smirking.

"There is a bathroom in the back next to the storeroom. The two out front were probably occupied, and Mr. Candy was in a code-red situation," Hayley surmised. "He must have switched to red wine after that, which would explain why he came into the storeroom to get a bottle and stumbled upon Jodie and Pia practicing witchcraft."

"What else do you want to tell us, Chet?" Sergio asked.

"That's it! It was just a stupid joke! I swear that's all I did!"

Mona shook her head in disgust. "What a rotten, despicable thing to do! I am ashamed of you right now, Chet! Where on God's green earth did you learn such a thing?"

Chet stared at his mother, slack-jawed. "From you, remember? You told all us kids that story from when you were in high school, and you slipped Ex-Lax in your soccer coach's water bottle because he benched you for three games after you deliberately kicked a girl on the opposing team in the shins so you could steal the ball away!"

"I was trying to teach you a lesson about what *not* to do when you're angry!" Mona argued.

"But—" Chet protested before Mona cut him off.

"Do as I say, not as I do! You're grounded until your eighteenth birthday!" Mona roared.

Another deafening silence.

Even Dr. Reddy knew well enough not to comment.

Chapter Nine

Sergio put an arm around Chet's shoulder. "Okay, son. We're done for now. You can go sit back down."

Chet bounded back to his chair in the corner, his phone in hand, to resume texting his friends.

"That's it? He's no longer a suspect?" Dr. Reddy scoffed.

"He came clean about the Ex-Lax," Sergio said.

Dr. Reddy folded her arms, agitated. "Exactly! If he was willing to poison a man, why abandon the credible possibility that the boy took it one step further and bludgeoned him to death?"

Sergio cocked an eyebrow. "Really, Dr. Reddy, I would hardly call a laxative poison."

"What if Mr. Candy was allergic to one of the ingredients. Would you be so dismissive then?"

"No, but he wasn't, and the Ex-Lax was not what killed him," Sergio patiently argued.

"Well, I, for one, think you are letting him off the hook far too easily," Dr. Reddy snorted. "He has already told us his motive. Mr. Candy unceremoniously kicked him out of jazz band, and the kid was thirsty for revenge."

Chet sighed loudly in the corner, dismayed to find all the attention in the room was still on him.

Mona lunged forward, red-faced with fury. "First you accuse my Jodie of corrupting your innocent daughter. Now you're accusing my son of murder? I've had it with you, lady!"

Hayley reached out and grabbed Mona's sweatshirt, forcefully pulling her back.

Mona whipped around to Hayley. "She's out of line, Hayley! Chet can be a prankster and pig-headed and lazy like his father, but he's a good boy, for the most part!" She then pointed a finger at Chet in the corner. "But you're still grounded!"

"A mother is always blinded by the love for her children," Dr. Reddy said to no one in particular.

Chet had heard enough. He shot back up to his feet and yelled at Dr. Reddy, eyes blazing, "I didn't get anywhere near Mr. Candy after I gave him the hot chocolate! I bet you can't say that, can you?"

It took a moment for Dr. Reddy to realize Chet was addressing her, but when she did, she huffed and threw him a haughty look. "I am quite sure I have no idea what you are talking about!"

"I saw you," Chet growled, eyes narrowing. "I saw you chasing after Mr. Candy. I was sitting right here. You were right in front of me and didn't even notice me, and I heard you threaten him!"

"That is a bald-faced lie! The boy is obviously just making things up to take the heat off himself," Dr. Reddy cried.

"You said you were going to do everything in your power to get him fired, or something like that," Chet said.

"Is that true, Doctor?" Sergio asked.

"No, I . . ." Dr. Reddy glanced around the room, unnerved by all the faces focused on her. "I mean . . . It was *nothing*!"

"I think you'd better explain," Sergio said. "And, please, don't leave anything out."

"There is nothing to explain! We simply had a disagreement, that's all."

She wanted to leave it there, but she instinctively knew that was going to be impossible. After mulling her options, Dr. Reddy was resigned to the fact that she was not going to be able to remain silent or simply brush it off. "Fine. My oldest daughter, Nina, has been struggling in Mr. Candy's music appreciation class, so I requested a meeting at the high school to discuss the situation with him. I told him Nina would do some extra-credit work in order to catch up. I thought we had resolved the situation. Nina worked exceedingly hard to bring her grade up, and I thought she had succeeded, but he still gave her a terribly unfair grade."

"He failed her?" Hayley asked.

"No." Dr. Reddy was so upset that she was near tears. "He gave her . . ." She choked on her words, almost unable to get them out. "He gave her a *B plus*."

Mona busted up laughing. "B plus? You're talking like that's the end of the world! I would be the proudest mother in the world if just one of my kids came home with a B plus! Hell, I'd throw a party if they came home with a C minus!"

Dr. Reddy bristled. "She deserved an A."

"That must have made you very angry," Sergio suggested.

"Yes, frankly, it did. Nina worked hard to improve her grade. We have very high expectations for her and her future, and a B plus was not going to help get her into Harvard. Mr. Candy's obstinance was going to potentially cost my daughter her future!"

Hayley was flabbergasted. "Do you honestly believe a B plus in music appreciation is going to hurt Nina's chances of getting into a good school?"

"Yes, I do, as a matter of fact," Dr. Reddy snapped. "I don't want her going to just a good school. I want both my daughters going to the *best* schools. A world-class college education is the first stepping-stone to a life of success."

Hayley glanced over at Pia, who was quietly listening to her mother, taking it all in. Hayley felt sorry for the poor girl, who, much like her older sister, had to be under intense pressure to perform perfectly, even in middle school.

"Look, Doctor, I understand you're a passionate advocate for your daughters. I have read all about you hang-glider parents," Sergio said.

There was another momentary pause before Randy tugged on Sergio's Mummy costume. "Helicopter."

Sergio turned to him, confused, then glanced toward the ceiling. "What? I don't hear anything." He turned to the others. "Do any of you hear a helicopter?"

"No, Sergio. Helicopter parents. That's what they call hard-driving, overprotective parents."

"What did I say?"

"Hang glider."

"My mistake. I grew up hang gliding in Brazil. You get my meaning! Parents who hover around trying to control everything!"

"I am not ashamed of taking a keen interest in the lives of my children," Dr. Reddy said defensively.

"Nor should you be," Sergio said. "I am just curious to know why you did not share this dispute you had with Mr. Candy earlier."

"Why should I? I told you, it meant nothing," Dr. Reddy said, suddenly getting flustered. "Okay, yes, I was mad, but not enough to bash him in the back of the head with a sledgehammer! I didn't say anything, because I knew if I did, I would immediately be a suspect, and I didn't want to have to deal with all that nonsense!"

"Too late!" Liddy interjected.

Dr. Reddy gave her a withering look.

"Now you know how it feels!" Chet blurted out with a self-satisfied smirk, not bothering to look up from his phone.

As Dr. Reddy's meltdown continued to worsen, the front door to the restaurant blew open, and King Kong suddenly came crashing inside, shocking everyone. He roared and pounded his chest as if he was about to grab Fay Wray and climb to the top of the Empire State Building and swat at airplanes.

Dr. Reddy screamed as Jodie and Pia both stared, wide-eyed and entranced. Even Chet glanced up from his phone to take in the sight of a gorilla suddenly in the restaurant, but then casually went back to texting.

The gorilla reached up and removed his head, revealing Bruce, whose face was sweaty and his hair matted. "Man, it's really hot inside this ape mask!"

Liddy turned and whispered into Hayley's ear. "Is it wrong for me to be oddly attracted to Bruce in that gorilla suit?"

"I really don't want to have that discussion with you, Liddy," Hayley said before emphasizing, "*ever*."

Bruce set the gorilla head down on a table. "Sorry I'm so late for the party. I've been at the hospital, waiting for Clara Beaumont to regain consciousness."

"Is she going to be all right?" Hayley asked.

Bruce nodded. "Doctor said she's in stable condition and should make a full recovery. They were worried she broke a hip from that nasty spill down the stairs, but thankfully that didn't happen. She does have a fractured elbow and a couple of nasty bruises. She finally woke up about ten minutes ago."

"Was she able to identify who broke into her house?" Sergio asked.

Bruce nodded again. "Lenny Bash."

Hayley gasped. "I know Lenny! He used to work here as a busboy. He started when the previous owner, Chef Romeo, ran the place and stayed on a while after I took over before he quit."

"Why did he quit?" Liddy asked.

"I'm not really sure. He never told me why; he just said he wanted to move on," Hayley explained.

"Sounds like he wanted to move on to a life of crime!" Mona added.

"Mona's right," Bruce said. "Lenny has had quite a few run-ins with the cops lately, built up quite a record. He's been shoplifting and writing bad checks all over town."

"So do you think Lenny has been the one breaking into all the houses lately?" Liddy asked.

"It's starting to appear that way," Bruce said. "Like I said, he's been a regular in the *Island Times* 'Police Beat' section for some time now for his petty crimes. But he may have stepped up his game to burglary—and now, unfortunately, assault."

"And he is still on the loose," Dr. Reddy shuddered.

Bruce turned to Sergio. "Donnie has put out an APB. I saw him at the hospital, and he wanted me to assure you that he is on top of this and has everything under control. They're going to find Lenny, so he wanted me to make sure you stay right here and enjoy yourself."

Bruce finally noticed all the glum faces in the room.

"Hey, I thought this was supposed to be a party! You're all acting as if somebody just died!"

Island Food & Cocktails
by
Hayley Powell

I recently ran into a classmate from my childhood, Sabrina Merryweather, at the town's Fourth of July parade. Sabrina now lives in Arizona, but was back on the island for a two-week vacation to visit with her family. What strikes me about Sabrina now is how much she has changed in the ensuing years since high school—or, more specifically, how much her *memory* has changed. You see, Sabrina is always excited to see me and catch up whenever she wings her way back to Maine, and she stubbornly maintains that we were "the bestest of best friends" when we were teenagers.

This could not be further from the truth.

There is a lot of revisionist history going on in Sabrina's brain. Case in point: the week of Halloween when we were juniors at Mount Desert Island High School. I remember it as if it was yesterday.

My two BFFs, Liddy and Mona, and myself had just sat down at a table in the school cafeteria to eat lunch. Everyone had been buzzing all day about a big, blow-out Halloween party that was supposedly happening that weekend. I found myself getting excited until I heard who was hosting the event—Sabrina Merryweather! Her parents were going to be out of town that weekend. My heart sank because I knew there was no way I would be receiving an invitation. Sabrina had made no secret about her intense dislike for me, for reasons I was never clear about. Mona thought she was jealous of me and was always trying to compete with me, but I had no ill will toward her at all. I just thought she didn't like my personality. But whatever.

Sabrina waltzed into the cafeteria carrying a stack of envelopes, followed by her faithful posse of three girls, who tried to dress exactly the same as their beloved queen bee.

We watched Sabrina glide around the cafeteria, magnanimously bestowing her envelopes upon the lucky chosen few, deliberately sidestepping our table to make a point, although it was pretty obvious to everyone she was snubbing us.

When her stack dwindled down to just three envelopes, she circled back toward us, and for a moment, I thought we were dead wrong and were about to receive invites to the party. But then, true to form, Sabrina stopped right in front of us, handed me all three envelopes, and said with a cruel smile slapped on her face,

"Could you hand those to Robert, Mike, and Tom behind you. I can't reach them."

I could feel my face reddening, but I was not about to give her the satisfaction of showing any emotion whatsoever. I simply shrugged and said, "Sure."

As I handed the envelopes to Robert, Sabrina cooed, "I really hope you can come, Robert!"

We all knew Sabrina had a wild crush on Robert Shields. She had been chasing him around the whole semester, shamelessly plotting ways to get him to ask her out, but so far failing in her single-minded mission. I would not have been surprised if the whole Halloween party idea had been hatched just as a ploy to get him over to her house, albeit along with about thirty other kids from our class.

Having been shut out of Sabrina's soirée, I suggested to Liddy and Mona that they come over to my house for a sleepover that weekend; we'd watch a bunch of scary movies on DVD and stuff ourselves with a ton of Halloween candy that my mother had bought. Liddy and Mona both thought that was a fabulous idea, but then Mike and Tom stood up behind us and came over and asked Liddy and Mona to be their dates for Sabrina's party. I knew they would decline out of solidarity, so I found myself jumping into the conversation and accepting on their behalf because I knew they would have more fun at a party than watching my little brother, Randy, run crying from the room because he was so scared of *Candyman* on TV.

That's when Robert, out of the blue, asked, "What about you, Hayley. Would you like to go together?"

You could have heard a pin drop.

Liddy had to reach over and gently close my mouth by raising my chin up with her hand. When I could not find my voice to answer Robert's question, Mona finally groaned, "Yes, Robert; yes, she would!"

"Great," he said with a laconic, sexy smile. "See you Saturday."

I could hardly breathe, and I felt faint, but I managed to get through the rest of the lunch period without making an utter fool of myself.

Needless to say, I was overjoyed with excitement. But, to be honest, I was also a little nervous about how Sabrina might react when I showed up unexpectedly at her party, on the arm of the boy she currently was intensely obsessed with.

On the invitation, Sabrina requested that everyone come as their favorite movie dance couple because she detested the typical scary Halloween costumes with all the blood and gore, claiming she got nauseous at the sight of blood. Looking back on that now, I find it rather odd, since she ultimately became a prominent medical examiner and dissected people for a living.

Robert and I decided to go to the party as Patrick Swayze and Jennifer Grey (Johnny and Baby from *Dirty Dancing*).

Of course, when we arrived at Sabrina's house a few days later, I should have known that about seventy-five percent of the party-goers would be dressed as Johnny and Baby, especially since the movie was still so popular, years after its release. Yes, there were a smattering of Dannys and Sandys from *Grease*, a Fred and Ginger from *Top Hat* (movie geeks who knew about those really old flicks on TCM), and a couple of white leisure suits paying tribute to John Travolta from *Saturday Night Fever*, but mostly there were just a whole lot of Johnnys and Babys pretty much everywhere you looked.

I spotted Sabrina as leather-clad bad girl Sandy from *Grease* and was relieved she hadn't noticed me yet, but then Robert suddenly grabbed me by the hand and dragged me toward her. "Let's say hi to Sabrina!"

Well, when our hostess turned around to see us approaching—hand in hand, mind you—let's just say, if looks could kill, I would have been dead on the floor.

It only got worse from there.

Robert appeared oblivious to the simmering tension as Sabrina tried keeping a fake innocuous smile planted on her face, although she was slicing and dicing me with insanely furious eyes.

I had to get away. "You two chat. I'm going to go to the ladies' room. Which way is it?"

Sabrina pointed down the hall and growled, "That way."

I was off.

There was a line of girls waiting, but a girl from my English class who had come up behind me said there was another bathroom farther down, off the laundry room, so I walked to that one with no line and went inside. I was just finishing up, washing my hands, when someone jiggled the doorknob.

"Be right out!" I said.

"No, you won't," someone answered.

I heard a click. I tried turning the door handle, but it wouldn't budge. Someone had locked the door from the outside. I kept jiggling the handle to no avail.

I suddenly heard Sabrina's enraged voice.

"This is for stealing my boyfriend, and having the gall to show up at my house and throw it in my face!"

And then there was silence.

She was gone.

And I was stuck in the bathroom off the laundry room that very few people knew about. I was trapped! My only hope was that Robert would eventually miss me and try to find me.

After about a half hour of pounding and yelling, I realized no one could hear me over all the music and noise. It was a tiny bathroom, and the heat was pumping through the vent. I was starting to sweat, and so I unbuttoned my blouse a couple of buttons, trying to stay cool. I could see in the mirror that my hair was a fright because I kept running my hands through it nervously, trying to come up with some kind of plan to escape.

Finally, like a miracle, I heard a click, and the door flew open. I was hoping it was Robert coming to my rescue, but actually it turned out to be Zach Rivers, one of the hulking high school football players, staring down at me. I tried to explain what had happened, but he didn't seem all that interested, so I gave up and just followed him back down the hall toward the living room.

The party was in full swing as we walked in, and then, quite unexpectedly,

Zach put his arm around me and pulled me close to him.

Well, that almost brought the whole room to a sudden standstill.

Hayley and Zach?

I noticed Robert had a disappointed look on his face.

Right next to him Sabrina was beaming, triumphant.

And that's when I knew I had been set up.

I learned later that, after Sabrina locked me in the bathroom, she enlisted Zach's help to execute her evil plan. She found Robert, who had been looking all over for me, and out of the kindness of her cold heart, she told him that she had seen Zach and me leaving together, but that she had no idea where we had gone, heavily suggesting we had snuck away to go somewhere and fool around!

She went on to add that she had heard this was not the first time I had done something as horrendous as ditching one boy for another, but not to worry because she was there to help him through his heartbreak, and thank God he found out in time what kind of person I really was!

My tousled hair, open blouse, and sweaty face only bolstered her ridiculous fake story. But, sadly, Robert bought it. And he didn't speak to me again. In fact, he and Sabrina started dating the following Monday.

Small consolation: Two months later, a hot Swedish foreign exchange student, Helga, arrived at school, and a smitten Robert dumped Sabrina to be with her, and he didn't bother to tell Sabrina. So I believe, in the end, there is such a thing as karma!

I never let that night dampen my enthusiasm for Halloween. Nowadays, I love hosting my own parties, and these next two yummy recipes are popular annual staples! I hope you love them as much as I do!

Boo Boozy Milkshakes

Ingredients
½ pint chocolate ice cream
½ pint vanilla ice cream
8 ounces chocolate milk
5 ounces bourbon

Combine ingredients in a blender, tailoring them to your liking. If you prefer a thinner shake, add a little more milk. If you like thicker, add more ice cream. Divide into 2 large glasses and enjoy.

Monster Meatball Sliders

For this recipe, you'll need 1 12-ounce jar marinara sauce, either one you've made or your favorite from the supermarket. You'll also need a package of 12 Hawaiian rolls or slider buns.

Turkey Meatballs Ingredients
(Note: to save time, you can use your favorite frozen meatballs)
1 pound ground turkey
1 egg, beaten
2 slices of bread, torn into small pieces
½ cup Italian bread crumbs
½ cup grated Parmesan cheese
½ cup panko crumbs
½ tablespoon Italian seasoning
½ tablespoon garlic powder
½ tablespoon dried basil
½ tablespoon dried parsley
1 teaspoon kosher salt
1 teaspoon ground pepper

Preheat oven to 375 degrees. Line a baking pan with foil and spray with cooking spray.

In a large bowl, add all of the ingredients and, with clean hands, combine them. Shape scoops of the meat mixture into 12 same-size meatballs. Place meatballs in a sprayed baking pan.

Bake in preheated oven for 20–25 minutes or until cooked through. You can cut one to check doneness. Add them to the warmed marinara sauce.

Assembling the Sliders
¼ cup butter
½ teaspoon garlic powder
1 teaspoon Italian seasoning
2 tablespoons Parmesan cheese
12 Hawaiian rolls or slider buns, sliced in half
2 cups shredded Mozzarella cheese
Butter, with Italian seasoning to taste
Parmesan cheese to taste

Use your favorite or homemade marinara sauce. On the stove, warm it in a pan big enough to hold the meatballs.

Preheat oven to 350 degrees.

In a small saucepan, melt the butter with the garlic powder and Italian seasoning, and set aside.

Butter a 9x13 baking pan and place the bottom halves of the Hawaiian rolls in the pan, then top each roll with a meatball, some extra sauce, and sprinkle the shredded Mozzarella evenly over the meatballs. Do this for all the rolls.

Carefully add the top halves of the rolls and gently press. Brush melted, seasoned butter over the tops of the rolls, then sprinkle the Parmesan cheese evenly over the tops.

Cover with tinfoil and bake in a preheated oven for 10 minutes. Remove the foil and put back in oven to bake for 5–7 minutes longer. Remove, slice, and serve warm.

Chapter Ten

As Sergio pulled Bruce aside to bring him up to speed on the dead body in cold storage that was currently lying inside the walk-in freezer, Hayley, Liddy, and Mona huddled together, all of them still rattled by the thought that there could be a cold-blooded killer lurking among them.

Hayley had discounted everyone in her mind, even Dr. Reddy, because she honestly could not conceive that any one of the guests left at her Halloween party was capable of such a malicious, violent act, especially the kids.

Nothing made any sense.

But who else could it have been, especially with the back door locked and all eyes on the front door the entire time?

Jodie tugged on Mona's sweatshirt. "Mommy, I'm tired. When can we go home?"

"Soon, baby, I promise. When Sergio says we can leave," Mona said, rubbing her daughter lightly on the head.

"But Pia got to go home. Why can't we?" Jodie whined.

"No, Jodie, Pia's right over there with her mom," Mona insisted.

"No, she's not," Jodie said.

They all looked over at the table near the front door, where Dr. Reddy and Pia had sat earlier. It was empty.

Liddy frantically glanced around the dining room. "Where did they go?"

"They couldn't have left out the front door. One of us would have seen them," Hayley said.

"They went out the back," Chet murmured, without taking his eyes off his phone.

"What? When?" Mona barked.

"Just now," Chet said, thumbs furiously tapping on his screen.

"Sergio! She's making a run for it!" Hayley cried, dashing out of the dining room toward the rear exit off the kitchen, next to the storeroom and pantry, where she came upon Dr. Reddy, clutching Pia's hand while sliding the bolt of the back door open to make her escape.

"Stop right there, Doctor!" Hayley exclaimed.

Dr. Reddy froze in place halfway out the door. Guilt was written on her face before she quickly masked it with indignation. "Don't be so dramatic, Hayley. I was just going to take Pia home. She's tired and needs some sleep. Don't panic; I was coming back. I was going to have my older daughter, Nina, babysit."

Hayley stared at her skeptically.

"My daughter has been through enough trauma for one

night. I am doing what's best for her. I should think Mona would do the same with her own child."

Sergio and Bruce suddenly appeared behind Hayley.

"I wasn't running away!" Dr. Reddy protested.

Liddy scampered in behind Sergio and Bruce, craning her neck, trying to see past the two much bigger men. "Yes, you were! The guilty always run!"

Dr. Reddy covered Pia's ears with her hands. "There is a dead body not twenty feet away from here. I will stay here all night if I have to, but this is no place for a child!"

"Dr. Reddy, as I have told you multiple times, no one is going anywhere, not yet. I called the county forensics team, and they're on their way, so we just need to sit tight until they get here. Hopefully, they can help us fill in a few of the blanks. I understand Pia is tired—we all are—but this is a crime scene, and your daughter is a potential witness, and so I insist on everybody's cooperation. Is that clear?"

Dr. Reddy's face flushed; her instinct was to argue some more, and she opened her mouth to protest, before sighing and slamming the door shut and sliding the bolt back into place.

"Can I at least get a cup of coffee to keep myself awake if we're going to spend a few more hours in this god-forsaken place?" Dr. Reddy groused.

She then marched back toward the dining room, dragging behind her a yawning Pia, who struggled to keep up with her mother's pace.

Sergio turned to Hayley and gave her an apologetic smile. "Do you mind?"

Hayley waved everyone out. "Go. Just make sure she doesn't try to duck out the front! I'll put a pot on."

Sergio and Liddy returned to the dining room to join the others.

Bruce hung back and gave his wife a comforting hug. "Long night, huh?"

"You could certainly say that," Hayley sighed wearily.

"I sure hope nobody mentions the corpse in the freezer in their Yelp review," Bruce joked.

"You better go help Sergio in case somebody else tries to make a break for it. I'll be right out with the coffee."

Bruce kissed Hayley softly on the lips.

She wrapped her arms around his neck. "Thanks, I needed that."

He winked at her and then bounded out of the kitchen in his gorilla suit.

Hayley took a deep breath, exhaled, then wandered into the pantry to fetch a package of coffee beans. She spotted it on the top shelf, grabbed it, and was turned halfway back around when something on the floor caught her eye.

It looked like a tiny piece of glass at first.

She set the coffee grounds down on a middle shelf and picked up a mini broom and dustpan to sweep it up, fearing someone might cut themselves on the broken glass, but as she bent down, it quickly became obvious the sparkling object wasn't glass.

It was a diamond embedded on a silver wedding band. Somebody at the party must have accidentally dropped it.

Hayley carefully picked it up and examined it.

Something was inscribed on the back of the band.

Forever Yours, Irving.

Irving.

She only knew one Irving in town. And that was the

late Irving Beaumont, who had died long ago. His widow, however, was still very much alive.

Clara Beaumont.

The poor elderly woman who was at this moment in the hospital recovering from a brutal attack during a home robbery.

How on earth did it get here?

It suddenly dawned on Hayley. Bruce had mentioned earlier that Clara Beaumont had told the police before passing out at her home that the robber had made off with her wedding ring.

This was it.

Engraved by her loving late husband, Irving.

And Lenny Bash had stolen it.

Which meant Lenny had been in this pantry at some point.

But how?

And why?

Why would Lenny Bash show up at Hayley's Halloween party with dozens of people present after having just robbed Clara Beaumont's house? There was the possibility that he had arrived in disguise—all the guests were wearing costumes, after all—but again, *why*? What would draw him here? Why would he risk hanging out in public where someone might recognize him, especially since he had no way of knowing whether or not Clara Beaumont had been able to identify him? Any rational burglar would no doubt go into hiding, lie low, and avoid the cops until he could skip town, not crash a party.

It made no sense.

And why was he in the pantry?

That's when Hayley noticed a few empty pans that had been shoved in the corner on the bottom shelf. She pulled one out and noticed small chunks of hamburger meat and crumbs of bread left on the bottom. She examined the other pan and found half of a mini pepperoni and bits of a flaky crust.

Or course!

Her missing food.

She had noticed that two pans of appetizers she had prepared for the party were missing earlier in the evening.

Her Mummy Meat Sliders and Pepperoni Pizza Pockets in the shape of jack-o'-lanterns!

Someone had scarfed them down right here in the pantry.

It had to be Lenny.

But what happened to him?

Where did he go?

On the video Randy had shot on his phone, all the guests had been accounted for as they left the restaurant. And the rear door was locked from the inside, which would have made it impossible for Lenny to flee from the back of the restaurant.

How could he have shown up at the party, chowed down on Hayley's food in the pantry, accidentally dropped Clara Beaumont's wedding ring at some point, and then just vanished into thin air?

This was a real head scratcher.

Hayley closed her hand around the diamond ring and was about to head back out to show Sergio what she had found when her eyes fell upon a deep scratch in the wooden floor of the pantry.

She bent down and ran her finger alongside it. What appeared so odd was the shape of the scrape. It was not your ordinary wear-and-tear scrape from heavy foot traffic or from someone dropping cans of food, causing damage to the floor. No, this scratch formed a large half circle that ran almost the full width of the pantry, almost as if in the shape of a rainbow.

What would cause a scratch like that?

Hayley looked around, failing to find any sharp object someone could have used to dig into the floor.

The shape reminded her of a door sagging from loose hinges scraping across the floor as someone tried to open it.

But the door to the pantry was at an opposite angle.

There was simply no way it would have been able to cause that scratch.

Her eyes settled on the back wall of the pantry.

Then she had a thought. She had seen enough movies set in gothic mansions to suspect that maybe . . . just maybe . . .

The thought made her chuckle.

No, she was being ridiculous.

But what if . . . ?

Hayley stood up and moved slowly to the back wall. She reached up, took hold of the top shelf, and gave it a good yank. Suddenly the wall began moving forward, creaking, as the bottom scuffed across the hardwood floor, following the pattern of the long half-circle scratch.

Hayley couldn't believe it.

The back wall of the pantry was a giant door.

Her new restaurant had a secret room!

Behind the wall, foreboding darkness.

Hayley poked her head in, squinting, able to make out an empty hallway that led down to a flickering light.

Hayley silently made her way down the hall toward the light until she came upon a small room that reminded her of a bunker where someone might hide to wait out the apocalypse. The light was from a couple of burning candles. There was a small, lumpy-looking cot in the corner. A rifle hanging on the wall. A few boxes of canned goods and supplies. And as she had expected, paper plates with a few of her Mummy Meat Sliders and Pepperoni Pizza Pockets jack-o'-lanterns.

There was no one in the room.

Whoever had been here was gone.

Or was he?

Hayley suddenly felt a rush of air against her neck.

As if someone was standing behind her, breathing.

She spun around.

A scream caught in her throat as she found herself face-to-face with Pennywise the Clown!

Chapter Eleven

As the creepy Pennywise, with his grotesque, distorted, evil smile and beady menacing eyes, advanced upon Hayley, she bolted forward, trying to push past him and out the door of the bunker.

But Pennywise anticipated the move and forcefully shoved her back as she tried ducking around him. Hayley stumbled and fell back on the cot as Pennywise slammed the door shut and locked it, effectively trapping her inside with him.

"You might as well take off that mask, Lenny. I know it's you," Hayley said, eyeing him warily, not sure what she would do in the event of a frontal attack.

Pennywise didn't say a word, but she could see his eyes blinking nervously behind the clown mask.

"I found the wedding ring you stole from Clara Beaumont's house in the pantry. I knew you had to be somewhere close by," Hayley explained matter-of-factly, desperately attempting to remain calm and not let on to Pennywise that she was seconds from fainting dead away from sheer fright.

Pennywise stood frozen by the door for a few moments, still refusing or afraid to say anything.

Hayley sighed. "Lenny Bash, take that mask off right now!"

The scary clown glared defiantly at Hayley some more, but then his white-gloved left hand slowly reached up and pulled the mask off, revealing Lenny's sweaty, troubled face.

He tried wiping the sweat off with the puffy arm of his clown costume, but the bunker was so hot, he didn't stay dry for long before more sweat beads rolled precipitously down his forehead.

"You shouldn't have come back here, Hayley," Lenny growled before picking up the sledgehammer from Randy's Annie Wilkes costume that had been leaning against the wall next to the door. "Everything would have been fine if you all had just gone home after cleaning up from the party."

"No, Lenny, no one was going to go home. Not until we figured out what was going on around here."

Lenny swallowed hard and raised the sledgehammer. "I don't want to hurt you . . . But I will if I have to . . ."

Hayley, sitting on the cot, leaned back against the wall, wanting to put as much distance from him as possible. She carefully eyed the door.

"Don't try to yell. This room is basically soundproof. No one out there will hear you," Lenny warned.

Hayley glanced around, taking in the shelves of canned food, a generator, a first-aid kit in the corner—all the supplies you would need for an underground bunker during a nuclear blast or zombie apocalypse. "What is this place? How did you find it?"

"I came across it by accident when I used to work here, back when Chef Romeo owned the place," Lenny said. "One night, after the restaurant closed and the boss thought everyone had gone home, I stayed behind because I was pumping myself up to ask Romeo for a raise. I went to his office, and he wasn't there, and that's when I saw the pantry wall was open, and there was this secret passage. It was the craziest thing! I thought things like this were only in the movies! I was curious, so I followed it down here to this room, where I found Chef Romeo stocking it with some canned goods! I surprised the hell out of him! At first, he was mad at me for snooping, but then he made me swear I'd never tell anybody about it!"

"How did Chef Romeo find it?"

"He didn't. He was the one who built it. The pantry and storeroom used to be three times the size they are now when he first bought the building, but Chef Romeo added the secret back wall and turned the rest of it into an escape room."

"But why? Was he worried Bar Harbor was going to be the target of an alien invasion or get hit by an asteroid? Normally, the biggest threat we have to face is an influx of obnoxious summer tourists and too many black flies."

"Chef Romeo told me when he moved here from New York, he left behind a few enemies, and so he wanted to know he had a safe hiding place in case they somehow found him up here," Lenny said.

Hayley knew the kid was speaking the truth.

She had been acutely aware from investigating the

mysterious circumstances surrounding his untimely death that the colorful, gregarious, and loud Chef Romeo Russo had suffered a few financial crises back in Brooklyn, using mob money to open a restaurant that went belly-up, raising the ire of his lenders when he couldn't pay it back as the interest skyrocketed every single day. Then, there was the astoundingly bad decision to get romantically involved with a mafia kingpin's wife; that certainly did not bring down the temperature of the already scalding-hot situation. It all resulted in the chef skipping town and starting anew in Maine, where he had hoped he would never be found. Unfortunately, a couple of adversaries from a very long list of individuals out to get the chef eventually did locate him, which resulted in his untimely demise. That's when Hayley took over the lease of the restaurant, changed the name to Hayley's Kitchen, and started a whole new business.

But at the time, she had no clue about any secret room. Not until now.

"How did Chef Romeo convince you to keep quiet about what you had found?"

"With a big wad of hundred-dollar bills," Lenny snorted. "He told me there was more where that came from if I stayed loyal to him and kept my mouth shut. I figured why not; I'd do anything he wanted as long as he kept throwing cash at me. But just my luck, he died right after that, and then you took over . . ."

"I always wondered why you didn't stay on, why you just up and quit . . ."

Lenny shrugged. "Big mistake, in retrospect. But at the time, I was just a dumb lug with money to burn. Why should I work when I could party, drink beer, smoke weed, chase girls? I even got myself a brand-new Harley Davidson, which I crashed into a telephone pole trying to do a wheelie three days after I bought it."

"And then you found yourself broke again," Hayley guessed.

"Who knew I could go through so much money that fast? I'd never had two cents to my name, so how was I ever going to be responsible with that kind of cash? My parents had already kicked me out; I had nowhere to go. I couldn't afford rent, so a couple buddies took me in for a while, but I couldn't stay with them forever, I got desperate . . ."

Hayley stood up from the cot. "So you began robbing houses for spare cash and jewelry you could pawn."

"I promised myself I was only going to do it once. Just once. So I would have enough to put down a deposit on a room to rent. I knew the Clements on Arata Drive up by the golf course were going to be out of town. I overheard Mrs. Clement talking to a friend at the Shop 'n' Save. It was so easy. I was in and out in no time. I had enough for rent and food for a whole month. But then, there was more partying, the money disappeared again, so I thought to myself, one more time, just one more time . . ."

"But it wasn't one more time. You kept going . . ."

"Like I said, it was always so easy . . ."

"Until it wasn't," Hayley said sharply.

Lenny's eyes flicked to the floor.

Hayley folded her arms. "Clara Beaumont was not supposed to be home tonight; she was supposed to be out of town visiting her sister, but she caught a cold and canceled her trip at the last minute, and that's when the two of you came face-to-face in her house . . ."

"I was coming up the stairs when I looked up and saw

her standing there at the top of the landing, holding a baseball bat in her hand. She had heard me break in through the kitchen window downstairs and was coming to investigate. I wasn't expecting to see anyone . . ." Lenny mumbled. "I swear, Hayley, I was more scared than she was . . ."

"What happened next?"

"Mrs. Beaumont started screaming and yelling, and the next thing I knew she was coming at me with the bat and taking whacks at me! You should see the nasty bruises I got on my arm. I was just trying to defend myself . . ." His voice quivered. "But . . ."

Hayley's heart sank as she anticipated what was coming next. "But what, Lenny?"

He looked up at Hayley, his face full of shame. "I was just trying to grab the bat away from her, but when I yanked it out of her hand, she somehow lost her balance, and that's when . . ."

"She tumbled down the stairs and hit her head on the hardwood floor at the bottom!"

"I didn't mean to hurt her! It was an accident!"

"But you didn't call for help; you just ran away and left her there!" Hayley snapped accusingly.

Lenny nodded. "Yes, I panicked. I didn't know what to do! This was the only place I knew where I could lie low for a while until the heat died down and I could sneak out of town without getting caught."

"But how did we not see you come in? We had eyes on the front door all night, and the back door was locked from the inside."

"I showed up when you were still setting up for the party; you had the back door open while you and Liddy and Mona were bringing in all the food. I waited until you went back to Mona's truck for another load, and then I was able to slip in, without any of you noticing, and hide back here in Chef Romeo's secret room."

That was why Lenny never showed up on Randy's video at any point during the party.

"I didn't think anyone would ever be able to find me," Lenny continued. "I didn't know I had dropped Mrs. Beaumont's wedding ring." Lenny sniffed and wiped his nose with his index finger, tears pooling in his eyes. "I swear on my life, Hayley, I never meant to kill Mrs. Beaumont!"

"You didn't."

Lenny's eyes widened in surprise. "What are you talking about? I saw her fall down the stairs and hit her head! There was blood!"

"You didn't kill Clara Beaumont, Lenny. She's recovering in the hospital. She may have a concussion, but she is going to live."

A wave of relief washed over Lenny's face. "Oh man, oh wow, I can't tell you how much better that makes me feel . . ."

"Yes, you can rest easy. But what about Boris Candy?"

Lenny's face went pale.

Hayley bravely took a step forward. "Did you murder him?"

Lenny began to slowly shake his head. "No . . . I . . ."

Hayley's eyes zeroed in on the sledgehammer at Lenny's side. She could make out traces of blood on it. "I can buy Mrs. Beaumont accidentally tripping and falling down the stairs, and I'm sure the police will as well. But explain to me how Mr. Candy *accidentally* ran his head into the flat edge of that sledgehammer, Lenny, because that one has me stumped."

Lenny glanced at the sledgehammer, noticing the blood for the first time. He knew he was caught. He raised his eyes, staring at Hayley, his face full of alarm and desperation, like a scared rabbit suddenly trapped in a hunter's cage.

That's when he menacingly raised the sledgehammer over his head.

Chapter Twelve

"What are you going to do, Lenny, bash me in the back of the head too, just like you did to poor Boris Candy?" Hayley cried.

Gripping the sledgehammer and waving it around in the air, Lenny vigorously shook his head. "No, no, you make it sound like I *wanted* to kill him, but I didn't. I had no choice!"

"Everyone has a choice, Lenny, and you made the wrong one," Hayley said. "And right now you have another choice to make. What are you going to do with that sledgehammer?"

Hayley held her breath.

Lenny stopped waving the weapon around threateningly but kept holding it above his head, staring up at it. Then he slowly lowered it to his side.

Hayley felt relieved that she had been spared for now,

but she was not going to take anything for granted. Her mind raced, desperate to come up with some kind of plan to escape this secret locked room.

"I can pretty much guess what happened next, Lenny," Hayley said softly, trying not to sound too aggressive, which might set him off again. "You were hiding out here after running away from Clara Beaumont's house, but you were hungry, you needed something to eat, and you probably didn't want to use up your food supply so early on," Hayley said, pointing to the shelf of canned goods above them. "On the other side of the wall, there was a party in full swing with lots of food, so you snuck out and snatched some pans of appetizers I had prepared when no one was around."

Lenny nodded. "The food smelled really good, and I was starving so bad, I decided to take the risk. And it worked. Nobody saw me. But then I got thirsty, I had a limited supply of bottled water back here, so I decided to grab some sodas from the coolers in the storeroom. But I couldn't get to them because those two little girls were pretending to be witches right next to the pantry. They would have spotted me the second I came out. So I stood behind the pantry wall, listening, waiting for them to finish up with their silly witch spells and return to the party. That's when I heard Mr. Candy come in to see the girls playing, and he yelled at them and upset them. After he left, they cast some kind of nasty spell on him. Then finally, I heard them leave. They never had a clue I was right behind the pantry wall listening to them the whole time."

"You figured it was safe to come out at that point to get your drinks, but then unexpectedly Mr. Candy returned . . ."

"Yeah, he came rushing in, like he was in a big hurry," Lenny said.

"That's because Mona's son, Chet, had just spiked his hot chocolate with Ex-Lax," Hayley explained. "He was running back here to find the bathroom since the two out front were occupied."

"At first, I didn't know who he was, in that evil clown getup."

"But Mr. Candy recognized you, and you could not have him telling anyone you were here, because the police might find out and surround the place, and you'd be trapped—"

"He tried to get past me; he looked so frantic, I didn't know he was rushing for the bathroom; I thought he was scared of me, knew what I had done, so I tried to stop him. There was a scuffle, and Mr. Candy started yelling. I wrestled him to the floor, tried to keep him quiet, begged him to stop making so much noise, but that just got him more upset and louder, and then he managed to squirm free. He tried to run, and that's when I saw the sledgehammer someone left in the kitchen leaning up against the wall . . ."

"So you grabbed it and chased after Mr. Candy and hit him in the back of the head to stop him from alerting anyone to your presence," Hayley said solemnly. "But Mr. Candy had no clue you had just robbed Clara Beaumont's house, or injured her, or were on the run from the law. Nobody did, not until Bruce showed up after the party was over with the news that Clara Beaumont had regained consciousness and identified you. So you killed the poor man for no reason."

"I . . . I didn't know that . . ."

"You dragged his body into the walk-in freezer to hide

it, but then you got an idea. Why not put on Mr. Candy's Pennywise costume so no one else would recognize you. You could walk around the party undetected and stock up on more food for your extended stay."

"I had no idea how long I would have to be holed up here; it could be weeks, maybe months. I couldn't risk leaving too early when everybody was still looking for me . . ."

All the pieces were finally coming together.

"That's why Mr. Candy was acting so strange around Sergio, after purposely trying to scare him earlier in the Pennywise costume, because it wasn't Mr. Candy. It was you," Hayley deduced. "After loading up and returning to this room, you were confident you had gotten away with it; nobody else saw you poking around. When Mr. Candy's body was found, there would be no witness to point the finger at you. The focus would be on the other party guests. You were home free."

"Until you found that damn ring," Lenny spit out. He took some time collecting his thoughts, figuring out his next move before he spoke again. Finally, his eyes flicked back to Hayley. "I'm sorry, Hayley, you've always been real nice to me, but I can't let you leave here and tell anyone where I am."

He took a menacing step toward her. He was even more intimidating in the frightening clown costume. He backed her up against the wall, then reached out with his white-gloved hands and shoved her down on the lumpy cot. Then he sprang across the room, grabbed some rope off the shelf and began binding her hands and feet as Hayley frantically searched the room for some means of escape. Unfortunately, she was trussed up before she had the opportunity to formulate any kind of workable plan.

She was now Lenny's prisoner.

"How long do you plan on keeping me here? My husband, my friends, they're just on the other side of the pantry wall; they're going to be searching for me."

Lenny picked up a roll of duct tape and pressed a piece across Hayley's mouth. "That's why you're going to stay nice and quiet here in the secret room. They call it that because nobody knows about it; it's a secret. And I'm going to make sure it stays that way."

Lenny bent down and lifted Hayley's feet up on the cot so she was in a prone position. "Why don't you get some rest? You're going to be here a while. But I swear, Hayley, when I do leave here and get out of town, I promise I will send word to your family where they can find you."

Hayley tried to say something, but her words were muffled underneath the duct tape.

"Since there's going to be two of us living here, we're going to need more food than what I've got stacked on the shelf. I think I saw another box of canned beans and vegetables in the storeroom. Wait here, I'll be right back."

He unbolted the lock on the door and hurried off.

Wait here?

Was he joking?

Where on earth could she go?

Hayley cranked her head around desperately.

There had to be some means of freeing herself.

Her eyes scanned the room, settling on the two burning candles bathing the room in a flickering orange light.

The flame.

It could burn through the ropes that tied her hands.

Hayley struggled to stand up, which was made all the more difficult with her hands bound behind her back and her feet tied together, but she managed, after a couple of tries, to remain upright without falling back down on the cot. She hopped over to one of the candles and spun around, dropping to her knees so her hands were on the same level as the burning candle. She stretched her arms out as far as they could go, wincing in pain, wishing she had paid more attention in the stretch class she had taken with Liddy that one time. The flame touched her outstretched finger and scalded her skin, causing her to emit a muffled yelp. She closed both hands into fists and prayed the flame would make contact with the rope and not her flesh. One of her fists accidentally bumped into the candle, nearly knocking it off the small table and onto the floor. She patiently tried again, and again, finally succeeding on the fourth attempt. She began to smell the smoke from the flame as it slowly burned through the ropes. She wrenched her wrists in opposite directions, feeling the rope start to loosen.

She was seconds away from freedom when Lenny suddenly appeared in the doorway of the room. "I smell something burning!" His eyes settled on Hayley trying to free herself. "What are you doing?"

He lunged across the room and roughly grabbed Hayley to stop her. Her hopes of escaping were dashed as he shoved her face-first up against the wall so he could inspect her hands, tied behind her back, to insure they were still secure.

Hayley craned her neck to see that, during the mêlée, the candle had been knocked off the table and onto the floor, where it rolled over on its side over to the cot, stopped by the army-issue gray blanket hanging down the side. The flame ignited the fabric, and the blanket caught fire, which quickly spread to the sheets and the mattress.

Hayley screamed through the duct tape over her mouth

and made frantic gestures with her head toward the fire, trying to warn Lenny.

Satisfied Hayley was bound to his satisfaction, Lenny finally became aware of black smoke in the air and spun around to see the cot on fire. With Lenny distracted, Hayley seized the opportunity to propel herself away from the wall, crashing into Lenny's body, which sent him flying across the room, tripping over his own two feet. He tried to grab the shelf to keep himself from falling, but the weight of his body dislodged the whole shelf from the wall. Stacks of canned food came raining down on him, smashing against his head until he was stretched out onto the floor, dazed and half-conscious.

As the flames grew, dancing up the wall above the cot, Hayley frantically tried screaming for help, but to no avail, not with the tape over her mouth and her hands and feet still tied.

She tried to wildly hop out of the room, but now the thickening black smoke threatened to overcome her. She felt light-headed, close to passing out. The whole building would soon be up in flames and destroyed.

She glanced down at Lenny.

He was still disoriented, rubbing his head, not fully aware that he too was about to succumb to smoke inhalation.

Then, suddenly, through the black smoke, Hayley saw King Kong burst through the room, look around, and then fling his massive, hairy body on top of the burning cot, effectively smothering the flames until they were snuffed out, except for a few burning pieces of fake fur left on the gorilla suit that he pounded out with his giant paws, like an ape in the jungle emulating Tarzan's cry by beating his chest.

Mona appeared in the doorway brandishing a fire extinguisher, which she used to spray white foam on the cot as well as Bruce's gorilla costume, just to be safe.

Sergio rushed in and pulled the tape off Hayley's mouth, then quickly began untying the ropes.

"Are you all right?" Sergio asked.

Hayley nodded as she coughed, waving away the last remnants of black smoke in the room, managing to choke out, "Yes, how . . . how did you find me?"

"We smelled smoke out in the dining room," Sergio explained. "And then we all fanned out to see where it could be coming from. Bruce noticed the black smoke billowing out from underneath the pantry wall. That's when he realized it was a door and not a wall. He followed the smoke down here to find you!"

"Thank you, King Kong!" Hayley gushed as she hugged Bruce, who was still inside his gorilla suit. "I always knew you were misunderstood."

"Come on, let's get you out of here," Bruce said gently as he guided his wife toward the door, his eyes falling to Lenny, who was writhing and moaning on the floor. "We'll leave Sergio to deal with him."

Sergio gave them a wink, then marched over and hauled Lenny to his feet, snapping handcuffs onto his wrists.

As Bruce escorted Hayley back up the narrow passage to the pantry, he turned and grinned. "I'm resisting the urge to pick you up and carry you out in my arms like Fay Wray."

"You are my hero, Bruce, but let's not push it. I can walk just fine."

He chuckled and leaned over and gave her a sweet kiss on the cheek. As they emerged from behind the pantry wall to the kitchen and storeroom where everyone else—

Liddy, Randy, Dr. Reddy, Jodie, Pia, and Chet—all waited anxiously for them, Hayley turned to Liddy and remarked, "I have to admit, Liddy, you were right about one thing."

"What's that?" Liddy asked, perplexed.

Hayley turned to her husband, sizing him up, and then said with a smile, "Bruce does look oddly sexy in his gorilla suit."

Chapter Thirteen

L enny Bash sat glumly in a chair, his hands cuffed behind his back, when Lieutenant Donnie finally arrived at the restaurant.

After reading Lenny his rights and calling the station
to have Donnie come over and escort Lenny to jail, Sergio had finally dismissed Dr. Reddy, who grabbed her
daughter firmly by the hand and huffily fled the scene,
much to everyone's enormous relief. Hayley announced
that Dr. Reddy would definitely not be invited back for
next year's Halloween party at Hayley's Kitchen.

"Are you seriously considering doing this again after
what happened this year?" Liddy asked.

"I'm an eternal optimist," Hayley explained. "Besides,
what are the odds that another fugitive will be hiding behind the walls of my restaurant this same time next year?"

"Given your track record, I'd say they're pretty good," Bruce cracked.

Donnie sadly shuffled over to Lenny, took him by the arm, and hauled him to his feet, muttering, "Okay, Lenny, let's go."

Sergio instantly noticed his young lieutenant's dispirited demeanor, and walked over and pulled him aside. "Everything okay, Donnie?"

"Yeah, Chief, I guess," Donnie shrugged.

No one in the dining room believed him for even a moment.

"Come on, Donnie, you can tell me. I know something's bothering you," Sergio said, patting him on the back.

He turned and lightly shoved Lenny back down in the chair before confiding to the boss, "I'm just a little bummed I wasn't the one to catch the perp. I really wanted to prove to you that I'm worthy of that promotion you gave me."

Sergio smiled warmly. "Donnie, there is no doubt in my mind I made the right decision about making you a lieutenant. You're one of my best officers. You're smart, loyal, a real good chicken."

Donnie looked up at Sergio, confused. "Sorry, Chief, what?"

"Chicken. A good chicken. It's another way of saying nice person, right?" Sergio said, turning to the others, who had no idea what he was talking about.

"Egg," Lenny mumbled from his chair.

Sergio spun around to Lenny. "What did you say?"

"Egg. The saying is, you're a good egg," Lenny sighed.

"Chicken. Egg. It's practically the same thing," Sergio snapped.

"No, it isn't," Lenny argued, shaking his head.

"Nobody asked you! You're under arrest! So just sit there and be quiet!" Sergio yelled, before turning his attention back to Donnie. "You're a good egg, Donnie. I'm real proud of you."

Donnie lit up. "Thanks, Chief. I'm going to work hard and be the best lieutenant this town has ever seen. I know I can do it because I've got a great role model in you to look up to. I can only hope to be as upstanding and trustworthy and, most importantly, brave as you . . ."

Someone came up behind Sergio and tapped him on the shoulder. He cranked his head around, and at the sight of Pennywise the Clown hovering close to him, Sergio let out a terrified high-pitched shriek so loud, Hayley thought her wineglasses might shatter.

Everyone burst out laughing, even Lenny, who wisely got himself under control and quickly clammed up after Sergio shot him a stern look of warning.

Sergio then grabbed the evil clown mask by the red hair and ripped it off, revealing Mona's son, Chet, who was giggling hysterically.

"Very funny, kid!" Sergio roared. "You want me to arrest you, too?"

"For what, making an officer of the law scream like a little girl?" Chet howled.

"That's enough, Chet; show the Chief some respect," Mona barked, attempting to be serious before she lost it all over again and guffawed, unable to catch her breath.

Lieutenant Donnie, trying his hardest not to join in on the raucous laughter and tick off the boss, hurriedly escorted Lenny out of the restaurant to his police cruiser.

"Come on, everybody. I'll finally put that pot of coffee

on, and we'll have a late-night snack of leftover Halloween treats," Hayley offered.

"I can't be drinking caffeine this late at night," Liddy said. "I won't be able to sleep a wink."

"There's hot chocolate left, if anyone wants some," Chet said with a mischievous grin.

"Thin ice, mister man," Mona growled, pointing a finger at her son. "You are on thin ice!"

Island Food & Cocktails
by
Hayley Powell

Another Halloween is finally behind us! This year, however, will definitely stand out as one to remember, especially given the sad passing of Mr. Candy, the school's music teacher. I hear his students are going to put on a band concert as well as a bake sale in his memory so they can purchase some new music stands for the band room, something that Mr. Candy had been requesting for some time.

It's no mystery that Mr. Candy had quite a sweet tooth, and the irony of his last name was not lost on anyone. Anyway, I thought I would make a candy pie as my own personal tribute and drop it off at the bake sale. This is the perfect recipe to share with you at this time of year because it will help you use up some of that leftover candy you may still have piled up from Halloween.

Speaking of a sweet tooth, I also have a pretty big one, and the other night, I found myself sitting in the living room scarfing down a bag of candy that I had bought for Halloween, but perhaps may or may not have forgotten to leave out on the front porch for the trick-or-treaters.

As I munched on a Kit Kat bar, I flash-backed to a memory from many years ago, when my brother, Randy, and I were little kids. It's a Halloween story he loves to tell this time of year at cocktail parties.

Randy was about eleven years old and had been planning for weeks to go out trick-or-treating with his friends to load up on candy, especially since Halloween was the only time of year that our mother would allow us to indulge; she did so for a week straight before she started worrying about our weight and cavities, and then she would confiscate whatever candy was left and donate it all to Housing for the Elderly, where she worked.

Randy and his buddies had been plotting their trick-or-treat route for weeks with military precision because they were expecting to each score a pillowcase full of sugary sweets. This year, Randy was secretly planning to hide at least half his haul where our mother wouldn't find it, so he could gorge himself well beyond the typical allotted week of inhaling our stashes, and Mom wouldn't be the wiser.

Unfortunately, Randy was so caught up in preparing for Halloween, he neglected all his household chores and responsibilities, and needless to say, our mother was growing increasingly frustrated. She warned Randy that he better stop dragging his feet or else. Of course, Randy promised he would get to the chores, but he never did.

So when Randy's math teacher called the house and informed our mother that he hadn't turned in two homework assignments and failed a pop quiz that week, well, that was the proverbial straw that broke the camel's back.

With one day to go before Halloween, Randy waltzed through the door that night for dinner, only to discover our mother standing in the middle of the room with her arms crossed and tapping one foot on the floor with her pursed-lipped, narrow-eyed expression that said, "You are in a world of trouble!"

Randy took one glance at her and knew he was in a code-red situation. He expected her to rant on and on about how irresponsibly he was acting. What he did not expect was for her to ground him for the whole week, allowing him to only go to school, and then he had to come straight home. He was also banned from all extracurricular activities and social events—including trick-or-treating!

Well, you can imagine there were elephant tears, lots of pleading, endless promises to bring his grades up, but this time, Mom didn't budge. I honestly thought she would. I overheard her on the phone, telling her friend Jane about it, and how she would have expected this kind of behavior from me, but not her normally well-behaved Randy. I should have been insulted, but as they say, when the shoe fits . . .

Anyway, Halloween arrived, and much to my surprise, Mom was still sticking to her guns. As I left with my friends, a crestfallen Randy had lost all hope of her changing her mind and stomped upstairs after dinner, slamming the door to his room not once, but twice, to make a point.

I met up with my posse, but after only a half hour going door to door with our plastic pumpkins, I decided to head home because I had been sniffling all day and wasn't feeling too well. I was walking down our street and could see a steady stream of kids going up and down the steps of our front porch as my mother handed out fistfuls of candy.

That's when I noticed a group of kids milling about around the back of our house. Curious, I snuck around to the other side and peeked around the corner to see what they were up to. Somebody had brought a ladder and had leaned it up against the house right under Randy's bedroom window. I could see him climbing down, his empty pillow case in hand. Somebody gave him a Frankenstein mask, and he put it on and zipped around to the front, where he joined a group of kids approaching our house to get some candy. After our mother dropped some candy bars in his pillow case, Randy broke off from the group, ran back around to his friends, returned the Frankenstein mask, and then borrowed a Harry Potter mask. Then he did the same thing all over again. Our mother was loading her own son up with candy and didn't even realize it!

Randy repeated this trick at least six more times, using a number of different masks, including Thor, Batman, Minnie Mouse, Lurch from *The Addams Family*, the Creature from the Black Lagoon, and the blue My Little Pony.

I had to admit, it was a genius plan. So clever, in fact, I was actually proud of his ingenuity, and so I decided not to rat him out.

But just when you think you've pulled one over on your parent, there always comes a surprise. Two days later, as I was coming downstairs for dinner, I heard Mom on the phone again with Jane.

"I know, Jane, I actually couldn't believe it was him. He must have come to the door four or five times before I finally figured out it was Randy. The mask was different every time, but I don't know of any other boy in the neighborhood who had a Pink Power Ranger patch on the front pocket of his jacket! I knew right then and there he was trying to pull a fast one."

I never did have the heart to break it to Randy that our mother knew all along what he had done that night because it has been his favorite story to recount over the years at Halloween parties.

Of course, I guess now, if he reads this column, he will finally know the cat is out of the bag.

So Happy Halloween, dear brother, and here's to many more!

With the arrival of fall, you can count on three things to never change.

• A drop in temperature, ushering in the colder months ahead.

• The annual return of the Pumpkin Spice latte.

• Store shelves stocked with bags and bags of candy corn.

Over the years, candy corn has become highly controversial; to me, there only seems to be two sides of the fence. You either love it or hate it! There really doesn't seem to be any middle ground, and I am definitely on the side of those who do *not* love it. That said, however, I thought that, for this column, instead of just ignoring it, for those of you who do love candy corn, I have an extra special cocktail recipe just for you!

So drink up, enjoy, and Happy Halloween!

Candy Corn Martini

Ingredients
2 ounces vodka
3 ounces sour mix
2 ounces pineapple juice
1 ounce Grenadine
Whipped cream for topping

Combine vodka, sour mix, and pineapple juice in a shaker with ice and shake well.

Strain into a martini glass and slowly pour the grenadine in so it settles on the bottom.

Top with whipped cream and enjoy.

No-Bake Candy Pie

This is a quick and simple, no-bake pie recipe that you can customize to your own personal preference with candy bars or loose candy. I love Heath Bars, so I freeze them, then smash them with a rolling pin to put in my pie. But I have a friend who loves Butterfingers, so she uses those instead. I have also used M&Ms, Reese's, and Snickers for variety. You name it, I have probably used it. Give it a try with your favorite leftover Halloween candy, and I know your kids will thank you!

Ingredients
1 8-ounce package cream cheese, at room temperature
1 8-ounce container of whipped topping, thawed
5 Heath Bars broken in pieces (save some to sprinkle on
    top of the pie or crunch more candy)
1 pre-made chocolate or graham-cracker pie crust

In a bowl, beat the cream cheese until smooth. Fold in the whipped topping. Add in your crushed candy, minus the candy for the topping. Spoon into the pie crust and smooth over, then sprinkle the reserved candy over the top. Refrigerate for 2–4 hours. Slice and serve!

SCARED OFF

Barbara Ross

Chapter One

"Aunt Julia, can you come and get us?" My thirteen-year-old niece, Page, was on the line, barely holding it together, a quivering voice with a sniffle at the end.

"I can hardly hear you." There was some kind of commotion in the background. "Are you still at Talia's?"

Another sniffle. "Yes."

"What's wrong?"

"Some older kids came. They brought some beers." More sniffles.

"I'm on my way."

I turned off the TV, shoved my feet into a pair of flats, grabbed my keys, and headed for the stairs. I hoofed it down the harbor hill toward my mom's house, where my car was stored in her garage. I was nervous, curious, but not panicked. Page was a sensible kid, mature for her age.

Surprised as I was by the call, I was confident she could handle herself until I got there.

As I went, I turned back to look at my place. My studio apartment was dark, as I intended, to discourage trick-or-treaters. Gus's restaurant on the first floor of the building was closed up tight. For two off-seasons, I had run a dinner restaurant in Gus's space with my boyfriend, Chris. But Chris and I were no longer, and neither was the restaurant. We'd talked about trying to carry on despite the change in our personal status and decided it would be too hard.

Mom's porch light was on and welcoming, even though it was almost ten o'clock and no one would still be trick-or-treating except the hardiest of teenagers. She was baby-sitting for my three-year-old nephew, Jack. I didn't stop to go inside but hurried around to the three-car garage at the back.

My sister, Livvie, and brother-in-law, Sonny, were in Portland, attending a Halloween party at a friend's house and then staying overnight in a hotel. It was the first time they'd been away without the kids since—honestly, it may have been the first time they'd ever been away without the kids. Livvie had been pregnant with Page when she and Sonny got married, so their domestic life started with a bang, like two teenagers shot out of a cannon. I really, really hoped whatever was going on with Page wouldn't require me to call them.

Page had declared herself too old for trick-or-treating. She and her best friend, Vanessa, were supposed to be having a sleepover at their new friend Talia's house. It had all been arranged by my sister. I was merely backup to the backup.

Busman's Harbor was quiet as the grave. As I drove down Main Street, the stores that were still open in the off-season had brightly lit windows displaying Halloween or harvest scenes, but no one was about. I drove cautiously nonetheless, wary of stragglers in costumes jumping out from between parked cars.

I saw the flashing blue lights of all three of Busman's Harbor's patrol cars as soon as I turned off Main onto Talia's street. Adrenaline surged, tensing my body and causing my heart to thrum in my chest. Whatever was going on was way more serious than I'd assumed. Every light in Talia's big Victorian house was on, which made it look like a demented jack-o'-lantern from the street. I screeched to the curb and jumped out, pelting toward the steps.

My friend Jamie Dawes, in his police uniform, opened the front door. "Whoa, Julia. The girls are fine."

I two-stepped, catching my breath. "Then why are you here? And why did Page call me to pick her up?"

"C'mon in, and see for yourself."

Jamie led me into a large front hallway, open to the third floor with a staircase winding along the walls. An enormous brass chandelier hung from the ceiling three stories above. The curtained French doors that presumably led to the front room were closed. I followed Jamie toward the back of the house.

The granite countertops and hardwood floor in the big kitchen were sticky with spilled, smelly beer. Potato-chip crumbs were dusted across the room, like feathers from a particularly vicious pillow fight. Most of the cabinet doors hung open. One had obviously served as Talia's parents' bar. It was empty except for a single, quarter-full bottle of gin tipped on its side.

"Did the other kids take off when you pulled up?" I asked.

"No. Something spooked them before we got here. We drove up the street to waves of teenagers, half of them in costume, running in the opposite direction. It was like the zombie apocalypse."

I laughed and relaxed. Jamie wouldn't be joking if Page was hurt.

Jamie flashed his familiar, comforting grin. He was a cop in this situation, but he was also an old friend. His mom and dad's yard backed onto my parents' property. Now he lived in the house alone. His parents had moved to Florida to be near his older sister. For three years, he'd been the newest member of Busman's Harbor's six-person police force, until a retirement had led to the hiring of a new "new guy" the previous spring.

"There wasn't a soul to be seen as I drove over," I told him. Through the back window I spotted flashlight beams bobbing in the backyard.

"Pete and the other guys are looking for stragglers," Jamie reassured me. "The girls are in the living room."

Chapter Two

Page, her best friend, Vanessa, and their hostess, Talia, were huddled on the formal, burgundy-colored couch, sobbing quietly. The tears unnerved me all over again. Page wasn't a crier. I ran to them and hugged each one, even Talia, whom I'd never met. "What on earth happened?"

Page was the brave one who spoke up. "We were having a sleepover," she said, and then stopped. I let the silence fall heavy between us and waited for the rest of the story. "We texted some girls in our class and invited them over," she finally admitted.

"Did you have permission to invite anyone else?" I could guess the answer.

"No." Page hung her head, her bright red curls falling across her freckled cheeks. A single tear fell from the end of her nose.

"It was just three girls," Vanessa added loyally. She would defend Page in any situation. They'd been best friends since Vanessa had moved to town three years earlier. Physically, they couldn't have been more different. Page was tall, taller than me already. She'd probably already attained her full height and had a swimmer's powerful body. Vanessa had long, tawny brown hair and improbable green eyes. She'd always been the shortest kid in their class and was still awaiting her growth spurt. But woe to anyone who was tempted to intimidate her based on her size. She was also, probably, my ex-boyfriend Chris's niece, but that mess was no longer my problem.

"Girls we know, our own age," Vanessa added.

I nodded. I was more than two decades older than these girls, but I remembered how these things went.

"They must have told other kids, even though they swear they didn't." Page was a little feistier than she'd been at first. Looking for scapegoats. "And then kids started coming."

"Boys," Vanessa said. "Big boys, with beers. And girls, like from the high school."

"Before we knew it, the house was full," Page continued. "Kids were everywhere, even in Talia's parents' bedroom." She made a gagging face. "The music was really, really loud, and they wouldn't turn it down, even when we asked them. And there was a fight."

"Not really a bad fight," Vanessa clarified. "Two boys were shoving and shouting in the backyard."

"Where are your parents?" I asked Talia. Livvie never would have agreed to a sleepover if she'd known no adults would be at home.

"At a party," Talia said. It was the first time she'd spoken. She was brown-eyed and brown-haired. Her height split the difference between Page and Vanessa. She looked like she'd been a good-looking child who was now passing through a mild, adolescent rough patch on her way to being a good-looking adult.

"Then who's in charge?" I asked.

"Mrs. Zelisko," Talia volunteered. "She lives upstairs."

"Oh." I had a passing knowledge of Mrs. Zelisko, a short, round, older woman I'd seen around town.

"We tried to find her," Page said, "when things got out of control, but we couldn't. We went to her apartment on the third floor, and she wasn't there. Like anywhere."

I looked at Jamie, who stood in the archway between the living and dining rooms. He held his arms out, palms upward. The cops hadn't found her either.

"And then the ghost came!" Talia said the words with maximum thirteen-year-old drama, and the other two squealed.

"The ghost?" I looked at Jamie. The slightest hint of a smile played on his lips.

"The ghost of Mrs. Zelisko!" Vanessa yelled.

"She was all dressed in white! Like a bride with a veil!" Talia screeched.

"Her face was white, like a clown, and she was flying," Page insisted.

The girls' eyes were bright, their voices high. "And all the kids who saw her screamed and ran." Vanessa was breathless.

"And then all the other kids, who didn't even see her, were screaming and running out the doors, too," Page added.

The girls went silent, staring at me through three sets of big, teary eyes.

"I think that brings us up-to-date," Jamie said. "I've called Talia's parents. They're on their way."

"Where's your overnight stuff?" I asked Page and Vanessa.

"Upstairs in Talia's room," Vanessa answered.

I glanced at Jamie, who nodded it was okay. "Why don't the two of you go and pack up? Talia, you go with them. I want to talk to Officer Dawes for a moment."

"There's no one up there," Jamie reassured them. "We've checked."

The girls rose from the couch. Faces strained, clinging together, they headed for the stairs. I followed Jamie back into the kitchen.

"How much trouble are they in?" I asked as soon as they were out of earshot. "Do I need to call Livvie and Sonny? I hate to interrupt their weekend if I don't have to."

Jamie surveyed the disaster of a kitchen. "This is clearly something that got out of hand. From what they told me, they didn't even know most of the kids who showed up." He put his palms down flat on the granite countertop and then jerked them away, rubbing the sticky stuff from his fingers. "They may be in huge trouble with their parents, but I don't think we'll be involved after tonight."

My shoulders relaxed, and I exhaled noisily. "Thanks," I said, meaning it. One of the great benefits of small-town life is knowing the local police.

"What's up with the flying?" I was tempted to change my assessment of my niece as a mature, level-headed kid.

"Darned if I know." Jamie drew his dark eyebrows together. He was one of those blue-eyed blonds with black brows and lashes and tannable skin. It was, as my sister said, *not fair*. "I don't know what they saw, but something frightened those kids into running out of here."

Jamie's partner, Pete Howland, entered through the kitchen door, his flashlight still on. His normally jovial face was twisted in a grimace. "You need to come see this," he said to Jamie.

"Excuse me." Jamie disappeared with Howland into the dark backyard.

Chapter Three

I looked around the big front hall while I waited for the girls. The three broad streets that climbed the hill in Busman's Harbor were lined with houses similar to this one. My mother lived in one. They were sea captains' houses, built in the days when ships and shipping dominated coastal life. The houses were designed to impress, even to intimidate. I'd never been in this one. The layout was different from the others I knew, but the feeling was the same.

Typical of these old houses, the ceilings on the first and second floor were high, maybe fourteen feet on the first floor and twelve on the second. The third-floor ceiling was lower, the space originally intended for servants. Added together, the ceiling of the open entrance hall towered almost forty feet above me. A staircase wound around the space. From a two-step landing to the left of the front door, the stairs turned and climbed up the wall. When they reached the second floor, there was another turn, and a balcony ran across the wall. I could see a doorway and a long hall off it. The girls' voices floated down from somewhere up there.

At the end of the balcony, there was another turn, and the stairs continued along a third wall to a small landing and a door on the top floor. The door was narrow and flat, obviously added long after the house was built to provide the tenant of the auxiliary apartment with privacy.

Where was the tenant? The girls' wild story aside, Mrs. Zelisko must have gone out, even though she'd been put in charge by Talia's irresponsible parents. My irritation rose.

The girls trooped down the stairs, Page and Vanessa each carrying a backpack and a bed pillow. Page's was in a pink pillowcase I recognized. Vanessa's was a teddy-bear print. They were still little girls in a lot of ways.

I was about to tell them to put their stuff in my car, but I hesitated. I didn't want to leave Talia alone with the police until her parents got home. Jamie was an old family friend to us but a stranger to her. She was clearly a nervous wreck, like the other two girls. I felt we should stay for moral support.

As I stood in the hallway, debating what to do, the back door opened, and Jamie reappeared, a flashlight in his hand, his mouth set. He beckoned me over. "Take Page and Vanessa home. This property is a crime scene. We're calling in the state police Major Crimes Unit."

From unfortunate experience, I knew what that meant. I looked into his eyes. "Please tell me it's not a kid."

Jamie shook his head. "Mrs. Zelisko."

* * *

At my mother's house, after consultation with Mom, I called my sister. No matter how discreet the cops were, word would certainly be flying around about the wild party. It wouldn't take long for news of the body to get out. We wanted to reach her before someone else did.

Livvie said they'd each had a couple of drinks at the party they'd attended and would drive back first thing in the morning. Even though I hated cutting their weekend short, I didn't protest.

The girls were either asleep or pretending to be in the "pink princess" bedroom Mom had decorated for Page when my dad was dying and Livvie and Page stayed over so often Mom thought Page needed her own room. Under intense questioning by Mom and me, Page and Vanessa had been polite, contrite, but not forthcoming. They knew they were in a whole lot of trouble.

Vanessa often stayed over when her mother, Emmy, worked the late shift at Crowley's, Busman's Harbor's nosiest, most touristy bar. At this time of year, the leaves were gone, and so were the tourists, so Crowley's was only open on Friday and Saturday nights. I'd texted Emmy to let her know Vanessa was at Mom's. She'd immediately sent a hurried thumbs-up. But small-town life being what it was, by the time she'd arrived at Mom's house two hours later, wild-eyed, she'd heard the whole story.

"What do we know about Mrs. Zelisko?" I asked Mom and Emmy. We were seated at Mom's kitchen table, and even though there was silence from upstairs, I kept my voice low. I knew from my own childhood that sound traveled up the back stairs.

"Not much, I'm afraid." My mother matched my hushed tone.

"I think," Emmy ventured, "she goes to Star of the Sea?" Star of the Sea was the local Catholic church.

Emmy was still in her Halloween costume, so it was hard to take her seriously. She was dressed as a cat. Not a sexy, cat-woman type cat, which would certainly have enhanced her tips. Instead, she wore something that looked like furry footie pajamas in what might have been a leopard, or tiger, or even calico print. The outfit had a hood with cat's ears on it, which Emmy wore up for warmth. My mother, true to the code of the thrifty Yankee housewife she'd become, never turned on the heat until November 1. The minutes were ticking rapidly toward that momentous date. Since I ran the family business, the Snowden Family Clambake, out of my dad's old office on the second floor of Mom's house, I could hardly wait for heat day to arrive.

"I think Mrs. Zelisko moved here five years or so ago," Mom ventured. "She's always rented the apartment on the third floor of that house."

"What did she do?" I asked. "Is she retired?" My hazy picture of Mrs. Zelisko included steel gray hair, an oval face with a prominent nose, and an extra chin. She had a hairy wart on one cheek near her ear. The perfect face for scaring children. She was short and cylindrical and wore black dresses so tight they looked like sausage casings. Though I could picture her, I couldn't guess her age.

"She's a bookkeeper," Mom said. "She takes care of the books for a lot of small businesses here in town. After your dad died and before you came home to run the clambake, I considered hiring her. Your dad always took care of the books, and I didn't think it was a strength of Sonny's."

My parents had founded the Snowden Family Clambake to keep the private island my mother had inherited in the family. From mid-June to mid-October, we loaded three hundred visitors on our tour boat, showed them the islands, lighthouses, seals, and eagles of Busman's Harbor, then took them briefly into the North Atlantic until we docked at Morrow Island. There we served an authentic Maine clambake meal; twin lobsters, the soft-shelled clams called steamers, corn on the cob, a potato, an onion, and a hard-boiled egg, all cooked under seaweed and salt-water-soaked tarps and over a roaring hardwood fire.

My brother-in-law had run the clambake for a few years after Dad died—and had nearly run it into the ground. It wasn't entirely his fault. There had been a recession, bad weather, and an ill-advised bank loan. The less said about those unhappy days the better. I had been called home to run the business. Four years later, I was still here. I'd thought I would marry Chris and make a life. Now, I had no idea what I was doing.

Mom, Emmy, and I talked about Mrs. Zelisko. What would bring a single woman in her . . . fifties? . . . to Busman's Harbor? If she wasn't in the tourist trade, if she didn't have friends or family locally, perhaps she simply liked living by the sea.

Eventually, Emmy took off. She lived on Thistle Island in a trailer parked on her old gran's property. Her four-year-old son, Luther, was a little too much for the elderly woman to handle when he was awake, so Emmy had to get some sleep and pick him up early in the morning.

Mom suggested I spend the night in my old room. I thought about my apartment, empty and dark, and agreed.

Chapter Four

In the morning, I was awakened by familiar sounds floating up the back stairs. Forks scraped across plates, water ran in the sink, and the murmur of adult voices, punctuated occasionally by the loud, querying voice of my nephew, Jack, came from the kitchen table. The sky visible through the windows was gray. Gusts of wind rattled the old, wooden frames. I snuggled under the covers for a few minutes before I got up.

Sort of dressed, in sweatpants and a T-shirt I found abandoned in my old bureau, I made my way down to the kitchen. Livvie and Sonny were already there. Someone, probably not my mom, had made a batch of scrambled eggs, and there was buttered toast on the counter. Everyone sat around the kitchen table except Jack, who had been excused and was careening around the circle formed by the dining room, living room, front hall, and kitchen.

"Jack, don't run," Livvie cautioned in a voice that sounded robotic and distracted.

Mom, Sonny, and Livvie ate and talked in subdued tones about all the construction in Portland. "Cranes everywhere," Sonny complained, but the traffic on the way home was, he said, "Light. Easy." Page sat at the table, silent and bent over, the eggs on her plate untouched.

"Good morning." Mom forced a tight smile. *Nothing to see here. Perfectly normal breakfast*, her expression said.

"I'm sorry you had to come home," I said to Livvie and Sonny, not sure how close to the elephant in the room I was supposed to get.

Sonny shrugged his big shoulders. "No problem. We'll do it a different time."

They wouldn't. "Did Emmy already pick up Vanessa?"

"First thing this morning," Mom confirmed.

I took some eggs from the pan, picked up a couple of pieces of toast, and sat down, still unclear on what I should or shouldn't say about the previous night.

"Mom, can I be excused?" Page asked.

"You didn't eat a thing," my mother said.

Livvie put a hand up, "It's okay."

"Can I go see Talia?"

"Talia's across the street," Mom explained to me. "The state police asked the Davies to stay somewhere else since their home is . . ."—she hesitated—"unavailable."

"You can say it," Page grumped. "I know there's a dead body there. I'm not a baby."

"So they've checked into the Snuggles," Mom finished.

The Snuggles Inn was run by Fee and Vee Snugg, neighbors, family friends, and honorary great aunts. I could see how the Davies family's situation would have appealed to Fee and Vee's big hearts.

Livvie answered Page's original question. "Lieutenant Binder and Sergeant Flynn have asked that you don't talk to Talia or Vanessa, even by phone or text, until they've taken your statement. Besides, your father and I haven't decided on your punishment yet."

The girls had looked so bedraggled the night before that I was tempted to say they'd been punished enough, but I kept my mouth shut. This was none of my business.

"I'm sorry about what happened," Livvie continued. "But you, Vanessa, and Talia invited those other girls over, something you were expressly forbidden to do."

Page looked wildly from one parent to the other and then made puppy-dog eyes at my mother, willing her to intervene. When Mom didn't take the bait, Page folded her arms across her chest but didn't leave the room.

I finished my eggs and gulped down a second cup of coffee. "I'm going across the street to talk to the Davies," I said.

"I'll come with you." Sonny pushed back his chair. "I have some questions. First up, how do they get off leaving the house when these girls are having a sleepover?"

"Dad!" Page shrunk into herself even further.

Livvie put a cautioning hand on her husband's arm. "Let's leave that discussion for later. We have more important things to deal with."

Sonny hesitated, but pulled his chair forward again, back under the table. "Okay, but these people have some explaining to do."

"Dad!"

Livvie walked me to the front door. "Are you going like that?"

I looked down at the sweatpants and T-shirt. "Casual visit," I said.

She followed me onto the porch. "Binder and Flynn said they'd come around ten to take Page's statement. Can you be here? You know those guys better than Sonny and I do, and you've been through this before."

"Of course," I said. "Anything you need."

Vee answered the door at the Snuggles, dressed as she always was in a skirt, blouse, hose, and heels. Today, appropriate to the season, the skirt was a wool plaid of deep oranges, browns, and yellows, and she wore a cardigan in the same deep orange over her crisp, off-white blouse. Her snow-white hair was in the neat chignon she always wore. I wondered if, after all these years, it grew that way. She was perfectly made up, which made me even more self-conscious about the sweats and T.

"Julia, what a delight. You've come to visit."

"Yes," I hesitated, "and no. I'm actually here to see the Davies."

Vee didn't miss a beat. "They're in the dining room. Or at least the adults are. I think Talia's in her room."

"Perfect. Thanks." I stepped through the door into the big front hallway and made for the swinging door to the dining room. I'd been in and out of that house so often since I was a child, I felt as comfortable there as I did in my mother's home or my own.

Talia's parents sat at the Snugg sisters' polished mahogany table with their backs to the door. They turned and rose at the sound of my footsteps.

"Howard Davies." He extended a hand.

"Blair Davies," she said and then offered her hand as well.

"Julia Snowden."

"You're Page's aunt," Blair said. "You came to the girls' rescue last night. We can't thank you enough."

My first impression was that Blair Davies was much older than her husband. He wore his brown hair long, with not a hint of gray. He had a youthful body, loose-limbed and lean. Her hair was completely white and fell to her shoulders. Her body was soft and pleasantly round. But as I looked from one face to the other, I saw the same lines around the eyes, the slight softening of skin at the chin. They were probably quite close in age. Late forties or early fifties, I guessed.

"Nice to meet you both. Unfortunately, I was too late for an actual rescue. I'm sorry I had to leave Talia alone with the police. They wouldn't let me take her."

"We pulled into the driveway moments after you left with Page and Vanessa. Talia was happy to see us, but of all the things that happened last night, I don't think spending a little time waiting with Officer Dawes was the traumatizing event," Howard said.

"How's Talia doing?" I asked.

"She's quiet and withdrawn," Blair answered. "It's a lot to process."

Howard Davies blew out air. "Sit, sit," he said, gesturing toward the dining table. "There's still coffee in the carafe."

I helped myself to coffee and cream in one of the Snugg sisters' china cups with the delicate pink roses painted on it, and sat across the table from the Davies. "Have you spoken to the police this morning?"

"They called to ask us to be available since they plan to come over later to interview Talia," Howard said. "They have crime-scene techs working at our house and in our yard. That's all we know."

"They asked if we knew who Mrs. Zelisko's next of kin would be," Blair added. "Unfortunately, we don't."

"We inherited her as a tenant," Howard explained. "She rented the third-floor apartment from the previous owners. We had no immediate use for the space, and it was nice to have a little cash coming in to help with the moving expenses. We welcomed Mrs. Zelisko staying on." He paused. "It's not like we interviewed her or selected her. The previous owners vouched for her. They told us she paid the rent on time, kept the place neat, didn't intrude in their family life. Her apartment didn't have a separate entrance, so she had to go through our living space to get to hers. It was a little awkward, but as the previous owners told us, she did her best to respect our privacy, and we respected hers."

"Did you get to know her at all?" I asked.

"A little," Blair answered. "We have a traditional Sunday meal, usually a roast or a casserole, served earlier than our normal workday dinner time. We invited her a few times. But our conversations tended to the general. Plans for the house, town events. She never talked about her past. We asked a few times. That accent." Blair paused and looked around the room, as if the source of the accent might be hiding in a corner. "She was polite, but not expansive."

"Where is the accent from?"

"Slovenia, she said," Howard answered.

"Talia is at an awkward age," Blair said. "She wasn't happy about the move. Thirteen is a terrible age to move

a kid. She's too old for a babysitter, but we were concerned about leaving her at night or for several hours on
her own."

"So we would ask Mrs. Zelisko to keep an eye on
her"—Howard picked up the story—"and tell Talia she
could go to Mrs. Zelisko if she needed anything when we
weren't home. It seemed to suit them both."

"Believe us"—Blair Davies looked straight at me,
begging for what? understanding? forgiveness?—"we
never, ever would have left your niece and her friend at
our home for a sleepover without adult supervision. We
thought it was three girls who'd be watching movies and
eating snacks. We're so thrilled Talia has made friends."

"I work at Emerson Laboratory," Howard said. "We
accepted an invitation to a Halloween party at the home
of one of my colleagues. We had lots of friends in Massachusetts, but moving here, especially during the season
when everyone is so busy, has been challenging. I have
work, and now Talia has school, but it's been hard on
Blair. So I jumped at the chance to go to this party. I
shouldn't have."

"We never imagined . . ." Blair's voice broke, and she
stared into her lap. "We are so sorry. Please tell your sister and brother-in-law how sorry we are."

Chapter Five

I shivered my way back to my apartment to shower and change into my fall uniform of jeans, a flannel shirt over a T-shirt, and work boots. On the way out the door, I grabbed my quilted vest off a hook by the staircase. The day was gray and chilly, a harbinger of the weather the rest of November would bring, if it wasn't worse.

As I walked back over the harbor hill, I saw the unmarked state police car belonging to Lieutenant Jerry Binder and his partner, Sergeant Tom Flynn, pull to the curb in front of my mother's house. I met the detectives on the front walk.

"Julia." Under his ski-slope nose, Jerry Binder's mouth turned up in a genuine smile. "You can't seem to stay out of trouble."

"Coincidence. I picked up my niece and her friend because Sonny and Livvie were out of town."

"Uh-huh." Tom Flynn didn't seem to find the fact that I kept turning up in their cases nearly so funny.

I led them to Mom's house and opened the front door. "Livvie has asked me to sit in on Page's interview, if that's okay."

Binder stepped across the threshold. "The more the merrier."

"Just keep quiet and let us drive," Flynn added. Completely unnecessarily in my opinion.

"We'll need to talk to you after," Binder said. "Since you were there when the body was discovered."

"I'm not sure what I can add to whatever Officers Dawes and Howland told you, but I'm happy to help in any way I can."

Livvie was in the kitchen. Mom had gone to work, and Livvie had sent Sonny and Jack home. I wasn't sure how she'd talked Sonny into not being present for his daughter's interview, but I was relieved. Things would go much more smoothly without Sonny's simmering temper and Jack's kinetic energy.

"Page!" Livvie called up the back stairs to her daughter. "Lieutenant Binder and Sergeant Flynn are here."

Page walked down the stairs, staring carefully at her feet. She was dressed in blue jeans and a nice shirt, and she'd made an attempt to tame her red curls, pulling them back in a ponytail.

"Hello." Page addressed the policemen.

"Shall we sit here?" Binder gestured to the kitchen table.

"Of course," Livvie said. "Anybody need anything? Coffee? Water?"

"Coffee would be nice," Binder said.

Flynn added, "Water, thanks."

I doubted they were thirsty. They probably wanted the atmosphere to appear more relaxed. Page was plainly miserable.

Livvie distributed the drinks, including a glass of water for Page, who hadn't requested it. Binder, sitting across from Page, leaned forward and put the elbows of his tweed sports coat on the table. Next to him, Flynn took out his notebook. Livvie sat next to Page. I took the chair at the end of the table.

Binder's sports coat looked comfy and lived-in, like Binder did. He was in his late forties; sandy hair ringed his bald head. He had two boys a little younger than Page. He was normally the good cop in these interviews, patient and understanding, while Flynn pushed aggressively for the details.

I hoped Flynn wouldn't push Page too hard. The cops were on the trail of a murderer, but Page was a kid. She'd met both detectives before, but in passing and never in a situation like this. Flynn, with his buzz-cut hair, military bearing, and gym-toned body, could be intimidating even when he didn't mean to be.

"Page," Binder said in his nice-dad voice, "we're going to ask you some questions about last night. It's very important that you're honest, even if you think your answer might get you or a friend of yours in trouble. Can you do that?"

Page nodded, face solemn.

"Nothing she says can get her in more trouble than she's already in." Livvie saw what Binder was doing.

"Okay," Binder said. "Let's begin. What time did you arrive at the Davies' house?"

Page looked at her mother, who nodded, encouraging her. "Vanessa's mom, Emmy, picked me up here before her shift started at Crowley's. It was around five o'clock, I think." Her voice had a soft, little-girl quality I hadn't heard in years.

"Sonny and I had left for Portland," Livvie said. "So Page was already here at Mom's."

Binder gave her a curt nod and turned his attention back to Page. "Who did you see at the Davies' house when you arrived?"

"Talia and her parents." Page continued in the same, barely audible tone. "And Vanessa, who came with me, of course."

"Both of Talia's parents were present when you arrived," Binder confirmed.

"Yes."

"Then what happened?"

"Mrs. Davies went over the rules. She said we could watch whatever we wanted on the TV, even if it was scary. She said there was pizza and salad for dinner and soda, which Talia was excited about because normally she's not allowed. Mrs. Davies said we could go into the family room; she'd take care of the trick-or-treaters."

"Did you see Mrs. Zelisko at any time when Talia's parents were still there?" Flynn asked.

"No. I never saw her at all, until . . ." Page's eyes again darted to her mother. Livvie nodded, her expression serious.

"We'll get to that." Binder steered the conversation kindly but firmly. "For now, let's keep talking about the time before the Davies left."

"We watched a movie, not a scary one. We could hear the doorbell ring, and Mrs. Davies complimenting all the little kids on their costumes while she gave out the candy. Then she heated up the pizza and called us to the kitchen to eat." Page drew a deep breath. "That's when she told us she and Mr. Davies were going out." Page picked up her water glass and took a long drink. "I was worried because I knew my parents wouldn't like that. But then Mrs. Davies explained that Mrs. Zelisko was upstairs, so I felt fine about it. A little later, Mr. and Mrs. Davies came into the back room to say goodbye to us. They said Mrs. Zelisko would be keeping her ears open, and we should go to her if we had any problems. And then they left."

"What time was that?" Binder asked.

"We'd been there maybe two hours?" Page didn't sound too sure.

"What did you do when they left?" Binder continued.

"At first, we started another movie, but we got bored, so then we started texting with some friends."

"Are these texts still on your phone?" Flynn asked.

"Yes."

"We'd like to see it, if that's okay."

"My mom has it."

Livvie retrieved the phone from her oversized pocketbook in the back hall. The rest of us were silent while we waited, though I had a million questions. Livvie entered the password and held out the phone. Flynn reached across the table and took it.

While Flynn examined the phone, Binder went on with the interview. "Who did you text with, Page?"

"Different friends from school. We were asking what

they were doing. Some went trick-or-treating; some handed out candy. Then we found out Jenna Warren was having a sleepover at her house with Kennedy and Lucy."

"I don't see that text here," Flynn said.

"It isn't on my phone. We were all on our own phones, checking in with different people. Talia was texting with Jenna and invited them over." Page paused, looking again at her mother. "I told her not to. But she said as long as we were quiet, Mrs. Zelisko wouldn't come downstairs, and no one would ever know."

Livvie looked at me, an amused squint to her eyes. Only a thirteen-year-old girl could believe six adolescent girls could remain quiet enough not to attract attention.

"And the three girls did come over," Binder said.

"Yes. Right away. Jenna only lives around the corner from Talia."

Flynn asked the girls' full names and wrote them down. I wondered if their parents knew they'd been at the Davies' or if the girls had snuck out and the parents were in for an unpleasant surprise.

"Then what happened?" Binder leaned farther forward and lowered his voice. We were getting to the hard part.

"Jenna did a group text to the whole world saying there was a party at Talia's and her parents weren't home." Page's voice quivered. "And then people started coming from everywhere, bringing beer. Big kids. High school kids. Jenna let the first group in, and after that we couldn't keep them out. They kept letting each other in."

"Did you know these kids?" Flynn asked.

"Some I know, like from swim team." Page had been on the Y swim team since she could dog-paddle. High school kids served as assistant coaches and lifeguards. "Some I recognized from school." Busman's Harbor had a combined middle and high school in the same building. The kids would pass each other in the halls. "Some were in costumes with creepy masks or makeup. Some I'm sure I've never seen before."

"How many kids would you say were there at the peak of the party?" Binder asked.

"Maybe a hundred?"

I doubted that was the actual number, but however many it was, it had seemed overwhelming to Page.

Binder didn't have to prompt her to continue.

"The party went on and on. Kids started wrecking the house. The music was really loud. There was a fight in the backyard. Someone threw up in the downstairs bathroom and didn't clean it up. People were in the bedrooms." Page shuddered. "Talia was crying. She knew she was in so much trouble. We didn't understand why Mrs. Zelisko didn't come downstairs and throw those kids out. Talia and I went up to get her."

At this point, both Binder and Flynn got very interested. They leaned in toward Page, whose eyes opened wide. She pushed her chair back a little.

"Did you see Mrs. Zelisko?" Flynn asked.

"There was no one in her apartment," Page said. "It was empty. We looked in every room that we could get in. Talia said maybe she forgot she was supposed to watch us and went out."

"Were there rooms up there you couldn't get into?" Binder asked.

"One door was closed. I thought it might be the bathroom. Talia wasn't sure. Mrs. Zelisko already lived there when Talia's family moved in, so Talia had never been in the apartment. We knocked and knocked. I tried the knob." Page's skin, already flushed behind her freckles, reddened more. "Normally I would *never*. But we were really scared. I couldn't open it."

"The door was locked from the inside?" Flynn tried to keep his normal bark in check.

"I don't know. The knob turned, but the door was stuck."

"Then what did you do?" Binder prompted.

"We went back downstairs. We couldn't find Vanessa. We shouted for her, but the house was so noisy. I got really nervous, so I called Aunt Julia." Page looked at me. "I didn't know what else to do."

"It's okay, sweetie," I said. "That's what I'm here for." Not only had Livvie and Sonny specifically asked me to provide backup in this instance, I thought it was generally the job description of an aunt to take those kinds of calls. I never wanted Page to hesitate to call me.

"What time did you call your Aunt Julia?" Binder asked.

"I don't know." Page sounded weepy, like not knowing the time was a personal failing.

Flynn scrolled through her phone. "Does nine forty-three sound right?"

"Yes," I said.

"Go on," Binder said to Page.

"The house was so crowded. There were people everywhere. There was a big group in the front hall, where Talia and I ended up when we came down the stairs from the apartment. Finally, I spotted Vanessa through the arch-way to the kitchen. I called out to her. A girl screamed and pointed up. And then everyone was screaming and point-ing. Mrs. Zelisko flew down from the ceiling! She was all dressed in white like a bride! Her face was white. She was a ghost! That's where she was when we were in her apartment. She was *dead."* Page burst into noisy tears. Livvie put an arm around her. The poor kid. The fanciful flying ghost story aside, whatever had happened had clearly been traumatizing. And something had happened. Mrs. Zelisko *was* dead.

"When you say she flew—" Flynn was at least making an effort to hide his skepticism.

"Flew like a bird," Page insisted, "from her apartment to the first floor."

"What happened when she reached the bottom?" Flynn asked.

"I don't know. There were too many people. Everyone was screaming and running out of the front door and the back door. I screamed too and pulled Talia outside. We ran to the corner of the block. That's where Vanessa fi-nally caught up to us."

Binder kept moving Page forward in the story. "What happened when you reached the corner?"

"Everyone else kept running, but Vanessa, Talia, and I stopped. We could see that the front door of Talia's house was wide open. Vanessa and I couldn't leave Talia. We could hear the police sirens. Besides, I'd already called Aunt Julia. So we went back."

"That was brave," Binder said.

Or foolish.

"Did you call the police?" I asked Page.

Flynn shook his head. "Neighbors. Multiple neighbors."

"Did you ever see Mrs. Zelisko or her ghost again?" Binder asked.

"No. Never. She wasn't in the hall when we got back to the house. The police came, and Aunt Julia came, and Vanessa and I came back to Grammy's house, and that was it."

Binder sat back in his chair. "Thank you, Page. You have been very, very helpful. Can you write down the names of everyone you remember seeing at the party?"

Livvie fetched a pad and pencil from beside Mom's landline, and Page labored, tongue sticking out through her lips. In the end, she had about twenty first and last names, ten more first names or nicknames. Binder and Flynn accepted it gratefully. It was as good a place as any to get started.

Flynn scrolled through Page's phone as she worked. "Did you take any photos of the party?"

Page looked at him like he was crazy. "Are you kidding?"

"Page, that's not the way we talk to Sergeant Flynn, or any grown-up," Livvie scolded.

"Are you on any social media? Could some of your friends have posted photos?"

"Instagram," Page answered. "I follow a lot of kids from school."

Flynn looked at Livvie, who nodded and then went back to the phone and scrolled. "There are lots of photos of the party." Flynn held the phone out to Page. "Take a look to see if it helps you remember anyone else."

Page took the phone and diligently scrolled. She added

three names to her list. When she was done, she handed the phone back to Flynn.

Flynn tried to give it back. "It's okay. If we need it again, we'll ask."

"Give it to my mom," Page said, resigned. She handed the list to Flynn and allowed herself to be hugged by her mother. I walked the detectives out to the front porch.

Chapter Six

"Do you have anything to add?" Binder asked me.

"No. Page did a good job on the parts where I was involved. Was she helpful?"

"Very. Especially the names she was able to provide." Flynn folded Page's list and put it in his notebook.

"Have you had any luck finding Mrs. Zelisko's next of kin?" I asked.

"Zero," Binder answered. "We can't find anything about her before she fetched up on your particular peninsula five years ago."

"Really? The feds must know something about her. When she immigrated, for sure."

"We're waiting to hear back from them. You're sure she was an immigrant?"

"She had a pronounced accent. Eastern European. She told the Davies she was from Slovenia."

Binder nodded. "We'll ask them about it. We're off to see them next. Across the street." He paused. "Of course, it's possible she immigrated years ago under a maiden name and Mr. Zelisko was someone who came and went subsequent to her arrival here."

"True. I don't think there's been a Mr. Zelisko since she arrived in town. I've heard she was a parishioner at Star of the Sea. It could be that someone there is a closer friend and knows more about her."

"Thanks," Binder said. "We're still searching her apartment, computer, and phone. Maybe there's some correspondence that will lead us in the right direction. In the meantime, we have to talk to Talia and Vanessa, and then get started on this list your niece gave us. Somewhere, there's an eyewitness."

"How did she die?" I asked.

"Awaiting autopsy results." Flynn was abrupt.

"But it definitely was murder?"

"No question," Binder answered.

"Was her body just lying in the backyard?"

"It was in the shed," Flynn said. "The killer had taken the trouble to hide it."

"What do you think about this whole crazy ghost thing?" I asked.

"I was going to ask you the same question." Binder wasn't amused. Murder was serious business.

The door of the Snuggles Inn opened, and Blair Davies strode onto the wide front porch. "Detectives?" she shouted in our direction.

"That's us," Binder called back. "Lieutenant Jerry Binder and Sergeant Tom Flynn. We're finishing up with Ms. Snowden, and we'll be right over."

"That's why I came out," Blair shouted. "I just got off the phone with Livvie. She told me Julia was present during Page's interview. I wondered if Julia could do the same for Talia. Livvie tells me Julia has some experience in these situations, and at least Talia knows her a little bit."

Binder looked at me and sighed. "I can't think of a reason why not. Julia, do you have time to join us?"

"Absolutely."

Blair led us through the inn to the dining room. Talia sat, slump-shouldered, next to her dad. Blair went around the table and took the chair on the other side of her. The detectives and I arranged ourselves across from them.

Vee Snugg bustled in from the kitchen. "Anyone need anything?" She knew Binder and Flynn from previous investigations, and neither Snugg sister ever missed a chance to check out Flynn's sports-jacket clad biceps.

"Miss Snugg." Binder rose and gave Vee a hug. Flynn also rose but stuck out a hand in self-defense. "Maybe some tea," Binder suggested. "And something for Miss Davies."

"Water, thank you," Talia said miserably.

While we waited for the tea, Binder steered the conversation toward the Davies' background. They had moved from Medview, Massachusetts, in June, right after school got out, so Howard could take a management job at Emerson Lab. These were prestigious, good jobs in Busman's Harbor, the kind Maine communities had too few of. The kind that could attract people from out of state to shore up our dwindling population.

Back in Massachusetts, Blair had been an elementary

school teacher, but she hadn't found a position since they'd relocated. "It's been challenging to make friends," she said. "Everyone here seems to know everyone already." She spread her hands out in front of her, a gesture taking in the whole town and all the people in it.

"That's why we accepted the Halloween party invitation," Howard explained, "so Blair could get to know some of my colleagues and their partners. We never should have." He shook his head with regret.

"We'll get to that," Binder said.

Vee and Fee and Fee's Scottish terrier, Mackie, arrived with the tea, Talia's water, and a plate of Vee's pumpkin cookies. "In case you're peckish."

If Vee was unsparingly glamorous, no matter the occasion, Fee was her opposite. Bent over from arthritis, she kept her steel-gray bangs out of her face with a pink plastic barrette. She never used makeup, and today she wore a brown corduroy skirt, a tan sweater, and the very footwear you picture when you hear the words "sensible shoes." Like her sister, she was smitten with Flynn. He had never done anything to encourage them, except for his daily, lengthy trips to the gym. I was convinced he toiled there for his own satisfaction and not for anyone's admiration of the results.

"Thank you," I said. Vee's pumpkin cookies had been a favorite since I was a kid. Fee bustled to the corner cabinet and distributed six small plates around the table. The heavenly smell of the big cookies was getting to me. They were shaped like pumpkins, and Vee had delicately decorated them with a lacey tracing of orange frosting to indicate the pumpkin shell and a green leaf peeping out from the stem.

"They're gluten-free," Vee said.

What the what?

"So you can eat one, Sergeant." She beamed at Flynn. "Or two."

Ohhh. Light dawned. Binder and Flynn had stayed at the B&B a number of times when they'd been in town on previous cases, and it had been source of endless frustration for Vee that Flynn never touched the goodies she painstakingly baked for their breakfasts. She had tried to tempt him with muffins, scones, and coffee cake, and he'd bypassed them all. Evidently, she'd decided that the only possible explanation was that he was gluten-intolerant.

I suspected he would object as much, if not more, to the light and dark sugar, chocolate chips, and sticks of butter that were in the delicious cookies. His body was a temple. But I had to give Vee points for trying.

I grabbed the cookie plate, took one to set a good example, and then started it around the table. At a minimum, the food would serve as an icebreaker. Talia was plainly miserable. She'd disobeyed her parents and gotten their home trashed. The senior Davies felt horribly guilty about leaving the girls to go to the party. And all of that and more had combined to set the stage for the murder of their tenant and the transformation of their home into a crime scene.

Everyone took a cookie until the plate made its way back around to Flynn, who was seated next to me. He held the plate in mid-air in front of him while Vee stared him down. Finally, he took the smallest cookie, which wasn't small, and the sisters withdrew.

My cookie was exactly as I remembered them from my youth—pumpkiny, and spicy, chocolatey and cakey, yet moist with a crunch from the walnuts that were in it. It perked me up considerably, and I thought Talia and Blair looked less droopy. Flynn's cookie sat untouched on his plate.

Binder got down to business. He asked first about the deceased. Mr. and Mrs. Davies gave the answers I already knew. Slovenian. Lived in the house when they bought it. Faithful attendee of Star of the Sea Catholic church.

"How about the previous owners?" Flynn asked. "The people who rented to her originally. Maybe they know more."

"They moved to Buffalo," Howard said. "I'll send you their contact information."

"Please." Flynn slid his business card across the table.

"Did Mrs. Zelisko tell you anything about Mr. Zelisko?" Binder asked. "If she was widowed or divorced?"

"Never," Blair answered. "Honestly, I wondered if there had been a Mr. Zelisko. I thought the 'Mrs.' might be more of an honorific."

A dead end. Binder appeared unperturbed. "Did she ever happen to mention what year she arrived in this country?" he asked. "Or maybe where she lived in the States before she moved to Busman's Harbor?"

All three Davies shook their heads.

"Or maybe where she lived immediately before coming to Busman's Harbor?" Flynn asked.

"No, nothing like that," Blair said.

"She didn't talk about her past," Howard added.

"Which was weird," Talia said, "because we talked about the past and where we moved from, like, all the time."

"I never really thought about it that way," Howard said, "but you're right, sweetheart."

Talia physically shook off the "sweetheart" with a flick of her hand, as if it was an annoying gnat.

"Did she pay rent by check or electronic transfer?" Flynn asked. "Our team has her laptop, and we'll find her bank account, but a check or account number could help us."

Howard colored slightly. "She paid in cash."

It wasn't an unusual arrangement for tenants in these auxiliary apartments to pay in cash. They usually got a discount for doing so, and the homeowner rarely reported the income to the IRS.

Binder steered the conversation to the previous night. Blair narrated the first part, up until the older Davies left for the party. Howard apologized again, profusely, for their bad judgment.

Talia took up the tale from there. In response to Binder's patient questioning, her telling of events matched Page's. Not so much so that it sounded rehearsed, but in all the important areas, their stories were the same. Even more than Page had, Talia grew more miserable as the story progressed and she described the party at her family home growing wilder and more out of control. As she talked, tears slid down her nose and fell onto the pink rosebuds on the china plate in front of her.

"It's okay." Blair rubbed her daughter's back. "We all make mistakes. No one could have foreseen everything that happened last night. The detectives just want to know about Mrs. Zelisko."

On the other side of Talia, Howard shifted his chair, his mouth turned down at the corners. He didn't seem inclined to let his daughter off so lightly. Perhaps no one

could have foreseen a murder, but the gathering of teenagers once word was on the street that the Davies weren't
home was entirely foreseeable.

Talia described the search for Mrs. Zelisko in more detail than Page had. She told how they'd looked in the sitting room and the bedroom, and had knocked at the
bathroom door.

"You're sure it was the bathroom," Flynn confirmed.

"Not sure, but it was right over my bathroom on the
second floor, and we hadn't seen one anywhere else in
the apartment."

"Makes sense," Binder said.

"We knocked and called, and she didn't answer," Talia
continued. "Page tried to open the door but couldn't."

"Did you look in the closets or under the bed?" Binder
pressed.

"No!" Talia sat up sharply. "I would *never*. It's her privacy."

"It's okay that you didn't," Binder assured her. "We
just want to be thorough."

Talia took a deep breath and continued. She described
the jammed-up gathering in the front hall. "And then
Mrs. Zelisko floated down the stairs!"

Floated, not flew, as Page had said. Flynn caught it
too. "She came down the stairs slowly?"

"She floated across the room," Talia explained as if to
someone not bright.

"I don't understand," Flynn persisted. "Did she come
down the bannister?"

Talia shook her head. "She was *old*." As if being old
made it impossible to consider that Mrs. Zelisko might
have slid down the bannister, but not impossible to consider that she might have floated through the air.

"How was she dressed?" Binder asked.

"She was all in white."

"Like a white dress?"

"No. Like white robes and a white veil. Like a nun. More like a nun in a white whaddyamacallit."

"Habit," Blair supplied.

"Habit," Talia repeated.

It didn't take long to wind up the rest of the story. The teenagers running out of the house. The police arriving. Me arriving and then leaving with Page and Vanessa. The Davies coming home. Flynn examined Talia's phone while Binder led the family through the denouement with businesslike precision.

The detectives thanked the family and stood. I did, too.

"I imagine you're anxious to get back to your home," Binder said to them. "We'll move as quickly as we can."

Blair shuddered. "To tell the truth, we're not in any hurry. Take your time."

Before they left, I watched Lieutenant Binder quietly fold a paper napkin around Flynn's uneaten cookie and slip it into the pocket of his sports coat.

I followed the detectives to their car. "What do you think?" I asked them.

"Those girls saw something in that hallway," Binder said. "But did they see a live woman or a dead one? That's the question."

Chapter Seven

Binder and Flynn got in their car and drove away. I suspected they were off to lunch at Gus's, but my strategy of standing in the street looking like I had nothing in particular to do didn't earn me an invitation.

I headed in the opposite direction, toward the Star of the Sea Catholic church. I walked down to the waterfront and crossed the wooden footbridge that connected the two sides of the inner harbor. In the summer, I might have lingered on the bridge to look out at the islands and the pleasure boats, but the November wind cut across the water. I stuck my hands in my vest pockets.

The inner harbor was the touristy part of Busman's Harbor, as opposed to the back harbor, where the lobster boats were moored. The east side was lined with fancy hotels and more recently built condo complexes. Above them loomed the bright white central steeple of the Star of the Sea.

The original, modest church had been built for the Irish servants of the wealthy "rusticators" who summered in Maine in the late nineteenth century, my mother's ancestors among them. When the town had been flooded with French Canadian immigrants, who moved here to work in the canneries, the current church was built. Now it served all the town's Catholics, from locals to snowbird retirees to summer families. They worshipped upstairs in the nave of the big church during the tourist season. In the off-season, when the summer people were gone and the snowbirds fled daily for warmer climes, services were held in the much more economically and successfully heated basement.

When I was young, there had been two full-time priests assigned to the Star of the Sea year-round. They lived in a house on the grounds, indulged by a devoted housekeeper. Now there was one part-time cleric, who rotated among three churches. He lived two towns away and seemed to show up in Busman's Harbor only when duty called, much to the disgruntlement of his more vocal parishioners.

But if their clerics registered as indifferent, the hard-core laity at the Star of the Sea did not let that affect their dedication. If anything, the priestly neglect revved them up. Which is why, as I approached the building, I was certain I would find the people I sought in the church hall on a Saturday afternoon.

Sure enough, I spotted Clarice Kemp across the big room, diligently pricing donated items for the church's main fundraiser, an auction that was nine months in the future. Clarice was the biggest gossip in Busman's Harbor. She'd recently retired from her job at the front desk of the Lighthouse Inn, a job that had put her at the nexus of town gossip, with sources ranging from the tourists staying in the rooms, to the locals eating in the dining room, to the yachters pulling up their boats outside. Now that Clarice had moved on from her life at the crossroads, I had heard she was spending her time at the Star of the Sea, another gossip hotbed, though it did confine her mostly to firsthand information about the town's Catholics.

There were a few other people in the room. Mike Parker—the "pipe charmer," as my family called him, since he somehow was able to keep the ancient plumbing at my mother's house up and running—and his wife, Doreen, were also pricing items. The half a dozen or so other people looked familiar, but I didn't know their names. I gave a wave and a smile to all and headed for Clarice.

"Julia, would you say this is mid-century modern?" She held out an enormous table lamp with a bulbous, oversized base inlaid with teal disks that might have been ceramic or plastic. The rest of the lamp was an unconvincing gold, except for the teal shade that spiraled from a wide bottom to a curlicued top.

"It sure is—" I groped for words.

"Ugly?" Clarice suggested.

"I was going to say grotesque."

"But is it *so* grotesque that it's somehow trendy or beautiful? I don't want some hipster from Brooklyn sweeping in here and thinking he's putting something over on us."

I laughed. "I haven't lived in New York City for going

on four years. I'm afraid I can't tell you what the hipsters will go for."

Clarice put the lamp back on the table. "I'll have Bev from Bev's Antiques take a look at it before I price it. What brings you here today?" Like a reporter, she moved us straight to the heart of the matter.

"I heard that Mrs. Zelisko was a parishioner here."

"Oooh," Clarice said. Her dreams of an original source had been realized. "I heard you were there when Pete Howland discovered the body."

The others in the room moved in closer. Needless to say, Mrs. Zelisko's murder was the number-one topic of conversation around town.

"Only tangentially," I assured her. "I happened to be at the Davies' house picking up my niece and her friend at the time."

"I heard there was a wild party," a woman said. "My friend lives on the street. Lots of college kids in revealing costumes having sex on the lawn and"—she lowered her voice—"*doing drugs*."

"I don't think it was as wild as all that," I protested. It didn't discourage them. The group closed in tighter. "The state police Major Crimes Unit is having trouble finding Mrs. Zelisko's next of kin," I continued, revealing my insider knowledge, which might or might not be a mistake in this situation. "And I thought maybe she had a close friend or friends here who might be able to help."

I let the suggestion sit while they looked at one another.

True to her role as a leader, Clarice spoke first. "Mrs. Zelisko was an absolute stalwart of the church. She was a professional bookkeeper, as you may know, and she gave generously of her time and talents. For example, she managed the books for this auction. At the end of the day, we sell over three thousand items—the big stuff in the main tent, the silent auction items, and the items we sell outright; sometimes we combine them into pretty baskets or boxes. It's a lot to keep track of, and I'm always so proud when we present the check with the proceeds to Father every year."

"Very admirable," I said. "But what I'm after is, did Mrs. Zelisko have any particular friends? Someone she may have confided in? The police need information about her family."

Clarice looked around the group and shook her head. "I never heard of any family. I had the impression she came to this country on her own."

"Then she'd have family back in her old country," I pointed out. "Or maybe even her husband's family. Someone who should be told about her death."

"She wasn't a person who made friends," a white-haired woman said. "She didn't have a car, and I offered to drive her to Hannaford several times. She never accepted."

That jibed with a memory I had of Mrs. Zelisko, climbing the harbor hill, string bags of groceries swinging at her sides.

"She was a little deaf," Doreen added. "I thought that might be why she avoided conversations."

Clarice nodded. "It took me a long time to catch on to that. She read lips quite well, but I'm sure it was tiring for her."

"I would say the people she was closest to were her clients," Mike the plumber said. "She kept the books for a lot of parishioners here."

"She approached us about her services," his wife added. "But I've always kept the books for the business."

"Who were her clients specifically?" I asked.

"Gleason's Hardware was one of the biggest," someone said, "and the most recent."

"Walker's Art Supplies," added another. "Barry Walker has been with her for a long time. I think he was one of her first clients."

"Gordon's Jewelry, for sure," Mike said.

"All owned by church members," Clarice said.

"Okay. I'll talk to them." A thought occurred to me. "Do any of you know her first name?"

"Uhm, Ellen?" Doreen ventured, though she didn't sound sure. "She didn't really use it."

"Helen?" Clarice suggested. "She always said it very quickly. And there was the accent."

"Or Eileen," someone else said.

"Irene," Mike put in. "It was definitely Irene."

"No, it wasn't," Doreen objected. "It definitely wasn't."

Chapter Eight

I said goodbye and thank you to the assembled group and made my way back downtown from the church, crossing over the footbridge.

There was no escaping the conclusion that Mrs. Zelisko valued her privacy. But why? Was it a natural reticence, perhaps caused by her hearing loss, or did something about her past make her reluctant to share personal information? Something about her past that was dangerous enough to get her killed.

It was very much the Maine way to let people keep themselves to themselves. Even Clarice Kemp, who would pass along any personal tidbit that came her way, wouldn't pry to get it, at least not with her subject directly. Our peninsula was, in a literal sense, the end of the road. It wasn't all that unusual for people to roll into town hoping to leave the past behind.

The footbridge left me off on the town pier right by the Snowden Family Clambake ticket kiosk. The little building always looked forlorn during the off-season, sitting alone on the concrete pier. I looked through the window to make sure no mail had been mistakenly put through the slot, but the tiny space was exactly as we'd left it when we'd cleaned up one last time and locked the door after Columbus Day.

From the pier, I walked a block to the corner of Main and Main, where Main Street crosses over itself after circling the harbor hill. On the first weekend in November, with Halloween over and the holiday season not yet begun, the street was deserted. The stoplight at the corner, the only one in town, was set to blinking yellow. Gordon's Jewelry was on the left-hand corner and Walker's Art Supplies and Frame Shop on the right. Unlike many of the shops on Main Street, both were open year-round. I went up the steps and opened the door of the jewelry shop.

Mr. Gordon, chubby and white-haired, was at his desk, bent over a velvet tray, a jeweler's loupe in his eye. The sound of the door opening caused him to sit up and turn in my direction.

"Julia, my dear. What brings you in on this chilly day?"

"Hi, Mr. Gordon. I've come to talk to you about your bookkeeper, Mrs. Zelisko. I'm sure you've heard."

He took the loupe off and replaced it with a thick pair of glasses. He gestured for me to sit on the wooden chair across from him. "I have indeed. Terrible tragedy. She was a fine woman." He looked genuinely saddened by the death.

I sat down. "Do you know much about her?"

"She's a member of Star of the Sea." He offered the one piece of information everyone seemed to have.

"I mean personally."

He hesitated. "Not really. When she came here, she was all business, no chitchat. I thought maybe she struggled with the language and that's why she avoided small talk. Then I realized she understood and spoke perfectly; she just didn't want to chatter. I didn't want to pry."

"How did you come to hire her?"

"When she first arrived in town, she joined the church. During a church auction committee meeting soon after she arrived, she introduced herself, said she was looking for clients." He took off his glasses and cleaned them rigorously with a soft cloth. "Alicia did the books for the business back then, but when it became too much for her, I remembered Mrs. Zelisko."

Mr. Gordon's wife, Alicia, had been very much his partner in life and in the jewelry business. She'd been a warm presence in the store, helping nervous boyfriends pick out engagement rings, sweethearts find something for their valentines, and happy tourists discover souvenirs that would remind them of their visit to the Maine midcoast. But a couple of years earlier, her mind had started to wander, not a good thing in a business that traded in the careful display and tracking of expensive goods. When Alicia was unable to help at all, Mr. Gordon still brought her to the store every day, where he could watch her and she could interact with people. Since the summer, even that had not been possible, and he'd hired someone to watch her at home. Mrs. Zelisko's interest in doing his bookkeeping must have seemed like a lifeline.

"It's all become so complicated," he was saying. "We used to keep our books in a paper ledger. But now it's all QuickBooks and this and that. We have to keep very close track of the sales tax, of course. We sell some high-end items here."

Sales tax, I knew from my own experience with our little gift store at the Snowden Family Clambake, was money a retailer collected and kept in trust on behalf of the state of Maine. The money didn't belong to the retailer and had to be passed on, along with a filing that accounted for it, in a timely manner. It was a simple process, but an important one.

"Mrs. Zelisko was wonderful," Mr. Gordon continued. "She took care of everything. I never worried a day about that aspect of the business when she was on the job. Which reminds me," he squinted over the top of his glasses. "I'll need to get my records back. I wonder when that will be."

"The police have Mrs. Zelisko's laptop," I told him. "They're trying to find her next of kin. Plus solve her murder, of course. I'm sure they'll make arrangements with her clients to get the information they need when they're done with it. You don't know, by any chance, who her next of kin might be?"

"No," Mr. Gordon answered slowly. "Like I said, we never discussed anything personal."

I stood up. "I figured. Do you know her first name? You paid her. I thought it might be on a check or a bank account."

"She had me pay her in her little company's name," he said. "I don't remember it. It's all automated, so I haven't looked at it since we set it up. Do you want me to look it up for you?"

"No, please don't trouble yourself." The police would have that information and more.

"As you please," Mr. Gordon responded. But he had already drifted back to the gems on his desk, the jeweler's loupe in his eye.

I crossed the street to Walker's Art Supplies and Frame Shop. Empty parking spots lined Main Street. During the season, a single empty space could spark a fistfight.

Walker's had been there as long as I could remember. Every June, when the school year was over and we prepared to move to Morrow Island, where our clambake was held, my mother brought Livvie and me to pick out colored pencils, pipe cleaners, tongue depressors, potholder loops, and clay for molding. Anything to keep us busy on rainy island days when the clambake didn't operate. Our morning at Walker's was like a second Christmas, even better because you got to pick out your own gifts. We loved it. None of the crafts took long-term with me, but Livvie spent her winters working at a pottery studio in town. She made the plates, lamps, and serving pieces the shop offered and painted them, too, with a delicate, controlled hand. It was a talent I envied.

I opened one of the double doors and entered Walker's familiar space. It was as different from Gordon's as possible. Gordon's was a tidy jewelry box, each piece displayed individually, uncrowded and locked up tight. Walker's was a double storefront. The long shelves that lined its walls were dusty and disheveled. Barry Walker claimed to know exactly where everything was, but he did not. Part of the fun of going to Walker's was hunting for the stuff of your dreams and finding a few things you hadn't thought about or even known existed but absolutely had to have the moment you discovered them.

Barry was on the right side of the big floor, the part of the store he used as his studio. In the off-season, he always painted like a frenzied squirrel. One canvas stood on his easel, while others, in various stages of completion, were scattered around that side of the shop, leaning against shelves and preventing patrons from getting near whatever goods were hidden behind them. Barry's paintings were angry abstract slashes in vibrant colors, the last thing most tourists wanted to purchase as a reminder of their mid-coast vacation. He would have done better with lobsters and lighthouses, which he was more than capable of painting, but Barry's only artistic interest was in pleasing himself.

He looked up when I stepped into the store. "Julia Snowden, as I live and breathe. What brings you here? Have a hankering to make your mom some new potholders?" He was a big, shambling man with long gray hair. He'd sported a day's growth of whiskers long before that look became fashionable. On the street, he was often mistaken for a homeless person, which didn't seem to bother him in the least.

I smiled at the tease. "That's Page's department now." Though Page had probably outgrown the task as well. "I wanted to talk to you about Mrs. Zelisko."

"Oh." Barry rubbed his brush with a cloth and then popped it into a jar of smelly liquid. "Darn shame."

"Yes, it is. I understand you were a client."

"A happy one. She was a lifesaver. I tried to keep up with the paperwork after Fran went to work at the home, but then it got ahead of me. I couldn't manage the quarterly filings with the IRS and the state. Five years ago, when Mrs. Zelisko joined our church and said she was available, I hired her on the spot. She started the next day. I'd gotten things in a terrible mess. It took her a while, but she untangled it."

Like Gordon's Jewelry, Walker's had started off as a mom-and-pop operation. But, in their case, revenue had dwindled during the recession and never completely returned. Fran Walker had taken a full-time job as an aid at a rehabilitation facility up the peninsula. It didn't surprise me that Barry had made a mess of their books.

"The police are looking for a next of kin. Did Mrs. Zelisko ever talk about her personal life?"

Barry shook his shaggy curls. "Never. Kept herself to herself, she did. I was always working when she was here, either tending to customers or painting. She respected my work and got down to hers. From time to time, she'd ask me about an expense or a particular sale we made, but that was it."

"Do you know her first name?" I asked him.

"Mrs.," he answered with a twinkle in his eye.

"Did you ever have any problem with the work she did? Anything at all?"

"In the beginning, it took us some time to get used to one another. I got a notice from the IRS that they hadn't received a quarterly payment. I asked Mrs. Zelisko about it. She said my payment had crossed in the mail with the notice and not to worry about it."

A tiny pit of concern opened in my belly. "And it never happened again?"

"Never," Barry said. "She said I shouldn't be bothered by those types of concerns, so after that, we used her address for any IRS correspondence. State of Maine, too." He gestured toward the counter behind the cash register that functioned as his desk. It was piled high with mail, papers, catalogs, and art supplies. "It was better if the paperwork went to her anyway."

I thanked Barry and went on my way, taking a last look at the rambling, shambling mess as I closed the door.

Gleason's Hardware was a large store and a going concern, busy from early in the morning, when contractors arrived to pick up their materials, until late into the afternoon. It was an old-fashioned store where the employees knew the stock and were always happy to provide helpful advice on any project you might be tackling.

There was a big-box store in Brunswick, but it was forty minutes away, too far for a plumber, electrician, or carpenter working on the peninsula to travel in the morning before going to a job. Too far for a handy homeowner or an unhandy one who simply wanted a drain cover for the kitchen sink or new blinds for the bedroom. Almost everyone in town had an account at Gleason's.

Gleason's had been run by the same family for five generations, and the only difference from then to now was that some of the goods had changed and you could no longer tie up your horse and buggy outside. The current proprietor was Al Gleason, a man in his mid-sixties who made even the work apron he and his employees wore look dapper. His son and daughter worked alongside him. Whenever I interacted with either of them, I had the impression they were thrilled to be in a position to carry on the family legacy.

The store was busy by Busman's Harbor off-season standards. I counted four employees and half a dozen customers wandering around in the big space. It took a while to find Al, but I kept asking. It turned out he was in his office at the back of the main floor.

"Julia." He peered over his reading glasses and the paper he'd been studying. "Can I help you find something?"

"I'd like to talk about Mrs. Zelisko."

"Ah." His smile disappeared. "I heard you were there when the body was found." He gestured to a stool in a corner of the office. "What can I tell you?"

"Anything at all. The police are looking for her next of kin. Did she ever speak about her family, or maybe a husband?"

"Never. We've only worked together for nine months or so. My brother-in-law Frank used to work here in the back office. He did all our bookkeeping. I hired Mrs. Zelisko when Frank retired."

I remembered Frank, a short, round man with a permanent squint. All he was missing was the green eyeshade.

"Once we got things set up," Al continued, "we didn't speak often and then mostly over the phone. The information she needed—employee timesheets, sales, inventory records—went to her electronically. Occasionally, she'd walk over with a document I needed to sign, but that was it."

"Did you ever have any trouble with her work?" I was thinking about Barry Walker's notice from the IRS.

"Never," he said, and then reconsidered. "Nothing except maybe the occasional timing thing. Let me put it this way, I had a lot more trouble with my brother-in-law when he did our books."

"Did you know Mrs. Zelisko's first name?" I asked.

"No. She did me the honor of calling me mister. I returned the respect."

Chapter Nine

Our ugly, modern town-hall-fire-station-police-head-quarters was on my route home from Gleason's. The parking lot out front was full. Several sullen teens, accompanied by a glowering parent or two, were entering or exiting. I couldn't imagine Lieutenant Binder and Sergeant Flynn were having a good day.

I decided to stop in and tell them what I'd learned, which admittedly wasn't much. Still, I thought every little bit might help. While some of the teens might turn out to be good witnesses, it was hard to believe one of the students at Busman's Harbor High had killed Mrs. Zelisko. What possible reason could they have? Unless the town was nurturing a budding serial killer.

As I'd guessed, Binder and Flynn were more than happy to squeeze me into their busy schedule. The civilian receptionist nodded that I should enter the multi-purpose room the detectives used as an office when they were in town. It was a cavernous space intended for large meetings and assemblies. The pair sat together at a plastic folding table on the far side of the room, Binder pecking at his laptop, Flynn bent over his notebook.

"Tough day so far?" I asked.

Binder wiped a hand from his chin up over his ski-slope nose and onto his bald head. "Brutal. The kids are mostly useless. They were drunk, or making out, or otherwise distracted. And the parents are *so* mad. About the party, about the drinking, and about having to take time out during their Saturday to come down here and sit through this."

"Have you interviewed all the kids who were at the party?"

He shook his head. "We still don't know who most of them are."

"People are terrible at estimating crowd size, and kids are notoriously worse," Flynn said. "The texts have been flying around all day, and now it's like Woodstock. Every kid in town was there or is saying they were there. We're going to be looking for these kids and taking statements for days."

"We ask each kid who else was there. But they're with their parents. They don't want to get their friends in trouble." Binder leaned back in the folding chair. "So while 'everyone' was there, we have the names of precious few."

"And we can't quit until we've found everyone."

"Because one of them might be the killer," I said.

"Yes, that, and we need some reliable witnesses."

"I've been talking to some people around town," I started. "Trying to find out what I can about Mrs. Zelisko's personal life."

Flynn sat forward. "And did you?"

"Absolutely not," I said. "She was active in the Star of the Sea Catholic church, as you've already heard. It seems she found most of her clients there. I've talked to a few at small businesses on Main Street. They all speak very well of her but know nothing about her next of kin, her husband's name, or even her first name."

"Ah." Binder picked up an envelope from his desk. "Apparently, it's Helene. If the billing department at her cell phone provider is to be believed. But that's as far as we've gotten. No next of kin yet, though we have her laptop and phone in the lab back in Augusta, so I hope we'll know something soon."

"Barry Walker at Walker's Art Supplies told me he has all his financial mail from the IRS and the state of Maine sent directly to Mrs. Zelisko," I said. "Did you find a lot of client mail?"

Flynn looked at Binder and then spoke. "Not so far. The crime-scene folks are still at the apartment. I'll tell them to be on the lookout, though I imagine most of it is electronic nowadays. I'm sure either the crime-scene people or the tech people will find it."

"Barry is particularly disorganized. It may have been something she did only for him," I told them.

Binder looked at his laptop and then back at me, anxious, I could tell, to get on with their busy day.

"Was Mrs. Zelisko really wearing a wedding dress or a nun's habit when she died?" I asked.

"She was dressed in a white nightgown and wrapped

in a white sheet," Binder answered, "when Pete Howland found her in the shed."

"Is the autopsy final? How did she die?" Sometimes they would tell me, depending on their mood and whether they thought I was helpful or in the way.

"Not final, but pretty definitive," Flynn said. "She was strangled. Though the body was pretty banged up. We should hear today whether that damage was pre- or post-mortem."

Would all those kids have heard nothing? I wanted to ask, but both men had stood.

"Thanks so much for coming in, Julia," Binder said, slowly and deliberately.

"Anytime," I said. "See you soon."

I looked around the cubicle wall that separated the reception area from the bullpen that all six of Busman's Harbor's sworn officers shared to see if Jamie wanted to grab lunch. There was no one in the room. I wasn't surprised. The local police had no doubt been drafted to help with the murder investigation, in addition to their usual duties. I was headed out the glass door into the cold when Emmy Bailey and Vanessa hurried up the walk.

"Julia, I'm so glad we ran into you." Emmy sounded mega-relieved. "Can you be present while Vanessa has her interview? Livvie said you were there for Page, and it really helped her stay calm. You have so much more experience with this."

I looked at Vanessa to see if this intrusion was welcome. She gave a tight but encouraging smile.

"Sure," I said. "Let's do this."

We walked along the corridor toward the multi-purpose room. "It's not hard, and the detectives won't be mean like they sometimes are on TV," I told Vanessa. "You're a witness, not a suspect. Tell the truth and be as accurate as you can, and you'll be fine."

Vanessa's shoulders, which had been somewhere in the vicinity of her ears, dropped visibly.

"We're here to see Lieutenant Binder and Sergeant Flynn," I told the civilian receptionist. "Emmy and Vanessa Bailey."

She glared at me. "And Julia Snowden," I added.

"Just a moment."

Binder and Flynn stood as we came in. "Ms. Bailey, Vanessa." Binder squinted at me in a way I hoped signaled amusement. "Ms. Snowden."

We acknowledged who we were. Binder and Flynn shook hands with Emmy and a flustered Vanessa and indicated they should sit on the other side of the plastic table. I dragged a chair over from the opposite side of the room and sat, too.

"I hope you don't mind I asked Julia to come," Emmy said.

"The more the merrier." Then Binder went through the same speech with Vanessa that he had given the other girls. She sat, unmoving, and looked him right in the eye.

Her story was the same as Page's and Talia's. The sleep-over, the invitation to the three girls, and then the party spiraling out of control. Unlike Page and Talia, who were taller, Vanessa was tiny. In a house crowded with older kids drinking, dancing, and horsing around, she'd been buffeted by the crowd and had ended up pushed into the kitchen. That's why she hadn't been with Page and Talia when they went upstairs looking for Mrs. Zelisko.

"Did you see anyone go out the back door?" Binder asked.

"Lots of people." Vanessa didn't hesitate. "People were going in and out the whole time. The backyard was, like, part of the party. Two boys were fighting out there, too."

Flynn read her a list of the kids they'd identified already and asked her if she'd seen them at the party. Vanessa answered, "yes," "no," or "I don't know who that is" in about equal measure.

Binder leaned forward, the fond father. "I get that you didn't know all the kids, but did you recognize them all, like from the hallways at school or around town?"

Vanessa shook her head. "I'm sure there were kids there from other schools." For the first time, she paused. "Maybe even, like, older kids. Not in school anymore."

Binder glanced at Flynn. "You think there might have been kids there who were beyond high school age?" It seemed like this was the first he was hearing this.

"Uh-huh. I think so. Some of them looked older."

What did that mean? Kids were terrible at judging ages.

"Did you recognize any of these older kids? Like maybe from working around town? Hannaford? The convenience store?" Binder's tone was still gentle.

Vanessa shook her head.

"Were they mostly boys or mostly girls, these older kids?" Flynn asked.

"Boys, I think. But I couldn't say definitely. There were a lot of people there."

"What happened after you ended up in the kitchen?" Binder asked.

"I heard Page calling from the living room. I couldn't reach her and Talia through all the people. They were in the archway between the living room and the front hall. I should have gone through the kitchen door into the hall, but I didn't know, so I-I . . ." Vanessa's speech slowed down, her confidence deserting her.

"It's okay," Binder said.

Emmy, who'd been silent and still during the interview to that point, laid a hand on her daughter's arm. "It's okay, sweetie. Nothing you say here is going to get you into trouble. More trouble," she amended.

"What happened then?" Binder brought her back to the point where she'd left off.

"Then Mrs. Zelisko fell down the stairs."

"She *fell* down the stairs?" Flynn attempted to clarify. Page had said "flew"; Talia had said "floated." Heaven knew what the other kids they'd spoken to had said, if they'd even been in the hallway when it happened.

"Not fell exactly," Vanessa said. "Everyone was screaming and shoving and running. When I got pushed into the hallway, Mrs. Zelisko was tumbling down that last set of stairs. Then she was at the bottom in a heap."

"What did she look like?" Binder asked.

"At the bottom of the stairs, she was all wrapped up like a mummy."

"What did you do then?" Binder kept the interview moving.

"I screamed and ran out like everyone else. I ran until I found Talia and Page at the end of the block. We decided to go back. There were still kids running in the other direction. Kids who probably weren't in the hallway when it happened. One kid knocked me over, right on my bum. It still hurts. But I got up and kept going."

"And when you got back to the house?" Binder prompted.

"The door was wide open."

"And Mrs. Zelisko?"

"Wasn't there." Vanessa's brave façade crumbled. Her voice quivered. Tears weren't far away.

"Did you see, at any time, either before you left the house or when you got back, anyone approach Mrs. Zelisko at the bottom of the stairs?" I could tell Binder was trying not to push her, but he needed to know.

"No!" Vanessa wailed. "I told you. I ran out as fast as I could. When I got back, she wasn't there. Nothing was there at all!" And then the tears did come.

Chapter Ten

Emmy and I had a hurried conference on the sidewalk in front of the police station. Page, Vanessa, and Talia were supposed to be grounded, but Emmy had to get to work. It seemed cruel to leave Vanessa, who was red-eyed and shaky, on her own. Page was still at Mom's house. I called Livvie, who'd gone home. She listened patiently and agreed the girls could be together now that they'd all had their interviews.

"Do you think they'll work each other up into a lather?" she asked me.

I glanced down the block, where Vanessa stood, awaiting a decision, her big, green eyes trained on me. "I don't know, but I think it's good for them to be together. They've had this traumatic experience. Not just Mrs. Zelisko, but the party. In some ways, they're the only ones who understand what they've been through."

"Okay," Livvie said. "I'll call Mom and let her know." She paused. "I'll call Blair Davies and invite Talia, too."

Emmy took off for Crowley's and her waitressing shift after giving Vanessa a fierce hug. "Promise you'll be good. I'll have my phone in my apron pocket, on vibrate. Here's yours." She reached into her bag and gave Vanessa her phone. With permission, Flynn had scrolled through it, as he had with Page and Talia's phones. "Call if you need me," Emmy said.

By the time Vanessa and I made it to Mom's house, Page was on the porch. Vanessa ran to her, and they hugged each other so hard Vanessa squealed. Across the street, the front door of the Snuggles Inn burst open. Talia flew out and ran across the street, pausing to look both ways, but otherwise her feet barely touched the ground. Page and Vanessa opened their arms to embrace her, and then all three of them went into the house.

Blair Davies came out the Snuggles front door and watched them go inside. She raised a hand in a dispirited wave and sat heavily in one of the two Adirondack chairs the sisters had left on the porch for late-season guests. I felt bad for her. It had been poor judgment to leave three girls with Mrs. Zelisko in charge, sure. But the Davies hadn't thrown the party or bought the beer. The whole thing had spiraled beyond their wildest imaginings. I crossed the street and sat down next to her.

Blair smiled, a small, tentative smile. Despite the events of the last day, we didn't really know each other.

"I appreciate your sister asking Talia to be with the other girls. She's been like a caged animal. I want to be mad at her. Inviting those friends over was clearly out of line. But all I can do is worry." As if to underline her concern, Blair rubbed her hands together, the universal sign for worry. And for being cold. Either was possible. "Howard's gone to work," she said. "Talia's with her friends. I don't know what to do with myself."

I tried to come up with ideas for her, though I suspected "helpful suggestions" wasn't what she was looking for. She was new in town, barred from her home, her tenant murdered. I opened my mouth to respond a few times but, on reviewing every possibility, thought better of it.

"Howard loves his work at the oceanographic lab," she said. "He's happy as a clam. Which is what he studies, by the way, clams. Talia had a hard summer. Seventh grade is a tough time to move a kid, particularly one who's lived in the same house and hung out with the same kids for almost her whole life. Particularly an only child. But now that she's settled into her new school and has found Page and Vanessa, she's much happier. Or she was until last night."

The cold seeped through the slats on the bottom of the chair. I would have loved to go home and get warm, but Blair clearly needed to talk.

"I'm the one who can't make the change," she continued. "The summer was great. Buy a big house in Maine and you'll discover friends you never knew you had. All summer people from our old hometown visited. And relatives we hadn't seen in years. The house was full and noisy. We went to the beach, took harbor cruises, toured the lighthouses and the botanical garden. We went out to your family's clambake once and loved it. Visiting friends gave us an excuse to learn about our new home."

The door opened, and Fee appeared on the porch, two folded blankets in contrasting plaids in her arms and Mackie at her heels. Wordlessly, she tucked a blanket around Blair and then one around me. I thanked her. Blair gave Fee a wan smile, and she and the dog disappeared back inside.

"It felt so strange not to go back to school. I miss it terribly," Blair said when the door to the inn had closed. "But I'll have to wait for someone to die to get a job around here." She stared into the middle distance. "Sometimes I would hear Mrs. Zelisko walking around in her apartment upstairs. She didn't have a separate entrance. She had to come and go through our house. Somehow that made it worse. I was alone all day, but I felt I had no privacy. She was there all the time. I couldn't forget her presence. It drove me crazy. That house, which I loved at first sight, has never felt like home. They say a house is not really your home until you've been alone in it. I never felt like I was."

"I've heard Mrs. Zelisko was deaf," I said. Maybe Blair had more privacy than she thought she did.

Blair shook her head. "Not deaf. A little hard of hearing. Sometimes I would call to her from across a room, and if she wasn't looking in my direction, she wouldn't hear me. And she kept her phone and TV up *loud*. But in conversation, face-to-face, she understood every word you said."

Blair shifted in her chair and drew the blanket tighter around her. "I wanted to tell Mrs. Zelisko to leave. I begged Howard. But he liked the money, even though we didn't need it. Our house in Massachusetts sold for way more than we paid here. And"—she paused—"he was concerned about where she would live."

Howard wasn't wrong. At this time of year, there would be plenty of places for Mrs. Zelisko to move, even at the rent I suspected she paid for a third-floor apartment without exterior access. But come June, she might well be out of luck. Every space would be rented to tourists for top dollar or used to house summer help.

"I'm glad Howard disagreed with me and we never asked her to move. I'm ashamed of myself for being so selfish." Blair put her head in her hands. "I'm sorry I wasn't nicer to Mrs. Zelisko. Maybe we could have been friends."

Mrs. Zelisko apparently hadn't had friends. Not in the way Blair meant. But it didn't seem like the right time to point that out.

I sat with Blair Davies for a long time, comfy under the Snuggles Inn blanket. I steered the conversation away from everything Mrs. Zelisko. I prattled on about all the fun things the town had planned for the rest of the season. The festival of Christmas trees. The lights at the botanical garden. The day we all got up at dawn to Christmas-shop in our pajamas.

Blair allowed herself to be jollied along. I could tell it was an effort to climb out of her gloom, but she made it, and we ended up laughing a lot. The sun grew dimmer. We wouldn't revert to standard time until that night, but on the eastern edge of the time zone, dark came early even before daylight saving time ended.

Eventually, it was too cold to sit even with the blankets. We stood and folded them, working together. Then we hugged. She went inside, and I trudged home to my apartment.

Chapter Eleven

It had been six months, but I still wasn't used to returning to an empty house. It wasn't so much that it was
empty. Chris worked long hours during the season, like I
did, and I often got home first. It was more that I hadn't
gotten used to coming home to a house where nothing
had been moved unless I moved it. Nothing had been
eaten unless I ate it. The bed hadn't been made unless I
made it. No wet towels in the bathroom. No size-eleven
work boots piled by the stairs. When Mrs. Zelisko had
been alive, Blair Davies had longed for an empty house.
Increasingly, I longed for a full one.

My mother had offered Le Roi, our Maine Coon cat, to
keep me company. He had belonged to the old caretakers
on Morrow Island. When they left, I took him, but he'd
regarded Chris as an interloper, and a battle of wills en-

sued. Which is to say Le Roi had done everything he was capable of to get rid of Chris, including, memorably, spilling my shampoo, spreading it all over the bathroom floor and then jumping repeatedly from the headboard onto Chris's head until he got out of bed, wandered into the bathroom, and nearly killed himself on the slippery floor. Attempted murder.

Finally, when Chris was unable to put his boots on in the morning without checking inside them, Le Roi had been removed to my mother's. It was an arrangement that suited all of us. I still got to see him every day when I went to work in the Snowden Family Clambake office on the second floor of my mother's house. In the summer, Le Roi lived with my sister on Morrow Island, where he wandered freely and begged for clams and pieces of lobster from any clambake customer with a soft heart.

I'd refused Mom's offer to return him. I could tell Le Roi loved it at her house and she loved having him. I didn't have the heart.

I grabbed my laptop, sat down on my beat-up old couch, with its view out the window to dusk settling over the back harbor, and searched for any sign of Mrs. Zelisko on the web. There was no website for her business and nothing about her online. She wasn't even in the photo of the Star of the Sea auction committee that appeared after their successful fundraiser year after year.

I snapped the laptop shut. What did I think I was doing? The police would have done this and more. But I felt so deeply curious about, and sorry for, Helene Zelisko. How did someone end up so isolated that even her "friends" at church didn't know her first name?

It wasn't like I was a social butterfly or given to deeply intimate relationships beyond my family and, formerly, my boyfriend. But this woman who lived alone, worked alone . . . It seemed to be a choice, but I couldn't help but wonder, was she hiding from someone? Someone who had found her and killed her?

My stomach rumbled. I hadn't eaten lunch. In the tiny kitchen alcove of the studio, I opened the refrigerator door. Light spilled onto the dark linoleum floor. A can of bacon fat, a limp bunch of celery, and a piece of cheddar cheese with mold on all sides stared back at me.

Chris was a wonderful cook, and when we'd run the dinner restaurant together, I'd never had to worry about my next meal. Or what to do with my time. I was busy every moment of every day, and I loved it.

The long winter loomed. The clambake business would be wound up when I closed the books on the season and divided the profits among Mom, Sonny and Livvie, Quentin Tupper, our silent investor, and me.

Hannaford closed at six o'clock in the off-season. If I was going to eat, I had to shop. I grabbed my keys and quilted vest and headed down the stairs. I walked through the dark restaurant to the back door and was surprised to see Page in the glow from the outside light, huddled in a sweatshirt that couldn't be keeping her warm enough.

"Page! You scared me. You shouldn't be out alone at night." I didn't elaborate. Murderer on the loose, Page a potential witness. But she understood what I meant. "Where are Vanessa and Talia?"

"I left them at Grammy's." She didn't wait for me but led me back to my own apartment.

"What's the matter?" She was pale and shaking. My stomach clenched as I wondered, after almost twenty-four hours of awful revelations, what could be upsetting her so much.

"I remembered something. Something I didn't tell the police."

I moved toward her. "That's okay, honey. Lieutenant Binder and Sergeant Flynn won't be mad. We'll go in the morning, and you can explain that you forgot."

"It's important." She paused. "And it's bad."

I waited for her to work up her nerve.

"Mr. Davies came home during the party. I saw him."

Now I was alarmed. "Howard Davies was at the house while the party was going on?"

"Yes." She squeaked out her answer. Then she found her voice. "I saw him going up the stairs from the first to the second floor. The hallway and staircase were filled with kids, and I thought it was so weird he didn't say anything. I called out to him, but it was so noisy. And then after it all happened, with the ghost of Mrs. Zelisko flying down from the ceiling and the police coming, it went right out of my head, and I've only just thought of it."

"What time was this?"

"I can't remember. The party was full-on, though."

"Was it before or after you and Talia went to look for Mrs. Zelisko?"

"Before." Her voice was stronger. "I'm sure before. Like, fifteen minutes before."

"If he was climbing the stairs, was his back to you?"

"Yes."

"Did you see his face?"

"No."

"Then why do you think it was him?"

"It looked like him from the back. And he had on the same clothes he was wearing when he left for his work party. Dad clothes, not kid clothes."

"Dad clothes?" I wasn't sure what Page thought that meant.

"A navy-blue sweater and those pants. Those tan pants."

"You mean khakis?"

"Like Quentin wears." She was losing patience with me.

Quentin Tupper, the silent investor in the Snowden Family Clambake, was probably the only man Page knew who wore khakis. Kids didn't wear them, unless it was part of a school uniform or under duress.

"Are you sure it was Mr. Davies?" I asked.

"No." And then she burst into tears.

I called Flynn to find out if the detectives were still in town. He and Binder were finishing dinner at Crowley's. They would meet us at the police station in fifteen minutes. I called Livvie to tell her what was going on. Then I called Mom to tell her Page was with me. We agreed she should keep Vanessa with her since Emmy was at work, but she should send Talia back to the Snuggles.

I hoped the walk to the police station would calm Page down, but she fretted the whole way. "What if it wasn't Mr. Davies? I could get him in so much trouble. I'm not sure."

"Lieutenant Binder and Sergeant Flynn are good at their jobs," I told her. "They'll talk to Mr. Davies. They'll interview the other guests who were at the work party to find out if he left at any time. They won't charge him with murder on your say so."

She stopped walking. "Maybe I shouldn't tell them. Won't Mr. Davies be so mad?"

"No. Mr. Davies wants to get to the bottom of this as much as anyone. He'll be happy to clear this up with the police." *Unless he was the murderer.* My voice was firm, though I wasn't one hundred percent sure of what I was saying. I didn't know Howard Davies from a hole in the wall. "Maybe he's already told the detectives he went home during the party. We don't know everything people have told them."

Page looked doubtful but started walking again.

Binder and Flynn did their best to make Page comfortable, even though the high ceiling and meeting-room-sized space of the multi-purpose room was intimidating. Responding to Binder's patient questions, she told the story to them exactly as she had told it to me. She was clear that she couldn't identify Howard Davies, though, "It really looked like him from the back. I was sure it was him at the time. He was wearing the same clothes."

When they were done, Binder took Page to the adjacent firehouse to find a treat in the firefighters' always well-stocked kitchen.

"What do you think?" I asked Flynn, as we stood in the dark hall waiting for them to return.

"She saw someone she thought was him, for sure. Davies is a young-looking guy, but he's in his early fifties. Would he look like a teenager from behind?"

"Probably not," I said. "Which means . . . ?"

"Which means if it wasn't Davies, there was a grown man mixed in among the teenagers at that party," Flynn concluded.

"Exactly what I was thinking. Have any of the other kids mentioned an adult male in the house?"

Flynn shook his head. "No. But they've been terrible witnesses. No one saw anything until Mrs. Zelisko flew through the air. Which every one of them claims they saw, by the way, even though not all of them were in the front hall when it happened."

"So she flew a few laps around the house and yard?"

He laughed. "So we've been told."

Binder and Page returned, then she and I walked back to Mom's. By the time we got there, the detectives' unmarked car was parked across the street, and Binder and Flynn were on the Snuggles Inn porch, asking to speak to Howard Davies.

Chapter Twelve

I woke up early, woolly-headed and confused. Then I realized the time had "fallen back" and my phone and laptop clocks had reset themselves overnight. The weather was still gray. I was tempted to stay in bed.

From downstairs at Gus's came the sounds of conversations, the scrape of the spatula across the grill, and the rattle of dishes being dumped into Gus's ancient dishwasher. Gus usually had three distinct crowds on Sunday. The before-church crowd, the no-church crowd, and the after-church crowd. I could tell by the amount of car-door slamming and yelling going on in the parking lot that other people were as messed up by the time change as I was.

I decided to see what I could discover about Howard Davies on the web. I found exactly what I would have expected before Page had revealed what she had seen.

There was an announcement in our local paper about Howard's new job at the oceanographic lab. Before that, in Medview, Massachusetts, Howard had played in a lot of tennis tournaments at a local club. Blair taught school, as she'd said. Talia was frequently on the honor roll at her old middle school and had had a lead in the school play.

A perfectly normal family. But how many normal families end up with a body in their shed?

I was about to give up when my cell phone buzzed. I didn't immediately recognize the number.

"Julia? Barry Walker." He was gasping, like it was hard to breathe.

"Barry, what is it?"

The sound of a deep inhalation followed by the slow release of breath traveled through my phone. "When we were talking yesterday, I got to worrying about my taxes. I left a message for the police that I needed my documents, but no one called me back. So this morning, I called the IRS. They have an emergency number, and I thought this was an emergency. I was on hold forever, but then an agent came on the line. He told me my federal taxes haven't been filed for years! Since the Zelisko woman took over my account. He couldn't tell me what I owed, of course, since he didn't have any of the paperwork, but he said the interest and penalties could really be piling up. I could owe more than the business is worth, even if I sold my building!"

The hysterical edge had crept back into his voice. I could understand why.

"You need to tell the state police about this," I said.

"*Why*?" Barry yelled through the phone. "If I tell them, they'll think I murdered her! If she wasn't dead, I'd be contemplating it right now."

"If Mrs. Zelisko was mismanaging your account, that's important information."

"Mismanaging? She wasn't failing to pay the taxes, like some kind of mistake or neglect. She was taking money from me, telling me she paid the taxes and then not paying them. She was stealing!"

Walker's always seemed to be barely hanging on. How much could Barry owe? It seemed more likely Mrs. Zelisko had been lying to him about the amounts and then pocketing the money. Even then, it couldn't be a lot of money, hardly worth risking your reputation for. Unless she was doing it to a lot of clients.

"I'm coming over," I said. "Give me half an hour."

But the time I opened the door of Walker's Art Supplies and Frame Shop, Al Gleason was already there, leaning against the high counter Barry used to cut the mats for his picture frames. Al's arms were crossed over his chest, and he was listening to an agitated Barry Walker.

Mr. Gordon scurried in behind me.

Al Gleason unfolded his arms and turned to me. "You were right on in what you guessed, Julia. My employees' withholding hasn't been paid in four months. Neither have their insurance premiums. I'd been getting notices, lots of them from the insurance company, but Mrs. Zelisko had changed the contact info, even the phone number. She was getting the calls about our non-payment."

"You were right about our store, too," Mr. Gordon said. "Sales tax hasn't been paid in months, even through the busy season." Christmas and Valentine's kept Gordon's Jewelry afloat in the winter, but the busy season was tourist season.

"Ugh," Mr. Gleason said sympathetically. "I'm guessing all that money isn't sitting in your bank account."

Mr. Gordon shook his head. "Not one penny of it. The money has disappeared."

"Maybe not." They all looked at me. "She's been stealing from Barry for five years." I didn't add that he was the most disorganized, the most trusting, and the most susceptible of the three of them. "I'm guessing she's been stealing long-term from others. I'd love to get a look at the books for the Star of the Sea auction. But if she started stealing from the hardware store and the jewelry store in the last four months, that means something has changed. Maybe she thought she was on the verge of being caught and she was planning to run somewhere. Or looking for a big hit so she could retire someplace warm. Maybe the police will find some of the money. It's not like she spent it on an extravagant lifestyle."

"Unless she had a gambling problem." Mr. Gordon looked miserable.

"If the money doesn't turn up during the police investigation, because they find out she was murdered for another reason, we can hire a forensic accountant to track it down," Al Gleason said.

I turned to Barry. "You see now that you have to talk to the police, right? There's safety in numbers. Lieutenant Binder and Sergeant Flynn won't suspect you specifically, because Mrs. Zelisko robbed a lot of people. More than the three of you in this room, I'm certain."

"Okay, okay," Barry said. "I agree. We talk to the police."

Chapter Thirteen

I called Binder and Flynn, who came right over. As the shop owners told the cops what they knew, I could see Flynn's eyes grow bigger. There must be dozens of people in town who had a motive to kill Mrs. Zelisko.

Binder asked the three men to come to the station to give formal statements after they closed up their shops for the day. Gleason had employees at the hardware store, who could cover him, so he said he'd be over in the afternoon. Mr. Gordon and Barry Walker would come by later.

Out on the sidewalk, Binder, Flynn and I stood in a tight circle against the wind, processing what we'd heard.

"This case gets weirder and weirder," Flynn said.

"And more and more complicated," Binder agreed. "By the way," he looked at me, "Howard Davies didn't leave his work party. It's not just his wife who vouches for him; we easily located plenty of witnesses. There were two cars in the host's driveway parked behind the Davies' car. The house where the party was is way out in East Busman's Village, too far to walk and make it back without his absence being noticed. No one can see how he could possibly have gotten home, even if he'd left."

Flynn stepped away from us to make a phone call. Binder looked at me. "The crime-scene techs are finished with the Davies' house. We're about to let the family move back in. Tom and I are going over for a last look while it's empty. Want to come?"

Flynn ended his call, and both men started down the sidewalk toward the Davies' house without waiting for my answer. They knew what it would be.

We stood on the big front porch while Flynn turned the key in the lock. Inside, the house was the same temperature as outside. If the Davies did that thing of not turning on the heat until November 1, it hadn't been on when they left Halloween night, and it still wasn't.

I knew it wasn't the job of the crime-scene techs to clean the house, but I was unprepared for the mess we found when we walked in. It felt like time had stopped and the party had just ended. It had only been two days earlier, yet it felt like weeks. This disheveled house with the Halloween decorations was from another time. It was terrible that the Davies had to come home to this.

We walked into the chilly hallway, then through the kitchen, which smelled so strongly of dried beer I had to hold my breath, and out into the yard. Flynn paced off the number of steps from the back stairs to the shed, coming up with twenty both times he did it.

Back inside, I followed the detectives as they roamed the first floor. The party had obviously raged principally in the kitchen and family room. The dining room was in less disarray, though there were overturned bottles and cans on the surface of the cherry dining table. The living room was in the best shape.

From there, we went back into the big entrance hallway. A glance around and then up to the ceiling confirmed my impressions of two days earlier. It was a towering space, made more dramatic by the staircase that ringed it and the large brass chandelier that hung down from the ceiling high above.

I stood on the second-story balcony while the detectives looked around the family bedrooms. I wasn't an officer of the law, so it felt like it would be a terrible invasion of the family's privacy for me to go in.

Then we climbed the stairs to Mrs. Zelisko's apartment. Evidence of the police search was all around us. In the sitting room, the top of the desk had been cleared, and the empty drawers hung open. The seat cushions of the love seat and easy chair were askew. In the tiny kitchen, the cupboard and all four drawers were empty, their contents left on the small table and the only chair, and in piles on the floor.

In the bedroom, the covers had been removed from the bed and left in a heap on top of the twin mattress. The bureau drawers hung open, Mrs. Zelisko's white underthings left in plain sight. I thought that, little as I knew her, Mrs. Zelisko would have been mortified. The small closet door was open. Inside hung five black dresses, two black jackets, and two black cardigans.

"Notice anything strange about this place?" Flynn asked me.

"There's nothing personal," I answered. The blank walls held no artwork or photos, and no empty hooks or light spots to indicate there had been any. "Were there any family photos on the tables or shelves that maybe your guys took?"

Flynn shook his head. "Zero."

"It's strange, because she spent so much time here," I said. "She worked at home, except at the rare times she went to her clients' businesses. Blair Davies said she heard Mrs. Zelisko moving around up here all day. She almost never went out except for errands and to services and meetings at the Star of the Sea."

"The papers we took from the desk and the laptop will help untangle some of this mess with her clients, but there was nothing personal there, either," Binder said.

"Weird," I said.

"And unhelpful," Binder added.

The last place we looked was the bathroom. "Mrs. Zelisko and her killer were hiding in here when Page and Talia came to look for her," I said.

"Yes, that's what we think, too," Flynn confirmed.

"Was she alive or dead at that point? Was she killed here or in some other room?"

Flynn shrugged. "Not clear."

"Why was she in her nightgown?" Binder wondered. "And why didn't she go downstairs when she heard all the noise?"

"She was hard of hearing," I told him. "I've heard differing accounts about how deaf she was." I peered through the doorway. "This bathroom looks so ordinary." The room was narrow and white. A clawfoot tub stood against one long wall. It had been fitted with a shower and a shower curtain holder. "Did you guys take the shower curtain?"

Binder walked into the room, looked around, and exited quickly. "We have it."

We returned to the landing at the top of the stairs. It

was so small the three of us could barely fit on it together. The railing height was barely up to my hip, and I'm short. It wouldn't be code in a modern house. I had an uncomfortable feeling as I looked over the edge. However she'd gone down—flew, floated, or fell—Mrs. Zelisko had a long trip.

Something small and fluttery on the elaborate chandelier far below caught my eye. "Wait, what's that?" Then more excited, I pointed. "I think I know what happened." I gave one little jump, then immediately stopped. The landing was precarious enough without any sudden moves.

I took a deep breath and rolled out a scenario. "Mrs. Zelisko is dead when the girls come upstairs. The killer hears them and drags the corpse into the bathroom. Then he's trapped. He has to get out of the house, and he decides he has to get Mrs. Zelisko out, too."

"Why?" Binder asked. "Why not sneak out himself and leave her for the Davies to find?"

"He must think the girls will be back, possibly at any moment. He can't risk them finding her while he's still making his escape."

"He's not a practiced killer," Flynn surmised. "He's panicking."

"He grabs the top sheet off her bed and ties it around her," I said. "He's going to pretend she's a ghost, a drunk ghost, and carry her out."

"He Weekend-at-Bernie's her!" The look on Binder's face was priceless.

"Except it doesn't go so well. She's small, but probably heavier and certainly more awkward to carry than he assumes," I continued.

Flynn got into the spirit of it. "He trips or loses hold of her, and she goes over the railing."

"And down into the front hall." Binder was buying it, or at least admitting the possibility.

"Not quite," I said. "She's hurtling down. Any kid who happens to be looking up, maybe talking to someone on the stairs above them, is going to see her and start screaming. Soon they're all screaming and running out the door. But Mrs. Zelisko doesn't make it to the floor. She catches on the chandelier, and the momentum swings her back and forth across the room. She falls off onto the stairs from the second to the first floor. She tumbles down from there, rolling the sheet back around her, and ends up on the landing. Depending on when a kid looks, she flies, floats, or falls."

"In a swirl of white fabric," Binder said.

"The kids have run off." Flynn continued the story. "The killer walks down the stairs, picks up the body, goes out the back door, and sticks her in the shed. He's bought a lot of time. The local cops don't find the body until after ten-fifteen. He could have been home by then."

"Or in a bar creating alibis," Binder said.

"Or off the peninsula and halfway to Route 95, if he wasn't from around here," I said.

"Wasn't from around here?" Flynn was surprised. "Based on our conversation with your shop-owner friends, there were probably a dozen people in town who may have wanted her dead. She couldn't cover her tracks forever."

We finally left the little landing and trooped down the stairs. "Something changed," I said. "Four months ago, she went from skimming a little extra from Barry Walker, a perfect mark, and probably some others like him, to embezzling sales tax from Mr. Gordon and employee withholding and insurance premiums from Gleason's. That was a much more dangerous game. She was bound to get caught."

"A much more lucrative game, too," Flynn said.

Binder stated the obvious conclusion. "She was preparing to run."

"Yes." We were downstairs in the hallway by then. "The question is, what changed four months ago?"

"The Davies moved to town," Flynn answered.

"The Davies moved to town, and Mrs. Zelisko no longer felt safe," Binder said. "The question is, why? We need to talk to them again."

Flynn fetched a ladder from the shed. He put gloves on, climbed up, and pulled the piece of fabric I'd spotted from the chandelier.

"Sheet fabric?" Binder asked from the ground.

"Uh-huh." Flynn climbed down.

"We need to get it to the lab to see if it matches the sheet the body was wrapped in, but I think Julia's solved a piece of the puzzle." Binder smiled at me. "Thank you."

Chapter Fourteen

I walked with Binder and Flynn back to the police station. As they were going in, Jamie came out.

"Julia! Great to see you. Want to have lunch?" He smiled like he was genuinely excited by the prospect.

"Sure. Do you have time?" Earlier in the fall, we had gone to lunch occasionally. I suspected Mom put him up to it, as a part of some "Dine with Poor Lonely Julia" program.

"I have to eat," he answered. "We're still rounding up kids who either were definitely at or were rumored to be at the party. And then, an hour ago, we got a list of Mrs. Zelisko's bookkeeping clients. We're calling all of them to set up meetings as well. I'm afraid they're getting some not great news."

"I heard."

He laughed. "I figured."

We walked toward Gus's, though we hadn't discussed where to eat. We entered via the front door, something I almost never did, and climbed down the stairs into the big room, where the open kitchen, counter and stools, and candlepin bowling lane were. Beyond it was the dining room with its booths, fake leather banquettes, and stunning views of the back harbor.

The restaurant was moderately busy with the Sunday lunch crowd, and I hurried through to an empty booth. I still felt really weird at Gus's. It wasn't like I was afraid of running into Chris. When you break up with someone in a town this small, you know you're going to run into them. Frequently. It was that the restaurant held so many memories. Chris and I had run the dinner restaurant there and eaten oh-so-many breakfasts. It was the place where we'd re-met when I'd moved back to town. The memories were in every corner of the space, and I couldn't shake them off.

"Howdy, stranger." Gus approached, order pad at the ready. No one in town except his wife knew how old he was, but he opened the restaurant at five in the morning to feed the fishermen and stayed open until after three, seven days a week, eleven months a year.

"I live upstairs," I pointed out.

"I give you your privacy." He sounded indignant. Gus did a great indignant. "You've been scarce down here."

"Busy," I said, which was a total lie. Without the dinner restaurant to run in the off-season, I wasn't busy enough.

"What'll you have?"

For lunch, Gus serves Maine hot dogs, which are bright red for some reason, hamburgers, grilled cheese, BLTs, and PB&J. In other words, things you could make for yourself at home. He accompanies them with the world's best French fries, and you can't do that at home.

"BLT," I said.

"Burger." Jamie didn't add rare, medium, or well-done. He was too experienced a diner to attempt to tell Gus how to cook a burger. You got 'em the way he made 'em, and you didn't complain.

When Gus left, I looked around to make sure we wouldn't be heard. Then I leaned toward Jamie. "I don't get it. I mean, you know how Mrs. Zelisko lived. Third floor walk-up, no car, five black dresses, and a couple of sweaters. There is no way she spent the money she'd been conning people out of all these years."

"For some thieves, the thrill is in the stealing," he said. "Not in spending the money. Not in the money at all."

I shook my head. "What I don't get is how it happened. She'd just gotten to town when Barry Walker hired her. Barry's disorganized, but she was handling his money. Why didn't he check her references?"

"The Star of the Sea Catholic church," Jamie answered. "She met people there, and they trusted her. Barry Walker was the perfect early mark. He was desperate for help. He didn't ask a lot of questions. With each new client, it got easier to get the next one. These people all knew one another. Each of them expected that *someone* had done the due diligence regarding references and such. If no one actually had, how would they know? After a while, it was embarrassing to ask."

"That's disgusting."

"Yup. It's called affinity fraud. The original Ponzi's victims were Italian-Americans from his own community. Bernie Madoff devasted Jewish foundations and charities. It's how con artists gain trust. We get notices at the station all the time. Scam going through the evangelical community. Someone pitching fraudulent investments at Elk's clubs. It's how it's done."

Gus arrived with our food, and the conversation turned to more cheerful topics. Jamie was going to Florida to see his parents for Thanksgiving. We made a plan to maybe see a movie sometime.

Gus came back, and we paid him in cash, the only tender he accepted as legal.

"Headed upstairs?" Jamie asked as he rose to leave.

"No. I'm going to Mom's. Page is still there. But before I do, I have an errand to run."

Gus waved as we walked back through the front room. "Don't be such a stranger."

Chapter Fifteen

On my way to Mom's, I stopped at our neighbors, the Goldsmiths. "Harley graduated from high school last year, right?" I asked June Goldsmith after we said hello. She'd been surprised to find me on her porch.

"She did. You would have been invited to the party, but I knew you'd be working out on Morrow Island."

I swiped with my hand to let her know not to stress about it. "Was Harley at that big party here in town on Halloween?"

"The one where Mrs. Zelisko was murdered? No, thank goodness. Harley's at UMaine Portland. She decided to stay on campus for Halloween weekend." June looked at me expectantly, wondering where the conversation was going.

"Did Harley leave her yearbook home, do you know? Could I borrow it overnight?"

Whatever June Goldsmith had expected me to say, that wasn't it. "I'll quickly check her room."

She returned within minutes with the book, bound in "Busman's High blue" faux leather, and handed it to me.

"I'll get it right back to you," I said.

"No hurry. I don't expect Harley home until Thanksgiving."

When I got to Mom's house, Page was at the kitchen table, textbook open, worksheet in front of her. School again tomorrow.

I sat down next to her. "Do you have a lot to do?"

She bit the eraser on her pencil. "Almost done." There was a sheet of math problems in front of her, and she appeared to have a couple left.

"Great. When you're finished, come find me."

Mom was in the sitting room off her bedroom, watching Sunday programming on PBS. "Julia, what are you doing here?"

"How come you still have Page?"

"She's upset. Sonny and Livvie both have work tomorrow. It's hectic in their house in the mornings. They thought it might be better if Page had some quiet time here and a little space before she had to go to school and see all those kids. There's bound to be a lot of chatter about the party and the murder. Livvie dropped clothes and her schoolwork off earlier. "

I thought about mornings at Livvie's house. Sonny would be long gone, off to help his father pull his lobster traps. Lobsters were scarce in November, and the weather would make work on the boat miserable, but the price the co-op paid was commensurately higher. Livvie would have her hands full getting Jack dressed and delivered to daycare before she went to her job at the pottery studio. She wouldn't have time to give extra attention to Page.

Livvie's busy life contrasted starkly with my own. Empty apartment. No restaurant to run. Empty. Dark. Still. What was I doing with my life?

"You didn't answer my question." Mom brought me back into the moment. "What are you doing here? You know you're always welcome, but you weren't expected."

There was never any point in trying to tiptoe around my mom. "The police still haven't identified all the kids who were at the party. I got a yearbook from June Goldsmith. I want to go through it with Page to see if she recognizes any of the photos as people who were there."

My mother pursed her lips and squinted at me. "Is that a good idea? I'm supposed to be letting Page settle down and get ready for the week."

"I think it is!" I left the room before she could object further.

Page and I met in her room, behind a closed door. I wasn't doing anything wrong, and Page seemed a whole lot happier about this activity than doing her homework, but I didn't want my mother to feel the need to interrupt.

I explained to Page that she hadn't seen Howard Davies at the party. "But," I said, "you did see someone. Someone dressed like they were older going up the stairs not long before you and Talia went to look for Mrs. Zelisko. I thought we could look through this yearbook to see if it was someone who's already graduated. Did you see his face at all?"

"I'm not sure. I may have seen it earlier, you know, before I saw his back going up the stairs."

We went slowly through the pages of the yearbook

containing the senior photos. Page shook her head, no, no, no, with each turn of the page. It didn't mean none of the kids had been at the party. It only meant she didn't recognize them, but it didn't represent progress. We looked at the rest of the book, including the photos of teams, clubs, performances. Page did recognize lots of those students and said some of them had been at the party. But in every case she'd already given the kid's name to Binder and Flynn.

When we closed the book, I sighed.

"Don't be sad, Aunt Julia," Page said. "Even if the man I saw wasn't Mr. Davies, he was a grown-up. He isn't going to be in this yearbook." Her face brightened, "Let's see if we can find anyone on my Instagram."

"Do you have your phone?" I was surprised.

"No." She rolled her eyes. "But I can sign onto my account from yours."

"Didn't Flynn ask you go through your social media on that first morning?"

"Yes, but I didn't know what I was looking for."

Page expertly signed onto her Instagram account from my phone and scrolled back in her feed to Friday night. The photos from her friends, taken in the thick of the action, were even more horrible than their leftover mess had caused me to imagine. Kids in gory, scary-looking costumes swilled from big liquor bottles, no doubt the ones stolen from the Davies. They danced in the dining room, made out in the corners, and threw up on the lawn.

There were no photos of the actual moment Mrs. Zelisko fell from above. It must have happened too fast. The kids had been stunned, and then they'd run.

Lots of the photos were pretty dark. It was hard to

make out faces. Squeezed in next to Page, I squinted at the screen, looking for a man in a navy sweater and khakis.

Then finally, she stopped scrolling. "Look!" She pointed to the edge of an image on her phone. "It's him!"

"How can you tell?" Only about a quarter of the figure was visible. The sliver of his face we could see was in profile. His hair was the same medium brown as Howard Davies's. The man in the photo gestured into the frame with a hand and an arm covered in a navy-blue sweater. One long khaki pant leg ended in a blue sock and brown loafer. Definitely not a kid, unless he'd come in costume as his father. I peered at what I could see of the man's face. He did look older, out of his teens. But it was hard to be sure with so little visible.

We scrolled quickly after that, looking for better photos of the same man. We switched to the profile page of the girl who had taken the original photo. Nothing turned up anywhere.

"We need to tell Lieutenant Binder and Sergeant Flynn about this," I told Page. "Maybe this girl has more photos on her phone she didn't upload."

"Okay." Page was losing steam.

"Text the photo to me along with the name of the girl who took the picture, and I'll send the info along to the detectives. They'll probably want to talk to you again."

"Sure."

Page did as I asked, but seemed deflated. Whether she was worried about about talking to the detectives again or school in the morning, I couldn't tell. I forwarded the text with a brief explanation to Binder and Flynn.

"I'm sorry all this happened," I said.

Page looked even more miserable. "It was our fault. If we hadn't texted those other girls . . . If there hadn't been a party . . ."

"You didn't murder Mrs. Zelisko." I was firm.

"But if we hadn't—"

"Aw, honey." I hugged her. "I don't know what happened to Mrs. Zelisko, but it's clearer and clearer she wasn't murdered by a kid at that party."

Page sniffled and nodded into my shoulder. I hoped Binder and Flynn would get back to me soon. We needed to get this case solved.

Chapter Sixteen

I didn't hear back from the detectives that night, but they were at Gus's restaurant when I came down from my apartment the next morning. For months, I'd been scuttling in and out through the back door, but in the spirit of desensitizing myself to the restaurant, I walked boldly through it.

Gus, unusual for a restaurateur, was not a fan of out-of-towners. But the state-police detectives had eaten there frequently enough that they'd wormed their way into his good graces, such as they were.

Binder called to me. "Julia, join us!" They already had their food in front of them, Binder, a western omelet, Flynn, as always, two soft-boiled eggs. Gus had also provided Flynn with two pieces of heavily buttered white toast. Flynn wouldn't eat it, but it came with the order, and Gus duly brought it. Flynn's abstemious ways bugged Gus as much as they bugged Vee Snugg. The detectives would probably be finished before I got served, but I sat down anyway.

"Thanks for the photo," Binder said. He pulled his phone from his jacket pocket and opened my text. He put on his reading glasses and squinted. "Not much to go on, but more than we had before."

Flynn also had his phone out. "Unknown victim, unknown suspect. This case gets better and better."

"We have an expert going through Mrs. Zelisko's laptop, trying to figure out how much she stole, who she stole it from, and how she did it," Binder said. "We sent the fabric we took from the chandelier to the lab. And we described what might have happened to the medical examiner. She's going to let us know if the injuries to the body are consistent with that scenario. We're making progress, but it feels like we're not."

"Too many possibilities," Flynn said. "Was it someone Zelisko stole from here in town, or maybe in her past life? But since we don't know anything about her past life, we don't know who that might have been. And then there's this guy." Flynn tapped the photo on his phone.

"Page says she's never seen him before, if that helps," I offered.

"It would have been more helpful if she had," Flynn groused.

After breakfast, I went back upstairs to my apartment. Flynn was right. We didn't know who Mrs. Zelisko was. And we didn't know where she'd come from.

Why had she stepped up the stealing four months ago?

The answer had to be that the Davies had arrived in town and become her landlords. What about the Davies had scared her to the point that she started planning to run, if that was what she was doing? Howard worked at the oceanographic lab. Blair was an elementary school teacher. Talia was thirteen. They were the opposite of scary.

The most logical answer was it had something to do not with who the Davies were, but where they came from.

I got out my laptop and settled onto my couch for a good search. Luckily, Medview, Massachusetts, had a local paper, and the local paper had put ten years of its archives online. That seemed like a fruitful avenue. I paid a little money, and I was in.

First, I tried searching for "Zelisko," though that was almost certainly not her name. "Embezzled" got me an article about a local manufacturing company whose treasurer had disappeared with millions. A compelling story, but not the one I was looking for. "Bookkeeper" got me a lot of links to old help-wanted ads.

I searched the edition for New Year's Day, five years back. Everyone agreed Mrs. Zelisko had arrived in Busman's Harbor around then. There was nothing of note in that day's paper, so I scrolled one week back, to December 25.

The format of the online paper immediately changed. Rather than a fully searchable online version, the archives from five years earlier and before were images of the actual paper that had been digitized and put online. This format, which I could skim, might be more useful.

Even though the paper was weekly, that still left a lot of pages to go through. I figured if Mrs. Zelisko had disappeared from Busman's Harbor, having stolen from a dozen town merchants, it would be a huge story in our

Gazette. So I decided to read backward through the issues of the Medview paper, examining front pages only.

By the time I finished looking at three years' worth, 150 front pages, I began to wonder if I was crazy. But I couldn't think of what else to do. Page was hurting, as were Vanessa and Talia. Barry, Mr. Gordon, and Al Gleason were angry, confused, and scared. And somewhere out there, there was probably a family, maybe a distant one, that deserved to know that Mrs. Zelisko, or whatever her name was, was dead.

I stood and stretched, rolling my head around on my shoulders to release the tension in my neck. Downstairs, Gus's was quiet, in the lull between breakfast and lunch. I got a glass of ice water from my kitchen and settled back onto the couch.

I was nine years back when I found it. A Mrs. Irene Chumley, who worked as a bookkeeper for many small businesses in Medview, had disappeared into the night, taking with her money that belonged to her clients and leaving them with a mountain of debt. Several former clients were quoted in the article—the owners of an appliance store, a shoe repair shop, a small dry-cleaning chain, and a delicatessen. None of those interviewed knew anything about Mrs. Chumley, except that she spoke with an Irish accent and was a devoted member and enthusiastic volunteer at St. Theresa's Catholic church in Medview.

My heart hammered in my chest. Finally, progress. Irene Chumley and Helene Zelisko had to be the same woman. They had the same M.O.

Now that I'd spotted the front-page article, I scrolled forward in time, examining the inside pages of the paper. There were follow-up stories about Mrs. Chumley. The local police had coordinated with the FBI. Tragically, several of the businesses she'd stolen from had failed, including the appliance store and the shoe repair shop.

Hands shaking, I called Flynn.

He didn't bother to say hello. "We're about to talk to the Davies about that photo you found. Do you want to come along? They're still at the Snuggles."

"I'll be right there. I have some information that may be helpful when you talk to them."

Binder and Flynn were already inside when I arrived at the Snuggles Inn. The Davies' bags, two carry-on-sized suitcases and a backpack, waited in the front hall. The family was packed and ready to go home.

Everyone was in the inn's formal living room. The Davies sat on the antique couch. The detectives were seated in straight-backed chairs across from them. Vee and Fee hovered in the background, dying to know what was happening. There was a fire going in the hearth. Mackie snoozed on the oriental carpet.

Howard Davies held a photo in front of him, a blown-up version of the one I'd texted to the detectives. Blair and Talia sat on either side of him. All three squinted as he turned the photo from side to side.

"I don't recognize him," Howard said. "I can certainly see why someone would think it was me. We were dressed almost identically."

Blair took the photo and brought it closer to her face. "He does look older. Too old to be at a teenage party, though I can't really tell how old."

"Talia, did you see this man at the party?" Binder asked.

"I don't think so."

"Page saw him going up the stairs fifteen minutes or so before you both went up to find Mrs. Zelisko," Binder said. "Does that help you remember?"

Talia shook her head. "No."

I cleared my throat. "I think I know something about Mrs. Zelisko. She worked in your old hometown of Medview as a bookkeeper." Binder and Flynn whipped their heads around to stare at me, but they didn't stop me, so I continued. "She called herself Mrs. Irene Chumley. She disappeared nine years ago, after stealing from her clients. Several businesses closed due to their losses. Does any of this sound familiar?"

"Well, I'll be." Howard sat back on the couch, clearly surprised by the news.

"We didn't live in Medview nine years ago," Blair explained. "We were still living in Boston then. We moved to Medview for the schools when Talia started kindergarten."

"You said you had a lot of visitors from Medview over the summer," I said. "Could any of them have been victims of Mrs. Zelisko—or Chumley, as she was? Were any of your guests small-business owners?"

"I don't think so." Blair spoke slowly, thinking. "Our visitors were neighbors, fellow teachers, parents bringing friends of Talia's." She stopped. Her eyes opened wide. "Howard, what did Warren and Sue Littlefield do before they retired?"

Howard sat up straighter. "I think they owned an appliance store in town. They don't talk about it. I gathered it ended badly."

"When they visited, did the Littlefields see Mrs. Zelisko?" I asked.

"Maybe," Blair said. "Yes. I remember it now. We were in our car, returning from the botanical garden. Mrs. Zelisko came down the front walk as we pulled into our driveway. I called out to her so I could introduce them, but she didn't hear me."

"Did the Littlefields see her?" Binder asked.

"I'm sure they did." The memory was coming back to her. Blair's words came out in a rush. "They asked about her. I explained she was our third-floor tenant. The strange thing was, Warren and Sue left soon afterward. I had thought they would stay for dinner. Warren said they didn't like to drive after dark. It wouldn't be dark for hours."

"When was this?" Flynn asked.

"The end of June," Blair said. "They were our first summer visitors."

"I hate to disappoint you, but they're not who you're looking for." Howard smiled a little. "They're in their late seventies."

The energy drained from the room like water from a bathtub when the plug was pulled. Flynn shut his notebook. "Probably not then." We sat silently for a moment.

"Wait," Howard said slowly. "I remember they had hoped their son would run the business after them. When it went belly-up, he went to work selling appliances in a big-box store."

"How old is the Littlefields' son?" Binder asked.

Chapter Seventeen

Two days later, I had coffee with Binder and Flynn at Gus's. The Massachusetts State Police had picked up Peter Littlefield at Maine's request, and the detectives had traveled the two hours south to interrogate him.

"He confessed instantly," Flynn said before I sat down.

"He couldn't wait to get it off his chest. He'd clearly been suffering since the night of the murder. I almost felt sorry for him," Binder said. "Almost."

"We interviewed the parents as well," Flynn said. "Warren and Sue Littlefield recognized Mrs. Zelisko—or Mrs. Chumley, as they knew her—when they visited the Davies. They were stunned speechless, made their excuses, and left."

Gus came over and took our order. Coffees for Binder and me, tepid water for Flynn. As always, Gus took Flynn's dietary regime as a personal affront. "Drink something brown and strong, man," he said. "Put some hair on that puny chest."

Even while sitting, Flynn managed to puff out his anything-but-puny chest. "Doing fine in that department," he said.

Binder waited for Gus to leave before he spoke. "On the way home from the Davies' house, the Littlefields agreed to do nothing. They were sure they'd never see a penny of their money. Losing the business had been a horrible ordeal. They wanted the past to remain in the past.

"But as the weeks went by, Mrs. Littlefield worried Mrs. Zelisko might be at it again. She fretted about all the people who would be hurt. She was desperate to call the authorities. Mr. Littlefield absolutely refused. They reached an impasse. Last week, Mrs. Littlefield decided to confide in their son, Peter, and ask him to help persuade his father."

"Telling Peter was a mistake." Flynn picked up the tale. "He went home and stewed. He'd expected to take over his parents' business. The store had been holding its own. The Littlefields had a reputation as people who really knew their stock, made great recommendations, and provided quality, timely installation and service. Peter saw a future where he'd make a nice living, be his own boss, and be a respected business owner in the community. He thought he was set."

"Then it all ended," Binder said. "He went to work in a big-box store selling the same appliances but for twelve dollars an hour."

"The more he stewed, the angrier he got," Flynn said.

"On Halloween night, he worked himself up into a state where he was determined to confront the woman he believed, not without reason, had caused his unhappiness."

Gus delivered the coffees, but not the despised glass of tepid water. Flynn would have to wait.

"Peter Littlefield swears he didn't plan to kill her," Binder continued when Gus turned and left without a word. "He wanted to talk to her, let her know what she'd done to his life. He thought it might get heated, but that was as far as it would go."

"Laying the foundation to avoid a first-degree-murder charge." Flynn was unimpressed by Littlefield's claim.

"So it was a complete coincidence he showed up on Halloween?" I asked.

"He was shocked when he pulled up to the Davies' house to discover there was a wild party in progress." Binder said. "But then he thought it might be a good cover if he was going to be yelling at her. He had some idea he would force her to return the money.

"He slipped into the house, which wasn't hard, given what was going on, and went up the stairs. Mrs. Zelisko was in her living room in her nightclothes. The television was on full blast. She didn't hear him come in. She seemed oblivious to the noise coming from downstairs. When he confronted her, she cut him dead, told him he'd never see a penny of the money she'd taken. She didn't try to deny what she'd done. She was calm, disdainful. He said that's what set him off. Before he knew it, he had strangled her."

"That's when Talia and Page came up the stairs toward the apartment, calling out for Mrs. Zelisko," Flynn said. "Mrs. Zelisko had turned off the television when she and Littlefield started their conversation. He said he almost had a heart attack when he heard the girls coming. He dragged the body into the bathroom and locked the door. He heard Page try to open it."

I shuddered, thinking how close my niece and her friend had come to a murderer. What would have happened if they had been able to open the bathroom door?

"The rest happened pretty much as you figured it," Flynn said. "The girls left, and he was stuck in the bathroom with a body. He did try to Weekend-at-Bernie's her. He wanted time to get as far away as possible. He tied the bedsheet around her and fireman-carried her out onto the landing. Mrs. Zelisko was tiny, but she was a dead weight. As he turned to close the apartment door behind him, he lost his footing, and she slipped off his shoulder and went over the low railing. He almost did, too. He watched in horror as she fell, got caught in the chandelier, and was swung over onto the staircase. He was sure he was done for."

"But by the time he got downstairs," Binder finished the story, "the house was empty. He picked her back up, slung her over his shoulder, and executed his original plan. He went out the back door and stuffed her in the shed. He was off the peninsula before Officer Howland discovered the body."

"It almost worked." Flynn shook his head. "He had no record, wasn't in any system, and had no apparent connection to 'Mrs. Zelisko.'"

"It might have worked if Julia hadn't found the connection," Binder said.

"And the photo," Flynn added.

My coffee was cold. I'd been so engrossed in the story, I'd forgotten to drink it. "Is there any hope my friends will get their money back?" I asked.

"Above our pay grade," Flynn answered. "Now that we know she was the target of a previous investigation, that part of the case is back at the FBI."

"The money is probably abroad," Binder said. "It will take a long time to get it back, if that ever happens. Your friends should get attorneys. The IRS and the state of Maine will negotiate some kind of terms for payment."

Not encouraging. "But her victims will have to pay."

"Yes."

"Where was Mrs. Zelisko in those four and a half years between when she left Medview and when she arrived in Busman's Harbor?" It was hardly relevant, but I was dying to know.

"The FBI believes she was in Exeter, New Hampshire, running the same old game. They have cases there. They're connecting the dots," Flynn answered.

"Who was she, really?" I asked.

Binder shook his head. "That we don't know yet."

So there might never be any notification of a next of kin. No one might ever know she had died. The murder was solved, but it didn't feel great. "So many victims," I said. "Three towns worth."

"That we know about," Flynn reminded me.

"And Warren and Sue Littlefield," Binder said. "When Sue realized her conversation with her son had started a chain of events that would end up with him in prison . . . You should have seen her reaction. It about broke my heart."

Chapter Eighteen

Ten days later, Mom gave a dinner party. She invited the Davies and the Snuggs, Emmy Bailey, Vanessa and Luther, Livvie, Sonny, Page and Jack, and me. "A way to fend off the dark," she said. "A welcome to new neighbors. It can be hard to make friends here."

Thirty-five years on, Mom was still the outsider, the summer person who lived on a private island who'd married the son of a local lobsterman. Blair's loneliness had captured her heart.

Sonny went over early to help Mom cook the chicken. Livvie brought a delicious pumpkin soup. I made a fall salad composed with pomegranate seeds and mandarin oranges. Vee turned up with one of her delicious apple pies. The Davies brought the wine.

Page and I set Mom's long dining room table. "How many?" I wondered aloud.

"Fourteen, plus Jack's booster seat," Mom called from the kitchen.

I counted and recounted. "Are you sure?" I shouted back.

"Yes!"

I shrugged and did as she asked.

A few days earlier, Barry Walker had called me. "Julia, can you help me out with the business?"

"Barry, I'm neither a tax attorney nor an accountant. You need an expert."

"I don't mean with that part of it," he said. "I mean with the business itself. You see how things are here. One more season, and I'll go under even without trying to repay the tax bill. You turned your family's clambake around. Come help me. I'll find some way to pay you something."

"Maybe you've found your winter job," Livvie said when I told her about it.

I laughed. "I don't think so. I took Barry's offer to pay as a statement of good intentions, not a promise I can take to the bank."

"Not just Walker's," Livvie said. "There are lots of businesses you could help in town. You went to school for it. You saved the Snowden Family Clambake."

"With a lot of luck and an investor," I pointed out.

"An investor was what we needed." Livvie put her fists on her hips, a sure sign I shouldn't bother arguing. "Think about it."

I smiled. She was relentless. "I will."

The three girls were thrilled to see one another and disappeared into Page's room. They were still on semi-lockdown. Page had to give her phone to Livvie every day when she got home from swim-team practice and didn't get it back until the next morning. I had heard the others were on similar restrictions.

When we finally gathered around the table, I had an intense longing for Chris to be beside me. But then I looked at the remarkable women surrounding me. My mom, a widow who'd rebuilt her life after a devastating loss. Fee and Vee, never married, running their own successful business. Emmy, divorced, making it work with two kids. And Blair and Livvie, married, raising children who were entering into their teenage years. Blair had left a job she loved for the sake of her husband's career. I hoped it would turn out to be worthwhile. I hoped she would find a place in Busman's Harbor.

There was still an extra place at the table. The back door opened, and Jamie came in, calling out, "Sorry I'm late." He entered the dining room as he shed his coat. "Thanks for inviting me."

Mom looked at me. "I hate the idea of him rattling around in that big old house all alone," she whispered.

It was the dark time between Halloween and Thanksgiving. The sun set at quarter past four in the afternoon. It was like entering a long tunnel.

But the candles burned brightly on the dinner table, and the conversation flowed easily. Mom raised her glass. "To old friends." She looked at the Snuggs and Jamie, who offered their glasses. "And new." She clinked with Howard Davies, who sat beside her. "Always remember the Snowdens are here if you need us."

"And we for all of you," Fee Snugg said.

"And we for all of you," Blair Davies added.

"And me for all of you." Jamie caught my eye and brought his glass to mine.

"Cheers!" Jack yelled and winged his sippy cup across the table, where it bounced off of Jamie's head.

"Whoa! That's not how we do it!" Sonny glowered, and Jack's face fell. "You'll get it, buddy," Sonny said more softly. "You'll get it soon."

RECIPES

Vee's Gluten-free Pumpkin Cookies

In the story, Vee Snugg makes her traditional pumpkin cookies gluten-free in an attempt to entice Sergeant Tom Flynn. In reality, you can make them either way. Vee's recipe is a twist on one that used to appear on the Libby pumpkin can. Lots of people make versions of these cookies, but I think Vee's are particularly delicious.

Ingredients

3½ cups Bob's Red Mill Gluten-Free All-Purpose Baking Flour (or standard all-purpose flour)
2⅓ cup old-fashioned oats
1¾ teaspoon baking soda
2 teaspoons pumpkin pie spice
1½ teaspoon salt
3½ sticks butter, softened
1¾ cup sugar
1¾ cup packed brown sugar
1 15-ounce can of pure pumpkin
2 large eggs
1¾ teaspoon vanilla abstract
1¾ cup chopped walnuts
1¾ cup chocolate chips
Decorator icing (optional)

Instructions

Mix flour, oats, baking soda, pumpkin pie spice, and salt in a medium bowl. In a large bowl, beat butter, sugar, and brown sugar until fluffy. Add pumpkin, eggs, and extract. Mix well. Gradually add flour mixture. Add nuts and chocolate chips.

Pre-heat oven to 350 degrees. Drop ¼ cup dough onto a parchment-covered baking sheet. Spread into a pumpkin shape about 1/4 inch thick. Continue until all dough is used.

Bake for 14–16 minutes, until firm and golden brown. Cool on baking sheets for 2 minutes and then remove to wire racks.

Decorate with icing when cool, if desired. Vee uses orange icing to outline the pumpkin ribs and green icing for the stem and leaves.

Makes 40 cookies.

Dear Reader,

I hope you enjoyed Julia Snowden's latest adventure in Busman's Harbor, Maine, as told in *Scared Off*. If this story was your first introduction to Julia, her family and friends, there are nine mystery novels, starting with *Clammed Up*. There are three additional novella collections, which also include stories by Leslie Meier and Lee Hollis, *Eggnog Murder*, *Yule Log Murder*, and *Haunted House Murder*. There are also two books in my Jane Darrowfield mystery series: *Jane Darrowfield, Professional Busybody*, and *Jane Darrowfield and the Madwoman Next Door*.

It doesn't happen often, but I got to write this tale of mayhem and murder in the season in which it is set. The lead-up to Halloween in 2020 was a decidedly scary time as parents debated whether trick-or-treating was safe. If their wild party had broken out this year, Page, Vanessa, and Talia would have been in even bigger trouble.

I hope that, as you read this story in a future I can barely imagine, you are preparing for hordes of children dressed in costumes to come to your door and then donning your own costume to go out to a party. If not, I wish for you a glass of warm cider, a plate of Vee's delicious pumpkin cookies, and a good book.

Sincerely,

Barbara Ross
Portland, Maine

I'm always happy to hear from readers. You can reach me at barbaraross@maineclambakemysteries.com, or find me via my website at www.barbararossauthor.com, on Twitter @barbross, on Facebook www.facebook.com/ barbaraann ross, on Pinterest www.pinterest.com/barbara annross and on Instagram @maineclambake. You can also follow me on Goodreads at https://www.goodreads. com/author/show/ 6550635.Barbara_Ross and on Book-Bub at https://www. bookbub.com/authors/barbara-ross.

Visit us online at
KensingtonBooks.com
to read more from your favorite authors,
see books by series, view reading
group guides, and more!

Visit us online for sneak peeks, exclusive
giveaways, special discounts, author content,
and engaging discussions with your fellow readers.

Betweenthechapters.net

Sign up for our newsletters and be the first
to get exciting news and announcements about
your favorite authors!
Kensingtonbooks.com/newsletter

Foxe's Book of Martyrs

U DELCI MOSTAY DUCHLA

Foxe's Book of Martyrs

Prepared by
W. Grinton Berry

BAKER BOOK HOUSE
Grand Rapids, Michigan

Reprinted by
Baker Book House Company

ISBN: 0-8010-3483-3

Tenth printing, June 1988
Eleventh printing, January 1989
Twelfth printing, October 1989

Printed in the United States of America

EDITOR'S PREFACE

ONLY a very few words of explanation are necessary to introduce this edition of Foxe's *Book of
Martyrs*, a work which used to hold a place in
thousands of households by the side of *The
Pilgrim's Progress* and the Bible, and which is well
fitted, at the present hour, to do great service for
Evangelical and Protestant truth.

Foxe is undoubtedly a vivid, powerful, truly
interesting writer with a style whose simplicity covers
elements both of tenderness and indignation; and
some of his narratives are among the finest in the
English language; but in his book, as he left it, he
did not always arrange his materials in the way
most likely to attract the reader of the present day.
His literary craftsmanship in the making of phrase,
sentence, and paragraph is noticeable; but he was
markedly deficient in literary *architectonics*. He
did not always build up his hewn stones into a
simple structure, the lines of which could at once be
taken in by the observer. An endeavour has been
made in this edition to remedy that defect. The
modern reader is won by clear and simple arrangement of what is placed before him; accordingly the
Editor has striven hard to merit the commendation
of having secured that.

The Editor believes that nothing essential has
been omitted in this edition, that he has conserved
everything in *The Book of Martyrs* that most

obviously makes for edification. Foxe, when he had the material, narrated at great length the examinations of the martyrs before their judges. Inevitably the same points of controversy emerge, the same questions are asked and the same answers given—again and again. The Editor of this edition has thought it necessary to avoid these repetitions, while having an anxious care that in the cases of the more illustrious martyrs—to each of whom a chapter is devoted—the truths for which they offered up their lives are fully and explicitly stated.

Further, the biographical part of Foxe's immortal work has in this edition been disentangled from the very lengthy dissertations on general religious history in which the illustrious author delighted. Foxe's plan was to tell his story under each reign, then when he came to the hour in which his hero struck upon the scene he pulled up, began to relate the biography of his subject from the beginning of his career, and, that done, returned to his main narrative. National history and personal biography were more mixed up than they need have been, and repetitions were frequent. These saltatory methods led to confusion, the biography did not stand out in sharp relief, the reader was not clearly pointed to it, and the general impression of the whole on his mind was blurred. The discursiveness of Foxe's work, in its original form, is also a bar to its hearty acceptance by the modern reader, for of all characteristics discursiveness is that of which the latter is most impatient. He likes narratives that are clean-cut, swift, full of movement, making straight for the point.

The Editor has kept these last-mentioned essential

EDITOR'S PREFACE

points in mind all the time of his preparation of this volume. The result, it is hoped, proves that Foxe's narratives, judged merely on literary grounds, are among the most graphic and the most readable in our literature. Add to that, that the great theme with which this famous book deals—the falsehood, aggressiveness, and intolerance of Romanism and its cruelty, which always merely waits its opportunity—are topics full of living significance at this hour, and it becomes reasonable to entertain hope that this volume may receive a great popular welcome and again nobly serve the cause for which it was written.

Perhaps it ought to be added that the Editor is quite aware that the Emperor Constantine, Wickliff, and Luther, whose lives are narrated in this book, were not martyrs in the current acceptation of the word. But the original meaning of martyr is witness, and these were assuredly witnesses whose testimony to the Gospel was of great value. Besides, every reader would have felt that the volume was imperfect without these sketches.

W. GRINTON BERRY

JOHN FOXE
THE MARTYROLOGIST[1]

JOHN FOXE was born at Boston, Lincolnshire, in
1516. He was a studious youth, and, aided by his
friends, was sent to Oxford when he was sixteen
years old. He became B.A. in 1537, probationer
Fellow of Magdalen College 1538, full Fellow 1539,
lecturer in Logic 1539-1540, and M.A. in 1543.
His intimate friends at Oxford included Hugh
Latimer and William Tyndale, and like them he
strongly favoured Protestantism. It was this fact
which led in 1545 to the resignation of Foxe and
five other Fellows of Magdalen.

On leaving Oxford he received temporary employment as tutor in the Lucy family at Charlecote,
Warwickshire. Early in 1547 he married at
Charlecote Church Agnes Randall, the daughter
of an old Coventry friend, and came up to London
to seek a livelihood. Before the end of 1548 Foxe
was appointed tutor to the orphan children of
Henry Howard, Earl of Surrey, who had been
executed in 1547. There were two boys, Thomas,
afterwards Duke of Norfolk, and Henry Howard,
afterwards Earl of Northampton, together with three
girls. Foxe joined his pupils at the castle of Reigate,
a manor belonging to their grandfather, the Duke of
Norfolk.

[1] This notice is a condensation of the account given in the
Dictionary of National Biography, vol. xx., by S. L. Lee.

BIOGRAPHICAL SKETCH

Foxe was ordained deacon by Ridley, Bishop of London, in St Paul's Cathedral, in 1550. Subsequently he preached at Reigate (though he had no pastoral charge there), being the first to preach Protestantism there. Meanwhile he was publishing theological tracts and reading much in church history.

When Queen Mary came to the throne in July 1553 an anxious time for Foxe began. The old Duke of Norfolk, a Catholic, was released from prison, and immediately dismissed Foxe from the tutorship of his grandchildren. The majority of Foxe's friends left England for the Continent at the first outbreak of persecution, and Foxe determined to follow them. He sailed from Ipswich to Nieuport, whence he proceeded to Strasburg, where he met his friend Edmund Grindal. He had brought with him in manuscript the first part of a Latin treatise on the persecution of Reformers in Europe from the time of Wycliffe to his own day. This volume, dealing mainly with Wycliffe and Huss, forms the earliest draft of *The Acts and Monuments* (so generally known as *The Book of Martyrs*), and was published in 1554.

After a stay of about a year at Frankfort, where Foxe came into intimate contact with the Scottish reformer, John Knox, he removed to Basle, where he suffered acutely from poverty. He found employment, however, as a reader of the press in the printing-office of Johann Herbst or Oporinus, an enthusiastic Protestant and publisher of Protestant books, who allowed Foxe adequate leisure for his own books.

Meanwhile Foxe was receiving through Grindal reports of the persecutions in England. Bradford's case was one of the earliest he obtained. When reports of Cranmer's examination arrived Foxe prepared then for publication. Grindal urged Foxe to complete at once his account of the persecutions of reformers in England as far as the end of Henry VIII.'s reign. He worked steadily, and in 1559 had brought his story of persecution down to nearly the end of Henry's reign. This work, which was in Latin, bears a dedication, dated September 1, 1559, to Foxe's old pupil, now Duke of Norfolk.

Foxe returned to England the same year, and early in 1560 Grindal, now Bishop of London, ordained him priest. He was engaged in translating the work above mentioned into English and in elaborating his information. The papers of Ralph Morice, Cranmer's secretary, had fallen into his hands together with much new material.

The Acts and Monuments was published on March 20, 1563. From the date of its appearance it was popularly known as *The Book of Martyrs*. Foxe forwarded a copy to Magdalen College, and received in payment £6, 13s. 4d. The success of the undertaking was immediate. The author was rewarded with a prebend in Salisbury Cathedral and with the lease of the vicarage of Shipton (May 11, 1563). Yet he still suffered from slenderness of means.

On the Good Friday after the publication of the papal bull excommunicating Queen Elizabeth (1570), Foxe, at Grindal's bidding, preached a powerful sermon at St Paul's Cross and renewed his attacks on the Catholics. A second edition of *The Acts and Monuments* was published in 1570. Convocation resolved that copies should be placed

ın cathedral churches and in the houses of archbishops, bishops, deacons, and archdeacons.

In 1575 Foxe energetically sought to obtain the
remission of the capital sentence in the case of two
Dutch Anabaptists condemned to the stake for their
opinions. He wrote to the Queen, Lord Burghley,
and Lord Chief Justice Manson, pointing out the dis-
proportion between the offence and the punishment,
and deprecating the penalty of death in cases of
heresy. A respite of a month was allowed, but
both the Anabaptists perished.

The third and fourth editions of *The Acts and
Monuments* were issued in 1576 and 1583 respec-
tively.

Foxe's health began to break up in 1586, and he
died, after much suffering, in April 1587. He was
buried in St Giles's Church, Cripplegate, London,
where a monument, with an inscription by his son
Samuel, is still extant.

Foxe was charitable to the poor, although his
own circumstances were frequently straitened, and
he was never well off; and he seems to have been
of a cheerful temperament. His wife survived
him eighteen years, dying in 1605. There were
at least five children of the marriage.

Foxe was a prolific author, but the work by
which he will ever be held in grateful remembrance
is *The Book of Martyrs*.

CONTENTS

CONTENTS

FOXE'S BOOK OF MARTYRS

THE PERSECUTION OF THE EARLY CHRISTIANS

CHRIST our Saviour, in the Gospel of St Matthew, hearing the confession of Simon Peter, who, first of all other, openly acknowledged Him to be the Son of God, and perceiving the secret hand of His Father therein, called him (alluding to his name) a rock, upon which rock He would build His Church so strong, that the gates of hell should not prevail against it. In which words three things are to be noted : First, that Christ will have a Church in this world. Secondly, that the same Church should mightily be impugned, not only by the world, but also by the uttermost strength and powers of all hell. And, thirdly, that the same Church, notwithstanding the uttermost of the devil and all his malice, should continue.

Which prophecy of Christ we see wonderfully to be verified, insomuch that the whole course of the Church to this day may seem nothing else but a verifying of the said prophecy. First, that Christ hath set up a Church, needeth no declaration. Secondly, what force of princes, kings, monarchs, governors, and rulers of this world, with their subjects, publicly and privately, with all their strength and cunning, have bent themselves against this Church! And, thirdly, how the said Church, all this notwithstanding, hath yet endured and holden its own! What storms and tempests it hath overpast, wondrous it is to behold: for the more evident declaration whereof, I have addressed this present history, to the end, first, that the wonderful works of God in His Church might appear to His glory; also that, the continuance and proceedings of the Church, from time to time, being set forth, more knowledge and experience may redound thereby, to the profit of the reader and edification of Christian faith.

At the first preaching of Christ, and coming of the Gospel, who should rather have known and received him than the Pharisees and Scribes of that people which had His law? and yet who persecuted and rejected Him more than they themselves? What followed? They, in refusing Christ to be their King, and choosing rather to be subject unto Cæsar, were by the said Cæsar at length destroyed.

The like example of God's wrathful punishment is to be noted no less in the Romans themselves. For when Tiberius Cæsar, having learnt by letters from Pontius Pilate of the doings of Christ, of His miracles, resurrection, and ascension into heaven, and how He was received as God of many, himself moved with belief of the same, did confer thereon with the whole senate of Rome, and proposed to have Christ adored as God; they, not agreeing thereunto, refused Him, because that, contrary to the law of the Romans, He was consecrated (said they) for God before the senate of Rome had so decreed and approved Him. Thus the vain senate (being contented with the emperor to reign over

YOU'RE INVITED TO:

Put on Love

COLOSSIANS 3:12-17

THE MBC&S CHRISTMAS BANQUET

Tuesday
December 4th

THE PUNISHMENT OF PILATE

them, and not contented with the meek King of
glory, the Son of God, to be their King) were
scourged and entrapped for their unjust refusing, by
the same way which they themselves did prefer.
For as they preferred the emperor, and rejected
Christ, so the just permission of God did stir up
their own emperors against them in such sort, that
the senators themselves were almost all destroyed,
and the whole city most horribly afflicted for the
space almost of three hundred years.

For first, the same Tiberius, who, for a great part
of his reign, was a moderate and a tolerable prince,
afterward was to them a sharp and heavy tyrant,
who neither favoured his own mother, nor spared
his nephews nor the princes of the city, such as
were his own counsellors, of whom, being of the
number of twenty, he left not past two or three
alive. Suetonius reporteth him to be so stern of
nature, and tyrannical, that in one day he recordeth
twenty persons to be drawn to the place of execution.
In whose reign through the just punishment of
God, Pilate, under whom Christ was crucified, was
apprehended and sent to Rome, deposed, then
banished to the town of Vienne in Dauphiny, and
at length did slay himself. Agrippa the elder, also,
by him was cast into prison, albeit afterward he was
restored.

After the death of Tiberius, succeeded Caligula,
Claudius Nero and Domitius Nero ; which three
were likewise scourges to the Senate and people
of Rome. The first commanded himself to be
worshipped as god, and temples to be erected in
his name, and used to sit in the temple among the
gods, requiring his images to be set up in all

3

temples, and also in the temple of Jerusalem; which caused great disturbance among the Jews, and then began the abomination of desolation spoken of in the Gospel to be set up in the holy place. His cruelty of disposition, or else displeasure towards the Romans, was such that he wished that all the people of Rome had but one neck, that he, at his pleasure, might destroy such a multitude. By this said Caligula, Herod Antipas, the murderer of John Baptist and condemner of Christ, was condemned to perpetual banishment, where he died miserably. Caiaphas also, who wickedly sat upon Christ, was the same time removed from the high priest's room, and Jonathan set in his place.

The raging fierceness of this Caligula had not thus ceased, had not he been cut off by the hands of a tribune and other gentlemen, who slew him in the fourth year of his reign. After whose death were found in his closet two small books, one called the *Sword*, the other the *Dagger*: in which books were contained the names of those senators and noblemen of Rome, whom he had purposed to put to death. Besides this *Sword* and *Dagger*, there was found also a coffer, wherein divers kinds of poisons were kept in glasses and vessels, for the purpose of destroying a wonderful number of people; which poisons, afterward being thrown into the sea, destroyed a great number of fish.

But that which this Caligula had only conceived, the same did the other two, which came after, bring to pass; namely, Claudius Nero, who reigned thirteen years with no little cruelty; but especially the third of these Neros, called Domitius Nero, who, succeeding after Claudius, reigned fourteen years with such fury and tyranny that he slew the most part of the senators and destroyed the whole order of knighthood in Rome. So prodigious a monster of nature was he (more like a beast, yea rather a devil than a man), that he seemed to be born to the destruction of men. Such was his wretched cruelty, that he caused to be put to death his mother, his brother-in-law, his sister, his wife and his instructors, Seneca and Lucan. Moreover, he commanded Rome to be set on fire in twelve places, and so continued it six days and seven nights in burning, while that he, to see the example how Troy burned, sang the verses of Homer. And to avoid the infamy thereof, he laid the fault upon the Christian men, and caused them to be persecuted.

And so continued this miserable emperor till at last the senate, proclaiming him a public enemy unto mankind, condemned him to be drawn through the city, and to be whipped to death; for the fear whereof, he, flying the hands of his enemies, in the night fled to a manor of his servant's in the country, where he was forced to slay himself, complaining that he had then neither friend nor enemy left, that would do so much for him.

The Jews, in the year threescore and ten, about forty years after the passion of Christ, were destroyed by Titus, and Vespasian his father, (who succeeded after Nero in the empire) to the number of eleven hundred thousand, besides those which Vespasian slew in subduing the country of Galilee. They were sold and sent into Egypt and other provinces to vile slavery, to the number of seventeen thousand; two thousand were brought with Titus in his triumph; of whom, part he gave to be devoured of the wild beasts, part otherwise most cruelly were slain.

As I have set forth the justice of God upon these Roman persecutors, so now we declare their persecutions raised up against the people and servants of Christ, within the space of three hundred years; which persecutions in number commonly are counted to be ten, besides the persecutions first moved by the Jews, in Jerusalem and other places, against the apostles. After the martyrdom of Stephen, suffered next James the holy apostle of Christ, and brother of John. 'When this James,' saith Clement, 'was brought to the tribunal seat, he that brought him and was the cause of his trouble, seeing him to be condemned and that he should suffer death, was in such sort moved therewith in heart and conscience that as he went to the execution he confessed himself also, of his own accord, to be a Christian. And so were they led forth together, where in the way he desired of James to forgive him what he had done. After that James had a little paused with himself upon the matter, turning to him he saith "Peace be to thee, brother;" and kissed him. And both were beheaded together, A.D. 36.'

Thomas preached to the Parthians, Medes and Persians, also to the Carmanians, Hyrcanians, Bactrians and Magians. He suffered in Calamina, a city of India, being slain with a dart. Simon, who was brother to Jude, and to James the younger, who all were the sons of Mary Cleophas and of Alpheus, was Bishop of Jerusalem after James, and was crucified in a city of Egypt in the time of Trajan the emperor. Simon the apostle, called Cananeus and Zelotes, preached in Mauritania, and in the country of Africa, and in Britain: he was likewise crucified.

Mark, the evangelist and first Bishop of Alexandria, preached the Gospel in Egypt, and there, drawn with ropes unto the fire, was burnt and afterwards buried in a place called there 'Bucolus,' under the reign of Trajan the emperor. Bartholomew is said also to have preached to the Indians, and to have translated the Gospel of St Matthew into their tongue. At last in Albinopolis, a city of greater Armenia, after divers persecutions, he was beaten down with staves, then crucified; and after, being excoriate, he was beheaded.

Of Andrew the apostle and brother to Peter, thus writeth Jerome. 'Andrew did preach, in the year fourscore of our Lord Jesus Christ, to the Scythians and Sogdians, to the Sacæ, and in a city which is called Sebastopolis, where the Ethiopians do now inhabit. He was buried in Patræ, a city of Achaia, being crucified by Ægeas, the governor of the Edessenes.' Bernard, and St Cyprian, do make mention of the confession and martyrdom of this blessed apostle; whereof partly out of these, partly out of other credible writers, we have collected after this manner: When Andrew, through his diligent preaching, had brought many to the faith of Christ, Ægeas the governor, knowing this, resorted to Patræ, to the intent he might constrain as many as did believe Christ to be God, by the whole consent of the senate, to do sacrifice unto the idols, and so give divine honours unto them. Andrew, thinking good at the beginning to resist the wicked counsel and the doings of Ægeas, went unto him, saying to this effect unto him: 'that it behoved him who was judge of men, first to know his Judge which dwelleth in heaven, and then to worship Him being known; and so, in worshipping the true God, to revoke his mind from false gods and blind idols.' These words spake Andrew to the proconsul.

But Ægeas, greatly therewith discontented, demanded of him, whether he was the same Andrew that did overthrow the temple of the gods, and persuade men to be of that superstitious sect which the Romans of late had commanded to be abolished and rejected. Andrew did plainly affirm that the princes of the Romans did not understand the truth and that the Son of God, coming from heaven into the world for man's sake, hath taught and declared how those idols, whom they so honoured as gods, were not only not *gods*, but also most cruel *devils*; enemies to mankind, teaching the people nothing else but that wherewith God is offended, and, being offended, turneth away and regardeth them not; and so by the wicked service of the devil, they do fall headlong into all wickedness, and, after their departing, nothing remaineth unto them, but their evil deeds.

But the proconsul charged and commanded Andrew not to teach and preach such things any more; or, if he did, he should be fastened to the cross with all speed.

Andrew, abiding in his former mind very constant, answered thus concerning the punishment which he threatened: 'He would not have preached the honour and glory of the cross, if he had feared the death of the cross.' Whereupon sentence of condemnation was pronounced; that Andrew, teaching and enterprising a new sect, and taking away the religion of their gods, ought to be crucified.

A LOVER OF THE CROSS

Andrew, going toward the place, and seeing afar off the cross prepared, did change neither countenance nor colour, neither did his blood shrink, neither did he fail in his speech, his body fainted not, neither was his mind molested, nor did his understanding fail him, as it is the manner of men to do, but out of the abundance of his heart his mouth did speak, and fervent charity did appear in his words as kindled sparks; he said, 'O cross, most welcome and long looked for! with a willing mind, joyfully and desirously, I come to thee, being the scholar of Him which did hang on thee: because I have always been thy lover, and have coveted to embrace thee.'

Matthew, otherwise named Levi, first of a publican made an apostle, wrote his Gospel to the Jews in the Hebrew tongue. After he had converted to the faith Æthiopia and all Egypt, Hircanus, their king, sent one to run him through with a spear.

Philip, the holy apostle, after he had much laboured among the barbarous nations in preaching the word of salvation to them, at length suffered, in Hierapolis, a city of Phrygia, being there crucified and stoned to death ; where also he was buried, and his daughters also with him.[1]

Of James, the brother of the Lord, thus we read:

James, took in hand to govern the Church with the apostles, being counted of all men, from the time of our Lord, to be a just and perfect man. He drank no wine nor any strong drink, neither did he eat any animal food; the razor never came upon his

[1] It should be understood that the accounts of the martyrdoms of apostles are mainly traditional.

9

head. To him only was it lawful to enter into the holy place, for he was not clothed with woollen, but with linen only; and he used to enter into the temple alone, and there, falling upon his knees, ask remission for the people; so that his knees, by oft kneeling (for worshipping God, and craving forgiveness for the people), lost the sense of feeling, being benumbed and hardened like the knees of a camel. He was, for the excellency of his just life, called 'The Just,' and, 'the safeguard of the people.'

When many therefore of their chief men did believe, there was a tumult made of the Jews, Scribes and Pharisees, saying; There is danger, lest all the people should look for this Jesus, as the Christ. Therefore they gathered themselves together, and said to James, 'We beseech thee restrain the people, for they believe in Jesus, as though he were Christ; we pray thee persuade all them which come unto the feast of the passover to think rightly of Jesus; for we all give heed to thee, and all the people do testify of thee that thou art just, and that thou dost not accept the person of any man. Therefore persuade the people that they be not deceived about Jesus, for all the people and we ourselves are ready to obey thee. Therefore stand upon the pinnacle of the temple, that thou mayest be seen above, and that thy words may be heard of all the people; for all the tribes with many Gentiles are come together for the passover.'

And thus the forenamed Scribes and Pharisees did set James upon the battlements of the temple, and they cried unto him, and said, 'Thou just man, whom we all ought to obey, this people is going astray after Jesus which is crucified.'

A TRUE WITNESS FOR CHRIST

And he answered with a loud voice, 'Why do you ask me of Jesus the Son of Man? He sitteth on the right hand of the Most High, and shall come in the clouds of heaven.'

Whereupon many were persuaded and glorified God, upon this witness of James, and said, 'Hosannah to the Son of David.'

Then the Scribes and the Pharisees said among themselves, 'We have done evil, that we have caused such a testimony of Jesus; let us go up, and throw him down, that others, being moved with fear, may deny that faith.' And they cried out, saying, 'Oh, oh, this just man also is seduced.' Therefore they went up to throw down the just man. Yet he was not killed by the fall, but, turning, fell upon his knees, saying, 'O Lord God, Father, I beseech thee to forgive them, for they know not what they do.' And they said among themselves, 'Let us stone the just man, James;' and they took him to smite him with stones. But while they were smiting him with stones, a priest, said to them, 'Leave off, what do ye? The just man prayeth for you.' And one of those who were present, a fuller, took an instrument, wherewith they did use to beat and purge cloth, and smote the just man on his head; and so he finished his testimony. And they buried him in the same place. He was a true witness for Christ to the Jews and the Gentiles.

Now let us comprehend the persecutions raised by the Romans against the Christians in the primitive age of the Church, during the space of three hundred years. Wherein marvellous it is to see and read the numbers incredible of Christian innocents that were tormented and slain. Whose kinds of punishments, although they were divers, yet the manner of constancy in all these martyrs was one. And yet, notwithstanding the sharpness of these so many and sundry torments, and also the like cruelness of the tormentors, such was the number of these constant saints that suffered, or rather such was the power of the Lord in His saints, that, as Jerome saith, 'There is no day in the whole year unto which the number of five thousand martyrs cannot be ascribed, except only the first day of January.'

The first of these ten persecutions was stirred up by Nero about the year of our Lord threescore and four. The tyrannous rage of which emperor was very fierce against the Christians, 'insomuch that (as Eusebius recordeth) a man might then see cities full of men's bodies, the old there lying together with the young, and the dead bodies of women cast out naked, without all reverence of that sex, in the open streets.' Many there were of the Christians in those days, who, seeing the filthy abominations and intolerable cruelty of Nero, thought that he was antichrist.

In this persecution, among many other saints, the blessed apostle Peter was condemned to death, and crucified, as some do write, at Rome; albeit some others, and not without cause, do doubt thereof. Hegesippus saith that Nero sought matter against Peter to put him to death; which, when the people perceived, they entreated Peter with much ado that he would fly the city. Peter, through their importunity at length persuaded, prepared himself to avoid. But, coming to the gate, he saw the Lord Christ come to meet him, to Whom he, worshipping,

said, 'Lord, whither dost Thou go?' To whom
He answered and said, 'I am come again to be
crucified.' By this, Peter, perceiving his suffering
to be understood, returned back into the city.
Jerome saith that he was crucified, his head
being down and his feet upward, himself so
requiring, because he was (he said) unworthy to
be crucified after the same form and manner as the
Lord was.

Paul, the apostle, who before was called Saul,
after his great travail and unspeakable labours in
promoting the Gospel of Christ, suffered also in this
first persecution under Nero. Abdias, declareth
that unto his execution Nero sent two of his
esquires, Ferega and Parthemius, to bring him word
of his death. They, coming to Paul instructing the
people, desired him to pray for them, that they
might believe; who told them that shortly after
they should believe and be baptised at his
sepulchre. This done, the soldiers came and led
him out of the city to the place of execution, where
he, after his prayers made, gave his neck to the
sword.

The first persecution ceased under Vespasian who
gave some rest to the poor Christians. After
whose reign was moved, not long after, the second
persecution, by the emperor Domitian, brother of
Titus. He, first beginning mildly and modestly,
afterward did so far outrage in pride intolerable,
that he commanded himself to be worshipped as
god, and that images of gold and silver in his
honour should be set up in the capitol.

In this persecution, John, the apostle and
evangelist, was exiled by the said Domitian into

Patmos. After the death of Domitian, he being slain and his acts repealed by the senate, John was released, and came to Ephesus in the year fourscore and seventeen; where he continued until the time of Trajan, and there governed the churches in Asia, where also he wrote his Gospel; and so lived till the year after the passion of our Lord, threescore and eight, which was the year of his age about one hundred.

Clement of Alexandria addeth a certain history of the holy apostle, not unworthy to be remembered of such as delight in things honest and profitable The words be these: When John was returned to Ephesus from the isle of Patmos, he was requested to resort to the places bordering near unto him. Whereupon, when he was come to a certain city, and had comforted the brethren, he beheld a young man robust in body, of a beautiful countenance, and of a fervent mind. Looking earnestly at the newly-appointed bishop, John said: 'I most solemnly commend this man to thee, in presence here of Christ and of the Church.'

When the bishop had received of him this charge, and had promised his faithful diligence therein, again the second time John spake unto him, and charged him as before. This done, John returned to Ephesus. The bishop, receiving the young man committed to his charge, brought him home, kept him, and nourished him, and at length baptized him; and after that, he gradually relaxed his care and oversight of him, trusting that he had given him the best safeguard possible in putting the Lord's seal upon him.

The young man thus having his liberty more, it

chanced that certain of his old companions and acquaintances, being idle, dissolute, and hardened in wickedness, did join in company with him, who first invited him to sumptuous and riotous banquets; then enticed him to go forth with them in the night to rob and steal; after that he was allured by them unto greater mischief and wickedness. Wherein, by custom of time, and by little and little, he, becoming more expert, and being of a good wit, and a stout courage, like unto a wild or unbroken horse, leaving the right way and running at large without bridle, was carried headlong to the profundity of all misorder and outrage. And thus, utterly forgetting and rejecting the wholesome doctrine of salvation which he had learned before, he entered so far in the way of perdition, that he cared not how much further he proceeded in the same. And so, associating unto him a band of companions and fellow thieves, he took upon himself to be as head and captain among them, in committing all kind of murder and felony.

It chanced that John was sent for to those quarters again, and came. Meeting the bishop afore specified, he requireth of him the pledge, which, in the presence of Christ and of the congregation then present, he left in his hands to keep. The bishop, something amazed at the words of John, supposing he had meant them of some money committed to his custody, which he had not received (and yet durst not mistrust John, nor contrary his words), could not tell what to answer. Then John, perceiving his perplexity, and uttering his meaning more plainly: 'The young man,' saith he, 'and the soul of our brother committed to your custody, I do require.' Then the bishop, with a loud voice sorrowing and weeping, said, 'He is dead.' To whom John said, 'How, and by what death?' The other said, 'He is dead to God, for he became an evil and abandoned man, and at length a robber And now he doth frequent the mountain instead of the Church, with a company of villains and thieves, like unto himself.'

Here the apostle rent his garments, and, with a great lamentation, said, 'A fine keeper of his brother's soul I left here! get me a horse, and let me have a guide with me:' which being done, his horse and man procured, he hasted from the Church, and coming to the place, was taken of thieves that lay on the watch. But he, neither flying nor refusing, said, 'I came hither for the purpose: lead me,' said he, 'to your captain.' So he being brought, the captain all armed fiercely began to look upon him; and eftsoons coming to the knowledge of him, was stricken with confusion and shame, and began to fly. But the old man followed him as much as he might, forgetting his age, and crying, 'My son, why dost thou fly from thy father? an armed man from one naked, a young man from an old man? Have pity on me, my son, and fear not, for there is yet hope of salvation. I will make answer for thee unto Christ; I will die for thee, if need be; as Christ hath died for us, I will give my life for thee; believe me, Christ hath sent me.'

He, hearing these things, first, as in a maze, stood still, and therewith his courage was abated. After that he had cast down his weapons, by and by he trembled, yea, and wept bitterly; and, coming to the old man, embraced him, and spake unto him with weeping (as well as he could), being even then baptized afresh with tears, only his right hand being hid and covered.

Then the apostle, after that he had promised that he should obtain remission of our Saviour, prayed, falling down upon his knees, and kissing his murderous right hand (which for shame he durst not show before) as now purged through repentance, and brought him back to the Church. And when he had prayed for him with continual prayer and daily fastings, and had comforted and confirmed his mind with many sentences, he left him restored to the Church again; a great example of sincere penitence and proof of regeneration, and a trophy of the future resurrection.

The causes why the Roman emperors did so persecute the Christians were chiefly these—fear and hatred.

First, fear, for that the emperors and senate, of blind ignorance, not knowing the manner of Christ's kingdom, feared and misdoubted lest the same would subvert their empery; and therefore sought they all means possible, how, by death and all kinds of torments, utterly to extinguish the name and memory of the Christians.

Secondly, hatred, partly for that this world, of its own natural condition, hath ever hated and maliced the people of God, from the first beginning of the world. Partly again, for that the Christians being of a contrary nature and religion, serving only the true living God, despised their false gods, spake against their idolatrous worshippings, and many times stopped the power of Satan working in their idols: and therefore Satan, the prince of this world, stirred up the Roman princes and blind idolaters to bear the more hatred and spite against them. Whatsoever mishappened to the city or provinces of Rome, either famine, pestilence, earthquake, wars, wonders, unseasonableness of weather, or what other evils soever, it was imputed to the Christians.

The tyrants and organs of Satan were not contented with death only, to bereave the life from the body. The kinds of death were divers, and no less horrible than divers. Whatsoever the cruelness of man's invention could devise for the punishment of man's body, was practised against the Christians—stripes and scourgings, drawings, tearings, stonings, plates of iron laid unto them burning hot, deep dungeons, racks, strangling in prisons, the teeth of wild beasts, gridirons, gibbets and gallows, tossing upon the horns of bulls. Moreover, when they were thus killed, their bodies were laid in heaps, and dogs there left to keep them, that no man might come to bury them, neither would any prayer obtain them to be interred.

And yet, notwithstanding all these continual persecutions and horrible punishments, the Church daily increased, deeply rooted in the doctrine of the apostles and of men apostolical, and watered plenteously with the blood of saints.

In the third persecution Pliny the second, a man learned and famous, seeing the lamentable slaughter of Christians, and moved therewith to pity, wrote to Trajan, certifying him that there were many thousands of them daily put to death, of which none did any thing contrary to the Roman laws worthy persecution. 'The whole account they gave of their crime or error (whichever it is to be called) amounted only to this,—viz. that they were accustomed on a stated day to meet before day-light, and to repeat together a set form of prayer to Christ as a God, and to bind themselves by an obligation—not indeed to commit wickedness ; but, on the contrary,—never to commit theft, robbery or adultery, never to falsify their word, never to defraud any man : after which it was their custom to separate, and reassemble to partake in common of a harmless meal.'

In this persecution, suffered the blessed martyr, Ignatius, who is had in famous reverence among very many. This Ignatius was appointed to the bishopric of Antioch next after Peter in succession. Some do say, that he, being sent from Syria to Rome, because he professed Christ, was given to the wild beasts to be devoured. It is also said of him, that when he passed through Asia, being under the most strict custody of his keepers, he strengthened and confirmed the churches through all the cities as he went, both with his exhortations and preaching of the Word of God. Accordingly, having come to Smyrna, he wrote to the church at Rome, exhorting them not to use means for his deliverance from martyrdom, lest they should deprive him of that which he most longed and hoped for. 'Now I begin to be a disciple. I care for nothing, of visible or invisible things, so that I may but win Christ. Let fire and the cross, let the companies of wild beasts, let breaking of bones and tearing of limbs, let the grinding of the whole body, and all the malice of the devil, come upon me; be it so, only may I win Christ Jesus!' And even when he was sentenced to be thrown to the beasts, such was the burning desire that he had to suffer, that he spake, what time he heard the lions roaring, saying, 'I am the wheat of Christ : I am going to be ground with the teeth of wild beasts, that I may be found pure bread.'

After the decease of the quiet and mild prince Antoninus Pius followed his son Marcus Aurelius, about the year of our Lord 161, a man of nature more stern and severe ; and, although in study of philosophy and in civil government no less commendable, yet, toward the Christians sharp and fierce ; by whom was moved the fourth persecution.

In the time of the same Marcus a great number of them which truly professed Christ suffered most cruel torments and punishments, among whom was Polycarp, the worthy bishop of Smyrna. Of whose end and martyrdom I thought it here not inexpedient to commit to history so much as Eusebius declareth to be taken out of a certain letter or epistle, written by them of his (Polycarp's) own church to all the brethren throughout the world.

Three days before he was apprehended, as he was praying at night, he fell asleep, and saw in a dream the pillow take fire under his head, and presently consumed. Waking thereupon, he forthwith related the vision to those about him, and prophesied that he should be burnt alive for Christ's sake. When the persons who were in search of him were close at hand, he was induced, for the love of the brethren, to retire to another village, to which, notwithstanding, the pursuers soon followed him ; and having caught a couple of boys dwelling thereabout, they whipped one of them till he directed them to Polycarp's retreat. The pursuers having arrived late in the day, found him gone to bed in the top room of the house, whence he might have escaped into another house, if he would ; but this he refused to do, saying, 'The will of the Lord be done.'

Hearing that they were come, he came down, and spoke to them with a cheerful and pleasant countenance : so that they were wonder-struck, who, having never known the man before, now beheld his venerable age and the gravity and composure of his manner, and wondered why they should be so earnest for the apprehension of so old a man. He immediately ordered a table to be laid for them, and exhorted them to eat heartily, and begged them to allow him one hour to pray without molestation ; which being granted, he rose and began to pray, and was so full of the grace of God, that they who were present and heard his prayers were astonished, and many now felt sorry that so venerable and godly a man should be put to death.

When he had finished his prayers, wherein he made mention of all whom he had ever been connected with, small and great, noble and vulgar, and of the whole catholic Church throughout the world, the hour being come for their departure, they set him on an ass and brought him to the city. There met him the irenarch Herod, and his father Nicetes, who taking him up into their chariot, began to exhort him, saying, 'What harm is it to say "Lord Cæsar," and to sacrifice, and save yourself?' At first he was silent : but being pressed to speak, he said, 'I will not do as you advise me.' When they saw that he was not to be persuaded, they gave him rough language, and pushed him hastily down, so that in descending from the chariot he grazed his shin. But he, unmoved as if he had suffered nothing, went on cheerfully, under the conduct of his guards, to the Stadium. There, the noise being so great that few could hear anything, a voice from heaven said to Polycarp as he entered the Stadium, 'Be strong, Polycarp, and play the man.' No one saw him that spake, but many people heard the voice. When he was brought to the tribunal, there was a great tumult as soon as it was generally understood that Polycarp was apprehended. The proconsul asked him, if he were Polycarp. When he assented, the former counselled him to deny Christ, saying, 'Consider thyself, and have pity on thy own great age'; and many other such-like speeches which they are wont to make:—'Swear by the fortune of Cæsar'— 'Repent'—'Say, "Away with the atheists."'

Then Polycarp, with a grave aspect, beholding all the multitude in the Stadium, and waving his hand to them, gave a deep sigh, and, looking up to heaven, said, 'Take away the atheists.'

The proconsul then urged him, saying, 'Swear, and I will release thee;—reproach Christ.'

Polycarp answered, 'Eighty and six years have I served him, and he never once wronged me; how then shall I blaspheme my King, Who hath saved me?'

The proconsul again urged him, 'Swear by the fortune of Cæsar.'

Polycarp replied, 'Since you still vainly strive to make me swear by the fortune of Cæsar, as you express it, affecting ignorance of my real character, hear me frankly declaring what I am—I am a

Christian—and if you desire to learn the Christian doctrine, assign me a day, and you shall hear.'

Hereupon the proconsul said, 'I have wild beasts; and I will expose you to them, unless you repent.'

'Call for them,' replied Polycarp; 'for repentance with us is a wicked thing, if it is to be a change from the better to the worse, but a good thing if it is to be a change from evil to good.'

'I will tame thee with fire,' said the proconsul, 'since you despise the wild beasts, unless you repent.'

Then said Polycarp, 'You threaten me with fire, which burns for an hour, and is soon extinguished; but the fire of the future judgment, and of eternal punishment reserved for the ungodly, you are ignorant of. But why do you delay? Do whatever you please.'

The proconsul sent the herald to proclaim thrice in the middle of the Stadium, 'Polycarp hath professed himself a Christian.' Which words were no sooner spoken, but the whole multitude, both of Gentiles and Jews, dwelling at Smyrna, with outrageous fury shouted aloud, 'This is the doctor of Asia, the father of the Christians, and the subverter of our gods, who hath taught many not to sacrifice nor adore.' They now called on Philip, the asiarch, to let loose a lion against Polycarp. But he refused, alleging that he had closed his exhibition. They then unanimously shouted, that he should be burnt alive. For his vision must needs be accomplished—the vision which he had when he was praying, and saw his pillow burnt. The people immediately gathered wood and other dry matter from the workshops and baths: in which service the Jews (with their usual malice) were particularly forward to help.

When they would have fastened him to the stake, he said, 'Leave me as I am; for he who giveth me strength to sustain the fire, will enable me also, without your securing me with nails, to remain without flinching in the pile.' Upon which they bound him without nailing him. So he said thus:—'O Father, I bless thee that thou hast counted me worthy to receive my portion among the number of martyrs.'

As soon as he had uttered the word 'Amen,' the officers lighted the fire. The flame, forming the appearance of an arch, as the sail of a vessel filled with wind, surrounded, as with a wall, the body of the martyr; which was in the midst, not as burning flesh, but as gold and silver refining in the furnace. We received also in our nostrils such a fragrance as proceeds from frankincense or some other precious perfume. At length the wicked people, observing that his body could not be consumed with the fire, ordered the confector to approach, and to plunge his sword into his body. Upon this such a quantity of blood gushed out, that the fire was extinguished. But the envious, malignant, and spiteful enemy of the just studied to prevent us from obtaining his poor body. For some persons suggested to Nicetes, to go to the proconsul, and entreat him not to deliver the body to the Christians, 'lest,' said they, 'leaving the crucified one, they should begin to worship *him*.' And they said these things upon the suggestions and arguments of the Jews, who also watched us when we were going to take the body from the pile. The centurion, perceiving the malevolence of the Jews, placed the body in the midst of the fire and burned it. Then we gathered up his bones—more precious than gold and jewels—and deposited them in a proper place.

In the same persecution suffered the glorious and most constant martyrs of Lyons and Vienne, two cities in France ; giving a glorious testimony, and to all Christian men a spectacle or example of singular fortitude in Christ our Saviour. Their history is set forth by their own churches, where they did suffer :—

The whole fury of the multitude, the governor, and the soldiers, was spent on Sanctus of Vienne, the deacon, and on Maturus, a late convert indeed, but a magnanimous wrestler in spiritual things ; and on Attalus of Pergamos, a man who had ever been a pillar and support of our church ; and lastly on Blandina, through whom Christ showed that those things that appear unsightly and contemptible among men are most honourable in the presence of God, on account of love to His name exhibited in real energy, and not in boasting and pompous pretences. For—while we all feared, and among the rest while her mistress according to the flesh, who herself was one of the noble army of martyrs, dreaded that she would not be able to witness a good confession, because of the weakness of her body ;—Blandina was endued with so much fortitude, that those who successively tortured her from morning to night were quite worn out with fatigue, owned themselves conquered and exhausted of their whole apparatus of tortures, and were amazed to see her still breathing whilst her body was torn and laid open. The blessed woman recovered fresh vigour in the act of confession; and it was an evident annihilation of all her pains, to say—'I am a Christian, and no evil is committed among us.'

Sanctus, having sustained in a manner more than human the most barbarous indignities, while the impious hoped to extort from him something injurious to the Gospel, through the duration and intenseness of his sufferings, resisted with so much firmness, that he would neither tell his own name, nor that of his nation or state, nor whether he was a freeman or a slave; but to every interrogatory he answered, 'I am a Christian.' This, he repeatedly owned, was to him both name, and country, and family, and everything.

The faithful, while they were dragged along, proceeded with cheerful steps; their countenances shone with much grace and glory; their bonds were as the most beautiful ornaments; and they themselves looked as brides adorned with their richest array, breathing the fragrance of Christ. They were put to death in various ways: or, in other words, they wove a chaplet of various odours and flowers, and presented it to the Father.

Maturus, Sanctus, Blandina, and Attalus, were led to the wild beasts into the amphitheatre to be the common spectacle of Gentile inhumanity. They were exposed to all the barbarities which the mad populace with shouts demanded, and above all to the hot iron chair, in which their bodies were roasted and emitted a disgusting smell. These after remaining alive a long time, expired at length.

Blandina, suspended from a stake, was exposed

as food to the wild beasts; she was seen suspended in the form of a cross and employed in vehement supplication. The sight inspired her fellow-combatants with much alacrity, while they beheld with their bodily eyes, in the person of their sister, the figure of Him Who was crucified for them. None of the beasts at that time touched her: she was taken down from the stake and thrown again into prison. Weak and contemptible as she might be deemed, yet when clothed with Christ, the mighty and invincible champion, she became victorious over the enemy in a variety of encounters, and was crowned with immortality.

Attalus also was vehemently demanded by the multitude, for he was a person of great reputation among us. He advanced in all the cheerfulness and serenity of a good conscience;—an experienced Christian, and ever ready and active in bearing testimony to the truth. He was led round the amphitheatre, and a tablet carried before him, inscribed 'This is Attalus the Christian.' The rage of the people would have had him dispatched immediately; but the governor, understanding that he was a Roman, ordered him back to prison: and concerning him and others, who could plead the same privilege of Roman citizenship, he wrote to the emperor and waited for his instructions. Cæsar sent orders that the confessors of Christ should be put to death. Roman citizens had the privilege of dying by decollation; the rest were exposed to wild beasts.

Now it was that our Redeemer was magnified in those who had apostatized. They were interrogated separate from the rest, as persons soon to be dismissed, and made a confession to the surprise of the Gentiles, and were added to the list of martyrs.

The blessed Blandina, last of all, as a generous mother having exhorted her children, and sent them before her victorious to the king, reviewing the whole series of their sufferings, hastened to undergo the same herself, rejoicing and triumphing in her exit, as if invited to a marriage supper, not as one going to be exposed to wild beasts. After she had endured stripes, the tearing of the beasts, and the iron chair, she was enclosed in a net, and thrown to a bull; and having been tossed some time by the animal, and proving quite superior to her pains, through the influence of hope, and the realising view of the objects of her faith and her fellowship with Christ, she at length breathed out her soul.

Now let us enter the story of that most constant and courageous martyr of Christ, St Lawrence, whose words and works deserve to be as fresh and green in Christian hearts, as is the flourishing laurel-tree. This thirsty hart, longing after the water of life, desirous to pass unto it through the strait door of bitter death, when on a time he saw his vigilant shepherd Sixtus, Bishop of Rome, led as a harmless lamb, of harmful tyrants, to his death, cried out with open mouth and heart invincible, saying, 'O dear father! whither goest thou, without the company of thy dear son? What crime is there in me that offendeth thy fatherhood? Hast thou proved me unnatural? Now try, sweet father, whether thou hast chosen a faithful minister or not? Deniest thou unto him the fellowship of thy blood?' These words with tears Saint Lawrence uttered, not because his master should suffer, but

THE CHURCH'S TRUE TREASURE

because he might not be suffered to taste of death's cup which he thirsted after.

Then Sixtus to his son shaped this answer: 'I forsake thee not, O my son, I give thee to wit, that a sharper conflict remaineth for thee. A feeble and weak old man am I, and therefore run the race of a lighter and easier death: but lusty and young art thou, and more lustily, yea more gloriously, shalt thou triumph over this tyrant. Thy time approacheth; cease to weep and lament; three days after thou shalt follow me. Why cravest thou to be partaker with me in my passion? I bequeath unto thee the whole inheritance.'

Let us draw near to the fire of martyred Lawrence, that our cold hearts may be warmed thereby. The merciless tyrant, understanding him to be not only a minister of the sacraments, but a distributor also of the Church riches, promised to himself a double prey, by the apprehension of one soul. First, with the rake of avarice to scrape to himself the treasure of poor Christians; then with the fiery fork of tyranny, so to toss and turmoil them, that they should wax weary of their profession. With furious face and cruel countenance, the greedy wolf demanded where this Lawrence had bestowed the substance of the church: who, craving three day's respite, promised to declare where the treasure might be had. In the meantime, he caused a good number of poor Christians to be congregated. So, when the day of his answer was come, the persecutor strictly charged him to stand to his promise. Then valiant Lawrence, stretching out his arms over the poor, said: 'These are the precious treasure of the church; these are the

29

treasure indeed, in whom the faith of Christ reigneth, in whom Jesus Christ hath His .mansion-place. What more precious jewels can Christ have, than those in whom He hath promised to dwell? For so it is written, "I was hungry and ye gave me to eat; I was thirsty, and ye gave me to drink; I was harbourless and ye lodged me." And again; "Look, what ye have done to the least of these, the same have ye done to me." What greater riches can Christ our Master possess, than the poor people, in whom He loveth to be seen?'

O, what tongue is able to express the fury and madness of the tyrant's heart! Now he stamped, he stared, he ramped, he fared as one out of his wits: his eyes like fire glowed, his mouth like a boar foamed, his teeth like a hellhound grinned. Now, not a reasonable man, but a roaring lion, he might be called.

'Kindle the fire (he cried)—of wood make no spare. Hath this villain deluded the emperor? Away with him, away with him: whip him with scourges, jerk him with rods, buffet him with fists, brain him with clubs. Jesteth the traitor with the emperor? Pinch him with fiery tongs, gird him with burning plates, bring out the strongest chains, and the fire-forks, and the grated bed of iron: on the fire with it; bind the rebel hand and foot; and when the bed is fire-hot, on with him: roast him, broil him, toss him, turn him: on pain of our high displeasure do every man his office, O ye tormentors.'

The word was no sooner spoken, but all was done. After many cruel handlings, this meek lamb was laid, I will not say on his fiery bed of iron, but on his soft bed of down. So mightily God wrought with his martyr Lawrence, so miraculously God tempered His element the fire; not a bed of consuming pain, but a pallet of nourishing rest was it unto Lawrence.

Alban was the first martyr that ever in England suffered death for the name of Christ. At what time Dioclesian and Maximian the emperors had directed out their letters with all severity for the persecuting of the Christians, Alban, being then an infidel, received into his house a certain clerk, flying from the persecutors' hands, whom when Alban beheld continually, both day and night, to persevere in watching and prayer, suddenly by the great mercy of God he began to imitate the example of his faith and virtuous life; whereupon, by little and little, he being instructed by his wholesome exhortation, and leaving the blindness of his idolatry, became at length a perfect Christian.

And when the aforenamed clerk had lodged with him a certain time, it was informed the wicked prince, that this good man and confessor of Christ (not yet condemned to death) was harboured in Alban's house, or very near unto him. Whereupon immediately he gave in charge to the soldiers to make more diligent inquisition of the matter. As soon as they came to the house of Alban he, putting on the apparel wherewith his guest and master was apparelled, offered himself in the stead of the other to the soldiers; who, binding him, brought him forthwith to the judge.

It fortuned that at that instant when blessed Alban was brought unto the judge, they found the same judge at the altars offering sacrifice unto devils, who, as soon as he saw Alban, was straightways in a great rage, for that he would presume of his own voluntary will to offer himself to peril, and give himself a prisoner to the soldiers, for safeguard of his guest whom he harboured; wherefore he commanded him to be brought before the images of the devils whom he worshipped, saying: 'For that thou hadst rather hide and convey away a rebel, than deliver him to the officers, that (as a contemner of our gods) he might suffer punishment of his blasphemy; what punishment he should have had, thou for him shalt suffer the same, if I perceive thee any whit to revolt from our manner of worshipping.' But blessed Alban, who of his own accord had betrayed to the persecutors that he was a Christian, feared not at all the menaces of the prince; but being armed with the spiritual armour, openly pronounced that he would not obey his commandment.

Then said the judge, 'Of what stock or kindred art thou come?' Alban answered, 'What is that to you, of what stock I come? If you desire to hear the verity of my religion, I do you to wit, that I am a Christian, and apply myself altogether to that calling.' Then said the judge, 'I would know thy name, and see thou tell me the same without delay.' Then said he, 'My parents named me Alban, and I worship the true and living God, Who created all the world.' Then said the judge, fraught with fury, 'If thou wilt enjoy the felicity of prolonged life, do sacrifice (and that out of hand) to the mighty gods.' Alban replieth, 'These sacrifices which ye offer unto devils, can neither help them that offer the same, neither yet can they accomplish the desires and prayers of their suppliants.' The judge, when he heard these words, was passing angry, and commanded the tormentors to whip this holy confessor of God, endeavouring to overcome with stripes the constancy of his heart against which he had prevailed nothing with words. And he was cruelly beaten, yet suffered he the same patiently, nay rather joyfully, for the Lord's sake. Then when the judge saw that he would not with torments be overcome, nor be seduced from the Christian religion, he commanded him to be beheaded.

Now from England to return unto other countries where persecution did more vehemently rage.

Pitiless Galerius with his grand prefect Asclepiades invaded the city of Antioch, intending by force of arms to drive all Christians to renounce utterly their pure religion. The Christians were at that time congregated together, to whom one Romanus hastily ran, declaring that the wolves were at hand which would devour the Christian flock; 'But fear not,' said he, 'neither let this imminent peril disturb you, my brethren.' Brought was it to pass, by the great grace of God working in Romanus, that old men and matrons, fathers and mothers, young men and maidens, were all of one will and mind, most ready to shed their blood in defence of their Christian profession.

Word was brought unto the prefect, that the band of armed soldiers was not able to wrest the staff of faith out of the hand of the armed congregation, and all by reason that Romanus so mightily did encourage them, that they stuck not to offer their naked throats, wishing gloriously to die for the name of their Christ. 'Seek out that rebel,' quoth the prefect, 'and bring him to me, that he may answer for the whole sect.' Apprehended he was, and, bound as a sheep appointed to the slaughter-house, was presented to the emperor, who, with wrathful countenance beholding him, said: 'What! art thou the author of this sedition? Art thou the cause why so many shall lose their lives? By the gods I swear thou shalt smart for it, and first in thy flesh shalt thou suffer the pains whereunto thou hast encouraged the hearts of thy fellows.'

Romanus answered, 'Thy sentence, O prefect, I joyfully embrace; I refuse not to be sacrificed for my brethren, and that by as cruel means as thou mayest invent: and whereas thy soldiers were repelled from the Christian congregation, that so happened, because it lay not in idolaters and wor-shippers of devils, to enter into the holy house of God, and to pollute the place of true prayer.'

Then Asclepiades, wholly inflamed with this stout answer, commanded him to be trussed up, and his bowels drawn out. The executioners themselves more pitiful at heart than the prefect, said, 'Not so, sir, this man is of noble parentage; unlawful it is to put a nobleman to so unnoble a death.' 'Scourge him then with whips,' quoth the prefect, 'with knaps of lead at the ends.' Instead of tears, sighs, and groans, Romanus sang psalms all the time of his whipping, requiring them not to favour him for nobility's sake. 'Not the blood of my progenitors,' said he, 'but Christian profession maketh me noble. The wholesome words of the martyr were as oil to the fire of the prefect's fury. The more the martyr spake, the madder was he, insomuch that he commanded the martyr's sides to be lanced with knives, until the bones appeared white again.

The second time Romanus preached the living God, the Lord Jesus Christ His well-beloved Son, and eternal life through faith in His blood, Asclepiades commanded the tormentors to strike Romanus on the mouth, that his teeth being stricken out, his pronunciation at leastwise might be impaired. The commandment was obeyed, his face buffeted, his eyelids torn with their nails, his cheeks scotched with knives; the skin of his beard was plucked by little and little from the flesh; finally, his seemly face was wholly defaced. The meek martyr said, 'I thank thee, O prefect, that thou hast opened unto me many mouths, whereby I may preach my Lord and Saviour Christ. Look; how many wounds I have, so many mouths I have lauding and praising God.'

The prefect astonished with this singular constancy, commanded them to cease from the tortures. He threateneth cruel fire, he revileth the noble martyr, he blasphemeth God, saying, 'Thy crucified Christ is but a yesterday's God; the gods of the Gentiles are of most antiquity.'

Here again Romanus, taking good occasion, made a long oration of the eternity of Christ, of His human nature, of the death and satisfaction of Christ for all mankind. Which done, he said, 'Give me a child, O prefect, but seven years of age, which age is free from malice and other vices wherewith riper age is commonly infected, and thou shalt hear what he will say.' His request was granted.

A little boy was called out of the multitude, and

set before him. 'Tell me, my babe,' quoth the martyr, 'whether thou think it reason that we should worship one Christ, and in Christ one Father, or else that we worship many gods?'

Unto whom the babe answered, 'That certainly (whatsoever it be) which men affirm to be God, must needs be one; and that which pertains to that one, is unique: and inasmuch as Christ is unique, of necessity Christ must be the true God; for that there be many gods, we children cannot believe.'

The prefect hereat clean amazed, said, 'Thou young villain and traitor, where, and of whom learnedst thou this lesson?'

'Of my mother,' quoth the child, 'with whose milk I sucked in this lesson, that I must believe in Christ.' The mother was called, and she gladly appeared. The prefect commanded the child to be hoisted up and scourged. The pitiful beholders of this pitiless act, could not temper themselves from tears: the joyful and glad mother alone stood by with dry cheeks. Yea, she rebuked her sweet babe for craving a draught of cold water: she charged him to thirst after the cup that the infants of Bethlehem once drank of, forgetting their mothers' milk and paps; she willed him to remember little Isaac, who, beholding the sword wherewith, and the altar whereon, he should be sacrificed, willingly proffered his tender neck to the dint of his father's sword. Whilst this council was in giving, the butcherly tormentor plucked the skin from the crown of his head, hair and all. The mother cried, 'Suffer, my child! anon thou shalt pass to Him that will adorn thy naked head with a crown of eternal glory.' The mother counselleth, the child is counselled; the mother encourageth, the babe is encouraged, and receiveth the stripes with smiling countenance.

The prefect perceiving the child invincible, and himself vanquished, committeth the blessed babe to the stinking prison, commanding the torments of Romanus to be renewed and increased, as chief author of this evil.

Thus was Romanus brought forth again to new stripes, the punishments to be renewed and received again upon his old sores. No longer could the tyrant forbear, but needs he must draw nearer to the sentence of death. 'Is it painful to thee,' saith he, 'to tarry so long alive? A flaming fire, doubt thou not, shall be prepared for thee by and by, wherein thou and that boy, thy fellow in rebellion, shall be consumed into ashes.' Romanus and the babe were led to execution. When they were come to the place, the tormentors required the child of the mother, for she had taken it up in her arms; and she, only kissing it, delivered the babe. 'Farewell,' she said, 'my sweet child; and when thou hast entered the kingdom of Christ, there in thy blest estate remember thy mother.' And as the hangman applied his sword to the babe's neck, she sang on this manner:

> All laud and praise with heart and voice,
>   O Lord, we yield to thee:
> To whom the death of this thy saint,
>   We know most dear to be.

The innocent's head being cut off, the mother wrapped it up in her garment, and laid it on her breast. On the other side a mighty fire was made, whereinto Romanus was cast, whereupon a great storm arose and quenched the fire. The prefect at length being confounded with the fortitude and courage of the martyr, straitly commanded him to be brought back into the prison, and there to be strangled.

THE STORY OF CONSTANTINE THE GREAT

IN the beginning of the tenth persecution, Dioclesian, being made emperor, took to him Maximian. These two, governing as emperors together, chose out two other Cæsars under them, to wit, Galerius and Constantius, the father of Constantine the Great.

Thus then Dioclesian, reigning with Maximian, in the nineteenth year of his reign began his furious persecution against the Christians, whose reign after the same continued not long. For it pleased God to put such a snaffle in the tyrant's mouth, that within two years after, he caused both him and Maximian to give over their imperial function, and so remain not as emperors any more, but as private persons.

They being now dispossessed, the imperial dominion remained with Constantius and Galerius, which two divided the whole monarchy between them : so that Galerius should govern the east countries, and Constantius the west parts. But Constantius, as a modest prince, refused Italy and Africa, contenting himself with France, Spain, and Britain, refusing the other kingdoms for the troublesome and difficult government of the same.

Galerius chose to him Maximian and Severus, as Cæsars. Likewise Constantius took Constantine his son Cæsar under him.

THE STORY OF CONSTANTINE

In the meantime, while Galerius with his two Cæsars were in Asia, the Roman soldiers set up for their emperor Maxentius, the son of Maximian who had before deposed himself. Against whom Galerius the emperor of the East sent his son Severus, which Severus in the same voyage was slain of Maxentius; in whose place then Galerius took Licinius.

And these were the emperors and Cæsars, who, succeeding after Dioclesian and Maximian, prosecuted the rest of that persecution, which Dioclesian and Maximian before began, during near the space of seven or eight years, which was to the year of our Lord 313; save only that Constantius, with his son Constantine, was no great doer therein, but rather a maintainer and a supporter of the Christians.

Which Constantius was a prince, very excellent, civil, meek, gentle, liberal, and desirous to do good unto those that had any private authority under him. And as Cyrus once said, that he got treasure for himself when he made friends rich, even so it is said that Constantius would oftentimes say that it were better that his subjects had the public wealth than he to have it hoarded in his own treasure-house. Also he was by nature sufficed with a little, insomuch that he used to eat and drink in earthen vessels (which thing was counted in Agathocles the Sicilian a great commendation); and if at any time cause required to garnish his table, he would send for plate and other furniture to his friends. In consequence of which virtues ensued great peace and tranquillity in all his provinces.

To these virtues he added a yet more worthy ornament, that is, devotion, love, and affection

40

towards the Word of God. By which Word being guided, he neither levied any wars contrary to piety and Christian religion, neither aided he any others that did the same, neither destroyed he the churches, but commanded that the Christians should be preserved and defended, and kept safe from all contumelious injuries. And when in the other jurisdictions of the empire the churches were molested with persecution, he alone gave license unto the Christians to live after their accustomed manner.

Constantius minding at a certain time to try what sincere and good Christians he had yet in his court, called together all his officers and servants, feigning himself to choose out such as would do sacrifice to devils, and that those only should dwell there and keep their offices; and that those who would refuse to do the same, should be thrust out and banished the court. At this appointment, all the courtiers divided themselves into companies: the emperor marked who were the constantest and godliest from the rest. And when some said they would willingly do sacrifice, others openly and boldly refused to do the same; then the emperor sharply rebuked those who were so ready to do sacrifice, and judged them as false traitors unto God, accounting them unworthy to be in his court, who were such traitors to God; and forthwith commanded that they only should be banished the same. But greatly he commended those who refused to do sacrifice, and confessed God; affirming that they only were worthy to be about a prince; forthwith commanding that thenceforth they should be the trusty counsellors and defenders both of his person and kingdom; saying thus much more, that they only were worthy to be in office, whom he might make account of as his assured friends, and that he meant to have them in more estimation than the substance he had in his treasury.

Constantius died in the third year of the persecution, in the year of our Lord 306, and was buried at York. After whom succeeded Constantine, as a second Moses sent and set up of God, to deliver His people out of their so miserable captivity into liberty most joyful.

He, Constantine, was the good and virtuous child of a good and virtuous father; born in Britain. His mother was named Helena, daughter of king Coilus. He was a most bountiful and gracious prince, having a desire to nourish learning and good arts, and did oftentimes use to read, write, and study himself. He had marvellous good success and prosperous achieving of all things he took in hand, which then was (and truly) supposed to proceed of this, for that he was so great a favourer of the Christian faith. Which faith when he had once embraced, he did ever after most devoutly and religiously reverence.

As touching his natural disposition and wit, he was very eloquent, a good philosopher, and in disputation sharp and ingenious. He was accustomed to say that an emperor ought to refuse no labour for the utility of the common-weal. An empire was given by the determinate purpose of God; and he to whom it was given, should so employ his diligence, as that he might be thought worthy of the same at the hands of the Giver.

I showed before how Maxentius, the son of Maximian, was set up at Rome by the prætorian soldiers to be emperor. Whereunto the senate, although they were not consenting, yet, for fear, they were not resisting. Maximian his father, who had before deprived himself, hearing of this, took heart again to resume his dignity, and laboured to persuade Dioclesian to do the same: but when he could not move him thereunto, he repaireth to Rome, thinking to wrest the empire out of his son's hands. But when the soldiers would not suffer that, of a crafty purpose he flieth to Constantine in France, under pretence to complain of Maxentius his son, but in very deed to kill Constantine. That conspiracy being detected by Fausta, the daughter of Maximian, whom Constantine had married, Constantine through the grace of God was preserved, and Maximian retired back: in his flight he was apprehended, and put to death.

Maxentius all this while reigned at Rome with tyranny and wickedness intolerable, much like to another Pharaoh or Nero; for he slew the most part of his noblemen, and took from them their goods. And sometimes in his rage he would destroy great multitudes of the people of Rome by his soldiers. Also he left no mischievous nor lascivious act unattempted.

He was also much addicted to the art magical, which to execute he was more fit than for the imperial dignity. Often he would invocate devils in a secret manner, and by the answers of them he sought to repel the wars which he knew Constantine prepared against him. And to the end he might the better perpetrate his mischievous and wicked attempts, he feigned himself in the beginning of his reign to be a favourer of the Christians; and thinking to make the people of Rome his friends, he commanded that they should cease from persecuting the Christians. He himself abstained from no contumelious vexation of them, till that he began at the last to show himself an open persecutor of them.

The citizens and senators of Rome being much grieved and oppressed by the grievous tyranny and unspeakable wickedness of Maxentius sent their complaints with letters unto Constantine, with much suit and most hearty petitions, desiring him to help and release their country and city of Rome; who, hearing and understanding their miserable and pitiful state, and grieved therewith not a little, first sendeth by letters to Maxentius, desiring and exhorting him to restrain his corrupt doings and great cruelty. But when no letters nor exhortations would prevail, at length, pitying the woful case of the Romans, he gathered together his army in Britain and France, therewith to repress the violent rage of that tyrant.

Thus Constantine, sufficiently appointed with strength of men but especially with strength of God, entered his journey coming towards Italy, which was about the last year of the persecution, 313 A.D. Maxentius, understanding of the coming of Constantine, and trusting more to his devilish art of magic than to the good-will of his subjects, which he little deserved, durst not show himself out of the city, nor encounter him in the open field, but with privy garrisons laid wait for him by the way in sundry straits, as he should come; with whom Constantine had divers skirmishes, and by the power of the Lord did ever vanquish them and put them to flight.

THE SIGN OF THE CROSS

Notwithstanding, Constantine yet was in no great comfort, but in great care and dread in his mind (approaching now near unto Rome) for the magical charms and sorceries of Maxentius, wherewith he had vanquished before Severus, sent by Galerius against him. Wherefore, being in great doubt and perplexity in himself, and revolving many things in his mind, what help he might have against the operations of his charming, Constantine, in his journey drawing toward the city, and casting up his eyes many times to heaven, in the south part, about the going down of the sun, saw a great brightness in heaven, appearing in the similitude of a cross, giving this inscription, *In hoc vince*, that is, 'In this overcome.'

Eusebius Pamphilus doth witness that he had heard the said Constantine himself oftentimes report, and also to swear this to be true and certain, which he did see with his own eyes in heaven, and also his soldiers about him. At the sight whereof when he was greatly astonied, and consulting with his men upon the meaning thereof, behold, in the night season in his sleep, Christ appeared to him with the sign of the same cross which he had seen before, bidding him to make the figuration thereof, and to carry it in his wars before him, and so should he have the victory.

Wherein is to be noted, good reader, that this sign of the cross, and these letters added withal *In hoc vince*, was given to him of God, not to induce any superstitious worship or opinion of the cross, as though the cross itself had any such power or strength in it, to obtain victory; but only to bear the meaning of another thing, that is, to be an admonition to him to seek and inspire to the knowledge and faith of Him Who was crucified upon the cross, for the salvation of him and of all the world, and so to set forth the glory of His name.

The day following this vision, Constantine caused a cross after the same figuration to be made of gold and precious stone, and to be borne before him instead of his standard; and so with much hope of victory, and great confidence, as one armed from heaven, he speedeth himself toward his enemy. Against whom Maxentius, being constrained perforce to issue out of the city, sendeth all his power to join with him in the field beyond the river Tiber; where Maxentius, craftily breaking down the Bridge called 'Pons Milvius,' caused another deceitful bridge to be made of boats and wherries, being joined together and covered over with boards and planks, in manner of a bridge, thinking therewith to take Constantine as in a trap.

But herein came to pass, that which in the seventh Psalm is written. 'He made a pit and digged it, and is fallen into the ditch which he made; his mischief shall return upon his own head, and his violent dealing shall come down upon his own pate:' which here in this Maxentius was rightly verified; for after the two hosts did meet, he, being not able to sustain the force of Constantine fighting under the cross of Christ against him, was put to such a flight, and driven to such an exigence, that, in retiring back upon the same bridge which he did lay for Constantine (for haste, thinking to get the city), he was overturned by the fall of his horse into the bottom of the flood; and there with the weight of his armour he was drowned: and his host drowned in the Red Sea. Pharaoh not unaptly seemeth to bear a prophetical figuration of this Maxentius.

For as the children of Israel were in long thraldom and persecution in Egypt till the drowning of their last persecutor; so was this Maxentius the last persecutor in the Roman monarchy of the Christians; whom this Constantine, fighting under the cross of Christ did vanquish, setting the Christians at liberty; who before had been persecuted now three hundred years in Rome.

In histories we read of many victories and great conquests gotten, yet we never read, nor ever shall, of any victory so wholesome, so commodious, so opportune to mankind as this was; which made an end of so much bloodshed, and obtained so much liberty and life to the posterity of so many generations.

Constantine so established the peace of the Church, that for the space of a thousand years we read of no set persecution against the Christians, unto the time of John Wickliff.

So happy, so glorious was this victory of Constantine, surnamed the Great. For the joy and gladness whereof, the citizens who had sent for him before, with exceeding triumph brought him into the city of Rome, where he was most honourably received, and celebrated the space of seven days together; having, moreover, in the market-place, his image set up, holding in his right hand the sign of the cross, with this inscription: 'With this wholesome sign, the true token of fortitude, I have rescued and delivered our city from the yoke of the tyrant.'

THE STORY OF CONSTANTINE

Constantine, with his fellow Licinius eftsoons set forth their general proclamation not constraining any man to any religion, but giving liberty to all men, both for the Christians to persist in their profession without any danger, and for other men freely to adjoin with them, whosoever pleased. Which thing was very well taken, and highly allowed of the Romans and all wise men.

I doubt not, good reader, but thou dost right well consider with thyself the marvellous working of God's mighty power; to see so many emperors confederate together against the Lord and Christ His anointed, who, having the subjection of the whole world under their dominion, did bend their whole might and devices to extirpate the name of Christ, and of all Christians. Wherein, if the power of man could have prevailed, what could they not do? or what could they do more than they did? If policy or devices could have served, what policy was there lacking? If torments or pains of death could have helped, what cruelty of torment by man could be invented which was not attempted? If laws, edicts, proclamations, written not only in tables, but engraven in brass, could have stood, all this was practised against the weak Christians. And yet, notwithstanding, to see how no counsel can stand against the Lord, note how all these be gone, and yet Christ and his Church doth stand.

JOHN WICKLIFF, THE MORNING STAR OF THE REFORMATION

ALTHOUGH it be manifest that there were divers before Wickliff's time, who have wrestled and laboured in the same cause and quarrel that our countryman Wicliff hath done, whom the Holy Ghost hath from time to time raised and stirred up in the Church of God, something to work against the bishop of Rome, to weaken the pernicious superstition of the friars, and to vanquish and overthrow the great errors which daily did grow and prevail in the world, yet notwithstanding, forsomuch as they are not many in number, neither very famous or notable, we will begin with the story of John Wickliff; at whose time this furious fire of persecution seemed to take his first original and beginning. Through God's providence stepped forth into the arena the valiant champion of the truth, John Wickliff, our countryman, whom the Lord raised up here in England, to detect more fully and amply the poison of the Pope's doctrine and false religion.

Wickliff, being the public reader of divinity in the University of Oxford, was, for the rude time wherein he lived, famously reputed for a great clerk, a deep schoolman, and no less expert in all kinds of philosophy; the which doth not only appear by his own most famous and learned writings, but also by the confession of Walden, his most cruel and bitter enemy, who in a certain epistle written unto Pope Martin V. saith, ' that he was wonderfully astonished at his most strong arguments, with the places of authority which he had gathered, with the vehemency and force of his reasons.'

It appeareth that this Wickcliff flourished about A.D. 1371, Edward III. reigning in England. This is out of all doubt, that at what time all the world was in most desperate and vile estate, and the lamentable ignorance and darkness of God's truth had overshadowed the whole earth, this man stepped forth like a valiant champion, unto whom that may justly be applied which is spoken of one Simon, the son of Onias : ' Even as the morning star being in the midst of a cloud, and as the moon being full in her course, and as the bright beams of the sun; so doth he shine and glister in the temple and Church of God.'

In these days the whole state of religion was depraved and corrupted: the name only of Christ remained amongst Christians, but His true and lively doctrine was as far unknown to the most part as His name was common to all men. As touching faith, consolation, the end and use of the law, the office of Christ, our impotency and weakness, the Holy Ghost, the greatness and strength of sin, true works, grace and free justification by faith, the liberty of a Christian man, there was almost no mention.

The world, forsaking the lively power of God's spiritual Word, was altogether led and blinded with outward ceremonies and human traditions; in these was all the hope of obtaining salvation fully fixed; insomuch that scarcely any other thing was seen in the temples or churches, taught or spoken of in sermons, or finally intended or gone about in their whole life, but only heaping up of certain shadowy ceremonies upon ceremonies; neither was there any end of this their heaping.

The Church did fall into all kind of extreme tyranny; whereas the poverty and simplicity of Christ were changed into cruelty and abomination of life. With how many bonds and snares of ceremonies were the consciences of men, redeemed by Christ to liberty, ensnared and snarled! The Christian people were wholly carried away as it were by the nose, with mere decrees and constitutions of men, even whither it pleased the bishops to lead them, and not as Christ's will did direct them. The simple and unlearned people, being far from all knowledge of the holy Scripture, thought it quite enough for them to know only those things which were delivered them by their pastors; and they, on the other part, taught in a manner nothing else but such things as came forth of the court of Rome; whereof the most part tended to the profit of their order, more than to the glory of Christ.

What time there seemed to be no spark of pure doctrine remaining, this aforesaid Wickliff, by God's providence, sprang up, through whom the Lord would first waken and raise up again the world, which was drowned and whelmed in the deep streams of human traditions.

This Wickliff, perceiving the true doctrine of Christ's Gospel to be adulterated and defiled with so many filthy inventions and dark errors of bishops and monks, after long debating and deliberating with himself (with many secret sighs, and bewailing in his mind the general ignorance of the whole world), could no longer abide the same, and at the last determined with himself to help and to remedy such things as he saw to be wide, and out of the way.

This holy man took great pains, protesting, as they said, openly in the schools, that it was his principal purpose to call back the Church from her idolatry, especially in the matter of the sacrament of the body and blood of Christ. But this boil or sore could not be touched without the great grief and pain of the whole world : for, first of all, the whole glut of monks and begging friars was set in a rage and madness, who, even as hornets with their sharp stings, did assail this good man on every side ; fighting, as is said, for their altars, paunches, and bellies. After them the priests and bishops, and then after them the archbishop, being then Simon Sudbury, took the matter in hand ; who, for the same cause, deprived him of his benefice, which then he had in Oxford. At the last, when their power seemed not sufficient to withstand the truth which was then breaking out, they ran unto the lightnings and thunderbolts of the bishop of Rome, as it had been unto the last refuge of most force and strength. Notwithstanding, the said Wickliff, being somewhat friended and supported by the king, bore out the malice of the friars and of the archbishop ; John of Gaunt, Duke of Lancaster, the king's son, and Lord Henry Percy, being his special maintainers.

The opinions for which Wickcliff was deprived, were these : That the Pope hath no more power to excommunicate any man, than hath another. That if it be given by any person to the Pope to excommunicate, yet to absolve the same is as much in the power of another priest, as in his. He affirmed, moreover, that neither the king, nor any temporal lord, could give any perpetuity to the Church, or to any ecclesiastical person; for that when such ecclesiastical persons do sin habitually, the temporal powers may meritoriously take away from them what before hath been bestowed upon them. And that he proved to have been practised before here in England by William Rufus; 'which thing' (said he) 'if he did lawfully, why may not the same also be practised now? If he did it unlawfully, then doth the Church err, and doth unlawfully in praying for him.'

Beside these opinions he began something nearly to touch the matter of the sacrament, proving that in the said sacrament the accidents of bread remained not without the subject, or substance, and that the simple and plain truth doth appear in the Scriptures, whereunto all human traditions, whatsoever they be, must be referred. The truth, as the poet speaketh very truly, had gotten John Wickliff great displeasure and hatred at many men's hands; especially of the monks and richest sort of priests.

Albeit, through the favour and supportation of the Duke of Lancaster and Lord Henry Percy, he persisted against their wolfish violence and cruelty: till at last, about A.D. 1377, the bishops, still urging and inciting their archbishop Simon Sudbury, who before had deprived him, and afterward prohibited him not to stir any more in those sorts of matters, had obtained, by process and order of citation, to have him brought before them.

The Duke, having intelligence that Wickliff should come before the bishops, fearing that he, being but one, was too weak against such a multitude, calleth to him, out of the orders of friars, four bachelors of divinity, out of every order one, to join them with Wickliff also, for more surety. When the day was come, assigned to the said Wickliff to appear, which day was Thursday, the nineteenth of February, he went, accompanied with the four friars aforesaid, and with them also the Duke of Lancaster, and Lord Henry Percy, Lord Marshal of England; the said Lord Percy going before them to make room and way where Wickliff should come.

Thus Wickliff, through the providence of God, being sufficiently guarded, was coming to the place where the bishops sat; whom, by the way, they animated and exhorted not to fear or shrink a whit at the company of the bishops there present, who were all unlearned, said they, in respect of him, neither that he should dread the concourse of the people, whom they would themselves assist and defend, in such sort as he should take no harm.

With these words, and with the assistance of the nobles, Wickliff, in heart encouraged, approached to the church of St Paul in London, where a main press of people was gathered to hear what should be said and done. Such was there the frequency and throng of the multitude, that the lords, for all the puissance of the High Marshal, with great difficulty could get way through; insomuch that the Bishop of London, whose name was William Courtney, seeing the stir that the Lord Marshal kept in the church among the people, speaking to the Lord Percy, said that if he had known before what masteries he would have kept in the church, he would have stopped him out from coming there; at which words of the bishop the duke, disdaining not a little, answered that he would keep such mastery there, though he said 'nay.'

At last, after much wrestling, they pierced through and came to Our Lady's Chapel, where the dukes and barons were sitting together with the archbishops and other bishops; before whom Wickliff, according to the manner, stood, to know what should be laid unto him. To whom first spake the Lord Percy, bidding him to sit down, saying that he had many things to answer to, and therefore had need of some softer seat. But the Bishop of London, cast eftsoons into a fumish chafe by those words, said he should not sit there. Neither was it, said he, according to law or reason, that he, who was cited there to appear to answer before his ordinary, should sit down during the time of his answer, but that he should stand. Upon these words a fire began to kindle between them; insomuch that they began so to rate and revile one the other, that the whole multitude, therewith disquieted, began to be set on a hurry.

Then the duke, taking the Lord Percy's part, with hasty words began also to take up the bishop. To whom the bishop again, nothing inferior in reproachful checks and rebukes, did render and requite not only to him as good as he brought, but also did so far excel in this railing art of scolding, that the duke blushed and was ashamed, because he could not overpass the bishop in brawling and railing, and, therefore, he fell to plain threatening; menacing the bishop, that he would bring down the pride, not only of him, but also of all the prelacy of England. 'Thou,' said he, 'bearest thyself so brag upon thy parents, who shall not be able to help thee; they shall have enough to do to help themselves'; for his parents were the Earl and Countess of Devonshire. To whom the bishop answered, that his confidence was not in his parents, nor in any man else, but only in God.

Then the duke softly whispering in the ear of him next by him, said that he would rather pluck the bishop by the hair of his head out of the church, than he would take this at his hand. This was not spoken so secretly, but that the Londoners overheard him. Whereupon, being set in a rage, they cried out, saying that they would not suffer their bishop so contemptuously to be abused. But rather they would lose their lives, than that he should so be drawn out by the hair. Thus that council, being broken with scolding and brawling for that day, was dissolved before nine o'clock.

After King Edward III. succeeded his son's son, Richard II., who was no great disfavourer of the way and doctrine of Wickliff. But the bishops now seeing the aged king to be taken away, during the time of whose old age all the government of the realm depended upon the Duke of Lancaster, and seeing the said duke, with the Lord Percy, the Lord Marshal, give over their offices, and remain in their private houses without intermeddling, thought now the time to serve them to have some vantage against John Wickliff; who hitherto, under the protection of the aforesaid duke and Lord Marshal, had some rest and quiet. Notwithstanding being by the bishops forbid to deal in doctrine any more, he continued yet with his fellows going barefoot and in long frieze gowns, preaching diligently unto the people. Out of whose sermons these articles were collected.

Articles collected out of Wickliff's sermons.

The holy eucharist, after the consecration, is not the very body of Christ.

The Church of Rome is not the head of all churches more than any other church is; nor that Peter had any more power given of Christ than any other apostle had.

The Pope of Rome hath no more in the keys of the Church than hath any other within the order of priesthood.

The Gospel is a rule sufficient of itself to rule the life of every Christian man here, without any other rule.

All other rules, under whose observances divers religious persons be governed, do add no more perfection to the Gospel, than doth the white colour to the wall.

Neither the Pope, nor any other prelate of the church, ought to have prisons wherein to punish transgressors.

Wickliff, albeit he was commanded by the bishops and prelates to keep silence, yet could not so be suppressed, but that through the vehemency of the truth he burst out afterwards much more fiercely. For he, having obtained the goodwill and favour of certain noblemen, attempted again to stir up his doctrine amongst the common people. Then began the Pharisees to swarm together striving against the light of the Gospel, which began to shine abroad; neither was the Pope himself behind with his part, for he never ceased with his bulls and letters to stir up them who otherwise, of their own accord, were but too furious and mad.

Accordingly, in the year of our Lord 1377, being the first year of King Richard II., Pope Gregory sendeth his bull directed unto the University of Oxford, rebuking them sharply, imperiously, and like a Pope, for suffering so long the doctrine of John Wickliff to take root, and not plucking it up with the crooked sickle of their catholic doctrine. Which bull, the proctors and masters of the University, joining together in consultation, stood long in doubt, deliberating with themselves whether to receive it with honour, or to refuse and reject it with shame.

The copy of this wild bull, sent to them from the Pope, was this : —

'It hath been intimated to us by many trustworthy persons that one John Wickliff, rector of Lutterworth, in the diocese of Lincoln, professor of divinity, hath gone to such a pitch of detestable folly, that he feareth not to teach, and publicly preach, or rather to vomit out of the filthy dungeon of his breast, certain erroneous and false propositions and conclusions, savouring even of heretical pravity, tending to weaken and overthrow the *status* of the whole Church, and even the secular government. These opinions he is circulating in the realm of England, so glorious for power and abundance of wealth, but still more so for the shining purity of its faith, and wont to produce men illustrious for their clear and sound knowledge of the Scriptures, ripe in gravity of manners, conspicuous for devotion, and bold defenders of the catholic faith; and some of Christ's flock he hath been defiling therewith, and misleading from the straight path of the sincere faith into the pit of perdition. Wherefore, being unwilling to connive at so deadly a pest, we strictly charge that by our authority you seize or cause to be seized the said John, and send him under trusty keeping to our venerable brethren the Archbishop of Canterbury and the Bishop of London, or either of them.'

I find, moreover, two other letters of the Pope concerning the same matter, the one directing that in case Wickliff could not be found, he should be warned by public citation to appear before the Pope at Rome within three months; the other exhorting the bishops that the King and the nobles of England should be admonished not to give any credit to the said John Wickliff, or to his doctrine.

The letters, being received from the Pope, the Archbishop of Canterbury and other bishops took no little heart; for, being encouraged by them, and pricked forward by their own fierceness and cruelty, it is to be marvelled at, with what boldness and stomach they did openly profess, before their provincial council, that all fear or favour set apart, no person, neither high nor low, should let them, neither would they be seduced by the entreaty of any man, neither by any threatenings or rewards, but that they would follow straight and upright justice and equity, yea, albeit that danger of life should follow thereupon. But these so fierce brags and stout promise, with the subtle practices of these bishops, who thought themselves so sure before, the Lord, against Whom no determination of man's counsel can prevail, by a small occasion did lightly confound and overthrow. For the day of the examination being come, a certain personage of the prince's court, and yet of no great noble birth, named Lewis Clifford, entering in among the bishops, commanded them that they should not proceed with any definite sentence against John Wickliff. With which words all they were so amazed, and their combs so cut, that they became mute and speechless. And thus, by the wondrous work of God's providence, John Wickliff escaped the second time out of the bishops' hands.

This good man ceased not to proceed in his godly purpose, labouring as he had begun; unto whom also, as it happened by the providence of God, this was a great help and stay, for that in the same year the aforesaid Pope Gregory XI. who was the stirrer up of all this trouble against him, turned up his heels and died. Whose death was not a little happy to Wickliff; for immediately after his decease there fell a great dissension between the Romish and the French Popes, and others succeeding them, one striving against another, that the schism thereof endured the space of thirty-nine years, until the time of the Council of Constance (A.D. 1417).

About the same time also, about three years after, there fell a cruel dissension in England, between the common people and the nobility, the which did not a little disturb and trouble the commonwealth. In this tumult Simon of Sudbury, Archbishop of Canterbury, was taken by the rustical and rude people, and was beheaded; in whose place succeeded William Courtney, who was no less diligent in rooting out heretics. Notwithstanding, Wickliff's sect daily grew to greater force, until the time that William Berton, Chancellor of Oxford, about A.D. 1381, had the whole rule of that University : who, calling together eight monastical doctors and four others, and putting the common seal of the University unto certain writings, set forth an edict, declaring that no man, under a grievous penalty, should be so hardy hereafter to associate themselves with any of Wickliff's abettors or favourers; and unto Wickliff himself he threatened the greater excommunication and farther imprisonment, and to all his fautors, unless that they after three-days' admonition or warning, canonical and peremptory (as they call it), did repent and amend. The which thing when Wickliff understood, forsaking the Pope and all the clergy, he thought to appeal unto the King's majesty ; but the Duke of Lancaster coming between forbade him, saying that he ought rather to submit himself unto the censure and judgment of his ordinary. Whereby Wickliff being beset with troubles and vexations, as it were in the midst of the waves, was forced once again to make confession of his doctrine.

Here is not to be passed over the great miracle of God's divine admonition or warning; for when the archbishop and suffragans, with the other doctors of divinity and lawyers, with a great company of babbling friars and religious persons, were gathered together to consult touching John Wickliff's books, when they were gathered together at the Black-Friars in London to begin their business upon St Dunstan's day, after dinner, about two of the clock, the very hour and instant that they should go forward, a wonderful and terrible earthquake fell throughout all England: whereupon divers of the suffragans, being affrighted by the strange and wonderful demonstration, doubting what it should mean, thought it good to leave off from their determinate purpose. But the archbishop (as chief captain of that army, more rash and bold than wise) interpreting the chance which had happened clean contrary to another meaning or purpose, did confirm and strengthen their hearts and minds, which were almost daunted with fear, stoutly to go forward in their attempted enterprise ; who then discoursing Wickliff's articles, not according unto the sacred canons of the holy Scripture, but unto their own private affections and men's traditions, gave sentence that some of them were simply and plainly heretical, others were erroneous, others irreligious, some seditious and not consonant to the Church of Rome.

Besides the earthquake aforesaid, there happened another strange and wonderful chance, sent by God, and no less to be marked than the other, if it be true, that was reported by John Huss's enemies. These enemies of his, amongst other principal points of his accusation, laid this to his charge at the Council of Constance ; that he should say openly unto the people as touching Wickliff, that at what time a great number of religious men and doctors were gathered together in a certain church to dispute against Wickliff, suddenly, the door of the church was broken open with lightning, in such sort, that his enemies hardly escaped without hurt. This thing, albeit that it were objected against Huss by his adversaries, yet, forsomuch as he did not deny the same, neither, if he so said, it seemeth that he

would speak it without some ground or reason, I
have not thought it good to leave clean out of
memory.

Of like credit is this also, which is reported of
Wickliff, that when he was lying very sick at London, certain friars came unto him to counsel him;
and when they had babbled much unto him touching
the catholic church, the acknowledging of his errors,
and the bishop of Rome, Wickliff, being moved
with the foolishness and absurdity of their talk, with
a stout stomach, setting himself upright in his bed,
repeated this saying out of the Psalms [cxviii. 17],
"I shall not die, but I shall live, and declare the
works of the Lord."

The Mandate of the Archbishop of Canterbury
   directed to the Bishop of London, against John
   Wickliff and his Adherents.

It is come to our hearing, that although, by the
canonical sanctions, no man, being forbidden or not
sent, ought to usurp to himself the office of
preaching, publicly or privily, without the authority
of the apostolic see or of the bishop of the place;
yet notwithstanding, certain, being sons of perdition
under the veil of great sanctity, are brought into such
a doating mind, that they take upon them authority
to preach, and are not afraid to affirm, and teach,
and generally, commonly, and publicly to preach, as
well in the churches as in the streets, and also in
many other profane places of our said province,
certain propositions and conclusions, heretical, erroneous, and false, condemned by the Church of God,
and repugnant to the determinations of holy church;
who also infect therewith very many good Christians,

causing them lamentably to err from the catholic faith, without which there is no salvation.

We therefore admonish and warn that no man henceforth, of what estate or condition soever, do hold, teach, preach, or defend the aforesaid heresies and errors, or any of them; nor that he hear or hearken to any one preaching the said heresies or errors, or any of them; nor that he favour or adhere to him, either publicly or privily; but that immediately he shun and avoid him, as he would avoid a serpent putting forth pestiferous poison; under pain of the greater curse.

And furthermore, we command our fellow-brethren, that of such presumptions they carefully and diligently inquire, and do proceed effectually against the same.

The chancellor the same time in Oxford was Master Robert Rygge; who, as it seemeth, favouring Wicklift's part, as much as he could or durst, many times dissembled and cloked certain matters, and oftentimes (as opportunity would serve) holpe forward the cause of the Gospel, which was then in great danger. When the time was come, that there must needs be sermons made unto the people, he committed the whole doings thereof to such as he knew to be greatest favourers of John Wickliff. The two proctors were John Huntman and Walter Dish; who then, as far as they durst, favoured the cause of John Wickliff. Insomuch that the same time and year, which was A.D. 1382, when certain public sermons should be appointed customably at the feast of the Ascension and of Corpus Christi to be preached in the cloister of St Frideswide (now

called Christ's Church), before the people, by the
chancellor aforesaid and the proctors, the doings
hereof the chancellor and proctors had committed to
Philip Reppyngdon and Nicholas Hereford.

Hereford, beginning, was noted to defend John
Wickliff openly, to be a faithful, good, and innocent
man; for the which no small ado with outcries was
among the friars. This Hereford, after he had long
favoured and maintained Wickliff's part, grew in
suspicion amongst the enemies of the truth; for as
soon as he began somewhat liberally and freely to
utter any thing which tended to the defence of
Wickliff, by-and-by the Carmelites and all the orders
of religion were on his top, and laid not a few
heresies unto his charge, the which they had strained
here and there out of his sermons, through the
industry of one Peter Stokes, a Carmelite, a kind
of people prone to mischief, uproars, debate, and
dissension, as though they were born for that
purpose. Much like thing do divers writers write
of the nature of certain spiders; that whatsoever
pleasant juice is in herbs, they suck it out, and
convert it into poison. But these cowled merchants
in this behalf do pass all the spiders, for whatsoever
is worst and most pestilent in a man, that do they
hunt out for, and with their teeth even, as it were,
gnaw it out; and of the opinions which be good,
and agreeable with verity, they do make schisms and
heresies.

After this, the feast of Corpus Christi drew near,
upon which day it was looked for that Reppyngdon
should preach, who in the schools had shown
forth and uttered that which he had long hidden
and dissembled, protesting openly that in all moral

matters he would defend Wickliff; but as touching
the sacrament, he would as yet hold his peace,
until such time as the Lord should illuminate the
hearts and minds of the clergy. When the friars
understood that this man should preach shortly,
these Babylonians, fearing lest that he would scarce
civilly or gently rub the galls of their religion,
convented with the Archbishop of Canterbury, that
the same day, a little before Philip should preach,
Wickliff's conclusions, which were privately condemned, should be openly defamed in the presence
of the whole University; the doing of which
matter was committed to Peter Stokes, friar,
standard-bearer and chief champion against Wickliff.

The chancellor having received the archbishop's
letters and perceived the malicious enterprise of the
Carmelite, was wonderfully moved against him, and
falling out with him and his like (not without cause)
for troubling the state of the University, said that
neither the bishop nor the archbishop had any
power over that University, nor should not have, in
the determination of any heresies. And afterward
taking deliberation, calling together the proctors,
with other regents and non-regents, he did openly
affirm that he would by no means help the Carmelite
in his doings.

These things thus done, Reppyngdon at the hour
appointed proceeded to his sermon; in the which,
he was reported to have uttered 'that in all moral
matters he would defend Master Wickliff as a true
catholic doctor. Moreover, that the Duke of
Lancaster was very earnestly affected and minded in
this matter, and would that all such should be
received under his protection'; besides many things

more, which touched the praise and defence of Wickliff.

When the sermon was done, Reppyngdon entered into St Frideswide's Church, accompanied with many of his friends, who, as the enemies surmised, were privily weaponed under their garments. Friar Stokes, the Carmelite, suspecting all this to be against him, and being afraid of hurt, kept himself within the sanctuary of the church, not daring to put out his head. The chancellor and Reppyngdon, friendly saluting one another in the church-porch, sent away the people, and so departed every man home to his own house. There was not a little joy throughout the whole University for that sermon.

John Wickliff returning again within short space, either from his banishment, or from some other place where he was secretly kept, repaired to his parish of Lutterworth, where he was parson; and there, quietly departing this mortal life, slept in peace in the Lord, in the end of the year 1384, upon Silvester's day. It appeareth that he was well aged before he departed, 'and that the same thing pleased him in his old age, which did please him being young.'

This Wickliff, albeit in his life-time he had many grievous enemies, yet was there none so cruel to him, as the clergy itself. Yet, notwithstanding, he had many good friends, men not only of the meaner sort, but also of the nobility, amongst whom these men are to be numbered, John Clenbon, Lewes Clifford, Richard Stury, Thomas Latimer, William Nevil, and John Montague, who plucked down all the images in his church. Besides all these, there was the Earl of Salisbury, who, for contempt in him noted towards the sacrament, in carrying it home to his house, was enjoined by Ralph Ergom, Bishop of Salisbury, to make in Salisbury a cross of stone, in which all the story of the matter should be written: and he, every Friday during his life, to come to the cross barefoot, and bareheaded in his shirt, and there kneeling upon his knees do penance for his deed.

And for the residue, we will declare what cruelty they used not only against the books and articles of John Wickliff, but also in burning his body and bones, commanding them to be taken up many years after he was buried; as appeareth by the decree of the synod of Constance, A.D. 1415, 'This holy synod declareth, determineth, and giveth sentence, that John Wickliff was a notorious heretic, and that he died obstinate in his heresy; cursing alike him and condemning his memory. This synod also decreeth and ordaineth that his body and bones, if they might be discerned from the bodies of other faithful people, should be taken out of the ground, and thrown away far from the burial of any church, according as the canons and laws enjoin.' This wicked and malicious sentence of the synod would require here a diligent apology, but that it is so foolish and vain, and no less barbarous, that it seemeth more worthy of derision and disdain, than by any argument to be confuted.

What Heraclitus would not laugh, or what Democritus would not weep, to see these so sage and reverend Catos occupying their heads to take up a poor man's body, so long dead and buried; and yet, peradventure, they were not able to find his right bones, but took up some other body, and so of a catholic made a heretic! Albeit, herein

Wickliff had some cause to give them thanks, that they would at least spare him till he was dead, and also give him so long respite after his death, forty-one years [1] to rest in his sepulchre before they ungraved him, and turned him from earth to ashes; which ashes they also took and threw into the river. And so was he resolved into three elements, earth, fire, and water, thinking thereby utterly to extinguish and abolish both the name and doctrine of Wickliff for ever. Not much unlike the example of the old Pharisees and sepulchre-knights, who, when they had brought the Lord unto the grave, thought to make him sure never to rise again. But these and all others must know that, as there is no counsel against the Lord, so there is no keeping down of verity, but it will spring up and come out of dust and ashes, as appeared right well in this man; for though they digged up his body, burnt his bones, and drowned his ashes, yet the Word of God and the truth of his doctrine, with the fruit and success thereof, they could not burn.

[1] The decree of the synod was not carried out until after the lapse of several years from its meeting.

A LEADER OF THE LOLLARDS: THE TROUBLE AND PERSECUTION OF THE MOST VALIANT AND WORTHY MARTYR OF CHRIST, SIR JOHN OLDCASTLE, KNIGHT, LORD COBHAM.

AFTER that the true servant of Jesus Christ, John Wickliff, a man of very excellent life and learning, had, for the space of more than twenty-six years, most valiantly battled with the great Antichrist of Europe, or Pope of Rome, and his diversely disguised host of anointed hypocrites, to restore the Church to the pure estate that Christ left her in at His ascension, he departed hence most Christianly in the hands of God, the year of our Lord 1384, and was buried in his own parish church at Lutterworth, in Leicestershire.

No small number of godly disciples left that good man behind him, to defend the lowliness of the Gospel against the exceeding pride, ambition, simony, avarice, hypocrisy, sacrilege, tyranny, idolatrous worshippings, and other filthy fruits, of those stiff-necked pharisees; against whom Thomas Arundel, the Archbishop of Canterbury (as fierce as ever was Pharaoh, Antiochus, Herod, or Caiaphas) collected, in Paul's church at London, a universal synod of all the papistical clergy of England, in the year of our Lord 1413 (as he had done divers others before), to withstand their most godly enterprise.

The principal cause of the assembling thereof,

was to repress the growing and spreading of the Gospel, and especially to withstand the noble and worthy Lord Cobham, who was then noted to be a principal favourer, receiver, and maintainer of those whom the bishop named Lollards; especially in the dioceses of London, Rochester, and Hereford, setting them up to preach whom the bishops had not licensed, and sending them about to preach : holding also and teaching opinions of the sacraments, of images, of pilgrimage, of the keys and church of Rome, repugnant to the received determination of the Romish Church. It was concluded among them, that, without any further delay, process should be awarded out against him, as against a most pernicious heretic.

Some of that fellowship who were of more crafty experience than the others, thought it not best to have the matter so rashly handled, but by some preparation made thereunto beforehand: considering the said Lord Cobham was a man of great birth, and in favour at that time with the King, their counsel was to know first the King's mind. This counsel was well accepted, and thereupon the archbishop, Thomas Arundel, with his other bishops, and a great part of the clergy, went straitways unto the King then remaining at Kennington, and there laid forth most grievous complaints against the said Lord Cobham, to his great infamy and blemish: being a man right godly. The King gently heard those blood-thirsty prelates, and far otherwise than became his princely dignity: notwithstanding requiring, and instantly desiring them, that in respect of his noble stock and knighthood, they should yet favourably deal with him; and that they would, if it were possible, without all rigour or extreme handling, reduce him again to the Church's unity. He promised them also, that in case they were contented to take some deliberation, he himself would seriously commune the matter with him.

Anon after, the King sent for the said Lord Cobham, and as soon as he was come, he called him secretly, admonishing him betwixt him and him, to submit himself to his mother the Holy Church, and, as an obedient child, to acknowledge himself culpable.

Unto whom the Christian knight made this answer: 'You, most worthy prince,' saith he, 'I am always prompt and willing to obey, forasmuch as I know you a Christian king, and the appointed minister of God, bearing the sword to the punishment of evil doers, and for safeguard of them that be virtuous. Unto you, next my eternal God, owe I my whole obedience, and submit thereunto, as I have done ever, all that I have, either of fortune or nature, ready at all times to fulfil whatsoever ye shall in the Lord command me. But, as touching the Pope and his spirituality, I owe them neither suit nor service, forasmuch as I know him, by the Scriptures, to be the great Antichrist, the son of perdition, the open adversary of God, and the abomination standing in the holy place.'

When the King had heard this, with such like sentences more, he would talk no longer with him, but left him so utterly.

And as the archbishop resorted again unto the King for an answer, he gave him his full authority to cite him, examine him, and punish him, according to their devilish decrees, which they called 'The Laws of Holy Church.' But forasmuch as the Lord

THE FURY OF ANTICHRIST

Cobham did not appear at the day appointed, the archbishop condemned him of most deep contumacy. After that, when he had been falsely informed by his hired spies, and other glozing glaverers, that the said Lord Cobham had laughed him to scorn, disdained all his doings, maintained his old opinions, contemned the Church's power, the dignity of a bishop, and the order of priesthood (for of all these was he then accused), in his moody madness, without just proof, did he openly excommunicate him.

This most constant servant of the Lord, and worthy knight, Sir John Oldcastle, the Lord Cobham, beholding the unpeaceable fury of Antichrist thus kindled against him, perceiving himself compassed on every side with deadly dangers, took paper and pen in hand, and wrote a confession of his faith, both signing and sealing it with his own hand: wherein he answered to the four chief articles that the archbishop laid against him. That done, he took the copy with him, and went therewith to the King, trusting to find mercy and favour at his hand.

The King would in no case receive it, but commanded it to be delivered unto them that should be his judges. Then desired he, in the King's presence, that a hundred knights and esquires might be suffered to come in upon his purgation, who he knew would clear him of all heresies. Moreover he offered himself, after the law of arms, to fight for life or death with any man living, Christian or heathen, in the quarrel of his faith; the King and the lords of his council excepted. Finally, with all gentleness, he protested before all that were present that he would refuse no manner of correction that

should, after the laws of God, be ministered unto
him; but that he would at all times, with all meekness, obey it.

Notwithstanding all this the King suffered him
to be summoned personally in his own privy chamber.
Then said the Lord Cobham to the King, that he
had appealed from the archbishop to the Pope of
Rome, and therefore he ought, he said, in no case
to be his judge. And having his appeal there at
hand ready written, he showed it with all reverence
to the King; wherewith the King was then much
more displeased than afore, and said angrily to him,
that he should not pursue his appeal; but rather he
should tarry in hold, till such time as it were of the
Pope allowed. And then, would he or nild he, the
archbishop should be his judge.

Thus was there nothing allowed that the good
Lord Cobham had lawfully required ; but, forasmuch
as he would not be sworn in all things to submit
himself to the Church, and so take what penance
the archbishop would enjoin him, he was arrested at
the King's commandment, and led forth to the Tower
of London.

When the day of examination was come, which
was the 23rd day of September, the Saturday after
the feast of St Matthew, Thomas Arundel, the
Archbishop, sat in Caiaphas' room, in the chapter-
house of Paul's, with Richard Clifford, Bishop of
London, and Henry Bolingbrook, Bishop of
Winchester. Sir Robert Morley, knight, and
lieutenant of the Tower, brought before him the
said Lord Cobham, and there left him for the time ;
unto whom the archbishop said these words: 'Sir
John, in the last general convocation of the clergy

of this our province, ye were detected of certain heresies, and, by sufficient witnesses, found culpable : whereupon ye were, by form of spiritual law, cited, and would in no case appear. Upon your rebellious contumacy ye were both privately and openly excommunicated. Notwithstanding we neither yet showed ourselves unready to have given you absolution (nor yet do to this hour), would ye have meekly asked it.'

Unto whom the Lord Cobham said that he desired no absolution ; but he would gladly, before him and his brethren, make rehearsal of that faith which he held and intended always to stand to. And then he took out of his bosom a certain writing concerning the articles whereof he was accused, and read it before them.

'As for images, I understand that they be not of belief, but that they were ordained since the belief of Christ was given by sufferance of the Church, to represent and bring to mind the passion of our Lord Jesus Christ, and martyrdom and good living of other saints : and that whoso it be, that doth the worship to dead images that is due to God, or putteth such hope or trust in help of them, as he should do to God, or hath affection in one more than in another, he doth in that, the greatest sin of idol worship.

'Also I suppose this fully, that every man in this earth is a pilgrim toward bliss, or toward pain ; and that he that knoweth not, ne will not know, ne keep the holy commandments of God in his living here (albeit that he go on pilgrimages to all the world, and he die so), he shall be damned : he that knoweth the holy commandments of God, and keepeth them to his end, he shall be saved, though he never in his life go on pilgrimage, as men now use, to Canterbury, or to Rome, or to any other place.'

Then counselled the archbishop with the other two bishops and with divers of the doctors, what was to be done; commanding him, for the time, to stand aside. In conclusion, by their assent and information, he said thus unto him: 'Come hither, Sir John: ye must declare us your mind more plainly. As thus, whether ye hold, affirm, and believe, that in the sacrament of the altar, after the consecration rightly done by a priest, remaineth material bread, or not? Moreover, whether ye do hold, affirm, and believe, that, as concerning the sacrament of penance (where a competent number of priests are), every Christian man is necessarily bound to be confessed of his sins to a priest ordained by the church, or not?'

This was the answer of the good Lord Cobham: that none otherwise would he declare his mind, nor yet answer unto his articles, than was expressly in his writing there contained.

Then said the archbishop again unto him: 'Sir John, beware what ye do; for if ye answer not clearly to those things that are here objected against you, the law of holy church is that we may openly proclaim you a heretic.'

Unto whom he gave this answer: 'Do as ye shall think best.' Wherewith the bishops and prelates were amazed and wonderfully disquieted.

At last the archbishop again declared unto him, what the Holy Church of Rome, following the saying of St Augustine, St Jerome, St Ambrose, and of the holy doctors, had determined in these matters : no manner of mention once made of Christ ! 'which determination,' saith he, 'ought all Christian men both to believe and to follow.'

Then said the Lord Cobham unto him, that he would gladly both believe and observe whatsoever holy Church of Christ's institution had determined, or yet whatsoever God had willed him either to believe or to do: but that the Pope of Rome, with his cardinals, archbishops, bishops, and other prelates of that church, had lawful power to determine such matter as stood not with His word thoroughly; that, would he not (he said) at that time affirm. With this the Archbishop bade him to take good advisement till the Monday next following (which was the twenty-fifth day of September), and then justly to answer, specially unto this point : Whether there remained material bread in the sacrament of the altar after the words of consecration, or not?

The Lord Cobham perceived that their uttermost malice was purposed against him, and therefore he put his life into the hands of God, desiring his only Spirit to assist him in his next answer. When the said twenty-fifth day of September was come Thomas Arundel, the Archbishop of Canterbury, commanded his judicial seat to be removed from the chapter-house of Paul's to the Dominic friars within Ludgate at London. And as he was there set, with a great sort more of priests, monks, canons, friars, parish-clerks, bell-ringers, and pardoners, Sir Robert Morley, knight, and lieutenant of the Tower, brought the good Lord Cobham, leaving him among them as a lamb among wolves.

A LEADER OF THE LOLLARDS

Examination of the Lord Cobham.

Then said the archbishop unto him: 'Sir John, we sent you a writing concerning the faith of the blessed sacrament, clearly determined by the Church of Rome, our mother, and by the holy doctors.'

Then he said unto him: 'I know none holier than is Christ and His apostles. And as for that determination, I wot it is none of theirs; for it standeth not with the Scriptures, but manifestly against them.'

Then said one of the lawyers: 'What is your belief concerning Holy Church.'

The Lord Cobham answered: 'My belief is, that all the Scriptures of the sacred Bible are true. All that is grounded upon them I believe thoroughly, for I know it is God's pleasure that I should so do; but in your lordly laws and idle determinations have I no belief. For ye be no part of Christ's Holy Church, as your open deeds do show; but ye are very Antichrists, obstinately set against His holy law and will. The laws that ye have made are nothing to His glory, but only for your vain glory and abominable covetousness. And as for your superiority, were ye of Christ, ye should be meek ministers, and no proud superiors.'

Then said Doctor Walden unto him: 'Swift judges always are the learned scholars of Wickliff!'

Unto him the Lord Cobham thus answered: 'As for that virtuous man Wickliff, I shall say here, before God and man, that before I knew that despised doctrine of his, I never abstained from sin. But since I learned therein to fear my Lord God, it hath otherwise, I trust, been with me: so much grace could I never find in all your glorious instructions.'

Then said Dr Walden yet again unto him: 'It were not well with me (so many virtuous men living, and so many learned men teaching the Scripture, being also so open, and the examples of fathers so plenteous), if I then had no grace to amend my life, till I heard the devil preach!'

The Lord Cobham said: 'Your fathers, the old Pharisees, ascribed Christ's miracles to Beelzebub, and His doctrine to the devil; and you, as their children, have still the selfsame judgment concerning His faithful followers. They that rebuke your vicious living must needs be heretics, and that must your doctors prove, when you have no Scripture to do it.' Then said he to them all: 'To judge you as you be, we need go no further than to your own proper acts. Where do you find in all God's law, that ye should thus sit in judgment on any Christian man, or yet give sentence upon any other man unto death, as ye do here daily? No ground have ye in all the Scripture so lordly to take it upon you, but in Annas and Caiaphas, who sat thus upon Christ, and upon His apostles after His ascension. Of them only have ye taken it to judge Christ's members as ye do; and neither of Peter nor John.'

Then said some of the lawyers: 'Yes, forsooth, Sir, for Christ judged Judas.'

The Lord Cobham said, 'No! Christ judged him not, but he judged himself, and thereupon went forth and so did hang himself: but indeed Christ said: "Woe unto him, for that covetous act of his," as He doth yet still unto many of you. For since the venom of Judas was shed into the Church, ye never followed Christ, neither yet have ye stood in the perfection of God's law.'

Then the archbishop asked him, What he meant by that venom?

The Lord Cobham said: 'Your possessions and lordships. For then[1] cried an angel in the air, as your own chronicles mention, Woe, woe, woe, this day is venom shed into the Church of God. Before that time all the bishops of Rome were martyrs, in a manner: and since that time we read of very few. But indeed since that same time, one hath put down another, one hath poisoned another, one hath cursed another, and one hath slain another, and done much more mischief besides, as all the chronicles tell. And let all men consider well this, that Christ was meek and merciful; the Pope is proud and a tyrant: Christ was poor and forgave; the Pope is rich and a malicious manslayer.'

Then a doctor of law, called Master John Kemp, plucked out of his bosom a copy of the bill which they had before sent him into the Tower by the archbishop's council, thinking thereby to make shorter work with him. 'My Lord Cobham,' saith this doctor, 'we must briefly know your mind concerning these four points here following. The first of them is this':—and then he read upon the bill: "The faith and determination of Holy Church touching the blessed sacrament of the altar is this; That after the sacramental words be once spoken by a priest in his mass, the material bread, that was before bread, is turned into Christ's very body, and the material wine is turned into Christ's blood. And so there remaineth, in the sacrament of the

---

[1] When Constantine endowed the Church.

altar, from thenceforth no material bread, nor material wine, which were there before the sacramental words were spoken ": Sir, believe you not this ? '

The Lord Cobham said : ' This is not my belief; but my faith is, as I said to you before, that in the worshipful sacrament of the altar is Christ's very body in form of bread.'

Then read the doctor again : ' The second point is this : Holy Church hath determined that every Christian man, living here bodily upon earth, ought to be shriven of a priest ordained by the Church, if he may come to him. Sir, what say you to this?'

The Lord Cobham answered and said : ' A diseased or sore wounded man hath need to have a sure wise chirurgeon and a true, knowing both the ground and the danger of the same. Most necessary were it, therefore, to be first shriven unto God, who only knoweth our diseases, and can help us.'

Then read the doctor again : ' The third point is this : Christ ordained St Peter the apostle to be His vicar here in earth, whose see is the Church of Rome, and He granted that the same power which He gave unto Peter should succeed unto all Peter's successors, whom we now call popes of Rome: by whose special power, in churches particular, be ordained prelates and archbishops, parsons, curates, and other degrees besides, to whom Christian men ought to obey after the laws of the Church of Rome. This is the determination of Holy Church. Sir, believe ye not this ? '

To this he answered and said : ' He that followeth Peter most nigh in pure living, is next unto him in succession ; but your lordly order esteemeth not greatly the lowly behaviour of poor Peter, whatsoever ye prate of him, neither care ye greatly for the humble manners of them that succeeded him till the time of Silvester, who, for the more part, were martyrs.'

With that, one of the other doctors asked him : ' Then what do ye say of the Pope ? '

The Lord Cobham answered : 'He and you together make whole the great Antichrist, of whom he is the great head ; you bishops, priests, prelates, and monks, are the body ; and the begging friars are the tail.'

Then read the doctor again : 'The fourth point is this : Holy Church hath determined, that it is meritorious to a Christian man to go on pilgrimage to holy places, and there specially to worship the holy relics and images of saints, apostles, martyrs, confessors, and all other saints besides, approved by the Church of Rome. Sir, what say you to this ? '

Whereunto the Lord Cobham answered : ' I owe them no service by any commandment of God, and therefore I mind not to seek them for your covetousness. It were best ye swept them fair from cobwebs and dust, and so laid them up for catching of scathe, or else to bury them fair in the ground, as ye do other aged people, who are God's images. It is a wonderful thing that saints now being dead should become so covetous and needy, and thereupon so bitterly beg, who all their life-time hated all covetousness and begging. But this I say unto you, and I would all the world should mark it, that with your shrines and idols, your feigned absolutions and pardons, ye draw unto you the substance, wealth, and chief pleasures of all Christian realms.'

Then said the archbishop unto him: 'Sir John, ye must either submit yourself to the ordinance of Holy Church, or else throw yourself (no remedy) into most deep danger. We require you to have no other manner of opinion in these matters, than the universal faith and belief of the Holy Church of Rome is. And so, like an obedient child, return again to the unity of your mother.'

The Lord Cobham said expressly before them all: 'I will no otherwise believe in these points than what I have told you here before. Do with me what you will.'

And with that the archbishop stood up and read a bill of his condemnation, all the clergy and laity vailing their bonnets: 'Forasmuch as we have found Sir John Oldcastle, knight, and Lord Cobham, not only to be an evident heretic in his own person, but also a mighty maintainer of other heretics against the faith and religion of the holy and universal Church of Rome; and that he, as the child of iniquity and darkness, hath so hardened his heart, that he will in no case attend unto the voice of his pastor; his faults also aggravated or made double through his damnable obstinacy, we commit him to the secular jurisdiction. Furthermore, we excommunicate and denounce accursed, not only this heretic here present, but so many else besides as shall hereafter, in favour of his error, either receive him or defend him, counsel him or help him, or any other way maintain him, as very fautors, receivers, defenders, counsellors, aiders, and maintainers of condemned heretics.

'And we give straight commandment that ye cause this condemnation and definitive sentence of excommunication concerning both this heretic and his fautors, to be published throughout all dioceses, in cities, towns, and villages, by your curates and parish priests, at such times as they shall have most recourse of people. Let the curate everywhere go into the pulpit, and there open, declare, and expound his process, in the mother-tongue, in an audible and intelligible voice, that it may be perceived of all men: and that upon the fear of this declaration also the people may fall from their evil opinions conceived now of late by seditious preachers.'

After the archbishop had read the bill of his condemnation before the whole multitude, the Lord Cobham said with a most cheerful countenance: 'Though ye judge my body, which is but a wretched thing, yet am I certain and sure, that ye can do no harm to my soul, no more than could Satan unto the soul of Job. He that created that, will of His infinite mercy and promise save it. I have, therein, no manner of doubt.'

He fell down upon his knees, and before them all prayed for his enemies, holding up both his hands and his eyes towards heaven, and saying, 'Lord God Eternal! I beseech Thee, of Thy great mercy sake, to forgive my pursuers, if it be Thy blessed will.'

After this, the bishops and priests were in great discredit both with the nobility and commons; for that they had so cruelly handled the good Lord Cobham. The prelates feared this to grow to further inconvenience towards them, wherefore they drew their heads together, and consented to use another practice somewhat contrary to that they had done before. They caused it to be blown abroad by their fee'd servants, friends, and babbling Sir Johns, that the said Lord Cobham was become a good man, and had lowly submitted himself in all things unto Holy Church, utterly changing his opinion concerning the sacrament. And thereupon, they counterfeited an abjuration in his name, that the people should take no hold of his opinion by any thing they had heard of him before, and so to stand the more in awe of them, considering him so great a man, and by them subdued.

When the clergy perceived that policy would not help, but made more and more against them, then sought they out another false practice : they went unto the King with a most grievous complaint, that in every quarter of the realm, by reason of Wickliff's opinions, and the said Lord Cobham, were wonderful contentions, rumours, tumults, uproars, confederations, dissensions, divisions, differences, discords, harms, slanders, schisms, sects, seditions, perturbations, perils, unlawful assemblies, variances, strifes, fightings, rebellious rufflings, and daily insurrections. The Church, they said, was hated. The diocesans were not obeyed. The ordinaries were not regarded. The spiritual officers, as suffragans, archdeacons, chancellors, doctors, commissaries, officials, deans, lawyers, scribes, and somners, were everywhere despised. The laws and liberties of Holy Church were trodden under foot. The Christian faith was ruinously decayed. God's service was laughed to scorn. The spiritual jurisdiction, authority, honour, power, policy, laws, rites, ceremonies, curses, keys, censures, and canonical sanctions of the Church, were had in utter contempt, so that all, in a manner, was come to naught.

And the cause of this was, that the heretics and lollards of Wickliff's opinion were suffered to preach abroad so boldly, to gather conventicles unto them, to keep schools in men's houses, to make books, compile treatises, and write ballads, to teach privately in angles and corners, as in woods, fields, meadows, pastures, groves, and in caves of the ground.

This would be, said they, a destruction to the commonwealth, a subversion to the land, and an utter decay of the King's estate royal, if remedy were not sought in time. And this was their policy, to couple the King's authority with what they had done in their former council, of craft, and so to make it, thereby, the stronger. For they perceived themselves very far too weak else, to follow against their enemies, what they had so largely enterprised. Upon this complaint, the King immediately called a parliament at Leicester. It might not, in those days, be holden at Westminster, for the great favour that the Lord Cobham had, both in London and about the city.

Thus were Christ's people betrayed every way, and their lives bought and sold. For, in the said parliament, the King made this most blasphemous and cruel act, to be a law for ever: that whatsoever they were that should read the Scriptures in the mother-tongue (which was then called Wickliff's learning), they should forfeit land, cattle, body, life, and goods, from their heirs for ever, and so be condemned for heretics to God, enemies to the crown, and most arrant traitors to the land. Besides this, it was enacted, that never a sanctuary, nor privileged ground within the realm, should hold them, though they were still permitted both to thieves and murderers. And if, in any case they would not give over, or were, after their pardon, relapsed, they should suffer death in two manner of kinds: that is; they should first be hanged for treason against the King, and then be burned for heresy against God.

Then had the bishops, priests, monks, and friars a world somewhat to their minds. Many were taken in divers quarters, and suffered most cruel death. And many fled out of the land into Germany, Bohemia, France, Spain, Portugal, and into the welds of Scotland, Wales, and Ireland; working there many marvels.

Sentence of death being given, the Lord Cobham was sent away, Sir Robert Morley carrying him again unto the Tower, where, after he had remained a certain space, in the night season (it is not known by what means), he escaped out, and fled into Wales. A great sum of money was proclaimed by the King, to him that could take the said Sir John Oldcastle, either quick or dead: who confederated with the Lord Powis (who was at that time a great governor in Wales), feeding him with lordly gifts and promises. About the end of four years, the Lord Powis, whether for greediness of the money, or for hatred of the true and sincere doctrine of Christ, seeking all manner of ways how to play the part of Judas, and outwardly pretending him great amity and favour, at length obtained his bloody purpose, and most cowardly and wretchedly took him, and brought the Lord Cobham bound, up to London; which was about the year of our Lord 1417, and about the month of December; at which there was a parliament assembled in London. It was adjudged, that he should be taken as a traitor to the King and the realm ; that he should be carried to the Tower, and from thence drawn through London, unto the new gallows in St Giles without Temple-Bar, and there to be hanged, and burned hanging.

Upon the day appointed, the Lord Cobham was brought out of the Tower with his arms bound behind him, having a very cheerful countenance. Then was he laid upon a hurdle, as though he had been a most heinous traitor to the crown, and so drawn forth into St Giles's field. As he was come to the place of execution, and was taken from the hurdle, he fell down devoutly upon his knees, desiring Almighty God to forgive his enemies. Then stood he up and beheld the multitude, exhorting them in most godly manner to follow the laws of God written in the Scriptures, and to beware of such teachers as they see contrary to Christ in their conversation and living. Then was he hanged up by the middle in chains of iron, and so consumed alive in the fire, praising the name of God so long as his life lasted ; the people, there present, showing great dolour. And this was done A.D. 1418.

How the priests that time fared, blasphemed, and accursed, requiring the people not to pray for him, but to judge him damned in hell, for that he departed not in the obedience of their Pope, it were too long to write.

Thus resteth this valiant Christian knight, Sir

A VALIANT CHRISTIAN KNIGHT

John Oldcastle, under the altar of God, which is
Jesus Christ, among that godly company, who, in
the kingdom of patience, suffered great tribulation
with the death of their bodies, for His faithful word
and testimony.

THE HISTORY OF MASTER JOHN HUSS

By the occasion of Queen Anne, who was a Bohemian, and married to King Richard II., the Bohemians coming to the knowledge of Wickliff's books here in England, began first to taste and savour Christ's Gospel, till at length, by the preaching of John Huss, they increased more and more in knowledge, insomuch that Pope Alexander V. hearing thereof, began to stir coals, and directeth his bull to the Archbishop of Prague, requiring him to look to the matter, and to provide that no person in churches, schools, or other places, should maintain that doctrine; citing also John Huss to appear before him. To whom the said John answering, declared that mandate or bull of the Pope utterly to repugn against the manifest examples and doings both of Christ and of His apostles, and to be prejudicial to the liberty of the Gospel, in binding the Word of God not to have free course; and, therefore, from this mandate of the Pope he appealed to the same Pope better advised. But, while he was prosecuting his appeal, Pope Alexander died.

After Alexander succeeded Pope John XXIII., who also, playing his part like a Pope, sought by all means possible to keep under the Bohemians, first beginning to work his malice upon the aforesaid John Huss, their preacher who, at the same time preaching at Prague in the temple of Bethlehem, because he seemed rather willing to teach the

Gospel of Christ than the traditions of bishops, was accused for a heretic.

The Pope committed the whole matter to Cardinal de Columna; who, when he had heard the accusation, appointed a day to John Huss, that he should appear in the court of Rome: which thing done, Wenceslaus, King of the Romans and of Bohemia, at the request specially of his wife Sophia and of the whole nobility of Bohemia, as also at the earnest suit and desire of the town and University of Prague, sent his ambassadors to Rome, to desire the Pope to quit and clearly deliver John Huss from that citation and judgment; and that if the Pope did suspect the kingdom of Bohemia to be infected with any heretical or false doctrine, he should send his ambassadors, who might correct and amend same, and that all this should be done at the sole cost and charges of the King of Bohemia: and to promise in his name, that he would assist the Pope's legates with all his power and authority, to punish all such as should be taken or found in any erroneous doctrine.

In the mean season, also, John Huss, before his day appointed, sent his lawful and meet procurators unto the court of Rome, and with most firm and strong reasons did prove his innocency; whereupon he so trusted, that he thought he should have easily obtained, that he should not have been compelled, by reason of the great danger, to appear the day appointed. But, when the Cardinal de Columna, unto whose will and judgment the whole matter was committed, would not admit any defence or excuse, John Huss's procurators appealed unto the Pope: yet, notwithstanding, this last refuge did not so much prevail with Cardinal de Columna, but that he would openly excommunicate. John Huss as an obstinate heretic, because he came not at his day appointed to Rome.

Notwithstanding, forsomuch as his proctors had appealed unto the Pope, they had other judges appointed unto them, as the Cardinals of Aquileia and of Venice, with certain others; which judges, after they had deferred the matter by the space of a year and a half, returned to the sentence and judgment of Cardinal de Columna, and, confirming the same, commanded John Huss's procurators, that they should leave off to defend him any more, for they would suffer it no longer: whereupon, when his procurators would not cease their instant suit, certain of them were cast into prison, and grievously punished; the others, leaving their business undone, returned into Bohemia.

The Bohemians little cared for all this; but, as they grew more in knowledge, so the less they regarded the Pope, complaining daily against him and the archbishop for stopping the Word of God and the Gospel of Christ to be preached, saying, that by their indulgences, and other practices of the court of Rome, they sought their own profit, and not that of Jesus Christ; that they plucked from the sheep of Christ the wool and milk, and did not feed them, either with the Word of God, or with good examples; teaching, moreover, and affirming, that the commandments of the Pope and prelates are not to be obeyed but so far as they follow the doctrine and life of Christ and of His apostles. They derided also and scorned the Pope's jurisdiction, because of the schism that was then in the church, when there were three Popes together, one striving against another for the papacy.

It happened by the occasion of Ladislaus, King of Naples, who was ravaging the Pope's towns and territories, that Pope John, raising up war against the said Ladislaus, gave full remission of sins to all those who would war on his side to defend the Church. When the bull of the Pope's indulgence was come to Prague, and there published, the King Wenceslaus, who then favoured that Pope, gave commandment that no man should attempt any thing against the said Pope's indulgences.

But Huss, with his followers, not able to abide the impiety of those pardons, began to speak against them, of which company were three certain artificers, who, hearing the priest preaching of these indulgences, did openly speak against them, and called the Pope Antichrist. Wherefore they were brought before the senate, and committed to ward: but the people, joining themselves together in arms, came to the magistrates, requiring them to be let loose. The magistrates, with gentle words and fair promises, satisfied the people, so that every man returning home to his own house, the tumult was assuaged: but the artisans, whose names were John, Martin, and Stascon, being in prison, were notwithstanding there beheaded. The martyrdom of these three being known to the people, they took the bodies, and with great solemnity brought them unto the church of Bethlehem: at whose funeral divers priests favouring that side, did sing on this wise; 'These be the saints, who, for the testament of God, gave their bodies.' And so their bodies were sumptuously interred in the church of Bethlehem, John Huss preaching at the funeral, much commending them for their constancy.

Thus this city of Prague was divided. The prelates, with the greatest part of the clergy and most of the barons who had any thing to lose, did hold with the Pope. On the contrary part, the commons, with part of the clergy and students of the University, went with John Huss. Wenceslaus the King, fearing lest this would grow to a tumult, being moved by the doctors and prelates and council of his barons, thought best to remove John Huss out of the city. And further to cease this dissension risen in the Church, he committed the matter to the disposition of the doctors and the clergy. They, consulting together, did set forth a decree, confirmed by the sentence of the King, containing eighteen articles for the maintenance of the Pope and of the see of Rome, against the doctrine of Wickliff and John Huss.

John Huss, thus departing out of Prague, went to his country, where he, being protected by the lord of the soil, continued preaching, to whom resorted a great concourse of people; neither yet was he so expelled out of Prague, but that sometimes he resorted to his church at Bethlehem, and there preached unto the people.

Moreover, against the said decree of the doctors John Huss answered with contrary articles as followeth.

The Objections of John Huss against the Decree of the Doctors.

False it is that they say the Pope and his cardinals to be the true and manifest successors of

Peter and of the apostles, neither that any other successors of Peter and of the apostles can be found upon the earth besides them: whereas all bishops and priests be successors of Peter and of the apostles.

Not the Pope, but Christ only, is the head; and not the cardinals, but all Christ's faithful people, be the body of the Catholic Church.

If the Pope be a reprobate, it is plain that he is no head, no nor member even, of the Holy Church of God, but of the devil and of his synagogue.

Neither is it true, that we ought to stand in all things to the determination of the Pope and of the cardinals, but so far forth as they do agree with the holy Scripture of the Old and New Testament.

The Church of Rome is not that place where the Lord did appoint the principal see of His whole Church: for Christ, Who was the head priest of all, did first sit in Jerusalem, and Peter did sit first in Antioch, and afterward in Rome. Also other Popes did sit, some at Bologna, some at Perugia, some at Avignon.

The prelates are falsifiers of the holy Scriptures who affirm and say, that we must obey the Pope in all things. For why? it is known that many Popes have been heretics, and one Pope was also a woman.

They fondly and childishly argue that the processes made against Master John Huss ought to be obeyed, because, forsooth, the whole body of the clergy of Prague have received them. By the same reason they may argue also, that we must obey the devil, because our first parents, Adam and Eve, obeyed him.

Unto these objections of John Huss the catholic doctors did answer in a long tedious process, the scope whereof principally tended to defend the principality of the Pope, and to maintain obedience to him above all other potentates in the world. Like as Christ is King of all Kings, and yet Charles may be King of France; so say they, Christ may be the universal head, and yet the Pope may be head under Him of the whole Church. While Christ walked here on earth in His bodily presence, He was Pope Himself and chief bishop, and so head of the Church here militant on earth. But because after He departed out of the world His body, which is the Church militant upon the earth, should not be headless, therefore He left Peter and his successors to His Church for a head in His place, unto the consummation of the world.

Thus then Master John Huss, being driven out of Prague, and, moreover, being so excommunicated, that no mass must be said where he was present, the people began mightily to grudge and to cry out against the prelates and other popish priests, accusing them as being simoniacs, covetous, proud; sparing not to lay open their vices, to their great ignominy and shame, and much craving reformation to be had of the clergy.

The King, seeing the inclination of the people, being also not ignorant of the wickedness of the clergy, under pretence of reforming the Church, began to require greater exactions upon such priests and men of the clergy as were known to be wicked livers. Whereupon they that favoured John Huss, complained of all, whomsoever they knew to be of the catholic faction, or enemies to John Huss; by reason whereof the priests of the popish clergy were brought, such as were faulty, into great distress, and such as were not faulty, into great fear, insomuch that they were glad to fall in, at least not to fall out, with the Protestants, being afraid to displease them. By this means Master Huss began to take some more liberty unto him, and to preach in his church at Bethlehem, and none to control him: by the same means the people received some comfort, and the King much gain.

Thus the popish clergy, while they went about to persecute John Huss, were enwrapped themselves in great tribulation, and afflicted on every side, as well of laymen, as of the evangelical clergy; nay, the women also and children were against them because of the interdict against John Huss.

The more the Pope's clergy were pinched, the more grudge and hatred redounded to John Huss, although he was no cause thereof, but only their own wicked deservings. And to help the matter forward, the Pope writeth letters to Wenceslaus, King of Bohemia, who was brother to Sigismund, the emperor, for the suppressing of John Huss and of his doctrine. 'We hear that in divers places under your dominion, there be certain who do follow and preach the errors of that arch-heretic Wickliff, whose books have been long since condemned in the general Roman council to be erroneous, heretical, and swerving from the catholic faith. Wherefore we do exhort your worship effectuously to show forth your regal power, both for the glory of God and defence of the catholic faith, as it becometh a catholic prince; whereby this heresy may be rooted out.'

During all this time of Pope John, there were three Popes reigning together, neither was yet the schism ceased, which had continued the space, already, of thirty-six years; by reason whereof a General Council was holden at Constance in A.D. 1414, being called by Sigismund the Emperor, and Pope John XXXIII. These three Popes were John, whom the Italians set up; Gregory, whom the Frenchmen set up; Benedict, whom the Spaniards placed. In this schismatical ambitious conflict every one defended his Pope, to the great disturbance of Christian nations. This Council endured three years and five months. Many great and profitable things to the glory of God and public profit might have been coucluded, if the rotten flesh of the churchmen could have bidden the salt of the Gospel, and if they had loved the truth.

Pope John was deposed by the decree of the Council, more than three and forty most grievous and heinous crimes being proved against him: as that he had hired Marcilius Parmensis, a physician, to poison Alexander, his predecessor; further, that he was a heretic, a simoniac, a liar, a hypocrite, a murderer, an enchanter, and a dice-player. Finally, what crime is it that he was not infected withal?

In this Council of Constance nothing was decreed or enacted worthy of memory, but this only, that the Pope's authority is under the Council, and that the Council ought to judge the Pope. And, as touching the communion in both kinds (bread and wine), although the Council did not deny but that it was used by Christ and His apostles, yet notwithstanding, by the same Council it was decreed to the contrary.

THE COUNCIL OF CONSTANCE

Which Council, although it was principally thought to be assembled for quieting of the schism between the three Popes; yet, notwithstanding, a great part thereof was for the cause of the Bohemians, and especially for John Huss. For before the Council began, the Emperor Sigismund sent certain gentlemen, Bohemians, who were of his own household, giving them in charge to bring John Huss, bachelor of divinity, unto the said Council. The meaning and intent thereof was, that John Huss should purge and clear himself of the blame which they had laid against him: and, for the better assurance, the Emperor did not only promise him safe conduct, that he might come freely unto Constance, but also that he should return again into Bohemia, without fraud or interruption; he promised also to receive him under his protection, and under safeguard of the whole empire.

John Huss, seeing so many fair promises and the assurance which the Emperor had given to him, sent answer, that he would come unto the Council. But before he departed out of the realm of Bohemia, and especially out of the town of Prague, he did write certain bills and caused them to be fastened upon the gates of the cathedral churches and parish churches, cloisters and abbeys, signifying unto them all, that he would go to the General Council at Constance there to declare his faith which he hath hitherto holden, and even at the present doth hold, and by God's help will defend and keep even unto death; wherefore, if any man have any suspicion of his doctrine, that he should declare it before the Lord Conrad, Archbishop of Prague; or, if he had rather, at the General Council, for there he would render unto every one, and before them all, an account and reason of his faith.

About the ides of October, 1414, John Huss, being accompanied with two noble gentlemen, Wenceslaus of Duba, and John of Clum, departed from Prague, and took his journey towards Constance. In all cities as he passed by, a great number of people did come unto him, and he was very gently received and entertained through all the towns of Germany, not only of his hosts, but of the citizens generally, and oftentimes of the curates; insomuch that the said Huss did confess, in a certain epistle, that he found in no place so great enemies as in Bohemia. And if it happened that there were any bruit or noise before of his coming, the streets were always full of people who were desirous to see and gratify him; especially at Nuremberg, where there were many curates who came unto him, desiring him that they might talk with him secretly, unto whom he answered: that he loved much rather to show forth his mind openly before all men than in hugger-mugger, for he would keep nothing close or hidden. So, after dinner, until it was night, he spake before the priests, senators, and divers other citizens, insomuch that they had him in great estimation and reverence.

The twentieth day after that he parted out of the town of Prague, which was the third day of November, he came unto Constance, and lodged at an honest matron's house, being a widow named Faithful, in St Gale's Street.

The morrow after, the noble men, Lord John de Clum, and Lord Henry Latzemboge, went to speak with the Pope, and certified him that John Huss was come, desiring that he would grant the said John Huss liberty to remain in Constance, without any trouble, or vexation, or interruption. Unto whom the Pope answered—that even if John Huss had killed his brother, yet would he go about, as much as in him lay, that no outrage or hurt should be done unto him during his abode in the city of Constance.

In this meantime, the greatest adversary that John Huss had, named Master Stephen Paletz, who was also a Bohemian born, was come unto Constance. The said Paletz did associate unto him one Michael de Causis, who was the first and bitterest accuser of the said John Huss. Paletz had been familiarly conversant with John Huss from his youth upward; but after that there was a bull brought unto Prague from Pope John XXIII. against the king of Apulia, named Ladislaus, the said John Huss withstood it openly, forsomuch as he saw that it was wicked and nought. Paletz, albeit that he had confessed at a certain banquet, in the presence of the said John Huss, that the said bull was contrary to all equity and right, yet, notwithstanding, forsomuch as he was bound unto the Pope by means of certain benefices received at his hand, he maintained and defended the said bull against John Huss.

As for Michael de Causis, the companion of Master Paletz, he was sometime the curate of New Prague: but he, not being content therewith, and seeking after a further prey, imagined a new device how to attain unto it; for he made a semblance that he had found out a new invention, whereby the mines of gold in Gilowy, which were perished and lost, might be set on work again. By this means he did so much with the King Wenceslaus, that he did put a great sum of money into his hands, to do that withal which he had promised. This honest man, after he had laboured certain days about it, perceiving that he brought nothing to pass, and that he was utterly in despair of his purpose, conveyed himself privily out of the realm of Bohemia with the rest of the money, and withdrew himself, as a worthy bird for such a nest, to the court of Rome.

These two jolly roisters, Stephen Paletz and Michael de Causis, drew out certain articles against the said Huss, saying, that they had gathered them out of his own writings, and especially out of his treatise which he had written of the Church. They trotted up and down, hither and thither, taking great pains to show the said articles unto the cardinals, bishops and monks, giving them to understand, that there were other matters of greater importance, which the said John Huss had committed against the holy constitutions, and other ordinances of the Pope and the church; which, if need were, they said they would propound before the Council. Through the kindling of this their fire, they did so incense the cardinals and the priests, that they all, with one mind, thought to cause the good man to be laid hands on.

The twenty-sixth day after the said Huss was come to Constance (during all which time he was occupied in reading, writing, and familiar talk with his friends), the cardinals, through the instigation of Paletz, and Michael de Causis, sent two bishops, to wit, the Bishops of Augsburg and of Trent, and with them the borough-master of Constance, and a certain knight, to the place where John Huss lodged, about dinner-time; who should make report unto him that they were sent by the Pope and his cardinals, to advertise him that he should come to render some knowledge of his doctrine before them as he had oftentimes desired, and that they were ready to hear him.

Unto whom John Huss answered, 'I am not come for any such intent, as to defend my cause particularly before the Pope and his cardinals, but that I would willingly appear before the whole Council, and there answer for my defence openly, without any fear or doubt, unto all such things as shall be required of me. Notwithstanding, forasmuch as you require me so to do, I will not refuse to go with you before the cardinals; and if it happen that they evil entreat or handle me, yet I trust in my Lord Jesus, that He will so comfort and strengthen me, that I shall desire much rather to die for His glory's sake, than to deny the verity which I have learned by His holy Scriptures.'

Wherefore it came to pass that, the bishops being instant upon him, and not showing any outward semblance that they bare any malice against him in their hearts (albeit they had privily laid garrisons both in the house where they were assembled, and also in other houses), John Huss took his horse which he had at his lodging, and went unto the court of the Pope and the cardinals.

When he was come thither, and had saluted the cardinals, they began to speak to him in this sort: 'We have heard many reports of you, which, if they be true, are in no case to be suffered; for men say, that you have taught great and manifest errors against the doctrine of the true Church; and that you have sowed your errors abroad through all the realm of Bohemia, by a long space of time; wherefore we have caused you to be called hither before us, that we might know how the matter standeth.'

Unto whom John Huss answered in few words: 'Reverend fathers! you shall understand that I am thus minded and affectioned, that I should rather choose to die, than I should be found culpable of one only error, much less of many and great errors. I am ready to receive correction, if any man can prove any errors in me.' The cardinals answered him that his sayings pleased them very well; and upon that they went away, leaving the said John Huss with Lord John de Clum, under the guard of the armed men, until four of the clock in the afternoon.

After that time the cardinals assembled again in the Pope's court, to take counsel what they should do with John Huss. Stephen Paletz and Michael de Causis, with divers others of their adherents, made earnest suit that he should not be let go at liberty again, and having the favour of the judges on their part, they bragged up and down in a manner as they had been mad men, and mocked the said John Huss, saying, 'Now we will hold thee well enough; thou art under our power and jurisdiction, and shalt not depart until such time as thou hast paid the uttermost farthing.'

A little before night, they sent the provost of the Roman court unto Lord John de Clum, to show him that he might return to his lodging; but as for John Huss, they had otherwise provided for him. When Lord John de Clum heard this news, he was wonderfully displeased, forasmuch as through their crafts, subtleties, and glosing words, they had so trained this good man into their snares; whereupon he went unto the Pope, declaring unto him all that was done; most humbly beseeching him, that he would call to remembrance the promise which he had made unto him and Lord Henry Latzemboge, and that he would not so lightly break his faith. The Pope answered, that all these things were done without his consent or commandment; and said further to Lord de Clum apart, 'What reason is it that you should impute this deed unto me, seeing that you know well enough that I myself am in the hands of these cardinals and Bishops?'

So the said Lord de Clum returned very pensiveful and sorry; he complained very sore, both privily and openly, of the outrage that the Pope had done; but all profited nothing. After this, the said John Huss was led to the house of the precentor of the church of Constance, where he was kept prisoner by the space of eight days; from thence he was carried unto the Jacobites, hard by the river Rhine, and was shut up in the prison of the abbey.

After he had been enclosed there a certain time he fell sore sick of an ague, by means of the stench of the place, and became so weak, that they despaired of his life. And for fear lest this good man should die in prison, the Pope sent unto him certain of his physicians to cure him. In the midst of his sickness his accusers made importunate suit to the principals of the Council, that the said John Huss might be condemned, and presented unto the Pope these articles:

He doth err about the sacraments of the Church,

and especially about the sacrament of the body of Christ, forasmuch as he hath openly preached, that it ought to be ministered openly unto the people under both kinds, that is to say, the body and blood. Moreover, it is affirmed by divers, that he hath taught both in the schools and in the church, or at the least that he doth hold this opinion, that after the words of consecration pronounced upon the altar, there remaineth still material bread in the sacrament.

He doth err as touching the ministers of the Church, forasmuch as he saith, that they cannot consecrate or minister the sacraments when they are in mortal sin. Moreover he saith, that other men beside priests may minister the sacrament.

He doth not allow and admit that the church signifieth the Pope, cardinals, archbishops, and the clergy underneath them.

He saith, that the Church hath no power of the keys, when the Pope, cardinals, and all other of the priests and clergy are in deadly sin.

He holdeth opinion that every man hath authority to invest and appoint any man to the cure of souls. This is evident by his own doings, forasmuch as many in the kingdom of Bohemia by their defenders and favourers, or rather by himself, were appointed and put into parish churches, which they have long ruled and kept, not being appointed by the apostolic see, neither yet by the ordinary of the city of Prague.

He holdeth opinion, that a man, being once ordained a priest or deacon, cannot be forbidden or kept back from the office of preaching. This is likewise manifest by his own doings, forasmuch as he himself could never be letted from preaching, neither by the apostolic see, nor yet by the Archbishop of Prague.

Moreover, when there were questions moved amongst the divines of the University of Prague upon the forty-five articles of John Wickliff, and they had called a convocation, and all the divines of Bohemia had concluded that every one of those articles was either heretical, seditious, or erroneous; he alone held the contrary opinion, that none of those articles were either heretical, seditious, or erroneous, as afterwards he did dispute, hold, and teach, in the common schools of Prague; whereby it is evidently enough foreseen, that he doth affirm those articles of Wickliff, which are not only condemned in England, but also by the whole Church.

Upon this accusation, they appointed three commissioners or judges; the Patriarch of Constantinople, the Bishop of Castel-a-mare, and the Bishop of Lebus; the which prelates heard the accusation and the witness which was brought in by certain babbling priests of Prague, confirmed by their oaths, and afterwards recited the said accusation unto the said Huss in the prison, at such time as his ague was fervent and extremely upon him.

Upon this, John Huss required to have an advocate to answer for him; which was plainly and utterly denied him. And the reason that the masters commissioners brought against it was this: that the plain canon doth forbid that any man should be a defender of him who is suspected of heresy. The vanity and folly of the witnesses was such, that if they had not been both the accusers and judges themselves, there should have needed no confutation.

Thus John Huss remained in the prison of the convent of the Franciscans, until the Wednesday before Palm Sunday; and in the mean season, to employ his time, he wrote certain books of the ten commandments, of the love and knowledge of God, of matrimony, of penance, of the three enemies of mankind, of the prayer of our Lord, and of the supper of our Lord.

The same day Pope John XXIII. changed his apparel, and conveyed himself secretly out of Constance, fearing the judgment by which afterwards he was deprived of his papal dignity by reason of most execrable and abominable forfeits and doings. This was the cause that John Huss was transported and carried unto another prison; for the Pope's servants, who had the keeping of John Huss, understanding that their master was fled, delivered up the keys of the prison unto the Emperor Sigismund, and to the cardinals, and followed their master the Pope. Then, by the consent of the Council, the said John Huss was put into the hands of the Bishop of Constance, who sent him to a castle on the other side of the river Rhine, not very far from Constance, where he was shut up in a tower with fetters on his legs, that he could scarce walk in the day-time, and at night he was fastened up to a rack against the wall hard by his bed.

In the mean season, certain noblemen and gentlemen of Poland and Bohemia did all their endeavour to purchase his deliverance, having respect to the good renown of all the realm, which was wonderfully defamed and slandered by certain naughty persons. The matter was grown unto this point, that all they who were in the town of Constance, who seemed to bear any favour unto John Huss, were made as mocking stocks, and derided of all men, yea, even of the slaves and base people. Wherefore they took counsel and concluded together to present their request in writing unto the whole Council, the fourteenth day of May, A.D. 1415; the tenor here ensueth:—

'When Master John Huss was freely of his own accord come unto Constance, under safe-conduct, he was grievously imprisoned before he was heard, and at this present is tormented both with fetters, and also with hunger and thirst. Master John Huss, neither being convicted nor condemned, no not so much as once heard, is taken and imprisoned, and is so weakened with thin and slender diet, that it is to be feared, lest that, his power and strength being hereby consumed and wasted, he should be put in danger of his wit or reason.

'Wherefore, we do wholly and most earnestly desire and require your reverences that both for the honour of the safe-conduct of our lord the King, and also for the preservation and increase of the worthy fame and renown both of the kingdom of Bohemia, and your own also, you will make a short end about the affairs of Master John Huss.'

The said barons and lords also presented a supplication unto the emperor: 'We most humbly require and desire your princely majesty, that you would interpose your good offices with the said most reverend fathers and lords, that they may effectually hear us in this our just petition.'

But what answer the emperor made hereunto, we could never understand or know; but by the process of the matter a man may easily judge, that this good emperor was led even unto this point, through the obstinate mischief of the cardinals and bishops, to break and falsify his promise and faith: and this was their reason whereby he was driven thereunto, that no defence could or might be given either by safe-conduct, or by any other means, unto him who was suspected or judged to be a heretic.

When John Huss was brought forth again before the whole assembly, a strange and shameful matter happened. They had scarcely read one article, and brought forth a few witnesses, but, as he was about to open his mouth to answer, all this mad herd began so to cry out upon him, that he had not leisure to speak one only word. The noise and trouble was so great and so vehement, that a man might well have called it a bruit of wild beasts, and not of men; much less was it to be judged a congregation of men gathered together, to determine so grave and weighty matters.

Some did outrage in words against him, and others spitefully mocked him; so that he, seeing himself overwhelmed with these rude and barbarous noises, and that it profited nothing to speak, determined finally with himself to hold his peace. From that time forward, all the whole rout of his adversaries thought that they had won the battle of him, and cried out all together; 'Now he is dumb, now he is dumb: this is a certain sign and token, that he doth consent and agree unto these his errors.' Finally, the matter came to this point, that certain of the most moderate and honest among them, seeing this disorder, determined to proceed no further, but that all should be put off until another time. Through their advice, the prelates and others parted from the Council for that present, and appointed to meet there again on the day after the morrow, to proceed in judgment.

On that day, which was the seventh of June, somewhere about seven of the clock, the sun a little before having been almost wholly eclipsed, this same flock assembled in the cloister of the friars minor, and by their appointment John Huss was brought before them, accompanied with a great number of armed men. Thither went also the emperor, whom the noble men, Lords Wenceslaus de Duba and John de Clum, did follow, to see what the end would be.

Then was read a certain article of accusation, in the which it was alleged, that John Huss had taught, and obstinately defended, certain erroneous articles of Wickliff's. To confirm their article, there was alleged that John Huss did withstand the condemnation of Wicklift's articles, the which had been first made at Rome. And afterward also, when the Archbishop of Prague, with other learned men, held a convocation at Prague for the same matter, he answered, that he durst not agree thereunto, for offending of his conscience, and especially for these articles : that Silvester the Pope, and Constantine, did err in bestowing great gifts and rewards upon the Church : also, that the Pope or priest, being in mortal sin, cannot consecrate nor baptize. ' This article,' said Huss, ' I have thus limited, so as I should say, that he doth unworthily consecrate or baptize, for that, when he is in deadly sin, he is an unworthy minister of the sacraments of God.' He did not consent that Wickliff's articles should be condemned, before sufficient reasons were alleged out of the holy Scripture for their condemnation.

'And of the same mind,' saith John Huss, 'are a great many other doctors and masters of the University of Prague; for when Sbinco the archbishop commanded all Wickliff's books to be gathered together in the whole city of Prague, and to be brought unto him, I myself brought also certain books of Wickliff's, which I gave unto the archbishop, desiring him, that if he found any error or heresy in them, he would note and mark them, and I myself would publish them openly. But the archbishop, albeit that he showed me no error nor heresy in them, burned my books, together with those that were brought unto him. He obtained a bull from the Pope that all Wickliff's books, for the manifold errors contained in them (whereof there were none named), should be taken out of all men's hands. The archbishop, using the authority of this bull, thought that he should bring to pass, that the King of Bohemia and the nobles should consent to the condemnation of Wickliff's books; but therein he was deceived. Yet nevertheless, calling together certain divines, he gave them in commission to sit upon Wickliff's books, and to proceed against them by a definitive sentence in the canon law. These men, by a general sentence, judged all those books worthy to be burned; which when the doctors, masters and scholars of the University heard report of, they, all together, with one consent and accord (none excepted but only they, who before were chosen by the archbishop to sit in judgment), determined to make supplication unto the King to stay the matter. The King, granting their request, sent by and by certain unto the archbishop to examine the matter. There he denied that he would decree any thing, as touching Wickliff's books, contrary unto the King's will and pleasure. Whereupon, albeit that he had determined to burn them the next day after, yet for fear of the King, the matter was passed over. In the meantime Pope Alexander V. being dead, the archbishop, fearing lest the bull which he had received of the Pope, would be no longer of any force or effect, privily calling unto him his adherents, and shutting the gates of his court round about him, being guarded with a number of armed soldiers, consumed and burned all Wickliff's books. Besides this great injury, the archbishop by means of this bull aforesaid, committed another no less intolerable; for he gave commandment, that no man after that time, under pain of excommunication, should teach any more in chapels. Whereupon I did appeal unto the Pope; who being dead, and the cause of my matter remaining undetermined, I appealed likewise unto his successor John XXIII.: before whom when, by the space of two years, I could not be admitted by my advocates to defend my cause, I appealed unto the high judge Christ.'

When John Huss had spoken these words, it was demanded of him, whether he had received absolution of the Pope or no? He answered, 'no.' Then again, whether it were lawful for him to appeal unto Christ or no? Whereunto John Huss answered: 'Verily I do affirm here before you all, that there is no more just or effectual appeal, than that appeal which is made unto Christ, forasmuch as the law doth determine, that to appeal, is no other thing than in a cause of grief or wrong done by an inferior judge, to implore and require aid and remedy at a higher judge's hand. Who is then a higher judge than Christ? Who, I say, can know or judge the matter more justly, or with more equity? when in Him there is found no deceit, neither can He be deceived; or, who can better help the miserable and oppressed than He?' While John Huss, with a devout and sober countenance, was speaking and pronouncing those words, he was derided and mocked by all the whole Council.

Then was there rehearsed another article of his accusation in this manner; that John Huss, to confirm the heresy which he had taught the common people out of Wickliff's books, said that he wished his soul to be in the same place where John Wickliff's soul was. Whereunto John Huss answered, that a dozen years before any books of divinity of John Wickliff's were in Bohemia, he did see certain works of philosophy of his, which, he said, did marvellously delight and please him. And when he understood the good and godly life of the said Wickliff, he spake these words.

This done, the said John Huss was committed to the custody of the Archbishop of Riga. But before he was led away, the Cardinal of Cambray, calling him back again in the presence of the emperor, said, 'John Huss, I have heard you say, that if you had not been willing of your own mind to come unto Constance, neither the emperor himself, nor the King of Bohemia, could have compelled you to do it.'

Unto whom John Huss answered: 'Under your license, most reverend father! I did say, that there were in Bohemia a great number of gentlemen and noblemen, who did favour and love me, who also might easily have kept me in some sure and secret place, that I should not have been constrained to come unto this town of Constance, neither at the will of the emperor, neither of the King of Bohemia.'

With that the Cardinal of Cambray even for very anger began to change his colour, and despitefully said: 'Do you not see the unshamefastness of the man here?'

And as they were murmuring and whispering on all parts, the Lord John de Clum, ratifying and confirming that which John Huss had spoken, said, that John Huss had spoken very well; 'for on my part' said he, 'who, in comparison of a great many others, am but of small force in the realm of Bohemia, yet always, if I would have taken it in hand, I could have defended him easily by the space of one year, even against all the force and power of both these great and mighty kings. How much better might they have done it who are of more force or puissance than I am, and have stronger castles and places than I have?'

After the Lord de Clum had spoken, the Cardinal of Cambray said, 'Let us leave this talk; and I tell you, John Huss! and counsel you, that you submit yourself unto the sentence and mind of the Council, as you did promise in the prison; and if you will do so, it shall be greatly both for your profit and honour.'

And the emperor himself began to tell him the same tale, saying, 'forasmuch as divers have told us, that we may not, or ought not, of right to defend any man who is a heretic, or suspected of heresy;

therefore, now, we give you counsel that you be not obstinate to maintain any opinion, but that you do submit yourself unto the authority of the holy Council, which thing if you do, we will give order that the Council shall suffer you to depart in peace, with an easy penance. Which thing if you, contrariwise, refuse to do, the presidents of the Council shall proceed against you. And, for our part, be ye well assured, that we will sooner make the fire with our own hands, to burn you withal, than we will suffer any longer that you shall maintain or use this stiffness of opinions, which you have hitherto used.'

The morrow after, which was the eighth day of June, the company assembled at the convent of the Franciscans. Thither was John Huss brought; and in his presence there were read the articles, which, they said, were drawn out of his books. Huss acknowledged all those that were faithfully and truly collected and gathered, to be his; of which sort there were but very few.

The Articles drawn from the books of John Huss, with his Answers to the same.

'Peter never was, neither is the head of the holy universal Church.'

Answer. This article was drawn out of these words of my book: 'All men do agree in this point, that Peter had received of the Rock of the Church (which is Christ), humility, poverty, steadfastness of faith, and consequently blessedness. Not as though the meaning of our Lord Jesus Christ was, when He said, "Upon this Rock I will build My

Church," that He would build every militant Church upon the person of Peter, for Christ should build His church upon the Rock which is Christ Himself, from whence Peter received his steadfastness of faith, forasmuch as Jesus Christ is the only head and foundation of every church, and not Peter.'

'If he that is called the vicar of Jesus Christ, do follow Christ in his life, then he is his true vicar. But, if so be he do walk in contrary paths and ways, then is he the messenger of Antichrist, and the enemy and adversary of St Peter, and of our Lord Jesus Christ, and also the vicar of Judas Iscariot.'

Answer. The words of my book are these: 'If he who is called the vicar of St Peter, walk in the ways of Christian virtues aforesaid, we do believe verily that he is the true vicar, and true Bishop of the Church which he ruleth; but if he walk in contrary paths and ways, then is he the messenger of Antichrist, contrary both to St Peter, and to our Lord Jesus Christ. And therefore St Bernard, in his fourth book, did write in this sort unto Pope Eugene: "Thou delightest and walkest in great pride and arrogancy, being gorgeously and sumptuously arrayed; what fruit or profit do thy flock or sheep receive by thee? If I durst say it, these be rather the pastures and feedings of devils than of sheep. St Peter and St Paul did not so; wherefore thou seemest by these thy doings to succeed Constantine, and not St Peter."' It followeth after, in my book, 'That if the manner and fashion of his life and living be contrary to that which St Peter used, or that he be given to avarice and covetousness, then is he the vicar of Judas Iscariot, who loved and chose the reward of iniquity, and did set out to sale the Lord Jesus Christ.'

'The papal dignity hath his original from the Emperors of Rome.'

Answer. Mark well what my words are: 'The pre-eminence and institution of the Pope is sprung and come of the emperor's power and authority; for Constantine granted this privilege unto the Bishop of Rome, and others after him confirmed the same : that like as Augustus, for the outward and temporal goods bestowed upon the Church, is counted always the most high King above all others; so the Bishop of Rome should be called the principal father above all other bishops.'

'No man would reasonably affirm (without revelation) either of himself or of any other, that he is the head of any particular Church.'

Answer. I confess it to be written in my book.

'The Pope's power as vicar is but vain and nothing worth, if he do not confirm and address his life according to Jesus Christ, and follow the manners of St Peter.'

Answer. It is thus in my book; 'That it is meet and expedient that he who is ordained vicar, should address and frame himself, in manners and conditions, to the authority of Him who did put him in place.'

'The cardinals are not the manifest and true successors of the other apostles of Jesus Christ, if they live not according to the fashion of the apostles, keeping the commandments and ordinances of the Lord Jesus.'

Answer. It is thus written in my book.

'A heretic ought not to be committed to the

secular powers to be put to death, for it is sufficient only that he abide and suffer the ecclesiastical censure.'

Answer. These are my words, 'They might be ashamed of their cruel sentence and judgment, especially forasmuch as Jesus Christ, Bishop both of the Old and New Testament, would not judge such as were disobedient by civil judgment, neither condemn them to bodily death.' A heretic ought first to be instructed and taught with Christian love and gentleness by the holy Scriptures. But if there were any, who, after gentle and loving admonitions and instructions, would not cease from their stiffness of opinions, but obstinately resist against the truth, such, I say, ought to suffer corporal or bodily punishment.

As soon as John Huss had spoken those things, the judges read in his book a certain clause, wherein he seemed grievously to inveigh against them who delivered a heretic unto the secular power, not being confuted or convicted of heresy: and compared them unto the high priests, Scribes and Pharisees, who said unto Pilate, 'It is not lawful for us to put any man to death,' and delivered Christ unto him : and yet notwithstanding, according unto Christ's own witness, they were greater murderers than Pilate. 'For he,' said Christ, 'who hath delivered Me unto thee, hath committed the greatest offence.' Then the cardinals and bishops made a great noise, and demanded of John Huss, saying: 'Who are they that thou dost compare unto the Pharisees?'

Then he said, 'All those who deliver up any innocent unto the civil sword, as the Scribes and Pharisees delivered Jesus Christ unto Pilate.'

'He that is excommunicated by the Pope, if he refuse and forsake the judgment of the Pope and the General Council, and appealeth unto Jesus Christ, after he hath made his appellation, all the excommunications and curses of the Pope cannot annoy or hurt him.'

Answer. I did make my complaint in my book, that they had both done me, and such as favoured me, great wrong; and that they refuse to hear me in the Pope's court. For after the death of one Pope, I did appeal to his successor, and all that did profit me nothing. And, therefore, last of all, I have appealed to the Head of the Church, my Lord Jesus Christ; for He is much more excellent and better than any Pope, to discuss and determine matters and causes, forasmuch as He cannot err, neither yet deny justice to him that doth ask or require it in a just cause; neither can He condemn the innocent.

'The minister of Christ, living according to His law, and having the knowledge and understanding of the Scriptures, and an earnest desire to edify the people, ought to preach; notwithstanding the pretended excommunication of the Pope. And moreover, if the Pope, or any other ruler, do forbid any priest or minister, so disposed, to preach, that he ought not to obey him.'

Answer. These are my words: 'That albeit the excommunication were either threatened or come out against him, in such sort that a Christian ought not to do the commandments of Christ, it appeareth by the words of St Peter, and the other apostles, that we ought rather to obey God than man.' Whereupon it followeth, that the minister of Christ, living according unto this law, ought to preach, notwithstanding any pretended excommunication; for God hath commanded us to preach and testify unto the people. Whereby it is evident, that if the Pope, or any other ruler of the Church, do command any minister disposed to preach, not to preach, they ought not to obey him.'

They objected unto him, that he had said, that such kind of excommunications were rather blessings.

'Verily,' said John Huss, 'even so I do now say again, that every excommunication, by which a man is unjustly excommunicated, is unto him a blessing before God. No Christian ought to doubt, but that a man sufficiently instructed in learning is more bound to counsel and instruct the ignorant, to teach those who are in doubt, to chastise those who are unruly, and to remit and forgive those that do him injury, than to do any other works of mercy.'

'There is no spark of appearance, that there ought to be one head in the spiritualty, to rule the Church, which should be always conversant with the militant Church.'

Answer. I do grant it. Christ is the Head of the spiritualty, ruling and governing the militant Church by much more and greater necessity than Cæsar ought to rule the temporalty; forasmuch as Christ Who sitteth on the right hand of God the Father, doth necessarily rule the militant Church as head.

'Christ would better rule His Church by His true apostles, dispersed throughout the whole world, without such monstrous heads.'

Answer. It is in my book as here followeth: 'We do verily believe that Christ Jesus is the head over every Church, ruling the same without lack or default, pouring upon the same a continual motion and sense.   The Church, in the time of the apostles, was far better ruled and governed than now is.   And what doth hinder, that Christ should not now rule the same better by His true disciples, without such monstrous heads as have been of late?'

When the articles were read over, together with their testimonies, the Cardinal of Cambray calling unto John Huss, said: 'Thou hast heard what grievous and horrible crimes are laid against thee, and what a number of them there are; and now it is thy part to devise with thyself what thou wilt do. Two ways are set before thee by the Council. First, that thou do meekly submit thyself unto the judgment of the Council, that whatsoever shall be there determined, thou wilt patiently bear, and suffer the same.   Which thing if thou wilt do, we will treat and handle thee with as great humanity, love, and gentleness, as we may.   But if as yet thou art determined to defend any of those articles which we have propounded unto thee, and dost desire or require to be further heard thereupon, we will not deny thee power and license thereunto: but this thou shalt well understand, that here are such manner of men, so clear in understanding and knowledge, and having such firm and strong reasons and arguments against thy articles, that I fear it will be to thy great hurt, detriment and peril.'

Unto whom, with a lowly countenance, John Huss answered: Most reverend fathers! I have often said that I came hither of mine own free will, not to the intent obstinately to defend any thing, but that if in any thing I should seem to have conceived a perverse or evil opinion, I would meekly and patiently be content to be reformed and taught. Whereupon I desire that I may have yet further liberty to declare my mind; whereof, except I shall allege most firm and strong reasons, I will willingly submit myself, as you require.'

Then said the Cardinal of Cambray : ' Forasmuch, then, as thou dost submit thyself unto the grace of this Council, this is decreed—First, that thou shalt humbly and meekly confess thyself to have erred in these articles which are alleged and brought against thee: Secondly, that thou shalt promise by an oath, that from henceforth thou shalt not hold, or teach, any of these articles : And last of all, that thou shalt openly recant all these articles.'

Upon which sentence, when many others had spoken their minds at length, John Huss said : ' I most humbly desire you all, even for His sake Who is the God of us all, that I be not compelled to do the thing which my conscience doth strive against, or which I cannot do without danger of eternal damnation : that is, that I should make revocation, by oath, to all the articles which are alleged against me. But if there be any man who can teach me contrariwise unto them, I will willingly perform that which you desire.'

Then said the Cardinal of Florence, ' John Huss, you shall have a form of abjuration, which shall be gentle, and tolerable enough, written and delivered unto you, and then you will easily and soon determine with yourself, whether you will do it or no.'

But John Huss constantly answered as before, insomuch that they said he was obstinate and stubborn. Thus they were all so grievous and troublesome unto him that he waxed faint and weary, for he had passed all the night before without sleep, through the pain of his teeth.

The Archbishop of Riga, unto whom John Huss was committed, commanded, that he should be carried again safely to prison. Then John de Clum following him, did not a little comfort him. No tongue can express what courage he received by the short talk which he had with him, when, in so great a broil and grievous hatred, he saw himself forsaken of all men.

After that John Huss was carried away, the emperor began to exhort the presidents of the Council in this manner following: 'You have heard the manifold and grievous crimes which are laid against John Huss, which are not only proved by manifest and strong witnesses, but also confessed by him; of which, every one of them, by my judgment and advice, hath deserved and is worthy of death. Therefore, except he do recant them all, I judge and think meet that he be punished with fire.'

The day before his condemnation, which was the sixth of July, the Emperor Sigismund sent unto him four bishops, accompanied with Lords Wenceslaus de Duba and John de Clum, that they should learn of him what he did intend to do.

When he was brought out of prison unto them, John de Clum began first to speak unto him, saying, 'Master John Huss, I am a man unlearned, neither am I able to counsel you, being a man of understanding: notwithstanding I do require you, if you know yourself guilty of any of those errors which are laid against you, that you will not be ashamed to alter your mind: if contrariwise, I would not that you should do any thing against your conscience, but rather suffer any punishment, than deny that which you have known to be the truth.'

Unto whom John Huss, turning himself, with lamentable tears said: 'Verily, I do take the Most High God for my witness, that I am ready with my heart and mind, if the Council can teach me any better by the holy Scripture, to alter my purpose.'

Then one of the bishops who sat by, said unto him, that he would never be so arrogant, that he would prefer his own mind before the judgment of the whole Council.

To whom John Huss answered: 'If he who is the least in all this Council can convict me of error, I will, with an humble heart and mind, perform whatsoever the Council shall require of me.'

'Mark,' said the bishops, 'how obstinately he doth persevere in his errors.'

And when they had thus talked, they commanded the keepers to carry him again to prison.

The next day after, which was Saturday, the sixth day of July, there was a general session holden of the princes and lords, both of the ecclesiastical and temporal estates, in the head church of the city of Constance, the Emperor Sigismund being president in his imperial robes and habit; in the midst whereof there was made a certain high place, being square about like a table, and hard by it there was a desk of wood, on which the vestments pertaining unto priesthood were laid for this cause, that before John Huss should be delivered over unto the civil power, he should be openly spoiled of his priestly ornaments.

When John Huss was brought thither, he fell down upon his knees and prayed a long time.

The proctor of the Council required that they might proceed unto the definitive sentence. Then a certain bishop, who was appointed one of the judges, repeated those articles which we have before remembered. John Huss went about briefly, with a word or two, to answer unto every one of them; but as often as he was about to speak, the Cardinal of Cambray commanded him to hold his peace, saying, 'Hereafter you shall answer all together, if you will.' Then said John Huss: 'How can I at once answer all these things which are alleged against me, when I cannot remember them all?' Then said the Cardinal of Florence: 'We have heard thee sufficiently.'

But when John Huss, for all that, would not hold his peace, they sent the officers who should force him thereunto. Then began he to entreat, pray, and beseech them, that they would hear him, that such as were present might not credit or believe those things to be true which were reported of him. But when all this would nothing prevail, he, kneeling down upon his knees, committed the whole matter unto God, and the Lord Jesus Christ. 'O Lord Jesu Christ! Whose Word is openly condemned here in this Council, unto Thee again I do appeal, Who when Thou wast evil entreated of Thine enemies, didst appeal unto God Thy Father, committing Thy cause unto a most just Judge; that by Thy example, we also being oppressed with manifest wrongs and injuries, should flee unto Thee.'

When he had spoken these words, one of them, who was appointed judge, read the definitive sentence against him:

THE SENTENCE OF THE COUNCIL

'Forasmuch as one John Huss, the disciple of John Wickliff, hath taught, preached, and affirmed the articles of Wickliff, which were condemned by the Church of God; especially resisting in his open sermons, and also with his adherents and accomplices in the schools, the condemnation of the said articles of Wickliff, and hath declared him, the said Wickliff, for the favour and commendation of his doctrine, before the whole multitude of the clergy and people, to be a catholic man, and a true evangelical doctor.

'Wherefore, this most sacred and holy Council of Constance, doth condemn and reprove all those books which the said John Huss wrote; and doth decree, that they all shall be solemnly and openly burned in the presence of the clergy and people of the city of Constance, and elsewhere; adding, moreover, that all his doctrine is worthy to be despised and eschewed of all faithful Christians. This sacred Synod doth straitly command, that diligent inquisition be made for such treatises and works; and that such as are found, be consumed with fire.

'Wherefore, this most sacred and holy synod, determineth, pronounceth, declareth, and decreeth that John Huss was and is a true and manifest heretic, and that he hath preached openly errors and heresies, despising the keys of the Church, and ecclesiastical censures. In the which his error, he hath continued with a mind altogether indurate and hardened by the space of many years, much offending the faithful Christians by his obstinacy and stubbornness, when he made his appeal unto the Lord Jesus Christ, as the Most High Judge.

'Whereupon the said synod judgeth him to be condemned as a heretic; and reproveth the said

appeal as injurious, offensive, and done in derision
unto the ecclesiastical jurisdiction; and judgeth the
said Huss not only to have seduced the Christian
people by his writings and preachings, neither to
have been a true preacher of the Gospel of Christ,
but also to have been an obstinate and stiffnecked
person, such a one as doth not desire to return
again to the lap of our holy mother the Church,
neither to abjure the errors and heresies which he
hath openly preached and defended. Wherefore
this most sacred Council decreeth that the said John
Huss shall be deposed and degraded from his priestly
orders and dignity.'

While these things were thus read, John Huss,
albeit he was forbidden to speak, notwithstanding,
did often interrupt them; and especially when he
was reproved of obstinacy, he said with a loud voice:
'I was never obstinate, but, as always heretofore,
even so now again I desire to be taught by the holy
Scriptures.' When his books were condemned, he
said, 'Wherefore have you condemned those books,
when you have not proved that they are contrary to
the Scriptures?' And oftentimes looking up unto
heaven, he prayed.

When the sentence and judgment were ended,
kneeling down upon his knees, he said: 'Lord
Jesus Christ! forgive mine enemies, by whom Thou
knowest that I am falsely accused, and that they
have used false witness and slanders against me;
forgive them, I say, for Thy great mercy's sake.'
This his prayer, the greater part, and especially the
chief of the priests, did deride and mock.

At last the seven bishops who were chosen out
to degrade him of his priesthood, commanded him to

put on the garments pertaining unto priesthood.
When he came to the putting on of the albe, he
called to his remembrance the white vesture which
Herod put on Jesus Christ to mock Him withal. So,
likewise, in all other things he did comfort himself
by the example of Christ. When he had now put
on all his priestly vestures, the bishops exhorted
him that he should yet alter his purpose, and provide
for his honour and salvation. Then he, being full
of tears, spake unto the people in this sort.

' These lords and bishops do exhort and counsel
me, that I should here confess before you all that I
have erred; which thing to do, if it were such as
might be done with the infamy and reproach of man
only, they might peradventure easily persuade me
thereunto; but now truly I am in the sight of the
Lord my God, without Whose great ignominy and
grudge of mine own conscience, I can by no means
do that which they require of me. With what
countenance then should I behold the heavens?
With what face should I look upon them whom I
have taught, whereof there is a great number, if,
through me, it should come to pass that those
things, which they have hitherto known to be most
certain and sure, should now be made uncertain?
Should I, by this my example, astonish or trouble so
many souls, so many consciences, endued with the
most firm and certain knowledge of the Scriptures
and Gospel of our Lord Jesu Christ and His most
pure doctrine, armed against all the assaults of
Satan? I will never do it, neither commit any such
kind of offence, that I should seem more to esteem
this vile carcase appointed unto death, than their
health and salvation.'

Then one of the bishops took away the chalice from him which he held in his hand, saying; 'O cursed Judas! why hast thou forsaken the counsel and ways of peace? We take away from thee this chalice of thy salvation.'

But John Huss received this curse in this manner: 'I trust unto God, the Father omnipotent, and my Lord Jesus Christ, for Whose sake I do suffer these things, that He will not take away the chalice of His redemption, but have a steadfast and firm hope that this day I shall drink thereof in His kingdom.'

Then followed the other bishops in order, who every one of them took away the vestments from him which they had put on, each one of them giving him their curse. Whereunto John Huss answered: that he did willingly embrace and hear those blasphemies for the name of our Lord Jesus Christ.

At last they came to the rasing of his shaven crown; but before the bishops would go in hand with it, there was a great contention between them, with what instrument it should be done; with a razor, or with a pair of shears. In the mean season, John Huss, turning himself toward the emperor, said: 'I marvel that forasmuch as they be all of like cruel mind, yet they cannot agree upon their kind of cruelty.' At last they agreed to cut off the skin of the crown of his head with a pair of shears.

And when they had done that, they added these words: 'Now hath the Church taken away all her ornaments and privileges from him. Now there resteth nothing else, but that he be delivered over unto the secular power.'

But before they did that, there yet remained

another knack of reproach; for they caused to be made a certain crown of paper, almost a cubit deep, on which were painted three devils of wonderfully ugly shape, and this title set over their heads, 'Heresiarcha.' Which when he saw, he said: 'My Lord Jesus Christ, for my sake, did wear a crown of thorns; why should not I then, for His sake, again wear this light crown, be it ever so ignominious? Truly I will do it, and that willingly.' When it was set upon his head, the bishop said: 'Now we commit thy soul unto the devil.' 'But I,' said John Huss, lifting his eyes up towards the heavens, 'do commend into Thy hands, O Lord Jesu Christ! my spirit which Thou hast redeemed.'

These contumelious opprobries thus ended, the bishops, turning themselves towards the emperor, said: 'This most sacred synod of Constance leaveth now John Huss, who hath no more any office in the Church of God, unto the civil judgment and power.'

Then the emperor commanded Louis, Duke of Bavaria, who stood before him in his robes, holding the golden apple with the cross in his hand, that he should receive John Huss of the bishops, and deliver him unto them who should do the execution; by whom as he was led to the place of execution, before the church doors he saw his books burning, whereat he smiled and laughed. And all men that passed by he exhorted, not to think that he should die for any error or heresy, but only for the hatred and ill-will of his adversaries, who had charged him with most false and unjust crimes. All the whole city in a manner, being in armour, followed him.

The place appointed for the execution was before the Gottlieben gate, between the gardens and the gates of the suburbs. When John Huss was come thither, kneeling down upon his knees, and lifting his eyes up unto heaven, he prayed, and said certain Psalms, and especially the thirty-first and fifty-first Psalms. And they who stood hard by, heard him oftentimes in his prayer, with a merry and cheerful countenance, repeat this verse: 'Into Thy hands, O Lord! I commend my spirit,' which thing when the lay-people beheld who stood next unto him, they said: 'What he hath done before, we know not; but now we see and hear that he doth speak and pray very devoutly and godly.' A certain priest sitting on horseback, in a green gown, drawn about with red silk, said: 'He ought not to be heard, because he is a heretic.' In the meantime, while John Huss prayed, as he bowed his neck backwards to look upward unto heaven, the crown of paper fell off from his head upon the ground. Then one of the soldiers, taking it up again, said: 'Let us put it again upon his head, that he may be burned with his masters the devils, whom he hath served.'

When, by the commandment of the tormentors, he was risen up from the place of his prayer, with a loud voice he said: 'Lord Jesu Christ! help me, that with a constant and patient mind, I may suffer this cruel and ignominious death, whereunto I am condemned for the preaching of Thy most Holy Gospel and Word.' Then, as before, he declared the cause of his death unto the people. In the mean season the hangman stripped him of his garments, and turning his hands behind his back, tied him fast unto the stake with ropes that were made wet. And whereas, by chance, he was turned towards the east, certain cried out that he should not look towards the east, for he was a heretic: so he was turned towards the west. Then was his neck tied with a chain unto the stake, which chain when he beheld, smiling he said, that he would willingly receive the same for Jesus Christ's sake, Who, he knew, was bound with a far worse chain. Under his feet they set two faggots, admixing straw withal, and so from the feet up to the chin, he was enclosed round about with wood.

But before the wood was set on fire, Louis, Duke of Bavaria, and another gentleman with him, who was the son of Clement, came and exhorted John Huss, that he would yet be mindful of his salvation, and renounce his errors. To whom he said: 'What error should I renounce, when I know myself guilty of none? For this was the principal end and purpose of my doctrine, that I might teach all men repentance and remission of sins, according to the verity of the Gospel of Jesus Christ: wherefore, with a cheerful mind and courage, I am here ready to suffer death.' When he had spoken these words, they left him, and shaking hands together, departed.

Then was the fire kindled, and John Huss began to sing with a loud voice: 'Jesu Christ! the Son of the living God! have mercy upon me.' And when he began to say the same the third time, the wind drove the flame so upon his face, that it choked him. Yet, notwithstanding, he moved awhile after, by the space that a man might almost say three times the Lord's Prayer. When all the wood was consumed, the upper part of the body was left hanging in the chain, which they threw down stake and all, and making a new fire, burned it, the head being first cut in small gobbets, that it might the sooner be consumed unto ashes. The heart, which was found amongst the bowels, being well beaten with staves and clubs, was at last pricked upon a sharp stick, and roasted at a fire apart until it was consumed. Then, with great diligence gathering the ashes together, they cast them into the river Rhine, that the least remnant of that man should not be left upon the earth, whose memory, notwithstanding, cannot be abolished out of the minds of the godly, neither by fire, neither by water, neither by any kind of torment.

This godly servant and martyr of Christ was burned at Constance, the sixth day of the month of July, A.D. 1415.

THE LIFE AND STORY OF THE TRUE SERVANT AND MARTYR OF GOD, WILLIAM TYNDALE,

WE have now to enter into the story of the good martyr of God, William Tyndale; which William Tyndale, as he was a special organ of the Lord appointed, and as God's mattock to shake the inward roots and foundation of the Pope's proud prelacy, so the great prince of darkness, with his impious imps, having a special malice against him, left no way unsought how craftily to entrap him, and falsely to betray him, and maliciously to spill his life, as by the process of his story here following may appear.

William Tyndale, the faithful minister of Christ, was born about the borders of Wales, and brought up from a child in the University of Oxford, where he, by long continuance, increased as well in the knowledge of tongues, and other liberal arts, as especially in the knowledge of the Scriptures, whereunto his mind was singularly addicted; insomuch that he, lying then in Magdalen hall, read privily to certain students and fellows of Magdalen college some parcel of divinity; instructing them in the knowledge and truth of the Scriptures. His manners and conversation being correspondent to the same, were such, that all they that knew him, reputed him to be a man of most virtuous disposition, and of life unspotted.

Thus he, in the University of Oxford, increasing

more and more in learning, and proceeding in degrees of the schools, spying his time, removed from thence to the University of Cambridge, where he likewise made his abode a certain space. Being now further ripened in the knowledge of God's Word, leaving that University, he resorted to one Master Welch, a knight of Gloucestershire, and was there schoolmaster to his children, and in good favour with his master. As this gentleman kept a good ordinary commonly at his table, there resorted to him many times sundry abbots, deans, archdeacons, with divers other doctors, and great beneficed men; who there, together with Master Tyndale sitting at the same table, did use many times to enter communication, and talk of learned men, as of Luther and of Erasmus; also of divers other controversies and questions upon the Scripture.

Then Master Tyndale, as he was learned and well practised in God's matters, spared not to show unto them simply and plainly his judgment, and when they at any time did vary from Tyndale in opinions, he would show them in the book, and lay plainly before them the open and manifest places of the Scriptures, to confute their errors, and confirm his sayings. And thus continued they for a certain season, reasoning and contending together divers times, till at length they waxed weary, and bare a secret grudge in their hearts against him.

Not long after this, it happened that certain of these great doctors had invited Master Welch and his wife to a banquet; where they had talk at will and pleasure, uttering their blindness and ignorance without any resistance or gainsaying. Then Master

Welch and his wife, coming home, and calling for Master Tyndale, began to reason with him about those matters whereof the priests had talked at their banquet. Master Tyndale, answering by the Scriptures, maintained the truth, and reproved their false opinions. Then said the Lady Welch, a stout and a wise woman (as Tyndale reported), 'Well,' said she, 'there was such a doctor who may dispend a hundred pounds, and another two hundred pounds, and another three hundred pounds: and what! were it reason, think you, that we should believe you before them?'

Master Tyndale gave her no answer, and after that (because he saw it would not avail), he talked but little in those matters. At that time he was about the translation of a book called *Enchiridion Militis Christiani*, which he delivered to his master and lady; after they had well perused the same, the doctorly prelates were no more so often called to the house, neither had they the cheer and countenance when they came, as before they had: which thing they well perceiving, and supposing no less but it came by the means of Master Tyndale, refrained themselves, and at last utterly withdrew, and came no more there.

As this grew on, the priests of the country, clustering together, began to grudge and storm against Tyndale, railing against him in alehouses and other places, affirming that his sayings were heresy; and accused him secretly to the chancellor, and others of the bishop's officers.

It followed not long after this, that there was a sitting of the bishop's chancellor appointed, and warning was given to the priests to appear, amongst

whom Master Tyndale was also warned to be there.
And whether he had any misdoubt by their
threatenings, or knowledge given him that they
would lay some things to his charge, it is uncertain;
but certain this is (as he himself declared), that he
doubted their privy accusations; so that he by the
way, in going thitherwards, cried in his mind heartily
to God, to give him strength fast to stand in the
truth of His Word.

When the time came for his appearance before
the chancellor, he threatened him grievously,
reviling and rating him as though he had been
a dog, and laid to his charge many things whereof
no accuser could be brought forth, notwithstanding
that the priests of the country were there present.
Thus Master Tyndale, escaping out of their hands,
departed home, and returned to his master again.

There dwelt not far off a certain doctor, that had
been chancellor to a bishop, who had been of old,
familiar acquaintance with Master Tyndale, and
favoured him well; unto whom Master Tyndale
went and opened his mind upon divers questions
of the Scripture: for to him he durst be bold to
disclose his heart. Unto whom the doctor said,
'Do you not know that the Pope is very Antichrist,
whom the Scripture speaketh of? But beware
what you say; for if you shall be perceived to be
of that opinion, it will cost you your life.'

Not long after, Master Tyndale happened to be
in the company of a certain divine, recounted for a
learned man, and, in communing and disputing with
him, he drave him to that issue, that the said great
doctor burst out into these blasphemous words, 'We
were better to be without God's laws than the

Pope's.' Master Tyndale, hearing this, full of godly zeal, and not bearing that blasphemous saying, replied, 'I defy the Pope, and all his laws;' and added, that if God spared him life, ere many years he would cause a boy that driveth the plough, to know more of the Scripture than he did.

The grudge of the priests increasing still more and more against Tyndale, they never ceased barking and rating at him, and laid many things sorely to his charge, saying that he was a heretic. Being so molested and vexed, he was constrained to leave that country, and to seek another place; and so coming to Master Welch, he desired him, of his good will, that he might depart from him, saying: 'Sir, I perceive that I shall not be suffered to tarry long here in this country, neither shall you be able, though you would, to keep me out of the hands of the spiritualty; what displeasure might grow to you by keeping me, God knoweth; for the which I should be right sorry.'

So that in fine, Master Tyndale, with the good will of his master, departed, and eftsoons came up to London, and there preached awhile, as he had done in the country.

Bethinking himself of Cuthbert Tonstal, then Bishop of London, and especially of the great commendation of Erasmus, who, in his annotations, so extolleth the said Tonstal for his learning, Tyndale thus cast with himself, that if he might attain unto his service, he were a happy man. Coming to Sir Henry Guilford, the King's comptroller, and bringing with him an oration of Isocrates, which he had translated out of Greek into English, he desired him to speak to the said Bishop of

London for him ; which he also did ; and willed him moreover to write an epistle to the bishop, and to go himself with him. This he did, and delivered his epistle to a servant of his, named William Hebilthwait, a man of his old acquaintance. But God, who secretly disposeth the course of things, saw that was not the best for Tyndale's purpose, nor for the profit of His Church, and therefore gave him to find little favour in the bishop's sight; the answer of whom was this: his house was full; he had more than he could well find : and he advised him to seek in London abroad, where, he said, he could lack no service.

Being refused of the bishop he came to Humphrey Mummuth, alderman of London, and besought him to help him: who the same time took him into his house, where the said Tyndale lived (as Mummuth said) like a good priest, studying both night and day. He would eat but sodden meat by his good will, nor drink but small single beer. He was never seen in the house to wear linen about him, all the space of his being there.

And so remained Master Tyndale in London almost a year, marking with himself the course of the world, and especially the demeanour of the preachers, how they boasted themselves, and set up their authority; beholding also the pomp of the prelates, with other things more, which greatly misliked him; insomuch that he understood, not only that there was no room in the bishop's house for him to translate the New Testament, but also that there was no place to do it in all England.

Therefore, having by God's providence, some aid ministered unto him by Humphrey Mummuth, and

certain other good men, he took his leave of the
realm, and departed into Germany, where the good
man, being inflamed with a tender care and zeal of
his country, refused no travail nor diligence, how,
by all means possible, to reduce his brethren and
countrymen of England to the same taste and
understanding of God's holy Word and verity,
which the Lord had endued him withal. Whereupon, considering in his mind, and conferring also
with John Frith, Tyndale thought with himself no
way more to conduce thereunto, than if the Scripture
were turned into the vulgar speech, that the poor
people might read and see the simple plain Word of
God. He perceived that it was not possible to
establish the lay people in any truth, except the
Scriptures were so plainly laid before their eyes in
their mother tongue, that they might see the
meaning of the text; for else, whatsoever truth
should be taught them, the enemies of the truth
would quench it, either with reasons of sophistry,
and traditions of their own making, founded without
all ground of Scripture; or else juggling with the
text, expounding it in such a sense as it were
impossible to gather of the text, if the right
meaning thereof were seen.

Master Tyndale considered this only, or most
chiefly, to be the cause of all mischief in the Church,
that the Scriptures of God were hidden from the
people's eyes; for so long the abominable doings
and idolatries maintained by the pharisaical clergy
could not be espied; and therefore all their labour
was with might and main to keep it down, so that
either it should not be read at all, or if it were, they
would darken the right sense with the mist of their

sophistry, and so entangle those who rebuked or despised their abominations; wresting the Scripture unto their own purpose, contrary unto the meaning of the text, they would so delude the unlearned lay people, that though thou felt in thy heart, and wert sure that all were false that they said, yet couldst thou not solve their subtle riddles.

For these and such other considerations this good man was stirred up of God to translate the Scripture into his mother tongue, for the profit of the simple people of his country; first setting in hand with the New Testament, which came forth in print about A.D. 1529. Cuthbert Tonstal, Bishop of London, with Sir Thomas More, being sore aggrieved, devised how to destroy that false erroneous translation, as they called it.

It happened that one Augustine Packington, a mercer, was then at Antwerp, where the bishop was. This man favoured Tyndale, but showed the contrary unto the bishop. The bishop, being desirous to bring his purpose to pass, communed how that he would gladly buy the New Testaments. Packington hearing him say so, said, ' My lord! I can do more in this matter, than most merchants that be here, if it be your pleasure; for I know the Dutchmen and strangers that have bought them of Tyndale, and have them here to sell; so that if it be your lordship's pleasure, I must disburse money to pay for them, or else I cannot have them: and so I will assure you to have every book of them that is printed and unsold.' The Bishop, thinking he had God ' by the toe,' said, ' Do your diligence, gentle Master Packington! get them for me, and I will pay whatsoever they cost; for I intend to burn and destroy them all at Paul's Cross.' This Augustine Packington went unto William Tyndale, and declared the whole matter, and so, upon compact made between them, the Bishop of London had the books, Packington had the thanks, and Tyndale had the money.

After this, Tyndale corrected the same New Testaments again, and caused them to be newly imprinted, so that they came thick and threefold over into England. When the bishop perceived that, he sent for Packington, and said to him, 'How cometh this, that there are so many New Testaments abroad? you promised me that you would buy them all.' Then answered Packington, 'Surely, I bought all that were to be had: but I perceive they have printed more since. I see it will never be better so long as they have letters and stamps: wherefore you were best to buy the stamps too, and so you shall be sure:' at which answer the bishop smiled, and so the matter ended.

In short space after, it fortuned that George Constantine was apprehended by Sir Thomas More, who was then Chancellor of England, as suspected of certain heresies. Master More asked of him, saying, 'Constantine! I would have thee be plain with me in one thing that I will ask; and I promise thee, I will show thee favour in all other things, whereof thou art accused. There is beyond the sea, Tyndale, Joye, and a great many of you: I know they cannot live without help. There are some that succour them with money; and thou, being one of them, hadst thy part thereof, and therefore knowest from whence it came. I pray thee, tell me, who be they that help them thus?'

'My lord,' quoth Constantine, 'I will tell you truly: it is the Bishop of London that hath holpen us, for he hath bestowed among us a great deal of money upon New Testaments to burn them; and that hath been, and yet is, our only succour and comfort.' 'Now by my troth,' quoth More, 'I think even the same; for so much I told the bishop before he went about it.'

After that, Master Tyndale took in hand to translate the Old Testament, finishing the five books of Moses, with sundry most learned and godly prologues most worthy to be read and read again by all good Christians. These books being sent over into England, it cannot be spoken what a door of light they opened to the eyes of the whole English nation, which before were shut up in darkness.

At his first departing out of the realm he took his journey into Germany, where he had conference with Luther and other learned men; after he had continued there a certain season, he came down into the Netherlands, and had his most abiding in the town of Antwerp.

The godly books of Tyndale, and especially the New Testament of his translation, after that they began to come into men's hands, and to spread abroad, wrought great and singular profit to the godly; but the ungodly (envying and disdaining that the people should be anything wiser than they, and, fearing lest by the shining beams of truth, their works of darkness should be discerned), began to stir with no small ado.

At what time Tyndale had translated Deuteronomy, minding to print the same at Hamburg, he sailed thitherward; upon the coast of Holland, he suffered shipwreck, by which he lost all his books, writings, and copies, his money and his time, and so was compelled to begin all again. He came in another ship to Hamburg, where, at his appointment, Master Coverdale tarried for him, and helped him in the translating of the whole five books of Moses, from Easter till December, in the house of a worshipful widow, Mistress Margaret Van Emmerson, A.D. 1529; a great sweating sickness being at the same time in the town. So, having dispatched his business at Hamburg, he returned to Antwerp.

When God's will was, that the New Testament in the common tongue should come abroad, Tyndale, the translator thereof, added to the latter end a certain epistle, wherein he desired them that were learned to amend, if ought were found amiss. Wherefore if there had been any such default deserving correction, it had been the part of courtesy and gentleness, for men of knowledge and judgment to have showed their learning therein, and to have redressed what was to be amended. But the clergy, not willing to have that book prosper, cried out upon it, that there were a thousand heresies in it, and that it was not to be corrected, but utterly to be suppressed. Some said it was not possible to translate the Scriptures into English; some, that it was not lawful for the lay people to have it in their mother tongue; some, that it would make them all heretics. And to the intent to induce the temporal rulers unto their purpose, they said that it would make the people to rebel against the king.

All this Tyndale himself, in his prologue before the first book of Moses, declareth; showing further what great pains were taken in examining that translation, and comparing it with their own imaginations, that with less labour, he supposeth, they might have translated a great part of the Bible: showing moreover, that they scanned and examined every title and point in such sort, and so narrowly, that there was not one *i* therein, but if it lacked a prick over his head, they did note it, and numbered it unto the ignorant people for a heresy.

So great were then the froward devices of the English clergy (who should have been the guides of light unto the people), to drive the people from the knowledge of the Scripture, which neither they would translate themselves, nor yet abide it to be translated of others; to the intent (as Tyndale saith) that the world being kept still in darkness, they might sit in the consciences of the people through vain superstition and false doctrine, to satisfy their ambition, and insatiable covetousness, and to exalt their own honour above King and Emperor.

The bishops and prelates never rested before they had brought the King to their consent; by reason whereof, a proclamation in all haste was devised and set forth under public authority, that the Testament of Tyndale's translation was inhibited —which was about A.D. 1537. And not content herewith, they proceeded further, how to entangle him in their nets, and to bereave him of his life; which how they brought to pass, now it remaineth to be declared.

In the registers of London it appeareth manifest how that the bishops and Sir Thomas More having before them such as had been at Antwerp, most studiously would search and examine all things belonging to Tyndale, where and with whom he hosted, whereabouts stood the house, what was his stature, in what apparel he went, what resort he had; all which things when they had diligently learned then began they to work their feats.

William Tyndale, being in the town of Antwerp, had been lodged about one whole year in the house of Thomas Pointz, an Englishman, who kept a house of English merchants. Came thither one out of England, whose name was Henry Philips, his father being customer of Poole, a comely fellow, like as he had been a gentleman, having a servant with him: but wherefore he came, or for what purpose he was sent thither, no man could tell.

Master Tyndale divers times was desired forth to dinner and supper amongst merchants; by means whereof this Henry Philips became acquainted with him, so that within short space Master Tyndale had a great confidence in him, and brought him to his lodging, to the house of Thomas Pointz; and had him also once or twice with him to dinner and supper, and further entered such friendship with him, that through his procurement he lay in the same house of the said Pointz; to whom he showed moreover his books, and other secrets of his study, so little did Tyndale then mistrust this traitor.

But Pointz, having no great confidence in the fellow, asked Master Tyndale how he came acquainted with this Philips. Master Tyndale answered, that he was an honest man, handsomely learned, and very conformable. Pointz, perceiving that he bare such favour to him, said no more, thinking that he was brought acquainted with him by some friend of his. The said Philips, being in the town three or four days, upon a time desired Pointz to walk with him forth of the town to show him the commodities thereof, and in walking together without the town, had communication of divers things, and some of the King's affairs; by which talk Pointz as yet suspected nothing. But after, when the time was past, Pointz perceived this to be the mind of Philips, to feel whether the said Pointz might, for lucre of money, help him to his purpose, for he perceived before that Philips was monied, and would that Pointz should think no less. For he had desired Pointz before to help him to divers things; and such things as he named, he required might be of the best, 'for,' said he, 'I have money enough.'

Philips went from Antwerp to the court of Brussels, which is from thence twenty-four English miles, whence he brought with him to Antwerp, the procuror-general, who is the emperor's attorney, with certain other officers.

Within three or four days, Pointz went forth to the town of Barrois, being eighteen English miles from Antwerp, where he had business to do for the space of a month or six weeks; and in the time of his absence Henry Philips came again to Antwerp, to the house of Pointz, and coming in, spake with his wife, asking whether Master Tyndale were within. Then went he forth again and set the officers whom he brought with him from Brussels, in the street, and about the door. About noon he came again, and went to Master Tyndale, and desired him to lend him forty shillings; 'for,' said he, 'I lost my purse this morning, coming over at the passage between this and Mechlin.' So Master Tyndale took him forty shillings, which was easy to be had of him, if he had it; for in the wily subtleties of this world he was simple and inexpert. Then said Philips, 'Master Tyndale! you shall be my guest here this day.' 'No,' said Master Tyndale, 'I go forth this day to dinner, and you shall go with me, and be my guest, where you shall be welcome.'

So when it was dinner-time, Master Tyndale went forth with Philips, and at the going forth of Pointz's house, was a long narrow entry, so that two could not go in a front. Master Tyndale would have put Philips before him, but Philips would in no wise, but put Master Tyndale before, for that he pretended to show great humanity. So Master Tyndale, being a man of no great stature, went before, and Philips, a tall comely person, followed behind him; who had set officers on either side of the door upon two seats, who might see who came in the entry. Philips pointed with his finger over Master Tyndale's head down to him, that the officers might see that it was he whom they should take. The officers afterwards told Pointz, when they had laid him in prison, that they pitied to see his simplicity. They brought him to the emperor's attorney, where he dined. Then came the procuror-general to the house of Pointz, and sent away all that was there of Master Tyndale's, as well his books as other things; and from thence Tyndale was had to the castle of Filford, eighteen English miles from Antwerp.

Then incontinent, by the help of English merchants, were letters sent, in favour of Tyndale, to the court of Brussels. Also, not long after, letters were directed out of England to the council at Brussels, and sent to the merchant-adventurers, to Antwerp, commanding them to see that with speed they should be delivered. Such of the merchants as were there at that time, being called together, required the said Pointz to take in hand the delivery of those letters, in favour of Master Tyndale, to the Lord of Barrois and others; which Lord of Barrois (as it was told Pointz by the way) at that time was departed from Brussels. Pointz did ride after the next way, and overtook him at Achon, where he delivered to him his letters; which when he had received and read, he made no direct answer, but somewhat objecting, said, there were of their countrymen that were burned in England not long before (as indeed there were Anabaptists burned in Smithfield); and so Pointz said to him, 'Howbeit,' said he, 'whatsoever the crime was, if his lordship or any other nobleman had written, requiring to have had them, he thought they should not have been denied.'

'Well,' said he, 'I have no leisure to write, for the princess is ready to ride.'

Then said Pointz, 'If it shall please your lordship, I will attend upon you unto the next baiting-place'; which was at Maestricht.

'If you so do,' said the lord, 'I will advise myself by the way what to write.'

So Pointz followed him from Achon to Maestricht, which are fifteen English miles asunder; and there he received letters of him, one to the council, another to the company of the merchant-adventurers, and another also to the Lord Cromwell in England.

So Pointz rode from thence to Brussels, and then

and there delivered to the council the letters out of England, with the Lord of Barrois' letters also, and received eftsoons answer into England of the same by letters which he brought to Antwerp to the English merchants, who required him to go with them into England. And he, very desirous to have Master Tyndale out of prison, let not to take pains, with loss of time in his own business, and diligently followed with the said letters, which he delivered to the council, and was commanded by them to tarry until he had other letters. A month after, the letters being delivered him, he returned, and delivered them to the emperor's council at Brussels, and tarried for answer for the same.

Philips, being there, followed the suit against Master Tyndale, and hearing that he should be delivered to Pointz, and fearing lest he should be put from his purpose, he knew no other remedy but to accuse Pointz, saying, that he was a dweller in the town of Antwerp, a succourer of Tyndale, and one of the same opinion; and that all this was only his own labour and suit, and no man's else, to have Master Tyndale at liberty. Thus Pointz was delivered to the keeping of two serjeants at arms.

Master Tyndale, still remaining in prison, was proffered an advocate and a procuror; the which he refused, saying that he would make answer for himself. He had so preached to them who had him in charge, and such as was there conversant with him in the Castle, that they reported of him, that if he were not a good Christian man, they knew not whom they might take to be one.

At last, after much reasoning, when no reason would serve, although he deserved no death, he was condemned by virtue of the emperor's decree, made in the assembly at Augsburg. Brought forth to the place of execution, he was tied to the stake, strangled by the hangman, and afterwards consumed with fire, at the town of Filford, A.D. 1536; crying at the stake with a fervent zeal, and a loud voice, 'Lord! open the King of England's eyes.'

Such was the power of his doctrine, and the sincerity of his life, that during the time of his imprisonment (which endured a year and a half), he converted, it is said, his keeper, the keeper's daughter, and others of his household.

As touching his translation of the New Testament, because his enemies did so much carp at it, pretending it to be full of heresies, he wrote to John Frith, as followeth, 'I call God to record against the day we shall appear before our Lord Jesus, that I never altered one syllable of God's Word against my conscience, nor would do this day, if all that is in earth, whether it be honour, pleasure, or riches, might be given me.'

THE HISTORY OF DR MARTIN LUTHER

WITH HIS LIFE AND DOCTRINE DESCRIBED

MARTIN LUTHER, after he was grown in years, being born at Eisleben in Saxony, A.D. 1483, was sent to the University, first of Magdeburg, then of Erfurt. In this University of Erfurt, there was a certain aged man in the convent of the Augustines with whom Luther, being then of the same order, a friar Augustine, had conference upon divers things, especially touching remission of sins; which article the said aged Father opened unto Luther; declaring, that God's express commandment is, that every man should particularly believe his sins to be forgiven him in Christ: and further said, that this interpretation was confirmed by St Bernard: 'This is the testimony that the Holy Ghost giveth thee in thy heart, saying, Thy sins are forgiven thee. For this is the opinion of the apostle, that man is freely justified by faith.'

By these words Luther was not only strengthened, but was also instructed of the full meaning of St Paul, who repeateth so many times this sentence, 'We are justified by faith.' And having read the expositions of many upon this place, he then perceived, as well by the discourse of the old man, as by the comfort he received in his spirit, the vanity of those interpretations, which he had read before, of the schoolmen. And so, by little and little, reading and comparing the sayings and examples of the prophets and apostles, with continual invocation of God, and excitation of faith by force of prayer, he perceived that doctrine most evidently. Thus continued he his study at Erfurt the space of four years in the convent of the Augustines.

About this time one Staupitius, a famous man, who had ministered his help to further the erection of a University in Wittenberg, being anxious to promote the study of divinity in this new University, when he had considered the spirit and towardness of Luther, called him from Erfurt, to place him in Wittenberg, A.D. 1508 and of his age the twenty-sixth. In the meanwhile Luther intermitted no whit his study in theology. Three years after, he went to Rome, and returning the same year, he was graded doctor at the expense of the Elector Frederic, Duke of Saxony: for he had heard him preach; well understanded the quickness of his spirit; diligently considered the vehemency of his words; and had in singular admiration those profound matters which in his sermons he ripely and exactly explained. This degree Staupitius, against his will, enforced upon him ; saying merrily unto him, that God had many things to bring to pass in his Church by him. And though these words were spoken merrily, yet it came so to pass anon after.

After this, Luther began to expound the Epistle to the Romans, and the Psalms: where he showed the difference betwixt the Law and the Gospel; and confounded the error that reigned then in the schools and sermons, viz., that men may merit remission of sins by their own works, and that they be just before God by outward discipline; as the

Pharisees taught. Luther diligently reduced the minds of men to the Son of God: as John Baptist demonstrated the Lamb of God that took away the sins of the world, even so Luther, shining in the Church as the bright daylight after a long and dark night, expressly showed, that sins are freely remitted for the love of the Son of God, and that we ought faithfully to embrace this bountiful gift

His life was correspondent to his profession; and it plainly appeared that his words were no lip-labour, but proceeded from the very heart. This admiration of his holy life much allured the hearts of his auditors.

All this while Luther altered nothing in the ceremonies, but precisely observed his rule among his fellows. He meddled in no doubtful opinions, but taught this only doctrine, as most principal of all other, to all men, opening and declaring the doctrine of repentance, of remission of sins, of faith, of true comfort to be sought in the cross of Christ. Every man received good taste of this sweet doctrine, and the learned conceived high pleasure to behold Jesus Christ, the prophets and apostles, to come forth into light out of darkness.

It happened, moreover, about this time, that many were provoked by Erasmus's learned works to study the Greek and Latin tongues; who, having thus opened to them a more pleasant sort of learning than before, began to have in contempt the monks' barbarous and sophistical learning. Luther began to study the Greek and Hebrew tongues to this end, that having drawn the doctrine of the very fountains, he might form a more sound judgment.

As Luther was thus occupied in Germany, which

was A.D. 1516, Leo X., who had succeeded after Julius II., was Pope of Rome, who, under pretence of war against the Turk, sent his pardons abroad through all Christian dominions, whereby he gathered together innumerable riches and treasure; the gatherers and collectors whereof persuaded the people, that whosoever would give ten shillings, should at his pleasure deliver one soul from the pains of purgatory; but if it were but one jot less than ten shillings, it would profit them nothing.

This Pope's merchandise came also to Germany, through the means of a certain Dominic friar named Tetzel, who most impudently caused the Pope's indulgences to be sold about the country. Whereupon Luther, much moved with the blasphemous sermons of this shameless friar, and having his heart earnestly bent with ardent desire to maintain true religion, published certain propositions concerning indulgences, and set them openly on the temple that joineth to the castle of Wittenberg, the morrow after the feast of All Saints, A.D. 1517.

This beggarly friar, hoping to obtain the Pope's blessing, assembled certain monks and sophistical divines of his convent, and forthwith commanded them to write something against Luther. And while he would not himself be dumb, he began to thunder against Luther; crying, 'Luther is a heretic, and worthy to be persecuted with fire.' He burned openly Luther's propositions, and the sermon which he wrote of indulgences. This rage and fumish fury of this friar enforced Luther to treat more amply of the cause, and to maintain the truth. And thus rose the beginnings of this controversy.

A WISE AND GODLY PRINCE

The good Duke Frederic was one, of all the princes of our time, that loved best quietness and common tranquillity; so he neither encouraged nor supported Luther, but often discovered outwardly the heaviness and sorrow which he bare in his heart, fearing greater dissensions. But being a wise prince, and following the counsel of God's rule, and well deliberating thereupon, he thought with himself, that the glory of God was to be preferred above all things: neither was he ignorant what blasphemy it was, horribly condemned of God, obstinately to repugn the truth. Wherefore he did as a godly prince should do, he obeyed God, committing himself to His holy grace and omnipotent protection. And although Maximilian the Emperor, Charles King of Spain, and Pope Julius, had given commandment to the said Duke Frederic, that he should inhibit Luther from all place and liberty of preaching; yet the duke, considering with himself the preaching and writing of Luther, and weighing diligently the testimonies and places of the Scripture by him alleged, would not withstand the thing which he judged sincere. And yet neither did he this, trusting to his own judgment, but was very anxious to hear the judgment of others, who were both aged and learned; in the number of whom was Erasmus, whom the duke desired to declare to him his opinion touching the matter of Martin Luther; protesting, that he would rather the ground should open and swallow him, than he would bear with any opinions which he knew to be contrary to manifest truth.

Erasmus began jestingly and merrily to answer the duke's request, saying, that in Luther were two great faults; first, that he would touch the bellies of monks; the second, that he would touch the Pope's crown! Then, opening his mind plainly to the duke, he said, that Luther did well in detecting errors, that reformation was very necessary in the Church: adding moreover, that the effect of his doctrine was true.

Furthermore, the same Erasmus, in the following year, wrote to the Archbishop of Mentz a certain epistle touching the cause of Luther: 'The world is burdened with men's institutions, and with the tyranny of begging friars. Once it was counted a heresy when a man repugned against the Gospels. Now he that dissenteth from Thomas Aquinas is a heretic: whatsoever doth not like them, whatsoever they understand not, that is heresy. To know Greek is heresy; or to speak more finely than they do, that is heresy.'

The godly and faithful Christians, closed in monasteries, understanding images ought to be eschewed, began to abandon that wretched thraldom in which they were detained.

Luther held especially in contempt these horned bishops of Rome, who arrogantly and impudently affirmed, that St Peter had not the charge alone to teach the Gospel, but also to govern commonweals, and exercise civil jurisdiction. He exhorted every man to render unto God that appertained unto God, and to Cæsar that belonged unto Cæsar; and said, that all should serve God. After that Tetzel, the aforesaid friar, with his fellow-monks and friarly fellows, had cried out with open mouth against Luther, in maintaining the Pope's indulgences; and that Luther again, in defence of his cause, had set up propositions against the open abuses of the same, marvel it was to see how soon these propositions were sparkled abroad in sundry and far places, and how greedily they were caught up in the hands of divers both far and near.

Not long after steppeth up one Silvester de Priero, a Dominic friar, who first began to publish abroad a certain impudent and railing dialogue against Luther. Unto whom he answered out of the Scriptures.

Then was Martin Luther cited, the seventh of August, by one Hierome, Bishop of Ascoli, to appear at Rome. About which time Thomas Cajetan, Cardinal, the Pope's legate, was then lieger at the city of Augsburg, who before had been sent down in commission, with certain mandates from Pope Leo, unto that city. The University of Wittenberg, understanding of Luther's citation, eftsoons directed letters to the Pope, in Luther's behalf. Also another letter they sent to Carolus Miltitius, the Pope's chamberlain, being a German born. Furthermore, good Frederic ceased not to solicit, that the cause of Luther might be freed from Rome, and removed to Augsburg, in the hearing of the Cardinal. Cajetan, at the suit of the duke, wrote unto the Pope ; from whom he received this answer :—

That he had cited Luther to appear personally before him at Rome, by Hierome, Bishop of Ascoli, auditor of the chamber ; which bishop diligently had done what was commanded him : but Luther, abusing and contemning the gentleness offered, did not only refuse to come, but also became more bold and stubborn, continuing or rather increasing in his former heresy, as by his writings did appear.

Wherefore he would that the Cardinal should cite and call up the said Luther to appear at the city of Augsburg before him; adjoining withal, the aid of the princes of Germany, and of the emperor, if need required; so that when the said Luther should appear, he should lay hand upon him, and commit him to safe custody: and after, he should be brought up to Rome. And if he perceived him to come to any knowledge or amendment of his fault, he should release him and restore him to the Church again; or else he should be interdicted, with all other his adherents, abettors, and maintainers, of whatsoever state or condition they were, whether they were dukes, marquisses, earls or barons. Against all which persons and degrees, he willed him to extend the same curse and malediction (only the person of the emperor excepted); interdicting, by the censure of the Church, all such lands, lordships, towns, tenements, and villages, as should minister any harbour to the said Luther, and were not obedient unto the see of Rome. Contrariwise, to all such as showed themselves obedient, he should promise full remission of all their sins.

Likewise the Pope directed other letters also at the same time to Duke Frederic, with many grievous words, complaining against Luther.

The Cardinal, thus being charged with injunctions from Rome, according to his commission, sendeth with all speed for Luther to appear at Augsburg before him.

About the beginning of October, Martin Luther, yielding his obedience to the Church of Rome, came to Augsburg at the cardinal's sending (at the charges of the noble prince elector, and also with his letters of commendation), where he remained three days before he came to his speech; for so it was provided by his friends, that he should not enter talk with the cardinal, before a sufficient warrant or safe-conduct was obtained of the Emperor Maximilian. This being obtained, eftsoons he entered, offering himself to the speech of the cardinal, and was there received of the cardinal very gently; who, according to the Pope's commandment, propounded unto Martin Luther three things, to wit,

I. That he should repent and revoke his errors.

II. That he should promise, from that time forward, to refrain from the same.

III. That he should refrain from all things that might by any means trouble the Church.

When Martin Luther required to be informed wherein he had erred, the legate answered that he had held and taught that the merits of Christ are not the treasure of indulgences or pardons, and that faith is necessary to him that receiveth the sacrament. Furthermore Luther protested that the merits of Christ are not committed unto men: that the Pope's voice is to be heard when he speaketh agreeable to the Scriptures: that the Pope may err: and that he ought to be reprehended. Moreover he showed, that in the matter of faith, not only the General Council, but also every faithful Christian is above the Pope, if he lean to better authority and reason.

But the cardinal would hear no Scriptures; he disputed without Scriptures; he devised glosses and expositions of his own head. Luther, being rejected from the speech and sight of the cardinal, after six days' waiting, departed by the advice of his friends, and returned unto Wittenberg; leaving an appellation to the Bishop of Rome from the cardinal, which he caused openly to be affixed before his departure. Cajetan writeth to Duke Frederic a sharp and a biting letter, in which he exhorteth the duke, that as he tendereth his own honour and safety, and regardeth the favour of the high bishop, he will send Luther up to Rome, or expel him out of his dominions.

To this letter of the cardinal the duke answereth, purging both Luther and himself; Luther, in that he, following his conscience, grounded upon the Word of God, would not revoke that for an error which could be proved no error. And himself he excuseth thus: that whereas it is required of him to banish him his country, or to send him up to Rome, it would be little honesty for him so to do, and less conscience, unless he knew just cause why he should so do; which if the cardinal would or could declare unto him, there should lack nothing in him which were the part of a Christian prince to do. And therefore he desired him to be a mean unto the Bishop of Rome, that innocency and truth be not oppressed before the crime or error be lawfully convicted.

This done, the duke sendeth the letter of the cardinal unto Martin Luther, who answered to the prince: 'I am not so much grieved for mine own cause, as that you should sustain for my matter any danger or peril. And therefore, seeing there is no place nor country which can keep me from the malice of mine adversaries, I am willing to depart hence, and to forsake my country, whithersoever it shall please the Lord to lead me.'

Here, no doubt, was the cause of Luther in great danger, being now brought to this strait, that both Luther was ready to fly the country, and the duke again was as much afraid to keep him, had not the marvellous providence of God, Who had this matter in guiding, provided a remedy where the power of man did fail, by stirring up the whole University of Wittenberg; who, seeing the cause of truth thus to decline, with a full and general consent addressed their letters unto the prince, in defence of Luther and of his cause; making their humble suit unto him, that he, of his princely honour, would not suffer innocency, and the simplicity of truth so clear as is the Scripture, to be foiled and oppressed by mere violence of certain malignant flatterers about the Pope.

By the occasion of these letters, the duke began more seriously to consider the cause of Luther, to read his works, and hearken to his sermons: whereby, through God's holy working, he grew to knowledge and strength; perceiving in Luther's quarrel more than he did before. This was about the beginning of December A.D. 1518.

Pope Leo, in the meantime, had sent forth new indulgences, with a new edict, wherein he declared this to be the catholic doctrine of the holy mother-church of Rome, prince of all other churches, that Bishops of Rome, who are successors of Peter, and vicars of Christ, have this power and authority given to release and dispense, also to grant indulgences, available both for the living and for the dead lying in the pains of purgatory: and this doctrine he charged to be received of all faithful Christian men, under pain of the great curse, and utter separation from all holy Church. This popish decree and indulgence, as a new merchandise or ale-stake to get money, being set up in all quarters of Christendom for the holy father's advantage, came also to be received in Germany about the month of December. Luther, hearing how they went about in Rome to pronounce against him, provided a certain appellation conceived in due form of law, wherein he appealeth from the Pope to the General Council.

When Pope Leo perceived, that neither his pardons would prosper to his mind, nor that Luther could be brought to Rome; to essay how to come to his purpose by crafty allurements, he sent his chamberlain, Carolus Miltitius (who was a German), into Saxony, to Duke Frederic, with a golden rose, after the usual ceremony accustomed every year, to be presented to him ; with secret letters also to certain noblemen of the duke's council, to solicit the Pope's cause, and to remove the duke's mind, if it might be, from Luther. But before Miltitius approached into Germany, Maximilian the Emperor deceased in the month of January, A.D. 1519. At that time two there were who stood for the election; to wit, Francis the French King, and Charles, King of Spain, who was also Duke of Austria, and Duke of Burgundy. Through the means of Frederic prince-elector (who, having the offer of the prefer-ment, refused the same), the election fell to Charles, called Charles V., surnamed Prudence: which was about the end of August.

In the month of June before, there was a public disputation ordained at Leipsic, which is a city under the dominion of George Duke of Saxony, uncle to Duke Frederic. This disputation began through the occasion of John Eckius, a friar, and Andreas Carolostadt, doctor of Wittenberg. This Eckius had impugned certain propositions of Martin Luther, which he had written the year before touching the Pope's pardons. Against him Carolostadt wrote in defence of Luther. Eckius again, to answer Carolostadt, set forth an apology, which apology Carolostadt confuted by writing. Upon this began the disputation, with safe-conduct granted by Duke George to all and singular persons that would resort to the same. To this disputation came Martin Luther, not thinking to dispute in any matter, but only to hear what there was said and done.

But, having free liberty granted by the duke, Luther was provoked, and forced against his will, to dispute with Eckius. The matter of their controversy was about the authority of the Bishop of Rome. Luther before had set forth in writing this doctrine : that they that do attribute the pre-eminency to the Church of Rome, have no foundation but out of the Pope's decrees, which decrees he affirmed to be contrary to the Holy Scriptures.

Against this assertion Eckius set up a contrary conclusion; saying, that they that succeeded in the see and faith of Peter, were always received for the successors of Peter, and vicars of Christ on earth. He contended that the supremacy of the Bishop of Rome was founded and grounded upon God's law.

Upon this question the disputation did continue the space of five days; during all which season, Eckius very unhonestly and uncourteously demeaned himself, studying by all means how to bring his adversary into the hatred of the auditors, and into danger of the Pope. The reasons of Eckius were these: 'Forasmuch as the Church, being a civil body, cannot be without a head, therefore, as it standeth with God's law that other civil regiments should not be destitute of their head, so is it by God's law requisite, that the Pope should be the head of the universal Church of Christ.'

To this Martin Luther answered, that he confesseth and granteth the Church not to be headless, so long as Christ is alive, Who is the only head of the Church; neither doth the Church require any other head beside Him, forasmuch as it is a spiritual kingdom, not earthly.

Then came Eckius to the place of St Matthew, 'Thou art Peter, and upon this Rock will I build My Church.' To this was answered, that this was a confession of faith, and that Peter there representeth the person of the whole universal Church. Also that Christ in that place meaneth Himself to be the Rock. Likewise they came to the place of St John, 'Feed My sheep;' which words Eckius alleged to be spoken, properly and peculiarly, to Peter alone. Martin answered, that after these words spoken, equal authority was given to all the apostles, where Christ saith unto them, 'Receive ye the Holy Ghost: whose sins soever ye remit, they are remitted.'

After this, Eckius came to the authority of the Council of Constance, alleging this amongst other articles: 'that it standeth upon necessity of our salvation, to believe the Bishop of Rome to be supreme head of the Church;' alleging moreover, that in the same Council it was debated and discussed, that the General Council could not err. Whereunto Martin Luther again did answer discreetly, saying, that of what authority that Council of Constance is to be esteemed, he left to other men's judgments. 'This is most certain,' said he, 'that no Council hath authority to make new articles of faith.'

The next year, which was 1520, the friars and doctors of Louvain, and also of Cologne, condemned the books of Luther as heretical; against whom Luther again effectually defended himself, and charged them with obstinate violence and malicious impiety. After this, within few days flashed out from Rome the thunderbolt of Pope Leo against the said Luther.

Another book also Luther wrote, addressed to the nobility of Germany, in which he impugneth and shaketh the three principal walls of the papists: I. No temporal or profane magistrate hath any power upon the spiritualty, but these have power over the other. II. Where any place of Scripture, being in controversy, is to be decided, no man may expound the Scripture, or be judge thereof, but only the Pope. III. When any Council is brought against them, they say, that no man hath authority to call a Council, but only the Pope. Moreover, in the aforesaid book divers other matters he handleth and discourseth: that the pride of the Pope is not to be suffered; what money goeth out of Germany yearly to the Pope, amounting to the sum of three millions of florins; that the emperor is not under the Pope; that priests may have wives; that liberty ought not to be restrained in meats: that wilful poverty and begging ought to be abolished: what misfortunes Sigismund the Emperor sustained, for not keeping faith and promise with John Huss and Jerome: that heretics should be convinced not by fire and faggot, but by evidence of Scripture, and God's Word: and that the first teaching of children ought to begin with the Gospel.

In this year moreover followed, not long after, the coronation of the new Emperor Charles V., which was in the month of October, at Aix-la-Chapelle. After which coronation, Pope Leo sent again to Duke Frederic two cardinals his legates, of whom one was Hierome Aleander, who, after a few words of high commendation first premised to the duke touching his noble progeny, and other his famous virtues, made two requests unto him in the Pope's name: first, that he would cause all books of Luther to be burned; secondly, that he would either see the said Luther there to be executed, or else would make him sure, and send him up to Rome, unto the Pope's presence.

These two requests seemed very strange unto the duke; who, answering the cardinals, said, that he, being long absent from thence about other public affairs, could not tell what there was done, neither did he communicate with the doings of Luther. As for himself, he was always ready to do his duty; first, in sending Luther to Cajetan the cardinal at the city of Augsburg; and afterwards, at the Pope's commandment, would have sent him away out of his dominion, had not Miltitius, the Pope's own chamberlain, given contrary counsel to retain him still in his own country, fearing lest he might do more harm in other countries, where he was less known. Forasmuch as the cause of Luther was not yet heard before the emperor, he desired the said legates to be a mean to the Pope's holiness, that certain learned persons of gravity and upright judgment might be assigned to have the hearing and determination of this matter, and that his error might first be known, before he were made a heretic, or his books burned: which being done, when he should see his error by manifest and sound testimonies of Scripture, Luther should find no favour at his hands.

Then the cardinals took the books of Luther, and openly burnt them. Luther, hearing this, in like manner called all the multitude of students and learned men in Wittenberg, and there, taking the Pope's decrees, and the bull lately sent down against him, openly and solemnly, accompanied with a great number of people following him, set them likewise on fire; which was the 10th of December A.D. 1520.

A little before these things thus passed between the Pope and Martin Luther, the emperor had commanded an assembly of the States of all the Empire to be holden at the city of Worms, the 6th day of January next ensuing; in which assembly, through the means of Duke Frederic, the emperor gave forth, that he would have the cause of Luther brought before him. Upon the 6th of March, the emperor, through the instigation of Duke Frederic, directed his letters unto Luther; signifying, that forasmuch as he had set abroad certain books, he, therefore, by the advice of his peers and princes about him, had ordained to have the cause brought before him in his own hearing; and therefore he granted him license to come, and return home again. And that he might safely and quietly so do, he promised unto him, by public faith and credit, in the name of the whole Empire, his passport and safe-conduct. Wherefore, he willed him eftsoons to make his repair unto him, and to be there present on the twenty-first day after the receipt thereof.

Martin Luther, after he had been first accursed at Rome upon Maunday Thursday by the Pope's censure, shortly after Easter speedeth his journey toward Worms, where the said Luther, appearing before the emperor and all the States of Germany, constantly stuck to the truth, defended himself, and answered his adversaries.

Luther was lodged, well entertained, and visited by many earls, barons, knights of the order, gentlemen, priests, and the commonalty, who frequented his lodging until night.

He came, contrary to the expectation of many, as well adversaries as others. His friends deliberated together, and many persuaded him not to adventure himself to such a present danger, considering how these beginnings answered not the faith of promise made. Who, when he had heard their whole persuasion and advice, answered in this wise: 'As touching me, since I am sent for, I am resolved and certainly determined to enter Worms, in the name of our Lord Jesus Christ; yea, although I knew there were as many devils to resist me, as there are tiles to cover the houses in Worms.'

The next day after his repair, a gentleman named Ulrick, of Pappenheim, lieutenant-general of the men-at-arms of the Empire, was commanded by the emperor before dinner to repair to Luther, and to enjoin him at four o'clock in the afternoon to appear before the Imperial Majesty, the princes electors, dukes, and other estates of the Empire, to understand the cause of his sending for: whereunto he willingly agreed, as his duty was. And after four o'clock, Ulrick of Pappenheim, and Caspar Sturm, the emperor's herald (who conducted Martin Luther from Wittenberg to Worms), came for Luther, and accompanied him through the garden of the knights-of-the-Rhodes' place, to the Earl Palatine's palace; and, lest the people that thronged in should molest him, he was led by secret stairs to the place where he was appointed to have audience. Yet many, who perceived the pretence, violently rushed in, and were resisted, albeit in vain: many ascended the galleries, because they desired to behold Luther.

Thus standing before the emperor, the electors, dukes, earls, and all the estates of the empire assembled there, he was first advertised by Ulrick of Pappenheim to keep silence, until such time as he was required to speak. Then John Eckius above mentioned, who then was the Bishop of Treves' general official, with a loud voice, said:

'Martin Luther! the sacred and invincible Imperial Majesty hath enjoined, by the consent of all the estates of the holy empire, that thou shouldest be appealed before the throne of his majesty, to the end 1 might demand of thee these two points.

'First, whether thou confessest these books here [for he showed a heap of Luther's books written in the Latin and German tongues], and which are in all places dispersed, entitled with thy name, be thine, and thou dost affirm them to be thine, or not?

'Secondly, whether thou wilt recant and revoke them, and all that is contained in them, or rather meanest to stand to what thou hast written?'

Luther answered: 'I humbly beseech the Imperial

Majesty to grant me liberty and leisure to deliberate; so that I may satisfy the interrogation made unto me, without prejudice of the Word of God, and peril of mine own soul.'

Whereupon the princes began to deliberate. This done, Eckius, the prolocutor, pronounced what was their resolution, saying, 'The Emperor's majesty, of his mere clemency, granteth thee one day to meditate for thine answer, so that to-morrow, at this instant hour, thou shalt repair to exhibit thine opinion, not in writing, but to pronounce the same with lively voice.'

This done, Luther was led to his lodging by the herald.

The next day, the herald brought him from his lodging to the emperor's court, where he abode till six o'clock, for that the princes were occupied in grave consultations; abiding there, and being environed with a great number of people, and almost smothered for the press that was there. Then after, when the princes were set, and Luther entered, Eckius, the official, spake in this manner: 'Answer now to the Emperor's demand. Wilt thou maintain all thy books which thou hast acknowledged, or revoke any part of them, and submit thyself?'

Martin Luther answered modestly and lowly, and yet not without some stoutness of stomach, and Christian constancy. 'Considering your sovereign majesty, and your honours, require a plain answer; this I say and profess as resolutely as I may, without doubting or sophistication, that if I be not convinced by testimonies of the Scriptures (for I believe not the Pope, neither his General Councils, which have erred many times, and have been

contrary to themselves), my conscience is so bound
and captived in these Scriptures and the Word of
God, that I will not, nor may not revoke any
manner of thing; considering it is not godly or
lawful to do any thing against conscience. Hereupon I stand and rest: I have not what else to
say. God have mercy upon me!'

The princes consulted together upon this answer
given by Luther; and when they had diligently
examined the same, the prolocutor began to repel
him thus: 'The Emperor's majesty requireth of thee
a simple answer, either negative or affirmative,
whether thou mindest to defend all thy works as
Christian, or no?'

Then Luther, turning to the emperor and the
nobles, besought them not to force or compel him to
yield against his conscience, confirmed with the Holy
Scriptures, without manifest arguments alleged to
the contrary by his adversaries. 'I am tied by the
Scriptures.'

Night now approaching, the lords arose and
departed. And after Luther had taken his leave of
the emperor, divers Spaniards scorned and scoffed
the good man in the way going toward his lodging,
hallooing and whooping after him a long while.

Upon the Friday following, when the princes,
electors, dukes, and other estates were assembled,
the emperor sent to the whole body of the Council
a certain letter, as followeth: 'Our predecessors,
who truly were Christian princes, were obedient to
the Romish Church, which Martin Luther impugneth.
And therefore, inasmuch as he is not determined
to call back his errors in any one point, we cannot,
without great infamy and stain of honour, degenerate

from the examples of our elders, but will maintain the ancient faith, and give aid to the see of Rome. And further, we be resolved to pursue Martin Luther and his adherents by excommunication, and by other means that may be devised, to extinguish his doctrine. Nevertheless we will not violate our faith, which we have promised him, but mean to give order for his safe return to the place whence he came.'

During this time, divers princes, earls, barons, knights of the order, gentlemen, priests, monks, with others of the laity and common sort, visited him. All these were present at all hours in the emperor's court, and could not be satisfied with the sight of him. Also there were bills set up, some against Luther, and some, as it seemed, with him. Notwithstanding many supposed, and especially such as well conceived the matter, that this was subtilely done by his enemies, that thereby occasion might be offered to infringe the safe-conduct given him; which the Roman ambassadors with all diligence endeavoured to bring to pass.

John Eckius, the archbishop's official, in the presence of the emperor's secretary, said unto Luther in his lodging, by the commandment of the emperor, that since he had been admonished by the Imperial Majesty, the electors, princes, and estates of the empire, and that notwithstanding, he would not return to unity and concord, it remained that the emperor, as advocate of the catholic faith, should proceed further: and it was the emperor's ordinance, that he should within twenty-one days return boldly under safe-conduct, and be safely guarded to the place whence he came; so that in the meanwhile he stirred no commotion among the people in his journey, either in conference, or by preaching.

Luther, hearing this, answered very modestly and Christianly, 'Even as it hath pleased God, so is it come to pass; the name of the Lord be blessed!' He thanked most humbly the emperor's majesty, and all the princes and estates of the empire, that they had given to him benign and gracious audience, and granted him safe-conduct to come and return. Finally he desired none other of them, than a reformation according to the sacred Word of God, and consonancy of Holy Scriptures, which effectually in his heart he desired : otherwise he was prest to suffer all chances for the Imperial Majesty, as life, and death, goods, fame, and reproach : reserving nothing to himself, but only the Word of God, which he would constantly confess to the latter end.

The morrow after, which was April the 26th, after he had taken his leave of such as supported him, and of the benevolent friends that oftentimes visited him, and had broken his fast, at ten o'clock he departed from Worms, accompanied with such as repaired thither with him.

It was not long after this, but the emperor to purchase favour with the Pope (because he was not yet confirmed in his Empire), directeth out a solemn writ of outlawry against Luther, and all them that took his part; commanding the said Luther, wheresoever he might be gotten, to be apprehended, and his books burned. In the meantime, Duke Frederic conveyed Luther a little out of sight secretly, by the help of certain noblemen whom he well knew to be faithful and trusty unto him in that behalf. There Luther, being close and out of company, wrote divers epistles, and certain books; among which he dedicated one to his company of Augustine friars, entitled, *De abroganda Missa*: which friars the same time being encouraged by him, began to lay down their private masses. Duke Frederic, fearing lest that would breed some great stir or tumult, caused the judgment of the University of Wittenberg to be asked in the matter.

It was showed to the duke, that he should do well to command the use of the mass to be abrogated through his dominion: and though it could not be done without tumult, yet that was no let why the course of true doctrine should be stayed, neither ought such disturbance to be imputed to the doctrine taught, but to the adversaries, who willingly and wickedly kick against the truth, whereof Christ also giveth us forewarning before. For fear of such tumults therefore, we ought not to surcease from that which we know is to be done, but constantly must go forward in defence of God's truth, howsoever the world doth esteem us, or rage against it.

It happened about the same time that King Henry VIII. wrote against Luther. In which book, first, he reproveth Luther's opinion about the Pope's pardons; secondly, he defendeth the supremacy of the Bishop of Rome; thirdly, he laboureth to refell all his doctrine of the sacraments of the Church.

This book, albeit it carried the King's name in the title, yet it was another that ministered the motion, another that framed the style. But whosoever had the labour of this book, the King had the thanks and the reward; for the Bishop of Rome gave to the said King Henry, and to his successors for ever, the style and title of *Defender of the Faith*.

Shortly after this, Pope Leo was stricken with sudden fever, and died shortly, being of the age of forty-seven years: albeit some suspect that he died of poison. Successor to him was Pope Adrian VI., schoolmaster some time to Charles the Emperor. This Adrian was a German born, brought up at Louvain, and as in learning he exceeded the common sort of Popes, so in moderation of life and manners he seemed not altogether so intemperate as some other Popes have been: and yet, like a right Pope, nothing degenerating from his see, he was a mortal enemy against Martin Luther and his partakers. In his time, shortly after the council of Worms was broken up, another assembly of the princes, nobles, and states of Germany was appointed by the emperor at Nuremberg, A.D. 1522.

Unto this assembly the said Adrian sent his letters, with an instruction unto his legate Cheregatus, to inform him what causes to allege against Luther.

Pope Adrian the Sixth, to the Renowned Princes of Germany, and to the Peers of the Roman Empire.

We hear that Martin Luther, a new raiser-up of old and damnable heresies, first after the fatherly advertisements of the see apostolic; then after the sentence also of condemnation awarded against him, and lastly, after the imperial decree of our well-beloved son Charles, elect Emperor of the Romans, and catholic King of Spain, being divulged through the whole nation of Germany; yet hath neither been by order restrained, nor of himself hath refrained from his madness begun, but daily more and more, ceaseth not to disturb and replenish the world with new books, fraught full of errors, heresies, contumelies and sedition, and to infect the country of Germany, and other regions about, with this pestilence; and endeavoureth still to corrupt simple souls and manners of men, with the poison of his pestiferous tongue. And (which is worst of all) hath for his fautors and supporters, not of the vulgar sort only, but also divers personages of the nobility; insomuch that they have begun also to invade the goods of priests contrary to the obedience which they owe to ecclesiastical and temporal persons, and now also at last have grown unto civil war and dissension among themselves.

Do you not consider, O princes and people of Germany! that these be but prefaces and preambles to those evils and mischiefs which Luther, with the sect of his Lutherans, do intend and purpose hereafter? Do you not see plainly, and perceive with your eyes, that this defending of the verity of the Gospel, first begun by the Lutherans to be pretended, is now manifest to be but an invention to spoil your goods, which they have long intended? or do you think that these sons of iniquity do tend to any other thing, than under the name of liberty to supplant obedience, and so to open a general license to every man to do what him listeth? They who refuse to render due obedience to priests, to bishops, yea, to the high bishop of all, and who daily before your own faces make their booties of church-goods, and of things consecrated to God; think ye that they will refrain their sacrilegious hands from the spoil of laymen's goods? yea, that they will not pluck from you whatsoever they can rap or reave?

Nay, think you not contrary, but this miserable calamity will at length redound upon you, your goods, your houses, wives, children, dominions, possessions, and these your temples which you hallow and reverence; except you provide some speedy remedy against the same.

Wherefore we require you, in virtue of that obedience which all Christians owe to God, and blessed St Peter, and to his vicar here on earth, that you confer your helping hands every man to quench this public fire, and endeavour and study, the best way ye can, how to reduce the said Martin Luther, and all other fautors of these tumults and errors, to better conformity and trade both of life and faith.   And if they who be infected shall refuse to hear your admonitions, yet provide that the other part, which yet remaineth sound, by the same contagion be not corrupted.   When this pestiferous canker cannot with supple and gentle medicines be cured, more sharp salves must be proved, and fiery searings. The putrefied members must be cut off from the body, lest the sound parts also be infected. So God did cast down into hell the schismatical brethren Dathan and Abiram; and him that would not obey the authority of the priest, God commanded to be punished with death. So Peter, prince of the apostles, denounced sudden death to Ananias and Sapphira, who lied unto God.   So the old and godly emperors commanded Jovinian and Priscillian, as heretics, to be beheaded. So St Jerome wished Vigilant, as a heretic, to be given to the destruction of the flesh, that the spirit might be saved in the day of the Lord.   So also did our predecessors in the Council of Constance condemn to death John Huss and his fellow Jerome, who now appeareth to revive again in Luther. The worthy acts and examples of which forefathers, if you shall imitate, we do not doubt but God's merciful clemency shall eftsoons relieve his Church.

These instructions of the Pope himself against Luther, I thought, Christian reader! to set before thine eyes. They cry, 'Heresy, heresy!' but they prove no heresy. They inflame kings and princes against Luther, and yet they have no just cause wherefore. They charge Luther with disobedience, and none are so disobedient to magistrates and civil laws, as they. They lay to his charge oppression and spoiling of laymen's goods; and who spoileth the laymen's livings so much as the Pope?

Now let us see what the princes answer to these aforesaid suggestions and instructions of Pope Adrian.

The Answer of the Noble and Reverend Princes, and of the States of the sacred Roman Empire, exhibited to the Pope's Ambassador.

They understand that his holiness is afflicted with great sorrow for the prospering of Luther's sect, whereby innumerable souls committed to his charge are in danger of perdition. The lord lieutenant, and other princes and states do answer, that it is to them no less grief and sorrow than to his holiness. But why the sentence of the apostolic see, and the emperor's edict against Luther, hath not been put in execution hitherto, there hath been causes great and urgent; as first, that great evils and inconveniences would thereupon ensue. For the greatest part of the people of Germany have

always had this persuasion, and now, by reading
Luther's books, are more therein confirmed, that
great grievances and inconveniences have come to
this nation of Germany by the Court of Rome: and
therefore, if they should have proceeded with any
rigour in executing the Pope's sentence, and the
emperor's edict, the multitude would conceive and
suspect in their minds this to be done for subverting
the verity of the Gospel, and for supporting and
confirming the former abuses and grievances, whereupon great wars and tumults, no doubt, would have
ensued. Unless such abuses and grievances shall
be faithfully reformed, there is no true peace and
concord between the ecclesiastical and secular
estates, nor any true extirpation of this tumult and
errors in Germany, that can be hoped.

Whereas the Pope's holiness desireth to be
informed, what way were best to take in resisting
these errors of the Lutherans, what more present
or effectual remedy can be had than this, that the
Pope's holiness, by the consent of the Emperor's
majesty, do summon a free Christian Council in
some convenient place of Germany, as at Strasburg,
or at Mentz, or at Cologne, or at Metz? and that
with as much speed as conveniently may be; in
which Council it may be lawful for every person
that there shall have interest, either temporal or
ecclesiastical, freely to speak and consult, to the
glory of God, and health of souls, and the public
wealth of Christendom, without impeachment or
restraint; whatsoever oath or other bond to the
contrary notwithstanding: yea, and it shall be every
good man's part there to speak, not only freely, but
to speak that which is true, to the purpose, and

to edifying, and not to pleasing or flattering, but simply and uprightly to declare his judgment, without all fraud or guile.

And as touching by what ways these errors and tumults of the German people may best be stayed and pacified in the meantime, the aforesaid lord lieutenant, with the other princes, thereupon have consulted and deliberated ; that forasmuch as Luther, and certain of his fellows, be within the territory and dominion of the noble Duke Frederic, the said lord lieutenant and other states of the empire shall so labour the matter with the aforenamed prince, Duke of Saxony, that Luther and his followers, shall not write, set forth, or print any thing during the said mean space.

That the said lord lieutenant and princes shall labour so with the preachers of Germany, that they shall not in their sermons teach or blow into the people's ears such matters, whereby the multitude may be moved to rebellion or uproar, or be induced into error. Also, that they shall move no contention or disputation among the vulgar sort ; but whatsoever hangeth in controversy, the same they shall reserve to the determination of the Council to come.

The archbishops, bishops, and other prelates within their dioceses shall assign godly and learned men, having good judgment in the Scripture, who shall diligently and faithfully attend upon such preachers : and if they shall perceive the said preachers either to have erred, or to have uttered any thing inconveniently, they shall godly, mildly, and modestly advertise and inform them thereof, in such sort that no man shall justly complain the truth of the Gospel to be impeached. But if the preachers, continuing still in their stubbornness, shall refuse to be admonished, and will not desist from their lewdness, then shall they be restrained and punished by the ordinaries of the place, with punishment for the same convenient.

Furthermore, the said princes and nobles shall provide and undertake, so much as shall be possible, that, from henceforth, no new book shall be printed, neither shall they privily or apertly be sold. Also order shall be taken amongst all potentates, that if any shall set out, sell, or print any new work, it shall first be seen and perused of certain godly, learned, and discreet men appointed for the same ; so that if it be not admitted and approved by them, it shall not be permitted to be published.

Finally, as concerning priests who contract matrimony, and religious men leaving their cloisters, the aforesaid princes do consider, that forasmuch as in the civil law there is no penalty for them ordained, they shall be referred to the canonical constitutions, to be punished thereafter accordingly ; that is, by the loss of their benefices and privileges, or other condign censures.

Let us return to the story of Luther, of whom ye heard before, how he was kept secret and solitary for a time, by the advice and conveyance of certain nobles in Saxony, because of the emperor's edict. In the meantime, while Luther had thus absented himself out of Wittenberg, Andreas Carolostadt, proceeding more roughly and eagerly in causes of religion, had stirred up the people to throw down images in the temples. Luther reproved the rashness of Carolostadt, declaring that their proceedings herein were not orderly, but that pictures and images ought first to be thrown out of the hearts and consciences of men; and that the people ought first to be taught that we are saved before God, and please him only by faith; and that images serve to no purpose : this done, and the people well instructed, there was no danger in images, but they would fall of their own accord. Not that he would maintain images to stand or to be suffered, but that this ought to be done by the magistrate; and not by force, upon every private man's head, without order and authority.

Albeit the Church of Christ (praised be the Lord) is not unprovided of sufficient plenty of worthy and learned writers, able to instruct in matters of doctrine; yet in the chief points of our consolation, where the glory of Christ, and the power of His passion, and strength of faith are to be opened to our conscience; and where the soul, wrestling for death and life, standeth in need of serious consolation, the same may be said of Martin Luther, among all this other variety of writers, what St Cyprian was wont to say of Tertullian, 'Da magistrum'; 'Give me my master.'

Those who write the lives of saints use to describe and extol their holy life and godly virtues, and also to set forth such miracles as be wrought in them by God; whereof there lacketh no plenty in Martin Luther. What a miracle might this seem to be, for one man, and a poor friar, creeping out of a blind cloister, to be set up against the Pope, the universal bishop, and God's mighty vicar on earth; to withstand all his cardinals, yea, and to sustain the malice and hatred of almost the whole world being set against him; and to work that against the said Pope, cardinals, and Church of Rome, which no king nor emperor could ever do, yea, durst ever attempt, nor all the learned men before him could ever compass : which miraculous work of God, I account nothing inferior to the miracle of David overthrowing the great Goliath.

Wherefore if miracles do make a saint (after the Pope's definition), what lacketh in Martin Luther, to make him a saint? who, standing openly against the Pope, cardinals, and prelates of the church, in number so many, in power so terrible, in practice so crafty, having emperors and all the kings of the earth against him; who, teaching and preaching Christ the space of nine and twenty years, could, without touch of all his enemies, so quietly in his own country where he was born, die and sleep in peace. In which Martin Luther, first to stand against the Pope, was a great miracle; to prevail against the Pope, a greater; so to die untouched, may seem greatest of all, especially having so many enemies as he had.

As he was mighty in his prayers, so in his sermons God gave him such a grace, that when he preached, they who heard him thought every one his own temptation severally to be noted and touched. Whereof, when his friends demanded how that could be; 'Mine own manifold temptations,' said he, ' and experiences are the cause thereof.' For this thou must understand, good reader! that Luther from his tender years was much beaten and exercised with spiritual conflicts. Hieronymus Wellerus, scholar and disciple of the said Martin Luther, recordeth, that he oftentimes heard Luther his master thus report of himself, that he had been assaulted and vexed with all kinds of temptations, saving only one, which was with covetousness; with this vice he was never, said he, in all his life troubled, nor once tempted.

Martin Luther, living to the year of his age sixty-three, continued writing and preaching about twenty-nine years. As touching the order of his death, the words of Melancthon be these, given to his auditory at Wittenberg, A.D. 1546:—

Wednesday last past, and the 17th of February, Dr Martin Luther sickened of his accustomed malady, to wit, of the oppression of humours in the orifice or opening of the stomach. This sickness took him after supper, with which he vehemently contending, required secess into a by-chamber, and there he rested on his bed two hours, all which time his pains increased; and as Dr Jonas was lying in his chamber, Luther awaked, and prayed him to rise, and to call up Ambrose his children's schoolmaster, to make a fire in another chamber; into which when he was newly entered, Albert, Earl of Mansfield, with his wife, and divers others at that instant came into his chamber. Finally, feeling his fatal hour to approach, before nine of the clock in the morning, on the 18th of February, he commended himself to God with this devout prayer: 'My heavenly Father, eternal and merciful God! Thou hast manifested unto me Thy dear Son, our Lord Jesus Christ. I have taught Him, I have known Him; I love Him as my life, my health, and my redemption; Whom the wicked have persecuted, maligned, and with injury afflicted. Draw my soul to Thee.'

HIS LAST WORDS

After this he said as ensueth, thrice: 'I commend my spirit into Thy hands, Thou hast redeemed me, O God of Truth!' 'God so loved the world, that He gave His only Son, that all those that believe in Him should have life everlasting.' Having repeated oftentimes his prayers, he was called to God. So praying, his innocent ghost peaceably was separated from the earthly corpse.

THE STORY, LIFE, AND MARTYRDOM OF MASTER JOHN HOOPER, BISHOP OF WORCESTER AND GLOUCESTER

John Hooper, student and graduate in the University of Oxford, after the study of the sciences, wherein he had abundantly profited through God's secret vocation, was stirred with fervent desire to the love and knowledge of the Scriptures: in the reading and searching whereof, as there lacked in him no diligence, joined with earnest prayer, so neither wanted unto him the grace of the Holy Ghost to satisfy his desire, and to open unto him the light of true divinity.

Thus Master Hooper, growing more and more, by God's grace, in ripeness of spiritual understanding, and showing withal some sparkles of his fervent spirit, fell eftsoons into displeasure and hatred of certain rabbins in Oxford, who began to stir coals against him; whereby, and especially by the procurement of Dr Smith, he was compelled to avoid the University; and removing from thence, was retained in the house of Sir Thomas Arundel, and there was his steward, till the time that Sir Thomas Arundel, having intelligence of his opinions and religion, which he in no case did favour, and yet exceedingly favouring the person of the man, found the means to send him in a message to the Bishop of Winchester, writing his letter privily to the bishop, by conference of learning to do some good upon him; but in any case requiring him to send home his servant to him again.

Winchester, after conference with Master Hooper four or five days together, when he perceived that neither he could do that good which he thought to him, nor that he would take any good at his hand, according to Master Arundel's request, sent home his servant again; right well commending his learning and wit, but yet bearing in his breast a grudging stomach against Master Hooper still.

It followed not long after this, as malice is always working mischief, that intelligence was given to Master Hooper to provide for himself, for danger that was working against him. Whereupon Master Hooper, leaving Master Arundel's house, and borrowing a horse of a certain friend (whose life he had saved a little before from the gallows), took his journey to the sea-side to go to France, sending back the horse again.

Master Hooper, being at Paris, tarried there not long, but in short time returned into England, and was retained of Master Sentlow, till the time that he was again molested; whereby he was compelled, under the pretence of being captain of a ship going to Ireland, to take the seas. And so escaped he (although not without extreme peril of drowning) through France, to the higher parts of Germany; where he, entering acquaintance with the learned men, was of them friendly and lovingly entertained, at Basil, and especially at Zurich, of Master Bullinger, being his singular friend. There also he married his wife who was a Burgonian, and applied very studiously to the Hebrew tongue.

When God saw good to give us King Edward to

reign over this realm, with some peace and rest unto
his Gospel, amongst many other English exiles who
repaired homeward, Master Hooper also, moved in
conscience, thought not to absent himself; but, seeing
such a time and occasion, offered to help forward the
Lord's work, to the uttermost of his ability. And
so, coming to Master Bullinger, and other of his
acquaintance (as duty required), to give them thanks
for their singular kindness and humanity toward him
manifold ways declared, with like humanity purposed
to take his leave of them. Unto whom Master
Bullinger spake on this wise :—

'Master Hooper,' said he, 'although we are
sorry to part with your company for our own cause,
yet much greater causes we have to rejoice, both for
your sake, and especially for the cause of Christ's
true religion, that you shall now return, out of long
banishment, into your native country again; where
not only you may enjoy your own private liberty,
but also the cause and state of Christ's Church, by
you, may fare the better; as we doubt not but it
shall.

'Another cause, moreover, why we rejoice with
you and for you, is this: that you shall remove not
only out of exile into liberty; but you shall leave
here a barren, a sour and an unpleasant country,
rude and savage; and shall go into a land flowing
with milk and honey, replenished with all pleasure
and fertility.

'Notwithstanding, with this our rejoicing one fear
and care we have, lest you, being absent, and so far
distant from us, or else coming to such abundance of
wealth and felicity, in your new welfare and plenty
of all things, and in your flourishing honours, where

ye shall come, peradventure, to be a bishop, and where ye shall find so many new friends, you will forget us your old acquaintance and well-willers. Nevertheless, howsoever you shall forget and shake us off, yet this persuade yourself, that we will not forget our old friend and fellow Master Hooper. And if you will please not to forget us again, then I pray you let us hear from you.'

Whereunto Master Hooper answered again that neither the nature of country, nor pleasure of commodities, nor newness of friends, should ever induce him to the oblivion of such friends and benefactors, 'and therefore,' said he, 'from time to time I will write unto you, how it goeth with me. But the last news of all, I shall not be able to write : for there' said he (taking Master Bullinger by the hand), 'where I shall take most pains, there shall you hear of me to be burned to ashes.'

Master Hooper, coming to London, used continually to preach, most times twice, at least once, every day ; and never failed. The people in great flocks daily came to hear his voice, as the most melodious sound and tune of Orpheus's harp, as the proverb saith ; insomuch that oftentimes when he was preaching, the church would be so full, that none could enter further than the doors thereof. In his doctrine he was earnest, in tongue eloquent, in the Scriptures perfect, in pains indefatigable.

Even as he began, so he continued unto his life's end. For neither could his labour and painstaking break him, neither promotion change him, neither dainty fare corrupt him. His life was so pure and good, that no kind of slander could fasten any fault upon him. He was of body strong, his health whole and sound, his wit very pregnant, his invincible patience able to sustain whatsoever sinister fortune and adversity could do. He was constant of judgment, a good justicer, spare of diet, sparer of words, and sparest of time: in house-keeping very liberal, and sometimes more free than his living would extend unto. He bare in countenance and talk always a certain severe grace, which might, peradventure, be wished sometimes to have been a little more popular in him: but he knew what he had to do best himself.

This, by the way, I thought to note, for that there was once an honest citizen, and to me not unknown, who, having in himself a certain grudge of conscience, came to Master Hooper's door for counsel: but, being abashed at his austere look, durst not come in, but departed, seeking remedy of his troubled mind at other men's hands. In my judgment, such as are made governors over the flock of Christ, to teach and instruct them, ought so to frame their life, manners, countenance, and external behaviour, as neither they show themselves too familiar and light, whereby to be brought into contempt, nor, on the other side, that they appear more lofty and austere, than appertaineth to the edifying of the simple flock of Christ.

At length, and that not without the great profit of many, Master Hooper was called to preach before the King's majesty, and soon after made Bishop of Gloucester. In that office he continued two years, and behaved himself so well, that his very enemies (except it were for his good doing, and sharp correcting of sin) could find no fault with him. After that, he was made Bishop of Worcester.

THE GARMENTS OF A BISHOP

But I cannot tell what sinister and unlucky contention concerning the ordering and consecration of bishops, and of their apparel, with such other like trifles, began to disturb the good and lucky beginning of the godly bishop. For notwithstanding that godly reformation of religion then begun in the Church of England, besides other ceremonies more ambitious than profitable, or tending to edification, they used to wear such garments and apparel as the popish bishops were wont to do: first a chimere, and under that a white rochet: then, a mathematical cap with four angles, dividing the whole world into four parts. These trifles, tending more to superstition than otherwise, as he could never abide, so in no wise could he be persuaded to wear them. For this cause he made supplication to the King's majesty, most humbly desiring His Highness, either to discharge him of the bishopric, or else to dispense with him for such ceremonial orders; whose petition the King granted immediately.

Notwithstanding, the bishops still stood earnestly in the defence of the aforesaid ceremonies; saying it was but a small matter, and that the fault was in the abuse of the things, and not in the things themselves: adding moreover, that he ought not to be so stubborn in so light a matter; and that his wilfulness therein was not to be suffered.

Whilst both parties thus contended more than reason would, occasion was given to the true Christians to lament, to the adversaries to rejoice. This theological contention came to this end: that the bishops having the upper hand, Master Hooper was fain to agree to this condition—that sometimes he should in his sermon show himself apparelled as the other bishops were. Wherefore appointed to preach before the King, as a new player in a strange apparel, he cometh forth on the stage. His upper garment was a long scarlet chimere down to the foot, and under that a white linen rochet that covered all his shoulders. Upon his head he had a geometrical, that is, a four-squared cap, albeit that his head was round. What cause of shame the strangeness hereof was that day to that good preacher, every man may easily judge.

Master Hooper, entering into his diocese, was so careful in his cure, that he left neither pains untaken, nor ways unsought, how to train up the flock of Christ in the true word of salvation. No father in his household, no gardener in his garden, nor husbandman in his vineyard, was more or better occupied, than he in his diocese amongst his flock, going about his towns and villages in teaching and preaching to the people.

The time that he had to spare from preaching, he bestowed either in hearing public causes, or else in private study, prayer, and visiting of schools. With his continual doctrine he adjoined due and discreet correction, not so much severe to any, as to them which for abundance of riches, and wealthy state, thought they might do what they listed. He spared no kind of people, but was indifferent to all men, as well rich as poor. His life, in fine, was such, that to the Church and all churchmen, it might be a light and example; to the rest a perpetual lesson and sermon.

Though he bestowed the most part of his care upon the flock of Christ, for the which He spent His blood; yet, nevertheless, there lacked no provision in him to bring up his own children in learning and good manners ; insomuch that ye could not discern whether he deserved more praise for his fatherly usage at home, or for his bishop-like doings abroad: for everywhere he kept one religion in one uniform doctrine and integrity. So that if you entered into the bishop's palace, you would suppose yourself to have entered into some church or temple. In every corner thereof there was some smell of virtue, good example, honest conversation, and reading of holy Scriptures. There was not to be seen in his house any courtly roisting or idleness ; no pomp at all ; no dishonest word, no swearing could there be heard.

As for the revenues of both his bishoprics, he pursed nothing, but bestowed it in hospitality. Twice I was, as I remember, in his house in Worcester, where, in his common hall, I saw a table spread with good store of meat, and beset full of beggars and poor folk : and I, asking his servants what this meant, they told me that every day their lord and master's manner was, to have to dinner a certain number of poor folk of the said city by course, who were served by four at a mess, with hot and wholesome meats ; and, when they were served (being before examined by him or his deputies of the Lord's prayer, the articles of their faith, and the ten commandments), then he himself sat down to dinner, and not before.

King Edward being dead, and Mary being crowned Queen of England, this good bishop was one of the first that was sent for to be at London. And, although the said Master Hooper was not ignorant of the evils that should happen towards him (for he was admonished by certain of his friends to get him away, and shift for himself), yet he would not prevent them, but tarried still, saying: 'Once I did flee, and take me to my feet; but now, because I am called to this place and vocation, I am thoroughly persuaded to tarry, and to live and die with my sheep.'

And when at the day of his appearance, which was the first of September 1553, he was come to London, he was received very opprobriously. He freely and boldly told his tale, and purged himself. But, in fine, it came to this conclusion, that by them he was commanded to ward; it being declared unto him at his departure, that the cause of his imprisonment was only for certain sums of money, for which he was indebted to the Queen, and not for religion.

The next year, being 1554, the 19th of March, he was called again to appear before Winchester, and other the Queen's commissioners. The Lord Chancellor asked whether he was married. 'Yea, my lord,' replied Master Hooper, 'and will not be unmarried till death unmarry me.' The commissioners began to make such outcries, and laughed, and used such gesture, as was unseemly for the place. The Bishop of Chichester, Dr Day, called Master Hooper 'hypocrite,' with vehement words, and scornful countenance. Bishop Tonstal called him 'beast:' so did Smith, one of the clerks of the council, and divers others that stood by.

Tonstal, Bishop of Durham, asked Master Hooper, whether he believed the corporal presence in the sacrament. And Master Hooper said plainly, that there was none such, neither did he believe any such thing. Then asked Winchester what authority moved him not to believe the corporal presence? He said, the authority of God's Word. Whereupon they bade the notaries write that he was married; and said, that he would not go from his wife, and that he believed not the corporal presence in the sacrament: wherefore he was worthy to be deprived of his bishopric.

The true Report of Master Hooper's Entertainment in the Fleet; written with his own Hand, the 7th of January, 1555.

The 1st of September, 1553, I was committed unto the Fleet from Richmond, to have the liberty of the prison; and, within six days after, I paid for my liberty five pounds sterling to the warden, for fees: who, immediately upon the payment thereof, complained unto Stephen Gardiner, Bishop of Winchester; and so was I committed to close prison one quarter of a year in the Tower-chamber of the Fleet, and used very extremely.

Then by the means of a good gentlewoman, I had liberty to come down to dinner and supper, not suffered to speak with any of my friends; but, as soon as dinner and supper was done, to repair to my chamber again. Notwithstanding, while I came down thus to dinner and supper, the warden and his wife picked quarrels with me, and complained untruly of me to their great friend the Bishop of Winchester.

After one quarter of a year and somewhat more, Babington the warden, and his wife, fell out with me for the wicked mass; and thereupon the warden resorted to the Bishop of Winchester, and obtained to put me into the wards, where I have continued a long time; having nothing appointed to me for my bed, but a little pad of straw and a rotten covering, with a tick and a few feathers therein, the chamber being vile and stinking, until by God's means good people sent me bedding to lie in.

On the one side of which prison is the sink and filth of all the house, and on the other side the town-ditch, so that the stench of the house hath infected me with sundry diseases.—During which time I have been sick; and the doors, bars, hasps, and chains being all closed, and made fast upon me, I have mourned, called, and cried for help. But the warden, when he hath known me many times ready to die, and when the poor men of the wards have called to help me, hath commanded the doors to be kept fast, and charged that none of his men should come at me, saying, 'Let him alone; it were a good riddance of him.'

I paid always like a baron to the said warden, as well in fees, as for my board, which was twenty shillings a week, besides my man's table, until I was wrongfully deprived of my bishopric; and, since that time, I have paid him as the best gentleman doth in his house; yet hath he used me worse, and more vilely, than the veriest slave that ever came to the hall-commons.

The said warden hath also imprisoned my man William Downton, and stripped him out of his clothes to search for letters, and could find none, but only a little remembrance of good people's names, that gave me their alms to relieve me in prison; and to undo them also, the warden delivered the same bill unto the said Stephen Gardiner, God's enemy and mine.

I have suffered imprisonment almost eighteen months, my goods, living, friends, and comfort taken from me; the Queen owing me by just account four score pounds or more. She hath put me in prison, and giveth nothing to find me, neither is there suffered any to come at me whereby I might have relief. I am with a wicked man and woman, so that I see no remedy (saving God's help), but I shall be cast away in prison before I come to judgment. But I commit my cause to God, Whose will be done, whether it be by life or death.

The 22nd of January following, 1555, Babington, the warden of the Fleet, was commanded to bring Master Hooper before the Bishop of Winchester, with other bishops and commissioners, at the said Winchester's house, at St Mary Overy's. The Bishop of Winchester moved Master Hooper earnestly to forsake the evil and corrupt doctrine (as he termed it) preached in the days of King Edward the Sixth, and to return to the unity of the catholic Church, and to acknowledge the Pope's holiness to be head of the same Church, according to the determination of the whole parliament; promising, that as he himself, with other his brethren, had received the Pope's blessing, and the Queen's mercy; even so mercy was ready to be showed to him and others, if he would condescend to the Pope's holiness.

Master Hooper answered, that forasmuch as the Pope taught doctrine altogether contrary to the doctrine of Christ, he was not worthy to be head thereof; wherefore he would in no wise condescend to any such usurped jurisdiction. Neither esteemed he the Church, whereof they call him head, to be the catholic church of Christ: for the Church only heareth the voice of her spouse Christ, and flieth the strangers. 'Howbeit,' saith he, 'if in any point, to me unknown, I have offended the Queen's majesty, I shall most humbly submit myself to her mercy; if mercy may be had with safety of conscience and without the displeasure of God.' Answer was made that the Queen would show no mercy to the Pope's enemies. Whereupon Babington was commanded to bring him to the Fleet again.

The 28th of January, Winchester and the commissioners sat in judgment at St Mary Overy's, where Master Hooper appeared before them at afternoon again; and there, after much reasoning and disputation to and fro, he was commanded aside, till Master Rogers (who was then come) had been likewise examined. Examinations being ended, the two sheriffs of London were commanded, about four of the clock, to carry them to the Compter in Southwark, there to remain till the morrow at nine o'clock, to see whether they would relent and come home again to the catholic Church.

So Master Hooper went before with one of the sheriffs, and Master Rogers came after with the other, and being out of church door, Master Hooper looked back, and stayed a little till Master Rogers drew near, unto whom he said 'Come, brother Rogers! must we two take this matter first in hand, and begin to fry these faggots?'

'Yea, sir,' said Master Rogers, 'by God's grace.'

THE COSTERMONGERS' CANDLES

'Doubt not,' said Master Hooper, 'but God will give strength.'

So going forwards, there was such a press of people in the streets, who rejoiced at their constancy that they had much ado to pass.

Upon the next day, they were brought again by the sheriffs before the said Bishop and commissioners. After long and earnest talk, when they perceived that Master Hooper would by no means condescend unto them, they condemned him to be degraded, and read unto him his condemnation. That done, Master Rogers was brought before them, and in like manner entreated, and so they delivered both of them to the secular power, the two sheriffs of London, who were willed to carry them to the Clink, a prison not far from the Bishop of Winchester's house, and there to remain till night.

When it was dark, Master Hooper was led by one of the sheriffs, with many bills and weapons, first through the Bishop of Winchester's house, and so over London-bridge, through the city to Newgate. And by the way some of the sergeants were willed to go before, and put out the costermongers' candles, who used to sit with lights in the streets: either fearing, of likelihood, that the people would have made some attempt to have taken him away from them by force, if they had seen him go to that prison; or else, being burdened with an evil conscience, they thought darkness to be a most fit season for such a business.

But notwithstanding this device, the people having some foreknowledge of his coming, many of them came forth of their doors with lights, and saluted him; praising God for his constancy in the true doctrine which he had taught them, and desiring God to strengthen him in the same to the end. Master Hooper passed by, and required the people to make their earnest prayers to God for him: and so went through Cheapside to the place appointed, and was delivered as close prisoner to the keeper of Newgate, where he remained six days, nobody being permitted to come to him, or talk with him, saving his keepers, and such as should be appointed thereto.

During this time, Bonner, Bishop of London, and others at his appointment, resorted divers times unto him to assay if by any means they could persuade him to relent, and become a member of their antichristian church. All the ways they could devise, they attempted: for, besides the allegations of testimonies of the Scriptures, and of ancient writers wrested to a wrong sense, according to their accustomed manner, they also used all outward gentleness and significations of friendship, with many great proffers and promises of worldly commodities; not omitting also most grievous threatenings, if with gentleness they could not prevail: but they found him always the same man, steadfast and immovable.

When they perceived that they could by no means reclaim him to their purpose with such persuasions and offers as they used for his conversion, then went they about, by false rumours and reports of recantations, to bring him and the doctrine of Christ which he professed, out of credit with the people. So the bruit being spread abroad, and believed of some of the weaker sort, by reason of the often resort of the Bishop of London and others, it at last came to Master Hooper's ears: wherewith he was not a little grieved, that the people should give credit unto false rumours. ' The report abroad (as I am credibly informed) is that I, John Hooper, a condemned man for the cause of Christ, should now, after sentence of death (being in Newgate, prisoner, and looking daily for execution) recant and abjure that which heretofore I have preached. And this talk ariseth of this, that the Bishop of London and his chaplains resort unto me. I have spoken and do speak with them when they come; for I fear not their arguments, neither is death terrible unto me; and I am more confirmed in the truth which I have preached heretofore, by their coming. I have left all things of the world, and suffered great pains and imprisonment, and, I thank God, I am as ready to suffer death, as a mortal man may be. I have taught the truth with my tongue, and with my pen heretofore; and hereafter shortly shall confirm the same by God's grace with my blood.'

Monday, the 4th of February, his keeper gave him an inkling that he should be sent to Gloucester to suffer death, whereat he rejoiced very much, lifting up his eyes and hands unto heaven, and praising God that He saw it good to send him amongst the people over whom he was pastor, there to confirm with his death the truth which he had before taught them; not doubting but the Lord would give him strength to perform the same to His glory. And immediately he sent to his servant's house for his boots, spurs, and cloak, that he might be in a readiness to ride when he should be called.

The next day following, about four o'clock in the

morning before day, the keeper with others came to him and searched him, and the bed wherein he lay, to see if he had written any thing; and then he was led by the sheriffs of London, and their officers, forth of Newgate to a place appointed, not far from St Dunstan's church in Fleet Street, where six of the Queen's guards were appointed to receive him, and to carry him to Gloucester, there to be delivered unto the sheriff, who, with the Lord Chandos, Master Wicks, and other commissioners, were appointed to see execution done.

The which guard brought him to the Angel, where he brake his fast with them, eating his meat at that time more liberally than he had used to do a good while before. About the break of the day he went to horse, and leaped cheerfully on horseback without help, having a hood upon his head under his hat, that he should not be known. And so he took his journey joyfully towards Gloucester, and always by the way the guard learned of him where he was accustomed to bait or lodge; and ever carried him to another inn.

On the Thursday following, he came to a town in his diocese called Cirencester, fifteen miles from Gloucester, about eleven o'clock, and there dined at a woman's house who had always hated the truth, and spoken all evil she could of Master Hooper. This woman, perceiving the cause of his coming, showed him all the friendship she could, and lamented his case with tears; confessing that she before had often reported, that if he were put to the trial, he would not stand to his doctrine.

After dinner he rode forwards, and came to Gloucester about five o'clock; and a mile without

the town was much people assembled, which cried
and lamented his estate, insomuch that one of the
guard rode post into the town, to require aid of the
mayor and sheriffs, fearing lest he should have been
taken from them. The officers and their retinue
repaired to the gate with weapons, and commanded
the people to keep their houses; but there was no
man that once gave any signification of any such
rescue or violence.

So was he lodged at one Ingram's house in
Gloucester; and that night (as he had done all
the way) he did eat his meat quietly, and slept his
first sleep soundly, as it was reported by them of
the guard, and others. After his first sleep he
continued all that night in prayer until the morning;
and then he desired that he might go into the next
chamber (for the guard were also in the chamber
where he lay), that there, being solitary, he might
pray and talk with God: so that all the day, saving
a little at meat, and when he talked at any time
with such as the guard licensed to speak with him,
he bestowed in prayer.

Amongst others that spake with him, Sir Anthony
Kingston, Knight, was one; who, seeming in time
past his very friend, was then appointed by the
Queen's letters to be one of the commissioners, to
see execution done upon him. Master Kingston,
being brought into the chamber, found him at his
prayer: and as soon as he saw Master Hooper, he
burst forth in tears. Master Hooper at the first
blush knew him not. Then said Master Kingston,
'Why, my lord, do you not know me, an old friend
of yours, Anthony Kingston?'

Hooper: 'Yes, Master Kingston, I do now know

you well, and am glad to see you in health, and do praise God for the same.'

Kingston : 'But I am sorry to see you in this case; for as I understand you be come hither to die. But, alas, consider that life is sweet, and death is bitter. Therefore, seeing life may be had, desire to live; for life hereafter may do good.'

Hooper : 'Indeed it is true, Master Kingston, I am come hither to end this life, and to suffer death here, because I will not gainsay the former truth that I have heretofore taught amongst you in this diocese, and elsewhere; and I thank you for your friendly counsel, although it be not so friendly as I could have wished it. True it is, Master Kingston, that death is bitter, and life is sweet: but, alas, consider that the death to come is more bitter, and the life to come is more sweet. Therefore, for the desire and love I have to the one, and the terror and fear of the other; I do not so much regard this death, nor esteem this life, but have settled myself, through the strength of God's holy Spirit, patiently to pass through the torments and extremities of the fire now prepared for me, rather than to deny the truth of His Word; desiring you, and others, in the meantime, to commend me to God's mercy in your prayers.'

Kingston : 'Well, my lord, then I perceive there is no remedy, and therefore I will take my leave of you : and I thank God that ever I knew you; for God did appoint you to call me, being a lost child.'

Hooper : I do highly praise God for it : and I pray God you may continually live in His fear.'

After these, and many other words, the one took leave of the other; Master Kingston, with bitter tears, Master Hooper with tears also trickling down his cheeks. At which departure Master Hooper told him that all the troubles he had sustained in prison had not caused him to utter so much sorrow.

The same day in the afternoon, a blind boy, after long intercession made to the guard, obtained license to be brought unto Master Hooper's speech. The same boy not long afore had suffered imprisonment at Gloucester for confessing of the truth. Master Hooper, after he had examined him of his faith, and the cause of his imprisonment, beheld him steadfastly, and (the water appearing in his eyes) said unto him, ' Ah, poor boy! God hath taken from thee thy outward sight, for what reason He best knoweth: but He hath given thee another sight much more precious, for He hath endued thy soul with the eye of knowledge and faith. God give thee grace continually to pray unto Him, that thou lose not that sight; for then shouldest thou be blind both in body and soul!'

The same night he was committed by the guard, their commission being then expired, unto the custody of the sheriffs of Gloucester, who, with the mayor and aldermen, repaired to Master Hooper's lodging, and took him by the hand.

Unto whom Hooper spake on this manner: ' Master mayor, I give most hearty thanks to you, and to the rest of your brethren, that you have vouchsafed to take me, a prisoner and a condemned man, by the hand; whereby to my rejoicing it is some deal apparent that your old love and friendship towards me is not altogether extinguished; and I trust also that all the things I have taught you in times past are not utterly forgotten, when I was here, by the godly King that dead is, appointed to be your bishop and pastor. For the which most true and sincere doctrine, because I will not now account it falsehood and heresy, as many other men do, I am sent hither (as I am sure you know) by the Queen's commandment to die; and am come where I taught it, to confirm it with my blood. And now, master sheriffs, I understand by these good men, and my very friends' (meaning the guard), 'at whose hands I have found so much favour and gentleness, by the way hitherward, as a prisoner could reasonably require (for the which also I most heartily thank them), that I am committed to your custody, as unto them that must see me brought to-morrow to the place of execution. My request therefore to you shall be only, that there may be a quick fire, shortly to make an end; and in the meantime I will be as obedient unto you, as yourselves would wish. If you think I do amiss in any thing, hold up your finger, and I have done: for I am not come hither as one enforced or compelled to die (for it is well known, I might have had my life with worldly gain); but as one willing to offer and give my life for the truth, rather than consent to the wicked papistical religion of the Bishop of Rome, received and set forth by the magistrates in England, to God's high displeasure and dishonour; and I trust, by God's grace, to-morrow to die a faithful servant of God, and a true obedient subject to the Queen.'

These words used Master Hooper to the mayor, sheriffs, and aldermen, whereat many of them lamented. Notwithstanding the two sheriffs were determined to have lodged him in the common gaol of the town, called Northgate, if the guard had not

made earnest intercession for him; who declared,
how quietly, mildly, and patiently, he had behaved
himself in the way; adding thereto, that any child
might keep him well enough, and that they themselves would rather take pains to watch with
him, than that he should be sent to the common
prison.

So it was determined he should still remain in
Robert Ingram's house; and the sheriffs and the
sergeants, and other officers, did appoint to watch
with him that night themselves. His desire was,
that he might go to bed that night betimes, saying,
that he had many things to remember: and so he
did at five of the clock, and slept one sleep soundly,
and bestowed the rest of the night in prayer.
After he got up in the morning, he desired that no
man should be suffered to come into the chamber,
that he might be solitary till the hour of execution.

About eight o'clock came Sir John Bridges, Lord
Chandos, with a great band of men, Sir Anthony
Kingston, Sir Edmund Bridges, and other commissioners appointed to see execution done. At
nine o'clock Master Hooper was willed to prepare
himself to be in a readiness, for the time was at
hand. Immediately he was brought down from his
chamber by the sheriffs, who were accompanied
with bills, glaves, and weapons. When he saw the
multitude of weapons, he spake to the sheriffs on
this wise: 'Master sheriffs,' said he, 'I am no
traitor, neither needed you to have made such a
business to bring me to the place where I must
suffer: for if ye had willed me, I would have gone
alone to the stake, and have troubled none of you
all.' A multitude of people assembled to the number

of seven thousand, for it was market-day, and many came to see his behaviour towards death.

So he went forward, led between the two sheriffs (as it were a lamb to the place of slaughter) in a gown of his host's, his hat upon his head, and a staff in his hand to stay himself withal: for the grief of the sciatica, which he had taken in prison, caused him somewhat to halt. He would look very cheerfully upon such as he knew: and he was never known, during the time of his being amongst them, to look with so cheerful and ruddish a countenance as he did at that present. When he came to the place appointed where he should die, smilingly he beheld the stake and preparation made for him, which was near unto the great elm-tree, over against the college of priests, where he was wont to preach. The place round about the houses, and the boughs of the tree, were replenished with people; and in the chamber over the college-gate stood the wolvish blood-suckers and turnelings, the priests of the college.

Then kneeled he down, forasmuch as he could not be suffered to speak unto the people. After he was somewhat entered into his prayer, a box was brought and laid before him upon a stool, with his pardon (or at least-wise it was feigned to be his pardon) from the Queen, if he would turn. At the sight whereof he cried, 'If you love my soul, away with it! if you love my soul, away with it!'

Prayer being done, he prepared himself to the stake, and put off his host's gown, and delivered it to the sheriffs, requiring them to see it restored unto the owner, and put off the rest of his gear, unto his doublet and hose, wherein he would have burned.

But the sheriffs would not permit that, such was their greediness; unto whose pleasures, good man, he very obediently submitted himself; and his doublet, hose, and petticoat were taken off. Then, being in his shirt, he took a point from his hose himself, and trussed his shirt between his legs, where he had a pound of gunpowder in a bladder, and under each arm the like quantity, delivered him by the guard.

So, desiring the people to say the Lord's prayer with him, and to pray for him (who performed it with tears, during the time of his pains), he went up to the stake. The hoop of iron prepared for his middle was brought, but when they offered to have bound his neck and legs with the other two hoops of iron, he utterly refused them.

Thus being ready, he looked upon all the people, of whom he might be well seen (for he was both tall, and stood also on a high stool), and in every corner there was nothing to be seen but weeping and sorrowful people. Then, lifting up his eyes and hands unto heaven, he prayed to himself. By and by, he that was appointed to make the fire, came to him, and did ask him forgiveness. Of whom he asked why he should forgive him, saying, that he knew never any offence he had committed against him. 'O sir!' said the man, 'I am appointed to make the fire.' 'Therein,' said Master Hooper, 'thou dost nothing offend me; God forgive thee thy sins, and do thine office, I pray thee.'

Then the reeds were cast up, and he received two bundles of them in his own hands, embraced them, kissed them, and put under either arm one of them, and showed with his hand how the rest should be bestowed, and pointed to the place where any did lack.

Anon commandment was given that the fire should be set to. But because there were put to no fewer green faggots than two horses could carry upon their backs, it kindled not by and by, and was a pretty while also before it took the reeds upon the faggots. At length it burned about him, but the wind having full strength in that place (it was a lowering and cold morning), it blew the flame from him, so that he was in a manner nothing but touched by the fire.

Within a space after, a few dry faggots were brought, and a new fire kindled with faggots (for there were no more reeds), and that burned at the nether parts, but had small power above, because of the wind, saving that it did burn his hair, and swell his skin a little. In the time of which fire even as at the first flame, he prayed, saying mildly and not very loud (but as one without pains), 'O Jesus, the Son of David, have mercy upon me, and receive my soul!' After the second was spent, he did wipe both his eyes with his hands, and beholding the people, he said with an indifferent loud voice, 'For God's love, good people, let me have more fire!' And all this while his nether parts did burn: for the faggots were so few, that the flame did not burn strongly at his upper parts.

The third fire was kindled within a while after, which was more extreme than the other two: and then the bladders of gunpowder brake, which did him small good, they were so placed, and the wind had such power. In the which fire he prayed with somewhat a loud voice, 'Lord Jesus, have mercy upon me; Lord Jesus, have mercy upon me: Lord Jesus receive my spirit.' And these were the last words he was heard to utter. But when he was black in the mouth, and his tongue swollen, that he could not speak, yet his lips went till they were shrunk to the gums: and he knocked his breast with his hands, until one of his arms fell off and then knocked still with the other, what time the fat, water, and blood, dropped out at his fingers' ends, until by renewing of the fire his strength was gone, and his hand did cleave fast, in knocking, to the iron upon his breast. So immediately, bowing forwards, he yielded up his spirit.

Thus was he three quarters of an hour or more in the fire. Even as a lamb, patiently he abode the extremity thereof, neither moving forwards, backwards, nor to any side: but he died as quietly as a child in his bed. And he now reigneth, I doubt not, as a blessed martyr in the joys of heaven, prepared for the faithful in Christ before the foundations of the world; for whose constancy all Christians are bound to praise God.

A FAITHFUL PARISH CLERGYMAN: THE HISTORY OF DR ROWLAND TAYLOR, HADLEY

THE town of Hadley was one of the first that received the Word of God in all England. The Gospel of Christ had such gracious success, and took such root there, that a great number of that parish became exceeding well learned in the Holy Scriptures, as well women as men, so that a man might have found among them many, that had often read the whole Bible through, and that could have said a great sort of St Paul's Epistles by heart, and very well and readily have given a godly learned sentence in any matter of controversy. Their children and servants were also brought up and trained so diligently in the right knowledge of God's Word, that the whole town seemed rather a University of the learned, than a town of cloth-making or labouring people; and (what most is to be commended) they were for the more part faithful followers of God's Word in their living.

In this town was Dr Rowland Taylor, who, at his first entering into his benefice, did not, as the common sort of beneficed men do, let out his benefice to a farmer, that shall gather up the profits, and set in an ignorant unlearned priest to serve the cure, and, so they have the fleece, little or nothing care for feeding the flock: but, contrarily, he forsook the Archbishop of Canterbury, Thomas

Cranmer, with whom he before was in household, and made his parsonal abode in Hadley, among the people committed to his charge; where he, as a good shepherd, dwelling among his sheep, gave himself wholly to the study of holy Scriptures. This love of Christ so wrought in him, that no Sunday nor holy-day passed, nor other time when he might get the people together, but he preached to them the Word of God, the doctrine of their salvation.

Not only was his word a preaching unto them, but all his life and conversation was an example of unfeigned Christian life and true holiness. He was void of all pride, humble and meek, as any child: so that none were so poor but they might boldly, as unto their father, resort unto him; neither was his lowliness childish or fearful, but, as occasion, time, and place required, he would be stout in rebuking the sinful and evil doers; so that none was so rich but he would tell them plainly his fault, with such earnest and grave rebukes as became a good curate and pastor. He was a man very mild, void of all rancour, grudge or evil will; ready to do good to all men; readily forgiving his enemies; and never sought to do evil to any.

To the poor that were blind, lame, sick, bedrid, or that had many children, he was a very father, a careful patron, and diligent provider; insomuch that he caused the parishioners to make a general provision for them: and he himself (beside the continual relief that they always found at his house) gave an honest portion yearly to the common alms-box. His wife also was an honest, discreet, and sober matron, and his children well nurtured, brought up in the fear of God and good learning.

He was a good salt of the earth, savourly biting the corrupt manners of evil men; a light in God's house, set upon a candlestick for all good men to imitate and follow.

Thus continued this good shepherd among his flock, governing and leading them through the wilderness of this wicked world, all the days of the most innocent and holy King of blessed memory, Edward the Sixth. But after it pleased God to take King Edward from this vale of misery unto his most blessed rest, to live with Christ, and reign in everlasting joy and felicity, the papists violently overthrew the true doctrine of the Gospel, and persecuted with sword and fire all those that would not agree to receive again the Roman Bishop as supreme head of the universal Church, and allow all the errors, superstitions, and idolatries, that before by God's Word were disproved and justly condemned.

In the beginning of this rage of Antichrist, a certain petty gentleman, called Foster, conspired with one John Clerk, to bring in the Pope and his idol-worship again into Hadley Church. For as yet Dr Taylor had kept in his church the godly church service and reformation made by King Edward, and most faithfully and earnestly preached against the popish corruptions, which had infected the whole country round about.

Therefore the foresaid Foster and Clerk hired one John Averth, parson of Aldham, a popish idolater, to come to Hadley, and there to begin again the popish mass. To this purpose they builded up with

DRAWN SWORDS AND BUCKLERS

all haste possible the altar, intending to bring in their mass again about Palm Monday. But this their device took none effect; for in the night the altar was beaten down : wherefore they built it up again the second time, and laid diligent watch, lest any should again break it down. On the day following came Foster and John Clerk, bringing with them their popish sacrificer, who brought with him all his implements and garments to play his popish pageant, whom they and their men guarded with swords and bucklers, lest any man should disturb him in his missal sacrifice.

When Dr Taylor, who, according to his custom, sat at his book studying the Word of God, heard the bells ringing, he arose and went into the church, supposing something had been there to be done, according to his pastoral office : and, coming to the church, he found the church doors shut and fast barred, saving the chancel door, which was only latched. Where he, entering in, and coming into the chancel, saw a popish sacrificer in his robes, with a broad new shaven crown, ready to begin his popish sacrifice, beset round about with drawn swords and bucklers, lest any man should approach to disturb him.

Then said Dr Taylor, 'Who made thee so bold to enter into this church of Christ to profane and defile it with this abominable idolatry?' With that started up Foster, and with an ireful and furious countenance said to Dr Taylor, 'Thou traitor! what dost thou here, to let and perturb the Queen's proceedings?' Dr Taylor answered, 'I am no traitor, but I am the shepherd that God, my Lord Christ, hath appointed to feed this flock : wherefore I have good authority to be here; and I command thee, in the name of God, to avoid hence, and not to presume here to poison Christ's flock.'

Then said Foster, 'Wilt thou, traitorly heretic, make a commotion, and resist violently the Queen's proceedings?'

Dr Taylor answered, 'I make no commotion; but it is you papists, that make commotions and tumults. I resist only with God's Word against your popish idolatries, which are against God's Word, the Queen's honour, and tend to the utter subversion of this realm of England.'

Then Foster, with his armed men, took Dr Taylor, and led him with strong hand out of the church; and the popish prelate proceeded in his Romish idolatry. Dr Taylor's wife, who followed her husband into the church, when she saw him thus violently thrust out of his church, kneeled down and held up her hands, and with a loud voice said, 'I beseech God, the righteous Judge, to avenge this injury, that this popish idolater doth to the blood of Christ.' Then they thrust her out of the church also, and shut the doors; for they feared that the people would have rent their sacrificer in pieces.

Thus you see how, without consent of the people, the popish mass was again set up with battle array, with swords and bucklers, with violence and tyranny.

Within a day or two after, with all haste possible, this Foster and Clerk made a complaint of Dr Taylor, by a letter written to Stephen Gardiner, Bishop of Winchester, and Lord Chancellor.

When the bishop heard this, he sent a letter to Dr Taylor, commanding him within certain days to come and appear before him.

BEARDING THE BISHOP

When Dr Taylor's friends heard of this, they were exceeding sorry and grieved in mind; which then foreseeing to what end the matter would come, came to him and earnestly counselled him to flee.

Then said Dr Taylor, 'Dear friends, I most heartily thank you, for that you have so tender a care over me. And although I know that there is neither justice nor truth to be looked for at my adversaries's hand, but rather imprisonment and cruel death: yet know I my cause to be so good and righteous, and the truth so strong upon my side, that I will, by God's grace, go and appear before them, and to their beards resist their false doings.'

Then said his friends, 'Master doctor, we think it not best so to do. You have sufficiently done your duty, and testified the truth both by your godly sermons, and also in resisting the parson of Aldham, with others that came hither to bring again the popish mass. And forasmuch as our Saviour Christ willeth and biddeth us, that when they persecute us in one city, we should flee into another: we think, in flying at this time ye should do best, keeping yourself against another time, when the church shall have great need of such diligent teachers, and godly pastors.'

'Oh,' quoth Dr Taylor, 'what will ye have me to do? I am now old, and have already lived too long, to see these terrible and most wicked days. Fly you, and do as your conscience leadeth you; I am fully determined (with God's grace) to go to the bishop, and to his beard to tell him that he doth naught. God shall hereafter raise up teachers of His people, which shall, with much more diligence and fruit, teach them, than I have done. For God will not forsake His church, though now for a time He trieth and correcteth us. As for me, I believe before God, I shall never be able to do God so good service, as I may do now; nor shall I ever have so glorious a calling as I now have, nor so great mercy of God proffered me, as is now at this present. Wherefore I beseech you, and all other my friends, to pray for me; and I doubt not but God will give me strength and His holy Spirit.'

When his friends saw him so constant, and fully determined to go, they, with weeping eyes, commended him unto God.

Dr Taylor, being accompanied with a servant of his own, named John Hull, took his journey towards London. By the way, this John Hull laboured to counsel and persuade him very earnestly to fly, and not come to the Bishop; and proffered himself to go with him to serve him, and in all perils to venture his life for him, and with him. But in no wise would Dr Taylor consent thereunto; but said, 'O John! shall I give place to this thy counsel and worldly persuasion, and leave my flock in this danger. Remember the good shepherd Christ, Which not alone fed His flock, but also died for His flock. Him must I follow, and with God's grace, will do.'

Shortly after Dr Taylor presented himself to the Bishop of Winchester, Stephen Gardiner, then Lord Chancellor of England. Now, when Gardiner saw Dr Taylor, he, according to his custom, reviled him, calling him knave, traitor, heretic, with many other villainous reproaches; all which Dr Taylor heard patiently, and at the last said unto him: 'My lord,' quoth he, 'I am neither traitor nor heretic, but a true subject, and a faithful Christian man; and am come, according to your commandment, to know what is the cause that your lordship hath sent for me.'

Then said the bishop, 'Art thou come, thou villain? How darest thou look me in the face for shame? Knowest thou not who I am?'

'Yes,' quoth Dr Taylor, 'I know who you are. You are Dr Stephen Gardiner, Bishop of Winchester, and Lord Chancellor; and yet but a mortal man, I trow. But if I should be afraid of your lordly looks, why fear you not God, the Lord of us all? How dare ye for shame look any Christian man in the face, seeing ye have forsaken the truth, denied our Saviour Christ and His word, and done contrary to your own oath and writing? With what countenance will ye appear before the judgment-seat of Christ and answer to your oath made first unto King Henry the Eighth of famous memory, and afterward unto King Edward the Sixth his son?'

The bishop answered, 'Tush, tush, that was Herod's oath, unlawful; and therefore worthy to be broken: I have done well in breaking it; and, I thank God, I am come home again to our mother the catholic Church of Rome; and so I would thou shouldest do.'

Dr Tayor answered, 'Should I forsake the Church of Christ, which is founded upon the true foundation of the apostles and prophets, to approve those lies, errors, superstitions, and idolatries, that the Popes and their company at this day so blasphemously do approve? Nay, God forbid. Let the Pope and his return to our Saviour Christ and His Word, and thrust out of the Church such abominable idolatries as he maintaineth, and then will Christian men turn unto him. You wrote truly against him, and were sworn against him.'

'I tell thee,' quoth the Bishop of Winchester, 'it was Herod's oath, unlawful; and therefore ought to be broken, and not kept: and our holy father, the Pope, hath discharged me of it.'

Then said Dr Taylor, 'But you shall not so be discharged before Christ, Who doubtless will require it at your hands, from Whose obedience no man can assoil you, neither the Pope nor any of his.'

'I see,' quoth the Bishop, 'thou art an arrogant knave, and a very fool.'

'My lord,' quoth Dr Taylor, "leave your railing at me, which is not seemly for such a one in authority as you are. For I am a Christian man, and you know, that 'he that saith to his brother, Raca, is in danger of a council; and he that saith, Thou fool, is in danger of hell fire.'

Then said the bishop, 'Thou hast resisted the Queen's proceedings, and wouldest not suffer the parson of Aldham (a very virtuous and devout priest) to say mass in Hadley.'

Dr Taylor answered, 'My lord, I am parson of Hadley; and it is against all right, conscience, and laws, that any man should come into my charge, and presume to infect the flock committed unto me, with venom of the popish idolatrous mass.'

With that the bishop waxed very angry, and said, 'Thou art a blasphemous heretic indeed, that blasphemest the blessed sacrament: and speakest against the holy mass, which is made a sacrifice for the quick and the dead.'

Dr Taylor answered, 'Nay, I blaspheme not the blessed sacrament which Christ instituted, but I reverence it as a true Christian man ought to do; and confess, that Christ ordained the holy communion in the remembrance of His death and passion. Christ gave Himself to die for our redemption upon the cross, Whose body there offered was the propitiatory sacrifice, full, perfect, and sufficient unto salvation, for all them that believe in Him. And this sacrifice did our Saviour Christ offer in His own person Himself once for all, neither can any priest any more offer Him, nor need we any more propitiatory sacrifice.'

Then called the bishop his men, and said, 'Have this fellow hence, and carry him to the King's Bench, and charge the keeper he be straitly kept.'

Then kneeled Dr Taylor down, and held up both his hands, and said, 'Good Lord, I thank thee; and from the tyranny of the Bishop of Rome, and all his detestable errors, idolatries, and abominations, good Lord deliver us: and God be praised for good King Edward.'

Dr Taylor lay prisoner almost two years. He spent all his time in prayer, reading the holy Scriptures, writing, preaching, and exhorting the prisoners, and such as resorted to him, to repentance and amendment of life.

On the 22nd of January 1555, Dr Taylor, and Master Bradford and Master Saunders, were again called to appear before the Bishop of Winchester, the Bishops of Norwich, London, Salisbury, and Durham; and there were charged again with heresy and schism: and therefore a determinate answer was required; whether they would submit themselves to the Roman Bishop, and abjure their errors; or else they would, according to the laws, proceed to their condemnation.

When Dr Taylor and his fellows heard this, they answered stoutly and boldly, that they would not depart from the truth which they had preached in King Edward's days, neither would they submit themselves to the Romish Antichrist; but they thanked God for so great mercy, that he would call them to be worthy to suffer for His Word and truth.

When the bishops saw them so boldly, constantly, and unmovably fixed in the truth, they read the sentence of death upon them.

Dr Taylor was committed to the Clink, and when the keeper brought him toward the prison, the people flocked about to gaze upon him: unto whom he said, 'God be praised, good people, I am come away from them undefiled, and will confirm the truth with my blood.' So was he bestowed in the Clink till it was toward night; and then he was removed to the Compter by the Poultry.

When Dr Taylor had lain in the said Compter a seven-night or thereabouts prisoner, the 4th of February, A.D. 1555, Edmund Bonner, Bishop of London, with others, came to degrade him, bringing with them such ornaments as do appertain to their massing-mummery. He called for Dr Taylor to be brought unto him; and at his coming, the bishop said, 'Master doctor, I would you would remember yourself, and turn to your mother, holy church; so may you do well enough, and I will sue for your pardon.'

Whereunto Master Taylor answered, 'I would you and your fellows would turn to Christ. As for me, I will not turn to Antichrist.'

'Well,' quoth the bishop, 'I am come to degrade you: wherefore put on these vestures.'

'No,' quoth Dr Taylor, 'I will not.'

'Wilt thou not?' said the bishop. 'I shall make thee ere I go.'

Quoth Dr Taylor, 'You shall not, by the grace of God.'

Then he charged him upon his obedience to do it: but he would not do it for him; so he willed another to put them upon his back. And when he was thoroughly furnished therewith, he set his hands to his side, walking up and down, and said, 'How say you, my lord? am not I a goodly fool? How say you, my masters? If I were in Cheap, should I not have boys enough to laugh at these apish toys, and toying trumpery?'

So the bishop scraped his fingers, thumbs, and the crown of his head.

At the last, when he should have given Dr Taylor a stroke on the breast with his crosier-staff, the bishop's chaplain said: 'My lord! strike him not, for he will sure strike again.' 'Yea, by St Peter will I,' quoth Dr Taylor. 'The cause is Christ's, and I were no good Christian, if I would not fight in my Master's quarrel.' So the bishop laid his curse upon him, but struck him not. Then Dr Taylor said, 'Though you do curse me, yet God doth bless me. I have the witness of my conscience, that ye have done me wrong and violence: and yet I pray God, if it be his will, to forgive you. But from the tyranny of the Bishop of Rome, and his detestable enormities, good Lord deliver us!' And when he came up to his chamber he told Master Bradford (for they both lay in one chamber), that he had made the Bishop of London afraid: 'for,' saith he laughingly, 'his chaplain gave him counsel not to strike me with his crosier-staff, for that I would strike again; and, by my troth,' said he, rubbing his hands, 'I made him believe I would do so indeed.'

The night after that he was degraded, his wife and his son Thomas and John Hull, his servant, resorted unto him, and were, by the gentleness of the keepers, permitted to sup with him. At their coming-in, they kneeled down and prayed, saying the litany. After supper walking up and down, he gave God thanks for His grace, that had given him strength to abide by His holy word. With tears they prayed together, and kissed one the other. Unto his son Thomas he gave a Latin book, containing the notable sayings of the old martyrs, and in the end of that he wrote his testament:

'I say to my wife, and to my children, The Lord gave you unto me, and the Lord hath taken me from you, and you from me: blessed be the name of the Lord! I believe that they are blessed which die in the Lord. God careth for sparrows, and for the hairs of our heads. I have ever found Him more faithful and favourable, than is any father or husband. Trust ye therefore in Him by the means of our dear Saviour Christ's merits: believe, love, fear and obey Him: pray to Him, for He hath promised to help. Count me not dead, for I shall certainly live, and never die. I go before, and you shall follow after, to our long home.

I say to my dear friends of Hadley, and to all others which have heard me preach; that I depart hence with a quiet conscience, as touching my doctrine, for the which I pray you thank God with me. For I have, after my little talent, declared to others those lessons that I gathered out of God's book, the blessed Bible. Therefore if I, or an angel from heaven, should preach to you any other Gospel than that ye have received, God's great curse upon that preacher!

Departing hence in sure hope, without all doubting of eternal salvation, I thank God my heavenly Father, through Jesus Christ my certain Saviour.'

On the morrow the sheriff of London with his officers came to the Compter by two o'clock in the morning, and brought forth Dr Taylor; and without any light led him to the Woolsack, an inn without Aldgate. Dr Taylor's wife, suspecting that her husband should that night be carried away, watched all night in St Botolph's church-porch beside Aldgate, having her two children, the one named Elizabeth, of thirteen years of age (whom, being left without father or mother, Dr Taylor had brought up of alms from three years old), the other named Mary, Dr Taylor's own daughter.

Now, when the sheriff and his company came against St Botolph's church, Elizabeth cried, saying, 'O my dear father! mother, mother, here is my father led away.' Then cried his wife, 'Rowland, Rowland, where art thou?'—for it was a very dark morning, that the one could not well see the other. Dr Taylor answered, 'Dear wife, I am here;' and staid. The sheriff's men would have led him forth; but the sheriff said, 'Stay a little, masters, I pray you; and let him speak to his wife:' and so they staid.

Then came she to him, and he took his daughter Mary in his arms: and he, his wife, and Elizabeth kneeled down and said the Lord's prayer. At which sight the sheriff wept apace, and so did divers others of the company. After they had prayed, he rose up and kissed his wife, and shook her by the hand, and said, 'Farewell, my dear wife; be of good comfort, for I am quiet in my conscience. God shall stir up a father for my children.' And then he kissed his daughter Mary, and said, 'God bless thee, and make thee His servant:' and kissing Elizabeth, he said, 'God bless thee; I pray you all stand strong and steadfast unto Christ and His Word.' Then said his wife, 'God be with thee, dear Rowland; I will, with God's grace, meet thee at Hadley.'

And so was he led forth to the Woolsack, and his wife followed him. As soon as they came to the Woolsack, he was put into a chamber, wherein he was kept with four yeomen of the guard, and the sheriff's men. Dr Taylor, as soon as he was come into the chamber, fell down on his knees and gave himself wholly to prayer. The sheriff then, seeing Dr Taylor's wife there, would in no case grant her to speak any more with her husband, but gently desired her to go to his house, and take it as her own, and promised her she should lack nothing, and sent two officers to conduct her thither. Notwithstanding she desired to go to her mother's, whither the officers led her, and charged her mother to keep her there till they came again.

Thus remained Dr Taylor in the Woolsack, kept by the sheriff and his company, till eleven o'clock; at which time the sheriff of Essex was ready to receive: and so they set him on horseback within the inn, the gates being shut.

JOYFUL AND MERRY

At the coming out of the gates, John Hull, before spoken of, stood at the rails with Thomas, Dr Taylor's son. When Dr Taylor saw them, he called them, saying, 'Come hither, my son Thomas.' And John Hull lifted the child up, and set him on the horse before his father: and Dr Taylor put off his hat, and said to the people that stood there looking on him, 'Good people, this is mine own son.' Then lifted he up his eyes towards heaven, and prayed for his son; laid his hat upon the child's head and blessed him; and so delivered the child to John Hull, whom he took by the hand and said, 'Farewell, John Hull, the faithfullest servant that ever man had.' And so they rode forth, the sheriff of Essex, with four yeomen of the guard, and the sheriff's men leading him.

And so they came to Brentwood, where they caused to be made for Dr Taylor a close hood, with two holes for his eyes to look out at, and a slit for his mouth to breathe at. This they did, that no man should know him, nor he speak to any man: which practice they used also with others. They feared lest, if the people should have heard them speak, or have seen them, they might have been much more strengthened by their godly exhortations, to stand steadfast in God's Word, and to fly the superstitions and idolatries of the papacy.

All the way Dr Taylor was joyful and merry, as one that accounted himself going to a most pleasant banquet or bridal. He spake many notable things to the sheriff and yeomen of the guard that conducted him, and often moved them to weep, through his much earnest calling upon them to repent, and to amend their evil and wicked living. Oftentimes also he caused them to wonder and rejoice, to see him so constant and steadfast, void of all fear, joyful in heart, and glad to die.

At Chelmsford met them the sheriff of Suffolk, there to receive him, and to carry him forth into Suffolk. And being at supper, the sheriff of Essex very earnestly laboured him to return to the popish religion, thinking with fair words to persuade him; and said, 'Good master doctor! we are right sorry for you. God hath given you great learning and wisdom; wherefore ye have been in great favour and reputation in times past with the council and highest of this realm. Besides this, ye are a man of goodly personage, in your best strength, and by nature like to live many years. Ye are well beloved of all men, as well for your virtues as for your learning: and me thinketh it were great pity you should cast away yourself willingly, and so come to such a painful and shameful death. Ye should do much better to revoke your opinions. I and all these your friends will be suitors for your pardon; which, no doubt, ye shall obtain.'

Dr Taylor staid a little, as one studying what answer he might give. At the last thus he said, 'Master sheriff, and my masters all, I heartily thank you for your good-will: I have hearkened to your words, and marked well your counsels. And to be plain with you, I do perceive that I have been deceived myself, and am like to deceive a great many of Hadley of their expectation.'

With that word they all rejoiced. 'Yea, good master doctor,' quoth the sheriff, 'God's blessing on your heart! hold you there still. It is the comfortablest word that we heard you speak yet. What!

should ye cast away yourself in vain? Play a wise man's part, and I dare warrant it, ye shall find favour.' Thus they rejoiced very much at the word, and were very merry. At the last, 'Good master doctor,' quoth the sheriff, 'what meant ye by this, that ye say ye think ye have been deceived yourself, and think ye shall deceive many a one in Hadley?'

'Would ye know my meaning plainly?' quoth he.

'Yea,' quoth the sheriff, 'good master doctor, tell it us plainly.'

Then said Dr Taylor, 'I will tell you how I have been deceived, and, as I think, I shall deceive a great many. I am, as you see, a man that hath a very great carcase, which I thought should have been buried in Hadley churchyard, if I had died in my bed, as I well hoped I should have done; but herein I see I was deceived: and there are a great number of worms in Hadley churchyard, which should have had jolly feeding upon this carrion, which they have looked for many a day. But now I know we be deceived, both I and they; for this carcase must be burnt to ashes: and so shall they lose their bait and feeding, that they looked to have had of it.'

When the sheriff and his company heard him say so, they were amazed, and looked one on another, marvelling at the man's constant mind, that thus, without all fear, made but a jest at the cruel torment and death now at hand prepared for him. Thus was their expectation clean disappointed.

At Lavenham, there came to him a great number of gentlemen and justices upon great horses, which all were appointed to aid the sheriff. These gentlemen laboured Dr Taylor very sore to reduce him to the Romish religion, promising him his pardon, 'which,' said they, 'we have here for you.' They promised him great promotions, yea, a bishopric, if he would take it: but all their labour and flattering words were in vain.

Coming within two miles of Hadley, Dr Taylor desired to light off his horse: which done, he leaped, and fet a frisk or twain, as men commonly do in dancing. 'Why, master doctor,' quoth the sheriff, 'how do you now?' He answered: 'Well, God be praised, good master sheriff, never better: for now I know I am almost at home. I lack not past two stiles to go over, and I am even at my Father's house.—But, master sheriff,' said he, 'shall we not go through Hadley?' 'Yes,' said the sheriff, 'you shall go through Hadley.' Then said he, 'O Lord! I thank Thee, I shall yet once or I die see my flock, whom Thou, Lord, knowest I have most heartily loved and truly taught. Lord! bless them, and keep them steadfast in Thy Word and truth.'

When they were now come to Hadley, and came riding over the bridge, at the bridge-foot waited a poor man with five small children; who, when he saw Dr Taylor, he and his children fell down upon their knees, and held up their hands, and cried with a loud voice, and said, 'O dear Father and good shepherd, Dr Taylor? God help and succour thee, as thou hast many a time succoured me and my poor children.'

The streets of Hadley were beset on both sides the way with men and women who waited to see him; whom when they beheld so led to death, with weeping eyes and lamentable voices they cried, saying one to another, 'Ah, Lord! there goeth our good shepherd from us, that so faithfully hath taught us, so fatherly hath cared for us, and so godly hath governed us. O merciful God! what shall we poor scattered lambs do? What shall come of this most wicked world? Lord strengthen him, and comfort him.'

And Dr Taylor evermore said to the people, 'I have preached to you God's Word and truth, and am come this day to seal it with my blood.'

Coming against the almshouses, which he well knew, he cast to the poor people money which remained of that which had been given him in time of his imprisonment. As for his living, they took it from him at his first going to prison, so that he was sustained all the time of his imprisonment by the charitable alms of good people that visited him. Therefore, the money that now remained he put in a glove and gave it to the poor almsmen standing at their doors to see him. And, coming to the last of the almshouses, and not seeing the poor that there dwelt, ready at their doors, as the other were, he asked: 'Is the blind man and blind woman, that dwelt here, alive?' It was answered, 'Yea, they are there within.' Then threw he glove and all in at the window.

Thus this good father and provider for the poor now took his leave of those, for whom all his life he had a singular care and study.

At the last, coming to Aldham-common, the place assigned where he should suffer, and seeing a great multitude of people gathered thither, he asked, 'What place is this, and what meaneth it that so much people are gathered hither?' It was answered, 'It is Aldham-common, the place where you must

suffer: and the people are come to look upon you.'
Then said he, 'Thanked be God, I am even at
home;' and so alighted from his horse, and with
both his hands rent the hood from his head.

When the people saw his reverend face, with a
long white beard, they burst out with weeping tears,
and cried, saying ' God save thee, good Dr Taylor!
Jesus Christ strengthen thee and help thee; the
Holy Ghost comfort thee.' Then would he have
spoken to the people, but the yeomen of the guard
were so busy about him, that as soon as he opened
his mouth, one or other thrust a tipstaff into his
mouth, and would in nowise permit him.

Dr Taylor thereupon sat down, and seeing one
named Soyce, called him and said, 'Soyce, I pray
thee come and pull off my boots, and take them for
thy labour. Thou hast long looked for them, now
take them.' Then rose he up, and put off his
clothes unto his shirt, and gave them away: which
done, he said with a loud voice, 'Good people! I
have taught you nothing but God's holy Word, and
those lessons that I have taken out of God's blessed
book, the holy Bible: and I am come hither this
day to seal it with my blood.' With that word,
Homes, yeoman of the guard, who had used Dr
Taylor very cruelly all the way, gave him a great
stroke upon the head. Then he kneeled down and
prayed, and a poor woman that was among the
people, stepped in and prayed with him: but her
they thrust away, and threatened to tread her down
with horses: notwithstanding she would not remove,
but abode and prayed with him. He went to the
stake, and kissed it, and set himself into a pitchbarrel, which they had set for him and so stood

with his back upright against the stake, with his hands folded together, and his eyes toward heaven, and so he continually prayed.

Then they bound him with chains, and the sheriff called one Richard Donningham, a butcher, and commanded him to set up faggots: but he refused to do it, and said, 'I am lame, sir; and not able to lift a faggot.' The sheriff threatened to send him to prison; notwithstanding he would not do it.

Then appointed he Mulleine, Soyce, Warwick, and Robert King, to set up the faggots, and to make the fire, which they most diligently did. Warwick cruelly cast a faggot at him, which lit upon his head, and brake his face, that the blood ran down his visage. Then said Dr Taylor, 'O friend, I have harm enough; what needed that?'

Furthermore, Sir John Shelton there standing by, as Dr Taylor was saying the psalm 'Miserere,' in English, struck him on the lips: 'Ye knave,' said he, 'speak Latin: I will make thee.'

At the last they set to fire; and Dr Taylor, holding up both his hands, called upon God, and said, 'Merciful Father of heaven, for Jesus Christ my Saviour's sake, receive my soul into Thy hands.' So stood he still without either crying or moving, with his hands folded together, till Soyce with a halbert struck him on the head that the brains fell out, and the corpse fell into the fire.

THE MARTYRS OF SCOTLAND

LIKE as there was no place, either of Germany, Italy, or France, wherein there were not some branches sprung out of that most fruitful root of Luther; so likewise was not this isle of Britain without his fruit and branches. Amongst whom was Patrick Hamilton, a Scotsman born of high and noble stock, and of the king's blood, of excellent towardness, twenty-three years of age, called abbot of Ferne. Coming out of his country with three companions to seek godly learning, he went to the University of Marburg in Germany, which University was then newly erected by Philip, Landgrave of Hesse. Using conference with learned men, especially with Frances Lambert, he so profited in knowledge and judgment that, through the incitation of the said Lambert, he was the first in all that University who publicly did set up conclusions there to be disputed of, concerning faith and works. Which young man, if he had chosen to lead his life after the manner of other courtiers, in all kind of licentious riotousness, should peradventure have found praise without peril or punishment; but, forsomuch as he joined godliness with his stock, and virtue with his age, he could by no means escape the hands of the wicked. For there is nothing safe or sure in this world but wickedness and sin.

Whoever saw the cardinals or bishops rage with their cruel inquisitions against riot, ambition, unlawful gaming, drunkenness, and rapines? But if any man were truly addict to the desire and study of godliness, confessing Christ to be his only patron and advocate, excluding the merits of saints, acknowledging free justification by faith in Christ, denying purgatory (for these articles Hamilton was burned), they spare neither age nor kindred, neither is there any so great power in the world, that may withstand their majesty or authority.

How great an ornament might so noble, learned, and excellent a young man have been unto that realm, being endued with so great godliness, and such a singular wit and disposition, if the Scots had not envied their own commodity!

This learned Patrick, increasing daily more and more in knowledge, and inflamed with godliness, at length began to revolve with himself touching his return into his country, being desirous to impart unto his countrymen some fruit of understanding which he had received abroad. Whereupon, persisting in his godly purpose, he took one of the three whom he brought out of Scotland, and so returned home without any longer delay. Not sustaining the miserable ignorance and blindness of that people, he valiantly taught and preached the truth, was accused of heresy, and, stoutly sustaining the quarrel of God's Gospel against the high priest and Archbishop of St Andrew's, named James Beaton, was cited to appear before him and his college of priests on the 1st of March, A.D. 1527. Being not only forward in knowledge, but also ardent in spirit, not tarrying for the hour appointed, he came very early in the morning before he was looked for; and there mightily disputing against

them, when he could not by the Scriptures be
convicted, by force he was oppressed. And so the
sentence of condemnation being given against him,
the same day after dinner, in all hot haste, he was
had away to the fire, and there burned.

And thus was this noble Hamilton, the blessed
servant of God, without all just cause, made away
by cruel adversaries, yet not without great fruit to
the Church of Christ; for the grave testimony of
his blood left the truth of God more fixed and confirmed in the hearts of many than ever could after
be plucked away: insomuch that divers afterwards,
standing in his quarrel, sustained the like martyrdom.

Within a few years after the martyrdom of Master
Patrick Hamilton, one Henry Forest, a young man
born in Linlithgow, who, a little before, had received the orders of Benet and Collet (as they
term them), affirmed that Master Patrick Hamilton
died a martyr. For this he was apprehended, and
put in prison by James Beaton, Archbishop of St
Andrew's, who, shortly after, caused a certain friar,
named Walter Laing, to hear his confession. When
Henry Forest had declared his conscience, how he
thought Master Patrick to be a good man and not
heretical, and wrongfully to be put to death, the friar
came and uttered to the bishop the confession that
he had heard, which before was not thoroughly
known. Hereupon it followed that, his confession
being brought as sufficient probation against him,
Henry Forest was concluded to be a heretic, equal
in iniquity with Master Patrick Hamilton, and given
to the secular judges, to suffer death.

When the day came for his death, and that he
should first be degraded, he was brought before the

clergy in a green place, being between the castle of St Andrew and another place called Monymaill. As soon as he entered in at the door, and saw the faces of the clergy, perceiving whereunto they tended, he cried with a loud voice, saying, ' Fie on falsehood! Fie on false friars, revealers of confession! After this day let no man ever trust any false friars, contemners of God's Word, and deceivers of men! ' After his degradation, he suffered death for his faithful testimony of the truth of Christ and of His Gospel, at the north church-stile of the abbey church of St Andrew, to the intent that all the people of Forfar might see the fire, and so might be the more feared from falling into the doctrine which they term heresy.

Within a year after the martyrdom of Henry Forest, or thereabout, James Hamilton, of Linlithgow; his sister Katherine Hamilton, the spouse of the captain of Dunbar; also another honest woman of Leith; David Straton, of the house of Lauriston; and Master Norman Gurley were called to the abbey church of Holyrood House in Edinburgh, by James Hay, Bishop of Ross, commissioner to James Beaton, Archbishop, in presence of King James the Fifth, who was altogether clad in red apparel. James Hamilton was accused as one that maintained the opinion of Master Patrick his brother; to whom the King gave counsel to depart, and not to appear: for in case he appeared, he could not help him; because the bishops had persuaded the King, that the cause of heresy did in no wise appertain unto *him*. And so Hamilton fled, and was condemned as a heretic, and all his goods and lands confiscated.

Katherine Hamilton, his sister, appeared upon the

scaffold, and being accused of a horrible heresy, to wit, that her own works could not save her, she granted the same; and after a long reasoning between her and Master John Spens, the lawyer, she concluded in this manner, 'Work here, work there; what kind of working is all this? I know perfectly, that no kind of works can save me, but only the works of Christ my Lord and Saviour.' The King, hearing these words, turned him about and laughed, called her unto him, and caused her to recant, because she was his aunt.

Master Norman Gurley was accused for that he said there was no such thing as purgatory, and that the Pope was not a bishop but Antichrist, and had no jurisdiction in Scotland. Also David Straton, for that he said, there was no purgatory, but the passion of Christ, and the tribulations of this world. And because, when Master Robert Lawson, vicar of Eglesgrig, asked his tithe-fish of him, he did cast them to him out of the boat, so that some of them fell into the sea; therefore he accused him, as one that should have said, that no tithes should be paid. These two, because, after great solicitation made by the King, they refused to abjure and recant, were condemned by the Bishop of Ross as heretics, and were burned upon the green side, between Leith and Edinburgh, to the intent that the inhabitants of Fife, seeing the fire, might be struck with terror and fear, not to fall into the like.

Not long after the burning of David Straton and Master Gurley, a canon of St Colm's Inche, and vicar of Dolor, called Dean Thomas Forret, preached every Sunday to his parishioners out of the Epistle or Gospel as it fell for the time; which then was a great novelty in Scotland, to see any man preach, except a black friar or a grey friar: and therefore the friars envied him, and accused him to the Bishop of Dunkeld (in whose diocese he remained) as a heretic, and one that showed the mysteries of the Scriptures to the vulgar people in English, to make the clergy detestable in the sight of the people. The Bishop of Dunkeld, moved by the friars' instigation, called the said Dean Thomas, and said to him, 'My joy, Dean Thomas, I love you well, and therefore I must give you my counsel, how you shall rule and guide yourself.' To whom Thomas said, 'I thank your lordship heartily.' Then the Bishop began his counsel after this manner:

Bishop: 'My joy, Dean Thomas! I am informed that you preach the Epistle or Gospel every Sunday to your parishioners, and that you take not the cow nor the uppermost cloth from your parishioners, which thing is very prejudicial to the churchmen; and therefore, my joy, Dean Thomas, I would you took your cow, and your uppermost cloth, as other churchmen do; or else it is too much to preach every Sunday: for in so doing you may make the people think that we should preach likewise. But it is enough for you, when you find any good Epistle, or any good Gospel, that setteth forth the liberty of the holy Church, to preach that, and let the rest be.'

The Martyr: 'My lord, I think that none of my parishioners will complain that I take not the cow, nor the uppermost cloth, but will gladly give me the same, together with any other thing that they have; and I will give and communicate with them any thing that I have; and so, my lord, we agree right well, and there is no discord among us. And whereas your lordship saith, It is too much to preach every Sunday, indeed I think it is too little, and also would wish that your lordship did the like.'

Bishop: 'Nay, nay, Dean Thomas, let that be, for we are not ordained to preach.'

Martyr: 'Whereas your lordship biddeth me preach when I find any good epistle, or a good Gospel, truly, my lord, I have read the New Testament and the Old, and all the epistles and the Gospels, and among them all I could never find an evil epistle, or an evil Gospel: but, if your lordship will show me the good epistle, and the good Gospel, and the evil epistle and the evil Gospel, then I shall preach the good, and omit the evil.'

Bishop: Then spake my lord stoutly and said, 'I thank God that I never knew what the Old and New Testament was; therefore, Dean Thomas, I will know nothing but my portuese and my pontifical. Go your way, and let be all these fantasies; for if you persevere in these erroneous opinions, you will repent it, when you may not mend it.'

Martyr: 'I trust my cause be just in the presence of God, and therefore I pass not much what do follow thereupon.'

And so my lord and he departed at that time. And soon after a summons was directed from the Cardinal of St Andrews and the Bishop of Dunkeld, upon the said Dean Thomas Forret, and others; who, at the day of their appearance, were condemned to the death without any place for recantation, because (as was alleged) they were heresiarchs, or chief heretics and teachers of heresies; and, especially, because many of them were at the marriage of a priest, who was vicar of Tulibothy beside Stirling, and did eat flesh in Lent at the said bridal. And so they were all together burned upon the Castle Hill at Edinburgh.

There was a certain Act of Parliament made in the government of the Lord Hamilton, Earl of Arran, giving privilege to all men of the realm of Scotland, to read the Scriptures in their mother tongue; secluding nevertheless all reasoning, conference, convocation of people to hear the Scriptures read or expounded. Which liberty of private reading lacked not its own fruit, so that in sundry parts of Scotland were opened the eyes of the elect of God to see the truth, and abhor the papistical abominations; amongst whom were certain persons in St John's-town.

At this time there was a sermon made by friar Spence, in St John's-town, otherwise called Perth, affirming prayer made to saints to be so necessary, that without it there could be no hope of salvation to man. This blasphemous doctrine a burgess of the said town, called Robert Lamb, could not abide, but accused him, in open audience, of erroneous doctrine, and adjured him, in God's name, to utter the truth. This the friar, being stricken with fear, promised to do; but the trouble, tumult, and stir of the people increased so, that the friar could have no audience.

At this time, A.D. 1543, the enemies of the truth procured John Charterhouse, who favoured the truth, and was provost of the said city and town of Perth, to be deposed from his office by the said governor's authority, and a papist, called Master Alexander Marbeck, to be chosen in his room, that they might bring the more easily their wicked and ungodly enterprise to an end.

On St Paul's day came to St John's-town, the Governor, the cardinal, the Earl of Argyle, with certain other of the nobility. And although there were many accused for the crime of heresy (as they term it), yet these persons only were apprehended: Robert Lamb, William Anderson, James Hunter, James Raveleson, James Finlason, and Helen Stirke his wife, and were cast that night in the Spay Tower.

Upon the morrow, when they were brought forth to judgment, were laid to their charge, the violating of the Act of Parliament before expressed, and their conference and assemblies in hearing and expounding of Scripture against the tenor of the said Act. Robert Lamb was accused, in special, for interrupting the friar in the pulpit; which he not only confessed, but also affirmed constantly, that it was the duty of no man, who understood and knew the truth, to hear the same impugned without contradiction; and therefore sundry who were there present in judgment, who hid the knowledge of the truth, should bear the burden in God's presence, for consenting to the same.

The said Robert also, with William Anderson and James Raveleson, were accused for hanging up the image of St Francis in a cord, nailing of rams' horns to his head, and a cow's rump to his tail, and for eating of a goose on Allhallow-even.

James Hunter, being a simple man and without learning, and a flesher by occupation, so that he could be charged with no great knowledge in doctrine, yet, because he often used that suspected company of the rest, was accused.

THE CRUEL PRIESTS

The woman Helen Stirke was accused, for that in her childbed she was not accustomed to call upon the name of the Virgin Mary, being exhorted thereto by her neighbours, but only upon God for Jesus Christ's sake; and because she said that if she herself had been in the time of the Virgin Mary, God might have looked to her humility and base estate, as He did to the Virgin's, in making her the mother of Christ: thereby meaning, that there were no merits in the Virgin, which procured her that honour, to be made the mother of Christ, and to be preferred before other women, but that only God's free mercy exalted her to that estate: which words were counted most execrable in the face of the clergy, and of the whole multitude.

James Raveleson aforesaid, building a house, set upon the round of his fourth stair the three-crowned diadem of Peter carved of tree, which the cardinal took as done in mockage of his cardinal's hat. After sentence given, their hands were bound, and the men cruelly treated: which thing the woman beholding, desired likewise to be bound by the sergeants with her husband for Christ's sake.

There was great intercession made by the town for the life of these persons to the Governor, who of himself was willing that they might have been delivered: but he was so subject to the appetite of the cruel priests, that he could not do that which he would. Yea, they menaced to assist his enemies and to depose him, except he assisted their cruelty.

The martyrs were carried by a great band of

armed men (for they feared rebellion in the town except they had their men of war) to the place of execution, which was common to all thieves, and that to make their cause appear more odious to the people. Every one comforting another, and assuring themselves that they should sup together in the Kingdom of Heaven that night, they commended themselves to God, and died constantly in the Lord.

The woman desired earnestly to die with her husband, but she was not suffered; yet, following him to the place of execution, she gave him comfort, exhorting him to perseverance and patience for Christ's sake, and, parting from him with a kiss, said, 'Husband, rejoice, for we have lived together many joyful days; but this day, in which we must die, ought to be most joyful unto us both, because we must have joy for ever; therefore I will not bid you good night, for we shall suddenly meet with joy in the Kingdom of Heaven.' The woman, after that, was taken to a place to be drowned, and albeit she had a child sucking on her breast, yet this moved nothing the unmerciful hearts of the enemies. So, after she had commended her children to the neighbours of the town for God's sake, and the sucking bairn was given to the nurse, she sealed up the truth by her death.

With most tender affection consider, gentle reader, the uncharitable manner of the accusation of Master George Wishart, made by the bloody enemies of Christ's faith. Ponder the furious rage and tragical cruelness of the malignant Church, in persecuting this blessed man of God; and, on the contrary, his humble, patient, and most godly answers made to them without all fear, not having respect to their boastful menacings and boisterous threats, but charitably and without stop of tongue answering, not changing his visage.

I thought it not impertinent somewhat to touch concerning the life and conversation of this godly man, according as of late it came to my hands, certified in writing by a certain scholar of his, named Emery Tylney, whose words here follow:

About the year of our Lord 1543, there was, in the University of Cambridge, one Master George Wishart, commonly called Master George of Benet's College, a man of tall stature, polled-headed, and on the same a round French cap of the best; judged to be of melancholy complexion by his physiognomy, black haired, long bearded, comely of personage, well spoken after his country of Scotland, courteous, lowly, lovely, glad to teach, desirous to learn, and well travelled; having on him for his clothing a frieze gown to the shoes, a black millian fustian doublet, and plain black hosen, coarse new canvass for his shirts, and white falling bands and cuffs at his hands.

He was a man modest, temperate, fearing God, hating covetousness; for his charity had never end, night, noon, nor day; he forbare one meal in three, one day in four for the most part, except something to comfort nature. He lay hard upon a puff of straw and coarse new canvass sheets, which, when he changed, he gave away. He had commonly by his bed-side a tub of water, in the which (his people being in bed, the candle put out and all quiet) he used to bathe himself. He loved me tenderly, and

I him. He taught with great modesty and gravity, so that some of his people thought him severe, and would have slain him; but the Lord was his defence. And he, after due correction for their malice, by good exhortation amended them and went his way. Oh that the Lord had left him to me, his poor boy, that he might have finished that he had begun! for he went into Scotland with divers of the nobility, that came for a treaty to King Henry.

If I should declare his love to me and all men; his charity to the poor, in giving, relieving, caring, helping, providing, yea, infinitely studying how to do good unto all, and hurt to none, I should sooner want words, than just cause to commend him.

To the said Master George, being in captivity in the Castle of St Andrews, the Dean of the same town was sent by the commandment of the cardinal and by his wicked counsel, and there summoned the said Master George, that he should, upon the morning following, appear before the judge, then and there to give account of his seditious and heretical doctrine.

Upon the next morning, the lord cardinal caused his servants to address themselves in their most warlike array, with jack, knapskal, splent, spear, and axe, more seeming for the war, than for the preaching of the true Word of God. And when these armed champions, marching in warlike order, had conveyed the bishops into the Abbey Church, incontinently they sent for Master George, who was conveyed unto the said church by the captain of the Castle, accompanied with a hundred men, addressed in manner aforesaid. Like a lamb led they him to sacrifice. As he entered in at the Abbey Church door, there was a poor man lying, vexed with great infirmities, asking of his alms, to whom he flung his purse. And when he came before the lord cardinal, the sub-prior of the Abbey, called Dane John Winryme, stood up in the pulpit, and made a sermon to all the congregation there assembled.

And when he ended his sermon, they caused Master George to ascend into the pulpit, there to hear his accusation. And right against him stood up one of the fed flock, a monster, John Lander, laden full of cursings written in paper : the which he took out—a roll, long and full of threats, maledictions, and words of devilish spite and malice, saying to the innocent Master George so many cruel and abominable words, and hitting him so spitefully with the Pope's thunder, that the ignorant people dreaded lest the earth would have swallowed him up quick. Notwithstanding Master George stood still with great patience, hearing their sayings, not once moving or changing his countenance.

When that this fed sow had read all his lying menacings, his face running down with sweat, and frothing at the mouth like a boar, he spit at Master George's face, saying, 'What answerest thou to these sayings, thou runnagate! traitor! thief! which we have duly proved by sufficient witness against thee?' Master George, hearing this, kneeled down upon his knees in the pulpit. When he had ended his prayer, sweetly and Christianly he answered to them all in this manner :

'It is just and reasonable, that your discretions should know what my words and doctrine are, and what I have ever taught, that I perish not unjustly, to the great peril of your souls. Wherefore, both for the glory and honour of God, your own health, and safeguard of my life, I beseech your discretions to hear me; and, in the mean time, I shall recite my doctrine without any colour.'

Suddenly with a high voice cried the accuser, the fed sow, 'Thou heretic, runnagate, traitor, and thief! it was not lawful for thee to preach. Thou hast taken the power at thine own hand, without any authority of the Church.'

Then all the congregation of the prelates, with their complices, said: 'If we give him license to preach, he is so crafty, and in the holy Scripture so exercised, that he will persuade the people to his opinion, and raise them against us.'

Master George, seeing their malicious intent, appealed from the lord cardinal to the Lord Governor, as to an indifferent and equal judge. To whom the accuser, John Lander, with hoggish voice answered, 'Is not my lord cardinal the second person within this realm, Chancellor of Scotland, Archbishop of St Andrews, Bishop of Mirepois, Commendator of Aberbroshok, *legatus natus, legatus à latere?*' And so, reciting as many titles of his unworthy honours as would have loden a ship, much sooner an ass, 'Is not he,' quoth John Lander, 'an equal judge apparently unto thee? Whom other desirest thou to be thy judge?'

To whom this humble man answered, saying: 'I refuse not my lord cardinal, but I desire the

Word of God to be my judge, and the temporal estate, with some of your lordships mine auditors, because I am here my Lord Governor's prisoner.'

Hereupon the prideful and scornful people mocked him. And without all delay, they would have given sentence upon Master George, had not certain men counselled the cardinal to read again the articles, and to hear his answers thereupon, that the people might not complain of his wrongful condemnation.

They caused the common people to void away, whose desire was always to hear that innocent man to speak. Then the sons of darkness pronounced their sentence definitive, not having respect to the judgment of God. And when all this was done and said, the cardinal caused his tormentors to pass again with the meek lamb into the Castle, until such time as the fire was made ready. When he was come unto the Castle, there came friar Scot and his mate, saying, 'Sir, ye must make your confession unto us.' He answered and said, 'I will make no confession unto you.'

When the fire was made ready, and the gallows, the lord cardinal dreading that Master George should have been taken away by his friends, commanded to bend all the ordnance of the Castle against that part, and commanded all his gunners to stand beside their guns, unto such time as he were burned. All this being done, they bound Master George's hands behind his back, and led him forth with their soldiers to the place of their wicked execution. As he came forth of the Castle gate, there met him certain beggars, asking of his alms for God's sake. To whom he answered, 'I want my hands, wherewith I should give you alms; but the merciful Lord, of His benignity and abundance of grace, that feedeth all men, vouchsafe to give you necessaries, both unto your bodies and souls.' Then afterwards met him two friars, saying, 'Master George, pray to our Lady, that she may be mediatrix for you to her Son.' To whom he answered meekly, 'Cease, tempt me not, my brethren!' After this he was led to the fire with a rope about his neck, and a chain of iron about his middle.

When he came to the fire, he sat down upon his knees, and rose again, and thrice he said these words, 'O thou Saviour of the world! have mercy on me. Father of heaven! I commend my spirit into Thy holy hands.' When he had made this prayer, he turned to the people, and said: 'For the Word's sake and true evangel, which was given to me by the grace of God, I suffer this day by men, not sorrowfully, but with a glad heart and mind. For this cause I was sent, that I should suffer this fire, for Christ's sake. Consider and behold my visage, ye shall not see me change my colour. This grim fire I fear not. I know surely that my soul shall sup with my Saviour Christ this night.'

The hangman, that was his tormentor, sat down upon his knees, and said, 'Sir, I pray you forgive me, for I am not guilty of your death.' To whom he answered, 'Come hither to me.' When that he was come to him, he kissed his cheek, and said, 'Lo! here is a token that I forgive thee. My heart, do thine office.' And then he was put upon the gibbet and hanged, and burned to powder. When that the people beheld the great tormenting, they might not withhold from piteous mourning and complaining of this innocent lamb's slaughter.

It was not long after the martyrdom of this blessed man of God, Master George Wishart, who was put to death by David Beaton, the bloody Archbishop and Cardinal of Scotland, A.D. 1546, the first day of March, that the said David Beaton, by the just revenge of God's mighty judgment, was slain within his own Castle of St Andrews, by the hands of one Leslie and other gentlemen, who, by the Lord stirred up, brake in suddenly upon him, and in his bed murdered him the said year, the last day of May, crying out, 'Alas! alas! slay me not! I am a priest!' And so, like a butcher he lived, and like a butcher he died, and lay seven months and more unburied, and at last like a carrion was buried in a dunghill.

After this David Beaton succeeded John Hamilton, Archbishop of St Andrews, who, to the intent that he might in no ways appear inferior to his predecessor, in augmenting the number of the holy martyrs of God, called a certain poor man to judgment, whose name was Adam Wallace. The order and manner of whose story here followeth.

There was set, upon a scaffold made hard to the chancelary wall of the Black-friars' Church in Edinburgh, on seats made thereupon, the Lord Governor. Behind the seats stood the whole senate. In the pulpit was placed Master John Lander, parson of Marbotle, accuser, clad in a surplice and red hood.

Was brought in Adam Wallace, a simple poor

man in appearance, conveyed by John of Cumnock, servant to the Bishop of St Andrews, and set in the midst of the scaffold. He was commanded to look to the accuser, who asked him what was his name. He answered, 'Adam Wallace.' Then asked he where he was born? 'Within two miles of Fayle,' said he, 'in Kyle.' Then said the accuser, 'I repent that ever such a poor man as you should put these noble lords to so great incumbrance this day by your vain speaking.' 'And I must speak,' said he, 'as God giveth me grace, and I believe I have said no evil to hurt any body.' 'Would God,' said the accuser, 'ye had never spoken; for you are brought forth for such horrible crimes of heresy, as never were imagined in this country before.'

Wallace answered that he said nothing but agreeing to the Holy Word as he understood; and thereby would he abide unto the time he were better instructed by Scripture, even to the death. 'If you condemn me for holding by God's Word, my innocent blood shall be required at your hands, when ye shall be brought before the judgment-seat of Christ.'

Then they condemned him and delivered him to the Provost of Edinburgh to be burned on the Castle Hill, who made him to be put in the uppermost house in the town, with irons about his legs and neck, and gave charge to Hugh Terry, an ignorant minister of Satan and of the bishops, to keep the key of the said house. The said Terry sent to the poor man two grey friars to instruct him, with whom he would enter into no communing. Soon after that were sent in two black friars, an English friar, and another subtle sophister, called Arbuthnot, with the which English friar he would have reasoned and declared his faith by the Scriptures; who answered, he had no commission to enter into disputation with him: and so left him.

Then was sent to him a worldly wise man, and not ungodly in the understanding of the truth, the Dean of Restalrig, who gave him Christian consolation, and exhorted him to believe the reality of the sacrament after the consecration. But Wallace would consent to nothing that had not evidence in the holy Scripture, and so passed that night in singing, and lauding God, to the ears of divers hearers, having learned the Psalter of David without book, to his consolation: for they had before spoiled him of his Bible, which always, till after he was condemned, was with him wherever he went.

After Hugh Terry knew that he had certain books to read and comfort his spirit, he came in a rage, and took the same from him, endeavouring to pervert him from the patience and hope he had in Christ his Saviour: but God suffered him not to be moved therewith.

All the next morning abode this poor man in irons, and provision was commanded to be made for his burning against the next day; which day came the Dean of Restalrig to him again, and reasoned with him; who answered as before, that he would say nothing concerning his faith, but as the Scripture testifieth, yea, though an angel came from heaven to persuade him to the same. Then after came in Hugh Terry again, and examined him after his old manner, and said he would gar devils to come forth of him ere even. To whom he answered, 'You should rather be a godly man to give me consolation in my case. When I knew you were come, I prayed God I might resist your temptations; which, I thank Him, He hath made me able to do: therefore I pray you, let me alone in peace.' Then he asked of one of the officers that stood by, 'Is your fire making ready?' who told him, it was. He answered, 'As it pleaseth God; I am ready soon or late, as it shall please Him.'

At his forthcoming, the Provost, with great menacing words, forbade him to speak to any man, or any to him. Coming from the town to the Castle Hill, the common people said, 'God have mercy upon him.' 'And on you too,' said he. Being beside the fire, he lifted up his eyes to heaven twice or thrice, and said to the people, 'Let it not offend you that I suffer death this day for the truth's sake; for the disciple is not greater than his Master.' The cord being about his neck, the fire was lighted, and so departed he to God constantly, and with good countenance.

Among the rest of the martyrs of Scotland, the marvellous constancy of Walter Mill is not to be passed over with silence; out of whose ashes sprang thousands, who chose rather to die, than to be any longer overtrodden by the tyranny of the cruel, ignorant, and brutal bishops, abbots, monks, and friars.

In the year of our Lord, 1558, this Walter Mill (who in his youth had been a papist), after he had been in Almain, and had heard the doctrine of the Gospel, returned into Scotland; and, setting aside all papistry, married a wife; which thing made him unto the bishops of Scotland to be suspected of heresy: and, after long watching, he was taken by two popish priests, and brought to St Andrews and imprisoned in the castle thereof. The papists threatened him with death and corporal torments, to the intent they might cause him to forsake the truth. But seeing they could profit nothing thereby, and that he remained firm and constant, they laboured to persuade him by fair promises, and offered unto him a monk's portion, for all the days of his life, in the Abbey of Dunfermline, so that he would deny the things he had taught, and grant that they were heresy; but he, continuing in the truth even unto the end, despised their threatenings and fair promises.

The said Walter Mill was brought to the metropolitan church of St Andrews, where he was put in a pulpit before the bishops to be accused. Seeing him so weak and feeble of person, partly by age and travail, and partly by evil entreatment, that without help he could not climb up, they were out of hope to have heard him, for weakness of voice. But when he began to speak, he made the church to ring again with so great courage and stoutness, that the Christians who were present were no less rejoiced, than the adversaries were confounded and ashamed. Being in the pulpit, and on his knees at prayer, Andrew Oliphant, one of the archbishop's priests, commanded him to arise, saying on this manner, ' sir Walter Mill, arise, and answer to the articles; for you hold my lord here over-long.' To whom Walter, after he had finished his prayer, answered, saying, 'Ye call me sir Walter, call me Walter, and not *sir* Walter; I have been over-long one of the Pope's knights. Now say what thou hast to say.'

Oliphant: 'Thou sayest there be not seven sacraments.'

Mill: 'Give me the Lord's supper and baptism, and take you the rest, and part them among you.'

Oliphant: 'Thou art against the blessed sacrament of the altar, and sayest, that the mass is wrong, and is idolatry.'

Mill: 'A lord or a king sendeth and calleth many to a dinner; and when the dinner is in readiness, he causeth to ring the bell, and the men come to the hall, and sit down to be partakers of the dinner; but the Lord, turning his back unto them, eateth all himself, and mocketh them:—so do ye.'

Oliphant: 'Thou deniest the sacrament of the altar to be the very body of Christ really in flesh and blood.'

Mill: 'As for the mass, it is wrong, for Christ was once offered on the cross for man's trespass, and will never be offered again, for then He ended all sacrifice.'

Oliphant: 'Thou preachedst secretly and privately in houses, and openly in the fields.'

Mill: 'Yea man, and on the sea also, sailing in a ship.'

Oliphant: 'Wilt thou not recant thy erroneous opinions?'

Mill: 'I will not recant the truth, for I am corn, I am no chaff: I will not be blown away with the wind, nor burst with the flail; but I will abide both.'

Then Oliphant pronounced sentence against him, that he should be delivered to the temporal judge, and punished as a heretic; which was, to be burned. Notwithstanding, his boldness and constancy moved so the hearts of many, that the provost of the town, called Patrick Lermond, refused to be his temporal judge; to whom it appertained, if the cause had been just: also the bishop's chamberlain, being therewith charged, would in no wise take upon him so ungodly an office. Yea, the whole town was so offended with his unjust condemnation, that the bishop's servants could not get for their money so much as one cord to tie him to the stake, or a tar-barrel to burn him; but were constrained to cut the cords of their master's own pavilion, to serve their turn.

Nevertheless, one servant of the bishop's more ignorant and cruel than the rest, called Alexander Somervaile, enterprising the office of a temporal judge in that part, conveyed him to the fire, where, against all natural reason of man, his boldness and hardiness did more and more increase, so that the Spirit of God working miraculously in him, made it manifest to the people, that his cause was just, and he innocently put down.

When all things were ready for his death, and he conveyed with armed men to the fire, Oliphant bade him pass to the stake. And he said, 'Nay! wilt thou put me up with thy hand, and take part of my death, thou shalt see me pass up gladly: for by the law of God I am forbidden to put hands upon myself.' Then Oliphant put him up with his hand, and he ascended gladly, saying, 'I will go to the altar of God;' and desired that he might have space to speak to the people, which Oliphant and other of the burners denied, saying, that he had spoken over

much; for the bishops were altogether offended
that the matter was so long continued. Then some
of the young men committed both the burners, and
the bishops their masters, to the devil, saying, that
they should lament that day; and desired the said
Walter to speak what he pleased.

And so after he made his humble supplication to
God on his knees, he arose, and standing upon the
coals, said on this wise:

'Dear friends! the cause why I suffer this day is
not for any crime laid to my charge (albeit I be a
miserable sinner before God), but only for the
defence of the faith of Jesus Christ, set forth in the
New and Old Testament unto us: for which as the
faithful martyrs have offered themselves gladly
before, being assured, after the death of their
bodies, of eternal felicity, so this day I praise God,
that He hath called me of His mercy, among the
rest of His servants, to seal up His truth with
my life: which, as I have received it of Him, so
willingly I offer it to His glory. Therefore, as
you will escape the eternal death, be no more
seduced with the lies of priests, monks, friars,
priors, abbots, bishops, and the rest of the sect
of Antichrist; but depend only upon Jesus Christ
and His mercy, that ye may be delivered from
condemnation.'

All that while there was great mourning and
lamentation of the multitude; for they, perceiving
his patience, stoutness and boldness, constancy and
hardiness, were not only moved and stirred up,
but their hearts also were inflamed. After his
prayer, he was hoisted up upon the stake, and
being in the fire, he said, 'Lord, have mercy on

me! Pray, people, while there is time!' and so he departed.

After this, by the just judgment of God, in the same place where Walter Mill was burnt, the images of the great church of the abbey, which surpassed both in number and costliness, were burned in the time of reformation.

THE LIFE, ACTS, AND DOINGS OF MASTER HUGH LATIMER, THE FAMOUS PREACHER AND WORTHY MARTYR OF CHRIST AND HIS GOSPEL

This old practised soldier of Christ, Master Hugh Latimer, was the son of one Hugh Latimer, of Thurkesson in the county of Leicester, a husbandman, of a good and wealthy estimation; where also he was born and brought up until he was the age of four years, or thereabout: at which time his parents, having him as then left for their only son, with six daughters, seeing his ready, prompt, and sharp wit, purposed to train him up in erudition, and knowledge of good literature; wherein he so profited in his youth at the common schools of his own country, that at the age of fourteen years, he was sent to the University of Cambridge; where, after some continuance of exercises in other things, he gave himself to the study of such divinity, as the ignorance of that age did suffer.

Zealous he was then in the popish religion, and therewith so scrupulous, as himself confesseth, that being a priest, and using to say mass, he was so servile an observer of the Romish decrees, that he had thought he had never sufficiently mingled his massing wine with water; he thought that he should never be damned, if he were once a professed friar; with divers such superstitious fantasies. In this blind zeal he was a very enemy to the professors of Christ's Gospel; as his oration made, when he proceeded Bachelor of Divinity, against Philip Melancthon and his works, did plainly declare.

Notwithstanding, such was the goodness and merciful purpose of God, that where he thought by that his oration to have utterly defaced the professors of the Gospel and true Church of Christ, he was himself by a member of the same prettily catched in the blessed net of God's Word. For Master Thomas Bilney, being at that time a trier out of Satan's subtleties, and a secret overthrower of Antichrist's kingdom, and seeing Master Latimer to have a zeal in his ways, although without knowledge, was stricken with a brotherly pity towards him, and bethought by what means he might best win this zealous, yet ignorant brother to the true knowledge of Christ. He came to Master Latimer's study, and desired him to hear him make his confession; which thing he willingly granted; with the hearing whereof he was, by the good Spirit of God, so touched, that he forsook his former studying of the school-doctors and other such fooleries, and became a true scholar of the true divinity. So that whereas before he was an enemy, and almost a persecutor of Christ, he was now an earnest seeker after Him, changing his old manner of calumnying into a diligent kind of conferring, both with Master Bilney and others.

After his winning to Christ, he was not satisfied with his own conversion only, but, like a true disciple of the blessed Samaritan, pitied the misery of others, and became a public preacher, and a private instructor, to the rest of his brethren within the University, by the space of three years, spending his time partly in the Latin tongue among the learned, and partly amongst the simple people in his natural and vulgar language. Howbeit, as Satan never sleepeth when he seeth his kingdom begin to decay, so likewise now, seeing that this worthy member of Christ would be a shrewd shaker thereof, he raised up his children to molest and trouble him.

Amongst these there was an Augustine friar, who took occasion, upon certain sermons that Master Latimer made about Christenmas 1529, to envy against him, for that Master Latimer in the said sermons, alluding to the common usage of the season, gave the people certain cards out of the fifth, sixth, and seventh chapters of St Matthew, whereupon they might, not only then, but always occupy their time. For the chief, as their triumphing card, he limited the heart, as the principal thing that they should serve God withal, whereby he quite overthrew all external ceremonies, not tending to the necessary beautifying of God's holy Word and sacraments. For the better attaining hereof, he wished the Scriptures to be in English, that the common people might thereby learn their duties, as well to God as to their neighbours.

The handling of this matter was so apt for the time, and so pleasantly applied of Latimer, that not only it declared a singular towardness of wit in him that preached, but also wrought in the hearers much fruit, to the overthrow of popish superstition, and setting up of perfect religion.

On the Sunday before Christenmas day coming to the church, and causing the bell to be tolled, he entereth into the pulpit, exhorting and inviting all men to serve the Lord with inward heart and true affection, and not with outward ceremonies: meaning thereby how the Lord would be worshipped and served in simplicity of the heart and verity, wherein consisteth true Christian religion, and not in the outward deeds of the letter only, or in the glistering show of man's traditions, of pardons, pilgrimages, ceremonies, vows, devotions, voluntary works, works of supererogation, foundations, oblations, the Pope's supremacy; so that all these either be needless, where the other is present, or else be of small estimation, in comparison.

It would ask a long discourse to declare what a stir there was in Cambridge, upon this preaching of Master Latimer. Belike Satan began to feel himself and his kingdom to be touched too near, and therefore thought it time to look about him, and to make out his men at arms.

First came out the prior of the Black Friars, called Buckenham, declaring that it was not expedient the Scripture to be in English, lest the ignorant might haply be brought in danger to leave their vocation, or else to run into some inconvenience: as for example, the ploughmam, when he heareth this in the Gospel, 'No man that layeth his hand on the plough and looketh back, is meet for the kingdom of God,' might peradventure, hearing this, cease from his plough. Likewise the baker, when he heareth that a little leaven corrupteth a whole lump of dough, may percase leave our bread unleavened, and so our bodies shall be unseasoned. Also the simple man, when he heareth in the Gospel, 'If thine eye offend thee, pluck it out, and cast it from thee,' may make himself blind, and so fill the world full of beggars.

Master Latimer, hearing this friarly sermon of Dr Buckenham, cometh again to the church, to answer the friar, where resorted to him a great multitude, as well of the University as of the town, both doctors and other graduates, with great expectation to hear what he could say: among whom also, directly in the face of Latimer, underneath the pulpit, sat Buckenham with his black-friar's cowl about his shoulders.

Then Master Latimer so refuted the friar; so answered to his objections; so dallied with his bald reasons of the ploughman looking back, and of the baker leaving his bread unleavened, that the vanity of the friar might to all men appear, well proving and declaring to the people, how there was no such fear nor danger for the Scriptures to be in English, as the friar pretended; at least this requiring, that the Scripture might be so long in the English tongue, till Englishmen were so mad, that neither the ploughman durst look back, nor the baker should leave his bread unleavened. 'Every speech,' saith he, 'hath its metaphors and like figurative significations, so common to all men, that the very painters do paint them on walls, and in houses.' As for example (saith he, looking toward the friar), when they paint a fox preaching out of a friar's cowl, none is so mad to take this to be a fox that preacheth, but know well enough the meaning of the matter, which is to paint out unto us, what hypocrisy, craft, and subtle dissimulation, lieth hid many times in these friars' cowls, willing us thereby to beware of them.

THE RAILING FRIARS

In fine, friar Buckenham with this sermon was so dashed, that never after he durst peep out of the pulpit against Master Latimer.

Besides this Buckenham, there was also another railing friar, not of the same coat, but of the same note and faction, a grey friar and a doctor, an outlandishman called Dr Venetus, who likewise, in his brawling sermons, railed and raged against Master Latimer, calling him a mad and brainless man, and willing the people not to believe him. To whom Master Latimer answering again, taketh for his ground the words of our Saviour Christ, 'Thou shalt not kill,' etc. 'But I say unto you, whosoever is angry with his neighbour shall be in danger of judgment : and whosoever shall say unto his neighbour, Raca (or any other like words of rebuking, as *brainless*), shall be in danger of council : and whosoever shall say to his neighbour, Fool, shall be in danger of hell fire.' He declared to the audience, that the true servants and preachers of God in this world commonly are scorned and reviled of the proud enemies of God's Word, which count them here as madmen, fools, brainless, and drunken : so did they, said he, in the Scripture call them which most purely preached and set forth the glory of God's Word. He so confounded the poor friar, that he drove him not only out of countenance, but also clean out of the University.

Whole swarms of friars and doctors flocked against him on every side, almost through the whole University, preaching and barking against him. Then came at last Dr West, Bishop of Ely, who preaching against Master Latimer at Barnwell Abbey, forbade him, within the churches of that

University, to preach any more. Notwithstanding that—so the Lord provided—Dr Barnes, prior of the Augustine friars, did license Master Latimer to preach in his church of the Augustines.

Thus Master Latimer, notwithstanding the malice of the adversaries, continued yet in Cambridge, preaching the space of three years together with such favour and applause of the godly, also with such admiration of his enemies that heard him, that the Bishop himself, coming in and hearing his gift, wished himself to have the like, and was compelled to commend him. Master Latimer, with Master Bilney, used much to company together, insomuch that the place where they most used to walk in the fields, was called long after, the Heretics'-hill. The society of these two, as it was much noted of many in that University, so it was full of many good examples, to all such as would follow their doings, both in visiting the prisoners, in relieving the needy, in feeding the hungry.

Master Latimer maketh mention of a certain history which happened about this time in Cambridge between them two and a certain woman then prisoner in the Castle or Tower of Cambridge. It so chanced, that after Master Latimer had been acquainted with Master Bilney, he went with him to visit the prisoners in the tower in Cambridge, and among other prisoners there was a woman which was accused that she had killed her own child, which act she plainly and steadfastly denied. Whereby it gave them occasion to search for the matter, and at length they found that her husband loved her not, and therefore sought all means he could to make her away. The matter was thus:

a child of hers had been sick a whole year, and at length died in harvest time, as it were in a consumption; which when it was gone, she went to have her neighbours to help her to the burial: but all were in harvest abroad, whereby she was enforced, with heaviness of heart, alone to prepare the child to the burial. Her husband coming home, and not loving her, accused her of murdering the child. This was the cause of her trouble, and Master Latimer, by earnest inquisition of conscience, thought the woman not guilty. Then, immediately after, was he called to preach before King Henry the Eighth at Windsor, where, after his sermon, the King's majesty sent for him, and talked with him familiarly. At which time Master Latimer, finding opportunity, kneeled down, opened his whole matter to the King, and begged her pardon; which the King most graciously granted, and gave it him at his return homeward.

By the means of Dr Buts, the King's physician, a singular good man, and a special favourer of good proceedings, Master Latimer was in the number of them which laboured in the cause of the King's supremacy. Then went he to the court, where he remained a certain time in the said Dr Buts' chamber, preaching then in London very often. At last, being weary of the court, having a benefice offered by the King at the suit of the Lord Cromwell and Dr Buts, he was glad thereof, and, contrary to the mind of Dr Buts, he would needs depart, and be resident at the same.

This benefice was in Wiltshire, under the diocese of Sarum, the name of which town was called West-Kington, where this good preacher did exercise himself to instruct his flock, and not only to them his diligence extended, but also to all the country about. In fine, his diligence was so great, his preaching so mighty, the manner of his teaching so zealous, that there, in like sort, he could not escape without enemies. He was cited to appear before William Warham, Archbishop of Canterbury, and John Stokesley, Bishop of London, Jan. 29, A.D. 1531. He was greatly molested, and detained a long space from his cure at home, being called thrice every week before the said bishops, to make answer for his preaching. At length, much grieved with their troublesome unquietness, which neither would preach themselves, nor yet suffer him to preach and do his duty, he writeth to the archbishop, excusing his infirmity, whereby he could not appear at their commandment, expostulating with them for detaining him from his duty-doing, and that for no just cause, but only for preaching the truth against the certain vain abuses crept into religion.

The story he showeth forth himself in a certain sermon preached at Stamford, Oct. 9, A.D. 1550: 'I was once,' saith he, 'in examination before five or six bishops, where I had much turmoiling. Every week thrice I came to examinations, and many snares and traps were laid to get something. Now God knoweth I was ignorant of the law, but God gave me answer and wisdom what I should speak. It was God indeed: for else I had never escaped them. At the last I was brought forth to be examined into a chamber hanged with arras, where I was wont to be examined: but now, at this time, the chamber was somewhat altered. For whereas before there was wont ever to be a fire in the chimney, now the fire was taken away, and an arras hanged over the chimney, and the table stood near the chimney's end.

'There was amongst the bishops that examined me one with whom I had been very familiar, and took him for my great friend, an aged man, and he sat next the table's end. Then, amongst all other questions he put forth one, a very subtle and crafty one, and such a one indeed, as I could not think so great danger in. And when I should made answer, "I pray you, Master Latimer," said one, "speak out; I am very thick of hearing, and here be many that sit far off." I marvelled at this, that I was bidden speak out, and began to misdeem, and gave an ear to the chimney; and, sir, there I heard a pen walking in the chimney behind the cloth. They had appointed one there to write all mine answers, for they made sure that I should not start from them: there was no starting from them. God was my good Lord, and gave me answer; I could never else have escaped it.'

The question to him there and then objected was this: 'Whether he thought in his conscience that he hath been suspected of heresy.' This was a captious question. There was no holding of peace would serve; for that was to grant himself faulty. To answer it was every way full of danger; but God, which alway giveth in need what to answer, helped him. Albeit what was his answer, he doth not express.

King Henry the Eighth with much favour embraced Master Latimer, and with his power delivered him out of the crooked claws of his enemies. Moreover, through the procurement partly of **Dr Buts**, partly of good Cromwell, he advanced him to the dignity of Bishop of Worcester, who so continued a few years, instructing his diocese, according to the duty of a diligent and vigilant pastor, with wholesome doctrine and example of perfect conversation duly agreeing to the same.

It were a long matter to stand particularly upon such things as might here be brought to the commendation of his pains; as study, readiness, and continual carefulness in teaching, preaching, exhorting, visiting, correcting, and reforming, either as his ability could serve, or else the time would bear. But the days then were so dangerous and variable, that he could not in all things do that he would. Yet what he might do, that he performed to the uttermost of his strength, so that although he could not utterly extinguish all the sparkling relics of old superstition, yet he so wrought, that though they could not be taken away, yet they should be used with as little hurt, and with as much profit, as might be. As for example, when it could not be avoided but holy water and holy bread must needs be received, he so instructed them of his diocese that in receiving thereof superstition should be excluded, charging the ministers in delivering the holy water and the holy bread, to say these words following:

Words spoken to the People in giving them Holy Water.

> Remember your promise in baptism;
> Christ His mercy and blood-shedding:
> By Whose most holy sprinkling,
> Of all your sins you have free pardoning.

PREACHING BEFORE THE KING

What to say in giving Holy Bread.

Of Christ's body this is a token,
Which on the cross for your sins was broken.
Wherefore of your sins you must be forsakers,
If of Christ's death ye will be partakers.

It is to be thought that he would have brought more things else to pass, if the time then had answered to his desire ; for he was not ignorant how the institution of holy water and holy bread not only had no ground in Scripture, but also how full of profane exorcisms and conjurations they were, contrary to the rule and learning of the Gospel.

As before, both in the University and at his benefice, he was tost and turmoiled by wicked and evil-disposed persons, so in his bishopric also, he was not clear and void of some that sought his trouble. One especially there was, and that no small person, which accused him to the King for his sermons. The story, because he himself showeth in a sermon of his before King Edward, I thought therefore to use his own words, which be these :

'In the King's days that dead is, many of us were called together before him, to say our minds in certain matters. One accuseth me that I had preached seditious doctrine. The King turned to me, and said, "What say you to that, sir ?"

'Then I kneeled down, and turned me first to my accuser, and required him. "Sir, what form of preaching would you appoint me to preach before a King? Would you have me for to preach nothing as concerning a King in the King's sermon? have you any commission to appoint me, what I shall preach?" Besides this, I asked him divers other questions, and he would make no answer to none of them all: he had nothing to say.

'Then I turned me to the King, and submitted myself to his grace, and said, "I never thought myself worthy, nor I never sued, to be a preacher before your grace; but I was called to it, and would be willing (if you mislike me) to give place to my betters: for I grant there be a great many more worthy of the room than I am. And if it be your grace's pleasure so to allow them for preachers, I could be content to bear their books after them. But, if your grace allow me for a preacher, I would desire your grace to give me leave to discharge my conscience."

'And I thank Almighty God (Which hath always been my remedy), that my sayings were well accepted of the King. Certain of my friends came to me with tears in their eyes, and told me they looked I should have been in the Tower the same night.'

Thus he continued in this laborious function of a bishop the space of certain years, till the coming in of the Six Articles. Then, being distressed through the straitness of time, so that either he must lose the quiet of a good conscience, or else forsake his bishopric, he did of his own free accord resign his pastorship. At what time he first put off his rochet in his chamber among his friends, suddenly he gave a skip on the floor for joy, feeling his shoulder so light. Howbeit, troubles and labours followed him wheresoever he went. For a little after he had renounced his bishopric, he was sore bruised and almost slain with the fall of a tree. Then, coming up to London for remedy, he was molested of the bishops, whereby he was again in no little danger; and at length was cast into the Tower, where he remained prisoner, till the time that blessed King Edward entered his crown, by means whereof the golden mouth of this preacher, long shut up before, was now opened again.

Beginning afresh to set forth his plough he laboured in the Lord's harvest most fruitfully, discharging his talent as well in divers places of this realm, as before the King at the court. In the same place of the inward garden, which was before applied to lascivious and courtly pastimes, there he dispensed the fruitful Word of the glorious Gospel of Jesus Christ, preaching there before the King and his whole court, to the edification of many. In this his painful travail he occupied himself all King Edward's days, preaching for the most part every Sunday twice. Though a sore bruised man by the fall of a tree, and above sixty-seven years of age, he took little ease and care of sparing himself. Every morning, winter and summer, about two of the clock, he was at his book most diligently.

Master Latimer ever affirmed that the preaching of the Gospel would cost him his life, to the which he cheerfully prepared himself. After the death of King Edward, not long after Queen Mary was proclaimed, a pursuivant was sent down into the country, to call him up, of whose coming, although Master Latimer lacked no forewarning, yet so far off was it that he thought to escape, that he prepared himself towards his journey before the said pursuivant came to his house. When the pursuivant marvelled, he said unto him—'My friend, you be a welcome messenger to me. And be it known unto you, and to all the world, that I go as willingly to

London at this present, called to render a reckoning of my doctrine, as ever I was at any place in the world. I doubt not but that God, as He hath made me worthy to preach His Word before two excellent princes, so will He able me to witness the same unto the third, either to her comfort, or discomfort eternally.'

When the pursuivant had delivered his letters he departed, affirming that he had commandment not to tarry for him; by whose sudden departure it was manifest that they would not have him appear, but rather to have fled out of the realm. They knew that his constancy should deface them in their popery, and confirm the godly in the truth.

Thus Master Latimer coming up to London, through Smithfield (where merrily he said that Smithfield had long groaned for him), was brought before the council, where he patiently bore all the mocks and taunts given him by the scornful papists. He was cast into the Tower, where he, being assisted with the heavenly grace of Christ, sustained imprisonment a long time, notwithstanding the cruel and unmerciful handling of the lordly papists, which thought then their kingdom would never fall; he showed himself not only patient, but also cheerful in and above all that which they could or would work against him. Yea, such a valiant spirit the Lord gave him, that he was able not only to despise the terribleness of prisons and torments, but also to laugh to scorn the doings of his enemies.

When the lieutenant's man upon a time came to him, the aged father, kept without fire in the frosty winter, and well nigh starved with cold, merrily bade the man tell his master, that if he did not look the better to him, perchance he would deceive him. The lieutenant of the Tower, hearing this, bethought himself of these words, and fearing lest that indeed he thought to make some escape, began to look more straitly to his prisoner, and so coming to him, chargeth him with his words. ' Yea, master lieutenant, so I said,' quoth he, 'for you look, I think, that I should burn; but except you let me have some fire, I am like to deceive your expectation, for I am like here to starve for cold.'

Many such like answers and reasons, merry, but savoury, coming not from a vain mind, but from a con tant and quiet reason, proceeded from that man, declaring a firm and stable heart, little passing of all this great blustering of their terrible threats, but rather deriding the same.

Thus Master Latimer, passing a long time in the Tower, from thence was transported to Oxford, with Dr Cranmer, Archbishop of Canterbury, and Master Ridley, Bishop of London, there to dispute upon articles sent down from Gardiner, Bishop of Winchester. The said Latimer, with his fellow-prisoners, was condemned, and committed again to prison, and there they continued from the month of April, to the month of October; where they were most godly occupied, either with brotherly conference, or with fervent prayer, or with fruitful writing. Albeit Master Latimer, by reason of the feebleness of his age, wrote least of them all ; yet oftentimes so long he continued kneeling in prayer that he was not able to rise without help. These were three principal matters he prayed for.

First, that as God had appointed him to be a preacher of His Word, so also He would give him grace to stand to his doctrine until his death, that he might give his heart blood for the same.

Secondly, that God of His mercy would restore His Gospel to England once again; and these words 'once again, once again,' he did so beat into the ears of the Lord God, as though he had seen God before him, and spoken to Him face to face.

The third matter was, to pray for the preservation of the Queen's Majesty that now is, at that time the Princess Elizabeth, whom even with tears he desired God to make a comfort to His comfortless realm of England.

The Lord most graciously did grant all those his requests.

First, concerning his constancy, even in the most extremity the Lord graciously assisted him. For when he stood at the stake without Bocardo-gate at Oxford, and the tormentors about to set the fire to him, and to the learned and godly Bishop, Master Ridley, he lifted up his eyes towards heaven with an amiable and comfortable countenance, saying these words, 'God is faithful, Which doth not suffer us to be tempted above our strength.'

How mercifully the Lord heard his second request in restoring His Gospel once again unto this realm these present days can bear record. And what, then shall England say now for her defence, which being so mercifully visited and refreshed with the Word of God, so slenderly and unthankfully considereth either her own misery past, or the great benefit of God now present? The Lord be merciful unto us.

Again, concerning his third request, it seemeth likewise most effectuously granted, to the great

praise of God, the furtherance of His Gospel, and to
the unspeakable comfort of this realm. When all
was so desperate that the enemies mightily flourished
and triumphed; when God's Word was banished,
Spaniards received, and no place left for Christ's
servants to cover their heads, suddenly the Lord
called to remembrance His mercy, and, forgetting
our former iniquity, made an end of all these
miseries. Queen Elizabeth was appointed and
anointed, for whom this grey-headed father so
earnestly prayed in his imprisonment: through
whose true, natural and imperial crown, the brightness of God's Word was set up again to confound
the dark and false-vizored kingdom of Antichrist,
the true temple of Christ re-edified, and the captivity
of sorrowful Christians released.

(A detailed account of the trial, condemnation,
and martyrdom of Bishop Latimer and Bishop Ridley,
begins on page 295.)

THE STORY OF BISHOP RIDLEY

Among many other worthy histories and notable acts of such as have been martyred for the true Gospel of Christ, the tragical story of Dr Ridley I thought good to chronicle, and leave to perpetual memory ; beseeching thee (gentle reader) with care and study well to peruse, diligently to consider, and deeply to print the same in thy breast, seeing him to be a man beautified with such excellent qualities, so ghostly inspired and godly learned, and now written doubtless in the Book of Life, with the blessed saints of the Almighty, crowned and throned amongst the glorious company of martyrs.

Descending of a stock right worshipful, he was born in Northumberlandshire; he learned his grammar with great dexterity in Newcastle, and was removed from thence to the University of Cambridge, where he in short time became so famous, that for his singular aptness he was called to be head of Pembroke-hall, and there made doctor of Divinity. Departing from thence, he travelled to Paris; at his return was made chaplain to King Henry the Eighth and promoted afterwards by him to the Bishopric of Rochester and so from thence translated to the see and Bishopric of London, in King Edward's days.

He so occupied himself by preaching and teaching the true and wholesome doctrine of Christ, that never good child was more singularly loved of his dear parents, that he of his flock and diocese. Every holiday and Sunday he preached in some place or other, except he were letted by weighty affairs. To his sermons the people resorted, swarming about him like bees, coveting the sweet flowers and wholesome juice of the fruitful doctrine, which he did not only preach, but showed the same by his life, as a glittering lanthorn to the eyes and senses of the blind, in such pure order that his very enemies could not reprove him in any one jot.

He was well learned, his memory was great, and he of such reading withal, that of right he deserved to be comparable to the best of this our age, as can testify his notable works, pithy sermons, and disputations in both the Universities, as also his very adversaries, all which will say no less themselves.

Wise he was of counsel, deep of wit, and very politic in all his doings. In fine, he was such a prelate, and in all points so good, godly, and ghostly a man, that England may justly rue the loss of so worthy a treasure.

He was a man right comely and well proportioned, both in complexion and lineaments of the body. He took all things in good part, bearing no malice nor rancour in his heart, but straightways forgetting all injuries and offences done against him. He was very kind to his kinsfolk, and yet not bearing with them any thing otherwise than right would require, giving them always for a general rule, yea to his own brother and sister, that they, doing evil, should seek or look for nothing at his hand, but should be as strangers and aliens unto him ; and they to be his brother and sister, which used honesty, and a godly trade of life.

He, using all kinds of ways to mortify himself, was given to much prayer and contemplation; for duly every morning, so soon as his apparel was done upon him, he went forthwith to his bed-chamber, and there, upon his knees, prayed the space of half an hour; which being done, immediately he went to his study, if there came no other business to interrupt him, where he continued till ten of the clock, and then came to the common prayer, daily used in his house. The prayers being done, he went to dinner, where he used little talk, except occasion by some had been ministered, and was it sober, discreet, and wise, and some times merry, as cause required.

The dinner done, which was not very long, he used to sit an hour or thereabouts, talking, or playing at the chess: that done, he returned to his study, and there would continue, except suitors or business abroad were occasion of the contrary, until five of the clock at night, and then would come to common prayer, as in the forenoon: which being finished, he went to supper, behaving himself there as at his dinner before. After supper recreating himself in playing at chess the space of an hour, he would return again to his study; continuing there till eleven of the clock at night, which was his common hour to go to bed, then saying his prayers upon his knees, as in the morning when he rose.

Being at his manor of Fulham, as divers times he used to be, he read daily a lecture to his family at the common prayer, beginning at the Acts of the Apostles, and so going through all the Epistles of St Paul, giving to every man that could read a New Testament, hiring them besides with money to learn by heart certain principal chapters but especially Acts xiii., reading also unto his household oftentimes Psalm ci., being marvellous careful over his family, that they might be a spectacle of all virtue and honesty to others. To be short, as he was godly and virtuous himself, so nothing but virtue and godliness reigned in his house, feeding them with the food of our Saviour Jesus Christ.

Remaineth a word or two to be declared of his gentle nature and kindly pity in the usage of an old woman called Mrs Bonner, mother to Dr Bonner, sometime Bishop of London. Bishop Ridley, being at his manor of Fulham, always sent for this said Mrs Bonner, dwelling in a house adjoining to his house, to dinner and supper, saying, 'Go for my mother Bonner'; who, coming, was ever placed in the chair at the table's end, being so gently entreated, as though he had been born of her own body, being never displaced of her seat, although the King's council had been present; saying, when any of them were there, as divers times they were, 'By your lordship's favour, this place of right and custom is for my mother Bonner.'

But how well he was recompensed for this his singular gentleness and pitiful piety after, at the hands of the said Dr Bonner, almost the least child that goeth by the ground can declare. For who afterward was more enemy to Ridley than Bonner? Who more went about to seek his destruction than he? recompensing this his gentleness with extreme cruelty; as well appeared by the strait handling of Ridley's own sister, and George Shipside her husband. Whereas the gentleness of Ridley did suffer Bonner's mother, sister, and other of his kindred, not only quietly to enjoy all that which they had of Bonner, but also entertained them in his house, showing much courtesy and friendship daily unto them, on the other side, Bishop Bonner, being restored again, currishly, without all order of law or honesty, by extort power wrested from the brother and sister of Bishop Ridley all the livings they had. And being not therewith satisfied, he sought to work the death of the foresaid Shipside, which had been brought to pass indeed, at what time he was prisoner at Oxford, had not God otherwise wrought his deliverance by means of Dr Heath, the Bishop of Worcester.

About the eighth of September, 1552, Dr Ridley, then Bishop of London, lying at his house at Hadham in Hertfordshire, went to visit the Lady Mary,[1] then lying at Hunsdon, two miles off; and was gently entertained of Sir Thomas Wharton, and other her officers, till it was almost eleven of the clock; about which time the said Lady Mary came forth into her chamber of presence, and then the said bishop there saluted her grace, and said, that he was come to do this duty to her grace. Then she thanked him for his pains, and, for a quarter of an hour, talked with him very pleasantly; said that she knew him in the court when he was chaplain to her father: and so dismissed him to dine with her officers.

After dinner was done, the bishop being called for by the said Lady Mary, resorted again to her grace, between whom this communication was. First the bishop beginneth in manner as followeth: 'Madam, I came not only to do my duty, to see your grace, but also to offer myself to preach before you on Sunday, if it will please you to hear me.'

[1] Afterwards Queen Mary.

At this her countenance changed, and, after silence for a space, she answered thus:

Mary: 'My lord, as for this last matter I pray you make the answer to it yourself.'

Bishop: 'Madam, considering mine office and calling, I am bound in duty to make to your grace this offer, to preach before you.'

Mary: 'Well, I pray you make the answer (as I have said) to this matter yourself; for you know the answer well enough. But if there be no remedy but I must make you answer, this shall be your answer; the door of the parish-church adjoining shall be open for you if you come, and ye may preach if you list; but neither I, nor any of mine, shall hear you.'

Bishop: 'Madam, I trust you will not refuse God's Word.'

Mary: 'I cannot tell what ye call God's Word: that is not God's Word now, that was God's Word in my father's days.'

Bishop: 'God's Word is all one in all times; but hath been better understood and practised in some ages than in others.'

Mary: 'You durst not, for your ears, have avouched that for God's Word in my father's days that now you do. And as for your new books, I thank God I never read any of them: I never did, nor ever will do.'

And after many bitter words against the form of religion then established, and against the government of the realm and the laws made in the young years of her brother (which, she said, she was not bound to obey till her brother came to perfect age, and then, she affirmed, she would obey them), she asked the bishop whether he were one of the council. He answered, 'No.' 'You might well enough,' said she, 'as the council goeth now-a-days.'

And so she concluded with these words: 'My lord, for your gentleness to come and see me, I thank you; but for your offering to preach before me, I thank you never a whit.'

Then the said bishop was brought by Sir Thomas Wharton to the place where they dined, and was desired to drink. And after he had drunk, he paused awhile, looking very sadly; and suddenly brake out into these words: 'Surely I have done amiss.' 'Why so?' quoth Sir Thomas Wharton. 'For I have drunk,' said he, 'in that place where God's Word offered hath been refused: whereas, if I had remembered my duty, I ought to have departed immediately, and to have shaken off the dust of my shoes for a testimony against this house.' These words were by the said bishop spoken with such a vehemency, that some of the hearers afterwards confessed their hair to stand upright on their heads.

What time King Edward, by long sickness, began to appear more feeble and weak, a marriage was concluded between the Lord Guilford, son to the Duke of Northumberland, and the Lady Jane, the Duke of Suffolk's daughter; whose mother, being then alive, was daughter to Mary, King Henry's second sister, who first was married to the French King, and afterward to Charles, Duke of Suffolk. The King, waxing every day more sick than other, whereas indeed there seemed in him no hope of recovery, it was brought to pass by the consent not only of the nobility, but also of the chief lawyers of the realm, that the King, by his testament, did appoint the aforesaid Lady Jane to be inheritrix unto the crown of England, passing over his two sisters, Mary and Elizabeth. The causes laid against Lady Mary were that it was feared she would marry with a stranger, and thereby entangle the crown: also that she would clean alter religion, bring in the Pope, to the utter destruction of the realm.

King Edward, not long after this, departed by the vehemency of his sickness, when he was sixteen years of age; with whom decayed in a manner the whole flourishing estate and honour of the English nation.

This Jane was forthwith published Queen at London, and in other cities where was any great resort. Between this young damsel and King Edward there was little difference in age, though in learning and knowledge of the tongues she was superior unto him. If her fortune had been as good as was her bringing up, joined with fineness of wit, undoubtedly she might have seemed comparable not only to your Aspasias, and Sempronias (to wit, the mother of the Gracchi), yea, to any other women beside, that deserved high praise for their singular learning; but also to the University-men, which have taken many degrees of the schools.

In the meantime, while these things were a-working at London, Mary, who had knowledge of her brother's death, writeth to the lords of the council a letter wherein she claimeth the crown. 'My lords, we require you, that of your allegiance which you owe to God and us, and to none other, forthwith, upon receipt hereof, do cause our right and title to the crown and government of this realm to be proclaimed in our city of London and other places.'

BISHOP RIDLEY

To this letter of the Lady Mary, the lords of the council made answer: 'This is to advertise you, that forasmuch as our Sovereign Lady Queen Jane is invested and possessed with the just and right title in the imperial crown of this realm, not only by good order of old ancient laws of this realm, but also by our late Sovereign Lord's letters patent, signed with his own hand, and sealed with the great seal of England: we must, therefore, as of most bounden duty and allegiance, assent unto her said grace, and to none other.'

This answer received, and the minds of the lords perceived, Lady Mary speedeth herself secretly away far off from the city, hoping chiefly upon the good will of the commons, and yet perchance not destitute altogether of the secret advertisements of some of the nobles. When the council heard of her sudden departure, and perceived her stoutness, and that all came not to pass as they supposed, they gathered speedily a power of men together, appointing an army, and first assigned that the Duke of Suffolk should take that enterprise in hand, and so have the leading of the band. But afterward, altering their minds, they thought it best to send forth the Duke of Northumberland, with certain other lords and gentlemen; and that the Duke of Suffolk should keep the Tower, where the Lord Guilford and the Lady Jane the same time were lodged.

Mary, in the meanwhile, tossed with much travail up and down, to work the surest way for her best advantage, withdrew herself into Norfolk and Suffolk, where she understood the Duke's name to be had in much hatred for the service that had been done there of late under King Edward in subduing the rebels; and there, gathering to her such aid of the commons on every side as she might, kept herself close for a space within Framlingham Castle. To whom first of all resorted the Suffolk men; who, being always forward in promoting the proceedings of the Gospel, promised her their aid so that she would not attempt the alteration of the religion, which her brother King Edward had before established by laws and orders publicly enacted, and received by the consent of the whole realm. Unto this condition she eftsoons agreed. Thus Mary, being guarded with the power of the gospellers, did vanquish the duke, and all those that came against her.

In the mean time, God turned the hearts of the people to her, and against the council. Which after the council perceived, and that certain noblemen began to go the other way, they turned their song, and proclaimed for Queen the Lady Mary.

And so the Duke of Northumberland was left destitute, and forsaken at Cambridge with some of his sons, and a few others, who were arrested and brought to the Tower of London, as traitors to the crown.

Mary, when she saw all in quiet by means that her enemies were conquered, followed up the 3rd day of August to London, with the great rejoicing of many men, but with a greater fear of more, and yet with flattery peradventure most great of feigned hearts. Her first lodging she took at the Tower, where the aforesaid Lady Jane, with her husband the Lord Guilford were imprisoned; where they remained waiting her pleasure almost five months. Lady

Jane Grey was executed on the 12th February, 1554. But the Duke, within a month after his coming to the Tower, being adjudged to death, was brought forth to the scaffold, and there beheaded.

Mary, besides hearing mass herself in the Tower, every day more and more discomforted the people, declaring herself to bear no good will to the present state of religion. Such whose consciences were joined to truth perceived already coals to be kindled, which after should be the destruction of many a true Christian man.

Divers bishops were removed, and others placed in their rooms; amongst whom was Dr Ridley. In the time of Queen Jane, he had made a sermon at Paul's Cross, so commanded by the council; declaring there his mind to the people as touching the Lady Mary, alleging the inconveniences which might rise by receiving her to be their Queen; prophesying—as it were before, that which after came to pass—that she would bring in foreign power to reign over them, besides subverting all Christian religion: showing that there was no other hope of her to be conceived, but to disturb and overturn all that, which, with so great labours, had been confirmed and planted by her brother. Shortly after this sermon, Queen Mary was proclaimed; whereupon he, speedily repairing to Framlingham to salute the Queen, had such cold welcome there, that, being despoiled of all his dignities, he was sent back upon a lame halting horse to the Tower.

About the 10th of March, Cranmer, Archbishop of Canterbury, Ridley, Bishop of London, and Hugh Latimer, Bishop also some time of Worcester, were conveyed as prisoners from the Tower to Windsor;

and from thence to the University of Oxford, there
to dispute with the divines and learned men of both
the Universities, Oxford and Cambridge, about the
presence, substance, and sacrifice of the sacrament.
The articles whereupon they should dispute were
these:

> First, Whether the natural body of Christ
> be really in the sacrament after the words
> spoken by the priest, or no?
> Secondly, Whether in the sacrament, after the
> words of consecration, any other substance
> do remain, than the substance of the body
> and blood of Christ?
> Thirdly, Whether in the mass be a sacrifice pro-
> pitiatory for the sins of the quick and the dead?

Dr Ridley answered without any delay, saying
they were all false; and that they sprang out
of a bitter and sour root. His answers were
sharp, witty, and very learned. He was asked,
whether he would dispute or no? He answered
that as long as God gave him life, he should not
only have his heart, but also his mouth and pen to
defend His truth: but he required time and books.
They said that he should dispute on Thursday, and
till that time he should have books. Then gave
they him the articles, and bade him write his mind
of them that night.

> The Report and Narration of Master Ridley, con-
> cerning the misordered Disputation had against
> him and his Fellow-Prisoners at Oxford.

I never yet, since I was born, saw anything
handled more vainly or tumultuously, than the

disputation which was with me in the schools at Oxford. Yea, verily, I could never have thought that it had been possible to have found amongst men recounted to be of knowledge and learning in this realm, any so brazen-faced and shameless, so disorderly and vainly to behave themselves, more like to stage-players in interludes to set forth a pageant, than to grave divines in schools to dispute. And no great marvel, seeing they which should have been moderators and overseers of others, and which should have given good examples in words and gravity, gave worst example, above all others, and did, as it were, blow the trump to the rest, to rave, roar, rage, and cry out. By reason whereof (good Christian reader) manifestly it may appear, that they never sought for any truth of verity, but only for the glory of the world, and their own bragging victory.

A great part of the time appointed for the disputations was vainly consumed in opprobrious checks and reviling taunts (with hissing and clapping of hands), to procure the people's favour withal. All which things, when I with great grief of heart did behold, protesting openly, that such excessive and outrageous disorder was unseemly for those schools, and men of learning and gravity, and that they which were the doers and stirrers of such things, did nothing else but betray the slenderness of their cause, and their own vanities: I was so far off, by this my humble complaint, from doing any good at all, that I was enforced to hear such rebukes, checks, and taunts for my labour, as no person of any honesty, without blushing, could abide to hear the like spoken of a most vile varlet, against a most wretched ruffian.

A RAGING MULTITUDE

At the first beginning of the disputation, when I should have confirmed mine answer to the first proposition in few words, afore I could make an end of my first probation, even the doctors themselves cried out, 'He speaketh blasphemies! he speaketh blasphemies!' And when I on my knees besought them, and that heartily, that they would vouchsafe to hear me to the end (whereat the prolocutor, being moved, cried out on high, 'Let him read it! let him read it!'): yet, when I began to read again, there followed immediately such shouting, such a noise and tumult, such confusion of voices, crying, 'Blasphemies! blasphemies!' as I, to my remembrance, never heard or read the like; except it be that one, which was in the Acts of the Apostles, stirred up of Demetrius the silversmith, and others of his occupation, crying out against Paul, 'Great is Diana of the Ephesians! great is Diana of the Ephesians!'

The which cries and tumults of them against me so prevailed, that I was enforced to leave off the reading of my probations, although they were short.

After the disputation, the Friday following, which was the 20th of April, the commissioners sat in St Mary's Church, and Dr Weston used particular dissuasions with every one of them, and would not suffer them to answer in any wise, but directly and peremptorily, as his words were, to say whether they would subscribe, or no. And first to the Archbishop of Canterbury, he said he was overcome in disputations. To whom the archbishop answered, that he was not suffered to oppose as he would, nor could answer as he was required, unless he would have brawled with them; so thick their reasons came one after another. Ever four or five did interrupt him, that he could not speak. Master Ridley and Master Latimer were asked what they would do: they replied, that they would stand to that they had said. Then were they all called together, and sentence read over them, that they were no members of the church: and therefore they, their fautors and patrons, were condemned as heretics.

After which, they answered again every one in his turn:

The Archbishop of Canterbury: 'From this your judgment and sentence, I appeal to the just judgment of God Almighty; trusting to be present with Him in heaven, for Whose presence in the altar I am thus condemned.'

Dr Ridley: 'Although I be not of your company, yet doubt I not but my name is written in another place, whither this sentence will send us sooner than we should by the course of nature have come.'

Master Latimer: 'I thank God most heartily, that he hath prolonged my life to this end, that I may in this case glorify God by that kind of death.'

After the sentence pronounced, they were separated one from another; the archbishop was returned to Bocardo, Dr Ridley was carried to the sheriff's house, Master Latimer to the bailiffs.

(A detailed account of the martyrdom of Bishop Ridley will be found in the next chapter.)

THE TRIAL, CONDEMNATION AND MARTYRDOM OF RIDLEY AND LATIMER.

AND thus hast thou, gentle reader, the whole life, both of Master Ridley and of Master Latimer, severally set forth. Now we couple them together, as they were together joined in one martyrdom.

Upon the 28th of September (1555), was sent down to Oxford a commission from Cardinal Pole to John White, Bishop of Lincoln, to Dr Brooks, Bishop of Gloucester, and to Dr Holyman, Bishop of Bristol, that they, or two of them, should have full power to judge Master Hugh Latimer, and Master Dr Ridley, for divers erroneous opinions, which they did maintain in open disputations had in Oxford. The which opinions if the named persons would recant, then they, the deputed judges, should have power to receive the said penitent persons, and forthwith minister unto them the reconciliation of the holy father the Pope. But if the said Hugh Latimer and Nicholas Ridley would maintain their erroneous opinions, then the said lords should pronounce them heretics, cut them clean off from the Church, and yield them to receive punishment.

Wherefore, the last of September, the said lords were placed and set in the divinity school at Oxford; and first appeared Master Dr Ridley. After his coming into the school, the cardinal's commission was read. But Dr Ridley, standing bareheaded, humbly expecting the cause of that his appearance, eftsoons as he had heard the cardinal named, and the Pope's holiness, put on his cap. 'The usurped supremacy, and abused authority of the Bishop of Rome, I utterly refuse and renounce. I may in no wise give any obeisance or honour unto him, lest my so doing might be a derogation to the verity of God's Word.'

The Bishop of Lincoln, after the third admonition, commanded one of the beadles to pluck Master Ridley's cap from his head. Master Ridley, bowing his head to the officer, gently permitted him to take away his cap. After this the bishop in a long oration exhorted Master Ridley to recant, and acknowledge the supremacy of the Pope.

Then Master Ridley said in this manner: 'As touching the saying of Christ, from whence your lordship gathereth the foundation of the Church upon Peter, truly the place is not so to be understood as you take it. For after that Christ had asked His disciples whom men judged Him to be, and they had answered, that some had said He was a prophet, some Elias, some one thing, some another, then He said, "Whom say ye that I am?" Then Peter said, "I say that Thou art Christ, the Son of God." To whom Christ answered, "I say, thou art Peter, and upon this stone I will build My Church;" that is to say, upon this stone—not meaning Peter himself, as though He would have constituted a mortal man, so frail and brickle a foundation of His stable and infallible Church; but upon this rock-stone—that is, this confession of thine, that I am the Son of God, I will build My Church. For this is the foundation and beginning of all Christianity, with word, heart, and mind, to confess that Christ is the Son of God.'

But the bishop, not attending to this answer, proceeded: 'We came not to reason with you, but must proceed, proposing certain articles, unto the which we require your answer directly, either affirmatively or negatively to every of them, either denying them or granting them, without further disputations or reasoning; the which articles you shall hear now; and to-morrow, at eight of the clock in St Mary's Church, we will require and take your answers.'

ARTICLES, JOINTLY AND SEVERALLY MINISTERED TO
DR RIDLEY AND MASTER LATIMER, BY THE
POPE'S DEPUTY

1. We do object to thee, Nicholas Ridley and to thee Hugh Latimer, jointly and severally; that thou hast affirmed, and openly defended and maintained, that the true and natural body of Christ, after the consecration of the priest, is not really present in the sacrament of the altar.

2. That thou hast publicly affirmed and defended, that in the sacrament of the altar remaineth still the substance of bread and wine.

3. That thou hast openly affirmed, and obstinately maintained, that in the mass is no propitiatory sacrifice for the quick and the dead.

After Master Ridley was committed to the mayor, the bishop commanded the bailiffs to bring in the other prisoner. Then Master Latimer bowed his knee down to the ground, holding his hat in his hand, having a kerchief on his head, and upon it a night-cap or two, and a great cap (such as townsmen use, with two broad flaps to button under the chin), wearing an old thread-bare Bristol frieze-gown girded to his body with a penny leather girdle, at the which hanged by a long string of leather his Testament, and his spectacles without case, depending about his neck upon his breast. After this the bishop began on this manner: 'What should stay you to confess that which all the realm confesseth, to forsake that which the King and Queen have renounced, and all the realm recanted. It was a common error, and it is now of all confessed: it shall be no more shame to you, than it was to us all. Therefore, Master Latimer, for God's love, remember you are an old man; spare your body, accelerate not your death, and specially remember your soul's health. If you should die in this state, you shall be a stinking sacrifice to God; for it is the cause that maketh the martyr, and not the death: consider that if you die in this state, you die without grace, for without the Church can be no salvation.' The bishop said that they came not to dispute with Master Latimer, but to take his determinate answers to their articles; and so began to propose the same articles which were proposed to Master Ridley.

The next day following (which was the first day of October), somewhat after eight of the clock, the said lords repaired to St Mary's Church, and after they were set in a high throne well trimmed with cloth of tissue and silk, appeared Master Ridley.

Then spake the Bishop of Lincoln: 'We came to take your determinate answers to our articles. If you have brought your answer in writing, we will receive it: but if you have written any other matter, we will not receive it.'

Then Master Ridley took a sheet of paper out of his bosom, and began to read that which he had written : but the Bishop of Lincoln commanded the beadle to take it from him. But Master Ridley desired license to read it, saying that it was nothing but his answer, but the bishop would in no wise suffer him.

Ridley : 'Why, my lord, will you require my answer, and not suffer me to publish it?'

Lincoln : 'Master Ridley, we will first see what you have written, and then, if we shall think it good to be read, you shall have it published; but, except you will deliver it first, we will take none at all of you.'

With that Master Ridley, seeing no remedy, delivered it to an officer, who delivered it to the bishop. After he had secretly communicated it to the other two bishops, he would not read it as it was written, saying, that it contained words of blasphemy; therefore he would not fill the ears of the audience therewithal, and so abuse their patience.

The Bishop of Gloucester and likewise the Bishop of Lincoln, with many words, desired Master Ridley to turn. But he made an absolute answer, that he was fully persuaded the religion which he defended to be grounded upon God's Word; and, therefore, without great offence towards God, great peril and damage of his soul, he could not forsake his Master and Lord God, but desired the bishop to perform his grant, in that his lordship said the day before, that he should have license to show his cause why he could not with a safe conscience admit the authority of the Pope. The bishop bade him take his license: but he should speak but forty words, and he would tell them upon his fingers. And eftsoons Master Ridley began to speak: but before he had ended half a sentence, the doctors sitting by cried that his number was out; and with that he was put to silence.

And forthwith the Bishop of Lincoln did read the sentence of condemnation, degrading Master Ridley from the degree of a bishop, from priesthood, and all ecclesiastical order; declaring him to be no member of the church: and committing him to the secular powers, of them to receive due punishment. Then Master Ridley was committed as a prisoner to the mayor.

Immediately Master Latimer was sent for, whom the Bishop of Lincoln desired to recant, revoke his errors, and turn to the catholic church.

'No, my lord,' interrupted Master Latimer, 'I confess there is a catholic church, but not the church which you call catholic, which sooner might be termed diabolic. It is one thing to say Romish church, and another thing to say catholic church: I must use here the counsel of Cyprian, who at what time he was ascited before certain bishops demanded of them sitting in judgment, which was most like to be of the Church of Christ, whether he who was persecuted, or they who did persecute? "Christ," said he, "hath foreshowed, that he that doth follow Him, must take up His cross. Christ gave knowledge that the disciples should have persecution and trouble. How think you then, my lords, is it most like that the see of Rome, which hath been a continual persecutor, is rather the Church, or that flock which hath continually been persecuted of it, even to death?"'

After Master Latimer had answered that he neither could nor would deny his Master Christ, and His verity, the Bishop of Lincoln desired Master Latimer to hearken to him: and then Master Latimer, hearkening for some new matter, the bishop read his condemnation; after which, the said three bishops brake up their sessions, and dismissed the audience. But Master Latimer required the bishop to perform his promise in saying the day before, that he should have license briefly to declare why he refused the Pope's authority. But the Bishop said that now he could not hear him, neither ought to talk with him. Then he committed Master Latimer to the mayor, saying, 'Now he is your prisoner, master mayor.'

And so continued Bishop Ridley and Master Latimer, in durance till the 16th day of October A.D. 1555.

Upon the 15th day in the morning, Dr Brooks, the Bishop of Gloucester, and the vice-chancellor of Oxford, Dr Marshal, with divers other of the heads of the University, came unto Master Irish's house, then Mayor of Oxford, where Dr Ridley was close prisoner. The Bishop of Gloucester told him for what purpose their coming, saying that yet once again the Queen's majesty did offer unto him her gracious mercy, if that he would come home to the faith which he was baptized in. If he would not recant they must needs proceed according to the law.

'My lord,' quoth Dr Ridley, 'as for the doctrine which I have taught, my conscience assureth me that it was sound, and according to God's Word;

the which doctrine, the Lord God being my helper, I will maintain so long as my tongue shall wag, and breath is within my body, and in confirmation thereof seal the same with my blood.'

'Seeing,' saith the Bishop of Gloucester, 'that you will not receive the Queen's mercy, we must proceed according to our commission to disgrading, taking from you the dignity of priesthood. So, committing you to the secular power, you know what doth follow.'

Ridley: 'Do with me as it shall please God to suffer you, I am well content to abide the same with all my heart.'

Gloucester: 'Put off your cap, Master Ridley, and put upon you this surplice.'

Ridley: 'Not I, truly.'

Gloucester: 'But you must.'

Ridley: 'I will not.'

Gloucester: 'You must: therefore make no more ado, but put this surplice upon you.'

Ridley: 'Truly, if it come upon me, it shall be against my will.'

Gloucester: 'Will you not do it upon you?'

Ridley: 'No, that I will not.'

Gloucester: 'It shall be put upon you by one or other.'

Ridley: 'Do therein as it shall please you; I am well contented with that, and more than that; "the servant is not above his Master." If they dealt so cruelly with our Saviour Christ, as the Scripture maketh mention, and He suffered the same patiently, how much more doth it become us His servants.'

They put upon Dr Ridley all the trinkets appertaining to the mass; and the same did vehemently inveigh against the Romish Bishop, and all that foolish apparel, insomuch that Bishop Brooks was exceeding angry with him, and bade him hold his peace. Dr Ridley answered that so long as his tongue and breath would suffer him, he would speak against their abominable doings, whatsoever happened unto him for so doing.

At which words one Edridge, the reader then of the Greek lecture, standing by, said to Dr Brooks; 'Sir, the law is, he should be gagged; therefore let him be gagged.' At which words Dr Ridley, looking earnestly upon him that so said, wagged his head at him, and with a sigh said, 'Oh well, well, well!' So they proceeded in their doings, yet nevertheless Dr Ridley was ever talking things not pleasant to their ears, although one or other bade him hold his peace, lest he should be caused against his will.

When they came to that place where Dr Ridley should hold the chalice and the wafer-cake, called the singing-bread, they bade him hold the same in his hands. And Dr Ridley said, 'they shall not come in my hands; for, if they do, they shall fall to the ground for all me.' Then there was one appointed to hold them in his hand, while Bishop Brooks read a certain thing in Latin law, the effect whereof was: 'We do take from you the office of preaching the Gospel.' At which words Dr Ridley gave a great sigh, looking up towards heaven, saying, 'O Lord God, forgive them this their wickedness!'

When all this their abominable and ridiculous degradation was ended very solemnly, Dr Ridley said unto Dr Brooks, 'If you have done, give me leave to talk with you a little concerning these matters.' Brooks answered and said, 'Master Ridley, we may not talk with you; you be out of the Church, and our law is, that we may not talk with any that be out of the Church.' Then Master Ridley said, 'Seeing that you will not suffer me to talk, neither will vouchsafe to hear me, what remedy but patience? I refer the cause to my heavenly Father, Who will reform things that be amiss, when it shall please Him.'

Then Master Ridley said, 'I pray you, my lord, be a mean to the Queen's majesty, in the behalf of a great many of poor men, and especially for my poor sister and her husband which standeth there. They had a poor living granted unto them by me, whiles I was in the see of London, and the same is taken away from them, by him that now occupieth the same room, without all law or conscience. Here I have a supplication to the Queen's majesty in their behalfs. You shall hear the same read, so shall you perceive the matter the better.' When he came to the place that touched his sister by name, he wept, so that for a little space he could not speak. After that he had left off weeping, he said, 'This is nature that moveth me: but I have now done.' Whereunto Brooks said, 'Indeed, Master Ridley, your request is very lawful and honest: therefore I must needs in conscience speak to the Queen's majesty for them.'

All things being finished, Dr Brooks called the bailiffs, delivering to them Master Ridley with this charge, to keep him safely from any man speaking with him, and that he should be brought to the place of execution when they were commanded.

The night before he suffered, as he sat at supper at Master Irish's (who was his keeper), he bade his hostess, and the rest at the board, to his marriage; 'for,' said he, 'to-morrow I must be married:' and so showed himself to be as merry as ever he was at any time before. And wishing his sister at his marriage, he asked his brother sitting at the table, whether she could find in her heart to be there or no. And he answered, 'Yea, I dare say, with all her heart:' at which word he said he was glad. At this talk Mistress Irish wept.

But Master Ridley comforted her, and said, 'O Mrs Irish, you love me not now, I see well enough; for in that you weep, it doth appear you will not be at my marriage, neither are content therewith. Indeed you be not so much my friend, as I thought you had been. But quiet yourself: though my breakfast shall be somewhat sharp and painful, yet I am sure my supper shall be more pleasant and sweet.'

When they arose from the table, his brother offered to watch all night with him. But he said, 'No, no, that you shall not. For I mind (God willing) to go to bed, and to sleep as quietly to-night, as ever I did in my life.'

Upon the north-side of the town, in the ditch over against Balliol-college, the place of execution was appointed: and for fear of any tumult that might arise, to let the burning of them, the Lord Williams was commanded, by the Queen's letters, to be there assistant, sufficiently appointed. And when every thing was in a readiness, the prisoners were brought forth.

Master Ridley had a fair black gown furred, and faced with foins, such as he was wont to wear being bishop, and a tippet of velvet furred likewise about his neck, a velvet night-cap upon his head, and a corner cap upon the same, going in a pair of slippers to the stake, between the mayor and an alderman.

After him came Master Latimer in a poor Bristol frieze frock all worn, with his buttoned cap, and a kerchief on his head, a new long shroud hanging over his hose, down to the feet.

The sight stirred men's hearts to rue, beholding the honour they sometime had, and the calamity whereunto they were fallen.

Master Doctor Ridley, as he passed toward Bocardo, looked up where Master Cranmer did lie, hoping belike to have seen him at the glass-window, and to have spoken unto him. But then Master Cranmer was busy with friar Soto and his fellows, disputing together, so that he could not see him. Master Ridley, looking back, espied Master Latimer coming after, unto whom he said, 'Oh, be ye there!' 'Yea,' said Master Latimer, 'have after as fast as I can follow.' So at length they both came to the stake. Dr Ridley, marvellous earnestly holding up both his hands, looked towards heaven. Then espying Master Latimer, with a wondrous cheerful look he ran to him, embraced, and kissed him; and comforted him, saying, 'Be of good heart, brother, for God will either assuage the fury of the flame, or else strengthen us to abide it.' With that went he to the stake, kneeled down by it, kissed it, and most effectuously prayed, and behind him Master Latimer kneeled, as earnestly calling upon God as he.

Then Dr Smith began his sermon to them upon this text of St Paul, 'If I yield my body to the fire to be burnt, and have not charity, I shall gain nothing thereby.' Wherein he alleged that the goodness of the cause, and not the order of death, maketh the holiness of the person; which he confirmed by the examples of Judas, and of a woman in Oxford that of late hanged herself. He ended with a very short exhortation to them to recant, and come home again to the church, and save their lives and souls.

Dr Ridley said to Master Latimer, 'Will you begin to answer the sermon, or shall I?' Master Latimer said, 'Begin you first, I pray you.' 'I will,' said Master Ridley.

Then, the wicked sermon being ended, Dr Ridley and Master Latimer kneeled down upon their knees towards my Lord Williams of Thame, unto whom Master Ridley said, 'I beseech you, my lord, even for Christ's sake, that I may speak but two or three words.' And whilst my lord bent his head to the mayor and vice-chancellor, to know whether he might give him leave to speak, the bailiffs and Dr Marshal, vice-chancellor, ran hastily unto him, and with their hands stopped his mouth, and said, 'Master Ridley, if you will revoke your erroneous opinions, and recant the same, you shall not only have liberty so to do, but also the benefit of a subject: that is, have your life.'

'Not otherwise?' said Master Ridley.

'No,' quoth Dr Marshal.

'Well,' quoth Master Ridley, 'so long as the breath is in my body, I will never deny my Lord Christ, and His known truth: God's will be done in me!'

Incontinently they were commanded to make them ready, which they with all meekness obeyed. Master Ridley took his gown and his tippet, and gave it to his brother-in-law, Master Shipside. Some other of his apparel that was little worth, he gave away; other the bailiffs took. He gave away besides, divers other small things to gentlemen standing by, pitifully weeping, as to Sir Henry Lea a new groat; and to divers of my Lord Williams's gentlemen some napkins, some nutmegs, and rases of ginger; his dial, and such other things as he had about him, to every one that stood next him. Some plucked the points off his hose. Happy was he that might get any rag of him.

Master Latimer very quietly suffered his keeper to pull off his hose, and his other array, which was very simple: being stripped into his shroud, he seemed as comely a person to them that were there present, as one should see; and whereas in his clothes he appeared a withered and crooked old man, he now stood bolt upright, as comely a father as one might lightly behold.

Master Ridley held up his hand and said, 'O heavenly Father, I give unto Thee most hearty thanks, for that Thou hast called me to be a professor of Thee, even unto death. I beseech Thee, Lord God, take mercy upon this realm of England, and deliver the same from all her enemies.'

Then the smith took a chain of iron, and brought

the same about both Dr Ridley's, and Master
Latimer's middles: and, as he was knocking in a
staple, Dr Ridley took the chain in his hand, and
shaked the same, and looking aside to the smith,
said, 'Good fellow, knock it in hard, for the flesh
will have his course.' Then his brother did bring
him gunpowder in a bag, and would have tied the
same about his neck. Master Ridley asked, what
it was. His brother said, 'Gunpowder.' 'Then,'
said he, 'I take it to be sent of God; therefore I
will receive it as sent of Him. And have you any,'
said he, 'for my brother'; meaning Master Latimer.
'Yea sir, that I have,' quoth his brother. 'Then
give it unto him,' said he, 'betime; lest ye come
too late.' So his brother went, and carried off the
same gunpowder unto Master Latimer.

Then they brought a faggot, kindled with fire,
and laid the same down at Dr Ridley's feet. To
whom Master Latimer spake in this manner:
'Be of good comfort, Master Ridley, and play the
man. We shall this day light such a candle, by
God's grace, in England, as I trust shall never be
put out.'

When Dr Ridley saw the fire flaming up towards
him, he cried with a wonderful loud voice, 'Lord,
Lord, receive my spirit.' Master Latimer, crying as
vehemently on the other side, 'O Father of heaven,
receive my soul!' received the flame as it were
embracing of it. After that he had stroked his face
with his hands, and as it were bathed them a little
in the fire, he soon died (as it appeareth) with very
little pain or none.

By reason of the evil making of the fire unto
Master Ridley, because the wooden faggots were

laid about the gorse, and over-high built, the fire burned first beneath, being kept down by the wood; which when Master Ridley felt, he desired then for Christ's sake to let the fire come unto him. Which when his brother-in-law heard, but not well understood, intending to rid him out of his pain (for the which cause he gave attendance), as one in such sorrow not well advised what he did, he heaped faggots upon him, so that he clean covered him, which made the fire more vehement beneath, that it burned clean all his nether parts, before it once touched the upper; and that made him often desire them to let the fire come unto him, saying, 'I cannot burn.' Which indeed appeared well; for, after his legs were consumed he showed that side towards us clean, shirt and all untouched with flame. Yet in all this torment he forgot not to call unto God, having in his mouth, 'Lord have mercy upon me,' intermingling his cry, 'Let the fire come unto me, I cannot burn.'

In which pangs he laboured till one of the standers by with his bill pulled off the faggots above, and where he saw the fire flame up Master Ridley wrested himself unto that side. And when the flame touched the gunpowder, he was seen to stir no more.

It moved hundreds to tears, in beholding the horrible sight; for I think there was none that had not clean exiled all humanity and mercy, which would not have lamented to behold the fury of the fire so to rage upon their bodies. Signs there were of sorrow on every side. Some took it grievously to see their deaths, whose lives they held full dear: some pitied their persons, that thought their souls had no need thereof. Well! dead they are, and the reward of this world they have already. What reward remaineth for them in heaven, the day of the Lord's glory, when he cometh with His saints, shall declare.

THE FIRES OF SMITHFIELD

An Account of some of the Martyrs that
with their Lives sealed their Testimony
there for the Protestant Faith

About the third year of King Henry I. the hospital
of St Bartholomew in Smithfield was founded, by
means of a minstrel belonging unto the King, named
Rayer, and it was afterwards finished by Richard
Whittington, alderman and mayor of London. This
place of Smithfield was at that day the place where
the felons and other transgressors of the King's
laws were put to execution.

John Badby, Artificer

In the year of our Lord 1410, on Saturday, being
the first day of March, the examination of one John
Badby, tailor, was made in a certain house or hall
within the precinct of the preaching friars of London,
before Thomas Arundel, Archbishop of Canterbury.
Which John Badby did answer, that it was impossible
that any priest should make the body of Christ, by
words sacramentally spoken.

The archbishop considering that he would in no
wise be altered, and seeing, moreover, his countenance
stout, and heart confirmed, so that he began to
persuade others as it appeared, pronounced the said

THE PRINCE'S INTERVENTION

John Badby an open and public heretic and delivered
him to the secular powers.

These things concluded by the bishops in the forenoon, in the afternoon the King's writ was not far
behind. John Badby was brought into Smithfield, and
there, being put in an empty barrel, was bound with
iron chains fastened to a stake, having dry wood put
about him. And as he was thus standing it happened
that the Prince, the King's eldest son, was there
present, who, showing some part of the good
Samaritan, began to essay how to save his life.

In the mean season the prior of St Bartholomew's
in Smithfield brought, with all solemnity, the sacrament
of God's body, with twelve torches borne before, and
so showed the sacrament to the poor man being at
the stake. And then they demanding of him how
he believed in it, he answered, that he knew well it
was hallowed bread, and not God's body. And then
was the fire put unto him. When the innocent soul
felt the fire, he cried 'Mercy!' calling belike upon
the Lord; with which horrible cry the Prince
being moved, commanded them to quench the
fire. This commandment being done, he asked
him if he would forsake heresy, which thing,
if he would do, he should have goods enough;
promising also unto him a yearly stipend out
of the King's treasury, so much as should suffice
for his sustentation.

But this valiant champion of Christ, neglecting the
Prince's fair words, as also contemning all men's
devices, being fully determined rather to suffer any
kind of torment, were it never so grievous, than so
great idolatry and wickedness, refused the offer.
Wherefore the Prince commanded him straight to

be put again into the fire. Even so was he nothing at all abashed at their torments, but persevered invincibly to the end.

WILLIAM SWEETING AND JOHN BREWSTER

William Sweeting, and John Brewster were both burned together, the 18th day of October, A.D. 1511. The chief case alleged against them was their faith concerning the sacrament of Christ's body and blood. There were other things besides objected, as the reading of certain forbidden books, and accompanying with such persons as were suspected of heresy. But one great and heinous offence counted amongst the rest, was their leaving off the painted faggots, which they were at their first abjuring enjoined to wear as badges during their lives, or so long as it should please their ordinary to appoint.

JOHN STILMAN

John Stilman was charged for speaking against the worshipping, praying, and offering unto images; as also for denying the carnal and corporal presence in the sacrament of Christ's memorial: and further, for that he had highly commended and praised John Wickliff, affirming that he was a saint in heaven.

He was delivered unto the sheriffs of London, to be openly burned, 1518.

THOMAS MAN

Thomas Man was apprehended for the profession of Christ's Gospel. He had spoken against auricular confession, and denied the corporal presence of Christ's body in the sacrament of the altar; he believed that images ought not to be worshipped, and neither believed in the crucifix, nor yet would worship it. For such like matters was he a long time imprisoned, and, at last, through fear of death, was content to abjure and yield himself unto the judgment of the Romish church. Thereupon he was enjoined, not only to make open recantation, but from thenceforth to remain as prisoner within the monastery of Osney beside Oxford, and to bear a faggot before the first cross, at the next general procession within the University. Howbeit not long after, the bishop having need of the poor man's help in his household business, took him out of the monastery, and placed him within his own house. All which notwithstanding, he fled, seeking abroad in other counties for work, thereby to sustain his poor life; he most commonly abode, sometimes in Essex, sometimes in Suffolk; where also he joined himself unto such godly professors of Christ's Gospel, as he there could hear of. But within few years after, he was accused of relapse, apprehended and brought before the Bishop of London. But because he would seem to do all things by order of justice, and nothing against law, he therefore appointed unto the said Thomas Man certain doctors and advocates of the Arches, as his counsellors to plead in his behalf. He was condemned as a heretic, and delivered to the sheriff of London sitting on horseback in Paternoster-row, before the bishop's door (A.D. 1518). The sheriff immediately carried him to Smithfield, and there, the same day in the forenoon, caused him to be 'put into God's angel,' 1518.

THE FIRES OF SMITHFIELD

JOHN FRITH

John Frith, a young man, had so profited in all
kind of learning and knowledge, that there was
scarcely his equal amongst his companions. He
had such a godliness of life joined with his doctrine,
that it was hard to judge in which of them
he was more commendable. At last he fell into
knowledge and acquaintance with William Tyndale,
through whose instructions he first received into
his heart the seed of the Gospel and sincere
godliness.

At that time Thomas Wolsey, Cardinal of York,
prepared to build a college in Oxford, marvellously
sumptuous, which had the name and title of Frideswide, but is now named Christ's-church. This
ambitious Cardinal gathered together into that
college whatsoever excellent thing there were in
the whole realm, either vestments, vessels, or other
ornaments, beside provision of all kind of precious
things. He also appointed unto that company all
such men as were found to excel in any kind of
learning and knowledge; among the which was
John Frith.

These most picked young men, of grave judgment
and sharp wits, conferring together upon the abuses
of religion, were therefore accused of heresy, and
cast into a prison, within a deep cave under the
ground of the same college, where their salt fish
was laid; so that, through the filthy stench thereof,
they were all infected, and certain of them, being
taken out of the prison into their chambers,
deceased.

John Frith with others, by the cardinal's letter,

who sent word that he would not have them so
straitly handled, were dismissed out of prison, upon
condition not to pass above ten miles out of Oxford.
Albeit this, his safety continued not long, through
the great hatred and deadly pursuit of Sir Thomas
More, who, at that time being Chancellor of
England, persecuted him both by land and sea,
besetting all the ways and havens, yea, and promising
great rewards, if any man could bring him any news
or tidings of him.

Thus Frith, being on every part beset with
troubles, not knowing which way to turn him,
seeketh for some place to hide him in. Thus
fleeting from one place to another, and often
changing both his garments and place, yet could
he be in safety in no place; no not long amongst
his friends; so that at last he was taken.

When no reason would prevail against the force
and cruelty of these furious foes, he was brought
before the Bishops of London, Winchester, and
Lincoln, who, sitting in St Paul's, ministered certain
interrogatories upon the sacrament of the supper
and purgatory. When Frith by no means could
be persuaded to recant, he was condemned by the
Bishop of London to be burned. When the faggots
were put unto him, he embraced the same; thereby
declaring with what uprightness of mind he suffered
his death for Christ's sake, 1533.

ANDREW HEWET BURNED WITH JOHN FRITH

Andrew Hewet, born in Feversham, a young man
of the age of four and twenty years, went upon a
holy-day into Fleet-street, towards St Dunstan's.

He met with one William Holt, who was foreman with the King's tailor, and being suspected by the same Holt, who was a dissembling wretch, to be one that favoured the Gospel, after a little talk had with him, he went into an honest house about Fleet-bridge, which was a bookseller's house. Then Holt, thinking he had found good occasion to show forth some fruit of his wickedness, sent for certain officers, who searched the house, and finding the same Andrew, apprehended him.

Andrew Hewet was brought before the Chancellor of the Bishop of London. When it was demanded of him what he thought as touching the sacrament of the last supper; he answered, 'Even as John Frith doth.' Then certain of the bishops smiled at him; and Stokesley, the Bishop of London, said, 'Why, Frith is a heretic, and already judged to be burned; and except thou revoke thine opinion, thou shalt be burned also with him.' 'Truly,' saith he, 'I am content therewithal.' Whereupon he was sent unto the prison to Frith, and afterwards they were carried together to the fire, 1533.

John Lambert

This Lambert, being born and brought up in Norfolk, studied in the University of Cambridge. After he had sufficiently profited both in Latin and Greek, and had translated out of both tongues sundry things into the English tongue, being forced at last by violence of the time, he departed beyond the seas, to Tyndale and Frith. There he remained the space of a year and more, being chaplain to the

English House at Antwerp, till he was disturbed by Sir Thomas More, and by the accusation of one Barlow carried from Antwerp to England; where he was brought to examination before Warham, the Archbishop of Canterbury.

Within short space after, the archbishop died; whereby it seemeth that Lambert for that time was delivered. He returned unto London, and there exercised himself about the Stocks, in teaching children both in the Greek and Latin tongue.

After that John Lambert had continued in this vocation, with great commendation, and no less commodity to the youth, it happened (1538) that he was present at a sermon in St Peter's Church at London. He that preached was named Dr Taylor.

When the sermon was done, Lambert went gently unto the preacher to talk with him. All the whole matter or controversy was concerning the sacrament of the body and blood of Christ. But Taylor desiring, as is supposed, of a good mind to satisfy Lambert, took counsel with Dr Barnes; which Barnes seemed not greatly to favour this cause.

Upon these originals Lambert's quarrel began of a private talk to be a public matter: for he was sent for by Archbishop Cranmer, and forced to defend his cause openly. For the archbishop had not yet favoured the doctrine of the sacrament, whereof afterwards he was an earnest professor. In that disputation, it is said that Lambert did appeal from the bishops to the King's majesty.

At last the King himself, all in white, did come as judge of that great controversy. On his right hand sat the bishops, and behind them the famous lawyers, clothed all in purple. On the left hand sat the peers of the realm, justices, and other nobles in their order; behind whom sat the gentlemen of the King's privy chamber. The manner and form of judgment was terrible enough of itself to abash any innocent; the King's look, his cruel countenance, and his brows bent into severity, did not a little augment this terror; plainly declaring a mind full of indignation. He beheld Lambert with a stern countenance; and then, turning himself unto his councillors, he called forth Dr Sampson, Bishop of Chichester, commanding him to declare unto the people the causes of this present assembly.

When he had made an end of his oration, the King, standing upon his feet, leaning upon a cushion of white cloth of tissue, turning himself toward Lambert with his brows bent, as it were threatening some grievous thing to him, said these words: 'Ho! good fellow; what is thy name?'

Then the humble lamb of Christ, humbly kneeling down upon his knee, said, 'My name is John Nicholson, although of many I be called Lambert.'

'What,' said the King, 'have you two names? I would not trust you, having two names, although you were my brother.'

'O most noble prince!' replied Lambert, 'your bishops forced me of necessity to change my name.'

And after much talk had in this manner, the King commanded him to declare what he thought as touching the sacrament of the altar.

Then Lambert, beginning to speak for himself, gave God thanks, Who had so inclined the heart of the King, that he himself would not disdain to hear and understand the controversies of religion.

YIELD OR DIE!

Then the King with an angry voice, interrupting his oration: 'I came not hither,' said he, 'to hear mine own praises thus painted out in my presence; but briefly go to the matter, without any more circumstance. Answer as touching the sacrament of the altar, whether dost thou say, that it is the body of Christ, or wilt deny it?' And with that word the King lifted up his cap.

Lambert: 'I answer, with St Augustine, that it is the body of Christ, after a certain manner.'

The King: 'Answer me neither out of St Augustine, nor by the authority of any other; but tell me plainly, whether thou sayest it is the body of Christ, or no.'

Lambert: 'Then I deny it to be the body of Christ.'

The King: 'Mark well! for now thou shalt be condemned even by Christ's own words, "This is my body."'

Then the King commanded Thomas Cranmer, Archbishop of Canterbury, to refute his assertion.

It were too long to repeat the arguments of every bishop; and no less superfluous were it so to do, especially forasmuch as they were nothing forcible.

At last, when the day was passed, and torches began to be lighted, the King, minding to break up this disputation, said unto Lambert in this wise: 'What sayest thou now, after all these great labours which thou hast taken upon thee, and all the reasons and instructions of these learned men? art thou not yet satisfied? Wilt thou live or die? what sayest thou? thou hast yet free choice.'

Lambert answered, 'I yield and submit myself wholly unto the will of your majesty.'

321

THE FIRES OF SMITHFIELD

Then said the King, 'Commit thyself unto the hands of God, and not unto mine.'

Lambert: 'I commend my soul unto the hands of God, but my body I wholly yield and submit unto your clemency.'

Then said the King, 'If you do commit yourself unto my judgment, you must die, for I will not be a patron unto heretics.' And, turning himself unto Cromwell, he said, 'Cromwell! read the sentence of condemnation against him.'

Of all other who have been burned at Smithfield, there was yet none so cruelly and piteously handled as this blessed martyr. For, after that his legs were burned up to the stumps, and that the wretched tormentors and enemies of God had withdrawn the fire from him, so that but a small fire were left under him, two that stood on each side of him with their halberts pitched him upon their pikes. Then he, lifting up such hands as he had, and his fingers' ends flaming with fire, cried unto the people in these words, 'None but Christ, none but Christ'; and so, being let down again from their halberts, fell into the fire, and there gave up his life, 1538.

STILE.

In the fellowship of these blessed saints and martyrs of Christ who innocently suffered within the time of King Henry's reign for the testimony of God's Word and truth, another good man cometh to my mind, not to be excluded out of this number, who was with like cruelty oppressed, and was burned in Smithfield about the latter end of the time of Cuthbert Tonstall, Bishop of London. His name was called Stile, as is credibly reported unto us by a worthy and ancient knight, named Sir Robert Outred, who was the same time present himself at his burning. With him there was burned a book of the Apocalypse, which he was wont to read upon. This book when he saw fastened unto the stake, to be burned with him, lifting up his voice, 'O blessed Apocalypse,' said he 'how happy am I, that shall be burned with thee!' And so this good man, and the blessed Apocalypse, were both together in the fire consumed, 1539.

ROBERT BARNES, THOMAS GARRET, AND WILLIAM JEROME.

When the valiant standard-bearer and stay of the Church of England, Thomas Cromwell, was made away, pity it was to behold what miserable slaughter of good men and good women ensued. For Winchester, having now gotten free swing to exercise his cruelty, wonder it was to see what troubles he raised in the Lord's vineyard. He made his first assaults upon Robert Barnes, Thomas Garret, and William Jerome, whom within two days after Cromwell's death he caused to be put to execution.

Robert Barnes was prior and master of the house of the Augustines, Cambridge. He did read openly in the house Paul's Epistles; because he would have Christ there taught and His Holy Word, he, in short space, made divers good divines. Thus Barnes, what with his reading, disputation, and preaching, became famous and mighty in the Scriptures. Suddenly was sent down to Cambridge a serjeant-at-arms who arrested Dr Barnes openly in the convocation-house, to make all others afraid. In the morning he was carried to Cardinal Wolsey at Westminster. Then, by reason of Dr Gardiner, secretary to the Cardinal, and Master Foxe, Master of the Wards, he spake the same night to the cardinal in his chamber of estate, kneeling on his knees.

Then said the cardinal to them, 'Is this Dr Barnes your man that is accused of heresy?'

'Yea, and please your grace; we trust you shall find him reformable, for he is both well learned and wise.'

'What! master doctor,' said the cardinal; 'had you not a sufficient scope in the Scriptures to teach the people, but that my golden shoes, my pole-axes, my pillars, my golden cushions, my crosses did so sore offend you, that you must make us ridiculous amongst the people? We were jollily that day laughed to scorn. Verily it was a sermon more fit to be preached on a stage, than in a pulpit; for at the last you said, I wear a pair of red gloves (I should say bloody gloves, quoth you), that I should not be cold in the midst of my ceremonies.'

And Barnes answered, 'I spake nothing but the truth out of the Scriptures, according to my conscience, and according to the old doctors.' And then did Barnes deliver him six sheets of paper written, to confirm his sayings.

The cardinal received them smiling on him, and saying, 'We perceive then that you intend to stand to your articles, and to show your learning.'

'Yea,' said Barnes, 'that I do intend, by God's grace, with your lordship's favour.'

The cardinal answered, 'Such as you are do bear us and the catholic church little favour. I will ask you a question: "Whether do you think it more necessary that I should have all this royalty, because I represent the King's majesty's person in all the high courts of this realm, to the terror and keeping down of all the wicked and corrupt members of this commonwealth; or to be as simple as you would have us? to sell all these things, and give them to the poor, who shortly will cast it against the walls? and to pull away this majesty of a princely dignity, which is a terror to all the wicked, and to follow your counsel in this behalf?"'

Barnes answered, 'I think it necessary to be sold and given to the poor. For this is not comely for your calling.'

Then answered the cardinal, 'Lo, Master Doctors! here is the learned wise man, that you told me of.'

Then they kneeled down and said, 'We desire your grace to be good unto him, for he will be reformable.'

Then said the cardinal, 'Stand you up! for your sakes, and the University, we will be good unto him. How say you, Master Doctor; do you not know that I am able to dispense in all matters concerning religion within this realm, as much as the Pope may?'

He said, 'I know it to be so.'

'Will you then be ruled by us, and we will do all things for your honesty, and for the honesty of the University.'

Barnes answered, 'I thank your grace for your good will; I will stick to the holy Scripture, and to

God's Book, according to the simple talent that God hath lent me.'

'Well,' said the cardinal, 'thou shalt have thy learning tried to the uttermost, and thou shalt have the law.'

After Barnes had continued in the Fleet the space of half a year, at length being delivered, he was committed to be a free prisoner at the Austin Friars in London; whence he was removed to Northampton, there to be burned. One Master Horne, having intelligence of the writ which should shortly be sent down to burn him, gave him counsel to feign himself to be desperate; and that he should write a letter to the cardinal, and leave it on his table, to declare whither he was gone to drown himself; and to leave his clothes in the same place; and another letter to the mayor of the town, to search for him in the water, because he had a letter written in parchment about his neck, closed in wax, for the cardinal, which should teach all men to beware by him. Upon this, they were seven days in searching for him, but he was conveyed to London in poor man's apparel; took shipping to Antwerp, and so to Luther.

The said Dr Barnes returned in the beginning of the reign of Queen Anne, as others did, and continued a faithful preacher, being all her time well entertained and promoted. After that, he was sent ambassador by King Henry VIII. to the Duke of Cleves, for the marriage of the Lady Anne of Cleves between the King and her, and well accepted in the ambassade, and in all his doings until the time that Stephen Gardiner came out of France.

Not long after, Dr Barnes, with his brethren,

were apprehended and carried before the King's majesty to Hampton Court, and examined. The King with many high words rebuked his doings in his privy closet. Unto whom when Barnes had submitted himself, 'Nay,' said the King, 'yield thee not to me; I am a mortal man;' and therewith rising up and turning to the sacrament, and putting off his bonnet, said, 'Yonder is the Master of us all, Author of truth; yield in truth to Him and the truth will I defend; and otherwise yield not unto me.' The King, seeking the means of his safety, at Winchester's request granted him leave to go home with the bishop, to confer with him. But, as it happened, they not agreeing, Gardiner sought, by all subtle means, how to entrap Barnes and his brethren. They were enjoined to preach three sermons the next Easter following; at which sermons Stephen Gardiner was present, either to bear record of their recantation, or trip them in their talk. Shortly after they were sent for to Hampton Court; from thence they were carried to the Tower, and never came out till they came to their death.

Now let us consider the story of Thomas Garret.

In the year of our Lord 1526, or thereabout, Master Garret, curate of Honey-lane in London, came unto Oxford, and brought with him Tyndale's first translation of the New Testament in English, the which he sold to divers scholars. News came from London that he was searched for as an heretic, and so he was apprehended and committed to ward. Afterwards he was compelled to carry a faggot in open procession from St Mary's church to Friswide's, and then sent to Osney, there to be kept in prison till further order was taken.

The third companion who suffered with Barnes and Garret, was William Jerome, vicar of Stepney. He was charged before the King at Westminster for erroneous doctrine.

One Dr Wilson entered into disputation with him, and defended, that good works justified before God. To whom Jerome answered, that all works, whatsoever they were, were nothing worth, nor any part of salvation of themselves, but only referred to the mercy and love of God, which direct the workers thereof.

Thus then Barnes, Jerome, and Garret, being committed to the Tower after Easter, there remained till the thirtieth day of July, which was two days after the death of the Lord Cromwell. Then ensued process against them. Whereupon all those three good saints of God were brought together from the Tower to Smithfield, where they, preparing themselves to the fire, had there at the stake sundry exhortations.

'Take me not here,' said Dr Barnes, 'that I speak against good works, for they are to be done; and verily they that do them not shall never come into the Kingdom of God. We must do them, because they are commanded us of God, to show and set forth our profession, not to deserve or merit; for that is only the death of Christ.'

One asked him his opinion of praying to saints. Then said Dr Barnes: 'Throughout all Scripture we are not commanded to pray to any saints. Therefore I cannot preach to you that saints ought to be prayed unto; for then should I preach unto you a doctrine of mine own head. If saints do pray for us, then I trust to pray for you within this half hour, Master Sheriff.'

Then desired Dr Barnes all men to bear him witness that he abhorred all doctrines against the Word of God, and that he died in the faith of Jesu Christ. The like confession made also Jerome and Garret. They, taking themselves by the hands, and kissing one another, quietly and humbly offered themselves to the hands of the tormentors; and so took their death with such patience as might well testify the goodness of their cause, and quiet of their conscience.—1540.

MISTRESS ANNE ASKEW, DAUGHTER OF SIR WILLIAM ASKEW, KNIGHT OF LINCOLNSHIRE

Here follow the examinations of Anne Askew, according as she wrote them with her own hand, at the instant desire of certain faithful men and women.

The First Examinaton before the Inquisitors, A.D. 1545.

Christopher Dare examined me at Sadler's Hall, and asked me, wherefore I said, I had rather to read five lines in the Bible, than to hear five masses in the temple. I confessed that I said no less; not for the dispraise of either the epistle or the Gospel, but because the one did greatly edify me, and the other nothing at all. He laid unto my charge, that I should say, If an ill priest ministered, it was the devil and not God. My answer was, that I never spake any such thing. But this was my saying: that whosoever he were that ministered unto me, his ill conditions could not hurt my faith, but in spirit I received, nevertheless, the body and blood of Christ. He asked me what I said concerning confession. I answered him my meaning, which was, as St James saith, that every man ought to acknowledge his faults to other, and the one to pray for the other. Then he sent for a priest who asked me, if I did not think that private masses did help the souls departed. I said, it was great idolatry to believe more in them, than in the death which Christ died for us.

Then they had me unto my Lord Mayor, who laid one thing to my charge, which was never spoken of me, but by them; whether a mouse, eating the host, received God or no? I made them no answer, but smiled.

Then the bishop's chancellor rebuked me, and said that I was much to blame for uttering the Scriptures. For St Paul, he said, forbade women to speak or to talk of the Word of God. I answered him that I knew Paul's meaning as well as he, which is, in 1 Cor. xiv., that a woman ought not to speak in the congregation by the way of teaching: and then I asked him how many women he had seen go into the pulpit and preach? He said he never saw any. Then I said, he ought to find no fault in poor women, except they had offended the law.

Then was I had to the Compter, and there remained eleven days, no friend admitted to speak with me.

The sum of my Examination before the King's Council at Greenwich.

They said it was the King's pleasure that I should open the matter unto them. I answered them plainly, I would not so do; but if it were the King's pleasure to hear me, I would show him the truth.

They said, it was not meet for the King to be troubled with me. I answered, that Solomon was reckoned the wisest King that ever lived, yet misliked he not to hear two poor common women, much more his grace a simple woman and his faithful subject.

Then my Lord Chancellor asked my opinion in the sacrament. My answer was this, 'I believe that so oft as I, in a Christian congregation, do receive the bread in remembrance of Christ's death, and with thanksgiving, according to His holy institution, I receive therewith the fruits, also, of His most glorious passion. The Bishop of Winchester bade me make a direct answer: I said, I would not sing a new song of the Lord in a strange land. Then the bishop said, I spake in parables. I answered, it was best for him, 'for if I show the open truth,' quoth I, 'ye will not accept it.' I told him I was ready to suffer all things at his hands, not only his rebukes, but all that should follow besides, yea, and all that gladly.

My Lord Lisle, my Lord of Essex, and the Bishop of Winchester required me earnestly that I should confess the sacrament to be flesh, blood, and bone. Then, said I, that it was a great shame for them to counsel contrary to their knowledge.

Then the bishop said he would speak with me familiarly. I said, 'So did Judas, when he betrayed Christ.' Then desired the bishop to speak with me alone. But that I refused. He asked me, why. I said, that in the mouth of two or three witnesses every matter should stand.

Then the bishop said I should be burned. I answered, that I had searched all the Scriptures, yet could I never find that either Christ, or His apostles,

put any creature to death. 'Well, well,' said I, 'God will laugh your threatenings to scorn.'
Then was I sent to Newgate.

My Handling since my Departure from Newgate.

I was sent from Newgate to the sign of the Crown, where Master Rich, and the Bishop of London, with all their power and flattering words went about to persuade me from God: but I did not esteem their glosing pretences.

Then came there to me Nicholas Shaxton, and counselled me to recant as he had done. I said to him, that it had been good for him never to have been born.

Then Master Rich sent me to the Tower, where I remained till three o'clock.

Then came Rich and one of the council, charging me upon my obedience, to show unto them, if I knew any manor woman of my sect. My answer was, that I knew none. Then said they unto me, that the King was informed that I could name, if I would, a great number of my sect. I answered, that the King was as well deceived in that behalf, as dissembled with in other matters.

Then commanded they me to show how I was maintained in the Compter, and who willed me to stick to my opinion. I said, that there was no creature that therein did strengthen me: and as for the help that I had in the Compter, it was by means of my maid. For as she went abroad in the streets, she made moan to the prentices, and they, by her, did send me money; but who they were I never knew.

They said that there were divers gentlewomen

that gave me money: but I knew not their names. Then they said that there were divers ladies that had sent me money. I answered, that there was a man in a blue coat who delivered me ten shillings, and said that my Lady of Hertford sent it me; and another in a violet coat gave me eight shillings, and said my Lady Denny sent it me: whether it were true or no, I cannot tell.

Then they did put me on the rack, because I confessed no ladies or gentlewomen to be of my opinion, and thereon they kept me a long time; and because I lay still, and did not cry, my Lord Chancellor and Master Rich took pains to rack me with their own hands, till I was nigh dead.

Then the Lieutenant caused me to be loosed from the rack. Incontinently I swooned, and then they recovered me again. After that I sat two long hours reasoning with my Lord Chancellor upon the bare floor; where he, with many flattering words, persuaded me to leave my opinion. But my Lord God (I thank His everlasting goodness) gave me grace to persevere, and will do, I hope, to the end.

Then was I brought to a house, and laid in a bed, with as weary and painful bones as ever had patient Job; I thank my Lord God therefor. Then my Lord Chancellor sent me word, if I would leave my opinion, I should want nothing; if I would not, I should forthwith to Newgate, and so be burned. I sent him again word, that I would rather die than break my faith.

The day of her execution being appointed, this good woman was brought into Smithfield in a chair, because she could not go on her feet, by means of her great torments. When she was brought unto the stake, she was tied with a chain, that held up her body. The multitude of the people was exceeding; the place where they stood being railed about to keep out the press. Upon the bench under St Bartholomew's Church sat Wriothesley, Chancellor of England; the old Duke of Norfolk, the old Earl of Bedford, the Lord Mayor, with divers others. Before the fire should be set unto them, one of the bench, hearing that they had gunpowder about them, and being alarmed lest the faggots, by strength of the gunpowder, would come flying about their ears, began to be afraid: but the Earl of Bedford declared unto him how the gunpowder was not laid under the faggots, but only about their bodies, to rid them out of their pains.

Then Wriothesley, Lord Chancellor, offered Anne Askew the King's pardon if she would recant; who made this answer, that she came not thither to deny her Lord and Master. And thus the good Anne Askew, being compassed in with flames of fire, as a blessed sacrifice unto God, slept in the Lord A.D. 1546, leaving behind her a singular example of Christian constancy for all men to follow.

John Lacels, John Adams, and Nicholas Belenian

There was, at the same time, burned with her, one Nicholas Belenian, priest of Shropshire; John Adams, a tailor; and John Lacels, gentleman of the court and household of King Henry. It happened well for them, that they died together with Anne

LEARNING GOD'S LAW

Askew: for, albeit that of themselves they were strong and stout men, yet, through the example and exhortation of her, they, being the more boldened, received occasion of greater comfort in that so painful and doleful kind of death: who, beholding her invincible constancy, and also stirred up through her persuasions, did set apart all kind of fear.

MASTER JOHN BRADFORD

John Bradford was born at Manchester in Lancashire. His parents did bring him up in learning from his infancy, until he attained such knowledge in the Latin tongue, and skill in writing, that he was able to gain his own living in some honest condition. Then he became servant to Sir John Harrington, knight, who, in the great affairs of King Henry the Eighth, and King Edward the Sixth, when he was treasurer of the King's camps and buildings, had such experience of Bradford's activity, expertness, and faithful trustiness, that above all others he used his service.

But the Lord had elected him unto a better function, to preach the Gospel of Christ. Then did Bradford forsake his worldly affairs and forwardness in worldly wealth, and give himself wholly to the study of the Scriptures. To accomplish his purpose the better, he departed from the Temple at London, where the temporal law is studied, and went to the University of Cambridge, to learn by God's law how to further the building of the Lord's temple. Within one whole year the University did give him the degree of a Master of Arts, and immediately after, the Master and Fellows of

335

Pembroke Hall did give him a fellowship; yea that man of God, Martin Bucer, oftentimes exhorted him to bestow his talent in preaching. Unto which Bradford answered always, that he was unable to serve in that office through want of learning. To the which Bucer was wont to reply, saying, 'If thou have not fine manchet bread, yet give the poor people barley bread, or whatsoever else the Lord hath committed unto thee.' And while Bradford was thus persuaded to enter into the ministry, Dr Ridley, Bishop of London, called him to take the degree of a deacon, obtained for him a license to preach, and did give him a prebend in his cathedral church of St Paul's.

In this preaching office by the space of three years, how faithfully Bradford walked, how diligently he laboured, many parts of England can testify. Sharply he opened and reproved sin, sweetly he preached Christ crucified, pithily he impugned heresies and errors, earnestly he persuaded to godly life. When Queen Mary had gotten the crown, still continued Bradford diligent in preaching, until he was unjustly deprived both of his office and liberty by the Queen and her council.

The fact was this: the 13th of August, in the first year of the reign of Queen Mary, Master Bourn, then Bishop of Bath, made a sermon at Paul's Cross, to set popery abroad, in such sort that it moved the people to no small indignation, being almost ready to pull him out of the pulpit. Neither could the reverence of the place, nor the presence of Bishop Bonner, who then was his master, nor yet the commandment of the Lord Mayor of London, whom the people ought to have obeyed, stay their rage; but the more they spake, the more the people were incensed. At length Bourn, seeing the people in such a mood, and himself in such peril (whereof he was sufficiently warned by the hurling of a drawn dagger at him), desired Bradford, who stood in the pulpit behind him, to come forth, and to stand in his place and speak to the people. Good Bradford, at his request, was content, and spake to the people of godly and quiet obedience: whom as soon as the people saw, they cried with a great shout,—'Bradford, Bradford; God save thy life, Bradford!' Eftsoons all the raging ceased, and quietly departed each man to his house. Bourn desired Bradford not to go from him till he were in safety: which Bradford, according to his promise, performed. For while the Lord Mayor and Sheriffs did lead Bourn to the schoolmaster's house, which is next to the pulpit, Bradford went at his back, shadowing him from the people with his gown.

The same Sunday in the afternoon, Bradford preached at the Bow Church in Cheapside, and reproved the people sharply for their seditious misdemeanour. Within three days, he was sent for to the Tower of London, where the Queen then was, to appear before the council. From the Tower he came to the King's Bench in Southwark: and after his condemnation, he was sent to the Compter in the Poultry in London: in which two places, for the time he did remain prisoner, he preached twice a day continually, unless sickness hindered him: such resort of good folks was daily to his lecture, that commonly his chamber was well nigh filled. Preaching, reading, and praying was his whole life. He did not eat above one meal a day; which was but very little when he took it; and his continual study was upon his knees. In the midst of dinner he used often to muse with himself, having his hat over his eyes, from whence came commonly plenty of tears dropping on his trencher. Very gentle he was to man and child.

Of personage he was somewhat tall and slender, spare of body, of a faint sanguine colour, with an auburn beard. He slept not commonly above four hours in the night; and in his bed, till sleep came, his book went not out of his hand. His chief recreation was in honest company, and comely talk, wherein he would spend a little time after dinner at the board; and so to prayer and his book again. He counted that hour not well spent, wherein he did not some good, either with his pen, study, or in exhorting of others. He was no niggard of his purse, but would liberally participate that he had, to his fellow-prisoners. And commonly once a week he visited the thieves, pick-purses, and such others that were with him in prison, unto whom he would give godly exhortation, and distribute among them some portion of money to their comfort. Neither was there ever any prisoner with him but by his company he greatly profited.

Walking in the keeper's chamber, suddenly the keeper's wife came up, as one half amazed, and seeming much troubled, being almost windless, said, 'O Master Bradford, I come to bring you heavy news.' 'What is that?' said he. 'Marry,' quoth she, 'to-morrow you must be burned; and your chain is now a buying, and soon you must go to Newgate.' With that Master Bradford put off his cap, and lifting up his eyes to heaven, said, 'I thank God for it; I have looked for the same a long time, and therefore it cometh not now to me suddenly, but as a thing waited for every day and hour; the Lord make me worthy thereof!'

They carried him to Newgate, about eleven or twelve o'clock in the night, when it was thought none would be stirring abroad: and yet, was there in Cheapside and other places (between the Compter and Newgate), a great multitude of people that came to see him, which most gently bade him farewell, praying for him with most lamentable and pitiful tears; and he again as gently bade them farewell, praying most heartily for them and their welfare. The next day at four a clock in the morning, there was in Smithfield a multitude of men and women; but it was nine a clock before Master Bradford was brought into Smithfield, with a great company of weaponed men, as the like was not seen at any man's burning. Bradford, being come to the place, fell flat to the ground, making his prayers to Almighty God. Then rising he went to the stake, and there suffered with a young man of twenty years of age, joyfully and constantly, whose name was John Leaf.

John Leaf

John Leaf was an apprentice to Humfrey Gawdy, tallow-chandler, of the parish of Christ-Church in London, of the age of nineteen years and above. It is reported of him that two bills were sent unto him in the Compter in Bread Street, the one containing a recantation, the other his confessions, to know to which of them he would put his hand. The bill of recantation he refused. The other he well liked of, and instead of a pen he took a pin, and pricking his hand, sprinkled the blood upon the said bill, willing to show the bishop, that he had sealed it with his blood already.

When these two came to the stake Master Bradford took a faggot in his hand, and kissed it, and so likewise the stake. Holding up his hands, and casting his countenance up to heaven, he said, 'O England, England, repent thee of thy sins, repent thee of thy sins.' Turning his head unto the young man that suffered with him, he said, 'Be of good comfort, brother; for we shall have a merry supper with the Lord this night.' And thus they ended their mortal lives, without any alteration of their countenance, being void of all fear. 1535.

Master John Philpot

Master John Philpot was a knight's son, born in Hampshire, brought up in the New College, Oxford. He was made Archdeacon of Winchester, and during the time of King Edward, continued to no small profit of those parts. When that King was taken away, and Mary his sister came in place, she caused a convocation of the prelates and learned men to be congregated to the accomplishment of her desire. In the which convocation Master Philpot sustained the cause of the Gospel manfully against the mass; for the which cause, he was called to account before Bishop Gardiner, and from thence was removed to Bonner and other commissioners, with whom he had sundry conflicts.

NO HERETIC BEFORE GOD

In the end the bishop, seeing his unmovable stedfastness in the truth, did pronounce the sentence of condemnation against him. 'I thank God', said Master Philpot, 'that I am a heretic out of your cursed church; I am no heretic before God. But God bless you, and give you grace to repent your wicked doings, and let all men beware of your bloody church.'

And so the officers delivered him to the keeper of Newgate. Then his man thrust to go in after his master, and one of the officers said unto him, 'Hence, fellow! what wouldst thou have?' And he said, 'I would go speak with my master.' Master Philpot turned him about, and said to him, 'To-morrow thou shalt speak with me.' Then the under-keeper said to Master Philpot, 'Is this your man?' and he said, 'Yea.' So he did license his man to go in with him; and Master Philpot and his man were turned into a little chamber on the right hand, and there remained a little time, until Alexander the chief keeper did come unto him; who, at his entering, greeted him with these words; 'Ah!' said he, 'hast not thou done well to bring thyself hither?'

'Well,' said Master Philpot, 'I must be content, for it is God's appointment: and I shall desire you to let me have your gentle favour; for you and I have been of old acquaintance.'

'Well,' said Alexander, 'I will show thee gentleness and favour, so thou wilt be ruled by me.'

Then said Master Philpot, 'I pray you show me what you would have me to do.'

He said, 'If you would recant, I will show you any pleasure I can.'

'Nay,' said Master Philpot, 'I will never recant, whilst I have my life, that which I have spoken, for

341

it is most certain truth; and in witness hereof I will seal it with my blood.'

Then Alexander said, 'This is the saying of the whole pack of you heretics.' Whereupon he commanded him to be set upon the block, and as many irons upon his legs as he could bear.

'Good master Alexander, be so much my friend, that these irons may be taken off.'

'Well,' said Alexander, 'give me my fees, and I will take them off: if not, thou shalt wear them still.'

Then said Master Philpot, 'Sir, what is your fee?'

He said four pound was his fees.

'Ah,' said Master Philpot, 'I have not so much; I am but a poor man, and I have been long in prison.'

'What wilt thou give me then?' said Alexander.

'Sir,' said he, 'I will give you twenty shillings, and that I will send my man for; or else I will my gown to gage.'

And with that Alexander departed from him, and commanded him to be had into limbo.

Then one Witterence, steward of the house, took Master Philpot on his back, and carried him down, his man knew not whither. Wherefore Master Philpot said to his man, 'Go to master sheriff, and show him how I am used, and desire master sheriff to be good unto me.' And so his servant went straightway, and took an honest man with him.

The sheriff took his ring off from his finger, and delivered it unto that honest man which came with Master Philpot's man, and bade him go unto Alexander, and command him to take off his irons, and to handle him more gently. And when they came to the said Alexander, and told their message from the sheriff, Alexander took the ring, and said,

'Ah! I perceive master sheriff is a bearer with him, and all such heretics as he is: therefore to-morrow I will show it to his betters.' Yet at ten of the clock he went in to Master Philpot, and took off his irons.

Upon Tuesday at supper, being the 17th day of December 1555, there came a messenger from the sheriffs, and bade Master Philpot make him ready, for the next day he should suffer. Master Philpot answered, "I am ready; God grant me strength, and a joyful resurrection.' And so he went into his chamber, and poured out his spirit unto the Lord God, giving Him most hearty thanks, that He of His mercy had made him worthy to suffer for His truth.

In the morning the sheriffs came, about eight of the clock, and he most joyfully came down unto them. And there his man did meet him, and said, 'Ah! dear master, farewell.' His master said unto him, 'Serve God, and He will help thee.' When he was entering into Smithfield, the way was foul, and two officers took him up to bear him to the stake. Then he said merrily, 'What! will ye make me a Pope? I am content to go to my journey's end on foot.'

When he was come to the place of suffering, he said, 'Shall I disdain to suffer at this stake, seeing my Redeemer did not refuse to suffer a most vile death upon the cross for me?' And when he had made an end of his prayers, he said to the officers, 'What have you done for me?' and every one of them declared what they had done; and he gave to every of them money. Then in the midst of the fiery flames he yielded his soul into the hands of Almighty God.

THE FIRES OF SMITHFIELD

About the 27th day of January in anno 1556, were burned these seven persons: Thomas Whittle, priest; Bartlet Green, gentleman; John Tudson, artificer; John Went, artificer; Thomas Browne; Isabel Foster, wife; Joan Warne, alais Lashford, maid.

What an evil mess of handling Whittle had, and how he was by Bishop Bonner beaten and buffeted about the face, by this his own narration sent unto his friend, manifestly may appear:—

'The bishop sent for me, out of the porter's lodge, where I had been all night, lying upon the earth, upon a pallet, where I had as painful a night of sickness as ever I had. And when I came before him, he asked me if I would have come to mass that morning, if he had sent for me. Whereunto I answered, that I would have come to him at his commandment, "but to your mass," said I, "I have small affection." At which answer he was displeased sore, and said I should be fed with bread and water. And as I followed him through the great hall, he turned back and beat me with his fist, first on the one cheek, and then on the other. And then he led me into a little salt-house, where I had no straw nor bed, but lay two nights on a table, and slept soundly, I thank God.'

Whittle, strengthened with the grace of the Lord, stood strong and immovable. Wherefore he was brought to the fire with the other six.

Master Bartlet Green was of a good house, and was sent unto the University of Oxford. By his often repairing unto the lectures of Peter Martyr he saw the true light of Christ's Gospel.

A BLOODSUCKING PRELATE

As he was going to Newgate there met with him two gentlemen, being his special friends, minding to comfort their persecuted brother : but their loving and friendly hearts were manifested by the abundance of their pitiful tears. To whom Green said, 'Ah, my friends! is this your comfort you are come to give me, in this my occasion of heaviness? Must I, who needed to have comfort ministered to me, become now a comforter of you?'

When he was scourged with rods by Bishop Bonner he greatly rejoiced, yet his shamefaced modesty was such, that never would he express any mention therof, lest he should seem to glory in himself, save that only he opened the same to one Master Cotton of the Temple, a friend of his, a little before his death.

He was first apprehended, but last of them condemned, which was the 15th day of January, and afterward burned with the other six martyrs, the 27th of January, 1556.

Thomas Brown dwelled in the parish of St Bride's in Fleet Street, and because he came not to his parish church, was presented by the constable of the parish to Bonner. Being had to Fulham he was required to come into the chapel to hear mass, which, refusing to do, he went into the warren, and there kneeled among the trees. For this he was greatly charged of the bishop, 'Brown, ye have been before me many times and oft, and I have travailed with thee, to win thee from thine errors; yet thou, and such like, do report, that I go about to seek thy blood.' To whom the said Thomas Brown answered again; 'Yea, my lord,' saith he, 'indeed ye be a bloodsucker, and I would I had as much blood as is water in the sea, for you to suck.'

And so he was committed to be burned.

Joan Lashford, was the daughter of one Robert Lashford, cutler, who was persecuted for the Gospel of God to the burning fire; and after him his wife; and after her, this Joan Lashwood, her daughter; who, about the age of twenty years, ministering to her father and mother in prison, was known to be of the same doctrine. Her confession was that she came unto no popish mass service in the church, neither would be confessed.

FIVE OTHER GODLY MARTYRS BURNED AT ONE FIRE

In this story of persecuted martyrs, next in order follow five others burned in the year of the Lord 1557, April the 12th: Thomas Loseby, Henry Ramsey, Thomas Thirtel, Margaret Hide, and Agnes Stanley: who were apprehended for not coming to their parish churches.

Thomas Thirtel answered unto Bishop Bonner, 'My Lord, if you make me a heretic, you make Christ and all the twelve apostles heretics.'

Margaret Hide said, ' My lord, I would see you instruct me with some part of God's Word, and not to give me instructions of holy bread and holy water, for it is no part of the Scripture.'

Agnes Stanley made this answer : ' My Lord, as for these that ye say be burnt for heresy, I believe they are true martyrs before God : therefore I will not go from my opinion and faith as long as I live.'

Altogether in one fire most joyfully and constantly

A STRIKING ANSWER

these five martyrs ended their temporal lives, receiving there-for the life eternal.

John Hallingdale, William Sparrow, and Richard Gibson

These three faithful witnesses of the Lord's testament were tormented and put to death, 18th of November 1557.

John Hallingdale said that Cranmer, Latimer, Ridley, Hooper, and generally all that of late had been burnt for heretics, were no heretics at all, because they did preach truly the Gospel: upon whose preaching he grounded his faith and conscience. William Sparrow answered Bishop Bonner, ' that if every hair of my head were a man, I would burn them all, rather than go from the truth.'

The Martyrs of the Islington fields

Secretly, in a back close, in the field by the town of Islington, were assembled together a certain company of godly and innocent persons, to the number of forty, men and women, who there virtuously occupied in prayer and in the meditation of God's holy Word. Cometh a certain man to them unknown; who, saluted them, saying, that they looked like men that meant no hurt. One of the company asked the man, if he could tell whose close that was, and whether they might be so bold there to sit. 'Yea,' said he, 'for that ye seem unto me such persons as intend no harm,' and so departed.

Within a quarter of an hour cometh the constable of Islington with six or seven other, one with a bow, another with a bill, and others with weapons; the which six or seven persons the said constable left a little behind him in a close place, there to be ready if need should be, while he, came through them. Looking what they were doing, he bade them deliver their books. They, understanding that he was constable, refused not so to do. With that cometh forth the residue of his fellows who bade them stand, and not depart. They answered that they would be obedient and go whithersoever they would have them; and so were they first carried to a brewhouse but a little way off, while that some of the said soldiers ran to the justice next at hand. But the justice was not at home; whereupon they were had to Sir Roger Cholmley. In the mean time some of the women escaped. In fine, were sent to Newgate twenty-and-two. These were in prison seven weeks before they were examined. Of these foresaid two-and-twenty, were burnt thirteen; in Smithfield seven, at Brentford six.

The names of these seven were Henry Pond, Reinald Eastland, Robert Southam, Matthew Ricarby, John Floyd, John Holiday, Roger Holland; only the examination of Roger Holland came to our hand.

This Roger Holland, a merchant-tailor of London, was first an apprentice with one Master Kempton, at the Black Boy in Watling Street, giving himself to dancing, fencing, gaming, banqueting, and wanton company. He had received for his master certain money, to the sum of thirty pounds; and lost every groat at dice. Therefore he purposed to convey himself away beyond the seas, either into France or into Flanders.

He called betimes in the morning to a servant in

the house, a discreet maid, whose name was Elizabeth,
which professed the Gospel, with a life agreeing
unto the same. To whom he said, 'Elizabeth, I
would I had followed thy gentle persuasions and
friendly rebukes; which if I had done, I had never
come to this shame and misery which I am now fallen
into; for I have lost thirty pounds of my master's
money, which to pay him, and to make up mine
accounts, I am not able. But I pray you, desire my
mistress, that she would entreat my master to take
this bill of my hand, and if I be ever able, I will see
him paid: desiring him that the matter may pass
with silence, for if it should come unto my father's
ears, it would bring his grey hairs oversoon unto his
grave.' And so was he departing.

The maid considering that it might be his utter
undoing, 'Stay,' said she; and having a piece of
money lying by her, given unto her by the death of
a kinsman, she brought unto him thirty pounds,
saying, 'Roger, here is thus much money ; I will let
thee have it, and I will keep this bill. But thou
shalt promise me to refuse all wild company, all
swearing and ribaldry talk ; and if ever I know thee
to play one twelvepence at either dice or cards, then
will I show this thy bill unto my master. And
futhermore, thou shalt promise me to resort every
day to the lecture at All-hallows, and the sermon at
Paul's every Sunday, and to cast away all thy books
of papistry and vain ballads, and get thee the
Testament and Book of Service, and read the
Scriptures with reverence and fear, calling unto God
still, for His grace to direct thee in His truth. And
pray unto God fervently, desiring Him to pardon thy
former offences, and not to remember the sins of thy

youth; and ever be afraid to break His laws, or offend His majesty. Then shall God keep thee, and send thee thy heart's desire.'

Within one half year God had wrought such a change in this man, that he was become an earnest professor of the truth. Then he repaired into Lancashire unto his father, and brought divers good books with him, and bestowed them upon his friends, so that his father and others began to taste of the Gospel, and to detest the mass, idolatry, and superstition; and in the end his father gave him a stock of money to begin the world withal, to the sum of fifty pounds.

Then Roger repaired to London again, and came to the maid that lent him the money to pay his master withal, and said unto her, 'Elizabeth, here is thy money I borrowed of thee; and for the friendship, good will, and the good connsel I have received at thy hands, to recompense thee I am not able, otherwise than to make thee my wife.' And soon after they were married, which was in the first year of Queen Mary.

After this he remained in the congregations of the faithful, until, the last year of Queen Mary, he, with the six others aforesaid, were taken.

And after Roger Holland there was none suffered in Smithfield for the testimony of the Gospel, God be thanked.

THE LIFE, STATE, AND STORY OF THE REVEREND PASTOR AND PRELATE, THOMAS CRANMER, ARCHBISHOP OF CANTERBURY

THOMAS CRANMER, coming of an ancient parentage, from the Conquest to be deducted, was born in a village called Aslacton in Nottinghamshire. He came in process of time unto the University of Cambridge; and was chosen fellow of Jesus college. The tongues and other good learning began by little and little to spring up again, and the books of Faber and Erasmus to be much occupied and had in good estimation. In whom Cranmer taking no small pleasure, did daily rub away his old rustiness on them, as upon a whetstone, until at the length, when Martin Luther was risen up, the more bright and happy days of God's knowledge did waken men's minds to the clear light of the truth; at which time, when he was about thirty years old, omitting all other studies, he gave his whole mind to discuss matters of religion. And, because he saw that he could not judge of these matters unless he beheld the very fountains thereof, before he would addict his mind to any opinion, he spent three whole years in reading over the books of holy Scriptures. After he had laid this foundation no less wisely than happily, when he thought himself sufficiently prepared, and being now instructed with more ripeness of judgment, like a merchant greedy of all good things, he gave his mind to read all kind of authors.

In the mean while, being addicted to no party or age, he weighed all men's opinions with secret judgment. He read the old writers, so as he despised not the new, and, all this while, in handling and conferring writers' judgments, he was a slow reader, but an earnest marker. He never came to any writer's book without pen and ink, but yet he exercised his memory no less than his pen. Whatsoever controversy came he gathered every author's sentence, briefly, and the diversity of their judgments, into common places, which he had prepared for that purpose; or else, if the matter were too long to write out, he noted the place of the author and the number of the leaf, whereby he might have the more help for his memory.

And so, being master of arts, and fellow of Jesus college, it chanced him to marry a gentleman's daughter: by means whereof he lost his fellowship there, and became the reader in Buckingham college. And for that he would with more diligence apply that his office of reading, he placed his said wife in an inn, called the 'Dolphin,' in Cambridge, the wife of the house being of affinity unto her. By reason whereof, and for his often resort unto his wife in that inn, he was much marked of some popish merchants: whereupon rose the report bruited abroad every where, after he was preferred to the Archbishopric of Canterbury, that he was but an hosteler, and therefore without all good learning.

Whilst this said Master Cranmer continued as

reader in Buckingham college, his wife died. The Master and fellows of Jesus college, desirous again of their old companion, chose him again fellow of the same college. In few years after he became the reader of divinity lecture in the same college, and in such reputation with the whole University, that, being doctor of divinity, he was commonly appointed one of the heads to examine such as yearly profess in commencement, either bachelors or doctors of divinity; by the approbation of these learned men the whole University licenseth them to proceed unto their degree; and by their disallowance the University rejecteth them, until they be better furnished with more knowledge.

Now Dr Cranmer, ever much favouring the knowledge of the Scripture, would never admit any to proceed in divinity, unless they were substantially seen in the story of the Bible: by means whereof certain friars, and other religious persons, who were principally brought up in the study of school authors without regard had to the authority of Scriptures, were commonly rejected by him; so that he was, for his severe examination, much hated, and had in great indignation. And yet it came to pass in the end, that divers of them, being thus compelled to study the Scriptures, became afterwards very well learned and well affected; insomuch, that when they proceeded doctors of divinity, they could not overmuch extol Master Doctor Cranmer's goodness towards them, who had for a time put them back, to aspire unto better knowledge and perfection.

While Dr Cranmer thus continued in Cambridge, the weighty cause of King Henry the Eighth, his divorce with the Lady Katherine dowager of Spain, came into question; which by the space of two or three years had been diversely disputed amongst the canonists and other learned men. It came to pass that Dr Cranmer, by reason that the plague was in Cambridge, resorted to Waltham Abbey, to one Master Cressy's house there, whose wife was of kin to the said Master Cranmer. He had two sons of the said Cressy with him at Cambridge as his pupils, wherefore he rested with the said two children, duringt hat summer-time, A.D. 1529. It chanced that the King had removed himself from London to Waltham for a night or twain, while Dr Stephen Gardiner, secretary, and Dr Foxe, almoner, were lodged in the house of the said Master Cressy.

When supper-time came, they all three doctors met together; and as they were of old acquaintance, the secretary and the almoner conferred with Dr Cranmer concerning the King's cause, what he thought therein.

Dr Cranmer answered, that in his opinion they made more ado in prosecuting the law ecclesiastical than needed. 'It were better, as I suppose,' quoth Dr Cranmer, 'that the question, whether a man may marry his brother's wife, or no? were decided by the Word of God, whereby the conscience of the prince might be quieted, than thus from year to year by frustratory delays to prolong the time. There is but one truth in it, which the Scripture will soon make manifest, being by learned men well handled, and that may be as well done in England in the Universities here, as at Rome. You might this way have made an end of this matter long since.'

The other two well liked of his device, and

conceived to instruct the King withal, who then was minded to send to Rome for a new commission. The next day, when the King removed to Greenwich, his mind being unquieted, and desirous of an end of his long and tedious suit, he called unto him Dr Stephen and Dr Foxe, saying unto them, 'What now, my masters,' quoth the King, 'shall we do in this infinite cause of mine? There must be a new commission procured from Rome; and when we shall have an end, God knoweth, and not I.' Dr Foxe answered, 'We trust that there shall be better ways devised for your majesty. It chanced us to be lodged at Waltham in Master Cressy's house this other night, where we met with an old acquaintance of ours, named Dr Cranmer. He thought that the next way were to instruct and quiet your majesty's conscience by trying your highness's question out by the authority of the Word of God, and thereupon to proceed to a final sentence.' The King said, 'Where is that Dr Cranmer? Is he still at Waltham?' They answered, that they left him there. 'Marry,' said the King, 'I will surely speak with him, and therefore let him be sent for out of hand. I perceive,' quoth the King, 'that that man hath the sow by the right ear: and if I had known this device but two years ago, it had been in my way a great piece of money, and had also rid me out of much disquietness.'

Whereupon Dr Cranmer was sent for. But when he came to London, he began to quarrel with these two his acquaintances, that he, by their means, was brought thither to be cumbered in a matter, wherein he had nothing at all travailed in study; and therefore most instantly entreated them, that they would make his excuse that he might be despatched away from coming into the King's presence. But all was in vain; for the more they began to excuse Dr Cranmer's absence, the more the King chid with them; so that, no excuse serving, he was fain to come to the court. 'Master doctor,' said the King, 'I pray you, and nevertheless because you are a subject, I charge and command you (all your other business set apart), to take some pains to see this my cause to be furthered according to your device, as much as it may lie in you, so that I may shortly understand whereunto I may trust. For this I protest before God and the world, that I seek not to be divorced from the Queen, if by any means I might justly be persuaded that this our matrimony were inviolable, and not against the laws of God; for otherwise there was never cause to move me to seek any such extremity: neither was there ever prince had a more gentle, a more obedient and loving companion and wife than the Queen is, nor did I ever fancy woman in all respects better, if this doubt had not risen; assuring you that for the singular virtues wherewith she is endued, besides the consideration of her noble stock, I could be right well contented still to remain with her, if so it would stand with the will and pleasure of Almighty God.'

Dr Cranmer besought the King's highness to commit the examining of this matter by the Word of God, unto the best learned men of both his Universities, Cambridge and Oxford. 'You say well,' said the King, 'and I am content therewith. But yet nevertheless, I will have you specially to write your mind therein.' After the King's departure, Dr Cranmer incontinent wrote his mind concerning the King's question ; adding to the same his opinion, that the Bishop of Rome had no such authority, as whereby he might dispense with the Word of God. When Dr Cranmer had committed this book to the King, the King said to him, 'Will you abide by this that you have here written before the Bishop of Rome?' 'That will I do by God's grace,' quoth Dr Cranmer, 'if your majesty do send me thither.' 'Marry,' quoth the King, 'I will send you even to him in a sure ambassage.'

And thus by means of Dr Cranmer's handling of this matter, in both the Universities of Cambridge and Oxford, it was concluded, that no such matrimony was by the Word of God lawful.

Whereupon a solemn ambassage was sent to the Bishop of Rome, then being at Bologna, wherein went Dr Cranmer and divers other learned men and gentlemen, A.D. 1530. And when the time came that they should declare the cause of their ambassage, the Bishop, sitting on high in his cloth of estate and in his rich apparel, offered his foot to be kissed of the ambassadors. The Earl of Wiltshire, disdaining thereat, stood still, and made no countenance thereunto, so that all the rest kept themselves from that idolatry. Howbeit, one thing is not here to be omitted, which then chanced by a spaniel of the Earl of Wiltshire. For he stood directly between the Earl and the Bishop of Rome, when the said Bishop had advanced forth his foot to be kissed. The spaniel straightway went directly to the Pope's feet, and not only kissed the same unmannerly, but took fast with his mouth the great toe of the Pope, so that in haste he pulled in his feet : our men smiling in their sleeves.

THOMAS CRANMER

Without any further ceremony the Pope gave ear to the ambassadors, who declared that no man could or ought to marry his brother's wife, and that the Bishop of Rome by no means ought to dispense to the contrary. Divers promises were made, and sundry days appointed, wherein the question should have been disputed; and when our part was ready to answer, no man there appeared to dispute in that behalf. So in the end, the Pope, making to our ambassadors good countenance, and gratifying Dr Cranmer with the office of the penitentiaryship, dismissed them undisputed withal.

This matter thus prospering on Dr Cranmer's behalf, Warham, Archbishop of Canterbury, departed this life, whereby that dignity then being in the King's disposition, was immediately given to Dr Cranmer, as worthy for his travail of such a promotion.

Upon this question of the marriage riseth another question of the Pope's authority. The new archbishop was not a little helped by his old collections and notes, which he used in studying: for all the weight of the business was chiefly laid on his shoulders. He therefore alone confuted all the objections of the papists. He showed that the Pope's lordship was brought in by no authority of the Scripture, but by ambitious tyranny of men; that the chiefest power in earth belonged to the Emperor, to Kings, and to other potentates, to whom the bishops, priests, popes, and cardinals, by God's commandment, were no less subject than other men of the commonwealth: that there was no cause why the Bishop of Rome should excel other bishops in authority, and therefore it were best that the ambitious lordship of this bishop, being driven out of England, should keep itself within his own Italy, as a river is kept within his banks.

Soon after the King and Queen, by the ecclesiastical law, were cited at Dunstable before the Archbishop of Canterbury and Stephen Gardiner, Bishop of Winchester, as judges, to hear the sentence of God's Word concerning the matter of their marriage. The King refused not to appear; but the Queen appealed to the Bishop of Rome. But forasmuch as the Pope's authority being banished out of the realm, and as by public authority it was enacted that no man should appeal out of the realm to Rome for any matter, the judges, making no delay, out of God's Word pronounced the marriage to be unlawful, and so made divorce. As the Pope's name and title were now abolished, the archbishop laboured also to banish out of the realm his errors, heresies, and corruptions. And not content therewith, he obtained of the King, partly by his own suit, and partly by other men's suit, that certain learned bishops should make a book of ecclesiastical institutions, which should be better purged from all popish superstitions. This book, by the title of the authors, they called *The Bishops' Book*. It appeareth that the Archbishop of Canterbury was not then well instructed in the doctrine of the sacrament, because there is granted a real presence. There was added also concerning worshipping of images, which article was none of the bishop's, but added and written by the King's hand.

The abolishing of monasteries now began to be talked of. The King's desire was, that all the abbey-lands should come to his coffers; the archbishop, and other men of the Church, thought it pertained more to Christian duty, that all the goods of monasteries (which were very great) should be put to the use of the poor, and erecting of schools. For which cause the King's will being somewhat bent against the archbishop and other maintainers of his doctrine, he set forth the Six Articles, containing the sum of popish religion, and by full consent of Parliament established them. What a slaughter by the space of eight years these Six Articles made, it were superfluous to repeat.

This Archbishop of Canterbury evermore gave himself to continual study; by five of the clock in the morning he was at his book, and so consuming the time in study and prayer until nine of the clock. He then applied himself (if the prince's affairs did not call him away) until dinner time to hear suitors, and to despatch such matters as appertained unto his special cure and charge, committing his temporal affairs unto his officers.

After dinner, if any suitors were attendant, he would very diligently hear them, and despatch them in such sort as every man commended his lenity and gentleness, although the case required that some while divers of them were committed by him to prison. And having no suitors after dinner, for an hour or thereabouts he would play at the chess, or behold such as could play. Then again to his ordinary study, at the which commonly he for the most part stood, and seldom sat; and there continuing until five of the clock, bestowed that hour in hearing the common prayer, and walking or using some honest pastime until supper time.

At supper, if he had no appetite (as many times he would not sup), yet would he sit down at the

table, having his ordinary provision of his mess
furnished with expedient company, he wearing on
his hands his gloves, because he would (as it were)
thereby wean himself from eating of meat, but yet
keeping the company with such fruitful talk as did
repast and much delight the hearers, so that by this
means hospitality was well furnished, and the alms-
chest well maintained for relief of the poor. After
supper, he would consume one hour at the least in
walking, or some other honest pastime, and then
again until nine of the clock, at one kind of study
or other; so that no hour of the day was spent in
vain, but the same was so bestowed, as tended to
the glory of God, the service of the prince, or the
commodity of the Church; which his well-bestowing
of his time procured to him most happily a good
report of all men, to be in respect of other men's
conversation faultless, as it became the minister of
God.

It is required, 'that a bishop ought not to be
stubborn:' with which kind of vice, without great
wrong, this archbishop in no wise ought to be
charged; whose nature was such as none more
gentle, or sooner won to an honest suit or purpose;
specially in such things, wherein by his word,
writing, counsel, or deed, he might gratify either
any gentle or noble man, or do good to any mean
person, or else relieve the needy and poor. Only in
causes pertaining to God or his prince, no man more
stout, more constant, or more hard to be won. Such
things as he granted, he did without any suspicion
of rebraiding or meed therefore: so that he was
rather culpable of overmuch facility and gentleness.

If overmuch patience may be a vice, this man may

seem peradventure to offend. For he had many cruel enemies, not for his own deserts, but only for his religion's sake : and yet whatsoever he was that sought his hindrance, either in goods, estimation, or life, and upon conference would seem never so slenderly to relent or excuse himself, the archbishop would forget the offence committed, and show such pleasure to him that it came into a proverb, 'Do unto my Lord of Canterbury displeasure, or a shrewd turn, and then you may be sure to have him your friend while he liveth.'

His quietness was such, that he never raged so far with any of his household servants, as once to call the meanest of them varlet or knave in anger, much less to reprove a stranger with any reproachful words.

How he was no niggard, all kind of people that knew him can well testify. And albeit such was his liberality to all sorts of men, that no man did lack whom he could do for, either in giving or lending ; yet nevertheless such was again his circumspection, that when he was apprehended and committed by Queen Mary to the Tower, he owed no man living a penny : whereas no small sums of money were owing him of divers persons, which by breaking their bills and obligations he freely forgave and suppressed before his attainder. When he perceived the fatal end of King Edward should work to him no good success touching his body and goods, he incontinently called for his officers, commanding them in any wise to pay where any penny was owing, which was out of hand despatched. And then he said, ' Now I thank God, I am mine own man.'

Certain of the Council attempted the King against

the archbishop, declaring plainly, that the realm was
so infected with heresies, that it was dangerous for
his highness further to permit it unreformed, lest
peradventure by long suffering, such contention
should ensue in the realm, and thereby might spring
horrible commotions and uproars, like as in some
parts of Germany: the enormity whereof they could
not impute to any so much, as to the Archbishop of
Canterbury, who by his own preaching, and his
chaplains, had filled the whole realm full of divers
pernicious heresies. The King would needs know
his accusers. They answered that forasmuch as he
was a councillor, no man durst take upon him to
accuse him; but, if it would please his highness to
commit him to the Tower for a time, there would
be accusations and proofs enow against him: for
otherwise, just testimony and witness against him
would not appear.

The King granted unto them that they should
the next day commit him to the Tower for his trial.
When midnight came, he sent Sir Anthony Denny
to Lambeth to the archbishop, willing him forthwith
to resort unto him at the court. The archbishop,
coming into the gallery where the King walked, and
tarried for him, his highness said, 'Ah, my Lord
of Canterbury! I can tell you news. For divers
weighty considerations it is determined by me, and
the council, that you to-morrow, at nine of the
clock, shall be committed to the Tower, for that
you and your chaplains (as information is given us)
have taught and preached, and sown within the
realm, a number of execrable heresies: and therefore
the council have requested me, for the trial of the
matter, to suffer them to commit you to the Tower,

or else no man dare come forth, as witness in these matters, you being a councillor.'

When the King had said his mind, the archbishop kneeled down and said, 'I am content, if it please your grace, with all my heart, to go thither at your highness's commandment. And I most humbly thank your majesty that I may come to my trial; for there be that have many ways slandered me : and now this way I hope to try myself not worthy of such report.'

The King, perceiving the man's uprightness, joined with such simplicity, said, 'O Lord, what manner a man be you! What simplicity is in you! Do you not know how many great enemies you have? Do you not consider what an easy thing it is to procure three or four false knaves to witness against you? Think you to have better luck that way than your Master Christ had? I see by it you will run headlong to your undoing, if I would suffer you. Your enemies shall not so prevail against you, for I have otherwise devised with myself to keep you out of their hands. Yet notwithstanding to-morrow, when the council shall send for you, resort unto them, and if they do commit you to the Tower, require of them, because you are one of them, a councillor, that you may have your accusers brought before them, and that you may answer their accusations before them, without any further endurance, and use for yourself as good persuasions that way as you may devise; and if no entreaty or reasonable request will serve, then deliver unto them this my ring (which then the King delivered unto the archbishop), and say unto them, "If there be no remedy, my lords, but that I must needs go to the

Tower, then I revoke my cause from you, and
appeal to the King's own person by this his token
unto you all," for ' (said the King unto the archbishop) ' so soon as they shall see this my ring,
they know it so well, that they shall understand
that I have resumed the whole cause into mine
own hands and determination, and that I have
discharged them thereof.'

The archbishop, perceiving the King's benignity,
had much ado to forbear tears.

On the morrow about nine of the clock before
noon, the council sent a gentleman-usher for the
archbishop, who when he came to the council-
chamber door, could not be let in; but of purpose
(as it seemed) was compelled there to wait among
the pages, lackeys and serving-men all alone. Dr
Buts, the King's physician, resorting that way, and
espying how my Lord of Canterbury was handled,
went to the King's highness, and said, 'My Lord
of Canterbury, if it please your grace, is well
promoted; for now he is become a lackey or a
serving-man : for yonder he standeth this half hour
without the council-chamber door amongst them.'
' It is not so,' quoth the King, ' I trow; the council
hath not so little discretion as to use the metropolitan
of the realm in that sort, specially being one of their
own number. But let them alone,' said the King,
' and we shall hear more soon.'

Anon the archbishop was called into the
council-chamber, to whom was alleged, as before
is rehearsed. The archbishop answered in like
sort as the King had advised him; and when he
perceived that no manner of persuasion or entreaty
could serve, he delivered them the King's ring,

revoking his cause into the King's hands. The whole council being thereat somewhat amazed, the Earl of Bedford with a loud voice, confirming his words with a solemn oath, said, 'When you first began this matter, my lords, I told you what would come of it. Do you think that the King will suffer this man's finger to ache? Much more, I warrant you, will he defend his life against brabbling varlets! You do but cumber yourselves to hear tales and fables against him.' And so incontinently upon the receipt of the King's token, they all rose, and carried to the King his ring.

When they were come to the King's presence, his highness with a severe countenance said unto them, 'Ah, my lords! I thought I had wiser men of my council than now I find you. What discretion was this in you, thus to make the primate of the realm, and one of you in office, to wait at the council-chamber door amongst serving men? I protest, that if a prince may be beholden unto his subject, by the faith I owe to God, I take this man here, my Lord of Canterbury, to be of all other a most faithful subject unto us.' And with that one or two of the chiefest of the council, making their excuse, declared, that in requesting his endurance, it was rather meant for his trial, and his purgation against the common fame and slander of the world, than for any malice conceived against him. 'Well, well, my lords,' quoth the King, 'take him and well use him, as he is worthy to be, and make no more ado.' And with that every man caught him by the hand.

But yet look, where malice reigneth, there neither reason nor honesty can take place. And therefore it was procured by his ancient enemies, that not only the prebendaries of his cathedral church in Canterbury, but also the most famous justices of peace in the shire, should accuse him. The articles were delivered to the King's highness by some of the council's means. When the King had perused the book, he wrapt it up, and put it in his sleeve ; and finding occasion to solace himself upon the Thames, came with his barge furnished with his musicians along by Lambeth bridge towards Chelsea. The noise of the musicians provoked the archbishop to resort to the bridge to salute his prince : whom when the King perceived, eftsoons he commanded the watermen to draw towards the shore, and so came straight to the bridge.

'Ah, my chaplain ! ' said the King to the archbishop, 'come into the barge to me.' The archbishop declared to his highness, that he would take his own barge and wait upon his majesty. ' No,' said the King, ' you must come into my barge, for I have to talk with you.' When the King and the archbishop, all alone in the barge, were set together, said the King to the archbishop, 'I have news out of Kent for you, my lord.' The archbishop answered, ' Good, I hope, if it please your highness.' 'Marry,' said the King, 'they be so good, that I now know the greatest heretic in Kent;' and with that pulled out of his sleeve the book of articles against both the said archbishop and his preachers, and gave the book to him, willing him to peruse the same.

When the archbishop had read the articles, and saw himself so uncourteously handled of the prebendaries of his cathedral church, and of such his neighbours as he had many ways gratified, the justices of the peace, it much grieved him; notwithstanding he kneeled down to the King, and besought his majesty to grant out a commission to whomsoever it pleased his highness, to try out the truth of this accusation. 'In very deed,' said the King, 'I do so mean; and you yourself shall be chief commissioner, to adjoin to you such two or three more as you shall think good yourself.' 'Then it will be thought,' quoth the archbishop to the King, 'that it is not indifferent, if it' please your grace, that I should be mine own judge, and my chaplains also.' 'Well,' said the King, 'I will have none other but yourself, and such as you will appoint: for I am sure that you will not halt with me in any thing, although you be driven to accuse yourself. And if you handle the matter wisely, you shall find a pretty conspiracy devised against you. Whom will you have with you?' said the King. 'Whom it shall please your grace to name,' quoth the archbishop. 'I will appoint Dr Belhouse for one, name you the other,' said the King, 'meet for that purpose.' 'My chancellor, Dr Coxe, and Hussy my registrar,' said the archbishop, 'are men expert to examine such troublesome matters.' 'Well,' said the King, 'let there be a commission made forth, and out of hand get you into Kent, and advertise me of your doings.'

The commissioners came into Kent, and there they sat about three weeks to bolt out who was the first occasion of this accusation; for thereof the King would chiefly be advertised. Every man shrunk in his horns, and no man would confess any thing to the purpose: for **Dr Coxe** and **Hussey**, being friendly unto the papists, handled the matter so, that they would permit nothing material to come to light. This thing being well perceived by one of the archbishop's servants, his secretary, he wrote incontinently unto **Dr Buts** and **Master Denny**, declaring that if the King's majesty did not send some other to assist my lord, than those that then were there with him, it were not possible that any thing should come to light: and therefore wished that **Dr Lee**, or some other stout man that had been exercised in the King's ecclesiastical affairs, might be sent to the archbishop.

Dr Lee was sent for by the King, and appointed the archbishop to name a dozen or sixteen of his officers and gentlemen, such as had discretion, wit, and audacity, to whom he gave in commission from the King, to search the purses, chests, and chambers of all those that were suspected to be of this confederacy, both within the cathedral church and without. Such letters or writings as they could find they should bring to the archbishop and him. Within four hours the whole conspiracy was made manifest!

Amongst others came to my lord's hands two letters, one of the suffragan of Dover, and another of **Dr Barber**, whom continually the archbishop retained as a counsellor in the law. These two men being well promoted by the archbishop, he used ever in such familiarity, that when the suffragan, being a prebend of Canterbury, came to him, he always set him at his own mess, and the other never from his table, as men in whom he had much delight and comfort, when time of care and pensiveness chanced. But that which they did, was altogether counterfeit, and the devil was turned into the angel of light, for they were both of this confederacy.

When my lord had gotten their letters into his hands, he called to him into his study the said suffragan of Dover and Dr Barber, saying, 'Come your ways with me, for I must have your advice in a matter.' When they were with him in his study altogether, he said to them, 'You twain be men in whom I have had much confidence and trust: you must now give me some good counsel, for I am shamefully abused with one or twain to whom I have showed all my secrets from time to time, and did trust them as myself. The matter is so now fallen out, that they not only have disclosed my secrets, but also have taken upon them to accuse me of heresy, and are become witnesses against me. I require you therefore, of your good advice, how I shall behave myself towards them. You are both my friends, and such as I always have used when I needed counsel. What say you to the matter?' quoth the Archbishop.

'Marry,' quoth Dr Barber, 'such villains and knaves (saving your honour) were worthy to be hanged out of hand without any other law.'

'Hanging were too good,' quoth the suffragan, 'and if there lacked one to do execution, I would be hangman myself.'

At these words, the archbishop cast up his hands to heaven, and said, 'O Lord, most merciful God, whom may a man trust now-a-days? Was never man handled as I am: but, O Lord, Thou hast ever-more defended me, I praise Thy holy name there-for!' And with that he pulled out of his bosom the two letters, and said, 'Know ye these letters, my masters?'

With that they fell down upon their knees, and desired forgiveness, declaring how they a year before were tempted to do the same; and so, very lamentably bewailing their doings, besought his grace to pardon and forgive them. 'Well,' said the gentle archbishop, 'God make you both good men! I never deserved this at your hands: but ask God forgiveness, against Whom you have highly offended. If such men as you are not to be trusted, what should I do alive? I am brought to this point now, that I fear my left hand will accuse my right hand.' And so he dismissed them both with gentle and comfortable words.

This was the last push of the pike that was inferred against the said archbishop in King Henry the eighth's days: for never after durst any man move matter against him.

Until the entering of King Edward, it seemed that Cranmer was scarcely yet throughly persuaded in the right knowledge of the sacrament; shortly after, he, being confirmed by conference with Bishop Ridley, took upon him the defence of that whole doctrine, to refute the error of the papists, that men do eat the natural body of Christ.

King Edward, when he perceived that his death was at hand, and knowing that his sister Mary was wholly wedded to popish religion, bequeathed the succession to the Lady Jane (being niece to King Henry the eighth), by consent of all the council and lawyers of this realm. To this testament of the King's, when all the nobles and judges had subscribed, they sent for the archbishop, and required him that he also would subscribe. But he said, that it was otherwise in the testament of King Henry, and that he had sworn to the succession of Mary, as the next heir; by which oath he was bound. He was judge of no man's conscience but his own: and as concerning subscription, before he had spoken with the King himself, he utterly refused to do it. The King said, that the nobles and lawyers counselled him unto it, and with much ado the archbishop subscribed. Not long after King Edward died, A.D. 1553, being almost sixteen years old. It was commanded that the Lady Jane should be proclaimed Queen: which thing much misliked the common people. Mary, shifting for herself, eftsoons prevailed; came to London; and caused the two fathers, the Duke of Northumberland and the Duke of Suffolk, to be executed. After that the Lady Jane, in age tender, and innocent from this crime, could by no means be turned from the constancy of her faith, she together with her husband was beheaded.

The Archbishop of Canterbury, though he desired pardon, could obtain none, insomuch that the Queen would not once vouchsafe to see him: for the old grudge against the archbishop for the divorcement of her mother, remained hid in the bottom of her heart. Besides this divorce, she remembered the state of religion changed; all which was imputed to the archbishop, as the chief cause thereof.

While these things were in doing, a rumour was in all men's mouths, that the archbishop, to curry favour with the Queen, had promised to say a mass after the old custom in the funeral of King Edward her brother: neither wanted there some which reported that he had already said mass at Canterbury. This rumour thinking speedily to stay, Cranmer gave forth a writing of his purgation. This bill lying openly in a window in his chamber, cometh in by chance Master Scory, Bishop of Chichester, who, after he had read the same, required of the Archbishop to have a copy. By the occasion of Master Scory lending it to some friend of his, there were divers copies taken out, and the thing published abroad among the common people; insomuch that every scrivener's shop almost was occupied in copying out the same. Some of these copies coming to the commissioners, the matter was known, and the archbishop commanded to appear.

Whereupon Dr Cranmer appeared before the said commissioners. A bishop of the Queen's privy council, bringing in mention of the bill, 'My lord,' said he, 'there is a bill put forth in your name, wherein you seem to be aggrieved with setting up the mass again: we doubt not but you are sorry that it is gone abroad.' To whom the archbishop answered, saying, 'I do not deny myself to be the very author of that bill. I had minded to have set it on Paul's Church door, and on the doors of all the churches in London, with mine own seal joined thereto.' When they saw the constantness of the man, they dismissed him.

Not long after, he was sent to the Tower, and condemned of treason. The Queen, when she could not honestly deny him his pardon, seeing all the rest were discharged, released to him his action of treason, and accused him of heresy; which liked the archbishop right well, and came to pass as he wished, because the cause was not now his own, but Christ's; not the Queen's, but the Church's. It was determined, that he should be removed to Oxford, there to dispute with the doctors and divines. Although the Queen and the bishops had concluded before what should become of him, it pleased them that the matter should be debated with arguments, that under some honest show of disputation, the murder of the man might be covered.

We now proceed to his final judgment and order of condemnation, which was the 12th day of September, 1555, and eighteen days before the condemnation of Bishop Ridley and Master Latimer. This thing let us consider: how unjustly these three poor prisoned bishops were handled, which when they were compelled to dispute, yet were not suffered to speak, but at their adversary's appointment. And if they began to make any preface, or to speak somewhat largely for themselves, by and by they were commanded from the high chair of master prolocutor to go to the matter. If they prosecuted their arguments anything narrowly, straightway they heard, 'Short arguments, master doctor! short arguments, master doctor!'

And, so condemned, they carried the archbishop to prison with a great number of spearmen and billmen.

Cranmer was of stature mean; of complexion pure and somewhat sanguine, having no hair upon his head, at the time of his death; but a long beard, white and thick. He was of the age of sixty-six when he was burnt; and yet, being a man sore broken in studies, in all his time never used any spectacles.

THE TRIAL AT OXFORD

After the disputations in Oxford between the doctors of both Universities, and the three worthy bishops, Cranmer, Ridley, and Latimer, they were judged to be heretics, and committed to the mayor and sheriffs of Oxford. But, forasmuch as the sentence given against them was void in law (for at that time the authority of the Pope was not yet received into the land), therefore was a new commission sent from Rome, and a new process framed for the conviction of these reverend and godly learned men.

At the coming down of the commissioners, which was upon Thursday, the 12th of September, 1555, in the church of St Mary, and in the east end of the said church at the high altar, was erected a solemn scaffold ten foot high, with cloth of state very richly and sumptuously adorned, for Bishop Brooks, the Pope's legate, apparelled in pontificals. The seat was made that he might sit under the sacrament of the altar. And on the right hand of the Pope's delegate beneath him sat Dr Martin, and on the left hand sat Dr Story, the King and Queen's commissioners, which were both doctors of the civil law, and underneath them other doctors, with the Pope's collector, and a rabblement of such other like.

The archbishop was sent for to come before them. He came forth of the prison to the church of St Mary, set forth with bills and glaves for fear he should start away, being clothed in a fair black gown, with his hood on both shoulders, such as doctors of divinity in the University use to wear, and in his hand a white staff. After he did see them sit in their pontificals, he did not put off his cap to any of them, but stood still till that he was called. And anon one of the proctors for the Pope called 'Thomas, Archbishop of Canterbury, appear here and make answer to that shall be laid to thy charge; that is to say, for blasphemy, incontinency, and heresy; and make answer here to the Bishop of Gloucester, representing the Pope's person.'

Being brought more near unto the scaffold, and spying where the King and Queen's majesty's proctors were, putting off his cap, he humbly bowing his knee to the ground, made reverence to the one, and after to the other.

That done, beholding the bishop in the face, he put on his bonnet again, making no manner of token of obedience towards him at all: whereat the bishop, being offended, said unto him, that it might beseem him right well, weighing the authority he did represent, to do his duty unto him. Whereunto Dr Cranmer answered, that he had taken a solemn oath, never to consent to the admitting of the Bishop of Rome's authority into this realm of England again; that he meant by God's grace to keep it; and therefore would commit nothing either by sign or token, which might argue his consent to the receiving of the same.

After they had received his answers to all their objections, they cited him to appear at Rome within fourscore days, to make there his personal answers: which he said, if the King and Queen would send him, he would be content to do. Thence he was carried to prison again, where he remained, notwithstanding that he was commanded to appear at Rome. But the Pope, contrary to all reason and justice, sent his letter unto the King and Queen to degrade and deprive him of his dignity : which thing he did not only before the eighty days were ended, but before there were twenty days spent!

Upon the receipt of this sentence definitive of the Pope, another session was appointed for the archbishop to appear the 14th day of February, before certain commissioners directed down by the Queen, the chief whereof was the Bishop of Ely, Dr Thirleby. With him was assigned Dr Bonner, Bishop of London, which two, coming to Oxford as the Pope's delegates, commanded the archbishop to come before them, in the choir of Christ's Church, before the high altar. They first began, as the fashion is, to read their commission, giving them full authority to proceed to deprivation and degradation of him, and so upon excommunication to deliver him up to the secular power.

Bonner, who, by the space of many years had borne, as it seemed, no great good will towards him, and now rejoiced to see this day wherein he might triumph over him, and take his pleasure at full, began to stretch out his eloquence, making his oration to the assembly after this manner :

'This is the man that hath ever despised the Pope's holiness, and now is to be judged by him : this is the man that hath pulled down so many churches, and now is come to be judged in a church : this is the man that contemned the blessed sacrament of the altar, and now is come to be condemned before that blessed sacrament hanging over the altar : this is the man that like Lucifer sat in the place of Christ upon an altar to judge others, and now is come before an altar to be judged himself.'

Bonner went on in his rhetorical repetition, beginning every sentence with, 'This is the man, this is the man,' till at length the Bishop of Ely divers times pulled him by the sleeve to make an end, and said to him afterward, when they went to dinner, that he had broken promise with him; for he had entreated him earnestly to use the archbishop with reverence.

This done, they began to bustle toward his degrading, and first to take from him his crosier-staff out of his hands, which he held fast and refused to deliver, and withal, imitating the example of Martin Luther, pulled an appeal out of his left sleeve under the wrist, which he there and then delivered unto them, saying, 'I appeal to the next General Council.' This appeal being put up to Thirleby the Bishop of Ely, he said, 'My lord, our commission is to proceed against you.'

When they came to take off his pall (which is a solemn vesture of an archbishop), he said, 'Which of you hath a pall, to take off my pall;' which imported as much as they, being his inferiors, could not disgrade him. Whereunto one of them said, in that they were but bishops, they were his inferiors, and not competent judges; but being the Pope's delegates, they might take his pall. And so proceeding took every thing in order from him, as it was put on. Then a barber clipped his hair round about, and the bishop scraped the tops of his fingers where he had been anointed, wherein Bishop Bonner behaved himself as roughly and unmannerly, as the other bishop was to him soft and gentle. Last of all they stripped him out of his gown into his jacket, and put upon him a poor yeoman-beadle's gown, full bare and nearly worn, and as evil favouredly made as one might lightly see, and a townsman's cap on his head; and so delivered him to the secular power.

After this pageant of degradation, then spake Lord Bonner, saying to him, 'Now are you no lord any more.' And thus, with great compassion of every man, was he carried to prison. There followed him a gentleman of Gloucestershire who asked him if he would drink. The archbishop answered, saying that if he had a piece of salt fish, he had better will to eat; for he had been that day somewhat troubled and had eaten little: 'but now that it is past, my heart,' said he, 'is well quieted.' Whereupon the gentleman gave money to the bailiffs that stood by, and said, that if they were good men, they would bestow it on him, 'for my Lord of Canterbury had not one penny in his purse to help him.'

While the archbishop was thus in durance (whom they had now kept in prison almost the space of three years), the doctors and divines of Oxford busied themselves all that ever they could to have him recant. And to the intent they might win him easily, they had him to the dean's house of Christ's Church, where he lacked no delicate fare, played at the bowls, had his pleasure for walking, and all other things that might bring him from Christ. They perceived what a great wound they should receive, if the archbishop stood steadfast; and again, how great profit they should get, if he, as the principal standard-bearer, should be overthrown. By reason whereof the wily papists flocked about him, with threatening, flattering, entreating, and promising. They put him in hope, that he should not only have his life, but also be restored to his ancient dignity, that there should be nothing in the realm that the Queen would not easily grant him, whether he would have riches or dignity. But if he refused, there was no hope of health and pardon; for the Queen was purposed, that she would have Cranmer a catholic, or else no Cranmer at all. At last the archbishop, being overcome, gave his hand.

The doctors and prelates without delay caused this recantation to be imprinted, and set abroad in all men's hands. All this while Cranmer was in uncertain assurance of his life, although the same was faithfully promised to him by the doctors. The Queen, having now gotten a time to revenge her old grief, received his recantation very gladly; but of her purpose to put him to death, she would nothing relent. Now was Cranmer's cause in a miserable taking, who neither inwardly had any quietness in his own conscience, nor yet outwardly any help in his adversaries. On the one side was praise, on the other side scorn, on both sides danger, so that neither he could die honestly, nor yet unhonestly live.

The Queen, taking secret counsel how to dispatch Cranmer out of the way (who looked for nothing less than death), appointed Dr Cole, and secretly gave him in commandment, that against the 21st of March, he should prepare a funeral sermon for Cranmer's burning.

Soon after, the Lord Williams of Thame, the Lord Chandos, Sir Thomas Bridges, and Sir John Brown, with other worshipful men and justices, were commanded in the Queen's name to be at Oxford at the same day, with their servants and retinue, lest Cranmer's death should raise any tumult.

Cole returned to Oxford, ready to play his part; who, the day before the execution, came into the prison to Cranmer, to try whether he abode in the catholic faith wherein he had left him. To whom Cranmer answered, that by God's gracc he would daily be more confirmed in the catholic faith; Cole giving no signification as yet of his death that was prepared. In the morning appointed for Cranmer's execution, the said Cole, coming to him, asked if he had any money; to whom when he answered that he had none, he delivered fifteen crowns to give to the poor: and so exhorting him to constancy in faith departed.

The archbishop began to surmise what they went about.

Then because the day was not far past, and the lords and knights that were looked for were not yet come, there came to him the Spanish friar, witness of his recantation, bringing a paper with articles, which Cranmer should openly profess in his recantation before the people, earnestly desiring him that he would write the said instrument with his own hand, and sign it with his name: which when he had done, the said friar desired that he would write another copy thereof which should remain with him; and that he did also.

The archbishop being not ignorant whereunto their secret devices tended, and thinking that the time was at hand in which he could no longer dissemble the profession of his faith with Christ's people, put secretly in his bosom his prayer with his exhortation written in another paper, which he minded to recite to the people, before he should make the last profession of his faith, fearing lest, if they had heard the confession of his faith first, they would not afterward have suffered him to exhort the people.

Soon after, about nine of the clock, the Lord Williams, Sir Thomas Bridges, Sir John Brown, and the other justices, with certain other noblemen that were sent of the Queen's council, came to Oxford with a great train of waiting men. Also of the other multitude on every side was made a great concourse, and greater expectation. They that were of the Pope's side were in great hope that day to hear something of Cranmer that should stablish the vanity of their opinion: the other part could not yet doubt, that he, who by continual study and labour for so many years had set forth the doctrine of the Gospel, either would or could now in the last act of his life forsake his part.

Cranmer at length cometh from the prison of Bocardo unto St Mary's church in this order: the mayor went before ; next him the aldermen ; after them was Cranmer brought between two friars, who, mumbling certain psalms, answered one another until they came to the church door, and there they began the song of Simeon, *Nunc dimittis*. Entering into the church, the friars brought him to his standing, and there left him. There was a stage set over against the pulpit, of a mean height from the ground, where Cranmer had his standing, waiting until Cole made him ready to his sermon.

The lamentable case and sight of that man gave a sorrowful spectacle to all Christian eyes that beheld him. He that late was Archbishop, Metropolitan, and Primate of England, and the King's privy councillor, being now in a bare and ragged gown, and ill favouredly clothed, with an old square cap, exposed to the contempt of all men, did admonish men not only of his own calamity, but also of their state and fortune. For who would not pity his case, and bewail his fortune, and might not fear his own chance, to see such a prelate, so grave a councillor, and of so long continued honour, after so many dignities, in his old years to be deprived of his estate, from such fresh ornaments to descend to such vile and ragged apparel, adjudged to die, and in so painful a death to end his life?

When he had stood a good space upon the stage, turning to a pillar adjoining, he lifted up his hands to heaven, and prayed unto God, till at the length Dr Cole, coming into the pulpit, began his sermon.

The latter part he converted to the archbishop, whom he comforted and encouraged to take his death well, by the example of the three children, to whom God made the flame to seem like a pleasant dew; adding also the patience of St Lawrence on the fire; assuring him that God, to such as die in His faith, either would abate the fury of the flame, or give strength to abide it.

With what great grief of mind Cranmer stood hearing his sermon, the outward shows of his body and countenance did better express, than any man can declare; one while lifting up his hands and eyes unto heaven, and then again for shame letting them down to the earth. A man might have seen the living image of perfect sorrow in him expressed. More than twenty times the tears gushed out abundantly, dropping down from his fatherly face. Pity moved all men's hearts, that beheld so heavy a countenance.

Cole, after he had ended his sermon, called back the people that were ready to depart, to prayers. 'Brethren,' said he, 'lest any man should doubt of this man's earnest conversion, you shall hear him speak before you; therefore I pray you, Master Cranmer, openly express the true profession of your faith, that all men may understand that you are a catholic indeed.'

'I will do it,' said the Archbishop, 'and that with a good will;' who began to speak thus unto the people: 'Forasmuch as I am come to the end of my life, whereupon hangeth all my life to come, either to live with my Master Christ for ever in joy, or else to be in pain for ever with wicked devils in hell, and I see before mine eyes presently either heaven ready to receive me, or else hell ready to swallow me up: I shall therefore declare unto you my very faith, without any colour or dissimulation; for now is no time to dissemble, whatsoever I have said or written in time past.

'I believe in God the Father Almighty, maker of heaven and earth. And I believe every word and sentence taught by our Saviour Jesus Christ, His apostles and prophets, in the New and Old Testament.

'And now I come to the great thing, which so much troubleth my conscience, more than any thing that ever I did or said in my whole life, and that is the setting abroad of a writing contrary to the truth; which now here I renounce and refuse, as things written with my hand, contrary to the truth which I thought in my heart, and written for fear of

death, and to save my life if it might be; and that
is, all such bills and papers which I have written or
signed with my hand since my degradation; wherein
I have written many things untrue. And forasmuch
as my hand offended, writing contrary to my heart,
my hand shall first be punished there-for; for, may
I come to the fire, it shall be first burned.

'And as for the Pope, I refuse him, as Christ's
enemy, and antichrist, with all his false doctrine.'

Here the standers-by, amazed, did look one upon
another, whose expectation he had so notably
deceived. Some began to admonish him of his
recantation, and to accuse him of falsehood. It
was a world to see the doctors beguiled of so great
a hope. I think there was never cruelty more
notably or better in time deluded; for they looked
for a glorious victory and a perpetual triumph by
this man's retractation. As soon as they heard
these things, they began to let down their ears, to
rage, fret, and fume; and so much the more, because
they could not revenge their grief—for they could
now no longer threaten or hurt him. For the most
miserable man in the world can die but once.

And when he began to speak more of the
sacrament and of the papacy, some of them began
to cry out, yelp and bawl, and especially Cole cried
out upon him, 'Stop the heretic's mouth and take
him away.' And then being pulled down from the
stage, Cranmer was led to the fire, accompanied
with those friars, vexing, troubling and threatening
him most cruelly. To whom he answered nothing,
but directed all his talk to the people.

When he came to the place where the holy bishops
and martyrs of God, Hugh Latimer and Nicholas

Ridley, were burnt before him, kneeling down, he prayed to God; and not long tarrying in his prayers, putting off his garments to his shirt, he prepared himself to death. His shirt was made long, down to his feet. His feet were bare; likewise his head. His beard was long and thick, covering his face with marvellous gravity.

Then the Spanish friars, John and Richard, began to exhort him and play their parts with him afresh, but with vain and lost labour. Cranmer, with steadfast purpose abiding in the profession of his doctrine, gave his hand to certain old men, and others that stood by, bidding them farewell.

And when he had thought to have done so likewise to Ely, the said Ely drew back his hand, and refused, saying, it was not lawful to salute heretics, and specially such a one as falsely returned unto the opinions that he had forsworn. And if he had known before that he would have done so, he would never have used his company so familiarly; and he chid those sergeants and citizens which had not refused to give Cranmer their hands. This Ely was a priest lately made, and student in divinity, being then one of the fellows of Brasenose.

Then was an iron chain tied about Cranmer. When they perceived him to be more steadfast than that he could be moved from his sentence, they commanded the fire to be set unto him.

And when the wood was kindled, and the fire began to burn near him, stretching out his arm, he put his right hand into the flame, which he held so steadfast and immovable (saving that once with the same hand he wiped his face), that all men might see his hand burned before his body was touched.

'HIS UNWORTHY RIGHT HAND'

His body did abide the burning with such steadfastness, that he seemed to move no more than the
stake to which he was bound; his eyes were lifted
up into heaven, and he repeated 'his unworthy
right hand,' so long as his voice would suffer him;
and using often the words of Stephen, 'Lord Jesus,
receive my spirit,' in the greatness of the flame, he
gave up the ghost.

ANECDOTES AND SAYINGS OF OTHER MARTYRS

W HEN sentence was given against Jerome of Prague a great and long mitre of paper was brought unto him, painted about with red devils; which when he beheld, throwing away his hood upon the ground amongst the prelates, he took and put upon his head, saying: 'Our Lord Jesus Christ, when He should suffer death for me, most wretched sinner, did wear a crown of thorns upon His head; and I, for His sake, instead of that crown, will willingly wear this mitre and cap.'—Constance, 1416.

—There came unto George Carpenter a certain schoolmaster of St Peter saying, 'My friend George! dost thou not fear the death and punishment which thou must suffer? If thou wert let go, wouldst thou return to thy wife and children?'

Whereunto he answered, 'If I were set at liberty, whither should I rather go, than to my wife and well-beloved children?'

Then said the schoolmaster, 'Revoke your former sentence and opinion, and you shall be set at liberty.'

Whereunto George answered: 'My wife and my children are so dearly beloved unto me, that they cannot be bought from me for all the riches and possessions of the Duke of Bavaria; but, for the love of my Lord God, I will willingly forsake them.'—Munich, 1527.

MARRIED TO THE STAKE

—And so going forth they came to the place of execution, where Anthony Peerson, with a cheerful countenance, embraced the post in his arms, and kissing it, said, 'Now welcome mine own sweet wife! for this day shalt thou and I be married together in the love and peace of God.' And pulling the straw unto him, he laid a good deal thereof upon the top of his head, saying, 'This is God's hat; now am I dressed like a true soldier of Christ, by Whose merits only I trust this day to enter into His joy.'—Windsor, 1543.

—As Giles Tilleman was brought to the place of burning, where he saw a great heap of wood piled, he required the greater part thereof to be taken away, and to be given to the poor: a little (said he) would suffice him. Also seeing a poor man coming by, as he went, that lacked shoes, he gave his shoes unto him ; better (said he) so to do, than to have his shoes burnt, and the poor to perish for cold. Standing at the stake, the hangman was ready to strangle him before ; but he would not, saying that there was no such need that his pain should be mitigated ; 'For I fear not,' said he, 'the fire ; do thou therefore as thou art commanded.' And thus the blessed martyr, lifting up his eyes to heaven in the middle of the flame, died, to the great lamentation of all that stood by.—Brussels, 1544.

—Peter Miocius was let down into a deep dungeon, under the castle-ditch, full of toads and filthy vermin. Shortly after, the senate began to examine him of certain articles of religion. To whom, as he was about to answer boldly and expressly to every point, they, interrupting him, bade him say in two

389

words, either yea or nay. 'Then,' said he, 'if ye will not suffer me to answer for myself in matters of such importance, send me to my prison again, among my toads and frogs, which will not interrupt me, while I talk with my Lord and my God.'—Dornick, 1545.

—Master Wingfield said to Kerby, 'Remember the fire is hot, take heed of thine enterprise, that thou take no more upon thee, than thou shalt be able to perform. The terror is great, the pain will be extreme, and life is sweet. Better it were betimes to stick to mercy, while there is hope of life, than rashly to begin, and then to shrink.'

To whom Kerby answered, 'Ah, Master Wingfield! be at my burning, and you shall say, there standeth a Christian soldier in the fire. For I know that fire and water, sword and all other things, are in the hands of God, and He will suffer no more to be laid upon us, than He will give us strength to bear.'—Ipswich, 1545.

—When the rope was put about Ann Audebert, she called it her wedding-girdle wherewith she should be married to Christ; and as she should be burned upon a Saturday, upon Michaelmas-even; 'Upon a Saturday,' said she, 'I was first married, and upon a Saturday I shall be married again.'—Orleans, 1549.

—About ten of the clock cometh riding the sheriff, with a great many other gentlemen and their retinue appointed to assist him, and with them Christopher Wade, riding pinioned, and by him one Margery Polley of Tunbridge; both singing of a psalm: which Margery, as soon as she espied afar off the multitude gathered about the place where he should suffer, waiting his coming, said unto him very loud and cheerfully, 'You may rejoice, Wade, to see such a company gathered to celebrate your marriage this day.'

Wade, coming straight to the stake, took it in his arms, embracing it, and kissed it, setting his back unto it, and standing in a pitchbarrel.

As soon as he was thus settled, he spake, with his hands and eyes lifted up to heaven, with a cheerful and loud voice, the last verse of Psalm lxxxvi. : 'Show some good token upon me, O Lord, that they which hate me, may see it, and be ashamed; because Thou, Lord, hast helped me, and comforted me.' The sheriff, often interrupted, saying, 'Be quiet, Wade! and die patiently.' 'I am,' said he, 'I thank God, quiet, master sheriff! and so trust to die.' Then the reeds being set about him, Wade pulled them, and embraced them in his arms, always with his hands making a hole against his face, that his voice might be heard, which they perceiving that were his tormentors, always cast faggots at the same hole, which notwithstanding, he still, as he could, put off, his face being hurt with the end of a faggot cast thereat. Then fire being put unto him, he cried unto God often, 'Lord Jesus! receive my soul;' without any token or sign of impatiency in the fire.—Dartford, 1555.

—When the time came that he should be brought out of Newgate to Smithfield, came to him Master Woodroofe, and asked him if he would revoke his evil opinion of the sacrament of the altar. Master Rogers answered and said, 'That which I have preached I will seal with my blood.

'Then,' quoth Master Woodroofe, 'Thou art a heretic.'

'That shall be known,' quoth Rogers, 'at the day of judgment.'

'Well,' quoth Master Woodroofe, 'I will never pray for thee.'

'But I will pray for *you*,' quoth Master Rogers.

His wife and children, being eleven in number, and ten able to go, and one sucking on her breast, met him by the way as he went towards Smithfield. This sorrowful sight of his own flesh and blood could nothing move him; but that he constantly and cheerfully took his death. When the fire had taken hold both upon his legs and shoulders, he, as one feeling no smart, washed his hands in the flame, as though it had been in cold water.—Smithfield, 1555.

—When the godly martyrs Master Cardmaker and John Warne were brought by the sheriffs to the place where they should suffer, the sheriffs called Cardmaker aside, and talked with him secretly so long, that in the mean time Warne had made his prayers, was chained to the stake, and had wood and reed set about him, so that nothing wanted but the firing; but still abode Cardmaker talking with the sheriffs.

The people which before had heard that Cardmaker would recant, on beholding this manner of doing, were in a marvellous dump and sadness, thinking indeed that Cardmaker should now recant at the burning of Warne. At length Cardmaker departed from the sheriffs, and came towards the stake, and, in his garments as he was, kneeled down and made a long prayer in silence to himself: yet the people confirmed themselves in their fantasy of his recanting, seeing him in his garments, praying secretly, and no semblance of any burning.

His prayers being ended, he rose up, put off his clothes unto his shirt, went with bold courage to the stake, and kissed it sweetly : he took Warne by the hand, and comforted him heartily; and so gave himself to be also bound to the stake most gladly. The people seeing this so suddenly done, contrary to their fearful expectation, as men delivered out of a great doubt, cried out for joy, saying, 'God be praised; the Lord strengthen thee, Cardmaker; the Lord Jesus receive thy spirit!'—Smithfield, 1555.

—When this good man, Rawlins White, while he was on his way to the stake, came to a place where his poor wife and children stood weeping and making great lamentation, the sudden sight of them so pierced his heart that the tears trickled down his face. But he soon after, as though he had misliked this infirmity of his flesh, began to be as it were altogether angry with himself; insomuch that in striking his breast with his hand he used these words : 'Ah flesh! stayest thou me so? wouldest thou fain prevail? Well, I tell thee, do what thou canst, thou shalt not, by God's grace, have the victory.' Then went he cheerfully and very joyfully, and set his back close unto the stake.—Cardiff, 1555.

—Thomas Hauker being bound to the stake, the fire was set unto him. In the which when he continued long, and when his speech was taken away by violence of the flame, his skin also drawn together, and his fingers consumed with the fire, so that now all men thought certainly he had been gone, suddenly, and contrary to all expectation, the blessed servant of God reached up his hands burning on a light fire, which was marvellous to behold, over his head to the living God, and with great rejoicing, as it seemed, struck or clapped them three times together. Which thing he had promised certain of his friends to do; and so, secretly between them, it was agreed, that if the rage of the pain were tolerable and might be suffered, then he should lift up his hands above his head towards heaven, before he gave up the ghost.—Coggeshall, 1555.

—A godly letter of John Bradford—'To my dear Fathers, Dr Cranmer, Dr Ridley, and Dr Latimer.

Our dear brother Rogers hath broken the ice valiantly, as this day, I think, or to-morrow at the uttermost, hearty Hooper, sincere Saunders, and trusty Taylor, end their course, and receive their crown. The next am I, who hourly look for the porter to open me the gates after them, to enter into the desired rest. God forgive me mine unthankfulness for this exceeding great mercy, that, amongst so many thousands, it pleaseth His mercy to choose me to be one, in whom He will suffer. Oh! what am I, Lord, that Thou shouldest thus magnify me, so vile a man and wretched, as always I have been? Is this Thy wont, to send for such a wretch and hypocrite, as I have been, in a fiery chariot, as Thou didst for Elias? Oh! dear fathers, be thankful for me, and pray for me, that I still might be found worthy, in whom the Lord would sanctify His holy name. And for your part, make you ready: for we are but your gentlemen-ushers: "The marriage of the Lamb is prepared, come unto the marriage." '—Smithfield, 1555.

THE VISION OF THREE LADDERS

—When Robert Samuel was brought forth to be burned, certain there were that heard him declare what strange things had happened unto him during the time of his imprisonment; to wit, that after he had been famished or pined with hunger two or three days together, he then fell into a sleep, as it were one half in a slumber, at which time one clad all in white seemed to stand before him, who ministered comfort unto him by these words: 'Samuel, Samuel, be of good cheer, and take a good heart unto thee: for after this day shalt thou never be either hungry or thirsty.'

No less memorable it is, and worthy to be noted, concerning the three ladders which he told to divers he saw in his sleep, set up toward heaven; of the which there was one somewhat longer than the rest, but yet at length they became one, joining (as it were) all three together.

As this godly martyr was going to the fire, there came a certain maid to him, which took him about the neck, and kissed him, who, being marked by them that were present, was sought for the next day after, to be had to prison and burned, as the very party herself informed me: howbeit, as God of His goodness would have it, she escaped their fiery hands, keeping herself secret in the town a good while after.

But as this maid, called Rose Nottingham, was marvellously preserved by the providence of God, so there were other two honest women who did fall into the rage and fury of that time. The one was a brewer's wife, the other was a shoemaker's wife, but both together now espoused to a new husband, Christ.

ANECDOTES AND SAYINGS

With these two was this maid aforesaid very familiar and well acquainted, who, on a time giving counsel to the one of them, that she should convey herself away while she had time and space, had this answer at her hands again: 'I know well,' saith she, 'that it is lawful enough to fly away; which remedy you may use, if you list. But my case standeth otherwise. I am tied to a husband, and have besides young children at home; therefore I am minded, for the love of Christ and His truth, to stand to the extremity of the matter.'

And so the next day after Samuel suffered, these two godly wives, the one called Anne Potten, the other called Joan Trunchfield, the wife of Michael Trunchfield, shoemaker, of Ipswich, were apprehended, and had both into one prison together. As they were both by sex and nature somewhat tender, so were they at first less able to endure the straitness of the prison; and especially the brewer's wife was cast into marvellous great agonies and troubles of mind thereby. But Christ, beholding the weak infirmity of His servant, did not fail to help her when she was in this necessity; so at the length they both suffered after Samuel, in 1556, February 19. And these, no doubt, were those two ladders, which, being joined with the third, Samuel saw stretched up into heaven. This blessed Samuel, the servant of Christ, suffered the 31st of August 1555.

The report goeth among some that were there present, and saw him burn, that his body in burning did shine in the eyes of them that stood by, as bright and white as new-tried silver.—Norwich, 1555 and 1556.

BLIND WOMAN'S BIBLE

—Suffered at the town of Derby a certain poor honest godly woman, being blind from her birth, and unmarried, about the age of twenty-two, named Joan Waste. This Joan was the daughter of one William Waste, an honest poor man, and by his science a barber, who sometime also used to make ropes. She was born blind, and when about twelve or fourteen years old, she learned to knit hosen and sleeves, and other things, which in time she could do very well. Furthermore, as time served, she would help her father to turn ropes, and do such other things as she was able, and in no case would be idle.

In the time of King Edward the Sixth, of blessed memory, she gave herself daily to go to the church to hear divine service read in the vulgar tongue. And thus, by hearing homilies and sermons, she became marvellously well affected to the religion then taught. So at length, having by her labour gotten and saved so much money as would buy her a New Testament, she caused one to be provided for her. And though she was of herself unlearned, and by reason of her blindness unable to read, yet, for the great desire she had to understand and have printed in her memory the sayings of the holy Scriptures contained in the New Testament, she acquainted herself chiefly with one John Hurt, then prisoner in the common hall of Derby for debts. The same John Hurt being a sober grave man, of the age of threescore and ten years, by her earnest entreaty, and being a prisoner, and many times idle and without company, did for his exercise daily read unto her some one chapter of the New Testament.

397

And if at any time the said John Hurt were otherwise occupied or letted through sickness, she would repair unto some other person which could read, and sometimes she would give a penny or two (as she might spare) to such persons as would not freely read unto her; appointing unto them aforehand how many chapters of the New Testament they should read, or how often they should repeat one chapter, upon a price.

Moreover, in the said Joan Waste this was notorious, that she, being utterly blind, could notwithstanding, without a guide, go to any church within the said town of Derby, or at any other place or person, with whom she had any such exercise. By the which exercise she so profited, that she was able not only to recite many chapters of the New Testament without book, but also could aptly impugn, by divers places of Scriptures, as well sin, as such abuses in religion, as then were too much in use in divers and sundry persons.

Nothwithstanding the general backsliding of the greatest part of the whole realm into the old papism again, this poor blind woman, continuing in a constant conscience, proceeded still in her former exercise.—Derby, 1556.

—Then both the bishops waxed weary of the said William Tyms, for he had troubled them about six or seven hours. Then the bishop began to pity Tyms' case, and to flatter him, saying, 'Ah! good fellow,' said they, 'thou art bold, and thou hast a good fresh spirit; we would thou hadst learning to thy spirit.'

'I thank you, my lords,' said Tyms, 'and both you be learned, and I would you had a good spirit to your learning.'—London, 1556.

A RUSE THAT FAILED

—Hugh Laverock, a lame old man and John Apprice, a blind man, were carried from Newgate in a cart to Stratford-le-Bow, and most quietly in the fire, praising God, yielded up their souls into His hands. Hugh Laverock, after he was chained, cast away his crutch; and comforting John Apprice, his fellow-martyr, said unto him, 'Be of good comfort, my brother; for my lord of London is our physician. He will heal us both shortly; thee of thy blindness, and me of my lameness.'—Stratford-le-Bow, 1556.

—There followed in this happy and blessed order of martyrs, burnt in one fire eleven men and two women, whose dwellings were in sundry places in Essex, and whose names hereafter follow:—Henry Adlington, Laurence Parnam, Henry Wye, William Hallywel, Thomas Bowyer, George Searles, Edmund Hurst, Lyon Cawch, Ralph Jackson, John Derifall, John Routh, Elizabeth Pepper, and Agnes George.

When these thirteen were condemned, and the day appointed they should suffer, they were divided into two parts, in two several chambers.

The sheriff came to the one part, and told them that the other had recanted, and their lives therefore should be saved, willing and exhorting them to do the like, and not to cast away themselves: unto whom they answered, that their faith was not builded on man, but on Christ crucified.

Then the sheriff, perceiving no good to be done with them, went to the other part, and said the like to them, that they whom he had been with before had recanted, and should therefore not suffer death, counselling them to do the like, and not wilfully to kill themselves, but to play the wise men; unto whom they answered as their brethren had done before, that their faith was not builded on man, but on Christ and His sure word.

Now when he saw it booted not to persuade (for they were, God be praised, surely grounded on the Rock, Jesus Christ), he led them to the place where they should suffer: and being all there together, most earnestly they prayed unto God, and joyfully went to the stake, and kissed it, and embraced it very heartily.

The eleven men were tied to three stakes, and the two women loose in the midst without any stake; and so they were all burnt in one fire, with such love to each other, and constancy in our Saviour Christ, that it made all the lookers-on to marvel.—Stratford-le-Bow, 1556.

—A blind boy, named Thomas Drowry, suffered martyrdom at Gloucester. Dr Williams, then Chancellor of Gloucester, ministered unto the boy such articles as are accustomed in such cases:

Chancellor: 'Dost thou not believe that after the words of consecration spoken by the priest, there remaineth the very real body of Christ in the sacrament of the altar?'

To whom the blind boy answered, 'No, that I do not.'

Chancellor: 'Then thou art a heretic, and shalt be burned. But who hath taught thee this heresy?'

Thomas: 'You, master chancellor.'

Chancellor: 'Where, I pray thee?'

Thomas: 'Even in yonder place;' pointing towards the pulpit.

Chancellor: 'When did I teach thee so?'

A TEMPTING OFFER

Thomas : 'When you preached a sermon to all men as well as to me upon the sacrament. You said, the sacrament was to be received spiritually by faith and not carnally and really, as the papists have heretofore taught.'

Chancellor : 'Then do as I have done, and thou shalt live as I do, and escape burning.'

Thomas : 'Though you can so easily dispense with yourself, and mock with God, the world, and your conscience, yet will I not so do.'

Chancellor : 'Then God have mercy upon thee ; for I will read the condemnation sentence against thee.

Thomas : 'God's will be fulfilled.'

The registrar being herewith somewhat moved, stood up, and said to the chancellor :

Registrar : 'Fie for shame, man ! will you read the sentence against him, and condemn yourself ? Away, away, and substitute some other to give sentence and judgment.'

Chancellor : 'No, registrar, I will obey the law, and give sentence myself, according to mine office.'
—Gloucester, 1556.

—Sir Richard Abridges sent for Julius Palmer to his lodging; and there friendly exhorted him to revoke his opinion, to spare his young years, wit, and learning. 'If thou wilt be conformable, and show thyself corrigible and repentant, in good faith,' said he, 'I promise thee, I will give thee meat and drink, and books, and ten pound yearly, so long as thou wilt dwell with me. And if thou wilt set thy mind to marriage, I will procure thee a wife and a farm, and help to stuff and frit thy farm for thee. How sayst thou ?'

Palmer thanked him very courteously, but very modestly and reverently concluded that as he had already in two places renounced his living for Christ's sake, so he would with God's grace be ready to surrender and yield up his life also for the same, when God should send time.

When Sir Richard perceived that he would by no means relent: 'Well, Palmer,' saith he, 'then I perceive one of us twain shall be damned: for we be of two faiths, and certain I am there is but one faith that leadeth to life and salvation.'

Palmer: 'O sir, I hope that we both shall be saved.'

Sir Richard: 'How may that be?'

Palmer: 'Right well, sir. For as it hath pleased our merciful Saviour, according to the Gospel's parable, to call me at the third hour of the day, even in my flowers, at the age of four and twenty years, even so I trust He hath called, and will call you, at the eleventh hour of this your old age, and give you everlasting life for your portion.'

Sir Richard: 'Sayest thou so? Well, Palmer, well, I would I might have thee but one month in my house: I doubt not but I would convert thee, or thou shouldst convert me.'

Then said Master Winchcomb, 'Take pity on thy golden years, and pleasant flowers of lusty youth, before it be too late.'

Palmer: 'Sir, I long for those springing flowers that shall never fade away.'—Newbury, 1556.

— Agnes Bongeor, who should have suffered with the six that went out of Mote-hall was kept back at the time, because her name was wrong written within the writ. When the said six were called out to go to their martyrdom and when the said Agnes Bongeor saw herself so separated from her prison-fellows, what piteous moan that good woman made, how bitterly she wept, what strange thoughts came into her mind, how naked and desolate she esteemed herself, and into what plunge of despair and care her poor soul was brought, it was piteous and wonderful to see; which all came because she went not with them to give her life in the defence of her Christ; for of all things in the world, life was least looked for at her hands.

For that morning in which she was kept back from burning, had she put on a smock, that she had prepared only for that purpose. And also having a child, a little young infant sucking on her, whom she kept with her tenderly all the time that she was in prison, against that day likewise did she send away to another nurse, and prepared herself presently to give herself for the testimony of the glorious Gospel of Jesus Christ. So little did she look for life, and so greatly did God's gifts work in her above nature, that death seemed a great deal better welcome than life.

Being in this great perplexity of mind, a friend of hers came to her, and required to know whether Abraham's obedience was accepted before God, for that he did sacrifice his son Isaac, or in that he would have offered him? Unto which she answered thus: 'I know,' quod she, 'that Abraham's will before God was allowed for the deed, in that he would have done it, if the angel of the Lord had not stayed him: but I,' said she, 'am unhappy, the Lord thinketh me not worthy of this dignity: and therefore Abraham's case and mine are not alike.'

'Why,' quod her friend, 'would ye not willingly have gone with your company, if God should so have suffered it?'

'Yes,' said she, 'with all my heart; and because I did not, it is now my chief and greatest grief.'

Then said her friend, 'My dear sister, I pray thee consider Abraham and thyself well, and thou shalt see thou dost nothing differ with him in will at all.'

'Alas, nay,' quod she, 'there is a far greater matter in Abraham than in me; for Abraham was tried with the offering of his own child, but so am not I: and therefore our cases are not alike.'

'Good sister,' quod her friend, 'weigh the matter but indifferently. Abraham, I grant,' said he, 'would have offered his son: and have not you done the like, in your little sucking babe? But consider further than this, my good sister,' said he, 'whereas Abraham was commanded but to offer his son, you are heavy and grieved because you offer not yourself, which goeth somewhat more near you, than Abraham's obedience did; and therefore before God, assuredly, is no less accepted and allowed in His holy presence.' After which talk between them, she began a little to stay herself, and gave her whole exercise to reading and prayer, wherein she found no little comfort.

In a short time came a writ from London for the burning, which, according to the effect thereof, was executed.—Colchester, 1557.

—Elizabeth Cooper being condemned, and at the stake with Simon Miller, to be burnt, when the fire came unto her, she a little shrank thereat, with a voice crying, 'Hah!' When the said Simon Miller heard the same, he put his hand behind him toward her, and willed her to be strong and of good cheer : ' for, good sister,' said he, ' we shall have a joyful and a sweet supper : ' whereat she, being as it seemed thereby strengthened, stood as still and as quiet as one most glad to finish that good work which before most happily she had begun.— Norwich, 1557.

Master Tyrrel with a certain of his company went into the chamber where the said father Mount and his wife lay, willing them to rise : ' for,' said he, ' you must go with us to Colchester castle.' Mother Mount, hearing that, being very sick, desired that her daughter might first fetch her some drink; for she was (she said) very ill at ease.

Then he gave her leave and bade her go. So her daughter Rose Allin, maid, took a stone pot in one hand, and a candle in the other, and went to draw drink for her mother : and as she came back again toward the house, Tyrrel met her, and willed her to give her father and mother good counsel, and advertise them to be better catholic people.

Rose : ' Sir, they have a better instructor than I; for the Holy Ghost doth teach them, I hope, which I trust will not suffer them to err.'

' Why,' said Master Tyrrel, ' art thou still in that mind, thou naughty housewife? Marry it is time to look upon such heretics indeed.'

Rose: ' Sir, with that which you call heresy, do I worship my Lord God ; I tell you troth.'

Tyrrel: ' Then I perceive you will burn, gossip, with the rest, for company's sake.'

Rose : ' No, sir, not for company's sake, but for my Christ's sake, if so I be compelled; and I hope

in His mercies if He call me to it, He will enable me
to bear it.'

So he, turning to his company, said, 'Sirs, this
gossip will burn: do you not think it?' 'Marry,
sir,' quoth one, 'prove her, and you shall see what
she will do by and by.'

Then that cruel Tyrrel, taking the candle from
her, held her wrist, and the burning candle under
her hand, burning cross-wise over the back thereof
so long, till the very sinews cracked asunder. In
which time of his tyranny, he said often to her,
'Why, wilt thou not cry? wilt thou not cry?' Unto
which always she answered, that she had no cause,
she thanked God, but rather to rejoice. He had
(she said) more cause to weep, than she, if he considered the matter well. In the end, he thrust her
from him violently.

But she, quietly suffering his rage for the time,
at the last said, 'Sir, have ye done what ye will
do?'

And he said, 'Yea, and if thou think it be not
well, then mend it.'

'Mend it!' said Rose; 'nay, the Lord mend you,
and give you repentance, if it be His will. And
now, if you think it good, begin at the feet, and
burn to the head also. For he that set you a work,
shall pay you your wages one day, I warrant you.'

And so she went and carried her mother drink,
as she was commanded.—Colchester, 1557.

—When these six constant martyrs had made their
prayers, they rose, and made them ready to the fire.
And Elizabeth Folkes, when she had plucked off
her petticoat, would have given it to her mother
(which came and kissed her at the stake, and ex-

horted her to be strong in the Lord): but the wicked there attending, would not suffer her to give it. Therefore, taking the said petticoat in her hand, she threw it away from her, saying, 'Farewell, all the world! farewell Faith! farewell Hope!' and so taking the stake in her arms, said, 'Welcome love!'

Now she being at the stake, and one of the officers nailing the chain about her, in the striking in of the staple he missed the place, and struck her with a great stroke of the hammer on the shoulder-bone; whereat she suddenly turned her head, lifting up her eyes to the Lord, and prayed smilingly, and gave herself to exhorting the people again.

When all the six were also nailed likewise at their stakes, and the fire about them, they clapped their hands for joy in the fire, that the standers-by, which were, by estimation, thousands, cried 'The Lord strengthen them; the Lord comfort them; the Lord pour His mercies upon them; with such like words, as was wonderful to hear.—Colchester, 1557.

—Master Rough, being at the burning of Austoo in Smithfield, and returning homeward again, met with one Master Farrar, a merchant of Halifax, who asked him, where he had been. Unto whom he answered, 'I have been,' saith he, 'where I would not for one of mine eyes but I had been.' 'Where have you been?' said Master Farrar. 'Forsooth,' said he, 'to learn the way.' And so he told him he had been at the burning of Austoo, where shortly after he was burnt himself.—Smithfield, 1557.

—After John Fetty had lain in the prison by the space of fifteen days, hanging in the stocks, sometimes by the one leg, and the one arm, sometimes by the other, and otherwhiles by both, it happened that one of his children (a boy of the age of eight or nine years) came unto the bishop's house, to see if he could get leave to speak with his father. At his coming thither, one of the bishop's chaplains met with him, and asked him what he lacked and whom he would have. The child answered, that he came to see his father. The chaplain asked again, who was his father. The boy then told him, and pointing towards Lollards' Tower, showed him that his father was there in prison.

'Why,' quoth the priest, 'thy father is a heretic.'

The child, being of a bold and quick spirit, and also godly brought up, and instructed by his father in the knowledge of God, answered and said, 'My father is no heretic; but you are an heretic, for you have Balaam's mark.'

With that the priest took the child by the hand, and carried him into the bishop's house, and there, amongst them, they did most shamefully and without all pity so whip and scourge, being naked, this tender child, that he was all in a gore-blood; and then they carried the child in his shirt unto his father, the blood running down by his heels.

At his coming unto his father the child fell down upon his knees, and asked him blessing. The poor man then, beholding his child, and seeing him so cruelly arrayed, cried out for sorrow, and said, 'Alas, Will! who hath done this to thee?'

The boy answered that as he was seeking how to come to see his father, a priest with Balaam's mark took him into the bishop's house, and there was

A CHILD'S DEATH

he so handled.   Cluney therewith violently plucked the child away out of his father's hands, and carried him back again into the bishop's house, where they kept him three days after.

Bonner, bethinking in himself of the danger which the child was in by their whipping, and what peril might ensue thereupon, thought better to discharge the said Fetty, willing him to go home and carry his child with him; which he so did, and that with a heavy heart, to see his poor boy in such extreme pain and grief.   But within fourteen days after the child died.—London, 1558.

INDEX

INDEX

INDEX